Brian Freeman is an internationally bestselling author of psychological suspense novels. His books have been sold in 46 countries and 20 languages. His debut thriller, *Immoral*, won the Macavity Award and was a nominee for the Edgar, Dagger, Anthony and Barry awards for best first novel. In 2013, *Spilled Blood* won the International Thriller Writers award for Best Hardcover Novel. *Season of Fear* is his second novel featuring Detective Cab Bolton.

Also by Brian Freeman

Spilled Blood
The Agency (writing as Ally O'Brien)

THE CAB BOLTON SERIES

The Bone House

THE JONATHAN STRIDE SERIES

The Cold Nowhere
The Burying Place
The Watcher
Stalked
Stripped
Immoral

Turn to Stone (A Jonathan Stride novella)
Spitting Devil (A Jonathan Stride short story)

SEASON OF FEAR

BRIAN FREEMAN

Quercus

First published in Great Britain in 2014 by Quercus Editions Ltd
This paperback edition published 2014 by

Quercus Editions Ltd
55 Baker Street
7th Floor, South Block
London
W1U 8EW

A CIP catalogue record for this book is available from the British Library

ISBN 978 1 78206 899 0
EBOOK ISBN 978 1 78206 898 3

10 9 8 7 6 5 4 3 2 1

Printed and bound in Great Britain by Clays Ltd, St Ives plc
Typeset by Ellipsis Books Limited, Glasgow

For Marcia
and in memory of
Ali Gunn

Sin crouches at your door.

It desires you, but you must overcome it.

Genesis 4:7

PROLOGUE

Ten Years Ago

He marched through the orange grove in quick, angry steps, crushing the litter of fruit that sweetened the night with a citrus perfume.

The sandy soil, still damp from the afternoon rain, modeled the design of the hard rubber treads on his boots. He made no effort to hide his trail. In the days ahead, they would follow his footprints back to where he had parked the stolen pickup truck. They would take photographs and make casts and review dozens of brands of footwear. They would tell the world that he bought Herman Survivors at Wal-Mart, like thousands of other hunters. They would find the GMC Sierra abandoned in the parking lot of a Sonny's Real Pit Bar-B-Q in Haines City, and the truck would lead them to the garage of a 1950s-era bungalow half a mile from the Gulf in Indian Rocks Beach. The owner, a snowbird from Wisconsin who spent his winters on the Florida coast, would be unaware that the truck was missing.

None of it would make any difference at all.

They would never find him.

A film of sweat from the sticky heat covered his body and festered under his black clothes. Trickles of moisture invited the mosquitoes and midges to feast on his face. He ignored the whine in his ears and the flutter of moth wings. He walked past the arrow-straight rows of trees like a soldier, focused on where he had to go and what he had to do.

Time was passing. He needed to hurry.

He saw the sanctuary high above him, cresting the hillside. The stone tower shimmered in the glow of spotlights. People could see it for miles from the swampy lowlands. The tower looked out of place, like something stripped from a European cathedral, too perfect and ornate for the scrub lizards and dripping Spanish moss of central Florida. Its pink marble shined like candy. Ceramic grilles adorned the stone, depicting flamingoes and baboons cavorting in Eden. Adam and Eve were pictured on the tower. So was the snake, whispering sweet nothings in Eve's ear.

Now he would crash the party in paradise. An invisible wraith. A bearer of death.

Kill the fortunate son.

'What are you doing?'

He stopped dead. The hot wind brought the orange trees to life. Clusters of ripe fruit swung from drooping branches. He looked back, but he was alone with the voice in his head.

'What's happening? I'm scared.'

He beat his forehead with a gloved fist to drive the memories away, but he found himself reliving the sensations regardless. The panic. The fear. Blackness and light whipping through his brain, faster than he could see. A shudder rippling through his body, a blow to the chest. And blood. So much blood, pooling and flooding like a crimson lake in the moonlight.

'Why is there so much blood?'

He remained motionless, waiting until the tiny voice went away. There was too much at stake to obsess over things he couldn't change. He couldn't afford to give in to emotions now. The only emotion he could allow into his heart was hatred. If he could channel his hatred, if he could taste its bitterness, he could do what he needed to do.

The orange grove ended at a slope that led to the hillside sanctuary. It was the highest mountain in a flat state. He climbed, with the tall grass crowding him. He beat away the insects now, because they had become insatiable, flocking around him like a biting cloud. Their whistling chatter was deafening. He used a penlight on the ground and saw lizards skittering back and forth across the trail ahead of him. He felt as if he were trudging through a primitive rain forest, thick with humid air that weighed on his chest.

Five minutes later, at the crest of the hill, he broke free onto a beautifully manicured lawn, where a garden party was underway. He saw the flicker of torches making silhouettes of the crowd assembled on the grass. Human noises burbled from the glitterati: laughter, rumbling voices, the clink of wine glasses. A hundred people, maybe more. Carillon bells played inside the tower, clanging out across the hilltop. The tune was familiar.

He slipped a hood over his head and steeled himself for the things to come. Awful, necessary things. He was a man with a mission. It was just that no one would know what that mission was.

'Birch wanted a magical night,' Diane Fairmont murmured as she studied the crowd from the raised dais that had been constructed on the lawn. 'I guess he got one.'

'I guess he did,' Tarla Bolton replied.

Tarla swept her long blond hair from her face. Her friend was right. The night really did sparkle. Below them, beautiful people wandered in and out of the dancing shadows like fairies. She saw tall men in suits and tuxedoes. They were all men with money, which was what every politician wanted at his event. Women wore summer dresses fluttering in the hilltop breeze. The younger ones spilled cleavage from silk. Older wives eyed the interlopers with sideways cynical stares.

They drank Chardonnay. They laughed. They inhaled the moist wind of the Florida night and smelled yellow jasmine. The bells of the tower played, reminding her of children banging spoons on old metal buckets.

'Do you know what the bells are playing?' Diane asked.

Tarla cocked an ear, letting her diamonds dangle, and then she laughed. 'It's probably something old and classical, but it sounds like Supertramp. Remember that song?'

'Which one?'

'"Goodbye Stranger."'

Diane's face soured at the irony. 'It's about one-night stands, isn't it? Birch probably asked them to play it.'

She turned away from Tarla and sat down in the chair behind the microphone. The loyal wife's chair. When Birch spoke, the cameras would all catch her there. Smiling. Applauding. The woman behind the man, dressed in a conservative ensemble, attractive but unthreatening. That was the image Birch wanted for her now. Voters didn't like trophy wives living in the governor's mansion.

Tarla watched her friend wither in the heat. Diane's skin was pale, not its typical gold from the summer sun. She'd spent most of the evening ducking the crowd. When Diane twisted her neck to stare at the pink tower, Tarla noticed a sharp stab of pain on her face. 'Are you all right?'

'It's nothing.'

'You don't look good,' Tarla said.

'I'm fine,' Diane insisted. 'Drop it, darling, please. The campaign is exhausting. I'm tired.'

Tarla weighed whether to push her friend, but she decided that now wasn't the time. She had several more days before she needed to be back on set in Mallorca, and she was staying with Diane in Birch's mansion, the way she did every summer. They could talk more later. Tonight was for politics. Tonight they had to wear masks.

Tarla and Diane had grown up together in the sleepy central Florida town of Lake Wales. They'd spent their earliest summers here in the Bok Sanctuary, swatting no-see-ums as they lay in the grass near the tower, talking about boys and dreams. Tarla knew that her best friend had always looked at her with naked envy since those days. Tarla was slim, blonde, tall. She'd escaped Lake Wales for Hollywood as a teenager and did what no real person should be able to do. She made it. She became an actress. She made movies and money. When the two girls both had out-of-wedlock sons at age twenty-one, Tarla could afford to shuttle her son Cab to movie sets around the world, while Diane relied on food stamps to feed Drew.

Birch Fairmont hired Diane as his secretary at Welsh Capital when Drew was ten. He chose her for her body and breasts as much as her Microsoft Excel skills. Age thirty, single mother, unapologetic about stealing a married man – which was what she did when Birch divorced his first wife. She had never pretended that her affair with him was anything but mercenary. She'd gotten exactly what she wanted: the mansion in the Mountain Lake Estates, the island vacations, the permanent security for her son. Though it had come with a steep price tag, which was written on Diane's face.

Tarla took the chair on the dais next to her friend. The other chairs were empty, but Birch and his entourage would soon fill them for the speech to the wealthy guests. Vote for me, but more than that, give me money. Not that Birch needed it. He'd funded most of his campaign from his own venture-capital millions.

'You heard they found that poor girl?' Diane asked.

'What girl?'

'The one who went missing. Alison, I think. Fourteen years old. It was in the news over the weekend. They found her body hidden in a ditch. Terrible.'

'Did you know her?'

'No, but I should write to her parents. Imagine what they're going through.'

Tarla didn't know what to say. She didn't understand the criminal mind; she couldn't comprehend how one person could inflict suffering on another. It mystified her that her only son had chosen to immerse himself in solving crimes. With his looks, Cab Bolton could have been an actor or model, but he investigated murders instead. Tarla hated it. She thought he had chosen his career as a kind of rebellion against her Hollywood world.

'I saw Drew this weekend,' Tarla said instead, thinking of mothers and children.

'Yes, he just got back home.'

'How is he?' she asked, knowing the answer, which was: *Not good*. Diane's son had battled drugs most of his life and had largely surrendered in his fight with addiction. It had been a source of heartache for Diane – and arguments with Birch – throughout their marriage.

'The doctors say he's better, but he's been better before,' Diane replied. 'Sooner or later, he starts again.'

'I know. I'm sorry.'

'You're lucky with Cab.'

'I am, but Cab's a loner like me. He shuts me out.'

'I don't know if that's true,' Diane said.

Tarla smiled. 'No? He spent more time with you than with me when he was here this summer. Avoiding his mother is his avocation.'

'He loves you, and he's a gem,' Diane lectured her, in a terse voice that said: *You've got everything.*

Tarla didn't protest. Diane was right.

Her friend's gaze landed on her husband in the crowd. Birch Fairmont was easy to spot. His voice was loud, his laugh exaggerated so that everyone could hear him. He had a lion's mane of gray hair that shone like wax under the torches, and a bronzed Florida tan. Normal people wilted under the humidity, but Birch glowed. He was big, with a prominent nose, plump cheekbones, jutting chin, and a stomach pushing over his belt. He wasn't tall, but he had charisma and confidence, the kind of magnetism that drew people to him. He was tailor-made to sell to the voters.

'Lyle and Caprice think he's really going to win,' Diane said.

Tarla was unimpressed. 'So I hear.'

'He got into the race as a protest. No one expected him to make any noise. Now Lyle says he's in the lead.'

'The incumbent died, and the new Dem is left of Nancy Pelosi,' Tarla scoffed. 'Chuck Warren, the Republican, cozies up to right-wing nutjobs. Birch looks like a statesman by comparison to those clowns.'

'It's a big thing,' Diane insisted. 'Caprice says this election could be the start of a national third party movement.'

Tarla laughed, which was the wrong thing to do, because she knew it annoyed her friend. 'That's what they said about that wrestler in Minnesota, too. Does Birch plan to shave his head and wear a feather boa?'

'It's not funny, Tarla,' Diane snapped. 'I believe in this.'

'I'm not questioning the message,' Tarla replied, 'just the messenger.'

Tarla refused to hold her tongue about Birch. She'd spent too many years seeing Diane locked up like a bird in a cage, singing when he told her to sing. She also knew that Diane was right. Birch might actually win. A scary thought. All the polls put him ahead, but polls didn't mean much two months before the election. The other parties wouldn't roll over. Chuck Warren was already hitting Birch on gun rights. The Democratic campaign manager, Ogden Bush, was promising an onslaught of negative ads. Tarla wasn't sure that Birch and his team knew how to play dirty enough to come out on top.

It was nine o'clock. The bells in the tower fell silent. Whispers swept through the crowd; the elegant guests looked around expectantly. Tarla saw Birch mounting the steps of the dais, with the yes-men of his campaign behind him. Birch's smile was wide and false. He was already in love with politics, the smell of power, the fawning operatives trailing in his wake. He wasn't the kind of man who would change Washington for the better. He'd be seduced by it like all the others.

Tarla had never liked Birch, and he knew it.

She stood up as he approached her. He was resplendent in his black suit, his teeth bleached as white as ivory. His eyes traveled over Tarla's silver beaded dress, diving into her cleavage like a spelunker in a cave. He put his arms around her in a bear hug, squeezing her full breasts. His hand fell to the small of her back, and she thought he would have cupped her ass if the media hadn't been there to watch him.

'Thank God there's a podium,' he whispered. 'You always give me such a hard-on, Tarla.'

'You're a pig,' she whispered back.

Birch laughed, as if they'd shared an intimate joke. *My dear friend, the Hollywood star.* He leaned down to kiss his wife's cheek, and his face was full of faux devotion. Tarla was an actress, and she knew acting when she saw it. He murmured in Diane's ear, and Tarla was close enough to hear what he said.

'For God's sake, Diane, you're not at a fucking funeral. Look like you're *happy*.'

Diane forced a half-smile onto her face for the cameras. Birch faced the podium and waved at the crowd with both arms. The assembly erupted with applause. Around him, two dozen donors and campaign staffers filled the empty chairs on the dais, clapping as they sat down. It was a warm night; their faces shined with sweat and were red from free booze. Tarla recognized most of them. Corporate orange growers. Disney executives. People with fat checkbooks.

Lyle Piper, Birch's chief of staff, hovered behind the candidate, barking instructions into a cell phone. His fiancée Caprice did the same. The applause continued; people repeatedly shouted Birch's name like a religious chant. Lyle was small next to Birch, with a slight frame and bird-like skinny fingers. He had thinning blond hair cut like a conservative CEO, and he acted the same way. In the times Tarla had met him, she didn't recall Lyle ever smiling. He was intense and preachy about everything from tax policy to cholesterol. Even so, he was less of a hypocrite than other politicians she'd met. He walked the walk about personal responsibility. Lyle had lost his parents four years earlier at age twenty-four, and since then, he'd been a surrogate father to two younger siblings. Not an easy job.

Lyle slipped an arm around Caprice's elbow. Lyle Piper and Caprice Dean were a political power couple in Florida, but they were idealistic in a way that only young people could be. They still thought they could change the world. They thought a new, centrist political party would be different from the other two. They thought Birch Fairmont would be the face of something that could tear down the extremes on both sides.

Tarla could have told them right then that they were naive.

Caprice leaned down to Diane. If Lyle looked older than his years, she looked younger. She was pretty and full-figured, with long dark hair, fresh-scrubbed skin without a hint of a Florida tan, and bookish black glasses propped high on her rounded nose. She wore a burgundy waistcoat, black slacks, and high heels smudged with mud. Her voice cracked with excitement. 'Isn't this great?'

'Wonderful,' Diane said, her own voice hollow.

The two political aides sat next to Diane on the dais. Birch raised his arms to quiet the crowd, but they may as well have been celebrating the balloon drop at a convention. It was Labor Day, and they had all seen the polls. They smelled momentum, which was like adrenaline in the veins of political junkies. This was their man. Birch Fairmont, candidate for the United States Congress in the 12th District from the newly formed Common Way Party.

Tarla kept an eye on Lyle Piper and was surprised by what she saw. The cameras had left him, and something black flitted across his face. He clasped his hands in his lap and stared at his leather shoes with a stony expression. Caprice grabbed his hand, and the mask of enthusiasm slipped momentarily from her face, too. Whatever they told the world, they both knew the truth about the candidate at the podium. They were dancing with a devil. That was politics.

'My good friends,' Birch said to a new round of cheers. The microphone broadcast his voice around the park. The tower shimmered a hundred yards away. The floodlights illuminated the stage, but the crowd was lost in shadows, and beyond them, on the fringe of the lawn, the world was black. The park disappeared into the surrounding jungle.

Tarla eyed Diane, who had a peculiar expression on her face. Her friend watched Birch with pride, fear, and hatred.

'My good friends,' Birch repeated.

More cheers.

'In less than two months, we will show America that we can choose something other than divisive rhetoric and empty slogans,' he continued, diving into his stump speech. 'That we can find consensus among our differences. That we can rely on good sense, not nonsense. That there really is a common way for all of us.'

Tarla saw Birch's photo on signs thrust into the air and waved by volunteers. The caption above his face read: *The Common Man.* She shook her head at the hubris of it all. Birch was many things, but he was not common. He was a businessman worth a hundred million dollars. Definitely not common.

'I need you with me!' Birch shouted.

He waited for an elevated energy in the voices of the crowd. That was how you built people into a frenzy of full-throated excitement, with each applause line louder than the one before. Instead, he got no reaction, except a low burst of uncomfortable clapping that died as quickly as it started.

Unsettled, Birch tried again.

'I need every one of you to be part of the common way!'

Heads turned, but no one cheered. Low voices murmured in an uneasy ripple. Birch was visibly annoyed. He looked over his shoulder at Lyle and mouthed: *What the hell?*

Like the rest of the crowd, Lyle's attention was focused elsewhere. He and everyone else had become aware of a man on the corner of the dais. He'd come from nowhere out of the shroud of the night. He was dressed completely in black: black long-sleeved nylon shirt, black tight jeans, black gloves over his hands, and – like a Dickens ghost – a black hood over his head. His presence froze them all into motionless silence. Tarla sucked in her breath as she saw him. She knew. Everyone knew.

Something bad was about to happen.

One person took action. She recognized him; he was the director of one of the largest corporate citrus farms in the area. Married. Father of three. He was on the dais in the second row, and he stood up and pushed to the front and marched toward the man in black. He got within ten feet before the man reached behind his belt with a gloved hand, which re-emerged holding a semi-automatic pistol. He lifted his right hand and calmly fired one shot into the head of the citrus farmer, who crumpled and slipped off the dais to the thick lawn.

The explosion, like unexpected thunder, woke up the crowd. Chaos descended. Screaming began; the audience turned en masse, like a wave, and stampeded toward the tower, where overgrown trails led out of the park.

The man in black was unaffected by the tumult. He was on a mission, marching along the front of the platform toward Birch Fairmont. The VIPs in the rows of chairs sat paralyzed, watching the violence unfold. A woman in the back row stood up to escape, but the man in black fired, hitting her in the shoulder, her torso blooming with red as she wailed and sunk to the wooden floor. No one moved again.

Smoke burned in Tarla's nose from the smell of the bullets. She found herself dizzy, seeing the man come closer. Birch had the look of a man on a falling plane, a man staring at his mortality seconds away. This instant, you are alive; the next instant, you will be dead. He faced the gunman with his fists clenched; he didn't run, because there was nowhere to go. His face went dark with frustration.

'You son of a–'

Birch didn't finish his curse. The man in black fired four times, one two three four, boom boom boom boom, each bullet streaking into Birch's chest, carving out ribs, organs, and blood. Birch staggered but didn't fall, and the man fired again, another round flush in the heart, and Birch's knees sagged. He grabbed for the podium, missed it like a blind man, and fell sideways, gasping out cherry-colored blood. His white shirt was crimson. His tanned face was ashen.

'*Birch!*' Diane screamed.

The man in black swung around and thrust the gun in Diane's face, but Tarla stood up and put herself between them. She had only one thought in her head, to protect her best friend. The barrel, inches away, fed smoke into her nose and mouth and made her choke. The metal almost touched her forehead. She couldn't see his eyes behind the black mesh, but she was close enough that she could smell his sweat and see the tiniest tremble in his hand. In her heels, she was taller than him. It was strange, what you noticed at a moment like that. He was a killer, but he was just a man.

She thought of her son, because she wanted him to be her last thought on this earth. Cab, six-foot-six, blond, funny, cynical, wicked smart, gorgeous. Cab, the one thing she had ever created in her life that gave her nothing but pure pride.

Then the gun was gone from her head. Gone, leaving her alive. Tarla could barely stand with nausea and relief. Birch's blood pooled around her feet. *It's over*, she thought, but she was wrong. The man in black pointed his gun at Lyle Piper. Lyle had a look of dazed confusion on his face, as if he had stumbled into a bad dream. Next to Lyle, Caprice's young voice warbled like a soprano, screaming out words that climbed into disbelief, almost unrecognizable.

'*What are you doing what are you doing what are you doing what are you doing?*'

Tarla watched in mute horror as the man fired again, one kill shot, no mercy. Just like that, Lyle keeled backward, and Caprice was spray-painted with blood and brain. He was dead, and she was alone.

One word, one scream, long and endless and riven with loss, wailed from the dais. '*No no no no no no no!*'

Vertigo descended on Tarla, overwhelming her senses. The world made circles, breaking up the way a kaleidoscope whirls and spins. She blinked once, and the gunman was gone, and she heard sirens and saw the multicolored flash of lights. She blinked again, and she was in a hospital bed miles away.

PART ONE

THE EXTREMES

1

'Chayla,' the union official said, stabbing the elevator button in the lobby of the Tampa Hyatt Regency. 'What the hell kind of name is that for a storm?'

His younger companion chuckled as he sipped a Starbuck's cappuccino, which left foam on his upper lip. 'Hey, it's better than Debby. Chayla sounds like some kind of evil witch, you know? Like she could seduce you and wipe out your home and you'd thank her for it. Debby, that's like being mugged by a Girl Scout.'

'Yeah, well, I don't care what name they give the things. This baby hits, we're talking hundreds of millions in damage. You guys are watching the weather maps?'

'Sure we are. Some models have landfall on the Gulf Coast by Wednesday of next week, but it could still turn north to New Orleans, and all we'll get is rain.'

The union official, whose name was Walter Fleming, poked a half-eaten chocolate donut at his well-dressed companion. As a rule, Walter didn't like hotshot political aides. They were too smart for their own good. Nobody could be as dumb as really smart people, particularly when they worked for the government. 'Just don't blow this, okay? Nothing loses votes faster than a messed-up disaster. Especially if it hits next Wednesday, huh? The Fourth of July?'

The political aide smirked behind his coffee cup. 'Relax, Walter. We're on it. Besides, if it comes our way, it's more work for your boys, right?'

Walter scratched his wiry gray crew-cut, which hadn't changed since his Marine days. 'It's not about that, and don't let anyone hear you talking that way.'

The two men wore lanyards and badges from the industrial union meeting at the Convention Center. Walter had been the number two man in the union's leadership hierarchy for more than fifteen years. He had no interest in the top job. The union leader had to wear expensive suits and put up with reporters and send out Twitter updates, whereas Walter could wear jeans and do the real political work behind the scenes. If anyone in Tallahassee wanted something important done without publicity, they knew who to call. Not the top dog. They called Walter.

The political aide – Brent Reed, thirty years old, curly black hair, goatee – had made the call to Walter when their poll numbers started going south. Reed was just the messenger boy. The call went much higher up the campaign food chain, but nobody at the top wanted to get their hands dirty. That was Walter's job. After fifty years in Democratic politics, ever since he was an eighteen-year-old kid, Walter knew everybody who mattered in Florida, and he knew how to get things done.

'Jeez, these elevators are slow,' Walter complained as they waited in the lobby.

'Yeah, there's never an electrical worker around when you need one,' Reed joked.

'Funny. That's real funny.'

Brent slid an iPhone out of his pocket and scrolled up the screen with his thumb. Walter figured he was probably checking his Facebook page, 'liking' some post about a Vegas vacation or a cat in a sweater. Dumb kids.

'Anyway, you can say you told me so,' Brent went on, fixated on his smartphone screen as he sipped his coffee. 'Looks like Diane Fairmont's numbers are for real. She's up three over Ramona Cortes in a three-way race. Eight over you-know-who.'

'I told you so. People haven't forgotten what happened to her husband ten years ago. Her favorability is, what, 65 percent? That's a lot better than our boy. He's down around 37 right now.'

'Maybe we should shoot his wife,' Reed joked again. 'He can compete with Diane for the sympathy vote.'

Walter eyed the hotel lobby, then bunched the silk lapel of Reed's suit coat in his beefy fist and hissed at the tall, slim aide. 'You want to read a remark like that in the papers? Keep your goddamn voice down.'

'Chill, Walter. There's no press around.'

'You better learn, there are spies *everywhere*. You have to talk like everything coming out of your mouth is going into an open mike. Haven't you figured out that this is a war? The Republicans cottoned on to that a long time ago, and the Common Way folks have done a hell of a good job of catching up.'

Brent shrugged. 'That's why we called you, isn't it?'

'It took you long enough.'

'Maybe so, but my people are getting nervous. They want to see some progress. What should I tell them?'

Walter shook his head. If he'd learned one thing in fifty years, it was that each new generation had to learn the old mistakes all over again. Give a kid a master's degree in public policy from FSU, and he was still a moron. Walter, who was six inches shorter than Brent Reed and a hundred pounds heavier, exhaled a cigar-tinged breath. 'We'll talk about this in my room. Not here.'

'Whatever.'

The elevator doors finally opened. A handful of hotel guests exited into the lobby. Most were delegates from the convention who greeted Walter like a celebrity. He pumped their arms and chatted them up, paying no attention to the impatient political aide with him. Brent held the doors open until the elevator's alarm buzzed, and then Walter shouldered inside and hit the button for the Hyatt's sixth floor with his fat thumb.

Just as the doors began to close, a bare arm slid between the narrowing gap, as if waving a magic wand. The doors reversed course, and a girl joined the two of them in the elevator compartment. Walter stuck out a sleeve of his tweed sport coat to keep the doors open until she was safely inside. She was young. Everybody looked young to Walter, but he figured she couldn't be more than twenty years old. She wasn't short, but she was anorexic-skinny: all bones, no curves, flat breasts. Her jaw worked; she was chewing gum. The girl wore a pink tank top that didn't even reach to her belly button, and her cut-off corduroy shorts were cut off so high that Walter could see the slope of both butt cheeks when she turned and faced the door. She pushed the button for the tenth floor.

'Wow,' Brent said.

Walter's idea of 'wow' was Kim Novak, but the girl in the elevator was cute, the way his youngest daughter was cute. She had pink-painted toenails poking out of flip-flops. Her hair was long, lush, and black; her face was pale and freckled, with a tiny oval mouth. A silver cross dangled from her right earlobe. He couldn't see her eyes, which were hidden behind sunglasses with leopard frames. She tugged on the strap of an oversized satchel purse, which was slung over one arm. She wore earbuds, and the music from the iPod squeezed into her skin-tight back pocket thumped so loudly that Walter could hear the screaming lyrics of the song. The girl hummed, and her hips swung rhythmically, and her head bobbed.

'What the hell is that noise?' Walter asked Brent. 'Is that supposed to be music?'

'Sounds like Rihanna. "Roc Me Out." Rihanna, that's a good name for a storm.'

'This girl is going to be deaf by the time she's thirty,' Walter said.

Brent's eyes were locked on the sway of the girl's shapely backside. 'What?'

'Forget it.'

'Anyway, I need to take something back to my people,' Brent went on. 'Do we have any dirt on Common Way yet?'

'Upstairs,' Walter repeated through gritted teeth.

'Oh, hell, you think this girl can hear a thing we say?' Brent raised his voice and called to her. 'Hey, sweetheart, rock me on the floor, okay? Man, that ass of yours could stop traffic.'

'Jesus, Brent!'

'Forget her, she's in her own world,' Brent told him, and he was right. The girl couldn't hear anything except Rihanna. She danced as the elevator ground upward. 'So?'

'Fine, we got nothing so far,' Walter said. 'I told you this was going to take time. We'll turn up something we can use, but we need to keep a low profile. If Common Way catches us spying, it's game over.'

'Were you able to get someone inside the campaign?'

'That's my business, not yours. And it's better for you if we keep it that way.' He added after a pause: 'Remember, Ogden Bush works for them now, not us. You don't want him connecting the dots. He knows me.'

'Bush. Fucking turncoat.'

'It's politics. We screwed him, he screws us. Sooner or later, we'll want him back on our side. In the meantime, sit tight, and let me do my job.'

'When do you plan to deliver? After the election? That won't do us much good.'

'We can't make shit up out of thin air. It's got to be legit.'

'Well, we're paying a lot of money, and we expect results. Something needs to happen soon.'

'What's the rush?' Walter asked.

'Our boy is watching the needle sink. He's not happy. He's about to make some decisions that none of us want.'

Walter took a moment to grasp Brent's meaning. 'Are you saying he's thinking of dropping out of the race?'

'Better to bow out than to get beaten. Live to fight another day, you know? He'd rather see Diane win than Ramona Cortes.'

'When?'

'Depends on Chayla. He doesn't want to announce until we see what happens to the storm. Plus, we've been thinking that you'd be able to dig up something that would be worth sticking around for. That's why we called you, Walter. So what do you want me to tell him?'

Walter rubbed his grizzled beard. 'Tell him to hang tight. Don't do anything stupid.'

'What if there's nothing to find?' Brent asked.

'There's dirt,' Walter insisted. 'These guys made a mistake somewhere, and we're going to throw it in their faces. But it won't make any difference if he's already out of the game.'

The elevator doors opened on the sixth floor. Walter stamped outside. He had Stoli in his room, and he needed a drink. He was angry with Brent; he was angry with the idiots in Tallahassee. Politics. The years passed, and nothing changed. Every election was a race to the bottom.

Brent tapped the young girl on the shoulder and held the elevator open with one hand. She didn't take off her sunglasses, but she popped an earphone out of her ear. 'Huh?'

'I like your music,' Brent said.

'Whatever,' the girl replied. She replaced the earphone before

Brent could say anything more. Walter smiled, and Brent looked deflated. The girl was good with a brush-off.

The odd thing was, as the doors closed, Walter studied the girl and thought: *I've seen you before.*

Peach Piper tugged the black wig off her head and shoved it inside her satchel purse along with her iPod.

Her real hair was blond, cut super-short in a page-boy style that barely swished across her freckled forehead. She whipped off her sunglasses. Her eyes were Atlantic blue. She yanked her tank top over her head – no bra – unzipped her short-shorts and shivered in the elevator in nothing but purple bikini panties. Eyeing the elevator buttons, she dug a Magic Kingdom T-shirt and loose white cargo pants out of her purse and practically jumped into them. She replaced her flip-flops with Crocs and her cross earring with a big gold hoop.

When she was done, she grabbed a crushable nylon backpack from inside the purse, squeezed the purse and her clothes inside, and shrugged the backpack onto both shoulders just as the elevator doors opened on the tenth floor. A black woman and her young son boarded the elevator, and the boy looked at Peach and giggled and whispered to his mother. Peach realized that her cargo pants were unzipped, and she discreetly tugged the zipper up as she pushed the button to return to the lobby.

The doors opened on the sixth floor again to let on two more convention delegates. She noticed with fleeting concern that Walter Fleming and Brent Reed remained in the hotel hallway. Fleming's back was to her. That was good, because the old union boss was the one Peach was worried about. He was smart and observant. Brent Reed was just a moron. He looked right at her in the elevator, and Peach gave him a big toothy smile, and he was completely oblivious.

He hadn't recognized her from the bar the previous night, either, when she was a redhead in a little black dress. Or from the food truck near the riverfront, when she was a Marlins fan with a baseball cap and gold tracksuit.

Peach rode the elevator down and wandered through the lobby. She exited into the hot June afternoon, jogged across the street through traffic, and made her way two blocks to a small park by the river. It was a perfect day, or as perfect as Tampa got during the sweaty summer, with a blue sky and Gulf breeze. She sat down on a bench between the palm trees, steps from the green water, and retrieved the Sony voice recorder from the side pocket of her satchel purse and plugged in her headphones. Rewinding, she listened to the elevator conversation between Fleming and Reed.

Hey, sweetheart, rock me on the floor, okay? Man, that ass of yours could stop traffic.

Moron.

Peach ran through the recording three times and then dialed the office number for the Common Way Foundation. The foundation was headquartered in a high-rise bank building only a few blocks away, but Peach actually worked in the foundation's opposition research department, which was squeezed into unmarked offices on the seedy end of downtown. The phone rang, and her brother Deacon answered on the second ring.

'Hey, Fruity,' he said.

'Hey.'

'Where are you?'

'Near the river. I'm coming back.'

'How'd you do?'

'Stalking Reed finally paid off.'

'He didn't make you, did he?'

Peach didn't answer.

'Sorry, I know that's an insult,' Deacon said, and she could hear his smile. 'So what did you find out?'

'You better call Caprice and have her talk to Ms Fairmont.'

'They're already at the media schmooze-fest at Diane's house. Is it important?'

'Yeah, I think so. Walter Fleming is coming after us. I think he's got some kind of spy inside Common Way.'

'Well, we figured. Is that it?'

'No, there's more,' Peach said. 'Tell her the Governor is thinking about dropping out of the race.'

2

Cab Bolton watched from the second-floor balcony as Diane Fairmont put on her political face for the television interviewer. She looked at ease in the spotlight. Natural. Warm. Comfortable in her own skin. She sat in an ornate chair near the fringe of a pond in her Tampa mansion's hilly gardens. Huge lily pads floated on the green water. A white swan lazily floated behind her and stirred ripples on the surface. Makeup people hovered around Diane like flies, making sure her skin didn't sweat, making sure she had the right flush for the camera.

The interviewer, an Asian man in his twenties, gestured at the swan and said something that made Diane laugh. Her smile looked sincere, and her dark eyes glittered with intelligence. She was in her mid-fifties now, like Cab's mother. She wore her golden brown hair in a sensible bob, shiny but not showy. Simple pearl earrings, but no other jewelry. Her suit was dark – serious, reliable – but her blouse was light blue – friendly, inviting. She kept her hands neatly folded in her lap and her legs pressed together. The entire look had probably been poll-tested.

Cab was surprised at how easily Diane had adopted a public image, because the woman he knew from his past had been a lonely introvert, hiding her emotional wounds. He wondered if her new persona was an act, but he was willing to believe that people didn't always stay the same as they aged. It had been a long time since he'd seen her. Their paths hadn't crossed since he spent a week at Birch Fairmont's house in June ten years earlier, during the summer that changed everything.

The summer that ended on Labor Day in death and blood.

He leaned on the white stone balcony, which was framed by columns that graced the front of the estate. The gardens below were lush with palm trees, weeping willows, gnarled oaks, and overgrown saw palmettos. Bronze sculptures of herons and fish dotted the lawns, and fountains sprayed out of the ponds like canopies. Through the web of greenery, he could just see the asphalt of Bayshore Boulevard beyond the estate walls and the calm water of Hillsborough Bay. They were inside the urban boundary of the Tampa peninsula, but this was a private world, carefully secluded from outside view by a stone wall and thick, carefully pruned hedges.

Even so, politics demanded that Diane invite the media to a meet-and-greet. Voters needed to size up their future governor. Hence the dark suit and sensible heels and understated appearance. Hence the softball questions from sympathetic talk-show hosts about her years as a single mother with a checkbook to balance. Yes, she was rich now, but she hadn't always been rich, and her life had been marred by more than its share of tragedy.

'Champagne, darling?' a sparkling voice asked.

His mother appeared on the balcony, surprising him. Tarla never gave any warning before she dropped into his life. She just appeared and disappeared. They'd arrived separately that evening at Diane's gated estate. Cab had driven more than 150 miles along Florida's west coast from his home in the beach town of Naples. Tarla lived much closer to Diane, on the top floor of a Gulf coast condominium in Clearwater half an hour away. He'd been looking for her since he got to the party, but Tarla was good at not being found until she wanted to be found.

'Sure, why not?' Cab said.

He took a sip from the crystal flute that Tarla handed him. The champagne was superb: dry and effervescent. Diane could afford the best, and it didn't hurt to make the media people a little drunk while they asked their questions.

'Do you know why they call Florida the Sunshine State?' Tarla asked, with a wicked little arch of her blond eyebrows.

'Why?'

'Because "Waiting to Die" looked like crap on the license plates.'

Cab rolled his cornflower-blue eyes. 'Do you really want to be making jokes like that when your best friend is running for governor? The eighty-five million senior citizens around here might not appreciate your sense of humor the way I do.'

'I'm practically a senior citizen myself, darling.'

'Please,' Cab told her. 'You're fifty-five, and you look like Naomi Watts.'

'Well, aren't you sweet.'

He wasn't lying. Tarla had retired from the movie business several years earlier, but she still looked like a Hollywood star. In truth, so did he. Anyone could see they were mother and son: matching eyes, matching sun-bleached blond hair, both with sharp, angular faces. Cab was six-foot-six with a long neck that emphasized his height. He had a gangly walk, not always graceful but easy to remember. He kept his short hair gelled, making spikes that sometimes resembled a sea urchin's shell. His nose was shaped like a ski jump, and he had a baby-smooth complexion that always looked as if he'd just shaved. He wore a one-carat diamond in his left earlobe, and he was particular about his tailored suits even on the most humid Florida day.

He could blend in on Rodeo Drive or South Beach, but he didn't really fit in at most crime scenes. That didn't bother him. If people wanted to underestimate him because of his looks, it made his job easier. The trouble was, he knew that he really didn't belong in the police world, as many of his colleagues regularly reminded him. He wasn't sure if he belonged anywhere. At thirty-five, he was still figuring out what he wanted to be when he grew up.

'I appreciate your being my date tonight,' Tarla said.

Cab grinned. 'I wouldn't miss it. Politicians and reporters are my two favorite kinds of people after serial killers.'

'Sarcasm doesn't suit you, Cab.'

'And yet I stick with it,' he replied.

'It's only two and a half hours from Naples to Tampa. Not such a long drive.'

'More like two in the Corvette,' he admitted.

'Well, see? I don't feel guilty. Unless I'm stealing you away from a romantic weekend with Wawa.'

'It's Lala,' Cab said, 'and you're not.'

'Ah.' Tarla sipped her champagne and fixed her son with knowing eyes. Her blond hair, which had never sported a gray root in her entire life, tumbled around her shoulders in curls that were casually messy. 'Everything still rosy there?' she asked.

'We're fine. Sorry to disappoint you.'

'Did I say I didn't like her?'

'You didn't have to. She's Catholic, Cuban, and Republican.'

'I have no problem with Cubans, darling,' Tarla replied, smiling.

'We're fine,' he repeated. 'Lala got pulled into a special assignment. I haven't seen much of her lately. We talk on the phone now and then.'

'Oh well, phone sex has its place in the world.'

Cab rubbed his forehead in exasperation. 'Seriously, Mother?'

'I'm teasing, darling. My, you really are crabby tonight.'

He drank his champagne without replying. He wouldn't have admitted it to Tarla, but his relationship with Lala had been strained for weeks. Lala Mosqueda was his sometimes partner on the Naples Police and his sometimes lover. They'd begun a relationship several months earlier. Lala was not a casual fling and not into casual sex, and that was a terrifying prospect for someone like Cab who had spent a dozen years not trusting any woman who came close to him. They were opposites in almost every way: Lala small, dark, and intense, fiercely religious and conservative; Cab absurdly tall and bird-like, blond, and generally unserious about everything except his work. Particularly religion and politics.

Even so, the two felt an attraction like magnets and steel. In the spring, Cab had traveled to Door County, Wisconsin, for an ugly, difficult murder investigation, and he'd spent much of the time driving the remote dirt roads, talking to Lala on his cell phone and realizing how much he missed her. When he came back to Naples, they'd tried being a couple again, but their relationship had been one step forward, one step back. It didn't help that she'd been away from Naples and mostly out of touch for several weeks. It also didn't help that his liberal, Los Angeles mother couldn't understand the attraction between her Hollywood son and a right-wing Cuban cop.

'Do you really think I look like Naomi Watts?' Tarla asked.

'I do.'

'My breasts are bigger than hers,' his mother said. 'Of course, mine have had a little help along the way.'

'I try not to think about it,' Cab said.

'Give me your honest opinion. Which one's perkier tonight?'

'Pass,' he replied.

Tarla laughed, a throaty chuckle that had made moviegoers and co-stars go weak in the knees for thirty years. Her body was still pencil thin; she worked out with the same frenzy she had when she was on screen. She leaned in and whispered, 'You realize I'm kidding, right?'

'Yes, I do.'

'Fine, give me your glass, I will find us more alcohol.'

His mother disappeared with a swish of apricot satin. Cab shook his head, because Tarla was Tarla, and there was nothing he could do to change her. He was still getting used to the idea of having his mother back in his life. For years, she'd lived in Hollywood and then London, while he bounced from the FBI to the police to private investigative work and back to the police in locales from Barcelona to Rhode Island. His inability to stay put had earned him the nickname Catch-a-Cab Bolton. However, he'd endured the sweaty Gulf coast for more than two years now: partly because he was tired of running, partly because of Lala.

Three months ago, Tarla had concluded that Cab was finally putting down roots. She'd moved from London to Florida without so much as a phone call to warn him of her arrival. He'd still been on his investigation in Door County when she showed up at his condo to find Lala, nude, stepping out of his shower. Things had gone downhill from there between the two women in his life.

He liked having his mother close to him, but he was also glad that he had convinced her to buy a Gulf-shore condo not far from Diane, rather than her original plan, which was to locate herself in Cab's building in Naples. Two hours along I-75 between them was just about right. He also couldn't blame his mother for all the trouble between him and Lala. He'd done a good job of pushing her out of his life.

Cab watched Diane's television interviews going on in the garden below him. He couldn't hear any of the back-and-forth, but he knew it was all about politics, which to Cab was nothing more than the art of helping voters decide which candidate was the better liar. The young Asian host had finished, and another reporter – a woman with coal hair who made him think of Lala – was settling in to take her turn. In the pause, Diane's gaze wandered, and her eyes met his in the dusky space between the lawn and the balcony. Her composure broke for only a moment. Ten years – it had been ten years. She nodded at him and gave him the smallest smile. He returned the acknowledgment.

That was all; that was the moment he'd dreaded for so long.

'She's born for this, isn't she?'

He turned toward the voice, actually grateful for the interruption. A man joined him on the balcony. 'I'm sorry?' Cab said.

'Diane. She's so smooth with the press. I told her she should have jumped into the race ten years ago. She would have won in a landslide. Who knows where she'd be now? Hell, maybe the White House.'

'Her husband had just been murdered,' Cab pointed out.

'Well, sure, that's my point. She was a shoo-in.'

The man craned his neck to stare up at Cab. Most people did. The man on the balcony was smaller by a foot, and he was forty but trying hard not to look more than thirty. His jet-black hair was tied in a long ponytail. He bulged with muscles, and he had a saddle-brown Florida tan. He was dressed in a black T-shirt, pastel green sport coat, white pants, and Topsiders with no socks. The big red button on his coat read, 'Governor Diane.'

'I know you, right?' the man said. 'You're Tarla's son, the detective.'

'That's me.'

'Garth Oakes,' the man told him, jutting out a hand. He had a rock-hard grip. 'I'm an entrepreneur. Fitness videos. You've probably seen my ads on TV. *Beat The Girth . . . With Garth!*'

Sometimes, living in Florida, Cab found himself wandering into a Carl Hiaasen novel. 'Sorry, I don't watch a lot of television.'

'Hey, well, never mind. If everybody looked like you, I wouldn't have a business, right?' Garth cradled a mug of herbal tea in his hand, with the string of the tea bag dribbling down the side. Cab smelled cinnamon and clove. 'I remember you from the bad old days in Lake Wales. You visited Birch's place that summer, right? You're like a giraffe, who can forget that.'

'Most people say I'm more like a heron,' Cab replied.

'A heron. Yeah, funny. I see it. Anyway, I was around there a lot back then. I did massages and workouts for Diane a few times a week. Part-exercise, part-therapy. Me and her, we're close. She really needed someone to talk to, you know? First there was Birch, and then she lost Drew a year later. One-two punch. That was rough, huh?'

'No doubt.'

'Me, I think it was worse losing her son than it was when Birch died. She spent hours crying on my shoulder. When she wasn't crying, she was talking about taking down the fucking drug dealers. Make 'em pay. You don't want to see that lady angry, I'm telling you. Not like I'm saying she wasn't upset about Birch. I mean, your husband gets murdered, that's a terrible thing, but Diane and Birch – well . . .' His voice trailed off.

'I don't think Diane would be too happy to hear you talking like this, Garth,' Cab pointed out.

'Oh, hey, just between us boys, right? Diane and Tarla are besties. I figure you're in on all of this crap.'

Cab put a hand on the man's shoulder. The fabric of the green sport coat felt cheap, like a thirty-dollar knock-off from a big box store. If Garth was selling fitness videos, he wasn't selling many of them. 'Excuse me, I have to go find my mother.'

'Yeah, sure, good talking to you.'

Cab left Garth on the balcony, sipping his tea and standing with his legs spread apart, like he owned the mansion. Inside, he found himself in a marble-floored hallway that stretched the length of the house. Double-wide doors led to a master bedroom. Diane's room. She had purchased the bayside mansion a few years earlier, when she moved from the small inland town of Lake Wales to the large coastal city of Tampa. There were too many memories in Lake Wales, she'd told Tarla. She associated the town with her childhood, with Birch's murder, with Drew's suicide. In Tampa, she could start fresh, in an estate a short drive from the Common Way Foundation headquarters. The foundation, launched with millions donated in the wake of Birch's assassination, had been the center of her life for a decade.

He stood in the doorway, spying on her suite. The artwork, the bedding, the heavy red wallpaper, all showed tropical birds. An overhead skylight cast a circle of light on the bed. There was no clutter in the room and nothing personal except for a photograph on the baroque nightstand of Diane's son Drew and another photo from childhood of Diane with Cab's mother. He saw no photograph of Birch Fairmont.

Cab headed for the end of the hallway, where white-carpeted stairs led to the first floor. As he descended the steps, he found himself face to face with an attractive woman heading in the opposite direction. She had alabaster skin and long, highlighted chestnut hair. Her face brightened as she saw him.

'Mr Bolton, there you are,' she said.

'Here I am.'

'Your mother said you were upstairs. I've been looking for you.'

Cab smiled warily. 'Oh?'

'My name is Caprice Dean. I'm the executive director of

the Common Way Foundation. Tarla probably mentioned that I wanted to speak to you tonight.'

'Actually, she didn't,' Cab said, 'but I'm usually the last to know when it comes to my mother.'

Caprice laughed. 'I understand how that goes.'

'What can I do for you, Ms Dean?'

'As it happens,' Caprice said, 'I want to hire you.'

They sat in a gazebo in the gardens, where the foliage made a quiet grove. Cab had counted at least fifty people in and around the estate, but the trail that led here was hidden from prying eyes. They both had champagne, fizzing with bubbles. The octagonal shelter was open to the air and situated in the flow of a damp bay breeze. Fountain grass bowed between the pillars.

'It's beautiful, isn't it?' Caprice said. 'It's so secluded here. That's what Diane likes about it. You could believe the city doesn't exist at all. Mind you, the barbarians are inside the gate tonight.'

'You mean the media?' Cab asked.

'Obviously,' she replied with a smirk.

'Well, if Diane values her isolation so much, why did she run for governor?' he asked. 'Politicians don't have a zone of privacy anymore. She knows that.'

Caprice nodded. 'You're right. It's open season on candidates these days. Honestly, we argued about it for a long time. I didn't think she should do it. I thought we should recruit someone else to be in the spotlight.'

'So why did she?' He smiled. 'I assume it wasn't solely the counsel of Garth Oakes.'

Caprice laughed. 'You've met Garth, have you? I'm not a fan, but Diane likes him. No, the campaign was Diane's call all the way. She felt it was her responsibility to lead the ticket.'

'Why were you opposed?' Cab asked.

'Oh, don't get me wrong. I thought we should be in the race, too. We've spent ten years at the foundation advancing our agenda from the outside. Influencing the debate. Supporting and opposing specific candidates. Now we're ready to get into the game.'

'In other words, the Governor is politically weak this year, and you hate the idea of a staunch conservative like Attorney General Cortes landing in Tallahassee.'

'That's true, too,' she acknowledged.

'Diane is ahead in the polls,' Cab pointed out. 'Isn't that a good thing?'

'It is, but there are also crazies who want to paint a target on her chest. Just like Birch.'

'You think she's at risk?'

'I do. That's why we'd like your help.'

'Oh? What kind of help?'

Caprice didn't answer right away. She pushed her champagne glass in a small circle on the marble table between them. A ringlet of lush brown hair fell across her forehead, and she brushed it back. Her eyes examined him curiously. 'You know, Tarla warned me about you.'

'Did she?'

'Yes, she said you were the least ideological person on the face of the earth.'

'Guilty,' Cab said.

'So you don't understand.'

'Understand what?'

'Why all of this matters.'

She said it intensely, with a serious face. She was passionate, just like Lala. He wondered why he found himself drawn to women who were so different from himself. Women who wore their hearts on their sleeve. Women who followed a cause with flags held high. Cab was nothing like that, but Caprice was obviously a true believer, and the truth was, he found her very attractive.

It was partly her looks. Younger, she would have been pretty; mature, nearing forty, she was beautiful. She had a smooth, soft face and dark, inquisitive eyes. He liked the whiteness of her skin, which was so un-Floridian. She was obviously comfortable with her body, which was fleshy in an erotic way, not stick skinny. She wore a midnight-blue dress that afforded a view of her strong legs well above her knees and of the swelling curves of her full breasts. She had an open, unflinching stare, not at all shy, not girly or cute. Her directness was as appealing to him as her physical features.

'It's not that I don't care,' Cab said.

'You just think all politicians are the same.'

'Exactly.'

'Well, we're not.' Caprice stood up and moved to the opposite side of the gazebo. Her movements had grace. She turned around, leaning back on the stone ledge. 'I was a political science major at UCF. I hated both parties, and I still do. They're all about ideology, not common sense. My boyfriend, Lyle, he felt the same way. We were both ambitious. We committed ourselves to the idea of an independent, centrist party that would truly compete against the Republicans and Democrats, not simply be a spoiler movement. With Birch's campaign, we thought we had taken the first step.'

'I'm sorry. I know what you lost that day.'

'With all due respect, Mr Bolton, you don't. I'm sure your mother told you what we went through on that dais, but you can't understand what it's really like to lose someone you love, to stand there covered in his blood and brains.'

Cab didn't reply. This wasn't a game of tit-for-tat, but in reality, he had lost someone he loved in a violent way, too. On a beach outside Barcelona, he had come face to face with a woman named Vivian Frost. He had never fallen so naively head-over-heels in love with anyone like Vivian, and he knew he never would again. He'd given up everything for her, including his job with the FBI, only to discover that she was partnered with a terrorist – that she'd been part of a conspiracy that led to the deaths of twenty-seven people in a bombing at a Spanish train station. She'd lied to him. Manipulated him.

There, on the beach, he'd shot her in the heart.

He knew what loss was like.

'Something like that changes you,' he said, joining her on the other side of the gazebo.

'Yes, it does,' Caprice agreed. 'Diane and I started the Common Way Foundation that same year. The violence outraged people around the country, and they supported us financially. The assassination was an attempt to silence what Lyle and Birch tried to do, and the foundation honored them and their principles. We stayed outside the process, but we took sides. We put a thumb on the scale. We pushed candidates and policy, and we didn't hesitate to rip both parties for their unwillingness to tell the truth. We learned our lesson.'

'Which was?'

'Play hardball,' Caprice said.

'Hardball. Is that why you hired a dirty tricks specialist like Ogden Bush for Diane's campaign?' Cab smiled and added: 'I may not be political, but I do read the papers, you know.'

Caprice winced at the man's name. 'Ogden was Diane's choice, not mine.'

'Still, he's a Democrat with a reputation for running fiercely negative campaigns, isn't he? Doesn't that fly in the face of your "we're not all the same" speech?'

'I suppose you could say that,' she agreed. 'Ogden fell out with the Dems a couple years ago, so he sells himself to the highest bidder. He was helpful to us on voting rights legislation last year. I didn't think we wanted him on the campaign, but Diane thought he could help her make inroads with liberal voters. In politics, we can't always be particular about who we sleep with.'

She leaned closer to him. Their shoulders brushed together.

'So what do you need me for?' he asked.

'I told you, Mr Bolton, I want to hire you.'

'Call me Cab,' he said.

Caprice's face softened. 'Okay. That's an unusual name. Why Cab?'

'Tarla was in a deli eating stuffed cabbage when her water broke.'

'How cute. Is that true?'

Cab smiled but didn't reply. He had no idea what was true. Tarla had never told him. Just like she had never told him who his father was. He'd made up stories over the years to fill in the gaps.

'You don't look much like any detective I've ever met,' Caprice went on. 'Do most Naples detectives have spiky hair like that?'

'It's a pomade from London.'

'I like it. The diamond earring?'

'A gift from a wealthy older woman.'

'And how tall are you? Eight feet?'

'About that.'

'Your suit looks like it costs what I make in a month at the foundation.'

'About that.'

'You don't apologize for having money, do you?'

'No. It is what it is. Tarla's wealthy, and she made me wealthy, which means I can do whatever I want. In my case, that usually means dealing with people doing ugly things.'

'Which is why I want to hire you.'

'I already have a job,' Cab said.

'Actually, I talked to your lieutenant in Naples. He didn't seem too upset to let me borrow you for a while.'

'I don't imagine he would be. He doesn't think I look much like a detective, either. Unfortunately, talking to my lieutenant behind my back makes me inclined to say no to whatever you have in mind. I don't like being manipulated, Ms Dean. That may be how things work at the Common Way Foundation, but it doesn't work with me.'

'Hear me out,' Caprice said, with a soft grip on his arm as he turned to leave. Her fingers were warm.

Cab shrugged. 'What do you want?'

'Diane's in jeopardy. I'm worried someone's planning another assassination attempt.'

'Hire a bodyguard.'

'I have.'

'So why do you need me?'

'I want you to find out what really happened ten years ago,' Caprice said, 'and whether it could happen again.'

'The FBI concluded that a right-wing militia group was behind the assassination. Its leader, Hamilton Brock, is in prison.'

'For tax fraud,' Caprice said, 'not for murder. No one talked, and they never determined exactly who pulled the trigger. The militia is alive and well even with Brock behind bars. You think he can't direct things from inside his cell?'

'Talk to the police. The FBI.'

'I've done that, and they're looking into it. However, one thing I've learned at the foundation is that we get better results when we do things ourselves. I don't want third parties I can't control. I want my own man.'

'You think you can control me?' Cab asked.

'I'd like to try,' Caprice replied, with a double entendre that neither of them missed.

Cab felt heat on the back of his dress shirt. 'I don't do security.'

'Security's not what I want. I want to know who wore that hood and pulled the trigger. Who killed Birch and Lyle? That's the only way we can stop them.'

'You're talking about digging into a ten-year-old crime after a massive investigation turned up nothing,' Cab said. 'There were no witnesses. There was no gun, no DNA. The militia stonewalled. This man was a ghost. I'm not sure why you think I'd be able to make inroads where the FBI failed. Besides, you're making a big leap. If there really is a credible threat against Diane today, chances are it has nothing to do with the past.'

'Sometimes it takes fresh eyes to see clearly, Cab. And I'm not wrong about the threat.' Caprice carried a satin clutch that matched her dress. She undid the clasp and reached inside. She withdrew a folded piece of paper and handed it to Cab. 'This arrived at the foundation last week.'

Cab unfolded the paper. It was a copy of a newspaper article from ten years earlier, featuring a photograph taken at the Bok Sanctuary in the wake of the murders. He saw bodies prone on the dais. Police. Shell-shocked survivors, including his mother, Diane, and Caprice, all of them ten years younger and ten years more innocent.

Someone had written across the photograph in a blood-red marker.

I'm back. Miss me?

3

City of Tampa.

The mural, like an oversized picture postcard, was painted on the brick wall of an ad agency building across the alley between Franklin and Florida Avenues in the northwest corner of downtown. Peach saw it every day when she squeezed her two-tone 1980s-era Thunderbird into spot 52. Each block letter spelling out the city's name featured a cartoon rendering of a different local tourist attraction. The Sulphur Springs Water Tower. The Plant Museum.

Places she'd never found time to visit.

The window was open, letting in the heavy evening air, making her clothes damp. Peach didn't mind; she hated the cold and loved the heat, even during the ferocious summer days. She stared at the mural, wondering why she'd never visited the Plant Museum in the years she'd lived here. Justin had told her once that the bronze sculpture of the Spinning Girl inside the museum looked like her, with her hair cut way up her forehead, her far-away eyes, and her breasts as shallow as Florida hills. She figured she should go see the sculpture sometime and see if it spoke to her. Maybe, in another life, she'd been the artist's model. Peach was a firm believer in reincarnation.

She left the engine running and turned on her radio. She hadn't felt like listening to music these past two weeks, but she could go for some Train or Bruno Mars or even Adele, although she was pretty much over Adele now. She punched the channel for the satellite pop blend, but instead of her sad songs, she heard some awful, screechy opera in a language that was probably German or Russian, where the words needed a lot of spit.

Justin.

Justin with his Beethoven T-shirts. He'd switched the channels on her radio again, and she was only finding out now. *I'm telling you, Peach, there's not a note of music worth listening to that was written after 1849.*

She shut off the radio and got out of the car. Next to her T-Bird, in spot 51, was a ten-year-old silver Mercedes SL convertible. For its age, it was in perfect condition, washed every week, sporty engine purring at eighty miles an hour on the back roads. Her brother Deacon babied it, just the way their older brother Lyle had. She ran the pad of her little finger along the chassis. Smooth. Lyle would have been pleased that the two of them still owned the car.

He'd only owned it for a month before . . .

Before.

Peach had been thinking about the past again. She'd been reminded two weeks ago how many people had been stripped out of her life. At age eight, she'd been orphaned when her parents died on a missionary trip in Colombia. At age twelve, she felt as if she'd been orphaned again when a soldier of the Liberty Empire Alliance gunned down her oldest brother Lyle, along with Birch Fairmont.

Now she was twenty-two, although people usually mistook her for a teenager. Now it had happened again. Another death. Another loss.

Peach felt numb.

She peered down the city streets. It was early evening, but it was June 29, a Friday, and it would still be light for hours. The streets weren't busy. There wasn't anything to bring out the after-work crowd in this sleepy section of the city. By habit, she checked the windows and balconies in the nearby apartment buildings to see if anyone was watching her. Deacon said she was paranoid, but she couldn't stop. When she decided she was alone, she veered across the parking lot to the office door.

The location of CWF Research was a drab, mostly windowless building with a brown metal roof. Half the building was vacant. The rest of the space was taken up by a cubicle farm owned by the foundation. She let herself in through double-wide doors on the side of the building facing Florida Street, only a block from the 275 freeway. The number was 1100, but the last zero had slipped sideways, making it look like an eye examining the traffic.

Peach hated being in the office. The space was claustrophobic, with dirty white paint on the walls. She didn't like being inside, sitting at a desk, making phone calls, clicking keys on a laptop. She liked the old ways of doing things. Paper. Film. At home, she didn't even use a computer or a tablet.

Once anything about you is digitized, you don't own it anymore. Soon you don't even own yourself. Justin.

She wanted to be where the people were. There was safety in numbers. She was desperately shy and had no real friends, but she liked watching people, studying them, analyzing them, listening to them. That was what she did best. Humint, Deacon called it. Human intelligence. Peach was their oppo girl. She was the one they sent when they needed someone who could blend into a crowd and come back with evidence of what their enemies were saying.

Peach didn't like thinking of other people as enemies, but that was what they were. They had proven that over and over again.

Inside the office, she stared over the beige fabric walls of the cubicles. She heard the cacophony of voices and the rattle of keys. It was campaign season, and everyone worked late. She followed the building wall toward her brother's office. The wall was taped over with news about politicians and policies. It was a low-tech bulletin board where researchers shared information that didn't necessarily make it online. Gaffes. Issues. Photographs. Things they could use against people.

She flopped down in Deacon's guest chair and rocked nervously back and forth. Her brother sat in front of his computer, and his fingers flew.

'Hey,' she said.

'Hey, good job today. You got the recorder?'

Peach reached into her pocket and handed him the Sony voice recorder that she'd used with Walter Fleming and Brent Reed.

'I'll run it through Dragon and get it back to you,' Deacon said.

'Uh-huh.'

'I talked to Caprice. She said to keep the lid on the news. She thinks if the story about the Governor breaks too early, it'll force him to deny it and stay in the race.'

'Duh.'

'You going back to the convention tomorrow?'

'Yeah, probably. I don't have anything else to do.'

Deacon stopped working and stared at his sister. 'Look, why don't you knock off for the day? Go home. Forget about the weekend. Someone else can cover it.'

'I don't know. Maybe.'

'Did you eat?'

'I had half a salad.'

'You need to eat.'

'Whatever,' Peach said. 'I'm not hungry.'

'I know you're upset.'

'I'm not upset. I'm nothing. That's what bugs me, you know? I don't feel a thing, and I don't know what to do about it.'

'I told you, go home,' Deacon said. 'Get some sleep. Or go work out. Go for a run.'

'Maybe,' she said again. 'You going home soon?'

'Later. I want to hit the gym.'

Deacon worked out every day. It was the only way to get past the stress of politics. He was skinny and strong, but he had a soft-edged face with unruly red hair and bedroom-blue eyes. He was a dead ringer for their father. Same long nose with a little hook. Same dreamy smile. He rarely shaved, giving him a stubbly strawberry beard. Women really went for Deacon. At the gym, girls homed in on him as if there were some kind of pheromone in his sweat. He never got serious about anyone, though. The two of them were all about work.

They'd lived together since Lyle was killed. Back then, Lyle had been their surrogate father. She and Deacon hadn't really been close during those years, because Deacon was an angry kid after their parents died. Angry at them. Angry at Lyle. Angry at the world. To Deacon, who was six years older, Peach was an annoying little girl, and he was a teenager with better things to do. That changed after Labor Day. At age eighteen, with money they inherited from Lyle, he bought a little house in Tampa, and Peach moved in with him. Caprice hired him to work at the new foundation. When Peach turned eighteen four years ago, she joined the foundation, too.

'Go on,' Deacon repeated. 'I'll see you at home. Make some tater tots or something.'

'Yeah, okay. See you later.'

Peach pushed herself out of the chair and navigated the maze to her own cubicle. The desk was uncluttered, and the monitor was dusty. There wasn't even a calendar on the cubicle wall. She had three photographs pinned up with thumbtacks. One was of Lyle next to his new Mercedes, in August of that last summer, looking fussy and proud. The other was of Deacon, two years back, on a Sunday outing to Honeymoon Island on the Gulf. Sunglasses, no shirt, tanned and fit. The last picture showed a man not much older than herself, with a pork pie hat, a handlebar mustache like a cartoon train robber, and a mock scowl for the camera. He was tall and beanpole skinny, with arms folded across his scrawny chest. He wore baggy jeans and a T-shirt showing *The Scream*.

Justin.

She got up and went to the next cubicle and sat down in his chair. There was nothing in the small space to remind her of him anymore. They'd taken everything away. The computer was new. The drawers were empty. They'd even removed the poster of Mozart on the wall and the kitten calendar she'd given him for Christmas. All that was left was his voice in her head.

Justin on Florida. *It's the cockroach capital of America. And there are lots of bugs, too.*

Justin on money. *My parents have money, and they're the unhappiest people you'll ever meet. They keep sending me money, because they want me to be unhappy, too.*

Justin on poetry. *The greatest poem ever is Blake's 'The Tyger.'*

Justin on sex. *Nothing screws up love faster than sex. So if we never have sex, we'll always be in love.*

They never had sex.

'Hello?'

Peach looked up when a voice interrupted her memories. A Hispanic woman in her mid-thirties stood in the opening of the cubicle. She held a cup of coffee in her hand and wore black glasses that looked straight out of Clark Kent and the 1950s.

'Who are you?' Peach asked.

The woman didn't have time to answer, because someone else appeared behind her and nudged her into the background the way an actor occupies center stage. The frown on Peach's face deepened.

'Oh, Peach, there are you,' Ogden Bush announced. 'Congratulations, I heard about your coup with Walter and Brent today.'

'You did?'

Bush smiled. He had the arrogant smile of a wolf living among chickens. 'I hear about everything. That's my job.'

His job was to direct opposition research for Diane's campaign. Target the Republicans. Target the Democrats. Plant media stories. Craft negative ads. He'd spent two months inside the building since Diane formally announced her candidacy. The activities of the political foundation had been unofficially swallowed up by the activities of the campaign, and they were squeezed together in the same space. Bush had hired his own staff who worked side-by-side with Peach, Deacon, and the other foundation employees. The political operative had his hand in everything now.

Peach didn't like him, but she didn't like many people. *We are alone, Peach. Alone and on our own.* Justin.

Ogden Bush had no allegiance to Diane or the foundation. He was a hired hand who followed the money. Ten years before, he'd been on the opposite side of the fence, working for the liberal Democrat against Birch Fairmont. Now he was on Diane's side, because she was the one paying the bills. Bush was clever and tough, but Peach didn't trust people who went where the wind blew.

He wasn't tall for a man, barely five-foot-nine, and he'd just turned forty. He had ebony skin. A generous-sized ruby ring adorned one finger. His coal eyes had the sharpness of a hawk that missed nothing, but he also had a way of looking through her, not at her, as if she were no more than prey. He kept a thin, neat mustache on his upper lip and a trimmed chin curtain along the pointed line of his face. His black hair was shaved short, with smudges of gray above both ears. He wore suits a size too small to emphasize his sleek, toned body. The suits were expensive and fashionable, because he wanted everyone to know how successful he was.

'People only pay attention to you if they know you can do something to them,' he'd told Peach when they first met. 'Good or bad, it doesn't matter.'

Bush squeezed the shoulder of the woman in the cubicle doorway. 'This is my newest researcher, Annalie Martine. Take her with you to the convention tomorrow. I'd like her in on the humint side of things.'

'I work alone,' Peach said.

'Take her with you,' Bush repeated, ignoring her protest. 'She'll be a quick study. She's got great references.'

Peach said nothing. She hated being paired with strangers. Bush knew it, but he didn't care.

'I figured Brent Reed's mouth would trip him up sooner or later,' Bush went on, his voice honey-smooth. 'What about Walter Fleming? Did he say anything of interest?'

'He talked about you,' Peach said.

'Oh?'

'He was concerned about you figuring out what he was doing. I think he's got a spy somewhere inside the campaign.'

'Well, that would be Walter's style,' Bush said. 'Don't worry, he's a crafty goat, but I know how he operates. Anyway, show Annalie the ropes, okay? I'm counting on you, Peach.'

Bush disappeared as his phone began to ring, and the musky cloud of his cologne went with him. Annalie gave Peach an apologetic smile. She looked uncomfortable. 'Sorry to drop in on you like this.'

Peach shrugged. 'Whatever.'

'Um.'

'What?' Peach asked, but then she realized she was sitting in Justin's chair and that Justin's chair now belonged to this new woman. This stranger. 'Sorry,' she said, getting up.

'No problem.'

Annalie didn't sit down. They stood in the cramped space together, barely two feet apart, eye to eye. They were the same height. Peach was skinny, but Annalie had curves under her black T-shirt and jeans. She would have looked younger and hotter if she'd lost the glasses and untied her black hair from the severe bun that was pulled back behind her head. She was pretty, with mellow golden skin and smoky eyes, but she wasn't trying to be attractive.

'I know it's hard when new people get dropped on you,' Annalie said. 'I'm lucky to be here. I need the job.'

'Ogden said you had hotshot references,' Peach said.

'Well, my father works for a big foundation donor.'

'You ever done oppo work before?' Peach asked.

'Sort of. I worked for a woman who did private detective work in Jacksonville. You know, cheating hubbies and stuff.'

'On the street or in the office?'

'A little of both.'

'You must have guts to take this job,' Peach said. 'You're not afraid that it's cursed or something?'

Annalie cocked her head. 'Cursed? I don't get it.'

'Ogden didn't tell you about the guy you're replacing?'

'No, he just said a position opened up on the research team. I figured the last guy quit or was fired or something.'

'He didn't quit,' Peach said. 'He didn't get fired. Justin was murdered two weeks ago.'

4

The sun sank into the Gulf waters, and Cab expected it to sizzle like an egg hitting a hot frying pan. The Florida sunsets never got old. The strips of clouds turned as pink as cut roses, and the sandbars took on rainbow colors. He cast his eyes down from the twentieth floor toward the white sand of Clearwater Beach. Swimmers and shell-hunters stood up to their ankles in the hot water, silhouetted by the sun. Around them, umbrellas dotted the beach like drips of bright paint.

He pulled out his phone and dialed Lala Mosqueda's number. The call went to voicemail, the way it always did lately. He'd left several messages. She hadn't returned them.

'Wawa?' said his mother. Tarla stood in the doorway between the sliding glass doors, still in the dress she'd worn to Diane's party.

'That stopped being funny a long time ago,' Cab said.

'I'm sorry, you're right.' His mother joined him on the balcony, leaning her bare elbows on the railing. The warm breeze off the water rustled her hair. 'So what does she call me? The Hollywood witch?'

'It rhymes with that,' Cab said.

'Well, good for her,' Tarla said, smiling. She added, as if she were checking on whether he wanted his coffee black: 'Are you in love with her, or is it just the sex?'

'Next subject.'

'Oh come on, darling.'

'I wasn't born with the love gene,' Cab told her, which was a lie. He'd been wildly in love with Vivian Frost in Barcelona. 'However, I'm also not into meaningless cheap flings.'

'I detect a little bit of an accusation in that statement.'

'Maybe you do.'

In his lifetime, he couldn't remember his mother seriously involved with anyone. She'd drifted from affair to affair, and she'd broken up more than one marriage. He loved his mother, but there were days when he didn't always like her. She was beautiful, and she was a loner, and he blamed her sometimes for making him the way he was.

In other words, he was a lot like her.

'I'm not trying to split the two of you up,' Tarla said. 'If you want to make it work with Lala, make it work. However, let's be honest, darling. I saw you with Caprice Dean this evening. There were sparks flying.'

'She's attractive. That's all it is.'

'Is that a sin? I've known Caprice for years. She's pretty, smart, serious, and she's going places. If Diane wasn't running this year, Caprice probably would, and as young as she is, I think she'd win. That's the kind of woman you belong with, Cab.'

'I really don't need romantic advice from you, Mother,' he said. 'Did you know Caprice wanted me to do investigative work for her when you asked me to come up this weekend?'

'She may have mentioned it,' Tarla said.

'So you lured me here under false pretenses.'

'Would you have come otherwise? Besides, this way I get to see you. I didn't leave London for the cultural life of Clearwater. The seafood is wonderful, and the boys on the beach are cute, but otherwise, it's a bit of a wasteland. I'm here because of you, Cab. Unless you'd prefer I go away.'

'I didn't say that,' Cab replied. 'I'm glad you're here.'

He wondered if that was completely true. They'd always had a close but co-dependent relationship, and sometimes he rebelled against it. Growing up, he had travelled with Tarla to movie sets all over the world, and although he had met famous people and stayed in amazing places, he felt homeless, as if he had no roots. Tarla was also intensely private, shutting him out from parts of her life, including the truth about his father. He'd learned to do the same. When he had a chance to leave, he did. At eighteen, he went to UCLA, graduated in three years, and to his mother's shock, he chose law enforcement when he could have chosen acting. She'd been prepared to find roles and open doors for him, but he didn't want the Hollywood life.

Now she was retired. Now they were together again, after nearly twenty years in different corners of the world. It was like starting over.

He turned and went inside. The condominium was ice-cold compared to the summer heat. He hadn't been to Tarla's place in several weeks, and she'd been decorating in the interim. The sprawling apartment looked like her. Cool. Modern. Expensive. It wasn't a place where you would sit down and put your feet up.

Tarla joined him from the balcony. She went to the bar and poured herself a glass of wine, and she held up the bottle with an inquiring glance. He shook his head. She drank more than he remembered.

'So why is Diane running for governor?' Cab asked. 'You always told me she didn't want to get her hands dirty. She wanted to work behind the scenes.'

Tarla shrugged. 'I'm not sure her heart is in it, but she saw an opportunity and couldn't say no. The Governor has been wounded by the kickback scandal involving his chief of staff. Ramona Cortes, the Republican, is another scary right-winger.'

'Ramona's not really so scary,' Cab said mildly.

Tarla's eyebrows arched toward heaven. 'You've met her?'

'She's one of Lala's cousins,' he said. 'One of about two hundred or so.'

'Charming. Well, Diane was getting pressure from foundation donors to get in the race to block her. They're afraid if Ramona becomes governor, she might decide to nuke Oklahoma.'

Cab smiled. 'Extremes are in the eye of the beholder. Do you really believe in the virginal purity of the Common Way Party?'

'Me? I'm a wild-eyed, woolly tree-hugger, you know that. A Democrat's Democrat. But Diane is my best friend, and she'd make a good governor. I believe that.'

Cab said nothing.

'I know you don't like her,' Tarla added, 'although I don't know why.'

'That's not true.'

His mother sat down next to him on a sofa that was black and umber, with striped hexagonal pillows. 'You've ducked every occasion where she and I were together. You didn't even come to Drew's funeral, though I basically ordered you to be there.'

'That was nine years ago, and I was busy with a murder investigation in Newport. I sent flowers.'

'Yes, how thoughtful,' Tarla snapped. 'Drew shot himself, for God's sake. Diane was hysterical. She tracked down that awful drug dealer in a bar and had to be physically restrained from attacking him.'

'I remember,' Cab said.

'I'm just saying, Diane has lived a life that's far more difficult than you or I have ever had to deal with. You don't have a clue of what she's gone through, Cab. She's a good person, and I want to support her in any way I can. If you can help, I wish you would.'

'I told Caprice I would look into it,' Cab said.

'You did?'

'I did.'

Tarla drank her wine and flushed a little with embarrassment. 'Oh. Well, good. Thank you.'

'I already have an appointment with Chuck Warren in the morning.'

'The fascist?'

Cab smiled. 'Not all Republicans are fascists.'

'Warren is.'

'Well, he was the Republican candidate for the Congressional seat ten years ago. After Birch was killed, he got tarred for being too cozy with right-wing extremists. I'd like to see what he says about what happened back then.'

'You really think he'll tell you the truth?' Tarla asked.

'No, but lies are more interesting. I usually learn more from lies than I do from the truth.'

'You live in a strange world, Cab.'

'No stranger than yours,' he said.

'True.' His mother smiled, but then her face darkened. 'Do you think Diane is in any danger?'

'I don't know. Threats to political candidates are dime-a-dozen, but this one is pretty specific.'

'Caprice thinks whoever killed Birch may be focused on Diane,' Tarla said.

'What do you think?'

'Me? I have no idea. How would I know?'

'You were there,' Cab said.

Tarla stood up and refilled her wine at the bar. 'I don't think you should waste your time on the past. Ten years is a long time ago. I doubt there's any connection.'

Cab joined her at the bar. 'You've never told me much about what happened to you that night.'

'I don't remember it,' she said. She pulled away from him, and the casualness in her voice was unconvincing. She was a bad actress when she played herself. 'I fainted, Cab. I woke up in the hospital. The night was erased from my brain.'

'You were inches away from the killer. Closer than anyone else who survived.'

'I don't remember him,' Tarla insisted. 'People tell me I protected Diane, but I don't even remember doing that.'

He kissed the top of his mother's head. 'I'm sorry. I know it must have been awful for you.'

Cab didn't push her for answers, because Tarla wasn't a person who could be pushed. If you poked her, she shrank like a turtle deeper into her shell. He also knew that his old axiom was right again. You could learn more from lies than you ever could from the truth.

Tarla was lying.

There was something about that night that she didn't want him to know.

5

The deer sprang out of nowhere, like a monster from the closet. It wasn't there, and then it was.

Peach gasped in surprise, and her foot dove for the brake. The Thunderbird jerked to a stop, throwing her against the safety belt. The young doe, momentarily frozen, stared curiously into the car's headlights, and when Peach switched the lights off, she saw its spindly legs clip-clop casually between the trees toward the lake.

See the little white cross? she'd told Justin on their weekend getaway to Lake Wales last month. *You have to be careful when you drive here.*

Peach closed her eyes.

When she touched her hands to her face, she realized she was crying. She pushed open the car door and climbed out into the darkness, her knees buckling. She grabbed the door to steady herself, then took uneasy steps into the grass. Insects descended on her, buzzing and biting. She looked around for the deer, but it had already disappeared toward the water. Her feet were wet. She imagined for a moment that she was standing in blood, but when she looked down at the dirt and pine needles, she saw that it was just rain pooled on the ground from an afternoon squall.

Peach was alone on the sprawling trails of Lake Seminole Park. She and Deacon lived in a pink bungalow on 98th Street in Seminole, which was a straight shot across the Gandy Bridge as she headed west out of Tampa. Their house, where they'd lived for ten years, was on the other side of the fence that marked the park's eastern border. She wasn't supposed to be in the park at night, but the security guards all knew who she was. To them, she was Peach Paranoid, but she was also the girl who had lost her parents in Colombia and her oldest brother in the Labor Day shooting. Let her be paranoid. Let her park wherever she wanted.

She didn't like to have her car seen at her house. She didn't want anyone knowing who she was or where she lived. Instead, she drove the T-Bird to the very end of the park's paved roads, near deserted picnic grounds. Twenty yards away, a sidewalk led to an open gate in the fence. She got out and slipped between the squat palm trees. She heard rustling and cackling from a brood of chickens that wandered in and out of the park from a nearby hobby farm. A peacock screamed not far away. She ducked through the gate and hugged the fence for another block until she was across the street from their house.

Overgrown oaks crowded the roof. The house dated to the 1960s and was surrounded by a warped wooden fence that Deacon was always promising to fix. The roof needed help, too; it was missing shingles from the last big storm, and it leaked over the toilet in her bathroom, dripping on her head. A sign warned trespassers against dogs, but they had never owned a dog. She didn't see the Mercedes in the driveway, and she didn't expect Deacon for hours.

She let herself inside. The house smelled of the fish she'd microwaved for dinner the previous night. The two of them weren't the best housekeepers, especially during campaign season. Junk mail and newspapers filled the counters and tabletops. The open wooden surfaces were gray with dust. Rather than turn on a light, she made her way in the dark toward her bedroom on the south side of the house, looking toward the park. There, she pulled the heavy curtains shut and switched on an overhead light.

Half a dozen white department store mannequins stared at her with empty eyes. She could see them in the full-length mirror, too, as if the bedroom were populated with ghosts frozen in odd poses. Deacon thought it was weird. She'd named them when she was a teenager: Ditty, Sexpot, Petunia, Rickles, Harley, and Bon Bon. They wore different wigs and outfits, suitable for disguises. A long-haired hippy. A blonde bombshell. A punk-tattooed biker chick with fire-red hair. She'd been all of those women in the past year.

She hadn't spent much time being herself.

Peach kicked off her Crocs and flopped backward onto her twin bed. She spread her arms and legs in an X and stared at the ceiling, which was webbed with hairline cracks in the plaster. She knew she should eat, but she wasn't hungry. All she wanted to do was sleep, but she hadn't slept for days.

Her phone rang. Sighing, she squeezed it out of her pocket. The number was blocked.

'Hello?'

'Is this Peach Piper?'

'Who is this?' she asked.

The Georgia-accented voice on the phone drawled at her. 'Ms Piper, my name is Detective Curtis Clay of the St Petersburg Police. I'd like to talk to you about a colleague of yours named Justin Kiel.'

They sat on the beach on the shore of Lake Wales, surrounded by children splashing in the water. Across the lake, they could see the expensive shore-side homes climbing the shallow hill, with manicured lawns that reminded her of antebellum plantations. The air was filled with the motor whine and gasoline smell of powerboats pulling inner tubes across the lake.

Peach wore a one-piece yellow swimsuit, and she had her arms wrapped around her knobby knees. Justin wore trunks that lay like a tarpaulin across his long, skinny legs. They were both damp from bobbing in the lake. He took off his pork pie hat and plopped it on top of her wet hair like a crown.

'There, that looks good,' he said.

Peach giggled. 'You're silly.'

As they sat with sand on their bodies, Justin took her hand, and in the silence, she realized: He's my boyfriend. They'd worked side-by-side at the foundation for a year, and she'd grown as close to him as she ever had to another person, but she'd never thought of it as being anything more. Except now it was.

Peach had never met anyone like him. He was quirky, with his little round hats and his old-fashioned mustache. He had a pimply face that most girls probably wouldn't like. Paper-straight bangs tickled his eyebrows. He was only two years older than she was, but he talked older, like someone who had lived a long time. He had an opinion about everything, delivered with the pompousness of a professor giving a lecture. He was hacker-smart about computers, but he kept almost his entire life off the grid. No cell phone. No credit cards, not even a checkbook. Cash only. He loved visiting antique stores and estate sales and buying hundred-year-old bric-a-brac – anything without a power cord, anything with dents and bruises and water stains, anything with a history of people who had owned it and had a story to tell.

All these years alone, and Peach had finally found a kindred spirit.

'So do you think I'm wrong?' she asked him. She realized she was nervous about what he would say.

'You are never wrong. About what?'

'Well, I mean, the celibacy thing.'

'You decided that a long time ago, right?' Justin said. 'It's what you believe in. I respect that.'

'Don't you want sex? Men always do.'

Justin scratched his head. His wet hair stood up like matchsticks. 'People can be really close without having sex. I think it's cool that you want something different.'

It wasn't the first time he'd told her that, but if they were really going to do this – boyfriend, girlfriend – she wondered if he'd feel that they needed to be physical. If she was going to do that with anyone, it was him, but the very idea of sex made her feel unclean. It was okay being naked, if he wanted that. It was okay kissing and holding. She'd just told herself as far back as she could remember that she would always be a virgin.

'Does it bother you being here?' Justin asked.

'What do you mean?'

'Lake Wales. Where your brother was killed.'

Peach hesitated. 'Yes.'

'I'm sorry. I shouldn't have suggested it.'

'No, that's okay, I told you I would come.'

'Have you been back since it happened?'

'I haven't, but it's a beautiful place. It should mean something other than death.'

'Do you remember that time?' he asked.

'Bits and pieces.' She thought about it, and then she said: 'My parents have mostly faded from my memory. Now Lyle is fading, too. I can't really hear him in my head anymore. He's going away. That's why I work at the foundation. It keeps a little bit of him alive.'

They were silent for a while. The intense sun dried their skin, and she could feel her face and shoulders pinking up and freckling. A jogger with a golden retriever ran along the shore in front of them, spattering water and damp sand.

'Do you like what we do?' Justin asked.

'Like it?'

'The work. Do you enjoy it?'

'I don't really think about that. I'm good at it. It's important.'

'Is it?'

She turned her head and shadowed her eyes with her hand to stare at him. 'What are you saying?'

Justin took a slow breath. 'It's just that some days I wonder who the good guys are and who the bad guys are, and whether there's any difference.'

'We're the good guys,' Peach said.

He smiled. 'You are, that's for sure.'

The sky was blue, but there was a cloud crossing his face. 'What's going on, Justin? Is something wrong?'

'No, nothing.'

He leaned closer and kissed her cheek without saying anything more. She was surprised. Usually, Justin beat a subject to death before he would let it go. He would talk and talk until she raised a white flag. Not this time. It made her a little unhappy. She didn't like the idea that he might be keeping something from her.

'I only got us one motel room,' he said. 'Are you okay with that?'

'Sure.'

'One bed?' he said.

'Yeah.'

'But no sex,' he told her. 'Don't worry.'

'I'm not worried.'

'You trust me that much?' he asked.

'You're about the only person in the world I trust,' Peach said. She stared at him with all the intensity she could find, because she wanted him to realize she was serious. 'You can tell me anything. You know that, don't you?'

'Did you know Mr Kiel well?' Detective Clay asked.

Peach lay motionless in bed, with the phone at her ear. The vacant eyes of the mannequins stared at her, wondering what she would say. She was silent for so long that the detective repeated the question.

'No,' she said finally. 'I didn't know Justin well at all. We were basically strangers.'

Her answer prompted an awkward pause. 'That wasn't what I heard.'

'Well, that's how it was.'

'You worked regularly with Mr Kiel, didn't you?'

'Sometimes.'

'But you were strangers?'

'We were colleagues,' Peach said. 'That's all.'

His drawl got a little cooler and less Georgia-friendly. 'Ms Piper, you do want to see us catch whoever did this to Mr Kiel, don't you?'

'Sure.'

'So if you can help us with information, you'll do that, won't you?'

'There's not much to tell.'

The detective breathed into the phone, like a sigh. 'Did you know that Mr Kiel sold drugs? He was a dealer?'

Peach wanted to scream. Her breath felt ragged in her chest. *He wasn't! That's a lie!* 'No.'

'Did you ever see him selling drugs? Or using drugs?'

'No.'

'Did he sell you drugs, Ms Piper?'

'No.'

'I'm not in narcotics. You can be honest with me.'

'I said no.'

'You're aware that Mr Kiel was shot in a drug sale gone bad, aren't you? Drugs were hidden in the motel room where his body was found.'

Peach felt the bed going round and round in circles. She got to her feet, made it to the wall, and slid down to the floor. Her free hand clenched into a fist. Her eyes squeezed shut.

'I only know what I read in the newspaper.'

'Do you know if Mr Kiel had any enemies?'

'I don't.'

'What were you and he working on when he was killed?'

Peach wiped her nose. 'What?'

'I said, what were you and he working on when he was killed?'

'Nothing.'

'You weren't working together?'

'No, I hadn't seen him in days. We hadn't talked.' That much was true. He'd dropped off the radar for a week. She'd been in a panic. *Where are you? What's going on?*

'Was Mr Kiel working on his own? Did he tell you anything about that?'

'No, nothing.'

He never said a word. Whatever was going on in his life, he'd left her out of it.

'Is there anything else you can tell me, Ms Piper?'

'No. I don't know anything.'

'Well, I appreciate your help.'

She thought he was being sarcastic with her. There was nastiness at the back of his throat. When he hung up, she pressed the phone to her lips and wondered why she'd lied to him. She did want Justin's murderer caught. She did know things that no one else knew. Without her, the police would write it off as another drug killing. A cocaine statistic. Everyone would believe that he was something that he wasn't.

Justin would say: *It doesn't matter, Peach. We all die, we're all dust. Legacy is a fiction.*

But it did matter.

She could tell them something important to help them find the truth. They were searching his apartment, but that wasn't where the answers were. He had another place, but she didn't know where it was. A safe house. A hideaway.

Peach looked up the number for the St Petersburg Police Department, and she called, still sitting on the floor. When the receptionist answered, she asked for Detective Curtis Clay. She would talk to him; she would give him what he wanted this time. Everything she knew.

'One moment, ma'am,' the woman on the phone told her. And then: 'What was that name again?'

'Detective Curtis Clay.'

'I'm sorry, ma'am, there's no detective working here by that name. Maybe you have the wrong location. You may want to try Tampa or one of the other Gulf cities.'

'He said it was St Pete,' Peach insisted.

'I'm very sorry, ma'am, we don't employ a Detective Clay. Would you like me to ask another—'

'It's my mistake,' Peach interrupted sharply. She hung up the phone.

6

Like thousands of other foreclosure homes around the Tampa peninsula, the house on Asbury Place was slowly becoming an eyesore. The previous owners had abandoned the property in April, leaving Florida to move in with family in Salisbury, North Carolina. Grass in the yard had grown six inches high, mixed with weeds that had gone to seed. The fifty-year-old elm tree bending over the roof had dropped thick crooked branches that littered the driveway. Rust stains dripped down the stucco from sagging gutters. The windows were boarded over and spray-painted with graffiti.

For the bank, the house was one more property on a long spreadsheet. It was the fifth house in the same neighborhood to suffer the same fate. No one had time to look after all of them.

The house was two blocks from the placid bay waters.

Two blocks from Diane Fairmont's walled estate.

That was the crazy democracy of Florida, where million-dollar mansions were next-door neighbors to garbage homes with pickups rusting on the lawn.

He'd parked half a mile away, near a condominium complex just off Bayshore Boulevard. No one would notice or remember his car. It was after midnight on a hot evening alive with the song of katydids. He followed the street beside the bay with a Dolphins baseball cap tugged low on his forehead. Sunglasses, even at night, covered his eyes. The headlights of a few cars lit him up from behind like a silhouette, but otherwise he was alone. At West

Alline, he followed the sidewalk in the darkness to the abandoned home on the corner.

Most of the other houses around him were unlit, but he heard the blare of party music from open windows half a block away. There were voices from people in the garden, but he couldn't see them, and they couldn't see him. The smell of cigarette smoke drifted down the street.

He dodged the fallen branches on the driveway. The front door was sheltered by overgrown hedges, and the lamppost near the steps had been shattered by rocks. NO TRESPASSING signs were posted on the door and the front windows. He'd first broken in three weeks ago, and since then he'd replaced the lock, so he had his own key. It would be weeks before the bank discovered the invasion. Or maybe the police would arrive first. Either way, by then it would be over, and he would be gone.

He let himself inside and closed the door behind him. The shut-up house was musty and hot. The power and water had long since been turned off, leaving the house to cook in the humid summer. He followed a hallway on his left through the mud room to an attached garage, where he slid a backpack off his shoulder and turned on an emergency lantern. Cockroaches scattered, disappearing under the metal shelves and into the rafters. Spider webs made silky nests in the corners. The concrete floor was smeared with oil where cars had been parked for years.

He'd hung a cork bulletin board on the nearest wall, covered with a collage of thumbtacked articles copied from Florida newspapers. Some were only weeks old. Some went back for years.

He studied the headlines.

FRANK MACY GETS EIGHT YEARS ON MANSLAUGHTER PLEA

ONE YEAR LATER, MORE TRAGEDY: FAIRMONT STUNNED BY SON'S SUICIDE

COMMON WAY FOUNDATION INFLUENCE GROWS – AND SO DOES CONTROVERSY

FAIRMONT TO ENTER GOVERNOR'S RACE

He removed a piece of paper from his backpack and pinned it up with the others. This article was new – only hours old – taken from the website of a local television station. It included a grainy photograph of Diane Fairmont from the video feed of an interview conducted in the garden of her estate.

Two blocks away.

He took a red marker from his backpack and drew a circle around Diane's head. With two quick slashes, he made cross-hatches, turning the circle into a target. He could smell the intoxicating aroma of the fresh ink. Like an artist, he scrawled a single word across her body.

Revenge.

He didn't have time to admire his handiwork. The frame of the house thumped with the weight of footsteps. Somewhere else in the house, muffled but unmistakable, he heard breaking glass.

Someone else was there. He wasn't alone.

He doused the lantern and stole inside, where his eyes adjusted to the shadows. The carpet was hard and worn under his boots. He listened and heard nothing, but something was different. The air pressure had changed; a window was open. He also smelled a noxious sweetness. Feces. Someone had used one of the waterless toilets.

He unsheathed a knife from a back pocket. The camouflage blade had saw teeth and curled to a fierce point. His hands were already securely covered in hospital gloves, leaving no prints.

Music filled the house with a teen-pop song by One Direction. The volume was loud enough that a neighbor might hear it and come to explore – or call the police. He traced the warbling boy-band music to a back bedroom, where the door was closed. He hid the knife behind his palm and silently twisted the door knob. He eased the door open.

A candle wavered on the floor, throwing off dancing light and a strawberry scent. The room was vacant of furniture, but he could see dents in the carpet where a bed had been placed. Flowered wallpaper had begun to bubble and curl as moisture got underneath it. A broken boarded window was pushed open, and he could see waving tree branches in the backyard. Sticky air blew through the bedroom. The music came from a battery-operated iPod dock at his feet, and he squatted and shut it off. He saw a wine bottled tipped on the floor, spilling Cabernet like blood. A wine glass lay broken beside it.

As the music stopped, a young girl appeared in the doorway of the walk-in closet next to him. Her feet were bare. She wore panties and a light blue mesh camisole. Her shoulder-length brown hair was dirty and curly. Her eyes flicked to the speakers, and then she saw him there, waiting for her.

'Oh, shit!'

She made a break for the window, but he was ready for her. He grabbed one wrist, twisted it, and yanked it behind her back. She howled in pain, but he clapped a gloved hand over her mouth.

'*Quiet.*'

'I'm sorry, I'm sorry!' she begged when he removed his hand. 'Jesus, I didn't know anybody was here!'

He shoved her toward the bedroom wall. 'Who are you?'

She folded her arms and danced on the balls of her feet. 'I'm Tina. Look, can I just go? With all these abandoned houses, I figured no one would care if I crashed here.'

'Why are you here? Where do you live?'

'I lived with my boyfriend until two days ago. Bastard threw me out because I ran up a 200-dollar cell phone bill. I mean, hello, who doesn't have unlimited texting these days?'

'How old are you?'

She shrugged. 'Nineteen.'

'How did you find this place?'

'I drove around looking for somewhere I could crash. The house looked empty. I said I was sorry, okay? You beat me to it. Fine. Take it, I'll go someplace else.'

'Did you tell anyone where you were?'

'Nobody, I swear, nobody else is going to crash your crib, man. I'm not looking to party. Besides, no phone, remember?'

He looked at her. She was young, foolish, and sweet. Half-teenager, half-woman. A tattoo of a sunflower peeked from her shoulder. Her skin had bikini tan lines. She misread his eyes, and her head cocked, and her mouth bent into a flirty grin. She took a strand of hair and twisted it around her finger.

'Hey, maybe we could figure something out,' she said. 'Like, maybe we could share the place.'

She bunched the lacy trim of her camisole with both hands and pulled it over her head, baring her chest. Her breasts were small, with chocolate brown, erect nipples and a tear-drop birthmark under her left cup. She tugged back and forth on the elastic of her panties, as if she were working the handlebars on a bicycle. When she peeled them halfway down her hips, he saw the curly fuzz of her pubic hair.

Tina bit her lip and came closer. 'Like what you see?'

He let the jagged knife slide down his hand, until the handle was in his grasp. The blade was an ugly, deadly thing. She didn't notice it.

'This could be like me paying rent, huh?' she said. 'What do you think?'

She really was cute, trying so hard to get what she wanted, which was a place to stay the night. He ran the gloved fingers of his other hand along her cheek, then into the hollow of her neck, then down to her right breast, which he cradled in his palm. His thumb flicked her nipple, and she purred.

'That would be great,' he said, 'except for one thing.'

She nestled against him, reaching for his zipper. 'What's that, lover?'

'DNA,' he said.

7

'It makes you wonder how they do it, right?' Chuck Warren asked. He gestured across the busy street, where a billboard featured an attractive thirty-something couple playing with three children in a Florida backyard. The tagline advertised a local doctor who performed vasectomies using no knife and no needle. 'I mean, what's the deal? Do they use garden clippers or what?'

'I'm not eager to find out,' Cab replied.

'You and me both. No snipping for me. Not that I'm looking to have more kids, but who knows? If I'm eighty, and I still have two marbles rolling around in my head, I might want to put my other marbles to good use.' He chuckled.

'Are you married, Mr Warren?'

'Divorced. Twice. It cost me the gross national product of Brazil both times. That's two and out for me. From now on, I drive, but I don't park. What about you, Detective? Are you married?'

'No.'

'And you've got money. Smart man. That's the way to keep it.'

Warren sipped coffee from a ceramic mug with his own face on it. It was Saturday morning, and Cab felt the Gulf heat tightening his eyes and shrinking his face like a mummy. The sharp creases in his charcoal suit were flattening like a wrinkled shirt in the shower. The two men stood on open green lawn in front of a radio station headquarters building, in the shadow of half a dozen enormous white satellite dishes. To their left, cars shot westward off the Tampa bridge to the crowded Gulf cities. Cab smelled dead fish wafting from the nearby beach.

One of the drivers on the highway spotted Chuck Warren and honked loudly. Warren waved back and gave a thumbs-up sign like a manic leprechaun. Two more drivers leaned on their horns in support, but another driver jerked an arm out his window at Warren with the middle finger extended.

Warren offered a cheery return salute. 'Socialist,' he said, laughing. He sat down on a bench near one of the satellite dishes. Balancing his coffee mug on the bench, he slid a cigar from the pocket of his navy sport coat and offered it to Cab, who shook his head. Warren lit the cigar, puffed, and picked up his coffee again. 'So do you listen to my show, Detective?'

'Sorry, no.'

'You a Socialist?'

'I'm a nothingalist.'

'I just figured, Hollywood mama and all, you had to be a crazy Dem.'

'No, just crazy.'

'Well, sooner or later, we all have to take sides,' Warren said.

The former Congressional candidate – and current radio talk show host – was in his early fifties but looked younger. He was about five-foot-eight. He had shock-white hair, as wiry as a brush, and a smooth face that had probably seen its share of Botox and plastic surgery. His cherubic expression – easy smile, twinkling brown eyes – belied his reputation for extreme rhetoric. He was, according to his website, a happy patriot, relentlessly cheery as he tore into left-wing politics. He had charisma. All once-and-future politicians did. As much as you could dislike a politician on television, Cab decided, it was hard to dislike one in person.

Warren crossed his legs. He wore dress slacks and tan loafers.

He looked to be in good shape for his age, but he had enough of a pooch to suggest that he liked steak dinners.

'So what can I do for you, Detective?' Warren asked. 'I love helping our boys in blue. Even ones with earrings.'

Cab smiled. Everyone mentioned the earring. 'I'm not here in an official capacity. Not as far as the Naples Police goes.'

'Well, in what capacity are you here?'

'There are concerns that Diane Fairmont may be at risk like Birch was ten years ago. Possibly from the same source. I'm trying to find out if that's true.'

Warren chuckled and shook his head. He didn't get angry; he got amused. 'What, is this part of her campaign strategy? Have you been conscripted by the folks at Common Way? I'm not really looking to be a political punching bag for that crowd. Been there, done that.'

'Are you still bitter about what happened ten years ago?' Cab asked.

Warren sucked on his cigar and blew out a sweet cloud of smoke. He had puffy Santa Claus cheeks. 'Not really.'

'It ruined your political career.'

'True, but it made me a millionaire.' Warren poked a thumb at the radio station behind him. 'Look, Detective, ten years ago I was the Republican candidate for Congress in the Twelfth District. It was my fourth run at it. I never cleared 45 percent. I was a nobody, an electrician with barely a dime to my name. Look at me now. Millions of people hang on my every word. Bill O'Reilly has me on speed dial. I've got a mansion on the inland waterway. I'm blessed to live in this country.'

'Except back then, you finally had a chance at winning the race, and Birch Fairmont took that away.'

Warren squinted into the beating sun. He slid out sunglasses from his pocket and put them on his face. 'Okay. Sure. Ten years ago, the Democratic incumbent dropped dead of a stroke. The Dems replaced him with a newbie liberal who suffered from foot-in-mouth disease. Talked about Fidel like he was some kind of George Washington. So yeah, I was running neck-and-neck in the polls.'

'Then Birch got in the race,' Cab said.

'That's right, he did. Or rather, Lyle Piper pushed him in. Lyle was the political brain behind Common Way. Him and Caprice Dean. Suddenly we had a three-way race, and Birch's numbers were pretty strong for a while. He got a lot of buzz, and buzz gets you free face-time on TV. Even so, I was going to win in the end. People have a way of coming home to their spouse after they have drinks with that pretty stranger in the bar.'

'You don't think Birch would have pulled it off? Everybody said he had the momentum.'

'No, I don't. The race was always going to be between me and the Dems. Ogden Bush was running their campaign, and the word on the street was that Ogden was going to bury Birch with negative ads. Pop his balloon. It would have worked, too. Birch's numbers were paper-thin.'

'What did you think when Birch was killed?'

Warren gulped coffee. His face on the mug had the same big smile. The Happy Patriot. 'I thought that was the end of my political career, and I was right. And no, I'm not minimizing what happened. It was terrible. However, I knew what it meant for my campaign.'

'Namely?' Cab asked.

'The mainstream media would blame me. They'd been trying to crucify me from the beginning. That Orlando reporter, Rufus

Twill, kept hyping bullshit stories about me and the Alliance. Chuck's a radical! Chuck's a right-wing extremist! Chuck's in bed with the Nazis! I knew the rest of the media would start talking about "hate speech" and calling this a political assassination and pointing fingers at me. Which is exactly what they did. Hell, some people thought I had Birch killed to get him out of the race.'

'Did you?' Cab asked with a small smile.

Warren grinned. 'I told you, I love cops. They can't resist asking gotcha questions. No, not true. See, if I wanted to get Birch out of the race, I would have set him up with a hooker a week or two before the election. I wouldn't have killed him. Dead people get sympathy. The last thing my campaign needed was Birch Fairmont made into a martyr.'

'The FBI think Hamilton Brock and the Liberty Empire Alliance were behind the assassination.'

'So they say.'

'You don't think so?'

'I think the feds conducted the most exhaustive investigation since Lincoln or Kennedy, and they didn't find a shred of real evidence linking Ham to the murders. That's a little funny, don't you think?'

'Hamilton Brock was a donor to your campaign. So were several of his lieutenants.'

Warren took the cigar and jabbed it at Cab, but without any malice in the gesture. The man relished the give-and-take of political debate. 'Well, first, I don't control who gives me money. Anybody wants to open a checkbook, I think that's their God-given American right, and I don't care what they believe. Second, Ham says those contributions were phony. He knew it would hurt me more than help me to have his group associated with my campaign.'

'And yet you obviously know him,' Cab said.

'Sure, I do. I've interviewed him on my show from the Coleman penitentiary. You ask me, Ham's a political prisoner. They needed to put someone away for the murders at Bok, so they trumped up tax charges against Ham in order to pretend they'd done their job.'

'You think he's innocent?'

'I do.'

'So who killed Birch?'

'I have no idea,' Warren said.

'Do you think Ham Brock knows?'

'You'll have to ask him. I'm not saying it couldn't have been some deranged sympathizer acting on his own. Maybe it was. I just don't think it was Ham or any of his boys. They're too smart. On other hand, there were also nasty rumors about Birch during the campaign.'

'Rumors?' Cab said.

'Oh, yeah, some ugly stories buzzed around the grapevine. Ogden was behind most of them, so who knows whether any of it was true. I didn't peddle the dirt myself, because it would have made things worse. After Labor Day, you couldn't say a bad thing about Birch. Getting killed makes you a saint. From what I hear, though, Birch was no saint.'

'How so?'

'Oh, let's just say that Birch and Diane weren't exactly one big happy family. That was all for the cameras.'

Cab stood up. He smoothed his suit and tugged the knot on his tie a little tighter. Warren remained sitting comfortably on the bench, with an arm slung around the back. Pungent smoke surrounded him like a halo.

'What about this year?' Cab asked. 'Feels like déjà vu all over again, doesn't it?'

'Politically? Sure it does. The Governor is cruising toward re-election, and then miraculously he gets bogged down in a corruption scandal involving his inner circle. The mainstream media pegs Attorney General Cortes as another crazy Tea Party Republican, just like me. Hell, Ramona was on Ham Brock's legal defense team, so she must be a radical extremist, right? And in marches Diane Fairmont of the Common Way Party to save the day. Like the Church Lady would say, how *conveeeeenient*.'

Cab cocked his head. 'Are you suggesting Diane had something to do with the scandal involving the Governor?'

Warren leaned forward with his elbows on his knees. 'I'm saying Common Way has built a reputation as a centrist organization that's above the fray, and that's a bunch of crap. They're as ruthless as either of the other parties. Come on, who did they bring in to handle oppo work when Diane got in the race? Ogden Bush riding a new horse with the same dirty ass. So don't tell me Diane Fairmont is anything other than politics as usual.'

'You do sound a little bitter.'

'I just believe in knowing my enemy.'

'Diane's your enemy?' Cab asked.

'This country has many enemies,' Warren replied, 'inside and out.'

'How well do you know her?'

'Well enough to hope she loses. Do *you* know her, Detective?'

'We've met,' Cab said.

The radio host opened his mouth, closed it, and chomped his lips over his cigar. Finally, he said, 'Word of advice from me to you. Don't trust her.'

'I'm not big on trusting anyone in politics,' Cab said. 'That doesn't mean she's not in danger.'

Warren leaned back against the bench. 'Maybe, maybe not. I'll leave that in your hands. If you ask me, the whole thing is probably a political ploy.'

'But?' he asked, hearing the man's hesitation.

'But let's face it. Common Way has bought itself a lot of friends over the years. They've bought a lot of enemies, too.'

Do you know her, Detective?

We've met.

Ten years ago.

The campaign had been in its infancy when Cab visited his mother while she was staying with Diane at Birch Fairmont's estate in Lake Wales. All of the political activity was happening elsewhere around the state. Cab never met Lyle Piper or Caprice Dean while he was there. He never saw Birch Fairmont that week in June. He was twenty-five years old, and his life was over.

He'd come from Barcelona, after the killing of Vivian Frost, after the internal security investigation that was kept tightly under wraps. No one wanted Cab or his story in the spotlight. His world had come to an end that summer, but he'd said nothing to Tarla, nothing to anyone, about what had happened. It was the beginning of his game of hopscotch, moving from place to place, jumping from job to job.

His mother had known that something was wrong, but she'd been unable to pry the truth out of him. In reality, she hadn't tried hard. She'd been busy filming television commercials, bolstering her millions with advertising sponsorships in anticipation of her retirement. Selling out, as she cheerfully put it. She'd been away most days, tramping around the orange groves with film crews.

Cab stayed at Diane's house, tunneling inside himself. He'd

spent the days reliving his time abroad, his relationship with Vivian, the things they'd said to each other, the lies she'd told. He'd been looking for an escape.

That was when Diane found him.

Diane, who was living in her own kind of hell with Birch.

There were nasty rumors.

Cab sat in his candy-red Corvette outside the radio station, and he remembered that week with more clarity than he wanted. It was a vivid week in a vivid, terrible year. They'd spent hours together. He'd listened to Diane talk about her life, the struggles with her son Drew, Birch's affairs. She was depressed. She was lonely. He was riven with guilt. They were primed for a mistake.

He remembered the afternoon that last day when she reached for him, and he reached back. They were both voracious with need, stripping off their clothes in the heat of her bedroom, with the summer air blowing inside. The two of them, naked, hungry. Her mound, moist as he kissed it. Her gasping scream as he entered her. She hadn't had sex with Birch in four years, she said. He hadn't had sex since Vivian, and he thought he could erase her memory in a single afternoon in Diane's bed. He remembered the lust of being inside her, this woman who was his mother's best friend, and he remembered the burning shame afterward.

He left Florida that night. He never saw her again.

He began to run.

Cab heard the vibrations of his phone over the purr of the Corvette's motor. He wondered if it was Lala, finally calling him back, but it wasn't. Her absence made him angry. He needed her.

'Cab, it's Caprice,' she said, her voice as fruity and intoxicating as a tropical drink.

'Yes, it is,' he said.

'What are you doing?'

'Actually, I'm about to drive to a federal penitentiary.'

'Hamilton Brock?'

'That's right.'

'Well, good luck. And thank you for helping Diane.'

Cab wondered if he'd ever really helped Diane, now or in the past. He remembered their eyes meeting the previous night, just for a moment. It brought back the guilt and shame. 'I guess I can't say no to my mother,' he said.

'Really? Here I thought you couldn't say no to me.'

Caprice was flirting with him, and he liked it.

'Are you checking on your new employee?' he asked.

'No, I wanted to see if you would go to dinner with me tonight.'

'Tonight?'

'It's Saturday, Cab. That's when people go out to dinner.'

'Is this work or a date?'

'Does it matter?'

'I guess not.'

He thought about Diane, and the recollection of the afternoon he'd spent with her was still arousing. He thought about Lala and the intensity of their relationship. Fire in bed. Arguments out of it. And for days now – silence.

'So?' Caprice asked. 'Shall we dance?'

'Yes, we shall.'

'Excellent. The Columbia in Ybor City at eight o'clock. Don't be late.'

8

Peach watched Annalie Martine from her Thunderbird. The newest foundation employee – the woman who'd replaced Justin – sat at a table outside an ice cream shop in Indian Shores. The Saturday noontime traffic on Gulf Boulevard was a parade of weekenders making a beeline for the sand. The strip mall where Annalie waited was tucked among pastel hotels and condos, and bikini-clad teenagers pushed and giggled past her toward the white beaches. Annalie lazily licked a single scoop of maplenut ice cream from a sugar cone.

She had let her hair down since the previous day. Literally. Lush and black, it cascaded to her shoulders. She wore stylish sunglasses that slid down her nose as her skin sweated in the heat. No more Clark Kent frames. She wore shorts and heels, and her legs were crossed. Her black tank top sported the letters DC in a block white font across her chest. The tank top dipped low, offering an ample view of cocoa-skinned cleavage.

Peach wandered across the parking lot. When she passed Annalie as she went inside the shop, the thirty-something woman glanced idly at her but made no sign of recognition. Peach wore a mousy-brown wig today, taken from the head of Bon Bon Mannequin, and the hair was bushy around her face. She wore big red sunglasses, jeans, and an untucked striped button-down blouse.

Inside, she ordered mocha-chip ice cream, took the cup outside, and sat in the chair next to Annalie.

'I'm sorry, I'm waiting—' the woman began, but then she stopped and said: 'Oh. Peach?'

'Hi.'

'It took me a second to recognize you.'

'That's the plan,' Peach said.

Annalie stripped off her sunglasses and pointed at herself with an inquiring glance. 'So, do I pass inspection? You said dress to get noticed.'

'Looking good.'

'Thanks.' Annalie licked her cone. 'You live near here?'

'Not too far.'

'Where's not too far?'

'A few miles.'

Annalie's eyebrows flickered. She didn't miss the fact that Peach wasn't offering specifics. 'Why did you want to meet so far west? We're heading back into the city, aren't we?'

Peach shrugged. 'Sorry, force of habit. I used to meet Justin here. He had a place on the Gulf a couple miles south.'

'Nice.'

'Parental money.'

'Well, I wouldn't know what that's like,' Annalie said with a sigh. 'Anyway, I came early and walked on the beach.' She tilted her chin toward the blue sky. 'Beautiful day, huh? It's like the calm before the storm. Everyone says Chayla will be bad.'

'Storms don't scare me,' Peach said.

'No? Me, I worry about waking up in Oz. Sounds like the weather people think Chayla will make landfall around the Fourth of July.'

'Unless it veers away. They never know.' Peach checked the time again. 'We should probably go. The convention takes an afternoon break in a couple hours. People will be outside smoking. We'll want to be listening.'

'Listening for what?'

'Whatever we hear,' Peach said. 'It's amazing what people will say. Do you smoke? You'll fit in better if you smoke.'

'Occasionally. What about you?'

'I don't smoke. I don't drink. But I can fake it.'

Annalie grinned: 'You don't drink, and you don't smoke. So what do you do?'

'What?'

'You know, that Adam Ant song? "Goody Two-Shoes"?'

'I don't know it.'

'Wow, I'm way too old,' Annalie sighed.

'Can you drive?' Peach asked.

Annalie pushed the last bite of her cone into her mouth with one finger and stood up. 'I'm the banged-up Corolla,' she said, pointing at a black car on the far side of the parking lot.

Peach finished her cup of mocha chip and deposited it in the wastebasket outside the store. She grabbed her backpack and followed Annalie to the old Corolla. When they got inside, Annalie looked sideways at her as she started the engine.

'I get the feeling you don't like me,' she said.

'I don't know you,' Peach replied.

'Is it because of me taking over from Justin? Was he like your gihow or something?'

'Gihow?'

'Guy I Hang Out With. Sounds better than partner or boyfriend or live-in or whatever.'

'Oh.' Peach felt herself shutting down at the mention of Justin's name. 'No, nothing like that.'

Annalie stared at her, as if she knew that Peach wasn't telling the truth. 'Okay.'

'Do you have a gihow?' Peach asked.

'Me? No way. No time.'

She said it breezily, but Peach didn't believe her. This woman was gorgeous. She had to be fending off passes from guys day and night.

They drove south on Gulf Boulevard, trailing a shuttle bus headed for Pass-a-Grille. She'd traveled this stretch of asphalt thousands of times: sometimes alone, sometimes with Deacon, sometimes with Justin. To Peach, this was Florida, with every building squeezed so tightly together that they looked as if they were holding their breath. The sidewalks were crowded with bare flesh. She saw turtle-like men with little heads jutting out of enormous torsos. Sagging old women in floppy hats. Boys with big bulges and girls with wiggling cheeks. Behind the buildings and parking lots, only steps away, the Gulf teased her, as motionless as glass, glinting with a million sun drops. There was hardly a wave cracking the surface now, but in a few days the Gulf would awaken like a monster and hurl itself against the land. Chayla.

Justin on storms. *Hurricanes make you feel small. It's good to feel small every now and then.*

'I looked up Justin's murder,' Annalie said. 'So it was a drug thing, huh?'

'That's what they say.'

'You don't think so?'

'I'm not a cop,' Peach said. 'I have no idea.'

'I just thought, you worked with him, you'd know something.'

'I don't know anything.'

They stopped at a stop light. Peach cracked the window, and a briny sea smell wafted inside. A crowd of teenage boys hooted at them as they ran through the crosswalk toward the beach.

'If Justin was your friend,' Annalie said, 'you must be sad. Or angry.'

'What do you mean?'

'I mean, you look like you're working pretty hard not to feel anything, which tells me you feel something big way down deep. I think you were close to Justin, and you won't say so.'

'You just met me,' Peach said. 'You don't know anything about me.'

Annalie accelerated again. The engine rattled.

'Your parents were killed when you were eight,' she said. 'Your oldest brother was murdered when you were twelve. The guy you worked with for a whole year just got shot selling cocaine. I guess I know some things, or at least how to find them. I'm a researcher, and I know how to read people's faces, too. You're not the mannequin you like to think you are.'

Mannequin.

It was probably nothing, but Peach didn't like that Annalie used that word. As if it were a message: I know you, I know what you keep in your bedroom. You can't hide from me. She didn't like being grilled for her secrets. Everyone wanted something from her these days, and it all involved Justin.

'Stop the car,' Peach said.

'Hey, sorry. I was out of line. I get in people's faces too much. It's a character flaw.'

'I said stop. Pull over.'

'Why?'

'I can't do this. Not now. Not today.'

'Look, Peach, I didn't mean anything–'

Peach pushed opened the door of the Corolla while it was still moving. Annalie jerked on the brakes, and horns wailed behind them. Peach undid the seat belt with clumsy fingers and spilled into the street, ignoring Annalie, who shouted at her. She left the car door hanging ajar and ran between the pink condos for the Gulf beach.

The water was hot. It didn't cool her down at all. Peach's bare toes squished in the wet sand. The cuffs of her jeans were soaked. She'd tied the laces of her Chuck Taylors together, and she spun the shoes from her hand like clunky tether balls. She walked, staring at the shells in the surf. She'd ran for a half-mile, ducking under fishing lines and dodging Frisbees that landed in the water. People looked at her because she was crying, but no one said anything. It was Florida. People broke up, and they went to the beach to cry.

Annalie was right. Peach had been lying to Deacon, and to herself, about feeling nothing. She'd been in love with Justin, and now he was gone, taken from her. Like her parents. Like Lyle. The emptiness was so great it made her want to swim into the deep water and drown herself. Justin had been someone she'd never anticipated, the one man she had ever invited to share her solitary existence. She had gotten up every morning, anxious to hear his voice and see his face. He made her smile.

They had sworn to be loyal to each other forever. No one else knew. Not Deacon or Caprice or Ms Fairmont or Ogden Bush. It was like being married, but better. They had something more sacred than love or sex.

That was what hurt the most, because Justin had betrayed her. He'd shut her out of what was happening to him and what he was doing. He'd gotten killed. She couldn't bear the loss of him, but even more than that, she couldn't bear not knowing *why*. It was not drugs. It was something else. Something he couldn't share with her.

Why?

Peach stood on the sand and stared at a four-story apartment building on the other side of the strip of beach, fifty yards away. The building was stucco, painted a fading color of red that got worn each season by the salt and wind. Balconies and picture windows, one above another, jutted over the dune. Wooden steps led down from the rear door. It wasn't a new building, but the condos were expensive. Everything was expensive here.

Justin's place.

This was why she'd come here. This was why she'd escaped from Annalie's car. She needed to see his apartment again. She needed to find out what he'd been hiding from her.

Peach trudged up the sand. She passed an old woman sprawled in a white plastic lounger under the shade of an umbrella. She had brown wrinkled flesh. Spanish music played from an old battery radio beside her. Peach knew her, because she was Justin's neighbor, a widow who lived one floor above him. Mrs Jabohnne. The old woman's eyes slitted open at the noise of Peach's footsteps, but she made no sign of recognition.

At the top of the beach, among flowers and long grass, Peach wandered under the shade of the first-floor apartment deck. Sand leached into the building's covered parking lot. She saw a faucet, and she turned on the water to wash her feet. When they were clean, she shoved her damp feet back into her sneakers. She still had Justin's key to let herself inside.

The building smelled musty. Bugs clung to the walls. She waited for the elevator, listening to it hum, and then took it to the second floor. Outside, in the open-air hallway, she turned right and opened the metal screen door. She let herself into Justin's apartment, which was stifling. More than eighty degrees. The apartment was dark, with the lights off and the vertical blinds in the living room mostly shut, letting in narrow cracks of sun. It still smelled like him. Justin loved scented oils, and the aroma of cherry blossoms permeated the space. She expected him to wander from the bedroom, towel knotted around his scrawny waist, toothbrush hanging out of his mouth like a cigarette.

He didn't.

The apartment was sparsely furnished. It had always been that way. He kept almost nothing personal here. None of his antiques. None of his papers or photographs or books. When they came here, he left his work in the car, but at some point when he was alone, the work disappeared. He put it somewhere. Not here. He'd been open about the fact that he had another place, but when she asked him about it, he'd said: *It's not safe for you to know. Not yet.*

Drugs, the police would say. That was where he kept his drugs. But they were wrong.

She needed to find out where he lived his other life. His safe house.

Peach passed the kitchen and went into the living room. He had leather sofas and a big television, and rocking chairs by the window that looked out on the beach. They'd sit there night after night, sipping tea, watching the sunsets. He'd read poetry to her and play classical music, no matter how much she said she hated it. It was all too dark, loud, and strong.

She stood by the windows, watching the water. Looking down, she saw a dead, desiccated salamander on the tile floor. She had no idea what she was looking for here. If the police hadn't found it, she wouldn't either. Maybe there was nothing to find, no clue to his secret, and yet she knew Justin. He would've left a message for her. Something.

Justin on life after death. *I want to come back and haunt you. Keep an eye open for me.*

She looked around the dusty apartment and willed him to make contact with her. She was here. She needed him. *What was it that you didn't want me to know? How do I find it?* She could tell from the clutter that the police had already pawed through the cabinets and drawers. Justin was typically very organized, and most of the apartment was in a state of chaos.

Or maybe it wasn't the police. Maybe it was someone else.

Peach wandered into the bedroom, which also faced the Gulf. Sheets had been ripped off the king bed and lay in a crumpled pile on the floor. The mattress had been knifed, exposing padding and springs. Looking for drugs. Looking for anything. On her left, double doors led to the deck. The apartment bathroom was there, too, where she would shower before bed and in the mornings. She'd practically lived here. That last week, when Justin disappeared, she'd spent every night waiting for him, and he never returned. He'd been somewhere else.

Where?

She picked her way around the debris. Justin kept a dresser on the wall opposite the bed, and the drawers had been removed and overturned. Clothes lay heaped on the floor. She recognized his T-shirts, his cut-offs, his boxer briefs, and his athletic socks. There were personal things, too, scattered on the tile. Tins of breath mints. Batteries. A wind-up Snoopy toy. Local restaurant menus. Even a box of condoms – unopened – which made her wonder if he'd been rethinking his willingness to remain celibate with her. Or maybe she hadn't been the only girl in his life. She didn't want to believe that.

Peach spotted a small book on the floor, and she bent and picked it up. It was old, bound in fraying green cloth, with embossed gold letters on the cover. She'd found it at an antiquarian bookshop months ago and purchased it for Justin as a gift. It was a book of poems by William Blake, his favorite poet. Every time she'd visited his apartment, it had been on his nightstand, next to his bed. The pages were delicate and yellowed.

She didn't have time to open the book to 'The Tyger.'

Instead, someone bellowed at her from the bedroom doorway. 'Put your hands in the air right now!'

Peach wheeled around in surprise. A big man filled the doorway, with a gun pointed at her chest. She gasped and thrust her hands upward with her elbows bent. The book was still in her hand.

'What the hell are you doing here?' the man demanded.

Peach struggled for something to say, but she said nothing. Behind her sunglasses, she studied the man. He was in his forties, with wavy blond-and-gray hair. He hadn't shaved. He wore a tan sport coat over a collarless black T-shirt, with navy slacks and black sneakers. His clothes fit snugly; his frame was heavy. A film of sweat made a mustache on his upper lip.

'Who are you?' he said, dragging aside a flap of his coat so she could see a gold badge dangling from his belt.

A cop?

No. She recognized the southern drawl in his voice. This was the man who had phoned her, claiming to be Detective Curtis Clay of the St Petersburg Police. He was a liar and a stranger, and looking at him, she knew that he was no cop. He was here for the same reason she was here. To find Justin's secrets.

'Whoa, chill, buddy. My name's Rebekah,' Peach said, modulating her own voice so it sounded like a New Yorker. 'I'm crashing with my mom in the condo upstairs. Could you put that gun away?'

The man who called himself Clay kept the gun pointed at her. 'I asked what you're doing here.'

'Jeez, I thought I smelled smoke. I figured I better check it out, you know? Mom's like the manager here. We've got snowbirds who are gone a lot, and she watches over things, so she's got a master key.'

'Bullshit,' he said. 'Tell me who you really are and what you're looking for.'

'Hey, I already said–'

'I know what you said. You're lying. How did you know Justin Kiel?'

'I didn't know him at all. I don't know who owns this place.'

He stared at her in the dim, dusty space. 'Show me your ID,' he said.

Peach shrugged, but she wasn't going to do that. 'Yeah, well, show me yours,' she said.

'Excuse me?'

'I'll show you mine if you show me yours.'

The man took a menacing step toward her. She could smell him as he came closer; he smelled of menthol, like the goopy pain patches she wore when she pulled a muscle. He holstered his gun. He dug in his coat pocket and came out with handcuffs, which dangled from his fingers.

'Maybe you'll feel like talking after a few hours in jail,' he said.

She didn't know where he planned to take her, but it wasn't jail.

Peach bolted. She dove into the bathroom and locked the door. The man chased after her, but he stumbled on the debris and fell with a loud curse. She yanked open the glass shower door. Inside the shower, a small window near the ceiling faced the beach. She reached as high as she could and was barely able to undo the lock and slide the window open. Noise and wet sea air rushed through the space.

The man's shoulder crashed into the locked bathroom door. It splintered and came off its frame, tumbling inward.

Peach grabbed the window ledge and pulled herself up the wall, but her shoes slipped on the tile. Her feet pedaled helplessly. She jumped, propping both hands against the frame and squeezing her elbows into the tight open space of the window, which was barely wide enough for her body. Her head jutted outside, then her shoulders and torso, and she could see the green water and the people on the beach and the sand and grass two stories below her.

She also saw Annalie Martine on the beach, running from the shoreline, arms waving, black hair flying.

Curtis Clay grabbed her ankles inside the shower stall and dragged her backward. Like a mustang at a rodeo, she bucked wildly, trying to dislodge him as she clung to the window frame. His grip was as tight as a bear trap, but when he yanked on her foot, her shoe came off. He stumbled, hitting the shower wall hard. The water turned on, blasting the stall, and when he lurched for her again, his feet slipped under him on the wet tile. He crashed down.

Peach squirmed through the window and threw herself outside.

She was free, she was falling. Her body twisted in mid-air. The Gulf dune roared up to meet her face.

9

I'm back. Miss me?

Cab unfolded a copy of the newspaper photograph that Caprice had given him, with the warning scrawled in the thick ink of a red Sharpie. He held the paper so that Hamilton Brock, the leader of the Liberty Empire Alliance, could see it. The two men sat in uncomfortable plastic chairs six feet apart. A video camera watched them from a corner of the ceiling.

'Who sent this?' Cab asked.

Brock's dark eyes flicked to the page and studied the ten-year-old photograph, but he said nothing. His face was devoid of expression.

'Bring back memories, does it?' Cab went on. 'Kind of like Springsteen, right? "Glory Days"?'

Brock's eyes refocused on Cab with barely veiled contempt, but he remained silent. So far, he hadn't said a word since Cab introduced himself. The hour-long drive north on I-75 to the Coleman Federal Correction Complex, which was located in Middle-of-Nowhere, Florida, in flatlands across from grazing cattle, felt like a waste of time. Brock had no interest in talking.

Cab had expected a hardened skinhead, but Hamilton Brock looked more like a suburban soccer dad. He was a high school football quarterback, ex-army, auto mechanic, father of four. At thirty-nine years old, he had neat black hair, no tattoos, and a physique that looked prison-lean, but not ripped. His face was carefully shaved. He sat with his hands folded in his lap and his long legs pressed together. His posture was perfect.

Ten years ago, Brock had been an all-American Wally World shopper with a 2,200-square-foot house in Bartow. His wife home-schooled their kids. They had annual passes to Disney World. At night, he'd recruited converts in the basement of a Lakeland church to a volunteer militia whose website advocated mass deportation of illegal aliens, an electrified fence on the Mexican border, a ban on Muslim immigration, defiance of the Internal Revenue Service, and – among blog posts Cab had reviewed – forced sterilization of welfare mothers who gave birth to a third child. The Liberty Empire Alliance had also stockpiled dozens of assault weapons, handguns, ammunition, plastic explosives, barbed wire, copper, canned goods, bottled water, and doses of the anthrax antibiotic Cipro in a U-Stor facility raided by the FBI in Fort Meade.

You never could tell.

Cab tapped a long finger on the newspaper article again. 'The Orlando reporter who wrote this? Rufus Twill. He wrote a lot about you and your group back then. Somebody repaid him by beating him within an inch of his life. Is that how you deal with people who don't see the world the way you do?'

The room was silent except for the rustle of the paper and the ticking of a decades-old clock high on the wall. Brock's mouth twitched. His head tilted a fraction, and he looked toward the floor and shook his head with disdain.

'Right, I don't get you, you're misunderstood,' Cab said. He waited until Brock met his eyes again, and he added: 'I know about your father, Mr Brock. Thirty-one years with the same company, and then his job was outsourced to India. He spent three years looking for another job and didn't find one. He shot himself when you were seventeen. You found the body.'

There was no emotion in Brock's face. The man had channeled his emotions into hatred long ago. He also had smart eyes, as penetrating as a snake's stare. Hatred and intelligence were a dangerous combination.

'Chuck Warren says you're innocent,' Cab went on. 'He called you a political prisoner.'

Brock showed the barest flicker of interest at the mention of the Republican's name. 'Mr Warren is correct. That's exactly what I am.'

'Oh, so you can talk,' Cab said. 'Good. Actually, I knew you could talk, because you've been on Warren's show. I was able to dig up the archives online. Here's one of my favorite quotes: "People accuse us of hoarding weapons because we want to overthrow the government. Not true. We need to be armed for when the government comes to overthrow us."'

The man's eyebrows arched with irony, and he cast his gaze around the prison visiting room.

Cab smiled. 'I get it. They really did come for you.'

'Yes, they did.'

'The jack-booted thugs of the FBI?'

Brock exhaled with a loud sigh. He leaned forward and spoke in an unusually quiet voice. 'You make jokes, Detective Bolton, but did you know that government officials with automatic weapons raided my home and the homes of half a dozen other patriots and kidnapped our children at gunpoint? Nineteen children hauled away and stripped from their parents. The oldest was eleven years old.'

'They wanted to make sure you didn't use the children as hostages. Human shields. It's been done before by extremist groups.'

Brock shook his head. He was talking now. He wanted to talk.

'The government was the one using children as hostages. Not us. This is the same government that waged a legal battle to have our children permanently taken from our custody and relocated under different identities so we could never find them again. Is that the America you serve, Detective?'

'The feds lost that fight,' Cab said, 'thanks to another branch of government called the American judiciary.'

'True enough. If you have children, I'm sure you will welcome a two-year battle against the behemoth of the federal government to enjoy the freedom to keep them. Not that we have many freedoms left in this country. Those of us who defend American values wind up here.'

'You're here because you didn't pay your taxes, aren't you?' Cab asked.

'I'm here as a scapegoat, because the government needed someone to blame for a murder they couldn't solve.'

That was what Cab expected Brock to say. It was the standard excuse of a guilty man. The trouble was, based on everything he'd read about this man, he expected him to be proud of what he'd done. To tell everyone, to take credit. Not to deny it and hide behind a lie.

'Most people think the government solved the murders,' Cab said, 'but they couldn't make the case because you and your allies stonewalled the investigation and destroyed records. Dozens of militia members disappeared. Including, most likely, the shooter.'

'We were standing up against a witch hunt,' Brock said. 'This was a vendetta.'

'Even Chuck Warren thinks the murders could have been committed by one of your Alliance members acting on his own.'

'That isn't true.'

'Actually, I believe you,' Cab said, 'because I don't think anyone in your group would go forward with a plan like that without your say-so.'

Brock nodded. 'That's why I know it wasn't one of us.'

'Are you really saying you didn't want Birch Fairmont dead?' Cab asked. 'Birch and the Common Way Party were ferocious enemies of your movement. Their policies on gun control and immigration were anathema to your group. Birch was a supporter of aggressive legal authority to combat domestic terrorists. That's what he called you, Mr Brock. Birch Fairmont said you and the Liberty Empire Alliance were the poster children for domestic terrorism. And he was on his way to joining the United States Congress, where he would have had considerable power to target groups like yours.'

'If you're asking me to say I'm sorry that Birch Fairmont was killed,' Brock said, 'I won't do that. He was an enemy of free people.'

'But you didn't kill him.'

'I'm not in the business of making martyrs of my enemies. That just gives them more power.'

'Do you know who did?'

'I assume it was someone who wanted *me* in *here*. They got their wish. They took down a patriot like Chuck Warren at the same time. Obviously, we had a mole inside the Alliance. Someone who was able to point the authorities at us. As it is, they had to settle for trumped-up tax charges when they couldn't link us to the murders.'

'So you think you and the Alliance were deliberately targeted. Set up as fall guys.'

Brock shrugged. 'Here I am.'

'Are you still the leader of the Liberty Empire Alliance?' Cab asked.

'I still have a voice,' Brock said in the same quiet, determined tone he had used from the beginning. 'They can lock me up, but they can't silence me until they put a gun to my head and pull the trigger. They can't change the truth of what I say. Did you know that in less than thirty years the founding race of this country will be in the *minority*? The takers are outbreeding us. This will no longer be America. It will be *Hispanica*.'

'I guess I better be nice to my girlfriend,' Cab replied. 'She's Cuban.'

Brock tensed. For the first time, Cab saw a flash of anger, as if rage bubbled under the man's skin.

'More jokes,' Brock said. 'Do you think this is funny? Millions of people feel the way we do. We have allies and converts everywhere. More and more people are hearing our message. Workers. Mothers. Fathers. Even police officers, Detective. And prison guards.'

Cab ignored the diatribe. Instead, he held up the newspaper photograph again. 'Let me ask you again. Who sent this?'

'I have no idea.'

'Is Diane Fairmont in danger?'

'If she is in danger, she has no one to blame but herself. People who try to stage a coup always the run the risk of the guillotine.'

'A coup?'

'That's what the Common Way Party is planning,' Brock said. 'That's what this campaign is about. She has been systematically erasing the obstacles on her way to power. If you don't think it's a conspiracy, you're naïve.'

'Ramona Cortes is the GOP candidate this year. She led your defense team nine years ago, didn't she?'

'Yes, she did. Real Americans all over this country contributed money for our defense. Ms Cortes was the best. However, it doesn't matter who represents you when the system is rigged to assure your guilt.'

'Are you still in touch with Ramona?'

'No.'

'But you share her politics,' Cab said. 'If it were a two-person race, if Diane were out of it, Ramona would be winning. You'd like that.'

Brock stood up. 'You're wasting your time. This election isn't about me or the Alliance. We're simply pawns. Just like last time. If we didn't exist, the Common Way Party would have had to invent us.'

'One more question,' Cab said. 'If you wanted Diane killed, could you arrange it? Could you make it happen from here?'

Brock smiled. 'Do you believe that if I wanted *you* dead, I could make sure you never walked out of this prison?'

The threat was so calm, so casual, and so real that Cab felt a chill. He didn't reply. He reached for a joke and didn't find one.

'Actually, I do believe that,' Cab admitted.

'See, that should tell you something,' Brock said, enjoying Cab's discomfort.

'What's that?'

'If I wanted to kill Diane Fairmont, she'd already be dead.'

10

The day washed away.

Peach and Annalie sat in cheap folding chairs on the beach at Honeymoon Island, which was connected to the Gulf coast by a causeway from the town of Dunedin. Peach propped her leg on a third chair. She'd twisted her ankle as she landed, and it was tightly taped with an athletic bandage she'd bought at Walgreens. Her other foot dipped in the hot surf. Her body ached, and she had scratches on her face and arms. Whenever she moved, she felt the grit of sand inside her clothes.

Annalie's phone rang, playing a song by Gloria Estefan. 'Rhythm is Gonna Get You.' Peach watched Annalie check the caller ID and ignore it. It wasn't the first call she'd ducked.

'Do you need to be somewhere? You don't have to hang out with me.'

'No, I don't need to be anywhere,' Annalie replied, shoving the phone back in her pocket. She wore a wide-brimmed yellow hat, and her face was shadowed from the sun. 'Saturday afternoon at the beach is pretty great, particularly since I thought I'd be working all day.'

She toasted Peach with a tilt of a warm beer bottle. Offshore, speedboats sliced the waves. The beach around them was crowded and noisy. Dozens of seagulls dodged the children and picked at the foam. Pelicans skimmed the surface with lazy wings. They sat in the midst of the calm water, near an uprooted palm tree half-buried in the sand. A cooling breeze took the edge off the heat, but when Peach closed her eyes, she felt the burn on her face.

'You change your mind about calling the police?' Annalie asked. 'If some guy's out there pretending to be a cop, they should know.'

'They'd say it was all about Justin and drugs,' Peach said. 'They'd figure that's why I was there, too. Besides, I can't get the police involved in anything without talking to Deacon and Ms Fairmont.'

'Justin was murdered. This isn't political.'

'Everything's political.'

Annalie shook her head. 'Well, it's your call. Just watch your back, okay? You can identify this guy, and he knows it. Maybe he's the one who killed Justin, did you think about that?'

'Yeah, I thought about it,' Peach said.

She'd thought about it, but she didn't believe it was true. She didn't think the killer would risk coming back, not after the police had already torn Justin's life apart. Whoever the man was in Justin's apartment, he was looking for answers, like her.

'You don't believe his death was about drugs, do you?' Annalie asked.

'I have no idea.'

'I'm stepping into his shoes, Peach. I have a right to know if I'm putting myself at risk.' Annalie reached out and put a hand on Peach's wrist. 'Do you know what Justin was working on before he was killed?'

'I don't.'

Annalie shivered, even in the heat. 'I have to tell you, all this dirt-digging we do gives me the creeps.'

'So why'd you take the job?'

'Why else? I need the money.'

'I thought your father worked for a big foundation donor.'

'He does, but he's not rich. Besides, I pay my own bills. I never had any interest in political crap, but after nine months without a job, I was running pretty low on cash. So my dad made a couple calls.'

'I assumed you had Washington ties,' Peach said.

'Why'd you think that?'

Peach pointed at Annalie's DC tank top, which was ringed with sweat on the hot afternoon. The woman looked down, as if she'd forgotten what she was wearing. She shook her head and smiled.

'Never been there. Somebody gave it to me.' She added: 'Listen, I know this isn't just a job for you. It's a cause. I get it.'

'You're right,' Peach said.

'That must have been awful for you and Deacon ten years ago.'

Peach watched the translucent green water. The waves swelled and broke in white ribbons. She saw a sailboat jutting like a shark's fin out of the distant horizon line. 'Yeah. It was even harder on him than me. I mean, just like that, Lyle was gone and Deacon had to take care of me. I didn't make it easy.'

'Seems like you guys get along now.'

'Oh, yeah. We couldn't be more different, but we're a team. It helps that we're working on Lyle's legacy. The Common Way Party was everything to Lyle. So much that he didn't always have a lot of time for us. Especially not that last summer.'

'I'm sorry.'

'Hey, campaigns are crazy. I get it now.'

'Do you know Diane Fairmont well?' Annalie asked.

Peach dipped a hand in the surf and let warm water spill through her fingers. 'I've met her. I don't know her well. She doesn't come over to the research wing very often. We're the dirty little secret that nobody wants to talk about.'

'Dirty?'

'Some people think so,' Peach said.

Annalie was quiet. A small Cessna flew over the beach, its motor whining. 'Can I ask you something?'

'What?'

'A few months ago, the Governor was looking unbeatable. He was way ahead of Ramona. Then his chief of staff got caught taking kickbacks from construction contractors, and his numbers tanked. Diane got in the race and vaulted ahead of both of them in the polls.'

'What's your point?' Peach asked.

'Is it possible that Common Way was involved?'

'What do you mean? The Governor is a sleaze. He surrounds himself with sleazy people.'

'You can be a sleaze and still be set up,' Annalie said.

'What are you saying? Do you think *I* had something to do with that? Because I didn't.'

'I never said you did, but sometimes special projects go on behind the scenes. People get recruited to do things they don't want to do.'

Peach's eyes widened. '*Justin?* That's who you mean, isn't it? You think Justin was involved in setting up the Governor's aide.'

'I don't know. Is it possible?'

'No!'

'And yet you don't think his death was about drugs.'

Peach stood up so fast that the chair spilled into the water behind her. Her leg buckled under her weight, and Annalie leaped to her feet and kept her from falling. Peach shrugged off the woman's help. She realized that she'd said far more to Annalie than she ever intended. Annalie was good. And smart. She knew a lot more about humint work than she was letting on.

'Let's go,' Peach said.

'I'm sorry. I had to ask. I need to know what I'm getting into.'

Peach splashed toward the wet, sandy fringe of the beach. Seagulls scattered into the air. 'You're wrong about Justin.'

Annalie grabbed her shoulder and stopped her. 'Maybe I am, but that doesn't explain why you went to Justin's apartment. What were you looking for?'

'Nothing.'

'Don't insult me, Peach. I know that's not true.' Annalie dug in a pocket. 'Were you looking for this?'

She held up a small book bound in fraying green cloth. Much of the gold lettering on the cover had flecked away. It was the book of poetry by William Blake that Peach had given to Justin. She'd thought she lost it when she fell from the apartment window. 'Give me that,' she said.

'There's an inscription,' Annalie told her. 'I looked through the book when you were in the drug store. "Then they followed / Where the vision led,/ And saw their sleeping child / Among tygers wild." That's from a poem called "The Little Girl Found." It's not a man's handwriting. Is it yours? Did you give Justin this book?'

'Give me that!' Peach repeated, ripping it out of her hand.

'The Little Girl Found. Is that you?'

'That's none of your business.'

'You loved Justin, didn't you?'

'I said, that's none of your business.'

'Did he love you?'

'Why do you care?' Peach asked. 'What difference does it make?'

'Because if he loved you, maybe he told you his secrets.'

'He didn't.'

'Are you sure?'

'I didn't find a thing in his apartment,' Peach said, and the bitterness was obvious in her voice.

'Justin wrote something in this book,' Annalie told her. 'It's on the page for the poem "The Tyger." Does that mean something to you?'

Peach's fingers tightened on the ragged cloth of the book. 'What did he write?'

'Look.'

Peach turned the brittle pages. She knew exactly where the poem was. She found it – *What immortal hand or eye / Could frame thy fearful symmetry?* – and Annalie was right. Someone had written a single word on the page. Not someone. Justin. It was his handwriting. There was no mistaking it.

The message had to be for her, didn't it? This was their poem. They'd read it over and over in bed, so many times, with such emotion that it was like the words of the poem had taken the place of sex between them. Every stanza was burned into her memory, and she could hear it in Justin's voice.

He wouldn't write on that poem to anyone but her. He'd written one word, but not a word. A name.

What made no sense was that it wasn't her own name on the paper.

Instead, Justin had written: *Alison.*

11

Cab couldn't take his eyes off Caprice.

The sconce lights, shaped like torches, played shadows across her white skin. She wore a sleeveless black dress, and her strong arms ended in manicured hands and scarlet nails. Her full brown hair covered the straps of her dress and swished in little curls across the slopes of her breasts. A double gold chain hugged her neck, and gold hoop earrings peeked out between the locks of her hair. Her deep red lips folded into a smile as he watched her.

'Like what you see?' she asked.

'I do.'

'I do, too,' Caprice said. 'You may have noticed I'm pretty direct.'

'So I gather.'

'You're tall, and you look like a movie star. People see you and think, he must be somebody. It turns me on to be seen with you.'

'Here I was thinking the same thing about you.'

Caprice didn't duck the compliment. She didn't bat her eyes at him and protest: *Me? At my age?* Instead, she took a sip of expensive Albariño and said: 'Oh, I know I turn you on.'

'Am I that transparent?' Cab asked.

'Yes, you are, but your mother called and told me.' Caprice laughed. 'How's that for a pick-up line?'

'Actually, it's not the first time I've heard it.'

She laughed again. He liked her laugh, which was confident and smart. 'Knowing Tarla, I bet not. She's a force of nature. Do you ignore her advice? Or are you one of those sons who protests and protests and then does what she wants anyway?'

'I'll let you know when I figure it out,' Cab said.

He glanced over the iron railing at the dining area below them, which looked like the patio of a Spanish villa in the romantic light. They were on the mezzanine, which was a narrow alcove at the top of a tiled staircase, with a dozen tables discreetly overlooking what was called the Don Quixote room. Cut flowers adorned the tables. The mosaic designs reminded him of Andalucía. The Columbia in Ybor City was a mammoth destination, but its subdivided dining rooms managed to feel intimate.

'Do you like the piquillos?' Caprice asked, dipping her little finger in Manchego cheese and licking it with her tongue.

'Superb.'

'I can't believe you've never been here. It's a Florida institution.'

'The waiters know you,' Cab said. 'Is this where you take all your men?'

Caprice tilted her head, as if debating whether to be honest. 'I do come here a lot. This is my favorite table.'

They were at the end of the mezzanine, largely invisible to others around them. 'Just like a cat,' he said. 'Keeping your back to the wall.'

'Actually, it's a spy's table,' Caprice said. 'I can look down and watch people, and they don't know I'm doing it.'

'You didn't answer my question,' Cab pointed out. 'Do you take all your men here?'

Caprice brushed one of her hands back through her hair. 'I mostly come here with lobbyists and donors to talk about policy. I don't have much time for romance. Frankly, I need to be careful about who I'm seen with. Politics is a public business.'

'And yet you're here with me,' Cab said.

'I wouldn't mind being photographed with you. I wouldn't mind doing a lot of things with you.' She took a crab croquette from one of the tapas plates in front of them. 'Don't misinterpret. I'm not in the market for a relationship, but I do like having someone who looks good in a tux when I have to go to events. And afterward, well . . .'

'Friends with benefits?'

'We don't even have to be friends. I have plenty of friends. Some men would call that the perfect arrangement.'

'Yes, they would.'

Caprice put a hand over his and rubbed his index finger in a provocative way. 'Am I embarrassing you? Like I told you, I'm direct. Usually, you get what you want by taking it, rather than asking.'

'Did I say I was complaining?' Cab asked.

'No, you didn't. Good.' She bit into the croquette and brushed Cuban cracker crumbs from her lips. 'Tarla said you run like hell from real relationships.'

'She'd say I run like hell from her, too,' Cab said. 'And she's probably right. Having a rich, famous, beautiful mother who wants to control your life isn't the unqualified blessing you might think.'

'I'm sure.'

'My girlfriend probably says I run from her, too,' Cab added.

Caprice left her hand where it was. 'Ah.'

'She's Cuban. She's a cop. Tarla doesn't approve.'

'I suppose she's beautiful.'

'She is.'

'Well, then why are you here flirting with me?' Caprice asked.

'Because Lala and I can't seem to make it work between us. I'll take most of the blame for that, but she and Tarla aren't entirely guilt-free. And to be candid, I find you very attractive, which makes it hard to say no.'

'Then say yes.'

'I'm having a good time,' Cab told her. 'Let's leave it at that for now.'

'Fair enough.'

Cab leaned back in his chair. He heard the throb of flamenco music and the click of castanets from somewhere in the restaurant. The aromas of mussels and chorizo rose from the table. 'It surprises me that there's no man in your life.'

'My career is my life,' she told him.

'Is that lonely?'

'Not for a driven woman like me. There hasn't been anyone serious since Lyle.'

'I'm sorry.'

Caprice traced a nail around the rim of her wine glass. Her eyes were reflective. 'Can I be honest with you? Lyle and I were never really romantic soul mates. We shared political values and ambition. It was a relationship of common interests. Which isn't to say that I didn't love him. I suppose that must sound awful, given what happened.'

'No. You were both young.'

'Yes, we were. Lyle was so rigid, too. Inflexible. That made it difficult. It's funny, because our whole mission as a third party is not to let ideology be the enemy of the greater good. I don't really blame him, of course. He felt so responsible in his personal life. He was trying to be a father to his younger siblings, and that was tough. Anyway, I swore to myself I wouldn't have that kind of relationship again, and when we got the foundation up and running, I never sought out opportunities. Too busy saving the world, I guess.'

'Married to the cause?' Cab asked.

'Something like that.' She read his face and added: 'I know. You don't believe in causes.'

'One man's cause is another's obsession. The Liberty Empire Alliance is a cause, too.'

'For evil, not good.'

'Who gets to say which is which?' Cab asked.

Caprice winked. 'Me.'

'You think we'd be better off with a benevolent dictatorship? Give the people what they need, regardless of what they want?'

'Maybe we would. I could think of worse people than us to overthrow the government, but let's try a third party first. A party where compromise and common sense aren't dirty words. A party that doesn't look for all-or-nothing solutions.'

Rather than argue, Cab took another garlic-and-chili shrimp. Caprice was right; he didn't believe in causes. Once you really believed in something, you could make excuses for anything. The ends always justified the means. It wasn't a long journey from Diane Fairmont to Hamilton Brock.

'Speaking of the Liberty Empire Alliance,' Cab said.

'Ah yes, you went to prison today. And you talked to Chuck Warren, too. How did those conversations go?'

'Pretty much as you'd expect.'

'Do you think Hamilton Brock is behind the threats against Diane?'

'He says if he wanted Diane dead, she'd already be dead. That may be true, but it doesn't mean Brock doesn't know or suspect who's doing this. As for Chuck Warren, he thinks the threats are just a political ploy.'

Caprice cocked her head. 'You mean, we made it all up to get sympathy for Diane?'

'Yes.'

'What do you think?'

'I'm assuming the threat is real until I prove otherwise. That doesn't mean I don't have doubts. If I find out you and your people are playing me, I won't hesitate to expose it.'

'I'd expect nothing less.' She added: 'So what's your next step?'

Cab reached inside the pocket of his suit coat. He still had a copy of the article there, with the threat scrawled across it. He unfolded the page and tapped the newspaper byline. 'Rufus Twill. He was an Orlando reporter. Some boys from the Liberty Empire Alliance nearly put him in a wheelchair a few years ago. I suspect he still keeps pretty close tabs on them.'

Caprice frowned. 'I don't like the idea of getting the media involved.'

Cab couldn't help where his mind went. He thought: *Or is that exactly what you want?* Press. News. Headlines. He wondered if he was a marionette, and if Caprice was a sexy puppeteer who was guiding him exactly where she wanted him to go. He shoved the article back in his pocket without replying.

'There's something else,' he told her. 'I need to talk to Diane.'

'Is that really necessary? Diane is busy with the campaign, and I don't control her schedule. I'm not sure how she can help you.'

'Neither am I, until I talk to her.'

She pursed her lips. 'The thing is, I didn't tell Diane that I was asking you to look into this. She's not convinced the threat is real. She doesn't want to be seen as exploiting what happened back then.'

'Well, real or not, I need you to set up a meeting,' Cab said. 'It doesn't have to be long. Fifteen minutes.'

'What do you hope to learn?'

'She was there when Birch was killed. She may remember something that would point me in the right direction.'

'Diane won't talk about the murders,' Caprice said. 'She doesn't give interviews about it.'

Cab pictured Diane's face in his head. He saw her eyes across the courtyard and the look that had passed between them the previous night. A look of remembrance, guilt, and desire. He remembered her ten years ago, too, when her eyes were closed and her mouth was contorted in pleasure, and her body was underneath his own.

'She'll talk to me,' he said.

Outside the Columbia, a black luxury sedan pulled to the curb to collect Caprice. The street was crowded. The driver, who had the heft of a bodyguard, got out and opened the rear door for her. Caprice balanced gracefully on the tips of her shoes to kiss Cab on the cheek. She whispered in his ear.

'Would you like to come home with me?'

'That's tempting,' he said, 'but I can't.'

She eyed the street around them. He thought she was looking for photographers. People watching them. Smartphones spying on them. She put her warm fingers around the back of his neck, and he bent down this time, and they kissed. Her tongue slipped between his lips. Her nails were sharp enough to leave scratches.

'Just so you know what you're missing,' she said.

Caprice got into the town car, and the driver shut the door. The car drove off, and Cab, still a little breathless and with the taste of lipstick on his mouth, dodged the traffic as he crossed the street. His red Corvette was parked at a meter in front of a brick building that sold hand-painted tile. The top was up. He unlocked the door and folded his stilt-like legs inside.

That was when he realized the car wasn't empty.

Lala Mosqueda sat in the passenger seat.

She said: 'Are you sleeping with her?'

Cab dangled his keys from his finger. 'Nice to see you, too.'

'I've been wondering whether you were serious about our

relationship,' Lala said. 'I guess I got my answer.' She pushed open the passenger door.

'Wait.' Cab reached across the car to take her hand.

She turned back to him and sat silently. Her dark eyes were on fire. The breeze outside had rustled her coffee-black hair, and it was a web across her golden face. She was dressed in black, making her almost invisible.

'I'm not sleeping with her,' he said.

'Why not? I could see the flush on her face. She wants you. She'd probably give you a hell of a ride.'

'You want to play games? Fine, I'll call her now. Funny thing is, she calls me back. There's not a lot of that going around.'

Lala's lips turned downward. 'I'm on a work assignment, you know that. I'm busy.'

'So why are you here? How did you find me?'

'You checked in on Facebook,' Lala said.

He smiled. 'Right. Damn that Zuckerberg.'

'I figured it was an invitation. Or a taunt.'

'Could be,' Cab said.

'So what, did you want to throw it in my face that you're seeing someone else?'

'I'm not seeing anyone. Including you, apparently.'

They sat in angry silence. They did that a lot. When they were together there was always heat, which was good when they were in bed and bad when they took out their resentment on each other. In some ways it was easier when they were apart. When he'd pursued a murder investigation in Door County in the spring, he couldn't stop thinking about her. Their longing for each other was palpable every time they talked. Then, when he came back to Naples, they'd fallen into their usual pattern. Reaching for each other and then pushing the other away.

Tarla didn't help. Tarla, with her cutting remarks, trying to drive a wedge between them. His mother feigned innocence, but she didn't like Lala, and Lala didn't like her.

He could feel the heat. As angry as they were, they wanted each other. He could almost feel her breasts cupped in his long fingers and hear her telling him what she wanted. If he reached for her, they would kiss, and then they would drive somewhere and make love, and minutes later, they would have their daggers out again. He wondered what it was between them, because it wasn't just physical. He knew her body as intimately as he'd known any woman; he'd long since memorized every tiny imperfection that made her perfect. The birthmark on the inside of her thigh. The ticklish, knobby bones of her knees. The crescents under her eyes when she'd slept badly that she covered with makeup. She was beautiful, but not in a Hollywood way like Tarla. She was real. She had a real job. She had family she loved and family she hated. She worried about real things: money, kids, storms, death. Being around her made him feel real, too.

'How's Tarla?' Lala asked, getting to the heart of the problem.

'Tarla is Tarla. She's never going to change.'

'Is she still making snarky comments about me?'

'Yes.'

'Do you want to tell me what she said?'

'No. I told her to knock it off, but she won't. We both know that.'

'We sure do,' Lala said.

'Is that why you didn't call back? Because I'm with her?'

'Partly. Of course, I didn't realize that a weekend with your mother also included tongue time with a leggy brunette.' She added: 'Let me guess. Tarla set you up with her.'

'Yes,' Cab admitted.

'Big surprise. Who is she?'

'Her name's Caprice Dean.'

Lala's head turned sharply. 'Are you kidding me? From the Common Way Foundation?'

'You know her?'

'She works with Diane Fairmont, right?'

Cab nodded. 'Tarla and Diane are best friends. I've told you that.'

'Well, you're playing in powerful circles, Cab. I guess that's where you belong.'

'Caprice asked me to do a job. It's not personal. I won't deny that she's attractive, and I won't deny that it's pretty clear there could be something there with her if I wanted it. I also won't deny that I'm pissed as hell that you've been ignoring me for weeks.'

'What's the job?' Lala asked.

'Someone may be targeting Diane Fairmont. There may be links to what happened to her husband ten years ago. The FBI and police are looking into it, but Caprice wanted someone working for her.'

'Or under her,' Lala said.

'Funny.'

'The feebs have the resources for this kind of case. You don't.'

Cab shrugged. 'True enough, but it's not that simple.'

'Because of your mother.'

'Right. Like I said, she and Diane are friends.'

'Diane is a candidate for governor. You have no idea what you're getting yourself into. This is a hornet's nest, Cab.'

'You may be right,' he admitted.

Lala opened the car door again. 'It was a mistake to come here. I'm sorry to ambush you.'

'Why did you?'

He felt her dark eyes on him. He saw the fullness of her lips, and he urgently wanted to kiss those lips. He missed her, and he felt like a fool.

'Because I believe there is something in you and me that is worth salvaging,' she told him.

'I do, too.'

'Then – and I can't stress this strongly enough – I suggest you *not* have sex with Caprice Dean.'

He chose not to take the bait. 'When can I see you again?' he asked.

'I don't know.'

'Nice.'

'I'm not trying to avoid you. I've got an assignment that's keeping me away from Naples. You know that.'

'Well, you've got my number,' Cab said, 'so call me maybe.'

Lala couldn't help herself. She laughed. She got out of the Corvette, and her movements were like a cat's. Her black clothes fit like a second skin. When she leaned back inside, her face had turned serious again. 'Does Tarla know about you and Diane? Your history together?'

'Only if Diane told her,' Cab said.

'Is it a problem for you?'

'Not so far, but I haven't seen Diane yet.'

'I meant what I said, Cab. Be careful. You may find yourself in over your head with these people. Even you.'

'I appreciate the advice.'

'No, you don't.' Lala shut the door, and she was gone.

12

Peach sat in the dark. It was past midnight. She didn't like air conditioning, and the house was damp and hot. She wore a spaghetti strap T-shirt and a roomy pair of Deacon's boxers she'd grabbed from the laundry. Her small feet were propped on the dusty living room coffee table, and her taped ankle throbbed. Sexpot Mannequin kept her company. Sexpot had hard nipples on crazy-big breasts, one arm cocked behind her head, and oddly muscular abs. She usually hung out in Peach's bedroom wearing a baby doll and a long blond wig.

The mannequin thing was strange. She knew that, but she didn't care. Some people collected stuffed animals. Some people dressed up Barbies. She liked having these faux women around, who were blank slates on which she could fashion new identities. They were her alter egos.

Justin on her mannequins. *I'm not sure they like me. I think they're worried I'll steal you away.*

Outside, headlights beamed through the picture window, and she heard the purr of the Mercedes engine. Deacon was home. She listened to his footsteps and then the rattle of the key as he let himself inside. He brought a smell of sweat with him; he'd been at the 24-hour gym. She said nothing, and he didn't see her in the living room shadows. He headed through the foyer to his bedroom at the back of the house, and a couple minutes later, she heard the loud bang of the pipes as he took a shower. Their bathrooms were old, and the water was rusty.

It was just the two of them. Peach and Deacon. They had the typical relationship of siblings who were close and not close, totally different and totally alike. They lived together; they worked together; they spent time together. Even so, he was six years older, and she still felt like a little kid around him. He had never tried to be a father to her, just an older brother with his own life. Unlike Lyle. When their parents died, Lyle had jumped into the role of fill-in dad, as if it were his calling. It changed him. It was weird how quickly Lyle aged in those years. Losing his hair. His voice deepening. Becoming so serious and strict.

She idolized Lyle, but that was the fuzzy glow of memory. He wasn't perfect. He'd often been harsh and judgmental with both of them. He could be neglectful, especially that last year, when politics constantly took him away. The Common Way Party was his priority then, not her. She remembered a long weekend in Tampa that last August. Deacon and Peach had gone on the road with Lyle, but instead of having fun in the city, Lyle had packed fundraising meetings into his schedule night and day, leaving them alone. Then, to make things worse, Peach contracted a case of pneumonia that left her hacking and feverish. Lyle acted as if it were her fault – like she was being sick just to inconvenience him. He'd insisted that Deacon drive her back to Lake Wales, and that had prompted a big argument, because Deacon wanted to stay. Then Deacon hit a deer on the road, damaging Lyle's precious new Mercedes. Another big argument. Peach had been practically delirious, but she had never forgotten the curses flying for days.

Those were among her last memories of Lyle, and she didn't like it that way.

The shower stopped. Not long after, Deacon turned on the light, making her squint. He stood in the living room doorway, with his muscular body wrapped in a worn bath towel.

'Fruity,' he said in surprise. 'I didn't know you were still up.'

'Couldn't sleep.'

He sat down on the old sofa next to her. She could feel warmth radiating from his skin, and his wavy red hair was damp. 'What's Sexpot doing in here?' he asked.

'Oh, you know her. She gets around.'

Deacon laughed. 'You get anything at the convention today?'

'Actually, I didn't go. The new girl, Annalie, hung out with me at the beach.'

'Good for you.' He pointed at her taped ankle. 'How'd you do that?'

'I stepped wrong in the sand. It's nothing. I'm fine.'

She thought about telling him about her visit to Justin's apartment – and her confrontation with the stranger pretending to be a St Petersburg detective – but she knew Deacon would be stern. He was overprotective, like Lyle, and he wouldn't like the idea of her sticking her nose into Justin's murder.

Was that what she was doing? She hadn't really admitted it to herself, but it was true. She didn't believe his death had anything to do with drugs. He'd been hiding something from her, and whatever it was had gotten him killed. She thought about Annalie. *Sometimes special projects go on behind the scenes. People get recruited to do things they don't want to do.*

'Can I ask you something?' she said.

'Sure.'

'Do you know what Justin was working on before he was killed?'

Deacon shook his head. 'No, Ogden pretty much had him under his thumb those last few weeks.'

'Ogden did?'

'Well, it looked that way. I saw Justin in his office a lot. You know how Ogden works. He keeps us walled off, so he can dodge the blame if things go wrong. Why? What's going on?'

Peach shrugged. 'It's nothing,' she lied. 'Annalie was wondering if she needed to follow up on any of Justin's projects.'

Deacon hesitated, as if deciding whether to believe her. Then he slapped her on the leg. 'Okay, I'm going to bed.' He got up, tightening the knot of his towel. 'You mind if I take Sexpot to my room? I like it when she watches me.'

'Ewww,' Peach said.

Her brother laughed. 'I'm kidding. Get some sleep.'

'I will. Hey, Deacon?'

'What?'

'Do you know anyone named Alison?'

He scrunched his mouth and thought about it. 'Alison? I don't think so. Who is she?'

'It's a name Justin mentioned.'

'Well, there's an Alison Kuipers at the law firm that Ms Fairmont uses. She signs off on legal questions for some of the jobs we do.'

'So if Justin had concerns about something, he would have called her?'

'Yeah, could be.'

'Thanks,' Peach said. 'It's not a big deal. I was just curious.'

Deacon mussed her hair, which he knew she hated. 'Go to bed, Fruity. It's late.'

'I will.'

Peach waited as Deacon returned to his bedroom. He turned off the light behind him, leaving her in darkness. The pale glow of a streetlight down the block made Sexpot's white limbs shimmer.

Peach wondered what it would be like to be empty at the core, dressed up so that people saw whatever they wanted to see.

Maybe that was her.

She waited half an hour without moving. It was past one in the morning. When she stood up, her twisted ankle protested, but she limped toward the front door. Not making a sound, Peach slipped out of the house, past the warped gates and the No Trespassing and Beware of Dog signs. She crossed the street in the humid haze and crept beside the fence guarding Seminole Park. The ground under her feet was damp. At the gate, she slipped into the bug-infested woods and slapped away insects that tried to fly up her nose. They swarmed her, as if they were trying to warn her away.

She ran to her Thunderbird.

She knew there was no going back now. She was all in.

The monitor on Peach's desk glowed in a rectangle of white light. Around her, the foundation research office was dark. She'd left the overhead fluorescent lights off. Her T-Bird wasn't parked in its usual spot, number 52, across from the Tampa mural. Instead, she'd parked outside an apartment building two blocks away, which wasn't visible from the office's double doors.

She didn't want anyone knowing about her late-night visit, but she knew she was leaving electronic footprints. That was the risk she had to take. If someone looked, they would see that her pass card had been used to enter the building at 1:52 a.m. If someone looked, they would also see that the dormant foundation computer account for Justin Kiel had been accessed at 1:57 a.m.

She knew his password. She hoped that no one had thought to completely deactivate his account, but when she keyed in *Tyger1827*, it was as if Justin had never died. His files were still there. His office e-mail was still there. She assumed the police had been through everything following the murder, but they were looking for evidence of drugs, suppliers, and customers. Peach knew there was nothing like that to find.

She ran a search of his files. *Alison.*

She ran a search of his e-mail. *Alison.*

Both searches elicited no results. She tried again with the last name that Deacon had given her – Kuipers – and got no hits again. If Justin had been in touch with the attorney at the foundation law firm, he'd done it offline. Peach knew him. He wouldn't have left digital records.

His e-mails made her sad. Many of them were to her. As she scrolled through his file of sent messages, she found herself smiling. Then crying. He wrote to her about work. He wrote to her about music and poetry. He wrote to her with his little philosophies about the world. He wrote to her every day, and then he didn't write to her at all. That last week, he dropped off the radar completely. As she studied his account, she saw that his last sent message was dated a week before he was killed. He hadn't been in the office those last several days.

However, Peach studied his mail folders and saw two draft messages. Unsent. When she opened the folder, she saw that both messages had been composed the evening before his death, and for some reason, he'd left them undelivered. She wondered where he had written them, because he hadn't been in the office that night. She'd been here herself, alone.

The first message was to her, and it included an attachment. Peach held her breath as she clicked on the draft e-mail, wondering what she would find. She expected something deep, something secret, that only she would be able to interpret.

Instead, the mail message said simply: *Cool place!*

She opened the attachment, which was a jpeg photograph taken with her own phone. She saw herself. Justin had taken a picture of her in front of a restaurant called The Crab Shack on Gandy Road. They'd eaten there several months earlier and spent hours over beer and Chesapeake-style blue crabs, hammering and picking meat from the tiny bodies. It was a happy memory. She looked carefree in the photo, with a big smile on her face, mugging and pointing her thumb over her shoulder. The restaurant, which was a tin-roof dive, was behind her, its exterior packed with kitschy decorations. A Landshark surfboard. A neon lobster in the window. Beer buckets and scrap metal crabs.

Peach studied the photo, and when the glow of her memory faded, she looked at it again and thought: *That's not right.*

Something was wrong, something odd, but the more she looked at it, the less she trusted her instincts. It was just an old photo. She'd seen it before. No big deal. And then she thought: *Why would Justin send me this again?* Why that photo? Why that night of all nights?

She sat in the darkness, but she had no answers. She clicked the Send button, and almost immediately her phone beeped as the e-mail arrived at her account.

Peach opened the second unsent message. This one was to Ogden Bush. It read simply: *I need to see you.*

Justin was trying to meet with Bush the night before he was killed, but he never sent the e-mail. Something secret was going on between Justin and Bush. That was what Deacon had suspected: *Ogden had him under his thumb.*

Peach logged off the account and switched off her monitor. The office was black, so she took a flashlight from her desk drawer. Following the light, she left her cubicle and made her way along the rear wall to Bush's office. The door was closed and locked, but that didn't matter. This had been Deacon's office until Bush bumped him out to a smaller desk during the campaign. Peach had a key, and she let herself inside.

The office smelled like Ogden Bush, which meant it smelled like heavy, expensive cologne. She cast her light around the room. Even in the short time he'd worked here, he'd filled the office with personal memorabilia. Photos of himself with Democratic politicians and Miami hip-hop celebs. Headlines from winning campaigns and from scandals that had engulfed his opponents. Plaques from Florida charities. College trophies for tennis. He carried his huge ego and his high-powered connections with him wherever he went.

Peach spotted the filing cabinet behind his desk. Using her flashlight, she quickly opened and shuffled through his desk drawers. She figured he kept a backup key in the office, and she was right. When she yanked open the bottom-most cubbyhole drawer, she found a silver key taped underneath it.

She opened the filing cabinet. The top drawer was stuffed with folders, seemingly in no order. She shuffled through them, but they were mostly historical, dealing with political maneuverings dating back for years. One of the folders was labeled with the name Chuck Warren. Another, immediately behind it, bore the name of Birch Fairmont. She was tempted to look, but for the time being she ignored them and moved to the second drawer.

The folder she wanted was at the front, as if it had been recently reviewed. The name on the tab said Justin Kiel. Peach pushed the tight folders apart and tried to squeeze the file on Justin out of the drawer, but before she could get it, she heard a muffled noise breaking the dead silence of the office. It was the street door opening and closing on the other side of the building.

Someone was coming inside.

Peach slammed the drawer shut. She switched off the flashlight and stumbled to Bush's office door. She pulled it closed behind her and crab-walked to the first open cubicle, where she threw herself inside, hugging the wall. Overhead, the fluorescent lights flickered to life, bathing the entire room in a bright, noon-time glow. She heard footsteps and whistling. Someone walked down the corridor, passing immediately next to the cubicle where she was hiding, and she recognized an aroma that she'd smelled only moments earlier.

Cologne.

Ogden Bush. He was here in the middle of the night.

She heard the man continue to his office door. His keys jangled in his hand. He pushed the key into the lock, but then she heard something that made her hold her breath. The door shoved open under his hand. It wasn't locked. She hadn't closed it completely when she made her escape.

The jangling stopped. The whistling stopped.

Bush retraced his steps. She could sense his closeness. He was so near her that she could hear the measured in-and-out noise of his breathing.

'Hello?' he called, his voice smooth and suspicious.

Peach waited. She kept as still as one of her mannequins.

'Is anyone there?' Bush demanded.

He waited, listening, as a full minute passed. Then another. Peach squirmed, uncomfortable in the tight space beside the cubicle wall. An overwhelming desire to pee made her squeeze her knees together. Finally, Bush turned back, and she heard him go into the office and close the door behind him. She decided to press her luck and get away, but as she unfolded her legs and crawled to the cubicle doorway, she heard his door open again. She didn't have time to hide. If he stopped, if he glanced inside the cubicle, he would see her.

Bush walked right by her. Short, suave, confident. He swung his briefcase in his hand, and he marched down the corridor without a sideways glance. He was whistling again. She saw his head bobbing in time to the tune on his lips. His suit looked as lush as silk, and his shoes had a mirror shine. Moments later, the office lights went off again, and she was alone, hugging her knees and staring into nothingness.

She gave him ten minutes to make sure he was gone. She knew she should leave quickly, but before she did, she checked Bush's office one last time. She unlocked the door. Unlocked the filing cabinet. Opened the drawer.

The file on Justin was gone.

Bush had taken it.

13

Cab parked his Corvette in a gravel driveway outside a white bungalow on the shore of Lake Hamilton, which was a long, slow drive from the Gulf in the center of the state. He climbed from the cold sports car into the afternoon heat. The temperature was in the nineties, and the sky over the lake was cloudless and baby blue. It was Sunday, July 1, and if the weather forecasters were right, Chayla would reach central Florida by Independence Day and surge ashore with sixty-mile-an-hour winds. Right now, the rotating storm, which looked like the Milky Way inching through the Caribbean, felt a long way off.

He wore a dark navy suit and burgundy-framed Gucci sunglasses. He'd polished his leather shoes that morning, and though the shine never lasted more than a day, Cab liked to keep them that way. Standing in the hot sun, with his hands in his pockets, he felt sweat gathering on his skin like a glaze brushed on St Louis ribs.

The house where Rufus Twill lived was old and unkempt. Spanish moss dripped from the trees and made decaying brown piles on the roof. The aluminum siding was crusted with dirt. Dead flowers drooped from clay pots dangling from the gutters. Twill, who'd spent twenty years as a reporter for an Orlando newspaper, was living on Social Security disability income now. He lived alone. Never married.

Cab rang the doorbell, and when no one answered he removed his sunglasses and peered through the oval window in the house's red front door. He could see through the small living room to the patio windows looking out on the lake, but he didn't see anyone inside. He wandered to the rear of the house, where a wide lawn, with overgrown grass and weeds, sloped toward the water. He saw a rickety dock with a new, brightly painted airboat tied to one of the posts. Twill lived on the southeast shore of the kidney-shaped lake, and Cab could see trees and thick marshes lining the far banks. He walked out to the dock and picked his way to the platform over the dirty, shallow water. Overhead, a bald eagle floated on the air in graceful circles.

His phone whistled in his pocket. Two voicemail messages had arrived during the drive inland. The first message was a familiar voice.

'*Cab, it's Caprice. I enjoyed last night. We should do it again. I set up a private meeting for you with Diane tonight at 9 p.m. Call me after if you want a late drink.*'

He thought about Lala's very specific suggestion not to have sex with Caprice. A late drink at her place would likely lead to bed. As appealing as that idea sounded, he decided he wouldn't call her. He hoped his willpower lasted through the evening.

The second voicemail message was a complete surprise.

'*Cab, this is Ramona Cortes. I believe we met briefly at a family wedding over the winter. I'd like to talk to you at lunch tomorrow. Let's say the Pilot House at the Tampa Yacht Club at 1 p.m. Call my aide if there's a problem.*'

Ramona had a slight hint of a Hispanic accent in her prosecutorial voice. Cab knew her enough to know that there was steel at the heart of her personality. Lunch with the Attorney General wasn't a request. It was an expectation. Drop everything, and be there.

Things were getting interesting.

Cab slid his phone into his pocket, but he didn't have time to think about what Ramona might want with him. Instead, a voice called to him from the end of the dock: 'Get those long arms in the air, friend.'

Cab turned around slowly. A small black man in his fifties stood in the overgrown grass. In one hand, he cradled a foot-long baby alligator. In the other, he held a grimy revolver with a wooden grip and eight-inch barrel that looked as if it hadn't been fired since the 1970s. Cab spread his fingers wide and cocked his forearms.

'I'm Detective Bolton, Mr Twill. We spoke on the phone.'

'Yeah, I talked to somebody. Let me see a badge and a photo ID, so I can see who you really are.'

Cab kept his hands up as he walked back along the dock, which shifted under his feet, almost throwing him into the lake. 'I hope I don't look like a member of the Liberty Empire Alliance,' he said.

'You'd be surprised.'

At the end of the dock, Cab peeled back the lapel of his coat and reached inside with two fingers to extract his wallet and badge. Twill leaned forward to study his credentials, and when he was satisfied, he shoved the big gun into his paint-streaked cargo pants.

'Can't be too careful,' Twill added.

'I understand. You should probably clean that gun. It's just as likely to blow up in your face as it is to shoot somebody else.'

Twill shrugged. 'It's not loaded. I hate guns.'

'I'm not a big fan either,' Cab admitted. 'Who's your friend?'

'This is Boots.' He used one finger to stroke the head of the alligator, which watched Cab with beady eyes and snapped its jaws.

'Alligator Boots,' Cab said. 'That's funny.'

'Boots could take your finger off if he were so inclined.'

'Well, one of my guiding principles in life is never to stick my fingers in an alligator's mouth,' Cab said.

Twill allowed a smile to crease his face. His skin was a light oak color, with mottled darker spots on his forehead. He wasn't tall, and he was skinny, with bony arms left bare by a loose gray tank top. He wore a Chicago Cubs baseball cap. One of his chocolate-brown eyes stared at Cab, and the other was fixed, like glass. A milky scar ran along the line of his misshapen chin.

'So what is it you want, Detective?'

'Are we off the record?' Cab asked.

'You don't have to worry about that. Since the beating, I don't write anymore. It scrambled my brain.'

'I'm sorry.'

'It is what it is. Like they say, the Lord closes a door, he opens a window somewhere else. I can't put two words together now, but I can play piano like some kind of Art Tatum. Or at least it feels that way to me. Stop by Cherry Pocket for dinner some Friday. You can judge for yourself.'

'I may do that.' Cab added: 'I suppose you can guess what I'd like to talk to you about.'

'Sure. Ham Brock, Chuck Warren, Birch Fairmont, all that ugly stuff back then. You realize about a thousand cops have gone down this road before you.'

'Well, do you mind going for a thousand and one?'

'I don't mind, but if it means giving up a source, even from a decade ago, I won't do that.'

'Understood.'

Twill pursed his lips. He glanced at his house and the surrounding woods, whose branches hung limply as if they were wilting in the humid air. 'How about we go out on the boat? My new toy. Let me just put Boots in his cage.'

'Do you think your house is bugged?' Cab asked, with a small smile.

Twill didn't smile back. 'You never know.'

The former reporter turned on his heel and headed up the lawn toward his back door. He walked with a pronounced limp. He wasn't gone five minutes before he returned to the dock, with a six-pack of Bud Light dangling from one hand. He and Cab boarded the airboat. Twill took the seat beside the rudder stick, and Cab sat next to him. Twill fired up the caged propeller, which howled like a Boeing jet, and smoothly guided the flat-bottom boat onto the lake.

As they reached open water, Twill accelerated. A cooling wind blew back Cab's styled hair, and spray dampened his suit. Twill secured his Cubs cap low on his forehead. He raced all the way to the far shore, where a large field of grassy marshes grew out of the water. Twill slowed and turned the boat directly into the tall grass, and the airboat easily slipped inside the wetland, obscured from view. Cab could see the muddy bottom; the lake was only six inches deep here. Lilypads and green algae dotted the surface. Black flies buzzed the boat. He saw a full-size alligator – at least seven feet – sunning itself on a sandbar among the reeds.

Twill cut the motor and popped open a beer. He offered one to Cab, who shook his head.

'I do this every day. Not so bad, huh? I used to live in Orlando and work for a living. Who needs that? Guess there has to be a fringe benefit to nine weeks in a coma.' He waved at the alligator. 'How's it going today, Rex? Swallow up any tourists?' Twill chuckled and took a slug of beer. 'So what kind of a name is Cab?' he asked.

'My mother was a big fan of the movie *Cabaret*,' Cab said.

'With Liza?'

'Right.'

'Hmm.' Twill drank more beer, and then he pulled a joint out of his pocket. 'You going to turn me in? It's medicinal. For the pain.'

'Do what you have to do,' Cab said.

Twill lit the joint and stretched out his legs. The marshland around them was a secluded nature preserve, walled off from the rest of the lake. Cab saw the walnut-sized head of a turtle poking out of the water. Nearby, a white heron darted its long neck into the ripples and emerged with a squirming fish.

'So when did it happen?' Cab asked.

Twill knew what he meant. 'Nine years ago this Wednesday.'

'The Fourth of July?'

'That's it. That also happens to be the day that Ham Brock and some of his buddies started serving their sentences for tax fraud, money laundering, and weapons violations. I guess their friends wanted to thank me for all the articles I'd done about the Alliance over the years. About six of them in hoods grabbed me out back of my apartment in Maitland. Took me in the trunk to a deserted section of the Ocala. I woke up in the hospital in September.'

'I'm sorry.' Cab didn't like that the Fourth of July – in three days – was an anniversary that had special meaning to Hamilton Brock and the members of the Liberty Empire Alliance.

'And here I am,' Twill went on.

'Do you still keep an eye on the Alliance?' Cab asked.

'One eye is all I've got.'

Cab winced. 'Yes, of course.'

'Never mind,' Twill replied, grinning. 'Sure I do. I never know when they might decide to come back and finish the job. I've got sources that keep me in the loop.'

'I was wondering if you'd heard any rumors about the Alliance targeting Diane Fairmont,' Cab said. He swatted away a particularly voracious fly. The heat was concentrated inside the grassy marsh, and he felt the sun cooking his long nose.

'Can't say as I have,' Twill told him.

'Nothing at all?' Cab asked.

'You sound like you were expecting a different answer.'

'I was.'

'Well, something like that would be kept way under wraps. Just because it hasn't hit my ears doesn't mean it's not happening. What are you thinking? The Alliance got rid of Birch, so now that Diane is in the race, why not get rid of her, too? Kind of a revenge thing?'

'Something like that.'

Twill rubbed the scar on his chin. He sucked on the joint, looking relaxed. 'What makes you so sure they got rid of Birch?'

Cab was surprised. 'You don't think the Alliance was involved? That's not what you said back then.'

'Oh, I was on a rampage about hate groups in those days. Still am. People don't take these domestic terrorists seriously, but they're plenty dangerous. The Islamists don't have a monopoly on crazy. Ten years ago, you had politicians like Chuck Warren coddling these boys and calling them patriots. I held his feet to the fire over that, and it cost him the election.'

'So what am I missing?' Cab asked. 'The Alliance had a major grudge against Birch over his political policies. They came after you for writing about them. Why do you now think Hamilton Brock may be innocent?'

'I never said innocent. Him and his crowd, they're bad, bad boys. Did one of them also put on a hood and shoot up the Bok? The FBI says yes. Me, well, I'm not so sure anymore.'

'What changed?'

Twill sighed and flicked the joint in the water. 'Let's say I know there's a difference between assassination and murder,' he replied.

Cab listened to the insects chattering. He began to understand why Twill preferred to talk in a place that was sheltered from electronic spies. 'Are you saying that you think the motive wasn't political?'

'I'm saying that whoever pulled the trigger knew the hammer was going to fall on the Alliance. Maybe it was those boys, maybe it wasn't. Honestly, I don't really care either way. You won't find me shedding any tears over Ham Brock taking the fall.'

'Except something must have put the idea in your head.'

Twill yanked his tank top over his baseball cap. 'Shit, it's hot. Ain't you roasting in that suit? Why do you wear something like that in Florida?'

'That's who I am,' Cab said.

Twill called to the alligator. 'It's who he is, Rex. You believe that? An idiot is who he is.'

Cab couldn't decide if Twill was drunk or stoned or simply ducking the subject. 'Somebody obviously told you something.'

'Hey, why tell stories about the dead? Birch is gone, right? That's probably for the best. A lot of people knew he was a son of a bitch. He would have gone down in flames sooner or later. Even his insiders were on to him. Lyle Piper called me the Saturday before Labor Day. Said we needed to have a talk.'

'About what?'

'I don't know. I was in the Keys that weekend. No phone. But I heard things after the murders that made me put two and two together.'

'So help me do the math,' Cab said.

Twill took a second beer can and rubbed the cool, damp aluminum over his chest. 'Okay, look, I'm not saying it means anything. People get mad, they blow off steam. You don't ruin somebody's life over that. That's why I never printed anything.'

'Who are you talking about?'

Twill sighed. 'You know that Diane had a son, right?'

'Drew,' Cab said.

'Right. Drew. He had big problems, okay? Heavy into drugs. Hanging out with some really bad people. He killed himself not too long after the murders. Thing is, Drew hated Birch Fairmont. I mean, *hated* him.'

'Who told you that?'

Twill put a finger on the side of his nose. 'Sources. I can't name names.'

'Okay, so Drew and Birch didn't get along. That's not exactly news when it comes to stepsons and stepdads.'

'Oh, this was more than not getting along. Believe me. Look, I didn't go searching for this. I was a reporter, and I was convinced that Ham Brock and the Alliance had gone off the deep end. I was hunting for proof to put the bastards away. This gal I talked to, she didn't want to tell me anything. It kinda spilled out. I don't think she told the police either.'

'Told them what?' Cab asked.

'A couple weeks before the murders, there was a problem at Birch's estate.'

'What kind of problem?'

'She wouldn't say. Or maybe she didn't exactly know, but it sounded mean. What she did know is that Drew was so wild about it that he got dropped into rehab. Know when he got out? Right before Labor Day. Interesting, huh?'

'But you don't know what happened,' Cab said.

'I don't. I looked for dirt, but nobody would talk. Even my original source got cold feet. She told me she didn't hear what she said she heard. Well, it ain't the kind of thing you're likely to make a mistake about.'

'What did she hear?'

Twill leaned closer to Cab. The beer and pot were on his breath.

'She told me she heard Drew screaming about how he was going to kill Birch Fairmont. This was right before he got shipped off to rehab. Quote unquote, he was going to blow his fucking head off.'

Rufus Twill waited until the tall detective disappeared around the front of his house. He stayed in the boat, which bobbed gently in the waves beside the dock. He took off his baseball cap and rubbed his sweaty hands through his hair. When he was sure that he was alone, he popped another beer and dug a phone out of his pocket. He dialed a number with one hand.

'It's Rufus,' he said.

'You shouldn't be calling me,' Ogden Bush replied.

'Yeah? Well, I thought you'd want to know. Somebody else is poking into the old shit. A detective named Bolton. He says he's working for Common Way. Just wondering if you'd heard about that.'

There was a long silence from the political operative. 'Interesting.'

'So they're keeping things from you, huh? Sounds like they don't necessarily trust you over there, Ogden.'

'Shut up, Rufus.'

'Hey, I didn't need to call. I'm doing you a favor.'

'I know. I appreciate it.'

'Yeah, well, appreciation don't come free. I like my new boat, but I was thinking, my truck's getting kind of old, too. Thought you might be able to do something about that.'

He could almost hear Bush grinding his teeth. 'I'll see what I can do. Now what did you tell the detective?'

'Oh, don't you worry about that,' Twill replied. 'I told him exactly what I told that kid Justin. Guess we'll see if Bolton winds up dead, too.'

14

'You okay, hun?'

Peach looked up from her plate of fried shrimp, which she hadn't touched. She sat at a long table in a corner of the Crab Shack restaurant, next to a lovey-dovey couple feeding each other bites of crab across the table. The Sunday afternoon crowd was noisy, and Peach had a headache.

'What?' she said.

'Just wanted to make sure you're all right,' the waitress repeated. 'You're not eating.'

Peach nibbled half-heartedly on a French fry. 'Oh, yeah, thanks. I don't have much of an appetite. Could you package this to go?'

'Sure, hun.' She added: 'Where's your friend?'

'My friend?'

'You came in here once before with a real nice guy. Had one of those old-fashioned mustaches. You guys looked so cute together.'

Peach tried to muster a smile. 'He's busy.'

The waitress put her hand on Peach's shoulder and gave her a just-us-girls look of sympathy, as if she'd blundered into the middle of a bad break-up. 'I understand, hun. I'm real sorry.'

Peach didn't say anything. All she could think about was that Justin wasn't here anymore. She could picture his face and hear his voice, but soon the memories would begin to fade. Like Lyle. Like her parents. She was holding on to a fraying lifeline, and eventually it would give way.

Justin on memory. *Everybody forgets everybody else. Fame doesn't buy you anything but a few years.*

When she'd paid her bill, Peach picked her way through the crowded tables and made her way outside. She stood near the entrance with the busy traffic on Gandy Road roaring in both directions behind her. This was where she'd been standing in the photograph that Justin had tried to send her. She could picture herself with the silly grin on her face, her thumb jerking toward the door as if she were hitchhiking. It was nothing special, just one moment in the history of all of their moments.

Why would he want to send it to her again? Why on that night?

Justin always had a plan. She dug out her phone and opened the attachment she'd forwarded to herself. With the screen in front of her, she flicked her eyes back and forth between the photo and the funky décor of the Crab Shack. Everything was the same. The neon in the windows. The giant plastic blue crab. The ship's rope tied between old driftwood. The yellow surfboard. Nothing had changed.

Except – no. That wasn't true.

The street number of the restaurant was hung on a little sign above the windows: 11400. However, the photo on her phone showed a completely different number: 10761. Justin had edited the photo. It was a skillful job; no one would notice the alteration if they weren't standing in front of the building. He was sending her a message, but what was he trying to tell her?

Looking at the restaurant, she spotted another tiny change in the photo. Between the words CRAB and SHACK on the roof sign was a little white house that was shaped like an arrow. The house was tilted to the left as she stared at it, but in the picture on her phone, the house – the arrow – pointed right. The actual sign was angled toward an open, empty field beside the restaurant, but the sign in the photo pointed in the opposite direction, toward a side street leading away from Gandy Road.

Suddenly, she could feel Justin guiding her. He wanted her to follow the arrow.

Peach jogged to the side street, which was San Fernando Drive. It was a nothing street, lined with telephone wires and crowded by palms and pines, but she stared at it now as if it were keeping secrets. She wandered down the middle of the street and found herself near a deserted industrial lot on the left. Everything was quiet, except for the shriek of birds. A quarter-mile down the road, she passed two run-down bungalows on large, unkempt lots. Cars and boats were strewn across weedy lawns. Evergreens towered over the houses and threw needles across the gravel. She passed another intersection. More remote houses. More trees. Badly fenced yards with children's toys. Gardens growing nothing. It was a typical old Florida neighborhood, where progress had stopped in 1955.

Ahead of her, the road ended at a concrete barricade. She walked all the way to the fence and saw only an abandoned road overgrown with brush. There was nothing here and nowhere else to go. Frustrated, she turned around, and that was when she spotted the mailbox on the last house on the road.

The number on the box was 10761.

Peach felt herself breathing faster.

It was a tiny white house, no more than a few hundred square feet, behind a four-foot chainlink fence surrounding a big lot. The lawn was scrub and dandelions. The house had a matchbox screened porch on the right, which enclosed the front door. Six identical windows faced the street; all the blinds were closed. Flowering bushes had been planted underneath the windows, but the vines were shriveled and dead. A bushy oak tree loomed over the entire house.

She was alone. The road was deserted, and the house was isolated among the empty lots. If you wanted to hide where no one would see you or find you, this was the perfect place. She checked the mailbox, but it was empty. Even so, she knew she was where Justin wanted her to be.

Peach climbed the low fence. The driveway was cracked and furry with weeds. At the porch, she opened the swinging door, disturbing the web of a large spider. There was no furniture on the concrete slab. Despite the shade, the porch was stifling. She knocked on the door to the house, but she didn't expect an answer, and she didn't get one. When she turned the knob, she found that the door was open. She stepped cautiously into a small living room.

This was Justin's house. His safe house. She saw all of his antiques, all of his quirky collectibles. She'd been with him when he bought many of them. This was where he kept his personal life, where no one could find his secrets. Or so he'd believed.

He was wrong. Peach was too late.

Someone had found the place before her. Someone had beaten her to it. The house had been searched. Antiques that may have hidden anything lay in shards on the floors. Books had been ripped apart; so had the chairs and sofas. There were holes punched in the walls. If there had been anything to find, it was gone. She wanted to cry. It was almost worse, finding this corner of Justin's life that she had never seen before and realizing that a stranger had already violated it. Her breath came raggedly. Her eyes felt full. The house smelled like him, but he was gone.

Peach crossed from the living room to the house's single bedroom. It was dark even in the daylight. The wooden floor groaned under her feet. There was a twin bed, with a mattress that had been slashed, and a state-of-the-art desktop computer that had been disassembled to remove its hard drive, leaving a hole. The monitor was smashed, exposing its interior components. A file cabinet was pushed against the wall, its drawers open and empty. He'd had pictures on the wall, but they'd been ripped apart, exposing the rear of the frames.

Nothing. They'd left her nothing.

She saw a table near the bedroom's only window, which looked out on the sorry lawn. Outside, she saw the mature oak tree with a canvas chair beneath it. A ladder in the dirt. A push lawnmower that had long since rusted into disuse. Inside, there was a coffee mug on the table. She could imagine Justin here, sipping tea, staring at the lonely brush, working on – what?

A photo frame lay on the floor near the table, its glass broken. The photo was still inside the frame. It was her. It was the same photo of Peach standing outside the Crab Shack restaurant.

Another message?

If so, she didn't understand it, because this photograph didn't contain the edits she'd seen on her phone. Maybe the picture was simply a reminder that he'd been in love with her. He'd kept it in his bedroom. He'd stared at her when he was here.

She felt like crying all over again.

Peach took a long, deep breath of hot, dusty air. There was no evidence to find here, nothing that would help her. She'd reached another dead end. However, as she took a last look around the bedroom, she spotted a tiny triangle of paper peeking out from under the file cabinet. When she pushed the empty cabinet aside, she jumped as a three-inch lizard made a frantic escape. She bent down and retrieved the paper.

Someone – Justin? – had taken a close-up picture of a newspaper article that been pinned to a cork bulletin board. It was impossible to tell where the photo had been taken. The article itself appeared to be nearly a decade old, copied from a Tampa newspaper.

FRANK MACY GETS EIGHT YEARS ON MANSLAUGHTER PLEA.

Only the opening paragraphs were legible in the photo:

Despite claims that the police had planted evidence against him, Tampa resident Frank Macy, 27, pled no contest to second-degree manslaughter charges today in the death of bartender Arnold White last February. Macy, who was already on probation for unrelated drug charges, was sentenced to eight years in prison.

White was assaulted in an alley behind the Spotted Dolphin, a bar in the Gulfside town of Pass-a-Grille on February 12. He later died of his injuries. One witness alleged that White had made sexual advances toward Macy on the night of the assault.

'This plea is a recognition of the fact that a jury trial would likely have resulted in Mr Macy's conviction of first-degree manslaughter, resulting in a significantly longer sentence,' said Ramona Cortes, Macy's defense attorney. 'We continue to believe that much of the evidence in this case was manufactured by authorities in an attempt to . . .

Peach read the fragment of the article six times, but she didn't understand it. She didn't know the name Frank Macy; she had never heard of him or the victim. The only name she knew was Ramona Cortes, who had been a high-profile defense attorney in Tampa before winning her first statewide election for Attorney General five years earlier. Everyone at the Common Way Foundation knew Ramona, because she and her Orlando firm had defended Hamilton Brock, too. Now she was the Republican candidate for governor.

Why did Justin think this article was important?

She studied the police photograph of Frank Macy. He was a stranger to her, not familiar at all, but he had an unusually soft, sensitive face. His dark hair was wavy and fell below his ears. He didn't look like a thug. He didn't have a tattooed face and square chin, a flat nose like a roadkill mouse, or mean dark eyes. Instead, he looked like a refugee from a boy band. His bedroom brown eyes said: *Look at me, little girl.* His skin just made you want to touch it. He looked lost.

Peach did some quick math in her head. Based on the date of the article, and the sentence he received, Macy would have been released from prison earlier this year. He was free.

It wasn't much, but it was something. She didn't know who Frank Macy was, or what Justin wanted with him, but she was going to find out.

15

The jungle-like garden in Diane Fairmont's Tampa estate was a mass of shadows. It was nine o'clock at night, but the summer days were long. Cab stood on the lawn, with the bone-white estate behind him. The air was ripe with dampness. A rabbit fed on the grass nearby, and gnats hovered in a cloud over the lily pond. He was procrastinating by not going inside. He felt nervous, like a twenty-something kid again. He'd avoided Diane for ten years, but he couldn't avoid her anymore.

What would they say to each other?

When the front door opened behind him, he shoved his hands in the pockets of his suit pants with unease. He expected to hear her voice, but instead, the voice was male and loud, breaking the silence like an earth-mover on a weekend morning.

'Hey, Detective!'

It was Garth Oakes. Fitness guru, masseur, would-be confidant and advisor for Diane. The man hopped down the steps and headed for Cab with an open-toed walk, his black ponytail swinging. He was dressed in pastels, as if *Miami Vice* had never gone off the air. White sport coat, collarless lavender shirt. The dusk made his skin as dark as a leather boot.

Garth thrust out his hand, and Cab shook it again.

'We met at the party on Friday,' Oakes said. 'Remember me?'

'Beat the Girth . . . With Garth,' Cab commented.

'You remember! Yeah, I don't care how many times I see myself on TV at three in the morning, it's still a kick. You here to see Diane?'

Cab nodded.

'She's running late,' Garth told him. 'We just wrapped up a massage, and she wanted to take a shower.'

'Okay.'

'Hey, I hear you're looking into some of these threats against her, huh? Way to go. Can't be too careful. Me, I'm always prepared.' Garth pulled aside the flap of his sport coat to reveal a ridiculously large automatic weapon holstered near his shoulder. 'People figure I'm like the Hulk, you know? Beat 'em off with my bare hands. Except a fist isn't much good if the other guy is packing. Nobody messes with Garth, baby. You try, you eat some lead sushi.'

Cab wasn't really listening, but he was pretty sure that Garth did say 'lead sushi.'

'I better get inside,' Cab said.

'Oh, sure. Hey, the campaign's going well, huh? You see the latest poll numbers? Some folks are saying the Governor may pack it in and get out of the race, but I don't think so. He probably figures the storm will give him a bump. Voters rally 'round the incumbent over that kind of thing.'

'They do.'

'He's going down, though.' Garth pointed at the 'Governor Diane' button pinned to his shirt. Or maybe it was pinned directly to the muscles on his chest. 'She's a shoo-in. Unless they find some nasty dirt, I say she wins by seven or eight points.'

'Dirt?' Cab asked.

'Well, politics ain't beanbag, right? You know they're out there looking.'

'Is there anything to find?'

Garth shrugged. 'There's *always* something to find. No saints and virgins in this business. I could tell you stories. Not that anyone could unzip my lips. You have to know how to keep secrets in my world.'

'What happens on the massage table stays on the massage table?' Cab asked.

'Ha, that's funny! Right! Believe me, once somebody lets you run your hands over their naked body, they figure they can tell you just about anything.'

'It's a good thing you're discreet.'

Garth crossed his fingers and thumped his heart. 'Believe it. People have tried to get crap out of me. Political people. Reporters, too. People know me and Diane are tight.'

'That's right. You said you were at her place in Lake Wales a lot, didn't you?'

'Yeah, I'm still in Lake Wales all the time. Got a lot of clients there.'

'What was it like at Birch's house back then?'

'Huh? Oh, ugly days. Ugly days.'

'Because of the murders?'

Garth flinched. 'Sure, of course. Because of the murders.'

'And then with Drew's suicide,' Cab added.

'Oh, yeah, even worse.'

'It must have been difficult,' Cab said, 'with Drew going in and out of rehab all the time. An emotional roller-coaster.'

'You know it. That was super-hard on Diane.'

'My mother said that Drew spent time in rehab right before the murders,' Cab went on.

'Oh, yeah. That was bad.'

'What happened?' Cab asked. 'I heard that Drew was really upset about something.'

Garth looked like a train slamming on the brakes before a crossing. 'Oh, well, who can tell with druggies, huh?'

'I heard he made threats.'

'Threats?'

'Like he was going to blow Birch's head off,' Cab said.

Garth laughed, which sounded like the nervous titter of a teenage girl. 'Oh, that was nothing. Kid was worked up. No big deal.'

'Except someone did shoot Birch,' Cab pointed out.

'I know, crazy, right? What are the odds? It's a crazy world.'

'Very crazy.'

Garth checked his phone and fiddled impatiently with the buttons. 'Well, I gotta run. I've got another rub-down tonight. One of the uniform chasers near Macdill. Here's my chance to find out the latest in navy secrets, right? Nice talking to you, Detective.'

'Same here,' Cab replied.

The masseur saluted and shouldered off toward the estate's main gate at a brisk pace. He looked back and smiled nervously when he saw that Cab was still watching him. He gave a little wave, but Cab thought he couldn't get away fast enough.

Diane was waiting for him in the first-floor study. It was a man's room in a woman's house, with wine-colored wallpaper and heavy, dark walnut on a wall of built-in bookshelves. It had a fireplace and wet bar. The armchairs looked weathered and not particularly comfortable. An oil painting of Birch Fairmont above the fireplace made him look like a Rockefeller.

'Hello, Cab,' Diane said.

He didn't know what to say, so he said nothing. He ran his fingers along the spines of the hardback books on the shelves. He could feel her eyes following him.

'Red or white?' she asked. She had two bottles of wine open on a silver tray. He didn't doubt that both were expensive.

'Red.'

'That's what I prefer, too,' Diane said, 'but I have to drink white now because of the campaign.'

Cab stopped and cocked his head, puzzled. She laughed and tapped a finger on her lips. 'Teeth,' she went on. 'Red wine stains the teeth. Doesn't look good on television.'

'Amazing,' Cab said.

'Yes, it's a different world, but you know that. Your mother faced the same thing all those years.'

'Yes, she did.'

'Sit down, won't you?' Diane asked. 'I don't bite.'

There were two armchairs, decorated in a floral pattern, on either side of the antique table on which Diane placed the wine glasses. His was a large, gently fluted bowl glass, in which she'd poured two inches of Cabernet. Hers was a crystal tulip, and she'd filled it with Sauvignon Blanc. He sat down, and she sat down. The two chairs were angled toward each other, and Cab had to bend his long legs awkwardly so as not to touch her.

Finally, he looked at her. She wasn't wearing makeup, and her face was flushed from the shower. Or maybe it was flushed because she was remembering when they were last together. She was older now – her skin not as taut, her brunette hair scrubbed of gray – but she was still elegant and attractive. She was casually dressed, but to Diane, casual meant a rose blouse, white satin slacks, and heels. He'd changed into a beige suit and narrow tie.

They clinked their glasses in a silent toast and drank. The Heitz Cabernet was superb.

'Tarla doesn't know,' Diane said. 'That was your first question, wasn't it?'

He nodded, because she'd read his mind. He realized that Diane was different now. More confident and mature, more open. The Diane of ten years ago wouldn't have bulled her way into that particular china shop.

'Why didn't you tell her?' he asked.

'I figured you didn't want me to. I assume you didn't tell her yourself.'

'You assume correctly.'

'I hope you don't feel guilty about what happened between us,' she said. 'Or worse, ashamed.'

'No.'

'Good. You'll never know what that afternoon meant to me.' After an awkward pause, she added: 'Or how it changed my life.'

There was nothing to say in reply, so again, he said nothing.

'Anyway, enough of that,' she said. 'It's over and done. We don't need to talk about it.'

'Okay.'

She glanced at the painting of Birch with emotions he couldn't read, and she drank more Sauvignon Blanc. 'So.'

'So.'

'Tarla tells me she's trying to set you up with Caprice,' Diane said.

Cab rolled his eyes. 'Well, you know my mother.'

'I do. You could do a lot worse, Cab. Caprice is brilliant, beautiful, driven. What we've done at Common Way is mostly thanks to her. Really, it should be her on the ticket, not me.'

'I don't exactly see myself as a politician's courtesan,' Cab said.

'Oh, with Caprice, I suspect you'd enjoy the experience,' Diane replied, smiling. 'However, it's your choice. You don't need all these middle-aged women interfering in your love life. Speaking of which, how is it for you having Tarla close to you again?'

'Challenging,' Cab said.

'So I gather. She has some choice words for your girlfriend. What's her name? Wawa?'

'Lala,' Cab said. 'No, they don't exactly get along. Lala met us for breakfast after Mass a couple months ago. Tarla said the Catholic Church should change its name to IHOP. International House of Pedophiles.'

'Your mother does speak her mind,' Diane murmured.

'Yes, she does.'

'She thinks you've spent your life running away from her.'

'No, just running,' Cab said, 'but she has a point.'

'So why do you do it?'

Cab sipped his wine. He had no intention of answering, but it was a good question. He usually avoided self-reflection the way he avoided yoga and Michael Bublé. He could have blamed Catch-a-Cab Bolton on Vivian Frost, the lover who'd betrayed him, the lover he'd killed; but the truth was, it had started long before her. He could have blamed Hollywood. He could have blamed Tarla, or his father, who didn't even exist for him. Any of those were easier than blaming himself.

'Are you planning to run away again?' Diane asked, when he ignored her question.

'My lieutenant in Naples would probably be happier if I did,' Cab said, smiling.

'Hiding behind jokes. Just like your mother. She loves you, you know. You have no idea how abandoned you've made her feel. You two have only each other, yet you chose to keep yourself thousands of miles away from her for years.'

Cab felt an urge to snap back at Diane. That was probably what she wanted. Instead, he tightened his grip on the wine glass and settled back into the chair. 'It's really supposed to be me asking the questions here.'

Diane laughed. 'Sorry. There I go again. It's just that she's my best friend.'

'I know. I love her, too, you realize.'

'Of course, you do.'

'Unfortunately, for Tarla, being a part of my life means trying to control me.'

'Well, rather than running away, you could try saying no.'

Cab smiled. 'Yes, I could.'

Diane had already drained most of the wine in her glass, and she refilled it. He knew she was nervous, even if she didn't show it. She lifted the bottle of red, but he shook his head. After she took another swallow – a large one – she put down the glass and gripped the arms of the chair a little too tightly.

'Caprice tells me you're looking into threats against me,' she said.

'That's right.'

'Is this real, or just an excuse for her to seduce you?' she asked.

'I don't think she needs an excuse,' Cab said. 'As for whether it's real, I suppose she showed you the note.'

Diane nodded. 'She did. Am I supposed to take it seriously? I really can't believe the Liberty Empire Alliance would be so bold as to try this again. It's gracious of you, Cab, but I think you're wasting your time. I have security. We have a very able police force, not to mention the FBI. I'm sure if there were any genuine threat, they would know about it, and they'd be able to deal with it.'

Cab felt as if he were being dismissed. 'You may well be right.'

'That's not to say I don't like having you around. I'm sure Caprice feels the same way.'

Her words had gotten faster, as if she were racing for a conclusion she didn't want to admit openly. She wanted him to stop investigating. She wanted him to quit.

'I do have some questions,' he said.

'Such as?'

'Do you really believe that the Liberty Empire Alliance killed Birch?'

Diane's jaw hardened. She looked offended. Or her offense was a convincing political act. 'That's your question? I watched one of their *soldiers* murder three people. Including my husband. It could have been me, too, and it could have been your mother, in case you've forgotten.'

'I haven't,' Cab said.

'Then clearly, my answer is yes. I was there. I saw it happen.'

'I'm sorry. I realize how horrible it was. If it's possible that the same person could be focused on you, then I want to follow any avenue to know who really pulled the trigger that night. That means finding out everything I can about the Labor Day murders.'

Diane shrugged. Her body language wasn't designed to encourage him.

'I've tried to talk to Tarla about the shooting,' he went on, 'but she won't say anything. I think she's keeping something from me.'

'Why do you think that?' Diane asked.

'I know my mother. Do you have any idea what it could be?'

'I don't. She and I don't talk about that night. We never have.'

'Tarla's meeting me at the Bok Sanctuary tomorrow afternoon,' Cab added.

'Whatever for?'

'Sometimes being back in a place where something bad happened will jar memories.'

'Maybe some memories are best left buried,' Diane said. 'I'd forget that night if I could.'

'Tell me something: was Drew there with all of you that night?'

'Excuse me?'

'I was wondering if your son was on the dais, too.'

'No, he wasn't.'

'Where was he?' Cab asked.

'Drew? He was home. He wasn't well. What does this have to do with anything?'

'Nothing. I just wondered how the trauma affected him. Were he and Birch close?'

Diane frowned. 'No.'

'Stepfather and stepson. It's never easy.'

She didn't respond well to his sympathy. 'No, it's not.'

'I heard that Drew had a bad episode shortly before the murders.'

'My son had drug problems for most of his life, Cab.'

'Yes, I know that. Was there anything that triggered that particular episode? Did something happen?'

Diane stood up, cutting him off. 'Addicts don't need triggers, I'm afraid. Look, Cab, I hate to be abrupt, but can we cut this short? I'm tired. The campaign is exhausting. I really don't want to talk about this anymore.'

'Of course.'

'I'm sorry I can't be more help. It's nice to see you again. Really.'

'It is.' Cab stood up, too.

'As I said before, this whole thing is probably a waste of your time. Caprice's heart is in the right place, but I wish she'd talked to me before hiring you. I would have told her not to bother.'

'I actually hope you're right about that,' Cab said. 'That would mean you're safe.'

She led him to the front door, and the parting was awkward. They didn't embrace. They didn't shake hands. She acted as if she couldn't wait for him to be gone, and she closed the door immediately behind him.

He found himself alone in the garden. It was night now. At the base of the steps, golden lanterns on white pillars illuminated the sidewalk, leading him away from the house. He made his way to the main gate, which was elaborately sculpted in wrought iron, with designs of herons and tree branches. The security guard let him out. Cab noted with satisfaction that the man was observant and tough, but he was only one man, and there were plenty of ways to breach the wall.

Cab stood outside in the midst of the dark urban neighborhood. The weather forecast was right. The night had changed. A west wind was blowing, and the air pressure had dropped. He could taste rain on his lips. He'd lived in Florida long enough to know that a storm was coming.

He studied the houses around him and felt uneasy. Some had lights, others didn't. The yards were a maze of fences and mature trees, all black in the darkness. Cars were parked along the curbs, leaving wide spaces between them. He couldn't see far, but he spent several minutes waiting and listening.

Eventually, he crossed the street to his Corvette, but it didn't change what he felt.

Somewhere around him were the eyes of a stranger. He was being watched.

16

He put down his binoculars and melted into the cover of the trees. The cop was smart; the good ones had a sixth sense when someone was spying on them. He watched the red Corvette scream away from Diane Fairmont's estate, and he wondered if the cop was going to be a problem.

He didn't want more death, but sometimes it was necessary. Like the girl who'd broken into the foreclosure house. Tina. Young, pretty, sweet. After he cut her throat, he'd dumped her body in a park near the Gulf shore. Eventually, they would match the blood on the carpet in the house and realize she'd been there, but by then, it wouldn't matter.

He only needed a few more days.

He thought about Justin Kiel. Justin was smart, too, like the cop. He'd put two and two together in a way that no one ever had. It could have been a disaster, but Justin had made the mistake of following him and trying to learn more. He was easy to spot, easy to trap.

All these years, his secret had been safe. Buried. Hidden. Until now. He should have expected it. Once the dirt was scraped off an old grave, there was always the risk that someone would stumble across it.

What's happening?

Why is there so much blood?

He squeezed his fists, pushing down his emotions. It was déjà vu. Ten years had changed nothing. All he could do was keep going.

He felt his throwaway phone vibrating in his pocket. He knew exactly who was on the other end of the line. He checked the neighborhood, and he was alone. He answered the phone: 'Do you have it?'

The man replied: 'Yes, I can get what you want. It isn't a problem.'

'Good.'

'This is serious firepower, friend,' the man said.

'Yeah, so?'

'I want to make sure this doesn't come back to haunt me.'

'Don't worry about that.'

'I'm someone who worries. Do you have the money?'

'Yes.'

There was a long pause. He could almost hear the calculations in the man's mind. Risk assessments. Greed. Eventually, greed always won out.

'Let's say Tuesday then,' the man said. 'The Picnic Island pier. After dark.'

'I'll be there.'

He hung up the phone. Everything was coming together now. Soon it would be Independence Day. Soon Chayla would roar like an animal across the land. The storm's violence would protect him. He would strike again, the way he had once before. And then they would finally have what they'd always wanted.

Power.

PART TWO

SOMETHING BAD

17

Cab expected the Pilot House at the Tampa Yacht Club to be crowded for Monday lunch. Instead, the room was empty. Attorney General Ramona Cortes sat alone at a table tucked into an oval cubbyhole at the back of the dining room. The walls around her were paneled in light oak and decorated with sailing flags. The bay windows were blocked by wooden shutters. Through the slats, he glimpsed the water.

Ramona put down her copy of the *Tribune* and got to her feet as he approached. 'Cab,' she said. 'What a pleasure to see you again. Thank you for coming.'

Cab smiled. 'I didn't think it was optional.'

'It wasn't. Not really.'

'No campaign aides?' he asked. 'Just us?'

'I like my privacy on certain matters.' Ramona gestured at the empty dining room. 'The restaurant is closed today, but they make an exception for me when I'm in town. I work out, and then I have lunch and dial for dollars. Fundraising is a never-ending process. Order whatever you want. I'm having tomato basil soup and grilled cheese.'

'That sounds delicious.'

A waiter hovered. Ramona held up two slim fingers, and he nodded and disappeared. A fresh iced latte sat in front of Cab's place setting. Apparently, his tastes were predictable. Ramona sipped club soda with a squeeze of lime from a highball glass.

The Attorney General was polite, but with a no-nonsense demeanor. When she smiled, it was with her lips; she didn't grin. She was in her early forties, small, with delicate hands and a trim physique. If there was any gray in her bobbed black hair, she'd erased it. She had a V-pointed chin and hooked nose, and her dark eyes were sharp and confident. She wore a tailored charcoal suit, which looked every bit as expensive as the one Cab was wearing.

Ramona had been extremely successful in two careers. She'd started as a private attorney in one of the state's largest law firms and then made the transition to the rough-and-tumble world of Florida politics. She had money, she had intellect, and she had the courage of her convictions. However, Cab had seen her on television, and he knew that she wasn't a gifted campaigner. She appeared aloof in public. Detached. She relied for her appeal on no-nonsense toughness. Her campaign slogan reflected the kind of person she was: *Ramona Cortes for a Strong Florida.*

'How's Lala?' she asked.

'She's fine. Busy with an assignment.'

'The two of you should visit me in Tallahassee sometime. A pool party around the holidays, maybe. Lala is my favorite cousin, you know.'

Cab wondered if Ramona knew that his relationship with Lala was on shaky ground. Among the Cubans he'd met, family was everything, and secrets were few. If Lala had said anything to anyone, it would have sped along the grapevine.

'We should do that,' he replied. He added with a smile: 'Although won't you be busy running the state by then?'

'That's my plan.' Ramona folded her hands neatly in front of her. 'You're probably wondering why I wanted this meeting.'

'I am.'

'I won't beat around the bush, Cab. My sources tell me you've gotten into bed with the Common Way Foundation. Is this true?'

He wondered if Lala had called her. 'I'm doing some work for them,' he acknowledged.

'What kind of work?'

'Private work,' he said.

Ramona studied him across the table. One of her index fingers tapped her other hand as precisely as a metronome. 'Actually, I was just being polite. I know exactly what they've asked you to do. You're investigating threats against Diane Fairmont. You're trying to determine whether there might be a link to the Labor Day murders ten years ago.'

'You're well informed.'

'Does that surprise you?'

'No,' Cab admitted.

'Let me tell you what's on my mind. I'd consider it a personal favor if you would resign from this investigation.'

'Resign?'

'That's right. Terminate your contract with Common Way.'

Before Cab could ask any of the dozens of questions that sprang into his head, Ramona was interrupted by a phone call. She excused herself and took the call, which turned out to be a long conversation. While the Attorney General was talking, the waiter returned with bowls of soup and grilled cheese ciabatta sandwiches. Ramona gestured for him to eat, and he did.

He'd finished half his sandwich by the time she got off the phone.

'I'm very sorry.'

'That's all right,' Cab said.

'I'm sure you have questions, but I can't answer many of them. I'm sorry. You'll have to take it on faith.'

Cab took a spoonful of soup. 'When a politician asks me to take something on faith, I find myself becoming agnostic.'

'I'm a lawyer, too,' Ramona said with a ghost of a smile. 'Does that help?'

'Even worse.'

'Here's what I can tell you. I've been kept apprised of these so-called threats against Diane. The FBI doesn't believe they can substantiate their veracity.'

'In other words, it's just a bunch of crackpots.'

'That's one possibility,' she said. 'Another possibility is that people at the Common Way Party have manufactured the threats. They may not be real at all.'

'You obviously don't like the people at Common Way,' Cab said. 'This couldn't have anything to do with the fact that Diane is pummeling you in the polls, could it?'

Ramona took a small bite of her sandwich and dabbed at her lips with the cloth napkin. She ate slowly, like a woman in no hurry. 'If you read the papers, you know that the spread in the polls is no more than a few points. Hardly pummeling.'

'Even so, I'm surprised you would take the threats lightly, given what happened to Birch Fairmont.'

She took his measure, the way a woman sizes up a man. Solid or not solid. Fake or sincere. Deep or shallow. 'May I speak confidentially, Cab?'

'By all means,' he said.

'I'm sure you know that before I was elected, I was a criminal attorney. I built a statewide reputation by taking on high-profile cases that received a great deal of media attention. That included Hamilton Brock and the Liberty Empire Alliance. Not a case that my political enemies will allow me to forget. Obviously, I won't say anything about the specifics of the legal matters, but I will tell you my personal belief that the threat from the Alliance was overblown in the media. Ogden Bush oversold them as radical domestic terrorists, and he had a specific political purpose in mind, namely, helping the Democrats. However, Brock and his associates were mostly paranoid blowhards who loved guns and spouted off about imaginary government plots. We're talking about plumbers and realtors. There were some thuggish characters among them perhaps, but not assassins.'

Cab thought about Brock in prison. He wasn't convinced that the man was a paper tiger. He also thought about Rufus Twill, with his limp and his one eye. The Alliance wasn't afraid of violence.

'So who killed Birch Fairmont?' Cab asked.

'I have no idea.'

'Then why do you assume the same person couldn't be targeting Diane?'

Ramona leaned across the table. 'Honestly? Because I believe the Common Way Party would do *anything* to elect Diane Fairmont as governor. Including falsifying threats if it would churn up sympathy among the voters. It's no surprise that they're trotting out the Alliance again, given my own professional history with them. Believe me, Cab, I know these people. I know Diane. Hamilton Brock isn't the only client of mine who was on the wrong side with her. These people are ruthless and dirty, and you shouldn't be working with them. They'll sacrifice you in a minute if it suits their purposes.'

Lala had told him the same thing. *You may find yourself in over your head with these people. Even you.* Chuck Warren had used similar language to describe the upstart party. Ruthless. Dirty.

One thing was certain. People were afraid of them.

'It's hard to believe that the Common Way Party could be any worse than what we've been getting from the other two parties for years,' Cab said.

'I disagree.'

'And you base this on what?'

Ramona shook her head. 'I'm afraid I can't say anything about that.'

'I've heard suggestions that Diane was somehow responsible for the scandal that enveloped the Governor this year,' Cab said. 'The Common Way people set up his aide. Do you think that's possible?'

'Yes, I do. And believe me, I'm no fan of the Governor.'

Cab eyed the Attorney General with surprise. 'That's a serious accusation.'

'We're under the cone of silence here. I'm telling you what I believe, not what I can prove. I really don't think that it's a coincidence that the Governor found himself knee-capped this year. When the Common Way people face opposition, they mow them down. That's what they've done on policy issues for a decade. They've been shaping a legislature to their views by targeting candidates and destroying those that oppose them. Now it's time for Diane to march in and take over.'

'Hamilton Brock called it a coup,' Cab said.

'I'm not sure he's wrong about that.'

'Do you think they've acted illegally? Or are you just complaining because they're better at the game than you are?'

'I think people complain about the government – as do I – but at least the actions of the government are largely transparent. There are watchdogs everywhere. An organization like Common Way has a huge endowment that allows them to wield influence behind the scenes with virtually no oversight. I think that kind of power offers an extraordinary temptation to cross the lines.'

'If you believe that's true, shouldn't you be investigating them?' Cab asked.

'What makes you think I'm not?'

Cab nodded. He put down his napkin on the plate and stood up. 'I appreciate the warning.'

'Will you do what I asked? Will you quit?'

'No, not yet. Not solely on your say-so. I'm sorry.'

Ramona stood up, too. She was a tiny dynamo next to him. 'You're making a mistake, Cab.'

'I'll tell you what I told them. If I discover that I'm being played, I'm out. Until then, I'm only interested in one thing. Making sure that Diane Fairmont doesn't suffer the same fate as her husband.'

The Attorney General frowned. 'This isn't about being played,' she said. 'If it were just that, I wouldn't care.'

'Then what is it?'

'A foundation employee named Justin Kiel was murdered recently,' she told him. 'The police concluded that the death was drug-related. I have reason to believe they are wrong.'

'Why is that?'

'For the time being, I can't say,' Ramona repeated. 'I'm just suggesting that you be careful.'

Cab shook his head. 'I hope you're not implying that Diane is somehow involved in a murder. I don't believe that for a moment. I'm no fan of politicians, but how many of them would really kill to get elected?'

The Attorney General sat down again and picked up her sandwich. 'More than you think, Cab. More than you think.'

18

'Frank Macy,' Peach said.

Deacon's fingers stopped clicking on his keyboard. 'Who?'

Peach slapped the paper she'd taken from Justin's safe house on the desk in front of her brother. 'This guy. He's got a long record. Drugs. Guns. Manslaughter. For some reason, Justin was interested in him. I'm betting there's a connection to his murder.'

Deacon picked up the paper and studied it. 'What is this? What does it have to do with Justin?'

'Justin kept a safe house for his computers and papers. Someone ransacked the place, but he missed this. I've been digging into Frank Macy all morning. He got out of jail earlier this year, but he's still in the area. He has an apartment near St Pete Beach. I'm going to find him.'

'Fruity, what the—' Deacon began. He stopped and stood up to look over the tops of the cubicle walls. When he sat down again, his voice was hushed. 'Let's not talk about this here.'

He led them past the cubicle farm. She could see the office for Ogden Bush on the far side of the building; the door was closed. Deacon guided her onto the street outside. It was a hot afternoon, but the wind had come alive, blowing garbage and dust around the pavement, making her blink. He walked quickly, and she struggled to keep up with him. They were in an area of derelict storefronts and barred windows. He led her three blocks to a small urban park that was little more than a square of dead grass and palm trees, with a row of green benches.

Deacon sat down. He was wearing an under-sized gray T-shirt, jeans, and dusty boots. He slipped sunglasses over his face and scratched his rust-colored stubble. 'Okay, you want to tell me what this is all about?'

'I want to know what really happened to Justin.'

'I get that, but why? I know you guys worked together, but I don't understand what you're doing.'

She took a breath. She was a private person, even around her brother, but she decided to tell him the truth. 'It was more than that.'

'What was?' Then Deacon tilted his head back and sighed. 'Oh, man. Really? You and Justin?'

'We were in love.'

'Hell's bells, why didn't you tell me, Fruity? No wonder you've been so upset.'

'It was something just for us,' Peach said. 'We didn't tell anyone.'

'Look, I'm sorry. I really am. I get it now, but I don't want you putting yourself in jeopardy over this. A murder investigation is for the police, not us.'

'I can't stop.' Peach felt her eyes welling with tears. She crumpled into her brother's shoulder and clung to his arm. The wind blew heat into her face like the open door of an oven. 'It's just one more thing, you know? One more thing they took away from me.'

He kissed the top of her head. 'Yeah, I know.'

'I loved Mom and Dad, and they died. I loved Lyle, and he died. I loved Justin, and he died. Maybe it's me.'

'It's not you.'

'Don't you get lonely without them?' she asked.

'Of course I do.'

'I miss Lyle,' she said. 'With everything going on, all the talk about Labor Day, I've been thinking about him a lot.'

'Me too.' Deacon chuckled. 'Except I also remember what an asshole he was.'

'Don't say that!' Peach exclaimed.

'Hey, he's gone, and I'm really sorry, but I'm not going to pretend that he was something other than what he was. He didn't treat us well. Everything else in the world was more important than we were.'

'He was responsible for us. That wasn't easy.'

'I'm not saying it was, but you didn't see what he was like. You were a kid then, but I wasn't.'

Peach frowned. In her heart of hearts, she knew Deacon was right, but she didn't like feeling that way. 'No, I saw it,' she said softly. 'I just don't like to remember him like that.'

'I get it. Remember him however you like. Believe me, I think about him every time I get into the Mercedes, but then I think: That car probably meant more to him than either of us did. I know that's harsh.'

'Yeah.' Peach sniffled.

'Now, you want to tell me what's going on? What have you been up to?'

Peach told him. She told him everything – about her late-night phone call from Curtis Clay, about her narrow escape from Justin's apartment with Annalie's help, about her late-night search of Ogden Bush's office, about her discovery of Justin's safe house, about the article she'd found about Frank Macy. It was a relief to say it out loud. To admit how much it meant to her to find the truth.

'Jesus,' he said she when she was finally done. 'You've been busy.'

She expected a lecture. Give it up. Let the police do their job. He didn't bother, because he knew she wouldn't listen.

'This guy in Justin's apartment, the one who claimed to be a cop,' he said. 'Who is he? Is there any way we can find him?'

Peach shook her head. 'I didn't recognize him.'

'He *sounds* like a private detective,' Deacon said.

'Working for who?'

'I don't know, but I'll pull some state photo records for you to look through. Maybe we can ID him that way.' Deacon hesitated, and he didn't look happy. 'You know, there's something you have to think about. I know you won't like it.'

'What?'

'This could still be all about drugs. Drug cases pull people out of the woodwork. Everybody smells money. This Curtis Clay, he could be hooked up with dealers looking for cash or dope.'

'What about the photo I found? What about Frank Macy?'

'You said it yourself,' Deacon reminded her. 'Macy's got a long track record with drugs. If Justin was involved with someone like that, then it's possible that Macy or one of his allies took him out. I just want you to be prepared if the truth about Justin is something you're not happy with.'

Peach was silent. She knew Deacon was right, but she didn't believe it. Then she said: 'I need to get close to Macy.'

'No way,' Deacon said. 'Doing research is one thing, but I don't want you going near this guy.'

'I'm not going to walk up to him and start asking questions! I listen. Nobody knows I'm around. If I can get close enough, maybe he'll say something. This is humint, this is what I do.'

'I know, and you're very good at what you do, but do you think this guy isn't? Don't believe his baby face. Criminals like Macy develop eyes in the back of their head.'

'I get it, but I need to know why Justin was interested in him. If it's *not* about drugs, then there's something else. What could it be? Macy's been out of circulation for eight years.'

Deacon hesitated. 'Okay, look, don't read too much into this.'

'Into what? Do you know something about him?'

'It's probably nothing, but I do know that Frank Macy has a connection to Diane. You may not remember. You were still pretty young.'

'What's the connection?' Peach asked.

'Do you remember Diane's son, Drew?'

'A little,' she said. 'I know he killed himself.'

Deacon nodded. 'I only met Drew a couple times, but Lyle talked about him a lot. He was afraid that Drew's behavior would undermine Birch's campaign. It's one thing that Birch's stepson had a big drug problem – that's bad enough – but he also hung out in Tampa clubs and got himself photographed in some compromising positions. And with the wrong kind of people.'

The wrong kind of people.

'Are you saying Drew knew Frank Macy?' Peach asked.

'Yeah, he did,' Deacon said. 'Macy liked to hang out with rich kids. He knew how to hook them up with street people. Drew and Macy were together a lot. First in college, then in Tampa and Lake Wales. Macy was Drew's drug dealer.'

19

Cab thought he'd become accustomed to the realities of fame, but it still surprised him that he couldn't go anywhere with his mother without her being recognized. Their afternoon at the Bok Sanctuary was no different. Tarla wore a white summer dress – loose, sheer but not overtly sexy – with a leather belt tied in a knot at her slim waist. Her blond hair was casual and messy, and she wore big sunglasses and almost no makeup. Even so, people began to whisper as soon as she arrived.

At the welcome desk inside the interpretive center, a hostess in her early sixties finally screwed up the courage to say: 'Are you . . . ?'

Tarla smiled. Moments later, she was signing autographs.

He didn't have anything to do while Tarla hobnobbed with her movie fans, so he spent his time examining the displays about Edward Bok, the author and editor who had built the tower and gardens in the late 1920s. It was a supremely lovely, peaceful place, designed to embody Bok's philosophy: 'Make you the world a bit better or more beautiful because you have lived in it.'

He knew that Tarla had made the world a better place during her stay. Looking at the glow on the faces of those who recognized her, he realized how much she and her movies had touched lives. He doubted that he would ever be able to say the same thing. Never married. No children. Spending his days delving into dark hearts.

It didn't feel like much of a legacy.

'Well,' Tarla said, appearing at his side again, slightly breathless. 'That was fun, wasn't it?'

'Yes, someone told me how exciting it was to meet Naomi Watts in person,' Cab replied.

'You're so funny, darling. Wicked but funny. You know, one of the women only had eyes for you. I may as well have been invisible.'

'Excuse me?'

Tarla inclined her head toward the welcome desk with a flirty flick of her eyebrows. Cab glanced in that direction and saw a woman in denim overalls staring intently at him. When their eyes met, she turned away. He didn't know her, but she was about his age, black and skinny, with reddish corn-rowed hair. The red T-shirt under her overalls advertised a local landscaping company.

'She looks quiet, but the quiet ones can surprise you,' Tarla said.

'You don't say.'

'I do say. I hear that librarians are ferocious in bed, for example.'

'Where exactly did you hear that?' Cab asked.

'Oh, it's true. What they lack in uncorrected vision they make up for in voluptuous curiosity.'

He knew better than to argue with his mother. He took a last look at the museum desk, where the black woman stared back at him again. Her puffy lips were pressed into a frown. She picked up a water tank as he watched her and headed outside to water the hanging flowers.

Cab offered Tarla his elbow, and she slung her arm through his as they left the welcome center and made their way uphill toward the tower. It was the top of the hour, and he heard carillon bells. The lawns around them were lush and manicured. Spanish moss swayed like a skeleton's arms as a stiff wind rustled the tree branches. Quivering red and pink flowers dotted the bushes. As they climbed, the concrete trail gave way to spongy dirt. Bamboo clusters leaned over the path. Where the ground leveled, they could see the pink stone tower and its elaborate metal grilles on the far side of an algae-laden pond.

They sat on a bench. The bells played a medieval carol. Tarla stared at the tower, which was full of memories for her, and the breezy self-assuredness in her face gave way to something more tentative. She could smile and make jokes, but she didn't want to be here.

'I know this is difficult for you,' Cab said.

'More than I expected,' Tarla admitted. 'I never came back here. After.'

'I'm not surprised.'

'It's a shame, because this was one of my favorite places as a child. Diane and I spent hours here. There were days in Hollywood where I would sit and think about what was going on at the tower at that very moment. Who was there. What the weather was like. What music might be playing. It got me through tough times, remembering this place.'

'Did you ever regret leaving home?' Cab asked.

'You mean, did I ever think about going back to Lake Wales? To my old life? Yes, many times. Even after I'd broken through, I had fantasies of going back. As soon as you leave something behind, you start to think of it as an easier, simpler time. Which it probably was.'

'Why did you leave in the first place?'

'Oh, you know me, Cab. I wasn't cut out for small-town life. What would I have done here? I couldn't steal a rich man like Diane. I didn't have it in me. Probably, I would have been one of those women back at the welcome center. I'm sure they're very fulfilled, but me, I would always have been on a low simmer, wishing I'd done something else.'

'How did Diane feel about your leaving?'

'She hated it. Hated me. At least for a while. However, when you chase a dream, you know you're giving something up. There's always a price. Your grandmother and I moved west, and a year later, she had a heart attack and died. I was alone. I really had no business making it on my own out there. I should have been ground into nothing. Most wannabes are. I was lucky. I never forget how lucky I was.'

Cab frowned. Somehow, it was painful for him to think of his mother alone in Los Angeles, with nothing and no one to rely on for support. Tarla touched his sleeve. When he looked at her, she took his hand.

'May I ask you something, Cab?'

'Of course.'

'Am I a bad mother?'

He was aware of the seriousness in her face and her fears over what he would say. 'Why on earth would you ask me something like that?'

'Hollywood types are not exactly known for their parenting skills, my dear. We can't all be Brad and Angelina. I dragged you around the world. I threw you into crazy social situations with no preparation. I couldn't help but notice that as soon as you had the opportunity to get away from me, you did.'

'I assumed you wanted me to follow in your footsteps,' Cab said.

'Guilty,' Tarla admitted. 'Nepotism is the new black when it comes to actors. You could well have outshined me.'

'I wanted to make my own footsteps, not follow yours. I was very much like you in that respect.'

'And how is that working out for you?'

'Not altogether well,' Cab admitted, smiling. 'I guess your shoes are hard to fill.'

Tarla laughed. 'Mine? Minuscule, compared to yours. Not just those size thirteen feet of yours. Imagine me raising a son who would actually do something worthwhile with his life.'

'Do you really mean that?' he asked.

His mother looked at him with genuine surprise. 'Are you serious? Of course I mean it.'

'Well, thank you,' Cab said.

'I apologize if it seems that I'm trying to run your life, darling. I'm afraid it comes with the territory. I could promise to quit, but you wouldn't believe me.'

'No, it's fine. As long as you don't mind when I pay no attention.'

Tarla grinned. 'Sooner or later, I'll wear you down. Which brings me to you and Caprice.'

Cab held up his hand. 'Enough.'

'Well, you can't blame me for trying.' She stood up and squared her shoulders. She waited as he got off the bench, too, and then added: 'So are you planning to stay in Florida?'

'I guess I am,' Cab said. 'I'm not sure I'll stay with the police, but I need a home base. This is actually a lovely place. And, as much as it pains me to admit it, I sort of like having you close by.'

'Well, you charmer you,' Tarla said. 'Come on, let's do this.'

'Are you ready?'

'As ready as I will be.'

They made their way to the tower, through the clutch of vines, past the webs of huge spiders, and finally broke onto the wide-open crest of the hillside. The bells above them had gone silent. The wind was loud and strong, like an ocean wave. He could see orange groves lining the land below them. That was where the killer had come from, an assassin in black marching through a cloud of citrus.

A wide path led from the tower itself, with soaring trees on either side, and ended in a broad swath of green lawn. 'This is where they built the dais,' Tarla said. 'Diane and I were the first to be seated. She wasn't feeling well.'

'Why not?'

Tarla shook her head. 'I don't know. She didn't say.'

'What about the assassin?'

'Nobody knew where he came from. However, we all knew what would happen when we saw him there. You could have asked anyone in the crowd. We knew people were going to die.'

'Did he say anything?' Cab asked.

'No.'

'Did anyone talk to him?'

'Birch swore at him before he was shot. Other than that, there was simply screaming.'

'What did Diane do?'

'Diane? Nothing that I remember. She was frozen. In shock.'

'Before the assassin shot Lyle, he turned toward Diane. You stood up and protected her.'

Tarla sighed. 'I told you, I don't remember that.'

'You're here now. You've never been back before. Close your eyes.'

She did, reluctantly. 'Sorry, Cab, I don't–'

'Don't talk.'

Tarla looked like a ghost, all in white with the wind mussing her blond hair. She inhaled, swelling her chest. The fabric of her dress fluttered. The two of them were alone, and except for the hillside breeze, the world was silent. No voices. No music. Sometimes it worked that way; sometimes the past could speak, if you invited it. He waited for her, and a minute passed, and then two minutes.

'I don't remember him,' Tarla said, 'but I remember what I felt.'

'What was that?'

'I remember thinking he was an ordinary man. How odd that was. I was taller than him. He just didn't seem like . . . I don't know.'

'A soldier?' Cab said softly.

Tarla opened her eyes. 'No, he certainly didn't seem like a soldier.'

'Do you remember anything else?'

'I'm afraid not.'

'I wonder if you felt like you knew him,' Cab said.

Tarla's face grew sharp. 'Knew him? What are you talking about?'

'Is it possible he wasn't a stranger?'

'He was wearing a hood,' she said. 'And how could it be anyone I knew? Who would do something like this?'

Cab debated whether to say anything at all. Then he said: 'Could it have been Drew?'

She reacted angrily. 'Drew? That's ridiculous, Cab! No, it wasn't Drew.'

'Someone overheard him threatening Birch shortly before Labor Day. He said he would kill him. Blow his head off.'

'I don't care what he said. Drew did not do this. He was in the pool at home when we left.'

'He could have gotten out of the pool.'

'And driven there how? Do you think Diane left him with car keys? He was just out of rehab. He wasn't going anywhere.'

She seemed certain of the truth, and he had to admit there was logic to what she said. He assumed that the FBI would have confirmed Drew's whereabouts as a standard check-a-box during their investigation. Even so, he wondered. Something made sense to him about Drew pulling the trigger. The whole affair felt personal.

Murder, not assassination.

'Why would Drew have threatened to kill Birch?' he asked.

'He was troubled, Cab. He was an addict. That doesn't make him a killer. He wasn't the type.'

'No one ever seems like the type.'

'I knew Drew. You didn't. I don't know why you're wasting your time with this, Cab. If you're trying to protect Diane, why aren't you back in Tampa? Whatever happened here was in the past. It's over, it's done. Why do you insist on reliving it?'

'Maybe because everyone tells me not to,' Cab said.

'Yes, you're stubborn. I get it. You're my son. Just please tell me you didn't raise this nonsense with Diane.'

'I asked where Drew was that night. That's all.'

'And you don't think she's smart enough to leap from A to B? Cab, you disappoint me. She deserves better from you than foolish accusations. Let it go.'

Cab felt slapped. He knew when Tarla was asked to go places she didn't want to go, she blustered and got angry. He didn't know why the next words popped into his head. Maybe he just wanted to hurt his mother.

'We slept together,' he told her.

Tarla stared at him. 'What? Who?'

'Diane and I. That summer. We slept together. Once. I left the next day.'

He did something he'd thought was impossible. He left his mother speechless. She opened her mouth, and it was as if she were staring at a blank cue card. She said nothing at all. The color drained from her beautiful face. This wasn't hurt; this was something much more profound. He'd damaged her in a way he couldn't comprehend.

She folded her arms across her chest. Head down, she stalked away from him.

'Wait,' he called after her.

Tarla didn't stop.

'Let's talk about this.'

His mother never looked back. She hurried down the trail to the tower and continued past it, where the downhill path swallowed her. She disappeared, and she wasn't coming back to him. He knew that.

He stared after her, utterly devastated.

It was an hour before Cab summoned the strength to leave the gardens. The clouds made it look darker and later than it was, but it was already early evening. He felt a hollowness in his stomach as he headed for his car.

'Mr Bolton?'

Cab was outside the gates when he heard the voice behind him. He turned. The black woman in overalls who had been staring at him when they arrived hovered near the bushes. She spoke softly, as if hesitant about approaching him. Her fingers played with her corn rows.

'Yes?' he said.

'You are Cab Bolton, aren't you? You're a detective.'

'I am.'

'My name is Gladiola Croft. Rufus Twill told me about you. He said you were looking into what happened here. He and I, we know each other pretty well. I told him things.'

'Things?' Cab asked.

'I used to work in Birch Fairmont's house,' she said. 'I was there that summer. Those murders? They didn't surprise me none. That man deserved what he got.'

20

The waitress at the Starfish Grill in St Pete Beach had the largest breasts that Peach had ever seen. They were like muskmelons overflowing in brown flesh out of a low-cut orange T-shirt that was tight enough to be body paint. When the girl, who called herself Steffi, bent over her to put an O'Doul's on a salted napkin, Peach was pretty sure she could see all the way to China at the bottom of her cleavage.

'Fire wings'll be right out,' Steffi told her with a toss of her blond hair. 'You want anything else?'

Peach was distracted. 'Uh, no, thanks.'

'They're super big, huh?'

'What?'

Steffi pointed to the indie-rock magazine overturned on the table in front of Peach. The Dutch band Rats on Rafts was featured on the cover.

'Oh,' Peach said, fighting the flush that crept onto her face. 'Oh, yeah.'

Steffi winked. She knew what Peach was thinking. 'I love them. That what you're listening to?'

A headphone wire snaked from under the magazine and wound its way to Peach's ear. 'No, Skynyrd.'

'Hey, classic,' Steffi said.

Peach nudged the magazine closer as the waitress disappeared. She wasn't listening to Skynyrd. The headphone was connected to a shotgun spy microphone and voice recorder hidden under the open pages. The microphone, pointed at a table nearest the white beach, amplified the conversation that Frank Macy was having with another man and two girls who didn't look much older than Peach. Frank and his male friend had pints of Guinness in front of them. The girls didn't look old enough to be drinking anything other than strawberry lemonade.

So far, they were talking about *Cosmopolitan* magazine and threesomes. Yuck.

Peach sipped her O'Doul's. She didn't drink, but she blended in readily enough at a beachside bar with a non-alcoholic beer in front of her. She'd taken her outfit from Harley Mannequin. Spiky black wig, streaked with red and blue. White Road Warrior tank top. Jean shorts with an oversized American Rebel belt buckle and fishnets down her legs. Black studded boots. She'd added thick blue eyeshadow, a nose ring, and a fake tattoo of chains and flames on her forearm.

The bar was half a block from Gulf Boulevard at the southern end of the peninsula between the Gulf and Tampa Bay. Steps away, waves roared over the sand, crashing in foam. The patio umbrellas rattled and flapped in the wind. So did the palm trees. There was no sun, only layer after layer of dark clouds. On the beach, surfers rode in on the swells, and teenage girls had their hair swirled into birds' nests. The dust of blown sand coated everything, including her tongue.

'*One of my buddies has a place on the beach,*' Macy said. '*I think we should take the party there.*'

'*Does he have a hot tub?*' one of the girls asked.

'*Hey, it's a zoning requirement to have a hot tub when you live on the beach. Didn't you know that?*'

His joke was greeted with giggles. Frank Macy was a hit with the young girls. Macy, sexy and suave, looked like a male model. Wavy hair, long and deliberately greasy. A plain white tee under an unbuttoned checked short-sleeve shirt. Red European pants. Weirdly smart, innocent eyes. His companion, who was Asian and had mostly avoided the conversation, was tougher and less sophisticated. Muscle shirt. Tattoos. Wild, ragged hair with a shaved railroad track.

'*I bet my colleague here can get us all happy and relaxed*,' Macy said.

The Asian man didn't smile. He drank his beer, and his eyes were stone.

Peach spotted a familiar face near the entrance to the bar. Annalie Martine scanned the tables, eyeing the crowd, which was mostly swimmers with wet towels slung over the backs of the wooden chairs, and beach hipsters with dirty hair and chains. She hunted for Peach, but didn't find her. Harley Mannequin had done her job.

Peach's phone vibrated on the table. She saw a text message.

Okay, I give up. Where are you?

Peach grinned and wiggled her fingers at Annalie across the bar. Her new colleague picked her way through the tables, watched by most of the men, including Frank Macy. Annalie's hair was loose again. She was dressed in black, but her golden legs were shapely below the fringe of her lycra shorts. Her biking shirt was a zipped sleeveless jersey. She wore fluorescent sneakers. She had a leather handbag, which she draped over the chair.

'One of these days, I'll spot you before you spot me,' Annalie said. There was a burble of noise hanging over the bar, but Annalie kept her voice low. Only Peach could hear her.

'If you do, I'm slipping,' Peach said.

Steffi thrust her immense breasts between them. Annalie ordered a Corona with lime.

'Wow, those things have to hurt,' Annalie said as the waitress headed for the taps. She cast a dubious eye around the bar. 'I didn't figure you for a boob 'n' lube kind of place. Big busts and tight short-shorts? Why are we here?'

'Work, not play,' Peach said.

Annalie noted the overturned magazine and the wire feeding into Peach's ear. 'So who are you after?'

Peach fingered the charm that dangled around Annalie's neck and smiled as if she were commenting on it. 'Table nearest the sand, two guys, two teenagers.'

Annalie cupped the charm in her palm. Her eyes swept the beach without her head turning toward the water. 'The cute one or the nasty one?'

'The cute one.'

'Who is he?'

'His name is Frank Macy,' Peach said.

She explained what she'd found at the safe house and shared a folder on Macy for Annalie to study. While Annalie reviewed the research, Steffi brought a bottle of Corona, with a lime wedge stuffed in the neck, and a basket of spicy chicken wings. Annalie squeezed the lime inside and upended the bottle with her thumb over the top. She finished reading the snippet of the article about Macy shown in the photograph, and like Deacon, she didn't look happy.

'I know guys like him,' Annalie said. 'They float from suburban cocaine parties to downtown immigrant trafficking. A sweet face doesn't mean a thing. I've known sweet faces to pour boiling water down the throats of their competitors. Don't mess with him.'

'I'm not messing. Just spying.'

'What's he saying?' she asked, drinking from her bottle of Corona, slim fingers around its neck.

Peach listened.

'*Now that is a hot, hot woman*,' Macy told the table. He meant Annalie.

'*She's old*,' one of the girls protested. '*She must be thirty*.'

'*Are you kidding? You can tell by the shape of her mouth. She's born to give blow jobs*.'

'He likes your smile,' Peach said.

'Nice. Exactly what are you hoping for? Do you think he's going to confess to Justin's murder between bites of fried pickles?'

'Maybe.'

Annalie bit into a chicken wing and licked around her lips with her tongue. 'I checked the reports on Justin's death. He was found at a dump of a motel next to the dog track, right? Three bullets in the head, execution-style. The police searched the room and found a brick of cocaine and ten thousand dollars squirreled away inside the guts of the microwave.'

'I know.'

'And now you're watching a known drug dealer.'

'A drug dealer with ties to Ramona Cortes. And Diane and her son.'

'Drugs are still the common denominator,' Annalie said. 'Are you sure Justin didn't have his fingers in the wrong pie?'

Peach opened her mouth to snap at Annalie, but she controlled herself. 'Well, that's why I'm here. I need to know what Justin wanted with Macy. I don't care where it leads. I just want the truth.'

'Even if the truth is what everyone says?' Annalie asked softly.

'Yeah, even that,' Peach replied. She couldn't resist adding: 'But it's not.'

An hour passed slowly at the bar. Peach drank her O'Doul's. Annalie drank her Corona. When they were done, they ordered two more, and when they finished the wings, they ordered quesadillas. She kept listening and recording Macy's conversation, but he stuck to rap singers, nightclubs, and sexual positions. He had nothing to say about politics, or Justin, or Diane Fairmont, and his hints at drugs were aimed at the girls. Annalie was right; he was too smart to say anything incriminating in public.

The beer was nonalcoholic, so maybe it was the wind and heat that made Peach feel buzzed. She and Annalie laughed and told jokes. She realized that she liked this woman, as different as they were. She felt comfortable around her, enough to start thinking about her as a friend. She didn't feel that way about many people. Hardly anyone, in fact.

Not knowing why she said it, she asked: 'Do you think I'm weird?'

Annalie scrunched her forehead, but nothing she did made her less pretty. 'Why would I think that?'

'I wear disguises. I'm a voyeur. I'm always listening to other people's business.'

'It's your job.'

'Well, yeah, but I'd probably do it anyway,' Peach admitted.

'Still not really weird,' Annalie said.

'I have mannequins at home. I collect them.'

'Male or female?'

'Uh, female. I name them, too.'

'Do you talk to them?' Annalie asked, grinning.

'No. Well, not in a long time.'

'That's a little weird, but still pretty low on the scale. Do they talk to you?'

'No.'

'Then you're good.'

'There's more. I'm weird about sex, too.'

Annalie smirked. 'Do tell.'

'I decided a long time ago that I wanted to be celibate.'

'Okay. Not what I was expecting, but okay.'

'I thought about it with Justin, but we never did.'

'Well, it doesn't sound weird to me,' Annalie said. 'It sounds sweet. Someday you may feel differently, but until then, do what you want. Or don't do what you want.'

'You have sex, right?' When Annalie hesitated, Peach added: 'Sorry, I'm being too personal. I'm not good with boundaries.'

'Don't worry about it. I'm not celibate, but I'm pretty conservative. I don't go jumping into bed. I have to be awfully close to a guy, and that hasn't happened a lot.'

'Is it worth it? It seems like sex causes nothing but problems.'

'You're right about that,' Annalie said.

Their conversation was interrupted. Near the beach, the two teenagers at Frank Macy's table got up, grabbing purses, headed for the bathroom. When Macy was alone with his Asian companion, he leaned closer, whispering, and Peach tried to adjust the microphone. At the same moment, the wind gusted, blasting static into her ear. She scowled, because the conversation became mostly inaudible.

She thought she heard the word 'gun.'

And two words that sounded like 'Picnic Island.'

The waitress Steffi appeared next to Macy with the check, and she murmured in his ear. He copped a discreet feel on her ass and gave her what looked like a hundred-dollar bill. Peach expected him to insert it in her cleavage. Macy and the Asian sauntered through the bar, passing so close to their table that she could smell his coconut body wash, and he gave Annalie an alluring, pretty-boy wink. He didn't seem to notice Peach.

'Did you get any of that?' Annalie asked when they were gone.

Peach rewound the recording. The words weren't any clearer the second, third, or fourth times. She told Annalie what she thought she'd heard, but she wasn't sure she was right, and she didn't know what any of it meant.

Annalie listened, too. 'I can't make out a thing.'

'No,' Peach said unhappily.

They waited five minutes, then paid their own bill and exited the bar into the narrow parking lot. The dead end street beside them led to a walkway across the grassy dunes down to the beach. Peach wasn't parked in the restaurant lot, but in a more deserted lot on the other side of the street.

Annalie got into her Corolla. 'See you tomorrow.'

'Yeah, see you,' Peach said. 'And thanks.'

She watched Annalie head toward Gulf Boulevard. She crossed the street, which was furrowed with cracked asphalt. The wind felt as if it would lift her off her feet. She walked with her head down, feeling oddly depressed. Her Thunderbird was near a dumpster at the back of the lot. She came around the driver's side and swung the door open.

Like fireworks, the base of her skull erupted in pain and light.

She felt herself flying – thrown across the interior of the car – her face colliding with the passenger window, like a brick against her forehead. Her head ricocheted with a blinding jolt of pain, and then something heavy landed on her back, squeezing air out of her lungs. A fist grabbed her shoulder like a vise and spun her over. She gasped for breath.

Frank Macy was on top of her, in her face. She tasted blood in her mouth. When she blinked, she had double-vision, seeing two of him. He looked as casually sexy as a lifeguard as he choked her with one hand and pressed the blade of a knife against her windpipe with the other.

'So who are you, little girl?' he demanded. 'And why are you watching me?'

Her mouth moved, but no words came out. His hand came away from her throat, and she could suck in air. His fingers dug in her pockets, front and back. He opened the glove compartment. He grabbed her purse and spotted the voice recorder, phone, and microphone inside.

'You're not police,' he said. 'Who are you?'

He pricked her with the knife, breaking skin, drawing blood. Any deeper, and he would slice her throat open. She felt saliva and acid welling in her mouth.

'I need answers, little girl. You've got two seconds, or I slit that pretty neck.'

He eased the pressure of the blade a tiny fraction, and she gagged and coughed. Sweat made her whole body wet. Tears leached from her eyes. She was going to tell him anything he wanted. Everything. She knew she would die anyway; he would suck out the truth, and then he would thrust in the knife. She felt dizzy with pain and terror; she saw flashes of bright color, like the after-image of the sun. Her brain throbbed in and out with her heartbeat.

'I work for Diane Fairmont,' she gasped.

Macy's face twisted in surprise. 'Fairmont? Is that really true?'

She nodded, and he laughed. He actually laughed. His teeth were perfect. 'All these years, and she's still scared of me.'

Peach said nothing.

'You know what?' Macy went on. He nuzzled her ear. '*She should be.*'

His hand pawed her the way a lover's would. He massaged her breasts as if he expected to arouse her. She squeezed her eyes shut. He pulled at her clothes, separating the seams, exposing her. He found her belt buckle and popped it. Her zipper snickered down.

Instinctively, she pressed her legs together. He was lean, but he was too strong for her. She tried to send her mind far away, but her mind had nowhere to go. His breath was sweet; he'd taken mints before assaulting her.

Someone screamed. It wasn't her own voice.

'Let her go! Get off her!'

Someone wrenched open the passenger door. Peach's torso spilled backward, and a hand caught her before she fell. She was conscious of Frank Macy rearing back, head banging on the hood as he ducked out of the other side of the car. Someone dragged her into the hot dusk, and in the swirling of pain and wind and color, she realized it was Annalie.

Annalie, holding her, propping her up.

Annalie, holding a gun that was trained on Frank Macy's face.

She heard the squeal of car tires. A black Lexus roared, appearing behind Macy. The driver's window was open, and Peach saw the Asian man from the bar, beckoning to Macy, a gun in his own hand. The two teenagers were in the back seat, looking terrified. It was a stand-off. Annalie didn't fire. The Asian man didn't fire. Macy took a tentative step backward, grinned, then opened the rear door of the Lexus and dove inside.

The car tore off toward the strip of road that fronted the Gulf.

The screech of tires faded. They were alone, the two of them, Annalie murmuring at her – are you okay, are you okay, are you okay. She still held the gun. Somewhere behind them, the surf sounded angry and loud.

Peach's entire body turned to rubber. She felt herself melting, drowning in an ocean of relief. She let out a huge sob and collapsed into Annalie's arms.

21

Gladiola Croft lived in the poor section of Lake Wales, in the shadow of the water tower. The houses looked like army barracks, all of them the same square one-story design and the same buff-and-brown color, like watery puke. She didn't invite him inside. There were two lawn chairs by the front door, and he sat in one of them, hoping the fraying vinyl straps would hold him. A cracked flower pot sat on the window ledge.

'You want some sweet tea?' she asked.

'I do.'

She disappeared into the small house, letting out the electronic noise of a video game being played inside. Teenagers on the steps of the next row house eyed him, his suit, and his Corvette. Telephone wires crisscrossed over his head, and dark clouds ran across the evening sky.

Gladiola returned, two ice-filled plastic glasses in her hand. He took the wet glass and drank a swallow. 'Excellent,' he said.

She squinted as the wind blew dust in her face. 'They say Chayla's gonna be bad.'

'Yes.'

'Wouldn't be too sorry to see this place blow away, but it's all we got.'

'I understand.'

She gave him a look, which told him she really didn't think he understood at all. It was the look that someone with no money gave someone who had plenty. He was familiar with it, and he didn't feel guilty anymore. Life was a lottery. There were losing tickets and winning tickets.

'How do you know Rufus Twill?' Cab asked.

'He's my uncle.'

Cab was surprised, but he could see the family resemblance when he looked at her face. 'Did Rufus grow up around here?'

'Yeah, but he got out, went to college. Mama always said Uncle Rufus was smart. Sly smart, somebody who knew the score. He did well for himself, writin' stories that got politicians into trouble. 'Least until he let those boys get the drop on him. They messed him up.'

'He says he plays the piano now. Have you heard him?'

Gladiola smiled. 'Yeah, he ain't bad. Not as good as he thinks he is, but he ain't bad.'

Cab wondered if people said the same thing about him. 'Rufus told me he had a source who overheard Diane's son Drew threatening Birch Fairmont. Was that you?'

'Yeah, that was me.'

'He said you took it back later.'

'I did that, you're right. I didn't want to get anybody into trouble.'

'So which is it?' Cab asked. 'Which story was true?'

'Drew, he said it. Yes, he did. Big as life. Mr Birch weren't there, though. It was just Drew and his mama and Mr Muscles.'

Cab cocked his head. 'I'm sorry?'

'The massage guy. He was always there.'

'Oh, Garth Oakes.'

'Yeah, that's him. Not so bad to look at, I guess. I mean, you're a lot easier on the eyes than him, but the man did fill out a T-shirt.'

'Garth was always there?'

'Oh, yeah. Some people like to rub shoulders with rich folks. Makes 'em feel special, I guess.'

'What about you, Gladiola? Why were you there?'

'That's my job. Was. I came three times a week to clean the house. Started when I was sixteen.'

Gladiola lit a cigarette. The wind took the smoke as soon as it escaped her lips. She was younger than Cab had first thought – maybe thirty – but she had a tired face. Her body was bony and small. As they sat in the lawn chairs, she kicked off her flat shoes and stretched her toes. She'd ditched her overalls inside, and she now wore plain cotton shorts below her red T-shirt.

Cab heard juvenile shouting inside the small house. 'You have kids?' he asked.

'Ya think? I got three.' Gladiola reached back and pounded on the door. 'Hey, knock it off! Don't make me come in there!'

'What do they do when you're at work?'

'They go to school, and that's where their asses gonna stay. My sister watches 'em after. She's got three of her own.'

'How long have you worked at the landscaping company?'

'A few years. When Ms Fairmont moved to Tampa, I decided I was sick of scrubbing toilets and figured I'd do something else.'

Cab finished his tea and put the plastic glass on the sidewalk next to his chair. He heard a bark and saw a wire-haired fox terrier scramble around the corner of the house. The dog eyed him suspiciously but then curled up next to Gladiola's legs. Its tongue lolled as it panted in the heat. The dog tentatively licked the side of Cab's damp glass, then knocked it over and dug a nose inside for the ice.

'So you spent a lot of time in the Fairmont house?' Cab asked.

'Sure did.'

'What was it like?'

She pursed her big lips. 'Weren't a real happy place.'

'How so?'

'Nobody got along. Not Mr Birch and his wife. Not Mr Birch and her son. It was a marriage for show. I always had two bedrooms to clean, know what I mean?' She reached down and scratched the dog's head. 'Didn't help that Mr Birch was a first-class pussy hound. Liked to rub up against anything with tits and an ass.'

'Did that include you?'

She swallowed tea and wiped her mouth. 'Yeah, he grabbed what he could when nobody was looking. I didn't like it, but I didn't want to get fired. I never let him poke me, if that's what you're saying.'

'Did Diane know what he was like?'

'Wives always know,' Gladiola said.

Cab thought about himself and Diane. He wondered if husbands knew when the shoe was on the other foot. 'Rufus said there was some kind of problem at the estate that summer.'

Gladiola nodded.

'When was this?' Cab asked.

'Guess it was a couple weeks before Labor Day.'

'And what happened?'

'It's not like I know the details,' Gladiola said. 'I wasn't in the room.'

'You know something.'

She played with her hair. Her eyes were tired. 'It was a Saturday night. Ms Fairmont had some kind of brunch thing on Sunday, so I was cleaning. The house was quiet. Most nights that summer, it was like a train station, people everywhere, 'cause of the campaign. But there was some money thing over in Tampa, and most of the campaign folks were there.'

'So who was in the house?' Cab asked.

'Guess it was me and Mr Birch and Ms Fairmont. And the muscle man.'

'Garth was there?'

'Oh, yeah. Like I said, he was always there.'

'What about Drew?'

She shook her head. 'He was off partying. Drinking. Drugs. Whatever he did in those days.'

'So what happened?' he asked again.

'I was in the dining room, and I heard shouting. Real loud. Real angry. Mr Birch and his wife, they were upstairs, and they were going at it.'

'What were they saying?'

'Couldn't hear that. All I heard were their voices thumping in the walls. Must have been, I don't know, fifteen or twenty minutes. Then . . .'

'Then what?' Cab asked.

Gladiola eyed him and gave a little shiver. 'Screaming.'

'What was going on?' he asked.

'Weren't too hard to guess. Mr Birch was walloping on his wife. It was something bad.'

'What did you do?'

'I froze,' she said. 'I don't know how long it lasted, but then it went god-awful quiet. Few minutes later, Mr Muscles came in, looking all white, told me to get the hell out, not to say a word to nobody. That's what I did.'

'Did you tell anyone?' Cab asked.

'Nope.'

'When were you next in the house?'

'Couple days, I guess. There weren't no brunch. They cancelled it. I came around my usual day, and it was like nothing had happened. Ms Fairmont went out of her way to say everything was fine. She didn't look fine, though. I mean, she sat in a chair and didn't get up once while I was there. In her bedroom, too, the sheets weren't the same. I always changed the sheets, but this time, somebody else did. Like, I don't know, maybe there was something on them they didn't want nobody to see.'

'Like what?'

'Like blood maybe.'

Cab frowned. 'What about Drew?'

'He stormed in while I was there. Practically foaming at the mouth. High as a kite, swearing up and down about what a bastard Mr Birch was, how he was gonna blow his fucking head off. They got me out of there fast, but I heard what I heard. Oh, yeah.'

'Except later you said you didn't,' Cab said.

Gladiola looked nervously at her bare feet. 'Like I said, why make trouble for people?'

'Did they pay you?'

'What?'

'Did they pay you not to say anything?'

Her lips scrunched up. 'Yeah.'

'Who paid?' Cab asked.

'Ms Fairmont. After the murders, when all the police were nosing around.'

'How much?'

'Thousand bucks. I shut my mouth fast.'

Cab thought about it. The bribe may have been an innocent mistake on Diane's part. She was protecting her son from police scrutiny and a media frenzy. Even if Drew wasn't involved in the murders, the suspicion would have destroyed him. She was probably thinking about her fundraising efforts for the Common Way Foundation, too. A wife-beater didn't make much of a martyr.

Diane was already becoming a very practical politician.

'And yet here you are,' Cab said.

'Say what?'

'You're talking. Telling me what happened. Why?'

'Rufus said you was a detective,' Gladiola said. 'Figured somebody should know about this.'

'Ten years later, you suddenly decide to spill your guts? While Diane Fairmont is in the middle of a campaign for governor? I find the timing of your crisis of conscience very convenient, Gladiola. Did you go to Diane looking for more money? Did she say no?'

Her face flashed with anger. 'I didn't do that!'

'What about your uncle? Did Rufus give you money?'

She slapped the aluminum frame of the lawn chair, and the fox terrier yelped and bolted. 'So what if he did? Rufus helps me out sometimes when he can. I got nothing!'

'So what will I find if I go inside? A new flat-screen? An Xbox?'

Gladiola said nothing, but he knew he was right.

'I like that brand new airboat your uncle had, too,' Cab went on. 'Did Rufus think I wouldn't notice that?'

He stood up and smoothed his tie and slipped sunglasses over his face again, although it was nearly dark. 'I really don't like people playing games with me, Gladiola. Rufus sent you after me like a drone strike. He and his friends are out to embarrass Diane Fairmont. Tell him I won't do his dirty work for him.'

He headed for his Corvette across the mostly dead lawn.

'I wasn't lying!' Gladiola shouted after him, her voice a loud screech. 'It happened just like I said.'

He didn't look back. He jangled his keys on his finger.

'Ain't no game either,' she went on, even louder. 'You watch yourself, huh? That first boy, they killed him.'

Cab stopped in his tracks. He pulled off his sunglasses. He slid his keys in his pocket, spun on his heels, and marched back up to

Gladiola. She was small but defiant, staring up at him from the lawn chair.

'What did you say?' he asked.

'You heard me.'

'Did you tell your story to someone else?'

'Sure did. 'Bout a month ago. Boy was asking questions about Mr Fairmont and that last summer, just like you. I told him 'bout that weekend and what happened. He was real excited, he was. Said it could be something important. Now he's dead.' She put a finger to her head and pulled the trigger.

'Who was he? What was his name?'

Gladiola folded her arms across her chest, and her jaw jutted out insolently on her face. 'Twenty bucks. 'Cause you thought I was lying.'

Cab took his wallet and retrieved a fifty-dollar bill. He opened her hand, put it inside, and closed her warm fingers over it. He didn't say a word, but his eyebrows arched in anticipation.

Gladiola smirked, looking pleased with herself.

'Weird-looking boy,' she said. 'Funny little round hat and one of those curly mustaches. Said his name was Justin.'

22

Peach waited with Annalie while she recovered from the assault by Frank Macy. The fear eased, and so did the nausea. Annalie disinfected the cut on her forehead. She was still in pain – her muscles ached, and her head throbbed – but now that she was safe, she wanted to be alone. Annalie, who'd come back after spotting a man in a red Cutlass staking out the parking lot, offered to stay with her. It took Peach until it was almost dark to convince her that she was fine.

When she headed north on Gulf Boulevard in her Thunderbird, she noticed Annalie following in her Corolla, all the way to the east-bound turn-off at Walshingham Road. Typically, Peach would have turned there, too, on her way back to Seminole Park, but she didn't want to be followed anymore, and she wasn't ready to go home.

She kept driving through Indian Rocks Beach and finally turned east. She was still dizzy, and the pain got worse as she drove. Twenty minutes later, she found herself on the Frankenstein bridge headed back to Tampa. It was dark by the time she reached the city streets. The car, almost without her guiding it, took her to Diane Fairmont's estate. The dark water of the bay was on her left. Across the street, the house was invisible behind the wall and the overgrown trees.

She got out of the car. Her skin was bruised and tender. She crossed Bayshore, and it never even occurred to her to walk down the side street to the main gate. Instead, she pushed into the brush and found a gnarled oak whose branches hung over the wall. Like a monkey, she climbed, swinging her legs onto the lowest branch and pulling herself up, setting off a loud exodus of birds. Twelve feet above the ground, she found a limb sturdy enough to support her weight, and she inched along the bough with the wall below her. When she was clear, she let her body dangle, and then she dropped. The ground was soft.

There were no sirens or alarms. No running feet. She beat away the mosquitoes and stamped through the bushes until she reached the open grass. Garden lights sparkled like fairies. She heard the splashing water of a fountain. Something loud snuffled near the ground – a raccoon, which watched her with glowing eyes and a hunched back. Everything else around her was pitch black. The estate was fifty yards away, and Peach headed for the marble steps.

She rang the bell, hearing rich Westminster chimes inside. A minute passed, and someone opened the door cautiously. She recognized Garth Oakes, who had his hand inside a coat, as if reaching for a gun. His clothes barely contained his muscles. His eyes pored over her and then narrowed with recognition.

'You're Deacon's sister, aren't you? What the hell are you doing here?'

'I want to see Ms Fairmont.'

'How'd you get inside?'

She didn't answer. Garth let her in, and she kicked off her shoes, rather than track mud along the hardwood floor. She felt small and dirty in her torn clothes. He led her to a corner room, brightly lit, with piano music playing softly from hidden speakers. A wall of windows looked out on the gardens, but the exterior was dark. Diane Fairmont was inside. So was Caprice. They sat on opposite sides of a round table with laptops in front of both of them.

Caprice assessed her condition with a single glance and got to her feet.

'Peach, what happened to you? Are you okay?'

Diane remained seated. She had half-glasses on her face, and she studied Peach from over the tops of the frames as if she were looking at a homeless waif who had dropped into her parlor. Peach realized what she must look like in her bedraggled disguise. She tried to talk and couldn't. She felt overwhelmed. It had seemed so important to be here, and now she had no idea what to say.

'You're hurt,' Caprice went on. 'What's going on? Does Deacon know you're here?'

Peach shook her head mutely.

Garth and Diane traded looks across the room. 'You want me to get her out of here?' he asked.

Caprice interrupted sharply. 'Don't be stupid, Garth. This girl works for me. Peach, do you want to sit down?'

'No,' she said finally. Looking around the elegant room, she decided that she didn't belong here. 'No, he's right. I'll go. I don't know why I came.'

'Something happened to you. What is it?'

'I just wanted to ask Ms Fairmont something,' she stuttered. She looked at Diane and found the question spilling out of her. 'I wanted to know if Justin was working on a project for you when he was killed.'

Peach didn't know what she expected. She didn't know what Diane would say. She had no idea how much it would hurt when Diane looked at her blankly and said, 'Who?'

She didn't know who Justin was. He'd worked for her, he'd lived, he'd died, and he was still a stranger to her. To Peach, it was as bad as a slap in the face.

'Justin was part of our research group,' Caprice explained softly.

'He was killed recently. The police suspected drug trafficking was involved.'

Diane's face tightened, as if blood and air had been sucked from her cheeks, and her eyes grew hard. 'If he sold drugs, he's no loss to this world,' she snapped, her voice bitter.

'They're wrong about him,' Peach said. 'I think his death had something to do with a man you know. Frank Macy.'

Peach wasn't prepared for Diane's reaction. The woman shut the cover of her laptop so hard that it sounded like the crack of a gunshot. Her entire body shook with fury as she jabbed her finger at Peach. '*Frank Macy*? How dare you say that name to me? Do you know what that man did to me? To my son?'

Peach felt staggered. She wanted to turn and run. 'He said you should be afraid of him. I thought I needed to tell–'

Diane slashed the air with her hand, cutting Peach off. Her face red, she stormed past Peach and left the room without a word. Like a servant, Garth followed on her heels. Peach and Caprice were alone. The piano music kept playing, oddly peaceful in the aftermath of Diane's outburst.

'I'm sorry,' Peach murmured.

Caprice put an arm around her shoulder. 'Frank Macy is a sensitive subject with Diane. You probably don't know about her son–'

'I do. I know.'

'Then you can understand how she feels. And why drug dealers get no sympathy from her.'

'Justin wasn't a drug dealer,' Peach said. 'I don't know what he had to do with Macy, but it wasn't drugs.'

'Well, regardless, Macy is someone to stay away from, Peach. It's for your own safety, but it's for the campaign, too. You know how the media works. They'll grab things and turn them into stories. We can't have that.'

'No.'

'Should I call Deacon?' Caprice asked. 'He can come get you.'

'No, I can drive.'

'Are you sure? You don't look good.'

'I'm sure.'

Caprice kept a protective arm around Peach's shoulder as she led her back to the hallway. At the door, Caprice followed her onto the porch. Peach stared into the gardens and found she was reluctant to go. Not yet. Not now. Reading her mind, Caprice gestured at a wrought-iron bench near the pond, and they both sat there, feeling the mist of the fountain. The breeze rustled Caprice's hair. Peach thought she was one of the prettiest women she'd ever met. It was easy to understand why Lyle had wanted to marry her.

'How are you, really, Peach?' Caprice asked. 'We don't get much chance to talk anymore. I feel bad about that.'

'I'm okay. Lonely sometimes.'

'After the campaign, I'll try to do better. I miss you. I see Deacon, but not you.'

'I know you're busy.'

Peach knew that Caprice felt responsible for her. It wasn't her job, but it was nice that she felt that way. If she and Lyle had married, Caprice would have been her sister-in-law, but Lyle had wanted Peach to think of Caprice as part-sister, part-mother, part-friend. She appreciated everything Caprice had done for her over the years, but she'd never felt quite that close to her. Deacon was the one who had drunk the Kool-Aid, signed on with Common Way, and devoted his life to the cause. Peach had simply been swept up in his wake.

'How's your work?' Caprice asked.

'Okay, I guess.'

'Deacon tells me you're very good at it.'

'Thanks.'

'I know it hasn't been easy for you,' Caprice said. 'Do you get out much? Do you have friends?'

'Not really. I'm too busy most of the time. It's okay, I don't mind being alone.'

'It's easy to tell yourself that even when it's not true. You shouldn't close yourself off. Lyle wouldn't like it.'

'I know.'

'Deacon says you've been thinking a lot about Lyle.'

'Yeah. Some.'

'I did that for a long time, too,' Caprice said, 'but there comes a time when it's not healthy to dwell on the past.'

'Oh, I just – I just wish I'd been nicer to him at the end. Things were pretty rocky that summer for all of us. I feel bad about that.'

'Don't. Lyle wouldn't want you to feel that way. You were just a girl.'

Peach smiled, even though the memory didn't cheer her up. 'There was this one weekend. You probably don't even remember. I was so sick. Pneumonia. I had to go back home early from Tampa. Lyle was afraid I was going to throw up in his Mercedes. Actually, I think I did. Deacon took me to Mr Fairmont's house that night.'

'I do remember,' Caprice said.

'Yeah. I was pretty delirious. It was really bad. All that blood.'

Caprice cocked her head. 'Blood?'

Peach looked at her. 'What?'

'You said blood.'

'Did I? That's weird.' She shook her head. 'No, phlegm. Nasty green stuff. Yuck. I was coughing up phlegm for days. That's what I meant to say.'

23

Walter Fleming took a huge bite of fish taco and grabbed a paper napkin to wipe his mouth. He always stopped at Taco Bus when he was in Tampa. He was parked under a tree at the back of the lot in his Chevy Tahoe, behind smoked windows. It was after midnight, but the Taco Bus – which literally dished out food from a renovated school bus – was open 24/7, and there was plenty of late-night traffic from urban kids lined up for carne asada.

Walter wore jeans and a black polo shirt. The baseball cap on his dashboard had a union logo, which was why he wasn't wearing it. He didn't want people remembering him.

The three-day union meeting at the downtown convention center was over. He'd stayed an extra day in the city, but he needed to head back to Tallahassee by morning. He wanted to be in the office before Chayla made landfall across the central coast. Storms were unpredictable, and nobody in politics liked events they couldn't control. That was how you lost elections.

He heard rapping on the window and unlocked the truck. The passenger door of the Tahoe opened, and Ogden Bush climbed in beside him. Walter cast a jaundiced eye on the man's two-thousand dollar suit and the gold watch hugging his slim wrist. The cloud of the man's cologne made him want to crack the window. Bush looked dressed for a club in South Beach.

'That's what you wear, Ogden?' he said. 'We're trying not to get noticed.'

Bush shrugged. 'I came straight from the Common Way office.'

Walter grunted and took another big bite of swai fish, which was flaky and delicious. 'Where's Curtis?' he asked, brushing crumbs out of his beard.

'He's in line. He wanted some *camarones*.'

Walter eyed the mirror. He spotted the forty-something private detective at the food truck window, and he frowned, seeing the man chat up three teenage girls. Curtis Ritchie's car, a red Cutlass, was parked nearby. Walter was paranoid about being seen – or, worse, taped or photographed – but as a rule, he insisted on in-person meetings when he needed to talk about political business. Phones, computers, e-mails, tablets, they all scared the hell out of him. You could never delete any of it. Sooner or later, someone would dig up the bits and bytes, and it would be all over the news. Besides, he liked seeing people's faces. You could read a lot in faces about who was scared and who was lying.

'How's the Governor?' Bush asked him.

'Nervous.'

'Yeah, he should be.'

'Are there any surprises coming that I should know about?' Walter asked.

Bush shook his head. 'No. They're watching him and his people, but so far, there aren't any new shitstorms.' He added: 'One of their spies caught you and Brent talking at the convention. That could have been bad. Good thing you covered for me.'

Walter shrugged. He knew who it was. The girl in the elevator. Damn, those people were smart. He'd warned Reed about underestimating Common Way. 'Don't worry, nobody knows about our arrangement,' he said. 'Not even the Governor. Not yet.'

'Let's keep it that way,' Bush replied. 'If people find out I'm playing both sides of the street in this race, that's bad for business.'

'We're the ones who have everything to lose, Ogden. For you it's just about money.'

Bush smiled, and even in the darkness of the car, his teeth were white. He brushed lint from his lapel. 'Not true. I want back in, you know that.'

Walter finished his taco and crushed the paper wrapper into a ball. He didn't like Ogden Bush. He didn't like dealing with double agents and moles, but that was the price of the political game. The ends justified the means. Young people got into the game with high-minded ideals, but sooner or later the smart ones realized that winning dirty was a hell of a lot better than losing clean. There was no prize – and no power – for the ones who came in second.

His relationship with Ogden Bush went back more than a decade. In those days, Bush was a newcomer. Smart, ambitious, but young and untested. When the 12th District incumbent dropped dead that year, Bush bucked the party establishment by helping a far-left state senator win the primary. He did it by trashing Walter's own hand-picked candidate, but Walter didn't hold grudges. He respected brass-knuckle tactics and people who took risks. Bush would have been a pariah if his candidate had lost, and they both knew it. Instead, Labor Day happened, and Bush hung the Liberty Empire Alliance like an albatross around Chuck Warren's neck. The Dem won. Bush became a star.

Even so, Walter knew that Bush's arrogance would catch up with him sooner or later. Two years ago, Bush backed a black Senate candidate who was forced out of the race over allegations of cocaine use. Bush called it racism, and his accusations split the party and cost them the election. Party leaders excommunicated him. His business dried up.

Walter knew how badly Bush wanted to get back inside the party after two years in the wilderness. That gave him leverage. When Bush wormed his way into Diane's campaign, Walter approached him with a deal he couldn't refuse: Become a spy. Pass along dirt they could use against Diane. If the Governor won, Walter would make sure that Bush got taken off the party shit list. If Diane won anyway, Bush could grab credit for steering the campaign.

Politics.

'What's their plan for Chayla?' Walter asked.

'Lay low. Ride out the storm. They'll have Diane show up at Red Cross sites and hand out soup and cookies. Lots of photographs. It'll be a wait-and-see thing on the government response. If things go smoothly, they'll congratulate the Governor – you know, this is no time for partisan divisions. If things go badly, they'll let surrogates roast him for incompetence.'

Walter nodded. He'd expected all of that.

The back door of the Tahoe opened. Curtis Ritchie climbed inside, carrying an order of spicy shrimp, which he peeled awkwardly with one hand. He leaned between the front seats, carrying an aroma of garlic and cayenne, mixed with the cigarette smoke clinging to his clothes.

'Shit, these are good. I wanted a taco, but the girls said these were better.'

Walter twisted far enough to see the detective's face. Ritchie carried a heavy load of blond stubble, and his unruly hair looked as if it hadn't been washed in a couple days. 'You want to flirt with teenagers, Curtis, do it on someone else's time.'

'I'm divorced. I'm a free man again. I like to shop around.'

Walter snorted. 'Like those *chicas* would give you the time of day.'

He had been married for almost five decades. He still appreciated the appeal of young girls, but to him they were like something you admired in a museum. He'd seen too many middle-aged politicians self-destruct over affairs with pretty aides. Sometimes he thought every man who ran for office should be castrated first. There would be fewer distractions, and they might actually get something done.

'So what do we know?' Walter asked. 'Tell me something.'

Ritchie popped a shrimp in his mouth and licked his fingers. 'My alter ego, Detective Curtis Clay of the St Pete Police, is still asking questions. You can't rush these things.'

Walter held up a hand to stop him. 'Knock it off about that. I'm sure you're kidding, because if you were really doing anything illegal, like impersonating a cop, I'd have to shut this operation down and get your license pulled. Right? I asked Ogden to make it damn clear that we were paying for investigative services only. If I'm ever asked to put my hand on a Bible in court, that's what I'm going to say.'

Ritchie smirked. 'Yeah, of course, I was kidding. I'm a kidder.'

'So what do we know?' Walter repeated.

'So far, nothing much,' Ritchie said. 'You wanted real dirt. That takes time.'

Walter shook his head in frustration. He'd told Brent Reed to be patient, but patience wasn't one of his own virtues. His blood pressure was always high, no matter how much medicine he took.

'Look, Walter,' Bush said, taking a shrimp from Ritchie's basket, 'we both know what the people at Common Way are like. You can't win as often as they do without crossing the line. I don't know if it's bribes or wiretapping or what, but there's something to find. I can't dig into it myself, because we can't have anyone finding out about our special relationship. That's why we have Curtis here.'

'Yeah, and what is Curtis here doing besides eating shrimp?'

Ritchie grinned. 'It's really good shrimp.'

'What about this kid Justin you told me about?' Walter asked. 'What's the deal with him?'

'Rufus tipped me off that Justin Kiel was asking questions about the Labor Day murders,' Bush replied. 'I asked Justin why, but he clammed up. I told Curtis to start checking him out, but somebody shot the kid in the head before we could figure out what he was doing.'

'Who did it?' Walter asked, staring at Curtis Ritchie.

Ritchie's brow furrowed. 'Don't know. I was following him, but the kid was smart. I think he made me. He went underground, and I lost him.'

'The police think the murder was a drug thing, but it smells funny,' Bush added. 'He's asking about Birch Fairmont, and then he gets popped? Makes you wonder.'

'Is there something hinky about the Labor Day murders?' Walter asked. 'Something the FBI missed?'

Bush shrugged. 'Hard to say. Rufus has it in his head that Diane's son was involved. If he was, and she knew, that's huge. Back then, I wanted everyone focused on Chuck Warren and Ham Brock, because we needed to crush Chuck in the polls. Now? It wouldn't hurt to have some ugly rumors about Diane and Drew.'

'Sounds risky to me,' Walter said. 'Her son killed himself. We don't need to generate any more sympathy for her.'

'Common Way's got someone looking into this, too,' Bush added. 'His name's Cab Bolton. He's a Naples cop. Caprice went around me and hired him herself.'

'Why would she do that?'

'Supposedly, there are threats against Diane, and he's trying to track down the source. Of course, Caprice is smart. She may be trying to make sure there are no unexploded bombs in Diane's past. Like Drew.'

Walter jabbed a finger at Curtis Ritchie. 'If there are any bombs like that, it's your job to find them, so we can blow them up ourselves.'

'Hey, I'm on it,' Ritchie assured him. 'I've been keeping an eye on one of their researchers. Peach Piper. She's been digging into whatever happened to Justin, too.'

'Piper? As in Lyle's sister?'

'That's her. I was following her earlier today, and she led me to somebody interesting. She's been tracking a drug dealer named Frank Macy. Smooth character but a real whack job. He got out of prison on a manslaughter gig earlier this year.'

Walter shrugged. 'Macy. Is that name supposed to mean something to me?'

Bush leaned across the seat and grinned. 'I looked him up. F rank Macy sold drugs to Diane's son Drew ten years ago. Small world, huh? As a little bonus, guess who his lawyer was? Ramona Cortes.'

That was the first thing Walter had heard in days that put him in a better mood. 'I like it,' he said. 'I like it a lot.'

Ritchie finished the last of his shrimp. 'Yeah, we figured you would. Macy could be our missing link to all sorts of shit. With any luck, he'll beat a path right back to Diane and Ramona. Maybe we can take down both of those bitches.'

24

'Do you always carry a gun?' Peach asked.

Annalie punched the pause button on the remote control. The playback on the sixty-inch television in the Common Way conference room froze, leaving the Governor with his mouth open in front of the electricians at the union convention. It was Tuesday morning, and the two of them were reviewing hours of video footage gathered at campaign events, hunting for gaffes that could be used in campaign ads.

'It's Florida,' Annalie said. She hefted her purse up and down as if she were working out with weights. 'Even Mickey Mouse probably carries a piece.'

'Well, I'm glad you came back to check on me. Thanks.'

'No problem. I didn't want to take any chances. That guy in the red Cutlass was watching you. I don't know if he was connected to Macy or not, but he definitely had his eyes on you.'

Peach got up and paced. Inside the conference room, the stale cold air made her shiver. Outside, the building rocked, and the walls groaned. She wondered who the man in the Cutlass was. She was a spy, and she didn't like being spied upon herself.

'I talked to one of my contacts about Macy,' Annalie added. 'There's not much buzz about him, but he had eight years in prison to make connections. He could be into anything.'

'Yeah.'

'What exactly did Diane say when you mentioned him?'

'She got furious. She thinks Macy was the one who got Drew hooked on drugs. Though I don't know why that would matter to Justin.'

Peach sat down again. Annalie said nothing.

'And then there's Alison,' Peach went on. 'Justin wrote her name in the poetry book. He must have wanted me to find it. She must be important, too.'

'You don't know who she is?'

'Deacon thought she might be a lawyer for the foundation, but I can't find evidence that Justin ever contacted her.' She added after a pause: 'You would have liked Justin. There was something deep about him that you don't find in a lot of people.'

Annalie brushed her raven hair out of her eyes. 'Well, if you liked him, I'm sure I would have liked him, too. You seem to be a pretty good judge of people.'

'No, I don't think I know people at all,' Peach said. 'I keep them away. Caprice says I'm too closed off.'

'You've been through a lot.'

'Yeah. It's hard to get close to people. And even harder to trust people.' She dragged words out of herself. 'I mean, I don't really know you, do I? I like you, but I don't know anything about you.'

Annalie smiled, as if she knew it was hard for Peach to say something like that. 'What do you want to know?'

'I don't know. Where'd you grow up?'

'Near Bonita Springs.'

'Are your parents alive?'

'Yes.'

Peach nodded. 'People think it's odd when I ask that, but I don't really know what that's like, you know? To have parents.'

'I know.'

'Did you go to college?'

'UCF.'

'I never wanted to go to college,' Peach said. 'What did you do after you graduated?'

'Partied. Ran up debt. Experienced the joys of minimum wage.'

They both laughed. Most Florida grads could tell the same story, spending the decade after school as beach bums. Even so, Peach watched Annalie fiddle with a pen on the table, and an unwelcome thought leaped into her head: *You're lying to me.* She had no idea why Annalie would lie about her past, or what she was hiding from her. Or maybe she was just being Peach Paranoid again.

'Well, like I said, you would have liked Justin. He would have liked you, too.'

'That's sweet.'

They were silent. Annalie looked uneasy.

'So Justin never said anything to you about Frank Macy?' she continued. 'The name never came up?'

Peach shook her head. 'No.'

'Show me the photo again,' Annalie told her. 'The one you found in Justin's safe house. Do you still have it?'

Peach slid the paper from her pocket and unfolded it. Annalie studied it carefully, and she pointed to the edges of the picture.

'Here's what I don't understand. This isn't a copy of the article itself. The article was pinned up somewhere. See the cork paneling on the side? That looks like a bulletin board.'

Peach had seen that, too. 'So?'

'So where was this taken?'

'I have no idea.'

'You were in Justin's safe house and his apartment,' Annalie said. 'Could it have been in there?'

'I don't think so. Maybe this was inside Frank Macy's apartment. I could get in and search it.'

'No, you will *not* do that,' Annalie told her firmly. 'If anyone goes in there, it's me. I'm the one with the gun, remember?'

'Yeah, okay,' Peach said, but she seethed with frustration. She needed a direction. She needed to do something. It was as if Justin were in the corner of the drab conference room, his arms folded, shaking his head at her in disappointment underneath his pork pie hat. *Hey, come on, Peach, I'm counting on you.*

The phone in the conference room rang. Peach knew she should get it, but she couldn't move. She stared at Justin in the corner as if he were real, with that I-know-everything smirk on his face. In her imagination, he winked at her and jabbed a finger at the phone as if he were pointing a gun.

You're going to want to take that call, Peach.

Annalie reached across the table and grabbed the receiver.

'Hello?' And then: 'What's his name?'

Annalie hung up the phone, her features dark with concern.

'What is it?' Peach asked.

'There's a detective out front who wants to talk to you about Justin.'

'Is it Curtis Clay?' Peach asked. 'The fake cop?'

Annalie shook her head. 'No, this one's real. His name is Cab Bolton.'

25

Cab sized up the young woman in front of him. She was pretty in a Carey Mulligan way, with page-boy blond hair and freckles. Her tiny mouth was constantly changing expressions, and her blue eyes had a luminous intensity. Her expression was severe and suspicious, like a yipper dog growling to protect its turf. She obviously had a paranoid streak, because he didn't think anyone had ever studied his identification more carefully. After holding it up to the light and comparing his photograph, she called the Naples Police to get a description of him.

Finally, she hung up.

Cab smiled at her. 'So? Am I me?'

'They said if my head came up higher than your neck, it wasn't you.'

'I hope they mentioned the earring, too. And the hair gel.'

'They said it was a pomade from London.'

'They obviously know me too well,' Cab said. 'So now that you know who I am, how about you tell me who you are.'

She sat on the other side of the conference table with her hands folded in front of her. The oversized armchair made her look small. 'Peach Piper.'

Cab heard the name and made the connection. 'As in Lyle Piper?'

'My brother.'

'I'm sorry.'

Peach shrugged. 'What do you want, Detective Bolton?'

Cab didn't answer immediately. His eyes wandered around the conference room. He spotted the frozen video on the television, and as he did, Peach reached for the remote control and shut it off. The Governor's face disappeared. He glanced out the window behind him at the cubicle farm and saw dozens of earnest workers in their twenties with bad haircuts. The room hummed with the white noise of air conditioning.

He noted the arrangement of papers around him and realized that Peach hadn't been alone in the conference room. Someone had been here with her, but whoever it was had left quickly.

'What exactly do you people do here?' he asked. 'This place is kind of shabby for a big-name foundation, isn't it?'

'We do research.'

'What kind of research?'

'Political research,' Peach said.

Cab nodded. The girl didn't want to give him details. 'I get it. Secret, world-changing stuff, huh? You could tell me, but then you'd have to kill me?'

'Something like that,' Peach replied.

'I thought opposition research was about catching politicians saying stupid things. How tough can that be? It's like shooting fish in a barrel, isn't it?'

Peach didn't reply, but her lips twitched with the tiniest of smiles, as if she were finally succumbing to his charm. 'You still haven't told me what you want.'

Cab didn't answer right away. He liked to meander with witnesses, which usually made them nervous and anxious to talk. Silence made people uncomfortable, especially around cops. However, as young as this girl was, she didn't rattle easily or open her mouth. Behind her paranoia, Peach was obviously smart.

'I asked at the desk to talk to someone who knew Justin Kiel,' he told her. 'They sent me to you.'

'Why are you interested in Justin?'

'I think you know why. He was murdered.'

Peach played with the television remote control in her hand. 'Well, yes, he was, Detective, but he wasn't murdered in Naples. The crime took place in St Petersburg. So how does this involve you?'

Cab smiled again. No doubt about it – she was smart.

'I'm not actually investigating the murder itself,' Cab admitted. 'Not for the police, anyway.'

'So you're a private citizen, and I'm a private citizen. That means I don't have to answer any of your questions, right?'

'Yes, you're right. Then again, I'm also working for your boss.'

Peach hesitated. 'Ms Fairmont?'

'And Caprice Dean,' Cab said.

'What did they hire you to do?'

Cab said nothing, and the girl nodded at the irony. 'Yeah, okay, you could tell me, but then you'd have to kill me,' she said.

'Something like that,' Cab replied.

'Why do you care about Justin? The police say he was killed in some kind of drug deal gone bad.'

'Do you believe that?' Cab asked.

'Do you?'

Cab studied the girl's defiant face. He'd come in here expecting to play cop games with her, but instead, she was playing cop games with him. He decided to be honest and see how she dealt with the truth. 'No,' he said.

Peach couldn't hide the intensity of her reaction. It wasn't surprise or curiosity. It was *exhilaration*. With one word, he had changed something inside her. She leaned forward with a strange excitement, as if, suddenly, she knew her place in the world. She'd been vindicated.

'If it wasn't drugs, what was it?' Peach asked.

'You tell me.'

She was silent. Around them, the walls shook with the wind. 'I have no idea,' she said finally.

Peach was lying. As always, lies told him more than the truth. She knew more than she was letting on, but whatever she knew, she was reluctant to tell him. He was a stranger.

'How well did you know Justin?' he asked.

'We worked together, that's all.'

Cab heard the translation in his head: *We were close. Very close.* He wondered exactly how close. Were they friends? Were they lovers? He thought that her skin flushed at the very sound of his name.

'What did you two work on?'

'Research.'

'Oh, right. Your lips are sealed. I know you have to be careful about telling people what you do, but we're on the same team, Peach. I'm not the enemy. If you and Justin were digging into something that got him killed, you should tell me.'

'Justin and I weren't working together before he was killed,' Peach said. 'I can't tell you anything.'

'What about computer records?'

'The police took everything. You'd have to talk to them.'

'Is there anyone else in the office who would know something?'

'Ogden Bush is the liaison to the campaign. You could talk to him.'

'Is he here?'

'No.'

'Then I guess I'm talking to you,' Cab said.

'I already said I can't help you.'

Peach gathered her files around her, as if the conversation was over. Cab thought about who this girl was. Peach Piper, sister of Lyle Piper. A decade earlier, she would have been a child, grieving the loss of her brother. The summer when Birch Fairmont was assassinated had changed her life profoundly. It had to be in her consciousness every day.

'One more question,' he said. 'This one's not about Justin.'

She was suspicious. 'Okay.'

'Who killed your brother?' Cab asked.

Peach stared at him. 'What kind of question is that?'

'I imagine it's a question you think about all the time. Who do you think murdered Birch Fairmont and Lyle Piper?'

'I don't know who pulled the trigger. It was some right-wing fanatic from the Liberty Empire Alliance. Maybe it was Ham Brock himself.'

'You believe that's what happened?' Cab said.

'Of course. That's why I'm here.'

'That's very noble.'

'Don't patronize me,' Peach snapped. 'You wouldn't be sarcastic if someone from your family had been murdered.'

'I wasn't being sarcastic, I was being sincere. And I nearly did lose a family member that day, although I know that isn't the same thing.'

Peach's eyes narrowed with recognition. 'Bolton? You're related to Tarla Bolton?'

'I'm her son.'

Her face softened. 'I'm sorry. I didn't realize.'

'That's okay. I usually don't advertise it.'

'Everybody says your mother saved Ms Fairmont that day. She was very brave.'

'Well, my mother rarely thinks before she acts,' Cab said. 'Sometimes the results are better than others.'

'It was a terrible day,' Peach said.

'Were you there?'

'No. Thank God. I couldn't have handled seeing it happen.'

Cab leaned across the conference table, which meant he was almost in Peach's face. She looked very young. 'Did you spend a lot of time at Birch Fairmont's estate that summer?'

'Sure. Lyle was there all the time because of the campaign.'

'What do you remember?'

'Not much. Deacon and I spent a lot of time in the pool. I read a lot. I was just a kid.'

'You strike me as a kid who would notice things,' Cab said.

'Like what?'

'Like something bad happening.'

'I don't know what you mean,' Peach replied.

'Do you remember anything about Birch and Diane?'

'No. They weren't together a lot. Birch was on the road. Ms Fairmont was alone.'

'Did you talk to her much?'

'Oh, no, hardly ever.'

'What about Diane's son? Drew?'

He saw a slight tic in Peach's face. 'What about him?'

'Did you know him?'

Peach shook her head. 'Why are you asking about him?'

'No reason.'

He let the silence linger. Staring at her, he thought she was telling the truth this time. She didn't know Drew. Even so, something about Drew's name had elicited a reaction, and she was obviously curious about why he'd brought it up. It was the same message as before: *I could tell you things, but I won't.*

She didn't trust him. Not yet.

Cab thought about Gladiola Croft's story. Something had happened two weeks before Labor Day between Birch and Diane. An argument. A fight. Maybe it didn't mean anything at all; maybe Drew's threat to kill his stepfather was just twenty-something angst. Or maybe this was all a game by Rufus Twill – and the shadowy people pulling strings behind him – to create a scandal that would tarnish Diane's campaign.

He would have been willing to believe the story was just a convenient lie, except for one thing.

Justin Kiel was dead. That was real.

'Two weeks before Labor Day, something very ugly happened at Birch's estate,' Cab told Peach. 'Do you know anything about that? It was a Saturday night.'

'No, if it's the weekend I'm thinking about, I was sick. Pneumonia. I don't remember much. I'm sorry.'

'I'm asking because of Justin,' he told her.

'How does this involve Justin?'

Definitely friends, Cab thought, watching her face. *Probably lovers.*

'Justin was in Lake Wales shortly before he was killed. He was asking questions about the Labor Day murders.'

'*What?* No, that can't be right.'

'You didn't know? He didn't tell you about it?'

'No, he didn't,' Peach said. She looked dazed, as if a wave had washed her away. 'He didn't say anything like that.'

He lowered his voice, but he held her blue eyes with his own. 'You understand why I'm worried, don't you? Someone killed Justin. It happened *two weeks ago*. Maybe the police are right, and this was a drug-related murder, but I don't like coincidences. I don't like the fact that Justin was looking into Birch's murder, only to wind up dead himself. I want to know what he found, because if it was enough to get him killed, then something is going on. Something is going on *right here and now.*'

Peach stood up. 'Stop,' she said. 'Just stop. Please.'

'Peach, if you know anything–'

'I don't,' she insisted.

'I need you to trust me.'

'I don't know you,' she said.

'Listen to me. Someone killed Lyle and Birch. Someone killed Justin. They may not be finished yet.'

'I have to go. I'm sorry.'

Peach held up her hands and backed away from him. He may as well have been holding a gun. Like a spooked deer, she bolted from the office without another word, leaving him alone.

Cab eased back in the reclining chair, frustrated, and let out his breath in a sigh. He didn't like walking away with nothing. He'd learned to trust his instincts, and his instincts told him that Peach knew more about the past than she'd told him. She probably knew more than she really understood.

He wished he had Lala with him. Lala had a way of connecting with young women that Cab never had.

His eyes scanned the conference room table. Peach had left her files behind her. He had no interest in spying on the inner workings of the Common Way Foundation, but he noticed a half-folded piece of paper on the desk, tented and face down, as if Peach had been looking at it before he arrived. Curious, he used a fingertip to slide the paper toward him.

Cab unfolded it and read it. He didn't understand what the photograph showed him, but by instinct, he didn't like it. Something about this single piece of paper in his hand felt dangerous. And important.

He saw a name he didn't recognize. Frank Macy.

And a name he did. Ramona Cortes.

26

Peach knew where she needed to go. Lake Wales.

She drove inland. Highway 4 was jammed with cars. There had been no evacuation ordered for Chayla's landfall, but some coastal residents weren't taking any chances with the storm.

It took her twice as long as it usually would to reach the exit at Lakeland, where she headed southeast toward Bartow. The farther she drove into the back country on the quiet two-lane highway, the more she retreated into her past. The land between towns was untouched by time. Flat, empty green fields. Fruit stands selling mesh bags of oranges out of barrels. Billboards advertising gun shows. The sky was a depressing charcoal overhead.

She thought about what Cab Bolton had told her.

Justin had been in Lake Wales before he was killed. They'd been there together barely a month earlier, and then he'd *gone back* without saying a word about it. He'd started asking questions about the Labor Day murders. That was his secret.

Why?

Part of her was angry at him. He'd lied and kept her in the dark. Their trip to Lake Wales was supposed to be a chance to talk about who they were, about life, love, sex, and the future. Their future. She'd even thought about breaking her vow that weekend and letting him take her virginity, but in the end, he'd been the one to say no, and she loved him even more for it.

She wondered how that same man could have deceived her. She wondered if he'd had an ulterior motive about the trip from the beginning.

When she'd left Lake Wales with Deacon years earlier, she had never wanted to see the town again. Justin had been the one to persuade her to return with him, but with each mile they drove, emotions rushed back. Memories flooded her, disconnected images that made no sense and left her deeply anxious. She was haunted by grief, loneliness, and loss. Through it all, Justin was there beside her.

Now she was going back again. Alone. She needed answers.

Ten miles outside town, when the first spatter of rain struck her windshield, she saw a cross in the long grass by the highway shoulder. Flowers decorated it, and the paint was fresh. Someone still honored whoever had died there. It was nice to think you could die and not be forgotten.

That had been her marker. That was where she'd pulled off the road with Justin.

'Why are we stopping?' he asked.

Peach didn't answer. She let the dust settle before climbing out of the car into the humid morning. They were alone here, early on Sunday, with nothing but the buzz of crickets rising from the fields and the black splotches of hawks circling in the blue sky.

She sat on the hood of the car. The metal was hot underneath her jeans. Justin came and joined her.

'See the little white cross?' she told him. 'You have to be careful when you drive here.'

Justin nodded, but he didn't understand.

'It's terrible how you see them everywhere,' she went on, 'and you know that every cross means somebody was lost.'

Peach breathed in the moist air. The sun was merciless. She realized that all her muscles were wound up into tight little knots. Her knees drummed relentlessly, making the car shake. She didn't want to go home again. She didn't want to be back in Lake Wales.

'We don't have to do this,' Justin murmured.

'I know.'

The world was absolutely still. She stared past the sagging telephone wires. Brown and white dots of cattle interrupted the green fields. Trees of uneven height lined the horizon. Some looked as tall as giants.

'You'd think I'd remember everything, wouldn't you?' she said. 'I don't. It's more like photographs in my head.'

'What do you remember?' he asked.

Peach took his hand and squeezed it tightly. 'A policewoman broke the news to me. I was at Birch's estate. I'd spent the evening there in one of the spare bedrooms, and I'd fallen asleep. They were all supposed to come back later. Lyle, Caprice, Birch, Ms Fairmont, her friend Tarla the movie star. Instead, none of them did. The police woke me up. They were all over the house. She told me that Lyle – she told me he was gone. So was Birch. I turned on the television, and that was all anyone could talk about.'

'You were alone?' Justin asked.

'Deacon was at our apartment, but he came and joined me. It was hours before anyone else got back, and they didn't talk to us. That was it. That's how your whole life changes.'

He took her hand, and he kissed each of her fingertips. She wanted to cry, but she had no tears.

'It was supposed to be a treat for me. I'd been so sick, and now that I was feeling better, Lyle said I could stay up for the party when they came home. I think he felt bad. He'd been angry for weeks. Me, Deacon, Caprice, he was yelling at all of us. This was a way to make it up to me.'

'Why was he so mad?'

She shrugged. 'That was Lyle. He had a temper. I understand campaigns now better than I did then. All the intensity. All the pressure. And that was the very first campaign for the Common Way Party. Lyle had everything riding on that race. He and Caprice had been planning it for years.'

A truck passed them on the rural highway. It was so big and fast that the vibration nearly slid them off the hood of the car. The truck carried fruit; she smelled a wave of citrus in its wake.

'People drive so fast,' Peach said, shaking her head. She closed her eyes. 'Poor Lyle, that last month was a nightmare.'

'How so?'

'Oh, it was my fault,' Peach said, with a tiny laugh. 'There was some big political fundraiser in Tampa in August, and Lyle had to go. He took me and Deacon with him. I really, really wanted to see the city. Deacon wound up like a babysitter, which he didn't like, and Lyle didn't have five minutes to spend with us. Then I got sick on Saturday night. Puking, hacking, burning up. It was really bad. Lyle acted like I was doing it just to annoy him. I wanted to go back home, and I was screaming and crying about it, and Lyle told Deacon to take the car and drive me back to Lake Wales. Deacon wanted to stay, so they yelled at each other, and then I yelled at both of them. Real nice. Anyway, Deacon finally drove me back, but that was a mess, too, because he hit a deer, which banged up Lyle's precious Mercedes. By the time we got back, I was so sick I was almost delirious, and Deacon was so rattled he could hardly walk straight. So he took me to Birch's estate to get help.'

She was quiet.

Justin said, 'Peach?'

And then: 'Are you okay?'

'Yeah.' She shrugged. 'Yeah.'

'What is it?'

'We walked into the middle of something there,' she said.

'What?'

'I don't know. My doctor was already at the estate when we arrived. Dr Smeltz. He said it was pneumonia, that it was lucky we got there when we did. I think my fever was like 104. Deacon was freaked out about the car, so he wasn't any help. I remember Caprice putting me to bed and kissing my head. She was very sweet. I woke up two days later, I think, or that's how it felt. Lyle was there when I did.'

'What did he say?'

'Nothing. I said I was sorry about being sick, I was sorry about the car, but he didn't say anything. I felt horrible, like I'd caused all the problems. I mean, I was twelve, I didn't know any better . . . except . . .'

'Except what?' Justin asked.

'I don't know. Something had changed.'

'I don't understand.'

'I'm not sure I do, either. Everyone was different. It's like I went to sleep that Saturday night, and when I woke up, nobody was the same. Lyle hardly talked to anyone. I'm not sure he ever slept. Ms Fairmont, I didn't see her at all. She was practically invisible. Birch drank all the time. There was this weird blackness hanging over everyone in the house. It felt like . . . it felt like something was going to happen. And then it did. I know that sounds crazy, but when the policewoman woke me up that night, it's like I already knew. I was expecting it.'

'You couldn't have been expecting anything like that,' Justin said.

'You wouldn't think so, would you? But she didn't have to say a word. I had this premonition. I think I even said it out loud before she did.'

'Said what?'

Peach frowned. 'I said, "They're dead, aren't they?"'

Finally, she drove into Lake Wales. Its deserted downtown streets felt like echoes of a ghost town. She saw no one. She drove past the Walesbilt Hotel, painted sea-foam green. It had once been a glamorous destination, but it was abandoned now, a fenced-off ruin with broken and boarded-up windows and deep cracks riddling the stucco. She and Justin had thought about breaking in at night, like urban explorers. Instead, they'd sat outside, eating fried chicken in her car and studying the destruction wrought by marauders and storms.

She'd thought she would always remember that weekend with Justin as one of the great moments of her life. It had felt like the beginning of something, but instead, it was the end. A few weeks later, he was gone. Now she wondered whether their romantic getaway had been nothing but a cover for whatever he was hiding from her.

Days later, he went back to Lake Wales.

Days later, he started digging into the past of a killer named Frank Macy.

He'd kept secrets from her all along. It made her feel bitter; it made her feel like a child.

And yet – *and yet* – he'd left clues for her, too. Just for her. Breadcrumbs that no one else could find. Part of her whispered that he was trying to protect her.

Part of her whispered that he had done it all for her. That he was trying to answer the question that had haunted her for ten years.

27

'Cab,' Caprice said. 'What an unexpected treat.'

She got up from behind her desk at the headquarters of the Common Way Foundation, which was on the other side of downtown from the shabby building that housed the foundation's research department. Her corner office was located near the pencil-top of the Sun Trust tower. Floor-to-ceiling windows looked out on the skyline in two directions. Westward, he could see the cloud mass marking the fringe of Chayla as it marched toward the coast. It was a dark day. The building swayed almost imperceptibly with the gusts.

Caprice's brunette hair was pulled tightly back, and her white skin and soft face were emphasized by amber teardrop earrings. She wore a gray business suit, with a skirt that fell just below her knees. Her heels were tall. Her serious eyes became flirtatious as she leaned in and kissed him on the cheek.

'To what do I owe the pleasure?' she asked.

'I have questions,' Cab said.

Caprice smiled. 'Of course you do. You are just full of questions.'

He strolled on the plush carpet to the windows overlooking the city. Caprice stood next to him, close enough that her hips brushed against his. He was very conscious of her presence.

'The storm will be here soon,' Caprice said. Her eyes were on him, not the sky.

'Yes, it will.'

He sat at a round glass table near the window. Caprice took the chair next to him. She smiled, waiting for him to start. The toes of her shoe casually rubbed his pant leg. She knew she made him uncomfortable, and he was pretty sure she liked the power she held.

'I just met Peach Piper,' Cab told her.

'Did you? Peach is a sweet girl, but don't underestimate her. She's wicked-smart. You could sit right next to her and not even realize it because of her disguises.'

'She was telling me about a foundation employee named Justin Kiel,' he said.

'I'm not surprised. Deacon says that Peach was quite sweet on Justin.'

'I'm wondering why you didn't tell me about Justin yourself. A member of your research team was murdered two weeks ago. You didn't think that was useful information in evaluating potential threats against Diane?'

'The police didn't raise any security concerns about the crime,' Caprice replied. 'They said it was drug-related. One dealer shoots another. Honestly, I wanted it kept under the radar as much as possible. It's not a great campaign story when an employee of the foundation turns out to be connected to drug trafficking.'

'I'm not sure it's that simple,' Cab said. 'Justin was looking into the Labor Day murders before he was killed.'

Caprice's brow furrowed with concern. 'Are you sure about that?'

'I am. Was he working for you?'

'No, of course not.'

'I thought maybe you hired him before you hired me.'

She shook her head. 'I didn't.'

'If he was killed because he was asking questions about Birch's death, then the threat against Diane is real and serious. I think you should increase security around her.'

Caprice nodded. 'I will. Do you know if Justin discovered anything that would help you?'

'Not yet.' He added: 'I'm not the only one interested in Justin's death. Ramona Cortes asked to see me. She mentioned Justin, too. She doesn't think his murder was drug-related.'

'Ramona,' Caprice said, shaking her head. 'Well, I doubt she knows anything more about the case than you or me. She's just stirring the pot. Anything that might embarrass Diane would draw Ramona like a magnet.'

'Do you know her personally?'

'Of course. Remember, I'm a lawyer, not just a pretty face. We go back a long way. Lyle and Ramona were classmates in law school, before their political paths diverged. She's very ambitious. People think the Attorney General is supposed to be above politics, when in fact it's one of the most political positions in any state. It's no surprise that so many top elected officials started out as AGs. You have the power of prosecution and you have a platform to get lots of publicity for what you do. Believe me, Ramona wants Diane out of the race any way she can, because she thinks she can beat the Governor head to head.'

'She tried to talk me out of working for you,' Cab said.

'I bet she did.'

'She has a pretty Machiavellian view of Common Way. She thinks you're not above using ruthless political tactics.'

Caprice smiled. 'We're not.'

'Within the law?'

'Naturally within the law, but we play to win. I don't apologize for that. The other parties are simply upset that we're getting better at the game than they are. Don't let sour grapes from Ramona concern you.'

Cab didn't doubt that Caprice was right about Ramona. In dealing with politicians, every word, every smile, every truth, every lie, was layered with motives. He didn't need to ask who was trying to play him, because everyone was. They all had their own agendas.

'Does the name Frank Macy mean anything to you?' Cab asked. 'He was an old client of Ramona's who went to prison on manslaughter charges a few years ago.'

'Did Peach tell you about him?' Caprice asked.

'Not directly, but she had some information about him with her.'

'Yes, Peach showed up at Diane's last night, talking about Macy. Diane didn't take it well. Drew hung out with Frank Macy in college. He was a drug dealer, one of those street-smart scholarship students who know how to capitalize on rich friends by using their urban contacts. Smart but tough. On some level, I think Diane always blamed Macy for Drew's death. Peach thought that Justin was interested in Macy, too.'

Cab's expression hardened. 'Justin was looking at Frank Macy? Macy was Drew's drug dealer? And you still didn't call me about any of this?'

Caprice reacted with obvious annoyance. 'You don't get it, do you, Cab? We are running a statewide political campaign. Drug killings do not help us. Someone like Frank Macy is poison. If his name is linked to Diane's in the media, our poll numbers drop. So no, I don't want you looking at him. I don't want Frank Macy within ten miles of anyone from Common Way. Was he involved in Justin's death? I have no idea. Frankly, I don't care, but if you want my political opinion, think about this. If Ramona Cortes wanted to attack Diane, an old client like Frank Macy would be a great way to do it. Macy wouldn't need to be connected to the murder at all. Just planting his name would hurt us. Has it occurred to you that Ramona might be behind all of this? That she might be manipulating you and Peach to sabotage Diane?'

'It has,' Cab said.

'Then maybe you should stop listening to her and focus on what I hired you to do.'

Caprice showed the sharpness of her teeth for the first time. She was a dominatrix, accustomed to getting what she wanted. He felt the allure. He knew exactly what a relationship with her would be like. He had no illusions that he would be the one in charge. She could take a strong man and drive him mad.

'Sorry,' she said, putting her smile back on. 'That's my passion coming through.'

'I realize that.'

'Remember, politics means nothing to you, but it's everything to me.'

'I realize that, too.'

She was the coquette again. 'Forgive me?'

Cab smiled. 'Of course.'

'I didn't mean to treat you like an employee. It's a bad habit of mine. Honestly, I have to confess, I was thinking about other things when I hired you. I wanted to get to know you better. Not that you're not good at what you do, but you're very attractive.'

'The feeling is mutual.'

'It sounds callous, but I don't really care about your girlfriend. If she can't keep you, that's her problem. I'd like to see more of you.'

'Believe me, I'm tempted,' he said, 'but it will have to wait until this business is done.'

'Because you work for me?' she asked, her eyes gleaming. 'Are you afraid of sexual harassment?'

'Not at all.'

'Maybe you should be.'

'I'm not worried,' Cab explained, 'because I don't work for you anymore.'

He watched Caprice inhale sharply, her nostrils flaring with anger. 'Is this a joke, Cab? Because it's not funny.'

'It's not a joke. I have a new client.'

'Who?' she demanded. 'So help me, if Ramona Cortes—'

'It's not Ramona.'

'Then what is this about?'

'I guess you could say my client is Justin Kiel.'

Caprice leaned across the table, pointing a blood-red fingernail in his direction. 'Oh, come on, Cab, what kind of nonsense is this? I asked you to help Diane. She's your mother's best friend. Do you care so little about her?'

'On the contrary. I care about her a great deal. If Justin Kiel was killed because he was asking questions about the Labor Day murders, then I need to know exactly what he found, because I want to protect Diane. But I can't do that if I have to be concerned with how my investigation fits into your political calculations.'

'I said I was sorry,' Caprice snapped.

'I know you did, but you're not sorry in the least. That's okay. You have your priorities. I have mine.'

Caprice frowned. 'So what does this mean? You keep working on the case, but I don't have to pay you for it?'

'Pretty much. Think of it as a sound business deal.'

'How can I argue with that?' she asked.

'You can't.'

'Then I guess we're done,' she concluded.

'Not quite. Now you're a witness.'

'Excuse me?'

'Justin wanted to know what happened ten years ago. So do I. Let's start with a fight between Birch and Diane a couple weeks before Labor Day. It was a Saturday night. It was so bad that Drew ended up threatening Birch's life, and he wound up in rehab. He got out of rehab just days before the murders. I'd like to know exactly what went on in that house.'

'I don't know,' Caprice replied.

'I think you do. Peach said you were there.'

She was silent for a moment. 'Diane would not want you looking into this, Cab,' she said softly.

'Maybe not, but I have no choice. I'm heading back to Lake Wales right now. I'm going to find out what's going on sooner or later. You might as well tell me.'

'I'm asking you to drop it. Please. As a friend, not as an employer.'

'I can't do that. I'm sorry. I don't care what this does to the campaign.'

'Well, I do care. So does Diane.'

'What really happened that Saturday night, Caprice? What are you people hiding?'

She stood up languidly from her chair. Every movement she made had grace; her body was a seamless extension of her sexuality. She leaned toward him, close enough to engulf him in a sweet breath of perfume. With a little smirk, she took his earlobe in her mouth and bit him.

'Go to hell, Cab,' she whispered.

28

The rain lashed the windshield of her Thunderbird. An ash tree bowing over the roof of the Lake Wales Library twisted in the wind like a drunken dancer. Peach opened the car door, which wrenched out of her hand. She ran for the library entrance, and in the doorway, safe from the downpour, she smoothed her hair, adjusted her fake black glasses, and made sure that her tan blouse was properly tucked into her brown skirt.

She looked like a librarian. Everyone was more comfortable talking to people who looked like they did.

Peach knew that Justin would have come here first. He always said that libraries held the answers to every question that could be asked in the world. If he was digging into the events in Lake Wales, he would have started at the Lake Wales Library. Someone was bound to remember him.

Inside, the thump of rain on the roof was as loud as thunder. The building was mostly empty. She saw a lone librarian at the registration desk eyeing the oversized front windows as they shook in the wind. The woman was in her fifties, plump, with strawberry hair and a round face.

Peach gave her a shy smile. 'Hello.'

'Can I help you?' The woman's voice had a trace of a German accent.

'Oh, well, I don't know. It's personal.'

'Yes?'

'My boyfriend was here a few weeks ago,' Peach said. 'I was hoping someone here talked to him.'

The librarian came up to the counter. 'And what is this about?'

Peach displayed a photograph on her phone of her and Justin near the lake just blocks from the library. Arms around one another; big smiles. 'See, that's us,' she said.

The woman squinted. The picture softened her, because it was two young people who were obviously in love. Peach could also tell from her expression that she remembered Justin, with his weird mustache and hat.

'You saw him, didn't you?' Peach asked.

'Well, yes, I do remember him,' the librarian admitted. 'A young person with an old-fashioned mustache like that, so unusual. He was funny, too. He had a lot to say about life. I liked him.'

Peach nodded. Her eyes stung with tears, which she didn't need to fake at all. 'He was a philosopher.'

'Oh, dear,' the librarian replied immediately. 'Did something happen?'

'He died.'

The woman grabbed her hand. 'I'm so sorry, how awful for you! He was just a boy. How can I help you?'

'Well, you can't, probably. Justin was a writer, like me. He was doing a story for an Orlando magazine about the tenth anniversary of the Labor Day murders – you know, with Diane Fairmont running for governor now. I'd like to finish the article for him, but I can't make heads or tails of his notes, so I'm trying to follow in his footsteps. Re-create his research. That's why I'm here.'

'I see.'

It wasn't entirely a lie, and Peach sold it with the sweetness of her face. 'Anything you can tell me would be such a help,' she said.

'Well, yes, he said he was doing a story about those terrible murders,' the woman said. 'He asked me if I lived here back then, but I'm afraid I only came to town five years ago, so I couldn't help him.'

'Did he talk to anyone else?'

'Maybe a couple of our volunteers, but they're not here today.'

'Oh. I understand.'

'He was in the library for a long time,' the librarian told her. 'He spent much of it in our microfiche section. I think he was going through all of the newspapers from back then. He made a lot of copies.'

'You don't know what he copied, I suppose.'

'No, I'm sorry, patrons make their own copies. I can show you our newspapers, however, if you'd like.'

'Yes, okay,' Peach said.

The librarian guided her to a row of carrels stocked with microfiche readers, near the windows that looked out on the fierce rain. She pulled out a drawer in a nearby filing cabinet. With a quick glance, she took a box from the back of the drawer and opened it to show her a stack of oversized negatives.

'These are the Lake Wales papers from August and September of that year. I believe that's where your young man started.'

Peach nodded. 'Thank you.'

'Do you need help with the machines?'

'No, I'm fine. Thank you so much. I appreciate your help.'

Peach sat down alone at a microfiche reader, and she quickly found the newspaper reports for the day after Labor Day. When she saw the headlines and photographs, her eyes blurred with tears, and her stomach squirmed, as if a great hole had opened up inside it. Instead of reading, she stared out the windows, hypnotized by the beat of the rain. She was glad there was no one else around.

It didn't really help her to know that Justin had studied the newspapers from ten years ago, other than to confirm that Cab Bolton was right. She didn't know what Justin would have learned, or what she hoped to discover by revisiting events that she had spent a long time trying to forget.

Her phone rang. She was grateful for the interruption.

'Fruity,' her brother said when she answered. The connection was bad; the storm was already eroding the quality of the signal.

'Hey.'

'I'm in the office, where are you?'

Peach hesitated. She didn't want to admit what she was doing. 'The library,' she said.

'Caprice told me about last night.'

'Yeah, I figured.'

There was a long pause. The connection flitted in and out, making him stutter. 'I am pretty pissed, you know that, right? Caprice said you made contact with Macy. Do you know what kind of man he is? He may look like Leo DiCaprio, but he's not.'

'I'm sorry. I didn't go there alone. Annalie was with me–'

'You could have gotten her killed, too!'

Peach felt like crying again. 'Don't yell at me, Deacon.'

Her brother went quiet. She thought for a moment that she'd lost the call, but then she could hear him breathing. 'I know. I'm sorry. Look, do you think I ignored what you said? I started investigating Macy myself as soon as you told me about him.'

'What did you find?' Peach asked.

'I hooked up with some of my contacts who know the Liberty Empire Alliance pretty well. Word is, their recruitment efforts are strong in the state prison system. If Macy spent eight years there, maybe they got to him.'

'You think he's tied in to Ham Brock?'

'I don't know. I'm still asking around.'

'Ramona Cortes represented both of them.'

'Yeah, I know. Interesting, huh? Look, I'm going to try to follow–' He stopped talking.

'Deacon?'

And then again: 'Deacon?'

She looked at her phone. The call was gone. She tried dialing his number, but she had no signal.

Peach fidgeted impatiently. Suddenly, Lake Wales felt far away from everything. She didn't know what she was doing here. She spent half an hour pretending to study the newspapers and hoping Deacon would call back, but when he didn't, she decided she should go. She put the box of microfiche on the shelf to be refiled. She headed for the exit door, but the librarian called to her.

'Did you find what you needed?'

Peach stopped at the desk and gave her a weak smile. 'Oh, yes, thanks. It was very helpful.'

'I'm so sorry again about your fiancé.'

'Thank you.'

'You be careful in the storm, okay? The best thing to do is find somewhere to hole up and let it all blow over.'

'Yes, you're right,' Peach said. She turned away, but as she did, she thought of another question. 'Oh, there's one other thing, if you don't mind. I was wondering, did Justin ask you anything about someone named Alison?'

The librarian stared at her. 'Alison? I don't think so. Do you have a last name?'

'I don't.'

'Do you know anything else about her?'

'I'm afraid not. Just the name Alison.'

Peach thought the woman looked suspicious, as if now this was all about exposing a boyfriend's affair.

'Well, he didn't say anything about that,' she said, her voice clipped.

'Okay. Thank you again.' She added: 'I appreciate your help. I'm sorry to bother you. Sometimes it's just nice to talk to someone who met him, even a stranger. It makes him feel not so far away.'

The woman's face lost its ice. 'Of course. You know, I do remember something. I didn't think about it at first, because your young man asked one of the other staff members about it, not me. I simply overheard him. He was looking for someone.'

'Do you remember who?'

The woman's brow furrowed. 'A doctor, I think. He was looking for a doctor who practiced around here ten years ago, and he was wondering if he was still in town. My associate looked it up for him.'

'What was his name?'

'Let me think. Wills? Wells? I'm sorry, I wish I'd paid more attention, but I didn't.'

'That's okay.'

Peach was disappointed, but then, with a strange little chill, she reached into her past and pulled out a name. It made no sense. It couldn't be him. Why would Justin want to know anything about him?

'Smeltz?' she murmured. 'Reuben Smeltz?'

The librarian's eyes widened with recognition. 'Why, yes! That was it! I'm sure that was his name.'

'And is he still alive? Is he still in town?'

'Let me check.' The woman tapped keys on her keyboard, and not even ten seconds later, she beamed. 'Yes indeed. Dr Smeltz has an office–'

'On East Park Avenue downtown,' Peach said. 'Near the old clock tower.'

She raised her eyebrows. 'You're right. That's exactly where it is. Do you know him?'

Peach didn't answer her, but yes, she knew Dr Reuben Smeltz. He was the man who treated her for pneumonia that night at Birch Fairmont's estate. He was her own doctor.

29

Garth Oakes jogged down the steps of the sprawling lakefront home in Lake Wales. He wore a form-fitting white T-shirt and baggy red nylon pants over his tree-trunk legs, and he carried a large nylon backpack. His black ponytail bobbed as he ran to his Subaru Outback. He dumped the pack in the rear and took a quick, hungry glance at the red Corvette parked immediately behind him. The rain was too heavy for Garth to see through the windshield, so Cab flashed his headlights at him.

Garth squinted, and then he ran for the passenger side of the Corvette and clambered into the sports car. He shook himself like a wet dog, releasing a spray of rain and an aroma of rosemary oil.

'Well, hey!' he said. 'Detective! This is a small world.'

'Not so small,' Cab admitted. 'I called your assistant. He said this is where you were.'

'Oh, cool, okay. Hope you weren't waiting too long.'

'Not long at all,' Cab said.

A gust of wind rattled the car. Wet leaves and garlands of Spanish moss blew across the chassis. A hundred yards away, the surface of the lake was dappled by the relentless downpour.

'Woo, what a storm, huh?' Garth exulted. 'And this is only the teaser. I've got to get back to Tampa before the roads get too bad.'

'I won't take a lot of your time.'

'Oh, don't worry about it, I'm fine.' The trainer nodded at the house across the street, which had manicured hedges and white columns adorning a long front porch. 'Been doing weekly massages for that lady for fifteen years. Hundred-dollar tip every time, but wow, it's like rubbing one of them shar pei dogs, know what I mean? Wrinkles everywhere. People think the massage biz is glamorous, like you spend your days oiling up women who look like Beyoncé. I mean, I'm not saying you don't get a hot twenty-something now and then, but they're never the ones who spread their legs and ask if you can give an *all-over* massage, know what I mean?'

Whenever Garth talked, Cab found himself practicing transcendental meditation to see if he could crowd out whatever the man was saying.

'Hey, want a power bar?' Garth asked, digging in his pocket and pulling out a chocolate protein bar. Cab shook his head, and Garth unwrapped it and took a big, chewy bite. 'Anyway, it's a living. I'd love to give up most of my personal clients and focus on my training videos, but I'm not there yet. Who knows, Diane gets in, maybe I get a publicity bump, you know?'

'Beat the Girth . . . With the Gov?' Cab asked.

Garth laughed, spitting granola onto the dashboard. His teeth were oddly purple against his Coppertone face. He'd been drinking wine, and he seemed a little drunk. 'I love it! I love it!'

Cab studied the wet, muscle-bound masseur. A hanger-on, that was how Gladiola Croft described him. Garth stayed close to Diane for the perks it brought him. Money. Access. Clients. Gladiola said he was always around that summer, and ten years later, he was still a fixture in Diane's life. Cab didn't think it was sexual. The vibe that Garth gave off was overtly gay. Even so, he appeared to be Diane's secret-keeper.

'Listen, Garth, I need your help with something,' Cab said.

The masseur nodded. 'Yeah, sure, what ya got?'

'Someone connected to the Common Way Foundation was murdered last month.'

'Oh, is this the guy that this chick Peach was talking about? I heard about that last night.'

'Justin Kiel,' Cab said.

'Okay, yeah, what about him?'

'Did you know who he was? Did you ever talk to him?'

Garth shook his head. 'Nope, never did.'

'Did anyone mention him to you? Did Diane?'

'No, she didn't even know who he was,' Garth said.

'What about a man named Frank Macy?' Cab asked.

Garth whistled. 'Oh, yeah, him I know. Don't mention him to Diane, she'll go crazy. Peach found that out.'

'Because of Drew?' Cab said.

'Right.'

'What was their relationship?'

'Oh, it was complicated.'

'How so?' Cab asked.

Garth finished his power bar, crumpled the wrapper, and shoved it in Cab's ashtray. 'Well, you gotta remember what Drew was like. I mean, here's a kid who grew up with nothing. Mom's dirt-poor. Hardly any food on the table. Then she marries a rich entrepreneur, and next thing you know, the kid's living in high so-ci-ety. Some kids can't adjust to that.'

Cab waited.

'Not that Drew was a bad kid,' Garth went on. 'I liked him. He just never had his head together.'

'How so?'

'Well, for starters, Drew was gay. He came to me for advice, because he couldn't deal with it. I mean, it's one thing to be a gay guy like me, buff and all. Nobody's going to mess around with me, hear what I'm saying?' He winked at Cab. 'Guess I'm not telling you anything about me that you haven't already figured out, huh?'

Cab smiled. 'No.'

'Don't suppose you play for the men's team.'

'Sorry.'

'Never hurts to ask. Anyway, Drew was skinny and shy. Kids in school tormented him. Vicious stuff. So did his stepdad.'

'Birch did?' Cab asked, frowning.

'Oh, yeah. Never in front of Diane, but Drew told me that Birch called him queer and fag and all sorts of other shit behind Diane's back. Kid *hated* Birch. Can't say as I blame him.'

'What about Frank Macy?'

'Drew met Macy in college. Lower-class background, but brainy, suave, and ruthless. Bad-ass package. Drew used to bring him to the estate in Lake Wales, like they were buddies. I think he liked the idea of hanging out with somebody who was cool and streetwise, you know? If I had to guess, Drew was probably super-attracted to Macy, too.'

'Macy's gay?' Cab asked.

'Doubt it. Even if he was, he wouldn't have looked twice at Drew. But there are plenty of so-called straight guys who don't mind having another guy suck their dick. As long as they're not the one on their knees, they figure it doesn't count. You ask me, Macy wouldn't have minded Drew taking the shine off when he didn't have any girls around. I think that would have messed with Drew's head in a big way.'

'Did Diane know any of this? Did you talk to her about it?'

'Later. Much later. After Drew ate that gun. It wasn't just the drugs that did him in. Drew told me that he and Macy had a falling-out. Macy said he was done with him. I'm thinking he was pretty cruel about it. That was the final straw for Drew, who was fragile to start with. It wasn't long after that he killed himself.'

Cab shook his head. This was worse than he thought. And more deadly. 'Did Macy and Drew hang out together that summer before the Labor Day murders?'

Garth nodded. 'Sure. I mean, it was a pretty sweet deal for Macy, huh? Rich kid always in need of a fix, plus an estate with a swimming pool and free booze. What's not to love?'

'Birch couldn't have been too happy about that during the campaign.'

'No shit. Lyle went ballistic about it, too. They were afraid the press was going to get wind of Macy. Birch and Diane argued about it, and Birch told Drew he never wanted Macy in his house again. Drew didn't care.'

'One more question, Garth. Birch and Diane. Two weeks before Labor Day. What really happened?'

The man's tanned face lost a couple shades of color. 'Hey, I really shouldn't talk about that.'

'If you think you're protecting Diane, you're not.'

'Yeah, but still. I've said too much.'

Cab leaned across the seat. 'There was an argument. Screaming. You came and told the maid to get out. Why? What did Birch do?'

'Look, I wasn't in the room,' Garth said. 'I assume the son of a bitch got rough with her.'

'How rough?'

'Rough enough that he told me to call a doctor and get him there fast. Then he told me to get the maid out of the house and get myself out, too.'

'What did you do?'

'Exactly what he said.'

'You didn't check on Diane?'

'I wanted to, but I didn't know what Birch would do. It was the worst I'd ever seen him. The guy had murder in his eyes.'

'Who else was in the house?' Cab asked.

'Nobody.'

'Who else knows about this?'

'Hardly anyone,' Garth said. 'I figure Lyle and Caprice found out, but they weren't going to tell anybody. Guess that's about all. Oh, and the doc. Reuben Smeltz. He was Diane's doctor.'

Cab made a note of the name.

'And Drew,' Cab said.

'Yeah, I don't know if Diane told him everything, but Drew could see she was hurt bad. She didn't appear in public again until Labor Day. People were starting to talk about it.'

'The stress drove Drew into rehab?'

Garth nodded. 'Yeah, he nearly killed himself with an overdose. Smeltz saved his life and got him back into treatment.'

'Do you think Drew was serious?' Cab asked.

'About what?'

'Killing Birch,' Cab said.

He expected a flat denial, but the masseur worked his mouth unhappily, like he was chewing something he couldn't swallow. 'Does it matter? Birch is dead. So's Drew.'

'It matters. Someone murdered Justin Kiel because he was asking the same questions.'

'Hey, I knew Drew,' Garth insisted. 'The kid wasn't up to something like that. Bad enough to gun down Birch, but those other people, too? No way he did that himself.'

'Okay. If he didn't pull the trigger himself, maybe he had help.'

'Like who?'

'Like Frank Macy,' Cab said. He saw a shadow in Garth's face as the masseur put two and two together. 'Come on, Garth. Is there something you're not telling me?'

'It's nothing,' he said. 'I saw something, but it's not important.'

'You obviously don't think that's true. What was it?'

Garth was silent, and he squirmed uncomfortably on the car seat. The wine had loosened his tongue, but not enough to get him to spill his secrets. Cab was losing patience.

'Look, Garth, I'm trying to protect Diane. Justin's dead. She may be at risk. I need your help if I'm going to keep her safe.' He didn't bother to add that if something happened to Diane, the gravy train ended for Garth. No more parties. No more hanging out in the mansion. No publicity bump for his exercise videos. Garth could connect the dots for himself.

'There's probably no connection,' the masseur finally replied. 'This happened weeks before Labor Day. Way back in July, I think.'

'What did?'

Garth hesitated. 'I heard gunshots.'

'Where?'

'In the orange groves near the estate. I checked it out. Drew had a gun. He was firing into the trees. Blasting away the fruit. I don't know, he might have been high. It wasn't a good scene, you know?'

'You never told anyone about this?'

'Are you kidding? No way. I didn't even tell Diane until later in the summer. I didn't want to get the kid in trouble.'

'Was Drew alone?' Cab asked.

Garth shook his head. He swallowed hard. 'No. No, he wasn't alone. That's the thing. Frank Macy was with him. It was Macy's gun.'

30

The knife was warm, heated by the dying man's severed entrails.

When he finally withdrew it from the body at his feet, torrents of rain poured into the wound. The rain spattered the blade, washing pink watery blood over his hands and onto the stone pier. The body below him twitched. The dying man's breath hacked and foamed; his heart still had a minute or two to beat, spurting rivulets that oozed into the bay.

The man with the knife breathed heavily. It had gone as planned, but it was never easy. First a blow from the flashlight to the other man's forehead, dizzying him. A jab to the throat. Ankle around ankle, driving him backward to the ground, his skull cracking on stone. And then the knife, opening him up, letting him bleed out.

The storm blotted out everything around him. He could barely see the beach, which was fifty yards away. The industrial buildings bordering the park were dark, deserted shapes. The agitated water slurped against the Picnic Island pier like a noisy blow job. Out in the channel, white lights outlined a giant ore tanker headed for safe harbor, but the ship appeared as disembodied as a ghost floating in darkness.

Below him, the man's eyes were fixed, like gray stones. It was almost over. He would spend eternity that way, with that same look of impotent, furious surprise. His mouth was stuck open. The blood no longer pulsed from the giant gash. The dead man's fingers were still curled around the aluminum pistol case, so he peeled them away, taking the handle of the case in his own hand. He had what he needed now. Everything was ready.

He pushed himself to his feet, staring at the body.

'Don't move!' a voice called to him above the rain.

Instinctively, he flicked up the heavy flashlight toward the sound. He saw a gun, twenty feet away, pointed at his chest. The man holding the gun squinted into the bright light. He was bulky, with blond hair plastered to his face. He wore a sport coat, dress pants, and sneakers. He looked middle-aged and soft.

This wasn't a moment for panic or fear, just cold calculations. Twenty feet wasn't an easy shot in the driving rain, but if he charged, he was dead. The man was a stranger, but his appearance was no accident. One of them had been followed. Himself or the dead man at his feet. It was bad either way.

The man with the gun came closer, rubbing his eyes. The rain was like a waterfall. The gun wobbled as he pointed it. 'He dead?' the man shouted, nodding at the body on the pier. 'That took balls!'

He didn't reply. The man had seen the murder play out. That was no good. He watched the man try to keep the gun steady and keep water out of his eyes. The flashlight was bright; it had to be a fat orange blob on his retinas now. The downpour made the man gulp and swallow.

'Looks like a gun case!' the man called, gesturing at the aluminum case. 'You planning on shooting somebody?'

'You,' he hollered over the howl of the storm.

The man's eyes widened nervously, but then his stubbly, fleshy face relaxed, and he chortled. He came even closer, until they were almost chest to chest. 'That's funny.'

'It's no joke. Who are you?'

'The name's Ritchie.'

'Better get the hell out of here, Ritchie.'

The man with the gun grinned at the hollow threat. 'Yeah? Maybe you haven't noticed, but your gun's inside a metal case, and mine's pointed at your chest. Now get on your knees.'

He assessed his options. There was a four-foot railing on one side of the pier. On the other side, the pier was open, inches above the swirling water. He didn't know how deep it was or what debris littered the bottom. As they confronted each other, the wind tore into both of their bodies, shoving them off balance. Rain threatened to drown them where they stood.

'Get on your knees!' Ritchie shouted again. 'Put the pistol case down.'

He squatted and put the aluminum case in front of him. Ritchie knelt down, and his blurred eyes, soaked by rain, flicked toward the pier as he groped for the handle of the case. The barrel of his gun dipped sideways.

That was the moment he needed.

With Ritchie off balance, he corkscrewed sideways, throwing himself off the pier. Ritchie's gun cracked above the storm. The bullet singed the flesh of his arm, but in the next moment, the water engulfed him, and he sank below the surface. The bay was warm and black. He kicked through the water, putting distance between himself and where he'd entered the bay. Somewhere above him, Ritchie fired again, and then again, but he knew the man was blind, seeing the after-image of the flashlight as if he'd been staring into the sun.

He felt the bottom; it wasn't deep. His head and then his torso rose out of the water like a sea monster. Ritchie was immediately above him. He seized the man's right ankle with both hands and levered his leg into the air. Ritchie toppled backwards. The gun blasted harmlessly toward the sky. Ritchie landed hard on the concrete pier, and he slithered out of the water and threw himself on top of the blond man, wrestling for the gun. He pinned Ritchie's wrist; the gun fired again, loud and hot. Ritchie landed a haymaker on the side of his skull, shunting him sideways, making the world spin. Heavy and strong, Ritchie rolled on top of him. The rain poured over their bodies.

The gun fired again, so close now that the explosion made his ear bleed. A bullet ricocheted on stone and metal, and something sharp cut his face. He grabbed Ritchie's wrist again, but the man outweighed him, and he could see the gun barrel push toward his face. He felt something in his pocket. Something sharp and solid. In a single seamless motion, he yanked out his knife and drove it sideways into the flesh of Ritchie's neck, until the hilt collided with cartilage and bone.

Ritchie howled. His fingers loosened. The gun fell.

He dislodged the big man with a heave of his fists, and Ritchie flopped over on his back, grabbing at the knife in his neck with both hands. The knife oozed out of his body, wet and slippery, and clattered on the pier. Ritchie gagged and clambered to his knees, pawing the ground for his gun, but it wasn't there. The killer already had the gun in his hand.

He watched Ritchie, who was choking on the blood that rose in his throat. The man scuttled on his hands and knees like a giant crab, limbs twitching, head jerking as torn nerves fired randomly at his brain. He put the hot barrel against Ritchie's skull and fired into his head. One shot, expelling bone, brain, and blood in a cloud. Ritchie became dead weight, collapsing. The second dead man on the pier. The second man he'd killed tonight.

He was soaked with bay water, rain, and sweat, but he had to move. He shoved Ritchie's gun into his belt. Bending over, he grabbed Ritchie's body with both hands and rolled him toward the edge of the pier, until the dead man fell free and splashed into the dark water and sank. He straightened up, his whole body aching. The bullet that grazed his arm had left a burn on his skin. He was still alone, surrounded by the tumult of the storm, but the noise was muffled in his ears. He stared into the bay, unable to see anything below the surface. They would find Ritchie eventually, but that didn't matter to him.

The other body was the one he needed.

He grabbed the dead man's ankles and dragged him toward the beach, letting the storm clean away the trail of blood.

PART THREE

CHAYLA

31

'You work late,' Cab said.

Dr Reuben Smeltz snorted. 'Paperwork,' he said. 'That's what medicine is about today. A thousand insurance companies with ten thousand forms and a hundred thousand codes. I delivered a baby last week. By the time I get the paperwork done, he'll be trying out for his sixth grade soccer team.'

'I guess the profession has changed a lot.'

'Profession? We're just mechanics now. Paid by the hour.' Smeltz slugged coffee from a foam cup and grimaced.

'It's still better than being a lawyer, though, right?' Cab asked.

Smeltz smiled. 'You do know how to look on the bright side of life, Detective.'

'That's what people tell me.' Cab glanced at the water-stained drop ceiling as the fluorescent lights flickered. A gust of wind rocked the windowless office. 'Anyway, I appreciate your seeing me. You must be anxious to get home.'

The doctor shrugged. 'Storms are storms. I've seen a lot worse than this.'

Smeltz was in his late sixties, medium-height and overweight. His hair was brown, but it was thinning, combed back and greased down to lay flat on his head. He had a jowly face and tiny circular glasses. He wore a pressed shirt and tie, and his white coat was hung on a rack near the office door. Papers were spread out in front of him, and he took occasional bites from a chicken-and-pear salad along with his coffee.

He sat behind a weathered oak desk. His leather armchair had splits in the seams where bits of yellow foam were escaping. Cab sat in front of the desk in an uncomfortable wooden chair that didn't encourage visitors to stay longer than necessary. The doctor had diplomas and photographs of patients on the wall behind him, reflecting a practice in Lakes Wales that dated back for decades. The wall on Cab's right was lined with filing cabinets, and each drawer was hand-labeled with letters of the alphabet.

The other wall, which had fake wood paneling, included a long table with a 1980s-era coffee-maker, a potted poinsettia, a bowl of round multicolored mints, and a surprisingly modern laser printer. A heavy door at the end of the wall featured a sophisticated combination lock.

'So you're from Naples?' Smeltz asked between bites of salad.

'Yes, I am.'

'My wife likes Naples. She thinks we should retire there. Get one of those high-rise condos.'

'They're very nice,' Cab said.

'Yes, except then all the seniors find out you're a doctor and they want free advice on everything from shingles to melanoma. For that, I may as well stay here.' He speared a piece of romaine lettuce with his fork. 'People ever tell you that you don't look much like a detective?'

'Regularly.'

'Cop or not, you realize I can't say a word about my patients.'

'Of course,' Cab said.

The rain on the roof sounded like a firing range. A drop of water squeezed through the ceiling and squished on the carpet.

The doctor got up and retrieved a large orange bucket, which he positioned under the leak.

'Old building,' he explained. 'I keep putting off replacing the roof.'

Another drop fell, making a loud *chunk* in the bucket.

'So you've got concerns about Diane Fairmont's safety,' Smeltz went on. 'True or not, that doesn't change anything. Diane was my patient, which means my lips are sealed, at least until she tells me otherwise. If you think you can weasel something out of me, don't try. That just annoys me. People have played those games with me for years.'

Smeltz grabbed a tissue and blew his potato-like nose. He crumpled the tissue, threw it away, and pumped a blob of alcohol sanitizer into his hand.

'Who's been asking you questions about Diane?' Cab asked.

The doctor chuckled. 'Oh, she's a popular topic. Sometimes it's reporters. Sometimes it's political types. Last month I had a man in here who was obviously a private detective. He hinted he would make it worth my while if I spilled some secrets. God knows who he was working for. The whole thing is a pretty sorry business, if you ask me, all these spies looking for dirt.'

'Diane's in the same business, isn't she? Common Way isn't shy about looking for dirt on its political opponents.'

'Maybe, but the lady has my vote.'

'You like her.'

'I do. Always have.'

'You mentioned reporters knocking on your door. Did one of them happen to be Rufus Twill?'

Smeltz smiled wide enough to show a row of aging teeth. He leaned back in his chair, which squealed in protest. 'Oh, sure, Rufus talked to me. He was a patient growing up, and I suppose he figured he could wheedle something out of me. I sent him packing without so much as a "No Comment."'

'What did Rufus want to know about Diane?'

'I suspect you already know, Detective, but if you don't, I'm not going to tell you. I'm sorry. I have a broad definition of privilege. I don't talk about my patients, and I don't talk about what other people say about my patients.'

Cab nodded. 'I imagine it had something to do with an incident between Birch and Diane shortly before the Labor Day murders.'

The doctor's face darkened. The bucket on the floor went *chunk* again. 'I told you, I have nothing to say.'

'Was Birch your patient, too?'

'No.'

'So he doesn't enjoy privilege.'

'That makes no difference,' Smeltz said.

'I just want to know what kind of man Birch was.'

The doctor rubbed the layer of fat gathered under his chin. 'If you're asking whether I cried when Birch was killed, I didn't.'

'I heard he was a bully and a son of a bitch.'

'I won't dispute that characterization,' Smeltz said.

'Were you surprised when he was killed?'

'Of course. Nobody expects terrorists to strike in their own backyard.'

'Some people think Birch's death was personal, not political.'

Smeltz narrowed his eyes. 'What are you implying?'

'I have a witness who overheard Diane's son, Drew, threatening to blow Birch's head off. He was seen with a gun that summer. And he got out of a stint in rehab just days before the murders.'

You can't honestly believe that Drew—' Smeltz exclaimed, but he stopped in mid-sentence. 'You're not going to goad me into saying anything, Detective. Drew was my patient, too. I'm not discussing him.'

'He's dead.'

'That doesn't change my obligations.'

Cab dug in his suit coat pocket for a piece of paper. 'You mentioned someone visiting you last month who looked like a private detective. Was this the man?'

He showed Smeltz a photograph of Justin Kiel taken from a newspaper article about his murder.

The doctor took the paper and shook his head. 'No, not even close. The man I spoke to was older and heavier.' Smeltz was about to hand the paper back to Cab when he looked at the photograph again. He didn't look happy. 'Wait a minute.'

'Do you know him?'

'Well, I recognize him, yes. He showed up when I was working late a few weeks ago. He works for a computer repair company. Apparently, my assistant called and said we were having problems with our computer. I'm always having problems with this damn thing.'

Cab nodded. Justin was clever. 'Did you leave him alone in your office?'

Smeltz thought about it. 'Actually, I did. Someone knocked on the outside door while he was working on the printer. It was a very annoying foreign person who was looking for directions and didn't seem to understand anything I was saying.' The doctor frowned and tapped the paper with a thick finger. 'Who is he? Are you saying this man was some kind of spy?'

'Yes, he was. Of a sort.'

Smeltz pounded his desk in annoyance. 'Was this about Diane again? If you find this man, I want to press charges.'

'I'm afraid you won't be able to do that. He was murdered.'

'Oh, my God!' Smeltz exclaimed.

Two drops fell from the ceiling in quick succession. *Chunk chunk.*

'His death is one of the reasons I'm concerned about Diane.'

The doctor looked flustered. 'Well . . . I hate to hear that, but I still can't tell you anything more than I have.'

'I appreciate your privacy concerns,' Cab went on, 'but if this man – Justin Kiel – was in your office, it's possible that he found something that contributed to his murder. Something in your files. I know that you want to protect your patients, but if Justin learned a secret about Diane or Drew—'

Smeltz shook his head. 'He didn't.'

'How can you be sure?'

'There's nothing about Diane or Drew on my computer. My computerized records don't go back that far.'

'What about hard copy files?' Cab asked, nodding at the row of file cabinets in the office.

'The files aren't there either,' Smeltz told him. 'I'm not a fool, Detective. Too many people have expressed interest in Diane for me to keep her papers in my ordinary files. Believe me, this man was only alone in my office for five minutes at most. He didn't find them. Nobody would find them.'

When Cab got back to the deserted main street of Lake Wales, the rain stung his face like a swarm of bees. He wore a black Burberry trench coat with the collar up and the belt tied at his waist. His wet blond hair lay messy and flat on his head. He endured the assault like a statue, frozen and tall. The night was black, and the wind carried a faint smell of oranges. He crossed the street beside the old marble clock tower and got into his Corvette, which was parked diagonally in front of a building for the *Lake Wales News*.

He was opposite a small plaza dotted with waving trees and a checkerboard sidewalk.

The downtown street wasn't a hive of activity in the best of times, but in the storm it was eerily quiet. Clouds of rain whipped between the old storefronts, taking on shapes like giant skeletons. The only light was the glow from the doctor's office, and as he watched, the light went black. Dr Smeltz was going home.

Cab turned on his engine. He didn't feel like making the long drive back to the coast. He decided to get a motel room, even though he knew the storm would be worse by morning. The rain, as bad as it was, was simply a preview of coming attractions. The real danger would begin tomorrow when the swirling body of Chayla nudged over land.

Tomorrow. The Fourth of July. Independence Day.

He backed out of the parking place and switched on his headlights. The beams captured the sheeting rain and the gray stone of the clock tower. He squinted. Just for an instant, he saw someone standing in the plaza. It was a young woman, alone, buffeted by the downpour. Water pooled like a lake at her feet. She was skinny, and without a coat, she was soaked to the bone. He couldn't see well enough to recognize her face, but there was something oddly familiar about her. He thought she was staring at him and that she knew who he was.

The wind gusted, the girl turned, and she vanished behind a curtain of rain. It was as if she'd never been there at all.

32

Peach waited until Dr Smeltz left his office.

She recognized the doctor's lumpy profile. He hadn't changed in the years since she'd seen him as a child. She had always liked him. He was gruff but had a sweet soul, and he had a special weakness for kids. Her appointments with him had always taken a long time, because he had Lego dinosaurs and Disney action figures for her, and he seemed to enjoy playing with them as much as she did. Or maybe that was just his way of making her feel at ease in a scary place.

Dr Smeltz bounded across the plaza, his multiple chins tucked against the rain, his brimmed hat dripping like a waterfall. He passed within ten feet of Peach, but he didn't see her. The doctor got into an Audi and drove away, his tires throwing up a wave of water. She figured he was going home to his house by the lake, with the huge front yard that stretched to the beach. Lyle had taken her there once. It was one of the last things they'd done together. He'd said she needed a follow-up visit for her pneumonia, but he didn't take her to the medical office. When they got to the doctor's house, Dr Smeltz didn't even examine her at all. Instead, she played on the lawn with Google, the doctor's Westie puppy, while Lyle and Dr Smeltz talked inside.

Lyle had never told her what they talked about, but afterward, he'd gone to see a lawyer in Orlando.

Peach stood in the rain. The Gulf storm was warm, but she felt chilled. The plaza was empty. So was the main street, now that the two men had left. She saw no traffic, but she kept an eye open for police cars stalking the downtown area. The doctor's building, which was low and built of tan brick and stucco, was deserted. The three tall windows facing the plaza were black. The wind nearly picked her up and carried her away. She hugged the trunk of a palm tree.

She thought about Cab Bolton. She'd spotted his car on the street, and she wanted to know where he was going. He'd seen her when he left the office, but she doubted that he would have recognized her in her disguise. She wondered what he wanted with Dr Smeltz. Him and Justin both. They had plucked this man from her past, and she didn't understand why.

Or did she?

Staring at the clinic where she had gone dozens of times as a child, she realized that she knew exactly what they were looking for. She heard Cab's voice in her head earlier that day. *Two weeks before Labor Day, there was a problem at Birch's estate. Something bad.*

And then another voice. Her own voice. Talking to Justin. *We walked into the middle of something.*

Deacon had driven her to Birch's estate on that awful Saturday night. The night of sickness and delirium. The night when they hit the deer. The night when her body was burning up and the nicest thing in the world was to have Caprice carry her to that lavish guest bedroom that smelled of vanilla and coconut and to see, hovering behind her, that smiling, fleshy, familiar face. Dr Smeltz. Her doctor. He would make everything better.

He was already there when we arrived.

That was the connection she'd failed to make all these years. Why would a child give it a second thought? He'd already been called to the house. Not for her. For something else entirely.

Something bad.

Justin must have found out, and Justin was dead. Had Cab Bolton found out, too? Had Dr Smeltz told him? It didn't matter. She needed to know for herself.

Peach grabbed her phone and shut off the power. She checked the downtown street. Awnings on the storefronts flapped madly, like baseball cards in a bicycle spoke. The trees bent down as if they were praying. Branches, leaves, and dirt spat through the air. She knelt in the plaza, which was lined with loose red bricks. It was easy enough to dig her fingers into the gaps and pry them free. She uprooted them and scattered them around the plaza the way the storm would. Gusts of wind could lift up rocks and hurl them like javelins.

She took one brick and walked ten more feet to the edge of the plaza, where she stood in front of the three floor-to-ceiling windows that looked in on the lobby of the clinic. *I'm sorry, Dr Smeltz.*

Peach hurled the brick into the center window. The glass shattered, caving inward, leaving shards on every side that looked like a shark's mouth. The crash banged loudly in her ears, but the howling wind drowned it out. No alarm sounded. No strobe lights flashed. She kicked some of the glass teeth out of the frame with the toe of her shoe and carefully squeezed through the hole into the building.

Rain flooded inside, pooling on the floor. The brick lay in the middle of the sandstone tile, surrounded by fragments that crunched under her feet. The water made the floor slippery, and she stumbled. Her skirt tore, and a gash opened on her knee. When she touched it, the cut stung, and her fingers came away with blood. She sucked them clean.

The waiting room was small. It smelled of antiseptic cleaner.

Behind the receptionist desk, she saw a door that led to the rest of the clinic. She'd been here many times, heard the young nurse call her name, and followed the woman nervously to the examining rooms in the back. Peach pushed through the wooden door, the way she had as a kid. When she closed it behind her, the hallway was black. She fumbled for a light switch and found it, and fluorescent lights flickered to life overhead. There were no windows; no one outside would see.

Most of the doors in the hallway were open. They led to different examining rooms. She saw cushioned tables on which she'd sat as a child, pedaling her legs. The doctor's little wheely chair. The cabinets where he'd grabbed bottles and needles. In one of the rooms, she saw green Legos that had been made into an alligator, and she smiled. Some things didn't change.

Dr Smeltz's name was on a plaque in the middle of one door. She opened it, stepped inside, and closed the door behind her, turning on the lights. The office smelled of Dr Smeltz, which meant it smelled of coffee and those little chocolate mints he kept for patients, but which he mostly ate himself. Peach saw a bowl of them on a table near his computer. She couldn't resist taking one and biting down on the candy shell. The taste brought a wave of memories.

Something in the office made a loud *chunk*, and she had to cover her mouth to keep from screaming. When it happened again, she saw rainwater dripping from the ceiling into an orange bucket. She giggled at her overreaction, but it reminded her that she had broken into an office building and was mounting an illegal search. She couldn't waste time.

She spotted the doctor's locked steel filing cabinets. Like she had in Ogden Bush's office, she did a search of the desk, and it took her less than five minutes to find a key. She unlocked the filing cabinet on the wall and opened the middle drawer, which was labeled with a handwritten D–F.

Peach pawed through bulging folders. The files were squeezed together so tightly that she could barely separate them. Dr Smeltz had been practicing in Lake Wales since the 1970s, and the spidery ink on some of the folders had faded. Papers were yellowed. The alphabetizing wasn't always perfect. Peach went from front to back, checking each folder, but found no files on Diane Fairmont. The name Fairmont didn't appear at all.

Ms Fairmont's maiden name was Hempl. Dr Smeltz had probably treated her before she married Birch. Peach repeated her search on the drawer labeled G-I, but again, the effort was fruitless. She began to feel frustrated, and her nervousness grew as time passed. The last cabinet on the wall had three unlabeled drawers. She checked them, but they were empty except for unmarked file folders and a box of markers. Finally, she unlocked the other filing cabinets on the wall and began to search all of the remaining drawers.

She expected to find her own medical file, but she never got there. She had reached the M files when she heard voices.

Peach froze, and her heartbeat soared with fear. Someone had spotted the broken window. She remembered that she'd left the outer hallway light on, which was *stupid, stupid, stupid.* She closed the drawer where she was searching and locked the cabinets with soft clicks. Her eyes traveled the room for a hiding place. She dove for the light switch, flicked off the office light, and groped her way to the desk. Finding it, she felt for the doctor's armchair and nudged it backward. The casters squeaked. Peach folded herself inside the small space under the desk, then pulled the chair as tightly against herself as she could. She held her breath.

She wondered if she'd been dripping on the floor, leaving a trail.

The office door opened, and the overhead lights came on again, harsh and bright. The voices got louder. There were two men. She heard their footsteps. At least one of them had a body odor problem.

'I'm telling you, the storm broke the window,' said one.

'Yeah? Did the storm turn the light on, too?' The second man had a Spanish accent.

'They probably forgot.'

The footsteps moved around the office. One of the men came up to the desk; she could see the shadow of his legs. He walked behind the desk; he was next to the chair. If he bent down, he would see her. She could have reached out and pulled up his sock, which had fallen to reveal a bare ankle.

'Nobody,' said the first man.

The second man grunted. He was the one who was close to her. 'Check the drug cabinet.'

'It's locked.'

'The book says always check the closet if there's an alarm. The combination is 0630.'

The second man moved away from the desk. Peach let out her breath in a slow, silent hiss. She heard the clicking of metal buttons, and the door to the supply closet opened. The floor was concrete; she could hear the difference in the sound of their footsteps.

'All clear here. Man, he's got a stash, huh?'

'He's a doctor, what do you expect?'

The two men returned to the office and locked the storage closet door.

'That it?' said the first man.

'We have to call Dr Smeltz,' his colleague replied.

'He's not going to be happy coming out in the storm.'

'He's not going to be happy seeing his window broken and his lobby looking like it's in the middle of Crooked Lake.'

'We hanging around?' asked the first man.

'You are. I'll go to the next call. I'll swing back and pick you up after the doc arrives.'

The first man muttered unhappily under his breath. Moments later, the office light went off. Peach waited, not moving. She heard footsteps receding in the hallway. The voices continued, muffled and distant, and then they went silent. She heard a door open and close.

Immediately afterward, a radio blared in the waiting room. Loud, hip-hop music. She wasn't alone. The first man had stayed behind, waiting for Dr Smeltz. She knew that the doctor would only need ten or fifteen minutes to make his way back to the clinic. She needed to be gone before he arrived.

Peach scrambled out from under the desk. She could still smell the mildewed aroma of sweat the men had left behind. Her instinct was to make an immediate break for the rear exit that led to the alley, but she still hadn't found a file for Diane Fairmont. Dr Smeltz didn't keep her file with his other patient records, but she realized that was no surprise. He would keep the records separate and secure. Even so, she didn't think he would keep the file off-site, in case he needed to access the information. There was only one room in the building that had a heavy door and a secure lock. That was the drug closet ten feet away from her.

The lock that opened with the combination 0630.

Peach wasted no time. She turned on the office light again and quickly keyed the buttons to gain access to the storage room. Inside, with a quick review of the room, she found herself disappointed. There were no filing cabinets. No lock boxes. The room was lined with metal shelves that were stocked with pharmaceuticals and medical supplies. She saw nowhere to hide files. Her face fell. The clock was ticking, and she needed to go.

Then she spotted a red metal chest shoved into a corner. It was two-feet by two-feet and twelve inches high. She'd almost missed it, because boxes of gauze and bagged patient gowns had been stacked on top of the lid. A small padlock latched the chest shut, and a handwritten sign had been taped to the front. The sign read, in bold black letters: BIO-HAZARD.

She stared at it, frowning. Why would a hazardous materials chest be covered up with supplies? Why a handwritten sign? She knew Dr Smeltz. He wasn't fussy about a lot of things, but he was particular when it came to the safety of his practice.

Peach crossed the room and used a hairpin to pop the tiny padlock. She shifted the clutter off the chest, undid the latch, and opened the heavy metal lid. There were no used needles or contaminated waste inside. Instead, the chest was empty except for two thick file folders.

One folder was labeled DIANE (HEMPL) FAIRMONT.

The second was labeled DREW HEMPL.

Peach stared at the folders and thought: *This is wrong.* However, she'd already left the line between right and wrong far behind her.

She gathered the files into her arms. Quickly, she relocked the chest and replaced the supplies, so it looked as if nothing had been disturbed. She hoped Dr Smeltz didn't look too carefully. Glancing at the clock on the wall, she shut the storage room door again.

Music thumped from the waiting room. It was Nicki Minaj. Peach switched off the lights and inched the office door open. The hallway lights were dark, but she pushed her face out to peek down the hallway, and she saw that the lobby door was open. A male voice rose above the music; the first man was on his cell phone. As she watched, he wandered into view, his back to her. He was tall and meaty, wearing a tight gray uniform.

Peach slipped into the hallway. A red EXIT sign glowed at the end of the corridor to her left. The medical files were snug under her right arm. Rain drummed on the roof above her. She backed up, keeping her eyes on the man in the lobby. Nicki sang about 'Beez in the Trap,' and the security guard did the worst white man's dance Peach had ever seen. He was still on the phone.

'Are you kidding? No way I'm apologizing to her. Okay, so I yelled at her kid. Big deal. She's lucky I didn't put my foot up his ass. Little twit was sticking peanut butter in my Blu Ray player! Is that supposed to be funny? I mean, the thing's completely f–'

He spun around, still dancing, and then he stopped dead.

Peach was a shadow halfway down the hallway, but he stared right at her. Their eyes met across the dark space. His mouth fell open in surprise.

'HEY!' he bellowed.

Peach turned and sprinted. Footsteps pounded behind her, but a scream and crash intervened as the man slipped in the pooled water and wiped out. She stole a look behind her; he was struggling to get up. He shouted curses after her, but she widened the gap and hit the emergency exit door with her shoulder. It flew open, and she bolted into the storm. Her heart was thumping, her mouth open, swallowing water that sprayed into her face. It was night, and the rainfall was a black shroud.

She was across the plaza before the man made it out of the building. She raced into the darkness and disappeared.

33

Cab perched his long legs on the motel bed, which took up most of the room. The motel had a musty, old-cigarette smell. He sat by the window with an open bottle of red wine in front of him. The hammering of rain on the glass was hypnotic. The wine was delicious; he always kept a bottle of Stags' Leap in the rear of the Corvette, in case of emergency.

Sitting alone in a cheap motel room in the middle of a storm definitely counted as an emergency. He was on his second glass.

He thought about what he had discovered so far and what it all meant.

Ten years ago, Birch Fairmont committed some unspeakable act that Diane and the people around her had kept a closely guarded secret to this day. Only two weeks later, an unidentified assassin shot three people at the Bok Sanctuary, including Birch. Back then, no one made a connection between the two events. Instead, the Liberty Empire Alliance got the blame for painting a target on Birch's chest. Hamilton Brock went to prison but claimed he was set up by a mole inside the Alliance. Chuck Warren lost the election but saw a conspiracy orchestrated by the Democrats and the media.

Conspiracy or not, the crime went unsolved.

Fast forward to now.

Rufus Twill, who had led the media wolf pack going after the Liberty Empire Alliance ten years ago, was singing a different song.

So was his niece, a former employee at the Fairmont household. They were both spreading rumors that Diane's son Drew hated Birch and wanted him dead. Drew also had a relationship with a hip, violent young drug dealer named Frank Macy. If Cab connected the dots, then maybe Birch's death wasn't what everyone originally believed. Or maybe he was being played, and this was just a new political conspiracy aimed at Diane.

Rufus Twill had an agenda in pointing a finger at Drew after all these years. That was obvious. He wasn't the kingpin; someone else was orchestrating the rumors. Money had changed hands. It felt like the usual election-year games – but Justin Kiel's death wasn't a game. He'd been executed.

Justin had found something that made him a mortal threat. He'd been asking questions about Birch's murder. He'd searched the office of Dr Reuben Smeltz. He'd followed the trail of Drew's drug dealer, Frank Macy. And he wound up with a bullet in his brain.

Definitely not a game.

Cab knew the least about Frank Macy of any of the players in this drama, but what he did know troubled him. Macy had a criminal record and access to guns. He also had connections to a woman who would very much like to see Diane's downfall. The Attorney General and Republican gubernatorial candidate, Ramona Cortes.

Cab didn't know what to believe anymore. He was in a shadow play, where he couldn't trust what his eyes told him. The wine swam in his head. His clothes were still wet; he was cold. The rain fired at the motel window like a machine gun. He picked up his cell phone and did what he always did when he couldn't sort out what was real and what was not.

He called Lala.

Signal was weak as the storm fought the satellites. He didn't expect an answer, but this time, on the second static-filled ring, he heard her voice.

'Hello, Cab.'

He almost forgot to say anything. Then he recovered. 'The storm's bad. Are you safe?'

'Yes.'

'Are you alone?'

God, what a stupid thing to say. He could hear her smile. 'Shouldn't I be asking you that question?'

'I have no interest in Caprice Dean,' he said.

'Liar.'

'Well, I have interest, but I'm taking your advice to heart.'

'Good.'

She was quiet and far away. The storm felt as if it were coming between them. He expected the call to drop and split them apart. He felt the physical distance and the desire for her body; it had been weeks since they'd made love. More than that, he felt ungrounded without her.

'Where are you?' she asked. 'At Tarla's place?'

'No, I'm in Lake Wales.'

'Because of Diane Fairmont?'

'Yes.'

Her words broke up. He held the phone near the window. 'What? I didn't hear that.'

'I asked if you'd found out anything.'

'Only that you were right. I'm swimming with sharks.'

'Well, your teeth are pretty sharp, too,' Lala said. 'I should know.'

Cab grinned. 'Nice memory for a man alone in a motel room. Tarla says we should try phone sex.'

'Yes, because sexual suggestions from your mother really turn me on.'

'You, too?'

He heard her laugh. He could always make her laugh. Then, as the silence drew out, he remembered where he was. 'Honestly?' he told her. 'I'm worried.'

'About what?'

'I have this feeling that the past is about to repeat itself, and I'm not going to be able to stop it.'

She didn't answer. He thought he'd lost her again. He wondered if she realized he'd been drinking.

'Lala?'

'Cab, if you find *anything at all*, I want you to call me.'

He was surprised by the intensity in her voice. 'I haven't. I have puzzle pieces that don't fit together. I have motives layered upon motives. None of it tells me who really killed Birch Fairmont. None of it tells me whether Diane is really in jeopardy.'

He waited for an answer, but didn't get one.

'I'm not working for Caprice anymore,' he went on. 'I want to know what's going on, but I can't do that with politicians trying to manipulate me.'

'I know how you feel. Really, I do.'

'Caprice wasn't happy. I think she wanted a detective boy-toy.'

He heard her laugh again. 'I hope you didn't quit because of me.'

'Partly.'

'I feel guilty about that. I don't own you.'

'Don't worry about it,' he said. 'I do have a problem, though.'

The static swallowed her voice again. When she spoke, she said, 'What problem?'

'I'm anticipating the return of Catch-a-Cab Bolton.'

'Oh.' Lala knew what his nickname meant. It was a symbol of his jackrabbit past. Never staying in one place. Never staying in one job. He was always chasing something or being chased. 'So are you going to leave Florida? Tarla won't be happy.'

'What about you?'

'This is about you, not me.'

'I didn't say I wanted to leave town. I'm saying I like the idea of working for myself. My vacation from the Naples Police is likely to become permanent. I don't think I was born to be part of a bureaucracy.'

'Okay.'

'I just want to make sure you understand that it has nothing whatsoever to do with you and me.'

'Okay.'

But he didn't think she believed him.

'Happy Independence Day,' he said.

'What?'

'It's past midnight. It's the Fourth of July.'

'You're right.'

'No fireworks this year. Chayla's spoiling the party.'

'I guess so.'

'Did you know that Independence Day is the anniversary of Hamilton Brock going to prison?' he asked.

'I didn't.'

'That bothers me. Anniversaries like that are dangerous. Except now I'm starting to wonder whether the Liberty Empire Alliance was involved in Birch's murder at all.'

He heard a knocking on his motel room door.

'I have to go,' he said. 'I ordered a pizza.'

'You?'

'Yes, me. There aren't many options here this late.'

'Pizza Hut doesn't put brie and spinach on their pies, you know.'

'So they told me,' Cab said.

'Listen, Cab, there's something you should know.'

'What?'

She didn't answer right away. He thought of a thousand different things she might say, and he wasn't sure how to reply to any of them.

'Nothing,' she went on.

'Are you sure?'

'I'm sure. Enjoy your pizza. But remember what I said. If you discover anything that doesn't feel right, I want you to call me right away.'

'Okay.'

'I mean it. Call me.'

'Yes, Mother.'

'Oh, that is so not funny.'

'Sure it is,' he said.

Cab hung up and put down his wine glass. He felt bad about bringing a pizza delivery guy out in the storm, but he was hungry, and the kid would like the tip. He couldn't believe they didn't put brie on their pizzas.

He grabbed his wallet out of his pocket and opened the motel room door, ushering in a wave of silver rain. It wasn't a teenager delivering his pizza.

Peach Piper stood on the doorstep.

34

'Well,' Cab Bolton said, as he ushered her into the motel room and closed the door. 'It's Peach, isn't it?'

'Yes.'

She watched the gangly detective slump into a chair by the window. He looked amused, rather than surprised, to see her here. He held up a half-empty bottle of wine. 'Want a glass? It's excellent, I promise.'

'I don't drink.'

'I have a pizza coming, if you're hungry.'

'Is it vegetarian?'

'It is, actually.'

She shrugged. 'I could eat.'

Peach shifted uncomfortably, dripping on the carpet. The room was dark. He noticed her glance at the light switch, and he leaned over with long arms and turned on the lamp. He gestured at the bed. 'You can sit down for the same price.'

'Okay.'

'I was about to swear that I have no evil intentions, but since you're the one who showed up in my motel room, shouldn't that be your line?'

Her lips twitched in a small smile. It was hard not to like this man. She sat primly on the end of the bed and put the two damp medical files next to her. His eyes studied the files curiously, but he didn't ask about them.

'You're soaked,' he said. 'I have an extra blanket in my trunk. Do you want it?'

'No, I'm okay. Thanks, though.'

Cab eased back into the chair and picked up his glass of wine. 'So.'

She knew he was waiting for her to explain. She didn't know what to say or even why she'd decided to come here. The arrival of the pizza gave her more time. Cab answered the door, paid the boy with what looked like a fifty dollar bill – no change – and propped open the white box on the table in front of him. He put a triangular slice on a paper plate and handed it to her, and when she took a bite, she decided she was ravenous. They finished more than half the pizza in silence.

He watched her the whole time, but his curious stare didn't bother her. His blue eyes were smart and ironic; so was his funny little grin. He was unusually handsome. Being so much younger than he was – at least ten years, probably fifteen – she didn't feel any attraction to him, but that didn't mean she couldn't appreciate a man who was very cute. It wasn't just his movie star looks. He projected an aura of being utterly comfortable in his own skin. As if he took the world seriously and himself not at all.

Of all the things she had to say, she finally said: 'So how tall are you?'

Cab threw back his head and laughed. She had the impression that he liked her, too. 'When I wear three-inch stilettos, I'm six-foot-nine,' he said.

She giggled. 'Well, you're tall even without them.'

'A little.'

'I suppose you're wondering–'

'Why you're here? Yes.'

'I saw your car from the highway,' she said.

'And so you just decided to say hi?'

'Not exactly,' she admitted.

He smiled at her. 'Let's see, that was you in the plaza near Dr Smeltz's office, right? I imagine you saw my Corvette in the parking lot at the foundation office today. So after you broke into the doctor's office to steal Diane Fairmont's medical file, you decided we were both after the same thing, and you made a leap of faith to trust me enough to share it with me. How am I doing?'

Peach's eyes widened. 'I – um . . .'

'By the way, I'm not psychic,' Cab told her. 'Dr Smeltz called me. He assumed I stole the file myself. He wasn't happy about his broken window, but he felt better when I offered to pay for the damage.'

'You did?'

'I did.'

'Oh.' Peach took a glance at the files. 'Did you tell him it was me?'

'I didn't know it was you, not until you showed up. By the way, you realize that what you did is against the law, right? If I were a cop, I would have to arrest you, but fortunately, I'm in the process of re-evaluating my career plans.'

'Oh,' she said again.

'Since you're not in cuffs, do you want to tell me why it was so important to get your hands on those files?'

He handed her another slice of pizza, but Peach wasn't hungry anymore. She was starting to feel young and stupid. 'I want to know what happened to Justin.'

'So do I.'

'He was looking for Dr Smeltz. I figured that he wanted what you did. He was trying to find out what happened between Mr and Mrs Fairmont.'

'And now you know,' Cab said. 'You've looked at the files, right?'

She nodded. 'It's really awful.'

'Tell me.'

Peach got up from the bed. She paced, her fingers laced together in front of her. She wasn't in disguise now. The rain had washed off her makeup. She'd changed back into her own oversized T-shirt and red jeans. It made her feel exposed. She didn't like anyone seeing who she really was.

Even so, she'd realized immediately that she couldn't keep the files to herself. Not when she saw what was in them.

'Dr Smeltz wrote it all down. He should have gone to the police, but Ms Fairmont begged him not to. She knew it would destroy her husband. It would have been the end of his campaign. It would have been the end of the Common Way Party. She didn't want that.'

Cab waited. She was grateful that he didn't rush her. Peach grazed the top of the file with her fingertips, as if it could burn her.

'Birch had been drinking. A lot.'

'That's usually how it starts,' Cab said.

'He knew that Ms Fairmont had been unfaithful. She'd had an affair.'

Cab said nothing, but Peach saw discomfort cross his face.

'They argued. There was a lot of shouting. Then he got physical. He started punching her. Kicking her. It was vicious. There was blood everywhere.'

Peach stopped and felt a sudden wave of nausea that was so strong it almost dropped her to her knees. She backed up to the wall and covered her mouth with her hand. Her eyes squeezed shut. She could smell her own panic and fear.

'Are you all right?' Cab asked, concerned.

'Yeah. It's just – so horrible that he could do that. She never said a word.'

'Even strong women sometimes stay silent,' Cab said.

'Drew found out,' Peach went on. 'He went crazy. He wanted to kill Birch. He was completely out of control. Dr Smeltz put him in rehab.'

'He got out right before Labor Day,' Cab said.

'Yes.'

'Still burning for revenge.'

'Yes.' Peach stared at Cab and whispered: 'Do you think Drew killed Birch? And my brother?'

'I don't know, Peach, but it's possible.'

She tried to imagine the horror Drew must have felt. The fury. He would have been about the same age then that Peach was now. An adult, but still tethered to his childhood.

'It was terrible, but I'm not sure I can bring myself to blame him,' she said. 'Birch nearly killed his mother. He murdered her unborn child. It must have driven Drew insane. How do you live with something like that?'

The room fell silent, except for the roaring of the rain, which was like a furious heartbeat. Peach stared at the floor, thinking of loss. Her loss. Ms Fairmont's loss. Things that couldn't be undone. She kept thinking about Ms Fairmont and felt a kinship with her that she'd never felt before. Knowing what she'd endured, she felt they were joined somehow.

Peach felt a chill from somewhere and realized it was Cab. When she looked at him, he was suddenly a stranger. He'd stood up from the chair, ghostly white, his handsome face stripped of life. She could see him trembling with an emotion that had opened up like a fissure in the earth. Anger. Or grief. Something inconsolable. He was not the same man he'd been moments earlier.

'What did you say?' he asked. 'Birch murdered her *child*?'

Peach realized she hadn't told him the worst part of the story.

It was as if she could barely say it out loud. 'Yes, Ms Fairmont was pregnant,' she explained. 'It was in her medical file. That was what started everything. Birch knew the baby wasn't his. That's when he started kicking her and when she started screaming. He was punishing her for what she'd done. By the time he stopped, she'd miscarried. She lost the baby.'

35

Tarla answered the door in a black silk nightgown and robe. Her feet were bare. Her bed hair was mussed. She was beautiful, but he could see a hint of age in her face, as if it were the first time he'd noticed that she was growing older. He hadn't seen her since their fight at the Bok Sanctuary, but her lips bent into a smile that was very much like his own. She was about to make a joke. Then she saw his expression, and everything changed. She knew, the way a mother always knows, that her son was in grievous pain.

'What is it, Cab?'

He pushed past her into the apartment, which was lit only by the kitchen light. The patio doors were opaque with rain. He was exhausted. The two-hour drive from Lake Wales to Clearwater in the storm, with his mind swirling, had left him numb. He wasn't able to cry.

'Did you know?' he asked.

Tarla stared at him. It was in her eyes: She knew exactly what was going on. She said nothing, because she was afraid of anything she might say. This was one of those fragile moments. Play it wrong, and the world would shatter. She was all too familiar with their history. She didn't want him to run away from her again.

'*Did you know?*' he repeated, harsh and demanding.

'Only when you told me about you and Diane,' Tarla replied calmly. 'Then I guessed.'

'But you knew she was pregnant. You knew she lost the child.'

Tarla put her palms together in front of her lips, as if she were praying, which he knew she was not. She didn't try to embrace him. They weren't touchy-feely like that, and she was smart enough to realize that this wasn't a situation that could be fixed with a hug. She sat down on the plush white sofa in the semi-darkness. 'Sit down, Cab,' she murmured.

'I'll stand.'

'Oh, for God's sake, sit down,' she snapped, but then she shook her head in annoyance with herself. 'I'm sorry, darling.'

Cab sat down in an armchair across from her. He leaned forward, his elbows on his knees.

'I found out much later,' Tarla told him. 'I didn't know back then. I knew something was wrong – I knew she'd been injured in some way – but I had no idea what had happened. She didn't say a word. How did you find out, Cab?'

'It doesn't matter.'

'I don't imagine Diane told you,' Tarla said.

'She didn't. When did she tell you?'

'After Drew killed himself. I'm not sure she meant to, but it spilled out with her grief.'

Cab nodded. 'What did she say?'

Tarla clenched her fists in anger. 'Birch assaulted her brutally. That monster. Honestly, I wish I'd known, I would have killed him myself. Imagine the two faces you need to do something like that to your wife and then stand up and proclaim yourself a political savior.'

'What else did she tell you?' he asked.

'She realized she was pregnant in July. It was a shock, of course. I gather she'd stopped bothering with protection. You get to your mid-forties without another child, and you start to assume—'

'Did she say who . . . ?'

'She only told me it wasn't Birch,' Tarla replied. 'They hadn't had sex in months. You have to believe me, Cab, she did *not* tell me who the father really was. I asked, of course, but she said she hadn't told him, and she said she would never tell anyone. She said . . .' Tarla stopped. 'Do you really want to hear what she said about it, darling?'

'I do.'

'She told me it was a one-time affair. Literally one-time. She said it was born out of her great need, and it was with a man who made her feel special for the first time in a long time.'

'And who ran away and avoided her for a decade,' Cab said bitterly.

'Well, what did you plan to do, Cab? Marry her? You may recall, she was already married at the time.'

'Is that supposed to make me feel better?' he asked. 'I'm angry at myself, but I'm angry at her, too. She never told me. Don't you think I had a right to know? The baby was mine, too.' It was strange how devastating those words were as he heard them on his lips.

'I understand, darling, but consider her situation. A married woman whose husband is running a political campaign? She finds herself pregnant by another man? Most women in her situation would have ended it. She didn't. She wanted the baby.'

'Was it a boy or a girl?' he asked quietly.

'I'm sorry, I don't know.'

A son or a daughter. That was the kind of question a single man didn't take much time to think about. He felt a wave of rage directed at Birch Fairmont. The man had murdered his child. If he'd known the truth back then, he might have killed Birch himself.

He had to remind himself: *Someone did.*

'She couldn't have expected to keep it a secret forever,' Cab said. 'Sooner or later, people were going to notice.'

'I think for a while she simply couldn't face it. She kept it from everyone as long as she could. I was her best friend, but she never told me. Birch was so caught up in the campaign, I doubt he saw what was happening to her. On the other hand, you're right, it couldn't last forever. So she decided to tell him.'

Cab knew how it went from there.

She told Birch that weekend. That Saturday night.

It was bad.

'That was when he assaulted her,' Cab murmured.

'Yes. The man cheated on her constantly, but let her have one affair and he couldn't handle it. She didn't want a divorce – that was the last thing she wanted. She told Birch the real father didn't know and never would. She said no one would ever think that the baby wasn't his. They could announce it. It would be a *boost* to his campaign. A little late-in-life miracle. Voters would love the idea.' Tarla carefully brushed a tear from each of her eyes. 'Well, you know how Birch reacted.'

Cab wanted to cry, but he felt empty. He had nothing inside.

'I'm so sorry, darling,' Tarla said. 'Really I am. If I had known, I would have told you. You deserved the truth.'

'It wouldn't have changed anything.'

'I suppose not.' His mother studied his sunken face and said: 'Does Diane know that you've found out about this?'

'No.'

'Are you going to tell her?'

'Do you think I should?' Cab asked.

'Yes, I do. I'm going over to Diane's place tomorrow to ride out Chayla with her. I could talk to her myself, but I think it's something you need to do. You have questions, and she's the only one who can answer them.'

'I have questions, but she won't like them,' Cab said.

'What do you mean?'

'She kept the story hidden. I need to know why.'

'Can you blame her?' Tarla asked. 'The media would have been incredibly hurtful. She deserved to grieve in her own way, not have her life blown up by scandal. That's still true today, Cab. Common Way is her life. Regardless of whether you're angry at her, you have no right to expose what happened and put everything she's worked for in jeopardy.'

'I'm not sure the secret is about politics. I'm not sure it ever was.'

'What on earth are you talking about?'

'Drew,' Cab said.

Tarla sprang to her feet. 'Oh, honestly, Cab, this again?'

The silk of her night clothes swished as she padded to the windows and stared out at the rain. The Gulf was invisible. He came up behind her and put a hand gently on his mother's shoulder.

'Drew threatened to kill Birch,' he said. 'Now I know he had a very powerful motive to do so.'

'I told you, he didn't do it. Leave it alone. What do you hope to accomplish?'

'Sometimes the truth is enough,' Cab said.

Tarla spun around, and strands of golden hair flew across her eyes. Her face was flushed as she shouted at him. 'Do you always have to be a fucking *policeman*?'

Cab was calm, but his mother looked embarrassed by her profane outburst. She turned back to the window and leaned against the cold glass with her forehead. He could see, in the blurry reflection, that her eyes were closed.

'Does it really even matter?' she murmured. 'Does it really matter after all these years? It's over. It's in the past.'

'Even if that were true, yes, it does matter. Birch wasn't the only one who was killed that night. Lyle Piper didn't deserve to die. The citrus farmer who tried to intervene, he didn't deserve to die.'

Tarla turned around, and she looked chastened. 'You're right, of course.'

'And I don't think it is over. Someone named Justin Kiel was murdered last month. I think it's because he was asking questions about the Labor Day killings.'

'How could that be?' Tarla asked. 'Even if Drew was involved, he died years ago.'

'Drew may have turned to someone else for help. Someone who is still alive. Someone who's trying to cover his tracks. Drew had a relationship with a drug dealer named Frank Macy, and he might have used Macy as part of the plot.'

Cab stopped as Tarla's face tensed with recognition. She was an actress and recovered almost immediately, but he didn't miss it. The name Frank Macy meant something to her. She knew who he was.

'Mother?' he asked. 'What do you know about Frank Macy?'

'Only that he was a friend of Drew's. I remember meeting him that summer.'

She shrank from the hardness in his eyes.

'What else?' he asked.

'Oh, darling, drop it. I got enough interrogations when I guest-starred on *Law & Order*. That Sam Waterston, he is yummy.'

'You're hiding something,' Cab said. 'You've been hiding something from me all along. What is it? Did you recognize the gunman? Was it Macy?'

'I told you, I don't remember a thing about that night.'

He took her chin gently between two fingers. 'Mother, this is not a game. This is not one of your movies. Innocent people have died, and they are still dying. You can't hide what you know. Not anymore.'

Tarla blinked back tears, and she wasn't acting. She was genuinely distressed. 'I can't say anything. Not to you. Don't you understand? You are a cop, darling. Whatever I tell you, I know you will have to act upon, and I can't allow that.'

Cab reached into his suit coat pocket. He pulled out his badge, and he put it in his mother's hand and closed her fingers around it. 'This is me resigning. I'm no longer a police officer. I'm a private citizen.'

'Cab, it isn't that simple.'

'It is. You *need* to tell me.'

Tarla turned away with his badge still clutched in her hand. She looked as if she would rather open the patio door and jump than open her mouth.

'I had no idea what I was seeing,' she said. 'I didn't give it any thought at all. It was only afterward that I wondered. I never said anything, but I've always wondered about it.'

'Was this on Labor Day?'

She shook her head. 'It was two days before.'

'Mother, what did you see?'

'That man,' Tarla replied. 'Frank Macy. I recognized him. It was in the garden of the estate, near a road coming out of the orange groves. I was taking a walk, and they didn't see me. They had no idea I was there. I saw an exchange of money between them. It was a large amount of money.'

Cab closed his eyes. He felt as if the pieces had finally come together. Two days before Labor Day, Drew paid Macy. This wasn't for drugs. This was for murder. Drew paid Frank Macy to kill Birch

Fairmont, and Macy chose to make it look like an act of domestic terrorism. And the dominoes began to fall.

'I wish you'd told me before,' he said quietly. 'This changes everything. Drew may be dead, but Frank Macy isn't. He's alive, and he's dangerous.'

Tarla shook her head. She looked stricken. 'You don't understand.'

'What?'

'It wasn't Drew,' she said. 'I didn't see Drew pay the money to Frank Macy. It was Diane.'

36

Peach left her T-Bird in Seminole Park, the way she always did. It was three in the morning, and with each hour, the storm got worse.

Cab Bolton had said almost nothing when he left her at the motel in Lake Wales. No explanations. No excuses. *I have to get back to Tampa right now. You can stay if you'd like. The room's paid for.* Then he sped away in his Corvette as if his entire life depended on it.

Peach had no desire to stay the night in Lake Wales. Instead, she went home. She'd followed Justin's trail, but now it had led her back where she started. She still had only one name circled in her brain, like a target. Frank Macy. He was closer than ever to the heart of everything. Somehow, Justin had made the mistake of getting in Macy's way.

Then she realized she had one more name that troubled her. The name she didn't understand at all. Alison.

Peach pulled a phone from her pocket. It was off; she'd turned it off before she went inside Dr Smeltz's office. When she turned it on, the phone was slow to reacquire signal. She finally was able to open her mobile browser and hunt for the name of the lawyer that Deacon had given her. Alison Kuipers. She found an entry for the woman at the Tampa law firm used by the Common Way Foundation, and she dialed the lawyer's direct number.

'This is Alison Kuipers. Please leave a message . . .'

Peach wasn't sure what to say. When she heard the beep, she left her number but no name. Then she added: 'Call me as soon as you can. It's about Justin Kiel.'

She hung up. As she did, her phone let out a noise like a wolf whistle. She had voicemail. When she checked her phone records, she saw that her brother Deacon had called while her phone was off. The call was three hours old.

She played the voicemail message and heard his voice, but it was muffled and strange. He was whispering.

'Fruity, it's me. Hey, listen . . . I got a call back from someone in state corrections. He says Frank Macy spent two years inside with a roommate named Truc. Vietnamese, gang affiliations in L.A. Truc is back on the street, and word is, he's involved in gun trafficking. High-capacity assault weapons. Give me a call as soon as you get this message, okay? There's something you should know about Macy and Diane, too . . .'

There was silence, and Peach thought that Deacon had hung up, but a moment later, he went on.

'Listen, if Macy really is involved in something, chances are he's not alone. Don't trust anybody.'

Peach climbed out of her car and was immediately drenched. She didn't run to dodge the rain; she didn't have the energy, and her twisted ankle throbbed. She felt carried by the wind at her back. She squished through loose mud to the hole in the fence and made her way to 98th Street. Their house was black. Deacon's Mercedes was parked in the driveway. He was home.

She kicked through running water in the street. It was dark brown with dirt and littered with pine needles, and it was already deep enough to carry debris from neighboring yards. She opened the gate in the warped fence – No Trespassing, Beware of Dog – and headed for the front door.

Give me a call as soon as you get this message, okay?

Ten feet away, she froze. Their front door was wide open.

The driving rain drowned out every other noise around her. Her eyes flicked to the windows, but she saw no movement behind the ratty curtains. Instinctively, she glanced over her shoulder. She was alone outside the house, but she didn't feel less afraid.

Peach had never owned a gun. She had never even held a gun in her hand, but she wished she had one now. Or she wished Annalie was with her, pointing her own gun at the open door.

She approached slowly. The door was broken just above the door knob. The frame was splintered, and the strike plate had been torn off. Someone had kicked their way into the house. Gusts of wind carried rain across the tiled foyer. She peered inside, but all she could see was a silver sheen reflecting on the floor. She reached around the door frame to flip the light switch, but the power was off.

Peach took two steps into the foyer. In the living room on her left, she could distinguish the stark white shape of Sexpot Mannequin, who was where she'd left her, in lingerie, strong arm cocked behind her head. Nothing looked disturbed. The timbers of the house shook. With the noise of the storm muffled, she listened again. She didn't think anyone was here, but the Mercedes was parked in the driveway. Her anxiety soared.

She called: 'Deacon!'

Her brother didn't answer.

She tiptoed toward his bedroom. The rainwater followed her, moving like a snake. The air was stale and still. She retrieved a tiny pen light on her keychain and cast a weak beam in front of her. She sweated under her wet clothes. Her hand trembled. The fluttering light illuminated the open door of Deacon's bedroom, and she saw something smeared across the wood. Getting closer, she touched it, and her finger came away sticky and red.

Blood.

'Oh, no,' she whispered. 'Oh, no, no, no, no.'

The flashlight lit up the bedroom. She moved it around to the bed, to the floor, to the bathroom. The room was empty, but she saw evidence of a fight. The sheets had been torn off the bed, and she saw more blood on the white mattress. She clasped both hands over her head in frustration and pulled at her hair. She bit her lip so hard that it split between her teeth.

She took her phone and dialed Deacon's number. There was no answer.

She dialed again. And again. Each time, she heard the call go to voicemail.

Peach ran from the house, leaving the broken door open behind her. She blinked, barely able to see through rain and tears. She held up her arms against the wind in her face, as if she could keep the gusts from blowing her away. Tree branches snapped and fell around her. She stumbled forward into the street, which was swollen with two inches of water, nearly knocking her off her feet.

She fought to the park and clambered inside her car. Her face was streaked with dirt. She was spattered with mud.

What to do, what to do, what to do.

Peach dialed 911. The circuits were overloaded, and the call failed. Half the city was declaring an emergency. Even if she got through, the police weren't coming. Not now. Not in the storm. She was on her own, and she needed help. *Don't trust anybody.* That was what Deacon had told her, but she couldn't listen to him now.

Peach dialed the phone.

'Annalie, it's me,' she said when she got voicemail. 'Deacon's missing. I need to see you right away. Please. Meet me at the office whenever you get this message. I'm going there now.'

37

Cab couldn't sleep.

He lay with his eyes open, staring at the ceiling. He was mostly undressed, on top of the duvet and sheets. The storm howled on the other side of the wall. The placid Gulf had become a monster, lashing the coast. Dawn was two hours away, but there would be no sun and barely any light when morning came. It was a dark day. Independence Day.

Boy or girl. He found himself going back to that question over and over. He'd lost a child, and he didn't even know if it had been a boy or a girl. Each wave of emotion that washed over him became something else as it retreated. His fury at Birch. His anger that Diane had kept the secret from him. His sympathy for her and what she'd suffered. His pain at the thought of how far she might have gone to avenge what her husband had done to her.

Cab felt responsible. He'd been the trigger. He'd set everything in motion. That one week, that one afternoon, had rippled far beyond the moment. A child had died. His child. And then others had been killed.

His fault.

He wondered how things might have been different. If Diane had carried the baby to term, would he still be in the dark? Would Birch be alive? He imagined himself seeing a ten-year-old boy – or girl – with ocean-blue eyes, taller than he or she had any right to be. Would the thought have flitted across his mind? Would there have been some kind of kinship, some connection, between the two of them?

Not that he would ever know. All he could do was speculate.

He had never thought about wanting children. He'd grown up as Tarla's only child, so he never spent time around babies. He'd never known his father, so he didn't know what that relationship could be like. In the early days with Vivian Frost in Barcelona, he had fantasized about a life with her, and maybe in the back of his mind that life had included kids. Her death – her betrayal – had hollowed out his desires for a long-term relationship. He couldn't imagine himself as a husband, let alone a father. A child never entered his consciousness.

Boy or girl.

Cab got out of bed and headed into the living room in his briefs. He thought about pouring himself a drink, but he already had a headache from the wine in Lake Wales. He watched wind and rain flooding through the halo of lights far below him. In the other high-rises, he could see a handful of apartments where the owners were awake, like him.

It was easier to think about work. About the puzzle. He knew what he had to do in the morning. He needed to talk to Caprice about Birch and Diane and the violence between them. He needed to see Diane, too.

He needed to hear about their child from her lips.

Cab turned in surprise as the doorbell chime rang through the condo. He noticed the clock and assumed it was Tarla. This was the guest apartment; Tarla lived in her own place next door. He really didn't want to talk to his mother again. They'd shared enough anger and secrets for one night. Even so, he went to the door and peered through the spyhole. It wasn't Tarla.

He opened the door.

Lala, her face wet from the rain and wet from crying, came through the door, closed it softly, and put her arms around him. She didn't say a word. She knew the truth, and her own heart was breaking. That was when he finally cried, too. He didn't sob; he didn't have the strength. Instead, tears welled in his eyes and spilled onto his cheeks in a slow trickle. She held him tightly, and he put his arms around her, too, and they stayed like that in a kind of bubble.

When she pulled away, she put her hands on his cheeks, which were damp.

'I'm so sorry.'

'How did you . . . ?' he asked, but there was only one answer. A very surprising answer.

'Tarla called me,' Lala said. 'She told me you were here. She told me – what you found out.'

Tarla. Just when he thought he couldn't stand his mother for one more day, she went and reminded him that she loved him.

'Is it possible that she really likes you?' Cab asked.

'It's possible that she knows you needed someone. Even me.'

He took her hand. It had been a long time since they'd held hands. Her grip was strong. She wanted him to feel her. It was a reminder to him that his attraction to Caprice was nothing but physical. Lala was different. Lala was more. That was what made her so attractive and so terrifying to him. That was why their relationship was in jeopardy. It could be deep, or it could be nothing at all, but it couldn't be something casual.

He didn't know what he wanted, and she knew it, but she didn't expect him to choose now.

'What did she tell you?' he asked.

'Just that Diane lost a child. Your child. That's all I needed to know.'

'There's more. I don't think the Labor Day murders were what everyone believed they were. Diane paid–'

Lala put a finger on his lips. She shook her head. 'Not now. Tomorrow, but not now. You have to let yourself grieve. Give yourself one night.'

'I never thought something like this would hit me so hard,' Cab admitted. He tried to smile and make a joke. 'Me as a father? It's a horrifying thought.'

'You do yourself a disservice to talk like that,' Lala said. 'I mean it, Cab. I don't want to hear that from you.'

He realized that he couldn't escape her seriousness. Nothing he did or said would make the situation less tragic. She could accept that reality, and he couldn't. She was the Mass-every-Sunday Catholic. She was the branch on a sprawling Cuban family tree. She had a community, and he had nothing except his mother, who was a loner like him. To Lala, loss like this was a part of life you faced and accepted, because more loss was always on the way. To him, it moved the earth.

He took her, and he held her.

She knew he needed her. She could feel his arousal blooming out of his grief. He touched her golden face, and her skin felt hot. Her black hair was wet and in disarray, and the messiness of it made him want to touch it and run his fingers through it, which he did. She took two steps backward and took the fringe of her black Door County tank top in her hands. He'd bought it for her months earlier; he was pleased that she was wearing it. She peeled it up her taut stomach and pulled it over her head, baring her full breasts for him. His hands were on her.

They came together, kissing. The time apart, the distance, the arguments, melted away. He knelt in front of her and removed the rest of her clothes. He kissed her stomach, kissed up her body to her face. Her fingers, with sharp nails, pushed his shorts down. They were naked; they were pressed together. It was the Fourth of July, and fireworks lit up their eyes. He had never needed a woman so much.

She led him to the bedroom. They lay facing each other, touching, but then she pulled him on top of her. Her knees bent, and her legs separated. He was trapped between her thighs; he was inside her. Everything else in the world finally fled his mind, and the only things left were her skin, breath, and wetness.

The storm raging outside sounded distant and unimportant, nothing but a summer rain.

Cab awoke two hours later. It was a short night, but he felt as if he'd slept forever.

It wasn't light outside. He could barely see. He stretched out a hand to the warm indentation on the mattress, but the bed was empty. Lala was gone. There was no note and no message on his phone. He pushed himself up, propped against a pillow. Through the doorway to the living room, he could see that her clothes were gone, too. The sensation of their lovemaking lingered with a satisfying ache on his body, but if it hadn't been for the faint essence of her perfume in the sheets, he wouldn't have been able to swear she had ever been there.

38

Annalie rapped her knuckles on the window of the Thunderbird, and Peach bolted awake. She shook herself, reached across the car, and unlocked the passenger door. Her friend scrambled inside out of the rain.

Peach stared at the downtown streets. It was early. Tampa was a ghost town. She was in her usual parking place, spot 52 in the lot outside the Common Way research office. Around them, the storm felt like a living thing. The lot was filling up like a lake, and if the water got much deeper, she was afraid that her car would float away.

Peach gave her a quick, earnest hug. 'I was afraid you wouldn't be able to get here.'

'We don't have a lot of time,' Annalie replied. 'In another three or four hours, everything on the coast will be impassable. You should be home, Peach, not here. It's not safe. What's going on? Your message said something about Deacon.'

'He's gone. They took him.'

'Who did?'

Peach took a breath and explained everything. She played his voicemail for Annalie, who frowned as Deacon talked about gun trafficking.

'You saw blood?' Annalie said quietly.

Peach nodded.

'You've tried calling him?'

'Over and over. No answer.'

Annalie was silent. The wind roared.

'If he was asking questions about Frank Macy, it's possible that Macy heard about it,' Annalie said finally. 'Someone could have tipped him off.'

'But what is Macy doing?' Peach asked. 'What's he up to?'

Annalie stared through the windshield. Drips of rain slid down her face. 'Whatever it is, it's not good.'

Peach folded her hands tightly together. 'You think he killed Deacon, don't you?'

'I have no idea, Peach,' Annalie said. 'I hope not.'

'We need to find Macy.'

Annalie grabbed her wrist. '*We* don't need to do anything. Not you.'

'I can't just sit here.'

'Go into the office. Go through Justin's e-mails. Go through Deacon's e-mails. See if you can find anything that would tell us what Macy is doing or where we can find him.'

Peach felt her face flush, and she opened her mouth to complain, but Annalie interrupted her. 'Listen to me, Peach. Please. You're emotionally involved. You're out of control. I don't blame you, but that's the way you make mistakes. Let me worry about Frank Macy. Let me find him. If you find anything that would help, you call me right away. Okay?'

Peach wanted to scream, but she knew Annalie was right. 'Yeah, okay. Keep me posted. Don't leave me in the dark.'

'I won't.'

Annalie got out of the car and ran to her Corolla. A few seconds later, she drove away, carving out waves of water as if she were parting the seas.

*

The more time Peach spent in the office, the more her frustration grew.

The foundation was closed for the holiday, but even if the office had been open, the storm would have kept everyone away. She worked in peace, listening to the walls rock. Her fingers flew on the keyboard, but she learned nothing. She went back through Justin's e-mails but didn't find anything that would explain what he had discovered. She knew Deacon's password, and she studied his e-mails, too, but there was nothing other than his usual campaign research.

She checked her brother's office voicemail. There was one new message from Caprice, which had come in the previous evening.

'*Deacon, it's me. Tried your cell phone, but couldn't reach you. Give me a call in the morning. I'm going over to Diane's, and we'll ride out the storm there. If you need me, I should be at the house by 10 a.m. or so.*'

No one had been able to reach Deacon. No one knew where he was.

She didn't know what to do next. She logged into Justin's account again and opened up the edited photograph taken outside the Crab Shack. He'd used the picture to guide her to his hideaway, but there was nothing left inside the house except the article about Frank Macy poking out from under a file cabinet. Whatever he wanted her to find, someone else had already found it and stolen it.

Then she remembered the photograph in the broken frame on the floor of the bedroom. It was the same photograph of herself that was attached to the e-mail. When she'd found the article about Frank Macy, she'd forgotten all about the photograph on the floor. If Justin wanted a picture of her in his hideaway, he had plenty of others to choose, but he'd used that one. She didn't think it was an accident.

He was trying to tell her something more.

She decided to go back to Justin's safe house. It was empty. No one would be there. She couldn't stay in the office any longer, doing nothing.

Before she logged out, however, she took another look at Justin's messages and saw the other e-mail he'd failed to send. The one to Ogden Bush.

I need to see you.

She grabbed her coat, but instead of leaving, she headed down the empty office corridor to Bush's office. She let herself inside, the way she had two days before, and unlocked the man's filing cabinets again. The file on Justin was still missing. She remembered a file on Birch Fairmont in another drawer, and that file suddenly took on new significance for her. She opened the other drawer, but the file on Birch was gone, too.

Bush had cleaned house.

She relocked the filing cabinets and did a search of the man's desk. She reviewed pink handwritten phone messages, copies of research reports that been gathered and written by the employees in the office, lists of media contacts around the state, and drafts of Diane's events calendar for the week ahead. Nothing looked unusual or suspicious. Bush wouldn't leave anything lying around that he didn't want someone to see. It was a dead end.

Then she saw that his voicemail light was flashing.

With only the slightest hesitation, Peach punched the speakerphone, and she heard a voice with a faint southern drawl fill the office. '*I need to talk to you right now. It's urgent.*'

It was a short message, but the voice was familiar. She'd heard it before. For a moment she struggled to place it, and then she knew. The recognition washed over her. The voice belonged to the man who called himself Curtis Clay, the man who'd pretended to be a

St Petersburg cop. The man who had held a gun on her and tried to put her in handcuffs in Justin's apartment.

That man. That fraud. He was in bed with Ogden Bush.

She clicked off the phone, but as she did, a silky voice called to her from the office doorway.

'What are you doing here, Peach?'

Ogden Bush had his hands on his hips. He wore a wet fedora. His raincoat dripped on the floor, and she could see a tailored black suit underneath it. His face was dark and curious, but he didn't sound angry. He was too smooth to blow up at her, and that made her trust him even less.

'You're a spy,' she said.

'Excuse me?'

'You're a spy. You've been spying on *me*.'

Bush's face melted into a politician's smile. He sat down in the guest chair and made no attempt to dislodge Peach from behind his desk. He crossed his legs, displaying wet shined shoes, and smoothed the creased lines of his suit pants.

'We're all spies at this place, Peach. Isn't that what you're doing, too? You didn't need to sneak in here. If you wanted answers about something, you could have talked to me. Exactly what do you want?'

Peach stabbed the button on Bush's phone. The short message played on the speakerphone. 'Who is he?' she asked.

'He's a contact of mine,' Bush said.

'He works for you.'

'Lots of people work for me. You work for me, too.'

'No, I work for Diane Fairmont.'

'We both do,' Bush said.

'That man calls himself Curtis Clay,' Peach went on. 'He called my home and pretended to be a cop. I caught him in Justin's apartment.'

'What were *you* doing in Justin's apartment?' Bush asked with a wink. 'You see? I told you, we're all spies. None of us is innocent.'

'Who is he?' she repeated.

Bush picked up a small pewter replica of the Bok tower from his desk and played with it between his fingers. He didn't answer. She smelled his cologne, and she watched his ruby ring glint under the light. His face was a mask, but she knew he was thinking fast. Looking for a way out.

'What do you know about Justin's death?' Peach asked.

'I only know what the police tell me, Peach.'

'I don't believe you. You kept a file on Justin. He wanted to talk to you the night before he was killed. Why did he want to see you?'

'I have no idea,' Bush told her calmly. 'We never spoke. This is the first I'm hearing about it. I think you should go home, Peach. The storm is getting bad. The office is closed. You shouldn't be here.'

'My next call is to Ms Fairmont. I'm going to tell her everything.'

Bush shrugged. 'She knows what I'm doing.'

'We'll see.'

Peach watched the man's face. She wasn't a poker player, but she knew a bluff when she saw it. She picked up the phone and punched the number for Ms Fairmont's house. Ringing buzzed through the speakerphone. Before there was an answer, Bush leaned casually across the desk and depressed the button on the receiver to cut off the call. 'All right, I think we can arrive at a compromise,' he said. 'The fact is, there are things that Diane is better off not knowing. Candidates think they want to know everything, but really, they don't. It's what we call plausible deniability.'

'I call it lying,' Peach said.

'Whatever. Okay, you want to know who that man is? His name is Curtis Ritchie. He's a private investigator, and yes, I use him from time to time. There's nothing unusual about it. It's common practice. I asked him to gather some information for me on Justin's activities.'

'He told me he was a St Petersburg cop.'

'I told Curtis to stay within the bounds of the law,' Bush said, 'but he's ex-police. Sometimes he forgets where the lines are drawn now that he's on his own.'

'Why were you spying on Justin?'

Bush continued to twist the pewter model between his graceful fingers. 'I found out that Justin was asking questions that were outside his job responsibilities here at the foundation. I was curious. I wanted to know why.'

'About the Labor Day murders.'

The man's eyebrows rose, as if she knew more than he expected. 'Yes.'

'Why do you care?'

'The only things that scare me in political campaigns are things I don't know.'

'Were you afraid something might come out that would make Ms Fairmont look bad?'

'If there was anything like that,' Bush said, 'I wanted to find out about it before our enemies did.'

Staring at him, Peach realized for the first time that she no longer had any idea who their enemies were. Once everything had seemed clear to her. Now she was caught in a labyrinth of ulterior motives. She didn't know whom to trust.

Deacon had already told her: *Don't trust anybody.*

'What did Curtis Ritchie find out?' Peach asked. 'He called you last night. His message said it was urgent.'

'I never reached him.'

'What was he doing?'

'He was following someone that you led him to,' Bush admitted. 'An unpleasant character named Frank Macy.'

Peach wanted to jump across the desk. '*Where?* Where is Macy?'

'I don't know. The last time I talked to Curtis, he said that Macy was in the industrial docks area, heading toward the Picnic Island pier. He thought Macy might be meeting someone. I haven't been able to reach him since then.'

39

Cab pulled into the cobblestoned driveway of Diane's estate. The wrought-iron gate ahead of him, sculpted with herons and vine leaves, was closed. He turned off the Corvette's engine. Rain gushed horizontally across the windshield. He saw no security staffing the gate or patrolling inside the wall. He didn't like that the exterior of the estate was deserted. The wall was built for privacy, not protection, and an intruder could easily get to the house without being challenged. He would have preferred to see men with guns outside.

His phone rang, and he saw the caller ID for Caprice Dean on the line.

'Good morning, Cab,' she said. 'What a beautiful day.'

'Is it?'

'Oh, you're not scared off by a little storm, are you?'

He could hear the grin on her lips as she teased him. He was disappointed that he still felt a physical reaction to the undercurrents in her voice. There were some women like that, women you had to work to resist.

'Apparently, the storm scared off the security at Diane's estate,' he replied.

A sheen of ice returned to her voice. 'Where are you?'

'In her driveway.'

'Cab, really? Do you have to bother Diane today?'

'I do,' he said.

He knew she wanted to snap at him, but was restraining her

temper. 'Well, I'm going to be over there myself in a couple of hours. If you're still there, I'm going to kick you out. Unless you can play nice and forget about work and just have cocktails with us, that is.'

'Not today, I'm afraid.'

'Your mother's coming, too.'

'Yes, she told me.' He added: 'You said you were going to increase security here at the house.'

'I did. We should have two men inside right now.'

'Inside,' Cab said.

'Yes, inside. Maybe you haven't noticed the torrential rain and sixty-mile-an-hour winds. Do you really expect me to have people standing outside in the storm?'

Cab frowned. 'No.'

'Well, good, can you get off my back? Not that I would typically complain about you being on my back.'

He didn't take the bait. 'What do you want, Caprice?'

'I wanted to apologize for yesterday.'

'That's not necessary.'

'I overreacted,' she went on. 'I'm not used to people telling me no. Actually, I enjoyed having you stand up to me. It makes me even more interested in you, personally and professionally.'

'Professionally, I'm in charge of solving crimes, and you're in charge of protecting your pretty political ass.'

'That sounds about right. And personally?'

'Personally, nothing is going to happen.'

She sounded disappointed. 'Don't I have a chance to persuade you? I can be very persuasive if you give me an opportunity. I'm not looking for a commitment. Neither one of us wants the white picket fence, do we? We're not signing up for marriage and kids.'

Kids. Cab thought again: *Boy or girl.* No, he didn't want a commitment, but he wanted more than he would find in bed with Caprice.

'I was going to call you today,' he said. 'I found out what happened between Birch and Diane.'

'No comment,' she said.

'I want to know if you and Lyle knew about it. I want to know *who else* knew.'

'And I repeat: No comment.'

'Fine. You won't talk. Let me tell you what I think. You and Lyle found out what happened that Saturday night. You knew exactly what Birch did to Diane. You knew you were running a monster on the ballot.'

Caprice's voice tensed with frustration. 'Cab, you are playing with fire here. This kind of scandal is exactly what Diane's enemies want, and it will do nothing to protect her. Do you really want to be a tool for Ramona Cortes?'

'You're talking about politics, Caprice, but I'm talking about murder. People died. Your *fiancé* died. Don't you care what really happened?'

'How dare you say something like that to me!' she exploded at him. 'I don't need you to lecture me about what I owe to those people. I know what happened. I know who was responsible for it.'

'Last chance. Did you and Lyle know what Birch did?'

'Yes, *of course* we knew!' Caprice hissed at him. 'Do you think we're idiots? Do you think we could spend all that time with a candidate and not realize he's a self-absorbed, cheating, abusive son of a bitch? News flash for you, Cab. So are half the politicians in Washington and Tallahassee. Birch would have fit right in.'

'Maybe so, but he never would have been elected if the truth had come out back then. He would have been crucified for what he did to Diane. It would have been the end of the Common Way Party before it even started.'

'You're right. That's true. It's true today, too. Why the hell do you think we kept it a secret? Why do you think it's *still* a secret? People like heroes and martyrs, Cab. They want the image, they don't want reality. Do you think anyone would thank you if you exposed what Birch did? That's not what they want to hear. The person you'd be hurting is Diane, because *victims* don't get elected governor.'

'But sometimes victims kill their abusers,' Cab said.

Caprice was silent. Then she said: 'What on earth are you talking about?'

'Diane paid money to Frank Macy two days before the murders. What was that money for?'

The silence dragged out again, even longer this time. 'I can't believe you'd even suggest something like that.'

'Diane was seen with Macy.'

'I don't care who saw what. Diane did not have Birch killed.'

'Are you sure?'

'Cab, do you think we could have kept what Birch did out of the press without Diane being involved? I talked to her personally. Just her and me, woman to woman. It was *her* choice to keep it a secret. It was her choice to go on with the campaign. You may find this hard to imagine, but she believes in Common Way, and she believed in it back then. She chose to stay silent about Birch, because she wanted him to win despite everything else. Do you think she would turn around and have him murdered?'

'Do you have another explanation?'

'I don't,' Caprice said, 'but I know Diane. She wouldn't do that. Besides, we're not just talking about Birch. Can you honestly tell me that you think Diane would let innocent people die?'

'Not if she knew what was going to happen. Maybe she didn't know.'

'You think she paid Frank Macy, but she didn't know what he was going to do?' Caprice asked.

'Macy's not an idiot. He's smart. He'd protect himself. Murder Birch, and people wonder why. They ask uncomfortable questions. But *assassinate* Birch and make it look like domestic terrorism? Now it's a political crime. Now there are fall guys. Ham Brock. Chuck Warren. The Liberty Empire Alliance.'

'You're wrong,' she said. 'Frank Macy sold drugs to Drew. Diane blames him for Drew's death. That's all I know. If she paid him, it wasn't for the reasons you think. It was something else. Maybe she just wanted him to go away.' She paused, and then she added harshly: 'And I'll tell you another thing. It's no accident that this is coming out now. Whatever went on between Macy and Diane, I'm certain that Ramona Cortes knows what it is. Ramona was Macy's lawyer. She wants it exposed, and she wants your fingerprints on this, not hers.'

'I still have to talk to Diane. I have to know what happened.'

'Do whatever you need to do, but I'm begging you to be discreet. The suspicion alone will destroy Diane if it becomes public.'

'You think I don't know that?' Cab asked.

'I think you do, but you don't seem to care.'

Cab wondered if that was true. Tarla had accused him more than once of being obsessed with answers, regardless of who got hurt. After Vivian Frost's betrayal, he'd come to believe that anyone in the world was capable of evil. He took it personally when people lied to him.

Maybe that was the problem. This was personal. Diane had never told him about the loss of his child, and he wanted to hurt her as a kind of revenge. He was ready to believe she was guilty of something terrible. He was ready to ruin her.

'I care about this more than you think,' Cab told her. 'I hate what Birch did to Diane.'

He waited for an answer but heard only thunder. 'Caprice?'

And then again: 'Caprice?'

Finally, she came back on the line. Her voice was different. She didn't sound like a politician anymore. 'Cab, we have a problem.'

'What is it?'

'Ogden Bush just called me on my other line. Peach was in his office a few minutes ago.'

'Peach? Why?'

'Apparently, someone broke into her house last night,' Caprice told him. 'Her brother Deacon is missing. Peach says Deacon was talking to his prison contacts about Frank Macy before he disappeared. Cab, I don't know exactly what happened ten years ago, but right now, I don't care. I'm more concerned with what's happening today. Get inside, and check on Diane.'

40

Peach crept along the scrub-lined gravel road through the docklands area. The pavement was invisible under the rippling water. Pebbles and sand cracked on her windshield like bullets shot by the fierce gales. Her wipers fought a losing battle against the rain, and she leaned forward, trying to see. A quarter mile ahead, the road split. A dead end led toward the port, where she could see a mammoth tanker docked in the water. To her left, a sign pointed toward Picnic Island Park. She headed that way, thudding across railroad tracks and driving slowly, unsure of the depth of the water underneath her tires. Ahead of her, palm trees and evergreens bowed toward the east, as if to say: *Run. Run that way. Run fast.*

The road ended at a crescent beach adjoining the bay.

The sprawling waterside park was the heel on the boot that made up the Tampa peninsula. Facing west, she stared at the narrowest point of the channel leading into Old Tampa Bay, across the water from the city of St Petersburg. The low-lying park was webbed with marshes and creeks. It was mostly wild and unkempt, matted with sea grass. Fuel tanks and mountains of crushed sandstone loomed in the industrial area bordering the park. A concrete pier jutted into the water beside a boat launch. Angry waves threw themselves over the pier, sending up twelve-foot clouds of spray.

She turned off the engine. The sky was black, like night. She could barely open her car door into the wind. When she stepped into three inches of water, she felt herself thrown backward by the force of the gusts. Her clothes were sodden. The rain pelleted her face; she had to shield her eyes. The noise of the storm was deafening, a shrieking chorus of water and wind.

At first, she thought the parking lot was empty, but then she spotted a car hidden inside a grove of trees. It was a red Cutlass, heavily dinged with years of abuse. The car was littered with wet leaves and had obviously been stranded here for hours. She staggered in a zigzag across the lot. Something slimy brushed her ankle, and she realized it was a fish, swept from the bay into the shallow lake that now covered the parkland. Better a fish than an alligator. She splashed forward onto spongy mud that sucked at her sneakers, and when she reached the abandoned Cutlass, she yanked open the door and piled inside.

The car smelled of smoke and French fries, despite an old pine air freshener dangling from the mirror. Its torn leather seats were buried under crumpled food wrappers and newspapers. A GPS navigator was suctioned to the dashboard. She spotted an old gallon milk jug one-third filled with a yellowish liquid, and her lip wrinkled in disgust.

Peach looked in the back seat. She saw a pair of binoculars and realized they were made for night vision. She spotted the corner of a laptop poking out from under a *Penthouse* magazine, and she needed two hands to lift the machine into the front seat. The laptop was a Toughbook, made for rugged use. She traced a USB cable plugged into one of the computer ports to a digital camera.

This was a stake-out car. A spy car.

She opened the glove compartment, which was crammed with electronic charger cables and receipts. She rifled through the pile of papers but didn't find any insurance information or owner records. She lifted the lid of the laptop and pushed the power button, but the battery was dead.

Peach flipped down the sun visor. She found a stack of more than a dozen identification cards tucked under an elastic strap. She pulled out the laminated cards and flipped through them. The card issuers were all different. State and county agencies. Trade associations. Corporations. Banks. The cards were fake, using a variety of aliases, but several of the cards included a photograph, and she recognized the man in the pictures.

It was Curtis Ritchie. Ogden Bush's private investigator. The man she knew as Curtis Clay.

Peach slid her phone from her pocket and called Annalie, and she was grateful when the woman answered. The connection was intermittent and ripped with static, but she could hear her.

'Peach, what is it? Are you okay?'

'I'm fine. I'm over in Picnic Island Park.'

Annalie's unhappiness cut through the line. 'I told you to stay in the office. What are you doing there?'

'The man who was following me in the red Cutlass, he's a PI named Curtis Ritchie. He works for Ogden Bush. Bush said that Ritchie was following Frank Macy last night, and the trail led here. I found the car, but he's nowhere around.'

'You should get out of there,' Annalie said. 'Right now.'

'There's no one here–'

'It doesn't matter. Someone may be coming back to get that car.'

'I need to see you,' Peach said.

'It's not safe to travel. The storm's getting worse.'

'*Please*. I'm going to Justin's safe house. Can you meet me there?'

There was a long pause, and she thought Annalie might say no. Then the woman replied: 'All right. It will take me an hour. Be careful.'

Peach hung up the phone.

She gathered up Ritchie's Toughbook and digital camera, and

she grabbed the charger cables from the glove compartment, hoping they matched the devices. She shoved the equipment under her shirt, which provided meager protection against the storm. The hardened plastic shells were cold on her damp skin. She opened the door and ducked out into the rain and kicked the door shut behind her.

Clutching the equipment against her body, Peach struggled back to her Thunderbird. She was nearly blind. Twice, the wind literally blew her to her knees. Pine needles whipped around her face, stinging like razors. The water at her feet swirled in foamy whirlpools, keeping her off balance. At her car, she dumped everything onto the passenger seat and heaved herself inside. She was shivering. She turned on the engine and blasted heat into the interior. The wipers shot back and forth.

She examined the electronic equipment, hoping it wasn't permanently damaged by the storm. When she checked the cables, she found a car charger with an adapter end that fit the laptop. She plugged it in and connected the power end to the car's cigarette lighter. The AC indicator on the damp machine turned green.

'Yes,' she murmured to herself.

Then she jumped so high her head struck the roof.

Someone rapped sharply on the driver's side window. Peach saw a man completely wrapped in a yellow slicker. His face was flushed and wet, and he looked as young as she was, with a pimply face. His hood was pushed down, and he wore a security officer's cap, robed in plastic. Behind him, ten yards away, she spotted a white SUV labeled PARK RANGER. The lights were on. The engine was running.

Automatically, Peach hit the lock on the car doors. The park policeman rapped on the window again. She lowered the window an inch, and he pressed his lips close to the gap and shouted to be heard.

'Ma'am, the park is closed.'

She smiled and shouted back. 'I was just leaving!'

'Are you okay? I saw you fall.'

'I'm fine! Thank you!'

His eyes traveled to the laptop and camera, and then he looked across the roof of the car to the border of the parking lot, where he spotted the Cutlass. She watched his eyes squint with suspicion.

'Ma'am, what are you doing down here?'

'What?' She pretended not to hear.

'Does that equipment belong to you, ma'am?' he demanded, pointing at the Toughbook on the seat.

'You mean the laptop? Of course.'

He frowned. 'Can you show me some identification, ma'am?'

'Is this necessary? I need to get home. I'm sorry – I didn't know the park was closed.'

'Your ID, ma'am,' he repeated.

Peach sighed and dug in her back pocket for her wallet. She slid out her driver's license and passed it through the crack in the window. Rain flooded down the glass inside the car.

'Turn off your car please, ma'am.'

'Look, officer, I'm cold and wet. I wasn't doing anything wrong. Can I please just have my license back?'

He didn't return her license. Instead, he pushed through the flooded park toward the Cutlass. She saw him peer inside and make a circuit around the vehicle. He opened the door, seeing what she saw: the clutter of a man who lived much of his life in his car. He popped the trunk release, checked it, and slammed it shut. He climbed inside the vehicle, and she remembered that she'd left Curtis Ritchie's roster of fake ID cards on the passenger seat in full view.

It didn't take long. The officer was smart enough to know that something was very wrong. He re-emerged into the storm, his face grim. He retreated from the car and headed straight for her. Peach knew where she was headed next. A prison holding cell.

She watched him come closer. As she debated what to do, she saw the park policeman pitch forward into the green water. He'd tripped on something snagged on the trunk of a palm tree. Whatever it was jutted above the surface like the back of a turtle. As he pushed himself up, the officer's arm disappeared under the water, and Peach watched with a weird sense of horror as his hand reappeared a second later, holding something at the end of his fingers.

It took her a moment, through the wild rain, to see that the policeman was clutching a fistful of hair. He was holding a head. A head, white and pale and dead, connected to a body.

She knew that face. It was Curtis Ritchie.

Peach screamed.

She shoved the Thunderbird into reverse and shot backwards, spinning the wheel. The car spun, as if she were riding a Tilt-a-Whirl. It turned, kicking up spray, its tires grinding on gravel and water. The engine coughed once and then roared. She shoved the gear down again, and she sped out of the park without looking back.

41

A bodyguard met Cab at the front door of Diane's estate. The man wasn't tall, but he was heavily muscled, and his brown eyes moved constantly, surveying Cab from head to toe and studying the estate's empty porch, where a curtain of rain spilled from the roof. He seemed competent. But he was one man, and it was a big house: he couldn't be everywhere at once.

'Where is she?' Cab asked.

'The sunroom.'

'Alone?'

'No, Garth Oakes is with her.'

'Do you have a partner here?' he asked the bodyguard.

The man shook his head. 'He was in an accident on his way up from Bradenton. I'm on my own.'

Cab frowned. One man.

'Stay alert,' he told him.

He hung up his Burberry trench coat and followed the bodyguard down the wood floor of the hallway. The house was warm. The sconce lights on the walls flickered. At the end of the hall, a wide oak door opened into an airy sunroom, but there was no sun. The room, on the corner of the house, featured a wall of floor-to-ceiling windows, including two patio doors leading out into the garden. The glass was silver with rain.

A chocolate-brown frieze decorated the floor, but the carpet ended twelve feet from the patio doors, where Italian marble took over. The wall on Cab's left was white, with stylized square panels and gold molding. A chandelier dripped crystal from the ceiling and was bright against the darkness of the morning. A claw-foot settee, with Tiffany table lamps on either end, was positioned on the wall on Cab's right. The room also included a breakfast nook near the tall windows.

Diane lay face down on a massage table that had been erected in the center of the room. She was naked, with a towel discreetly draped across her backside. Garth, his hands glistening with oil, kneaded the muscles in her neck with his thumbs, under the fringe of her bobbed brown hair. The sound of the door made Diane open her eyes. She saw Cab and didn't look surprised. Her eyes closed again.

'Give us a few minutes, will you, Garth?' she murmured.

'Oh, sure, of course.'

Garth wiped his hands on a towel. His tanned skin looked almost orange under the chandelier. He wore a silk lavender polo shirt, black-striped Zubaz, and Crocs that matched his shirt. He'd swapped his ponytail for a hair knot on top of his head.

'Hey,' he said to Cab.

The masseur was subdued. He grabbed a sport coat, which sagged with weight. Cab figured that the man's gun was shoved into one of the pockets. The masseur brushed by him as he left the room. Cab turned away to give Diane privacy, and he avoided the reflections in the windows. He heard her climb off the massage table and listened to the swish of fabric as she covered herself with a robe.

'I'm decent,' she murmured.

She sat in the breakfast nook near the patio windows. Her long fingers cradled a champagne flute, filled with a mimosa. She watched the storm assault the glass, and her face looked far away.

Cab took a seat across from her. 'It's not safe sitting so close to the windows.'

She shrugged. 'They're reinforced for storms.'

'Not for bullets,' he said.

She gave him a strange look. 'Is there a threat?'

'There may be.'

Diane showed no concern for her safety. She gave the French doors a curious look, as if seeing a gunman outside would be as interesting as seeing a lost doe. She was distracted, and he wondered if Tarla had called her. He wouldn't put it past his mother to give her best friend a warning. *Cab's coming. He knows.* As if reading his mind, Diane said: 'Dr Smeltz talked to me.'

'Ah.'

'Someone stole my medical files. He says it was you.'

'No, it wasn't me, but I was able to retrieve them. They're safe. You won't be reading anything in the papers.'

Diane didn't look comforted. Her face tightened with fury. 'Do you have any idea how violated I feel?'

'I think I do.'

Diane tugged the flaps of her robe tighter below her neck. Something about the gesture gave him a vivid and unwanted memory of their two bodies together. He wondered if the same image was in her own head. It had felt right at the time, but almost immediately, it had gone wrong.

'So,' she said. 'You know.'

'Yes, I know.'

She leaned her head back and stared at the ceiling. She was a powerful woman who looked powerless. 'I told you that afternoon changed my life.'

He said nothing.

'I suppose you're going to ask how I could have kept this from you,' she went on. 'It's a fair question. I've thought about it myself a great deal. Then and now.'

Cab shook his head. 'Obviously, I understand. I don't like it, but I understand.'

'Still, she was your child, too.'

He wasn't prepared for how that one sentence cut open his heart and left him bleeding. *She*. A girl. He'd been summoning his courage to ask the question, and now she had answered it for him. She recognized what she'd done, and her face filled with sincere distress. 'I'm sorry,' she continued. 'I didn't mean to break it like that, but I thought you would have seen it in my file.'

'I didn't look that closely.'

'Well, yes. She. A daughter.'

He shrugged. The gesture was false. 'A daughter I never would have known anyway. I suppose it doesn't matter.'

'Of course it matters, Cab!' Diane exclaimed. 'And for what it's worth, I apologize. Back then, I had no choice but to hide the truth from you, and from Tarla, too. It doesn't make it right, but you can appreciate the situation I was in. After that, well, I have no excuses to give you. You deserved the truth, but I never sought out the right moment. I didn't want to revisit what happened. Even so, a day doesn't go by that I don't think about her.'

His emotions betrayed him. Whatever he wanted to say lodged in his throat and went nowhere. His eyes felt wet.

'I never thought it compromised a strong man to cry,' she told him. 'I've had years to deal with this. It's new to you.'

Cab wanted to ask what he needed to ask and then escape. He cleared his throat. 'There are things I need to know.'

'I'm sure. It changes everything, doesn't it, knowing what a sick son of a bitch my husband was? Why do you think I've worked so hard to keep the truth hidden? I'd like to tell you that Birch was sorry for what he'd done. Maybe for a day or two, he was, but then he went back to being the man I knew. Utterly self-absorbed. Utterly heartless.'

'And yet . . .'

'And yet I covered for him. That's right. Was I weak? Back then, yes, I probably was. I thought it was my fault. That's the way victims are programmed to think. Besides, I was the one who invited you into my bed. I had to accept the consequences.'

'Not those consequences,' Cab said.

'No. Looking back, I was a fool about a lot of things. Some lessons are hard to learn.'

'Diane, I need to ask you about the murders,' he told her.

'It was *not* Drew,' she snapped. 'There's simply no way he was involved. Yes, I told my son what happened to me. Yes, he hated Birch. Did he want to kill him? I'm sure he did, but Drew didn't have the inner strength to do something like that. You're wrong, Cab.'

'I believe you. Drew wasn't the shooter. Whoever pulled the trigger had a calculating mind. He knew exactly what he was doing.'

'Then what else can I tell you?' Diane asked.

'Drew doesn't fit the profile of the murderer,' Cab went on, 'but Frank Macy does.'

Diane cocked her head in surprise. He tried to read her eyes to see whether the surprise was genuine or an act, but whatever she felt was quickly subsumed by her bitterness toward the man. Her knuckles tightened around the crystal glass in her hand.

'Why on earth would Macy kill Birch?'

'Maybe because someone paid him,' Cab said.

Diane slowly put down the glass. She closed her eyes for a long second. He could see her chest swell with a deep breath.

She pushed back her chair and got up, and she wandered into the dead center of the room, directly below the chandelier. She crossed her arms and stared at the floor. Her feet were bare on the brown carpet.

'Tarla saw us,' she said. 'She saw me with Macy, didn't she?'

'Yes, she did.'

'I thought I caught a glimpse of her on the trail. That poor dear. All these years, she wondered if I arranged to have Birch killed, and she never said a word to me about it. She never asked me for the truth.'

'She knew what Birch did to you.'

'Still, that's a true friend.' She looked up at Cab. 'I wasn't paying off Macy to commit murder. That's not what the money was for.'

'It was two days before Labor Day, Diane.'

'I know. I can understand your suspicion.'

'Then explain it to me. Why did you pay Frank Macy?'

He wasn't prepared for her answer.

'I wanted him to get me a gun,' Diane replied.

'A gun? Why?'

Diane sat down on the settee. She looked small with the windows framed behind her. 'That's a good question. I'm not entirely sure I know the answer. At the time, I planned to kill myself. I can't tell you the kind of despair I felt. I couldn't admit publicly what Birch had done to me, but I wasn't sure I could go on living with him. Knowing what he'd taken from me. I had visions of putting that gun in my mouth, but . . .'

'But what?' Cab asked.

'I have to be honest. I thought about killing Birch, too. Maybe I would have killed him and then killed myself. I don't know. However, I'd be lying if I said I wasn't thinking about murdering my husband.' She shook her head. 'Despite that, I didn't kill him.

Maybe with a few more days, I would have screwed up the courage and done it, but someone beat me to it.'

Cab could read her face. He knew she was telling him the truth. 'Did Macy get you the gun?'

'He did.'

'Do you still have it?'

A tear slipped down her cheek. 'No. Drew found it. It was the gun that he . . .'

Cab nodded. 'I'm sorry.'

'I blame Frank Macy for his death, but in the end, I have to blame myself, too.'

'Who else knows that Macy sold you a gun?' Cab asked.

'Only Macy and me, I assume. And now you and Tarla. Macy could have told someone, but it wouldn't have been in his interest to admit it. I'm sure the gun wasn't legally obtained.'

'What about Ramona Cortes?' he asked. 'Did she contact you? Did she try to use your transaction with Macy as leverage? Defense attorneys will use any ammunition available to them to get their client a better deal.'

'Indeed they will.'

'Did she?' he repeated.

Diane trembled, like a sapling caught in the storm. 'I don't know why you're asking about this. There's no reason to think Macy had anything to do with Birch's death. You should just drop it.'

Cab got up and walked over to her. The black windows felt dangerous. He knelt in front of the settee.

'Maybe Macy didn't kill Birch. Or maybe we're simply missing something. Either way, Macy is in the middle of whatever's going on right now. Justin was looking at him, and now Justin's dead. Deacon Piper is missing. The question is why.'

'*Deacon?*' Her face turned ashen. 'Deacon is missing? When? What happened?'

'Caprice says someone took him from his house last night.'

Diane's hand flew to her mouth. 'Oh, my God.'

She leaned forward and put her arms tightly around him. He could feel the curves of her body pressing on him through the thin robe. It was awkward; they felt like strangers. Strangers who had slept together. Who had conceived a child.

'What's going on, Diane?' he asked.

She took a deep breath. He had to remind himself who she was and what this meant to her. She was a candidate for the most powerful office in the state. There were people who would do anything to bring her down. And here he was, asking for her worst secrets.

'I did something illegal,' she murmured, as if speaking softly would make her innocent. As if the truth would still be hidden.

He gently eased her away from him. 'What did you do?'

'You have to understand my situation,' she said. 'After Drew died, I went crazy. I'd lost everything. I needed to blame someone. I became obsessed with Frank Macy. I wanted him punished, but nobody could stop him. I worked with the police to get drug charges filed, but he walked away with probation. All I could think about was getting him behind bars. It was like I couldn't go on with my life until I'd avenged Drew's death. I was willing to do anything in my power to put Macy away. And you know – by then – I had a lot of power. A lot of money. It made me think I could do whatever I wanted, and there would be no consequences.'

'What happened?' Cab asked quietly.

'There was a killing in the town of Pass-a-Grille. A bartender was assaulted and died of his injuries. There were no witnesses. It was in a bar that Frank Macy frequented. Macy *knew* the bartender. Don't you see, this was my chance. Finally, I *had* him. So I arranged to have DNA evidence planted in the alley and in Macy's apartment. Macy had no alibi. He was selling drugs that night. You have to love the irony, don't you? He must have suspected I was behind it. Ramona called me, and she didn't say it outright, but she made it clear that she thought I'd paid someone on the police to make sure Macy was framed. However, even she couldn't make this one go away. Macy took a plea and did eight years. Less than he deserved for what he did to Drew, but at least I had a measure of justice.'

Cab closed his eyes. 'Diane–'

'I know. It was wrong. You have to remember, I'm in politics. I convinced myself that the ends justified the means.'

'You didn't do this alone,' he said.

'No.'

'Who helped you? Was it someone with the police?' Then Cab realized that he already knew the answer. 'Deacon Piper,' he said softly. 'It was Deacon, wasn't it? He planted the evidence.'

Diane nodded. 'I needed a spy, you see. Someone I could trust. Deacon knew how to do these things. He handled everything for me. It was a private thing between the two of us. But if he really is missing–'

'Then it means Frank Macy knows what happened,' Cab said. 'He's out for revenge. On both of you.'

42

Dead eyes stared at him from inside the trunk of the car.

Through the overnight hours, rigor had made the body stiff, like an alabaster statue in a museum, fingers frozen into claws. He saw the webbed purple bruise on the forehead where the corner of the flashlight had fractured the skull. Hungry black bugs had already swarmed the hole in his abdomen and begun to feed. Pieces of intestine peeked between their wriggling bodies like a messy plate of pasta.

He retrieved the aluminum pistol case and blew two hitchhiking insects onto the garage floor with a puff of breath. He opened the case and retrieved the gun, which was cradled in gray foam. Checked it. Readied it. The butt felt smooth and sure in his gloved hand. As it had once before.

Ten years ago.

It felt as if he were back in the orange grove. He could feel himself marching in the sandy soil. The crickets chattered warnings that no one else understood. Each hot breath under the hood rebounded in his face. He remembered the sense of freedom as he broke into the clearing. Saw the lights beckoning him. Heard the swell of voices.

He remembered odd things from that night. The first to die, the citrus farmer, had crumbs in his mustache from something he'd eaten. No one had said a thing to him about it, and so he died with pastry on his face. What was his name? He didn't know; he hadn't even read the news reports. They say you always remember the first, the look on the face, the sounds of dying, the way the soul gets ready to flee the body. All of that was true, but of course, the man on the dais wasn't his first.

He remembered his first. He remembered Alison.

He replaced the pistol case in the car and shut the trunk, obscuring the body. When he checked the clock on his phone, he saw that it was ten o'clock. His nerves frayed. Acid rose in his throat. It was soon. It was almost time. Chayla was a bonus, as if the devil had a sense of humor.

He rehearsed everything that would happen next. Walk two blocks to the estate. Head for the lights of the sunroom, where they would be waiting for him, unaware. That was the most important part of what he needed to do, and yet it would take the least time. The hood. The explosions of the gun. The bodies falling. All of that would be over and done in seconds, and he would be on his way. He knew how it would go, because he had done it before.

Back to the foreclosure house for the last time. Take the car. Drive. Drive south, through the storm, on the deserted highways; drive all the way to the Everglades, the wilderness where bodies became food for the alligators. He could dump him there, and it would be over. His work would be done.

He stared at the newspaper articles thumbtacked to the bulletin board. His collection of greatest hits.

FAIRMONT TO ENTER GOVERNOR'S RACE

ONE YEAR LATER, MORE TRAGEDY: FAIRMONT STUNNED BY SON'S SUICIDE

FRANK MACY GETS EIGHT YEARS ON MANSLAUGHTER PLEA

COMMON WAY FOUNDATION INFLUENCE GROWS – AND SO DOES CONTROVERSY

He'd thought about leaving the articles behind to taunt the police, but he didn't think it was necessary now. They would know where the trail led. They would know, but just like ten years ago, they would find only roads that led nowhere.

He shoved the gun in his belt and removed a cigarette lighter from his pocket. With a flick of his thumb, he lit a flame, and then he yanked the first article from the wall, leaving behind a torn scrap of paper. He held a corner to the flame and watched the fire catch, running and spreading, incinerating the pulp to gray ash. As the fire neared his fingers, he let it fall to the floor, where he kicked at the ash with his toe and watched the fragments float. He pulled another article and burned it, and then another and another, and finally, the garage was redolent of smoke and fire, and the bulletin board was empty except for the one article on which he'd scrawled a single word.

Revenge.

'Ashes to ashes,' said a voice from the doorway.

43

Peach clenched the wheel as she flew across the Gandy Bridge.

She felt as if the wind under her tires would lift her like a Cessna and pitch her into the bay. Despite her efforts to keep the car straight, the heavy Thunderbird zigzagged back and forth between the lanes. She was alone heading west, with no more than a few stray headlights shining in the opposite direction as people escaped the Gulf. The rain belched from the sky, looking like a tsunami carrying the sea into her face. Individual drops sped like fleeing dots of light across her windshield. The normally placid bay surged with white foam, and waves as high as houses spewed across the low-lying bridge.

She breathed a sigh of relief when the causeway crossed back onto land. The storm surge had overrun the beaches, and she could see surf pawing at the shoulders of the highway. Justin's safe house was less than a mile west. When she spotted the Crab Shack restaurant, she turned left, splashing through four inches of rippling water as she drove to the very end of the deserted road.

No one else was around. She didn't see a light or a car anywhere. It was just her and the storm.

When she got out of the car, the water was up to her ankles. The limbs of the oak tree hanging over the house groaned with the wind. She mounted the fence with Curtis Ritchie's equipment bundled in her arms, and then she kicked her way toward the porch. The air was full of brine. Her lips tasted of salt. She wrenched open the screen door and watched a snake slither in panic down the concrete steps into the water.

Inside, dampness hung in the living room. She could see patches of black mold growing near the air vents. Cockroaches shot for the walls as she stood in the middle of the room, dripping on the carpet. Everything was as she remembered it, cluttered with the debris left by whoever had searched this place. She didn't think anyone had been here since her last visit. She checked the clock on her phone and wondered when Annalie would arrive.

Peach deposited Curtis Ritchie's laptop and digital phone on a bruised antique coffee table, marred with circular water stains. She studied the compact house and wondered if there was really anything to find here. The search had been thorough. She eyed the ceiling, but there was no crawlspace overhead. The drawers and cabinets in the kitchen were wide open. So was the refrigerator, which had been raided by bugs. The room smelled of spoiled meat.

She returned to Justin's bedroom, where she'd found the newspaper article that had led her to Frank Macy. It had been hidden under the filing cabinet. She toppled the filing cabinet with a crash, scattering more roaches. She'd thought there might be papers taped to the underside, but she was wrong. Frustrated, she sat on the ruins of Justin's mattress.

'You should have told me what you were doing,' she said aloud.

The photograph of herself in front of the Crab Shack restaurant was on the floor in its small broken frame. She bent down and retrieved it. Pieces of glass sprinkled to the carpet like jewels. She removed the photograph from the frame, but nothing was hidden behind it, and nothing was written on the back of the photo paper. It was a print he'd made at Walgreens. She examined the details in the photo, noting that this was the original, unlike the attachment he'd planned to send in his e-mail. The restaurant number was unaltered. So was the arrow on the roof.

She returned the photo to the frame and carefully picked away the remaining glass. She put it back on the little table in front of the window, the way Justin would have had it. He would have been able to stare it as he worked on his computer. She hoped that looking at her made him smile, but it wasn't a particularly flattering picture, with that big goofy smile on her face, hair greasy and unwashed, arm high in the air with her thumb pointing behind her. She remembered telling Justin that all she needed were checkered overalls, and she could have been standing outside a Bob's Big Boy restaurant.

Peach got up and went to Justin's laminate desk. The dismembered computer was unusable. So was the smashed monitor. She sat in his chair, which faced the window. If he'd left her something, it might have been small, like a flash drive, but she found nothing but dusty cables inside the desk drawers. She knew that whoever had been inside the house had stripped the place long before she got here.

The photo mocked her, as if she were laughing at herself. Then she noticed something unusual. In the photo, she was pointing backward with her thumb. The gesture highlighted the restaurant behind her, but as she stared at the photo from Justin's desk, she realized that she was pointing out the window. Outside. Not inside the house.

Peach got up from the desk. Ignoring the flood of rain, she unlocked the window and threw it open. She jutted her face outside, squinting into the downpour. She saw a lake surrounding the house, rather than the grass and weeds of the yard. The thick, decades-old oak tree was on her left, sprouting huge limbs over the roof. On her right was an old propane tank. Scrub brush in the nearby vacant land grew right up to the edge of the chainlink fence.

She climbed out the window and dropped into the water. The ground was mud under her feet. The bark of the old oak tree was furrowed with seams and knots, and she examined the larger gaps with her fingers to see if anything was shoved inside. When that proved fruitless, she picked up the empty propane tank, but it was no more than rusted debris. There was almost nothing else in the yard, except a telescoping ladder lying against the foundation. She dragged it out of the water and examined the underside of each step, but Justin hadn't hidden anything for her there.

It was another dead end.

The photograph was just a photograph, not a message.

Peach returned to the house and shut the window, but it caught on the frame and stayed open half an inch. She was soaked, and she knew she smelled like a wet dog. When she checked her phone again, she saw that Annalie was late. It had been almost ninety minutes since their phone call. When she returned to the living room, she peered through the blinds, hoping to see Annalie's Corolla arrive outside, but she saw only her own T-Bird parked out front. She dialed her friend's number on the phone again, but there was no answer. She didn't leave another message.

She sat on the torn cushions of the sofa. Drips of water splattered on the carpet. The broken antiques of Justin's life were in ruins around her. A baroque gold clock with cherubs. A child's rocking horse with chipped paint. A tapered, rose-colored bottle made of delicate glass. A laughing Buddha with a well-rubbed stomach. Nothing matched anything else. Justin had never cared about a theme for his collection; he simply bought pieces that spoke to him.

His books were scattered across the floor. Biographies of classical composers like Brahms and Haydn. Eclectic science books covering everything from astronomy to microbiology. Novels and essays from the eighteenth century. *Joseph Andrews. Rasselas. Gulliver's Travels.* There were titles in French that she didn't understand. It was all so . . . Justin.

One book caught her eye. She'd missed it before, because it was mostly covered under a record album of Bruno Walter conducting Beethoven's *Fidelio*. Sitting on the sofa, she spotted the green cloth cover of a small book of poetry. It was the same book – the same edition – of poetry by William Blake that she'd purchased for him as a birthday present. She frowned to think he'd already owned a copy, but he had never said a word about that when she gave it to him.

Peach got up from the sofa and picked up the volume. Without even thinking about it, she flipped to the page for 'The Tyger.'

He'd written something there, just as he had in the copy she'd found in his apartment. The handwriting was the same. She knew it all too well. This message was no more helpful than the name – *Alison* – she'd found on the same page in the book she'd given him.

The message said: *You already know the truth.*

Peach shook her head. 'No, I don't know,' she said aloud. 'Justin, I really don't know anything.'

In frustration, she threw the book against the wall, where the binding broke and yellow pages floated to the floor. She was sick of his mysteries. She was sick of his enigmas and codes. He hadn't trusted her enough to tell her what he was doing, and now she was left to pick up the pieces.

She sat down on the sofa again and opened the cover of Curtis Ritchie's laptop. She booted it up on battery power. The thumbnail for Ritchie's username on the login screen was a close-up photograph of a woman's breast. That pig. Frowning, she clicked on the thumbnail, and it asked her for a password. Peach swore. She knew nothing about the man, and she had no idea what he might have used as his password. Randomly, she picked things out of her head. 12345. ABCDEF. 00000. After ten unsuccessful tries, she slapped the lid shut.

This was getting her nowhere. She wondered again: Where was Annalie? She glanced toward the lonely street, which was drowning under the assault of the storm. A finger of worry crept up her spine.

She grabbed Ritchie's digital camera. There was only a single bar of power left on the battery indicator; she didn't have much time to examine it. She opened the file of photographs on the Micro SD card, which consisted of hundreds of pictures, and scrolled to the beginning.

The first picture she saw was of Justin.

He was on the beach behind his condominium. He wore ridiculously long swim trunks, and his feet were in the calm surf. He wore headphones connected to a white iPod in his hand. Probably listening to Mozart. Peach clicked to the next photograph. Justin again. And again. Ritchie had been stalking Justin everywhere he went. She saw Justin getting into his car in the office parking lot. Justin eating a Cuban sandwich at the Kooky Coconut. Justin at a St Pete antique mall. She saw herself, too. Ritchie had plenty of photographs of the two of them together. It made her heart ache, because scrolling through the pictures was like looking at a travel album of the final weeks they'd spent together.

It was also hugely invasive. Ritchie had photographed the two of them inside her house. He'd crept up to the window like a voyeur and snapped shots into her darkened living room. She saw the two of them snuggled together on her sofa. Justin clowning with

Harley Mannequin. Herself, laughing, with her hands over her ears, as he made her listen to a Strauss opera. They were moments frozen into her memory, but she felt cheated now, realizing she had shared them with someone else. Someone who was watching their every move.

She clicked through the rest of the photographs. Justin had successfully kept one aspect of his life secret. There were no pictures of his safe house. There was nothing to suggest that Ritchie knew where this house was, which meant that he hadn't been the one to search it. She wondered how Justin had concealed the location; he'd obviously come here often, and yet somehow he'd made sure that he wasn't followed. That was one advantage of being paranoid. You took precautions.

And yet everywhere else Justin had been, Curtis Ritchie had been there, too. She flipped forward and backward, going faster and faster, hypnotized by everything she saw. For a few brief moments, Justin was alive again.

Justin in Starbucks.

Justin in the produce aisle at Publix.

Justin on the sponge docks in Tarpon Springs.

Justin in Starbucks again.

Justin in Lake Wales. She recognized the environs. Ritchie had followed Justin on the secret trip he made to Lake Wales without her. She saw him at the library. At the Bok Sanctuary. Out on a deserted stretch of highway. Walking out of Dr Smeltz's office with a backpack slung over his arm.

The next photograph showed Justin in a parking lot near the doctor's office. He had something in his hand that looked like the same kind of medical file that Peach had retrieved from the locked supply closet.

What was the file? And where was it now? Whoever had searched his safe house must have found it and removed it.

She kept flipping through the pictures. The camera flashed a warning that the battery was almost dead. It would go black soon. When the camera died, she knew she would feel alone again. Looking at the pictures made her feel that Justin was with her.

Justin at the Pier.

Justin in an antiquarian bookstore.

Justin in Starbucks again.

He'd been in Starbucks a lot, which wasn't unusual, but something about the picture attracted her eyes. The photo was taken from outside, through the shop window. Justin was at a table with his back to the camera, but he wasn't alone. Someone else sat across from him, but all Peach could see when she zoomed in was an arm. A female arm. Justin was meeting a woman at the coffee shop.

Who?

She clicked to the next photograph, which was taken at the same Starbucks on the same day. Ritchie was inside now, at the counter. The angle was reversed. The off-kilter photo showed Justin from the front, and his companion's back was to the camera. Peach stared at the back of a woman's head. Stared at luscious, long dark hair.

Peach began to hear every breath in her chest. She felt dizzy. The throb of a headache split open her forehead. She didn't want to see the next photograph, but she had no choice. She knew what she would see, because she recognized the woman now. She watched the picture fill the small screen, and there she was.

Annalie.

Annalie was at the table with Justin.

PART FOUR

HIT AND RUN

44

The receptionist at the police department in St Pete Beach laughed at Cab over the phone. 'I'm sorry, could you say that again, Detective? I really want to be sure I heard you correctly.'

'You've got an ex-con named Frank Macy whose driver's license record indicates that he has an apartment in St Pete Beach,' he repeated. 'I'd like you to roll a couple uniforms over there to see if he's in his apartment now.'

'You want us to bring some bagels or scones over there with us?' the receptionist asked.

'That's funny,' Cab said. 'I appreciate your sense of humor. I know my timing isn't exactly perfect–'

'Perfect? Detective, maybe you haven't looked outside your window recently, but we have a tropical storm on top of our heads right now. If you look west, you'll probably see Dorothy and Toto blowing past you any minute. So as hard as you may find this to believe, we're not just sitting around the station watching repeats of *Burn Notice*. We're a little busy out here. And we don't have time to send our officers on babysitting detail for some ex-con.'

'I just want to know if he's *there*,' Cab insisted.

'Then I suggest you drive out here yourself and knock on his door,' she snapped. 'Now I've got about a hundred other calls on hold, and some of them may actually be important. Happy Fourth of July, Detective.'

She hung up.

Cab didn't blame her. Nothing would get attention today other than the storm.

He threw his phone on the passenger seat of the Corvette. He was still parked outside the wrought-iron gate of Diane's estate. The neighborhood around him was empty. Some of the residents had probably left town ahead of Chayla, and all the others were inside, cursing the fact that the storm had landed on a summer holiday. As he watched, the lights glowing in the palatial homes went dark. He didn't see lights anywhere now. Not on the street. Not inside Diane's estate. The power was out. The morning was already grim under the black sky, and the outage seemed to extinguish the last glimmer of life.

Cab got out of the car. Despite his black trench coat, he was already wet to his skin where the rain streamed under his collar. He shoved his hands in his pockets and studied the dense foliage closing in around the estate. The brick walls were overgrown with ivy. Trees knelt down and stretched out their branches on both sides of the walls.

He walked to the end of Coachman Street, where the elegant cobblestones ended. He followed the wall of Diane's estate, avoiding the rivers overflowing out of the curbs. Flying leaves made a kind of green snow in the air. Where the road turned, he found a row of compact bungalows on a tree-lined street. There were no cars anywhere. Everyone had pulled their vehicles inside the safety of their garages. He saw no lights here either. The outage covered the entire block.

Turning in the opposite direction, he followed Richards Street to where it ended two hundred yards later at Asbury Place. Nothing was different here. The area felt equally desolate and dark. No cars on the street in either direction. No power. He glanced at a house on the north side of the T-intersection that was obviously deserted, with boarded-up windows and NO TRESPASSING signs posted on the front door. Another foreclosure house among thousands in Florida.

Cab walked toward the bay, where the houses got larger again. He could see the wild panorama ahead of him, besieged by the storm. The thin trunks of the palm trees were bent over like question marks. A spiny frond slapped his face so hard that it felt like the cut of a knife, and when he touched his hand to his cheek, it came away with blood that was quickly washed clean by the driving rain. It was growing more and more unsafe to be outside in the storm. There were no perceptible threats in the neighborhood around him, but that didn't make him feel better. The threats that bothered him were the ones he couldn't see.

Cab returned along the sidewalk of Bayshore Boulevard to the corner of Diane's sprawling estate. He didn't see anyone on the streets. When he climbed into his Corvette, he realized that the sheer pounding of the storm had left his muscles aching and stifled his hearing. He glanced in the mirror and saw that the cut on his cheek had stopped bleeding. His blond hair lay flat on his head.

He grabbed his phone.

He scrolled through his recent calls and found the number from which Ramona Cortes had invited him to lunch. He dialed the number, but there was no answer on her private cell phone. He left a message asking her to call him, and then he found the number for the offices of the Attorney General in Tallahassee. It was a public holiday, but he suspected that the office would be staffed while Chayla was assaulting the Gulf coast in the middle of a statewide campaign. Three transfers later, he found himself connected to a senior aide to Ramona Cortes.

'I'm very sorry, Detective,' she told him, 'but Attorney General Cortes isn't in the Tallahassee office today.'

'I understand. It's important that I talk to her soon. We had lunch on Monday, and she asked me to stay in touch on an investigation

I'm running.' That was partly true, so he didn't feel guilty about fudging the facts.

'Let me see what I can do, Detective.'

Cab hung up, but before he could decide on his next move, his phone rang again. Not more than five minutes had passed.

'Detective Bolton? It's Jaci Muzamel. I'm Ramona's personal assistant. I understand you're trying to reach her.'

'I am.'

'I have instructions to put you through if you call. Ramona is still in Tampa for the campaign, but unfortunately, she's not reachable right now.'

Cab was surprised that Ramona had anticipated that he might call her again – and that she would consider it a priority to take his call. 'It would be helpful if I could talk to her as soon as possible,' Cab said. 'I know the storm is causing problems everywhere.'

'It is, but the storm's not really the issue. Ramona is very regimented about her workout routine. I'm not even sure a hurricane would keep her away from the club. She always turns off her phone. It's the one hour of the day she keeps to herself.'

Cab glanced up the street toward Bayshore Boulevard. 'Is that the Tampa Yacht Club? That's where I met her for lunch.'

'Actually, it is.'

'Well, I'm not far away from there,' Cab said. 'Would she mind if I drove over and met her in person?'

'I think that would be fine. She was adamant that she wanted to talk to you if you tried to reach her. I'll call ahead to the club and have them let you in.'

'I appreciate it,' Cab said.

He put down the phone and headed out on the deserted streets. The Tampa Yacht Club was only a mile away. He wondered if Ramona would still be happy to talk to him when she found out that he wanted to ask questions about an old client named Frank Macy.

45

Annalie.

Annalie had lied to her. She'd lied from the very beginning. She knew Justin.

Peach checked the date of the photograph on Curtis Ritchie's camera and saw that the picture had been taken only a week before Justin was killed. A week – just before he dropped off the radar. Annalie was part of the plot. Either she had killed Justin herself, or she knew who did. Then she'd wormed her way into a job at Common Way in order to find out what Justin knew.

Part of her mission was deceiving Peach. Pretending to protect her. Pretending to be her friend. All the while, Annalie had tracked everything that Peach was doing, and like a fool, Peach had played right into her game.

She thought about Deacon's message.

If Macy is involved in something, he's not doing this alone. Don't trust anybody.

She thought about Annalie's odd reticence in sharing details about her past. She'd written it off to her own paranoia, because she needed a friend. She'd overlooked all the signs that this woman knew more about Justin – and about herself – than someone from the outside should ever have known. She'd trusted Annalie.

A mistake. She stared at the living room in Justin's safe house, which had been searched from top to bottom, and she thought: Annalie was the one who searched the house.

And now Peach had invited her back here. Annalie – who always carried a gun and had shoved that gun into Frank Macy's face, as if they were strangers.

They weren't strangers. They were partners. Working together.

Peach had to get out of the house. She didn't want to be here when Annalie arrived. Her emotions would betray her. Annalie would take one look at Peach's face, and she would realize that Peach *knew*. If it were about anything else, she could wear a disguise, but this was about Justin. She couldn't stare at this woman and cover up her rage.

She grabbed Ritchie's digital camera and Toughbook. Before she left, she hurried back into the bedroom, grabbed the photo of herself out of the frame on the small table, and shoved it into her back pocket. That was private. That was between her and Justin, and she didn't want to leave it for anyone else to find.

It was time to go, but when she returned to the living room, she saw that she was too late. Blurred headlights flashed through the rain and cut across the walls. Through the blinds, she saw Annalie's Corolla pulling up in front of the house. Peach froze. The car door swung open, and Annalie ducked into the storm.

Peach stood in the middle of the living room, watching and waiting. Annalie hoisted one leg over the low fence, then the other, and she dropped into the rain-speckled lake surrounding the house. She examined the place with both hands on her hips. Her long black hair was plastered to her face and neck.

There was nowhere to hide. Annalie would see her if she tried to make a run for her Thunderbird. She also realized that she didn't want to run. Not now. Not from this woman. She wanted to confront her about what she'd done. She wanted to know who else was involved. She wanted answers.

Annalie headed for the porch, and Peach finally sprang into

action. Looking around for something to defend herself, she scooped up a pink glass bottle from the floor and clutched the neck in her fist. She stepped lightly to the bedroom and hid behind the open door. She held her breath, listening.

The wooden screen door opened and slammed shut on rusted hinges. Footsteps climbed the front steps. She heard the knob turning on the front door, and then the storm grew louder, as if it were inside the house with her.

Annalie called out: 'Peach? It's me.'

Her voice sounded normal. Friendly. When Peach didn't answer, Annalie called again, but her tone was deeper and more cautious. 'Peach? Are you here? Are you okay?'

Peach's fingers were slippery with sweat. The glass bottle was hard to hold. The storm hammered the roof above her, and the bedroom felt damp and hot. A cockroach crept up the wall near her face. She had to take a breath, and she tried to do it silently, but her chest felt tight with fear.

A sharp metallic click snapped the silence from the other room. She knew that sound, because she'd heard it often enough when Deacon was manipulating his own weapon. It was the slide of a semi-automatic handgun being racked. Annalie had her pistol in her hand and a round in the chamber. It was ready to fire.

'Peach?' she called again.

Annalie headed for the bedroom where Peach was hiding. Her squishy footprints sank into the wet carpet, one after another. At the doorway, she stopped. Peach couldn't see her, but she was so close that Peach could hear water dripping from her hair. The window was cracked open, causing the wind to whistle and moan. Rain spat through the gap.

Peach hoisted the bottle over her head.

Half of Annalie's body appeared beyond the door. Annalie faced the window, looking outside, not looking behind her. Her bare arm was cocked at the elbow, gun in her hand, her index finger bent on the trigger. Peach saw golden skin on the curve of her jaw. She recognized Annalie's beautiful face, and something flinched inside her. She didn't want to believe that this woman was her enemy.

Don't trust anybody.

She didn't have time to second-guess herself. Annalie felt the presence behind her and began to turn, and in the same moment, Peach swung the bottle down hard. The elegant glass cut awkwardly through the air and landed on Annalie's skull, breaking into pieces. The woman took a staggering step in pain and surprise. Her hand tensed; the gun went off, blasting a bullet into the bedroom wall, which erupted in dust and plaster. Annalie's eyes closed, and she crumpled, knees buckling. She pitched to the floor. The gun spilled from her hand.

She lay in the middle of the bedroom, limbs splayed, not moving. Glass shards surrounded her.

Peach rushed forward and grabbed the gun. Annalie's eyes blinked, and her breathing was loud. A wave of fury washed over Peach. Annalie was alive, and Justin was dead. She felt no sympathy for her. She didn't care what happened next, to either of them. Grabbing Annalie's arm and leg, she roughly shoved the woman over on her back. Peach stood over her, kicking away glass.

'Who are you? Tell me who are you! Tell me what you did to Justin!'

Peach crouched over Annalie. She jerked one hand back and slapped the woman sharply across the face, leaving a bloom of red. 'Tell me what you did! You bitch! You liar!'

A low moan rumbled from Annalie's throat as she tried to focus. Peach slapped her again, even harder.

'I saw you! You were with him! Did you kill him? Was it you? Tell me, *was it you?* If you were the one, so help me, I will pull this trigger right now. I will! I'll kill you myself!'

Annalie's jaw moved. Her eyes opened and closed. Staring at her, all Peach could see was Justin's face and then the photograph of the two of them together. Annalie and Justin. A week before he was murdered.

'Do you think I won't kill you? Do you think I'm just a kid? You played me from day one. Did you laugh at how easy it was to get me to trust you?'

Peach aimed away from Annalie's head, and she jerked on the trigger, too quickly, too heavily. The gun fired wildly into the floor, and the recoil forced her arm back and nearly made her fall. She cringed with the violence of the explosion. The bullet blew up splinters from the floorboard. Annalie's head rocked in agony as the shock waves cracked in her skull.

Peach knelt over Annalie, a knee on her chest. She held her tightly down.

'I'll do it,' she vowed. 'I will. I don't care.'

Annalie's breath stuttered. Her eyes blinked into narrow slits. The world had to be spinning, a hurricane of noise and light, but Annalie's mouth moved soundlessly, and a choked word gasped from her throat.

'Peach.'

Peach screamed at her again. 'You killed Justin! You bitch, you killed him! Did you kill Deacon, too? Are you the one?'

'Peach,' Annalie repeated, unable to say anything more.

'It was you!' Peach shouted. She couldn't stop herself. She couldn't think about right and wrong. The words bubbled out with spit and foam. 'It was you, it was you, it was you, it was you!'

Annalie tried to talk again, but Peach shoved the gun into the woman's open mouth. Between her red lips and her perfect teeth.

'This is what you did to Justin! *You blew his head off, and that's what I'm going to do you!*'

She slid her finger over the trigger. Nothing made sense anymore. Not the past. Not the future. There was only right now, her and Annalie and the gun. There was nothing in her world but the rain and the heat of this moment. Pull the trigger, and she was dead, and Justin was avenged, and maybe, maybe, she could have peace after everyone she had lost.

Pull the trigger. Pull the trigger.

She began to feel the pressure on her skin. The trigger pushed back at her finger. They did a little dance together. Finger and trigger. Pull. Pull. Pull.

That was when music interrupted her. Wildly improbable music. Gloria Estefan sang 'The Rhythm is Gonna Get You.'

Annalie's phone was ringing.

46

Cab sat at a multi-station weight machine in the fitness room at the Tampa Yacht Club. His trench coat and suit coat hung from a lat bar. His leather shoes were a lost cause. The club still had electrical power, and several flat-screen televisions in the empty room were tuned to CNN. He saw live reports of the ferocious surf hitting the Gulf near Clearwater. He wondered where his mother was and where Lala was.

He checked his phone. Fifteen minutes had passed. Ramona Cortes still hadn't arrived.

One of the club employees served him a bear claw and a bottle of water. The sugar helped keep him awake. His ears still rang from the noise of the storm. When he finished the pastry, he got up and went to the mirrored wall and adjusted the knot in his tie.

Over his shoulder, he saw the Attorney General join him in the fitness room. She was wet from the rain.

'Hello, Cab,' Ramona said. 'A little over-dressed for Pilates, aren't you?'

'I'm more of a Zumba man.'

'I'd like to see that,' she said, chuckling. 'Do you mind if I run while we talk?'

'Not at all.'

'This hour is sacred. Regardless of what else you do, you need to respect your body. As it is, I had to cancel my massage today, and I never miss that. My masseur is unavailable.'

Ramona was dressed in running shorts and a tank top. She had a towel draped around her neck, and she wore pink Nikes. She was a small woman, but her legs were muscled and shapely under the snug Lycra. Her arms looked strong. She climbed onto a treadmill and set it at a slow pace. Gracefully, she jogged along with the moving platform.

'So I hear you quit,' she called over the noise of the machine. 'Caprice must not be happy. She's a stubborn woman. She's accustomed to getting what she wants.'

'Funny, she says the same thing about you,' Cab said.

'I'm sure she does, and she's right. Anyway, I'm glad you took my advice.'

'Well, I decided I would live a happier life not working for politicians.'

'Astute choice,' Ramona said. She increased the speed of the machine, until she was running, not jogging.

'I'm still investigating the threat against Diane,' Cab said. 'I'm convinced it's real and imminent.'

Ramona gave him a sideways glance. 'Why do you think that?'

'Because I'm looking into someone with a considerable motive to harm Diane. He's someone from your past. A client named Frank Macy.'

If she found the name unexpected, she didn't show it. 'Frank? I really don't think you need to worry about him.'

'When did you last talk to him?'

'It's been several years. I severed ties to prior clients when I was elected. I knew he was released not too long ago, but that's all. Mind you, I know Frank, and it wouldn't surprise me if he's up to his old tricks again. Drugs. Guns. He likes having money to throw at the girls on the beach.'

'Frank had close ties to Diane's son. Drew Hempl. And he has a history with Diane, too.'

Ramona's lips pursed into a frown, but the speed of her run didn't change. 'Yes, I know he does.'

'What do you know about Frank's relationship with her?'

'Quite a lot, actually.'

Cab wondered how far to go. How much to say. 'Enough to get Diane into political trouble?'

'Yes,' she acknowledged. 'Probably enough to ruin her.'

'And yet nothing has been exposed. You're showing remarkable restraint when it comes to a political opponent.'

Ramona switched off the machine and slowed to a stop. She wiped her forehead with the towel. 'What are you suggesting, Cab?'

'Caprice suspects you're behind everything that's going on. She thinks you know damaging secrets about Diane and Frank Macy. You can't release anything about it yourself, so you're using me to bring it out into the open. Destroying Diane's political ambitions and furthering yours at the same time.'

'Do you believe her?'

'I don't believe any politician. That includes you.'

She chuckled. 'Well, you're right. For a politician, the agenda comes first. Ahead of friends, if we're lucky enough to have any. Even ahead of family, as much as it pains me to say so. As long as we get what we want, the ends justify the means.'

'That's what everyone tells me,' Cab said. 'Does that mean you'd jump at an opportunity to wipe out a political enemy? An opportunity with Frank Macy's name on it?'

Ramona sighed and pointed at Cab's bottle of water. She waggled her fingers at him, and he handed it over. She took a sip. 'Look, Cab, I'm not asking you to trust me. I'm asking you to look at it from my perspective, which is political self-interest. Frank Macy was my client, and any communication between him and me is still governed by attorney–client privilege. If I were to violate that privilege, I could be disbarred, which would be something of a political liability for the Attorney General of the State of Florida.'

Cab smiled. 'True enough.'

'Even if I wanted to find a way around privilege – say, by using a rich, handsome, ridiculously tall investigator to do my dirty work for me – I would still be putting my head on the chopping block. My connection to Frank Macy is a matter of public record. As soon as his name starts popping up in the media, so does mine. That's not politically helpful. So as much as Diane wants to keep her interactions with Frank a secret, you can be assured that I want to keep my name away from him, too.'

'Maybe so,' Cab said, 'but Frank's still a threat to Diane.'

Ramona climbed off the treadmill. She continued to drink Cab's water. 'Why are you so sure? You have no reason to think he was involved in the Labor Day murders, do you?'

'I thought I did, but apparently I was wrong about that,' Cab admitted.

'Ah.' Ramona chose her words carefully. 'In other words, you suspected that Diane or her son might have used the services of a third party to resolve the problem of an abusive husband.'

Cab's eyebrows rose. 'You know a lot.'

'It's an ongoing investigation, and I'm up to speed on all aspects of it. Our special agent friends have their flaws, but they did examine that angle in considerable detail back then and concluded there was nothing to it. It was kept out of the media out of deference to the family.'

'I see.'

'So that's why I consider Frank Macy to be a non-issue.'

Cab shook his head. 'There's more. Justin Kiel had a newspaper article in his safe house about Macy's manslaughter plea. So it appears that Justin was looking at Frank before he was killed. In addition, as of last night, Deacon Piper is missing. Someone broke into his house. He was talking to sources about Frank Macy earlier in the day.'

Ramona frowned. 'You're sure about Justin?'

'Yes.'

'That surprises me, but it's still a big leap to think that Frank was involved in his death. Or in Deacon's disappearance. What's the connection?'

Cab hesitated. He was handing Ramona a political bombshell by saying anything. 'Hypothetically?'

'If you wish.'

'Okay. Let's assume that you and Macy were correct that fraudulent evidence was used to implicate him in that manslaughter case in Pass-a-Grille. Let's also assume that if Diane was involved in planting evidence, she had help from someone inside Common Way. Someone like Deacon Piper. If Frank Macy suspected that Diane and Deacon stole eight years of his life, don't you think he'd do something about it?'

Ramona's eyes grew smoky. 'I knew I was right about Diane. I can't believe the arrogance of those people.'

'I'm speaking hypothetically.'

She shrugged. 'Yes, of course.'

'You see why I'm trying to find Macy. If Deacon is gone, Diane is next. I'd like you to pull strings to help me locate him.'

'Look, Cab, Frank is certainly capable of violence. I don't wear rose-colored glasses about some of my old clients. However, I don't see him targeting Diane or Deacon. He's not that foolish. He likes his breezy life too much to put it in jeopardy over a crazy scheme for revenge. And the situation with Justin Kiel is much more complicated than you realize.'

Cab stared at her. 'Why?'

'I can't say.'

'If this is about politics–'

'It's not,' she said. 'I can't discuss an ongoing criminal investigation.'

'Ramona, I need your help. If I'm right, time is very short.'

She frowned. 'This is extremely delicate. I need your assurance that nothing I say will make its way back to Common Way.'

'You have it,' Cab said.

Ramona sat on the edge of the treadmill. 'The fact is, I've long suspected that Common Way has engaged in illegal activity behind the scenes. Espionage. Blackmail. Maybe worse. What I've never been able to do is prove it. However, a few months ago, an employee in what I call the black ops area of Common Way approached my office.'

'An employee?' Cab asked. Then he said: 'Justin Kiel.'

Ramona nodded. 'Justin didn't like what was going on there. He had the same suspicions that I did. He believed that Common Way was illegally influencing legislative policy, candidate selection, elections, whatever. They were using money – and probably other criminal tactics – to get their way. Justin offered to be a double agent for me. To dig into the foundation's secrets. It all had to be handled with absolute confidentiality. I couldn't be directly involved. If Diane Fairmont discovered that I was using someone inside her organization to spy on her, the blowback would have thrown me out of the campaign and probably out of office altogether. So I recruited someone to serve as a go-between with Justin. I needed someone I could trust implicitly. And we began to gather information.'

'What did you find?' Cab asked.

'Plenty to be suspicious about, but no proof that would lead to indictments. We couldn't proceed without rock-solid evidence, and we didn't have it. And then a few weeks ago, Justin contacted his go-between to say that he had urgent new information. He didn't explain what it was – and he was murdered before he had a chance to share it.'

'His new information could have been about Frank Macy,' Cab said. 'Justin may have come across Macy's plans regarding Deacon and Diane.'

'Maybe, but I don't think so. I know you've been listening to this girl Peach Piper, but she was emotionally involved with Justin. It clouds her judgment. I'm sympathetic, but I think she's on the wrong track about Frank.'

Cab's eyes narrowed. 'How do you know so much about Peach and her investigation into Justin's death?'

'Because Justin was my own agent,' Ramona replied calmly. 'Do you think I would sit here and do nothing? He worked for me, and I want to know who killed him. I arranged to get another mole inside Common Way to investigate his death. I used Justin's go-between to work undercover. She was highly motivated, because she knew him. They were friends. She wanted to catch his killer as much as I did.'

'A mole,' Cab said. 'Undercover.'

'That's right.'

There was only one person Ramona would have used for a mission like that.

I needed someone I could trust implicitly.

Ramona said nothing more, but she didn't need to say a word. Cab knew exactly who it was. When you can't trust your friends, you turn to your family.

'Lala,' he said. 'You put Lala inside Common Way.'

He grabbed his phone and dialed.

47

Gloria Estefan sang, and Peach stared at the caller ID on Annalie's phone. What she saw made no sense at all.

Cab Bolton was calling Annalie.

She pushed herself to her feet, standing over Annalie's prone body. Her first paranoid thought was that Cab was part of the conspiracy, but she'd checked his identification. She'd called the Naples Police. He really was a detective. He really was one of the good guys.

Or was he?

Don't trust anybody.

'Hello?' she said.

There was a pause before he answered. When he did, she recognized his voice. 'Who is this?'

She tried to think, but confusion overwhelmed her. She said nothing.

'Hello?' Cab continued. 'Who's there?'

'It's Peach,' she murmured.

'Peach? How did you get this phone?'

'Why are you calling Annalie?' she asked.

'She's a friend of mine. Peach, is she there? Can I talk to her?'

Peach stared at the woman on the floor. Her eyes were open now, and her lips were moving, but Peach couldn't understand the words. 'She killed Justin,' Peach said into the phone.

'What? No, she didn't, Peach. She *didn't*. I promise you.'

'I have her gun.'

'Peach, let me talk to her. Please.'

'You people took Justin away from me, but you're done. It's over. You can't stop me.'

His voice grew urgent. 'Peach, *listen to me.*'

'No, you listen!' she shouted, losing control. 'I'm sick of people lying to me. Justin lied! He shut me out, and he lied! Now Annalie lied to me, too. Do you hear me? I'm sick of it! You're not going to get away with it anymore.'

'Peach, stop,' Annalie murmured at her feet.

'Peach, stop,' Cab told her, like an echo.

She pointed the gun at Annalie's head again. 'Why should I? Why shouldn't I just shoot her?'

Cab's words tumbled over the phone line. 'Peach, the woman that you know as Annalie is actually a police investigator named Lala Mosqueda. She is *not* part of any conspiracy. She did *not* kill Justin. She's been working undercover for the Attorney General to find out what really happened to him.'

Peach blinked. 'What?'

'She is not the enemy. She is on your side.'

'You're lying,' Peach said. 'You're all lying to me.'

'Peach,' whispered the woman at her feet. The stranger at her feet. 'I'm sorry. It's true. I'm a cop. I was working with Justin.'

Peach still held the gun in her hand. It was pointed at Annalie's head. Except Annalie wasn't Annalie.

'Why should I believe you?' she demanded.

The woman on the floor braced herself on her hands, her elbows bent. The barrel of the gun was an inch from her dark eyes. 'Because Justin was my friend, too. Because I want to catch whoever killed him as much as you do.'

Cab's voice came through the phone. 'She's telling you the truth, Peach.'

'I don't – I don't know . . .'

'My name is Lala,' the woman said to her. 'Is that Cab on the phone?'

Peach nodded mutely.

'Okay, listen to me. Slowly point my gun toward the wall. Please. Nice and steady. Don't make any sudden movements with it.'

Peach looked inside her heart. Annalie was Lala, and she didn't know who Lala was, but she realized that nothing had changed. She liked her. She didn't want to hurt her. She wanted to trust her – and Cab Bolton, too. Her whole arm trembled as she thought about what she'd been ready to do. The gun in her hand felt ugly and lethal. She could hardly hold it, and she swung her whole body in order to point the barrel at the wall.

'That's good. Give me the phone, okay?'

Peach handed the phone to her. The gun was still in her other hand.

'You know how to rack the slide,' Lala told her. 'Keep your finger off the trigger.'

Peach yanked the slide of the gun back and forth, and a gold cartridge popped from the barrel like a jack-in-the-box and fell to the floor. Lala closed her eyes and breathed easier. As Peach watched, Lala spoke into the phone.

'Cab Bolton,' she said. 'Get your ass over here.'

Cab squatted in front of Peach, who sat on the floor with her back against the wall and her arms wrapped tightly around her knees. Her eyes stared out the window at the storm. She looked even younger than she was.

'Don't be hard on yourself,' he said. 'You had no way of knowing. I didn't know, either.'

Lala winced as she held an ice pack to the back of her head. 'I wanted to tell you, Peach. Really. I'm sorry.'

'I almost killed you,' Peach murmured.

'Well, you didn't. Anyway, I understand how you must have felt, seeing me in those pictures. I feel stupid that Curtis Ritchie was able to get those photos without me realizing it.'

Cab got to his feet. 'Are you sure you're okay?' he asked Lala.

'I think so. It's just a nasty bump. I was woozy, but I didn't black out.'

'Still.' He took her face in his hand and moved his finger left and right in front of her nose to make sure that her eyes were properly focused. She stuck out her tongue at him, and then he leaned in and kissed her lips. 'I didn't have a chance to do that this morning,' he said.

'I said goodbye,' Lala told him, 'but you were asleep. Guess I wore you out.'

'I guess you did.'

Peach stared at them. 'So are you two–?'

'I keep him in my life to drive myself crazy,' Lala replied.

'I keep her in my life to drive my mother crazy,' Cab added.

Cab watched a little smile play across Peach's face. She found them funny.

'So why are we here, Peach?' Cab asked. 'You said this was Justin's hidey-hole, but you didn't know about this place until after he was killed?'

Peach shook her head. 'I knew he had a safe house, but he never told me where it was.'

Cab looked at Lala. 'What about you? Did you know about it?'

'No.'

He studied the wreckage of the house. 'Well, someone found it.'

'I don't think it was Curtis Ritchie,' Peach said. 'There were no pictures of this place on his camera. The trouble is, whoever searched it took everything. There's nothing left to tell us anything. It's a dead end.'

'How did *you* find this place?' Cab asked her.

He listened to Peach explain about the photograph attached to a draft e-mail from Justin and to the edits in the picture that had led her down San Fernando Drive to this house. She pulled a hard copy of the photograph from her back pocket and showed it to him.

'See? Justin kept this picture in a frame by the window. I thought maybe he was sending me another message, but I guess I was wrong. I couldn't find anything.'

'You said the photo in the e-mail was edited,' Cab said. 'What about this one?'

'I don't think so. The street number is the same now. So's the little house on the restaurant sign.'

'What about other changes?'

'I – I'm not sure I really looked.'

'Do you still have the original?' Cab asked.

Peach nodded. 'It's on my phone.'

She scrolled through her camera roll, clicked on a picture, and handed the phone to Cab. He stared at the image on the camera screen, then at the printed photo in his hand. He went back and forth several times, and at first he thought Peach was correct. The photos were identical.

Except . . .

'The vent,' Cab said.

Lala looked at him. 'What?'

'Justin added an exhaust vent on the roof of the restaurant. It's right above Peach. It's in the hard-copy print here, but the vent's not in the original photograph.'

Cab didn't have time to say anything more before Peach was on her feet and over to the bedroom window. She threw up the sash and practically jumped through the cramped space into the flooded yard. She pushed through the standing water until she could see the roof of the house, and then she pointed and screamed.

'There's a vent above the bedroom. Right above the bedroom! That can't be right!'

Peach ran for the side of the house, and Cab saw her struggling to mount a telescoping ladder against the frame. It fought her in the storm like a reluctant dance partner. When she finally slapped it under the roof line, he reached out through the open window with both hands and grabbed the ladder to steady it. The lightweight aluminum bucked and swayed as the wind tried to rip it out of his grasp.

'Be careful, Peach,' he called. 'I can't hold it.'

She climbed past him. He could see her legs and feet immediately in front of him as she pulled herself up onto the house's low roof. Her body thumped on the shingles over their heads. She shouted something he couldn't understand, and then a tortured twisting of metal screeched from above them. Cab saw an aluminum vent hood sail like a Frisbee across the yard. Peach's body reappeared in front of him. He hugged the ladder, but when she was halfway to the ground, a gust of wind wrenched it from his hands and threw it backward. Peach flew, landing flat on her back in the water.

'Peach!' Cab shouted.

He started to climb through the window himself, but she pushed herself to her feet. 'I'm okay, I'm okay! I've got something!'

She had a large plastic-covered package tucked snugly under her arm.

He helped her through the window back into the bedroom. She looked immensely pleased with herself, and he realized that the importance of this discovery wasn't about anything they might find inside the package. It was about her and Justin. In the end, he'd trusted her. He'd left something for her to find. Not anyone else. Her. He was still the young man she'd loved.

Peach reached out her arms and handed the package to Lala. 'You look,' she said.

The package was approximately twelve inches by fifteen inches, wrapped in heavy plastic and sealed with duct tape. It was damp with spray but otherwise undamaged. Cab could see a thick sheaf of papers and manila folders inside. Lala took the package to the mattress and used her fingernails to pick at the duct tape and peel the folds of plastic apart.

Cab saw a stack of photographs that had been produced on a home printer. He recognized the first page; it was a match for the article on Frank Macy that Peach had found under the filing cabinet. Justin was no fool. He'd anticipated that things might come to a bad end, and he'd made a backup of everything he'd discovered.

Lala didn't flip through the rest of the photographs immediately. Instead, she removed a thick manila folder, similar to the records that Peach had stolen from Dr Smeltz's office. Peach recognized it, too.

'Is that a medical file?' she asked Lala.

Cab saw Lala's brow wrinkle in confusion. 'Yes, it is.'

'Curtis Ritchie had a photograph of Justin outside Dr Smeltz's office,' Peach said. 'He'd stolen someone's file. Is it a duplicate of what I found? Is it Ms Fairmont's file?'

She shook her head. 'No, it's not hers.'

'Then whose is it?'

Lala looked at Peach. 'Yours,' she said.

48

Tarla tipped her champagne glass into the circle with Caprice and Diane. Their crystal glasses clinked together.

'To Governor Diane,' Tarla said with a smile.

Caprice repeated the toast, but Diane said nothing. Her smile was forced. They drank, and then Diane turned away toward the windows looking out on the garden. Candles lit the room, flickering and throwing shadows on the walls. The power was out.

Caprice leaned close to Tarla's ear. 'Do you know where Cab is?'

'No, I haven't talked to him.'

'You know how much I like him, Tarla, but he's going to ruin Diane's campaign if he's not more careful. He doesn't seem to appreciate the collateral damage we could face if certain things are exposed.'

'My son never met a sleeping dog he didn't want to wake up,' Tarla commented.

'Well, I'd still feel better with him in the house today.'

'Does Cab believe there's a serious threat?' Tarla asked.

'He can't be sure, but some bad things happened overnight. I'm worried.'

Tarla nodded and sipped champagne. Caprice wandered away to an armchair in the corner of the sunroom, where she tried to get storm updates on her cell phone. Signal came and went.

The threat of violence didn't feel real to Tarla. Something so foreign never felt real until it happened. It made her think about the warm Labor Day night ten years ago. A holiday then, a holiday now. Her only concerns then had been Diane's health, and her annoyance with Birch, and her frustration with Cab shutting her out of his life. Then, in the blink of an eye, blood had been spilled. People had died. A man who smelled of sweat and fear shoved the barrel of a gun in her face.

She didn't believe something like that could happen again. Could it?

She studied Diane, who was unusually quiet. They hadn't had any real chance to talk, and the unspoken things hung between them. Tarla felt guilty about what she'd told Cab. The money changing hands between Diane and Frank Macy. She felt angry, too, that Diane had never told her that the baby she'd lost had been fathered by Cab. Even between good friends, there were secrets that could cost everything.

Tarla approached Diane by the floor-to-ceiling windows and put a hand on her shoulder. Her friend looked back and acknowledged her. The silence between them seemed to carry all of their apologies, as if nothing else were needed. Each of them knew what the other was thinking. Sometimes it was strange to recall that they had been friends for more than four decades, ever since they were ten-year-olds lying side-by-side on the open lawns of the Bok Sanctuary and fantasizing about their futures. Neither of them could have imagined how the future would really turn out.

'Don't tell Caprice,' Diane murmured.

Tarla was concerned. 'What?'

Diane looked at her aide, whose back was to them on the other side of the sunroom. 'When the storm is past, I'm getting out of the race.'

'No! Why do that? You were born for this.'

'I've done things,' Diane whispered. 'Things that can't be undone.' She saw Tarla's face and added: 'Not Birch. Other things.

If I'm going to ask people to trust me as governor, I have to be able to trust myself.'

'You're making a mistake,' Tarla told her. 'The past doesn't matter. I know who you really are.'

'Do you? I don't even know myself anymore. Maybe it happens to every politician. I'm becoming the mask that I despise in every candidate from the other parties. We need someone authentic.'

Tarla squeezed her hand. 'Don't do anything rash. Give it time.'

Caprice called to them from a chair in the corner. 'You're on the air, Diane.'

She'd found a live stream on her phone. The local network superimposed a photograph of Diane over footage of surf pounding the beaches, and they played a voice-over of a phone interview she'd conducted earlier in the morning.

'No, I'll be right here in Tampa. I'm not going anywhere. The important thing is to put safety first, and that means supporting the first responders who are putting themselves at risk and going without sleep to help everyone in central Florida. If you don't need to be outside, stay home, and let those good people do their jobs.'

'Nice,' Caprice said.

The screen shifted to a shot of the Governor outside the Capitol building in Tallahassee. He had a similar message of support, pledging every available state resource to protecting the area and rebuilding from any storm-related damage. It was impossible not to notice that the sun was shining in the Panhandle. He was a long way from Chayla.

'Not so much as an umbrella,' Caprice added. 'That's going to hurt him. He can talk about not getting in the way of rescue efforts all he wants, but people will remember that you were here, and he wasn't.'

Diane said nothing, as if she were sick of political intrigue. She turned back to the windows. Behind them, Caprice muted her phone again, restoring silence except for the beat of the storm. Tarla could see their reflections against the glass in the darkness of the morning. The light of the candles aged both of them. They were two middle-aged women at that stage of life when they had to decide if they could forgive themselves for their mistakes.

'I told Cab things I probably shouldn't have,' Tarla admitted. 'I'm sorry.'

Diane's lips creased into something like a smile. 'Well, I didn't tell Cab things that I probably should. I guess that makes us even.'

'You could have told me. I wouldn't have judged either of you.'

'Keeping secrets is a hard habit to break,' Diane said.

Tarla heard her phone ringing in her purse on the breakfast table. She retrieved it and saw that her son was calling. 'Speak of the devil,' she told Diane. And then into the phone: 'Hello, darling. We were just talking about you. Are you going to join us?'

'Soon,' Cab said, but his voice crackled with static, as if he were far away. 'Is everything okay over there?'

'Perfectly fine. Just three lonely women against the world. The power's out, but we're making do.'

'You're alone?' Cab asked. 'Where's security?'

She struggled to hear him. 'Oh, I'm sure there are men with guns wandering around somewhere. And of course, we have Garth, in case there's a massage emergency.'

'I'll be there in less than an hour,' he told her. Before he hung up, he added: 'Mother, I don't say this often, but be careful. If anything at all unusual happens, call 911, and then call me.'

'You are so dramatic. I really wish you'd gone into acting.'

'I'm serious.'

She lowered her voice. 'I know you are, darling. I hear you. Get here soon.'

She hung up. Diane was watching her. 'What did he say?' she asked.

'He's on his way.'

Diane nodded. She took her empty champagne glass to the table and refilled it from a pitcher of mimosas. As she sipped the glass, she looked around the sunroom, and she seemed to notice for the first time that it was just the three women keeping vigil against the storm.

'Where's Garth?' she asked.

Cab put down the phone. 'There are no problems at Diane's place for now,' he said.

Peach wasn't listening. She held her medical records in her hands without opening the file. 'Why would Justin take this?' she asked Cab. 'Why would he care? And why hide it with these other things?'

'I don't know,' Cab told her. 'Sometimes boyfriends get curious about things they should leave alone.'

Peach shook her head. 'Not Justin. If he wanted to know something, he would have asked me. Plus, he meant for me to find this. He wanted me to see it.'

Cab couldn't pretend to understand. It was a piece of the puzzle that didn't fit, but he didn't have time to worry about it. Lala looked up from the other papers that Justin had hidden away inside the false vent on the roof. 'We may have bigger problems. Cab, take a look at this.'

Cab sat next to her on the bed. Lala showed him a copy of the photograph that he'd already seen, displaying the article about Frank Macy's manslaughter plea. Then she turned over more pages.

There were other copies of newspaper articles, all of them dealing with Diane Fairmont and her son and the Common Way Foundation. It was like an obsession, but it wasn't the articles themselves that bothered him. These weren't copies made from a newspaper. Someone had made copies of these articles and posted them on a wall like a macabre collection of trophies. Like warnings. It was the kind of collage he'd sometimes found after a stalker struck his victim.

He saw more photographs. These were taken inside an empty garage. The bulletin board was in the background, against a foreground of an oil-stained floor. And then more photographs, inside what appeared to be an abandoned house.

'What is this?' Cab asked, but he knew what it looked like. A staging ground. The lair of a killer.

He realized that he was staring at the reason that Justin had been murdered. Somehow, Justin had found this place. A place that no one was supposed to know about. Not until after more people had died.

'The bigger question is *where*,' Lala said. She could read his thoughts. She knew what these pictures meant.

She put the last photograph in front of him. It was an exterior shot of a dilapidated chocolate-brown house at a T-intersection, with a Bank Sale sign posted in the front yard. The branches of an old elm tree brushed the roof. The windows were boarded over with plywood.

'We need to go,' Cab told her, getting up.

'Do you know where it is?'

'I was just there,' he said. 'I saw it this morning. It's two blocks from Diane's estate.'

49

Garth checked every room on the first floor of the estate, but the security guard wasn't there. He'd seen him fifteen minutes earlier in the kitchen, with his gun on the table and a croissant in front of him. Now the croissant was half-eaten, and the security guard and his gun had both vanished. Candle wax oozed across a plate, but the candle had gone out, and he could smell smoke in the air.

When he checked his phone, Garth saw that he had zero bars of signal. He held it in the air and shook it, but the cell towers had finally gone down. He picked up the house phone and heard nothing. No dial tone.

They were an island now. Cut off.

He opened the front door and shouldered onto the porch. The storm wailed. The wind hurtled debris across the yard. He shouted the guard's name, but his own voice was like a whisper. The garden lights were off. It may as well have been the middle of the night.

Garth grabbed an oilskin slicker from the hall closet and shrugged his beefy torso into it. Before he zipped it, he removed his gun from his shoulder holster and shoved it inside one of the raincoat pockets. The coat had a hood, which he yanked over his head and tied with a knot under his chin. He shoved his feet into rubber boots. When he jogged down the steps into the deep water, he felt as if the bay had overrun the land and turned it all into a vast sea. The animal sculptures in the garden seemed to be drowning.

He bowed his head against the wind and pushed toward the back of the estate. The paths were invisible except for the humps of land jutting out of the water like the undulating tail of a monster. He left the open lawn and found himself in dense foliage. Trees fired leaves at him. Grit got in his mouth. The rain squirmed inside his slicker. The sheer force of the water in his face made it hard to breathe.

'Screw this!' Garth said aloud.

He turned around, using one arm to shield his face from the branches that whipped through the air like knife blades. He followed the fence hugging the border of the estate and then veered into the gardens. Mud sucked at his boots under the water, and he kept losing his balance, because he couldn't see the ruts of the ground below his feet. Finally, he felt hard cobblestones as he reached the driveway. He headed toward the house.

That was when he heard the shot.

It came from outside the property. The sharp bang was barely audible over the wail of Chayla screaming at him. He reversed course and ran toward the wrought-iron gate at the street. The two halves of the gate slammed wildly back and forth, open and closed, closed and open. Garth had to dive out of the way when one of the metal panels took aim at him like a baseball bat. When both halves swung open again, he hustled onto the street. He was outside the grounds now, and he saw the storm roaring out of the bay. The waves of rain came and came and came. The wind picked up everything in its path and swept it toward him.

He squinted, trying to see. He had no idea where the gunshot had come from. Ahead. Behind. Was it really a shot? Maybe someone had set off a firecracker for the Fourth of July.

No, it was definitely a shot.

Garth pulled his gun from his pocket. He splashed down the street, carried by the wind at his back.

'I don't hear sirens,' Cab said. 'I don't see any lights.'

Lala nodded in agreement. 'There's nobody coming.'

They were alone on Bayshore Boulevard. Waves crashed in twenty-foot surges that swept from the bay on their right and flooded through both lanes toward the houses that fronted the opposite side of the street. The sports car rode on water, not pavement.

'Try the security guard again,' Cab said.

Lala shook her head. 'No signal.'

The street was black. There was no light anywhere. He slowed in the deep water to keep the car from stalling, and he felt the tires bump up on the curb as he swerved, unable to keep a straight path. When he spotted the cross-street that led to the abandoned house, he swung the wheel left, and the Corvette fishtailed. He shot down the narrow cobblestoned street. Where the road ended, he parked on a soft shoulder. The brown roof of the foreclosed property was barely visible beyond a swath of mature elm trees. Cab got out, and Lala got out on the other side. They both had their guns in their hands.

A chainlink fence marked the eastern edge of the lot. Squat hedgerows grew beside it, giving them shelter. They stayed low. In the rain, they could barely see. He felt as if he were a passenger on the Maid of the Mist, engulfed by the spray of Niagara Falls. They crept close to the rust-stained stucco wall of the house. The front windows were nailed shut with plywood, and kids had spray-painted the boards with graffiti.

They reached the front door. It was locked.

Cab cupped his hands over Lala's ear. 'The garage,' he said.

He led her along the front sidewalk. Panicked lizards leaped from the bushes and skittered up the wall. Water cascaded down the slanted roof of the garage and sluiced over their heads. They slogged into the driveway, where they stood in front of a tan double-wide garage door. Cab pointed at Lala's gun, and she held it straight and ready as he bent down to yank the chrome handle. The door slid upward on its tracks with a bang.

A black Lexus sedan was parked in the middle of the concrete floor, facing the street. Cab approached on the left side of the car, and Lala shadowed him on the right. They met at the rear of the sedan. The garage was deserted.

'I know this car,' Lala murmured. 'It's Frank Macy's.'

Cab slid a penlight from his pocket and cast a beam around the garage. He spotted the cork bulletin board on the east wall and recognized it from the photographs Justin had taken. When he examined the bulletin board, he saw that only one article remained, thumb-tacked in the very center. He recognized a gauzy picture of Diane, and he saw the message written across the paper in red marker.

Revenge.

Gray ash lay at his feet. With the garage door open, the wind scattered the ash into a cloud. He bent down and could still see burnt fragments of paper that had survived the char. When he caught one, it was fresh and warm.

'Cab,' Lala said.

She crouched near the trunk of the car. He came closer, and he said, 'Yeah, I smell it, too.'

Cab opened the driver's door of the sedan and pulled the trunk release lever. The trunk popped open with a soft click. He heard Lala suck in her breath, and he knew what she'd found.

'Is it Deacon?' he asked.

Lala shook her head. Her face was screwed up in puzzlement.

He came around the back of the car. The first thing he saw was an aluminum pistol case, which was open and empty, with a slot in the foam where the gun had been. The next thing he saw were bugs crawling across a large sheet of plastic wrap, feeding on the belly of the body that stared up at him. He recognized the face.

It was Frank Macy.

50

Peach felt abandoned.

She'd wanted to go with Cab and Lala, but they had refused to let her join them in Tampa. They told her to go home, but she couldn't bear to set foot inside her own house. She couldn't stay here either, not when everything in this place reminded her of Justin. Cab had given her a key to his mother's condominium in Clearwater, but she didn't want to head west into the teeth of the storm. So she perched on Justin's sofa as stiffly as one of her mannequins, listening to Chayla beat on the house like a hip-hop singer.

Justin on hip-hip. *If Beethoven were alive today, he'd probably be a rapper. I think I'm glad he's dead.*

Justin.

Her medical file sat on the table in front of her, unopened. Her records. Her history. *Everything* about her was in there. Dr Smeltz had been her doctor from the day she was born, and he had been her doctor until she and Deacon moved to the Gulf. Really, he was still her doctor. She had never chosen a new physician; she hadn't seen a doctor in years. Other girls went to the doctor to deal with birth control, but that wasn't an issue for her.

Everything.

Like the time, after her parents died, when she'd gone crazy with a razor blade and cut herself on her stomach. Lyle had found her bleeding and rushed her to the hospital. She still had the scars.

They'd made her see a psychiatrist, but she hated the man's questions and his annoying patient voice. Couldn't he see that all she needed was for her parents to come back from their trip? When were they coming home?

Around that time, she found a mannequin sticking out of a Dumpster behind a Kohl's department store. Her first. Ditty. She'd called her that, because she kept hearing that John Mellencamp song in her head – the one with the little ditty about Jack and Diane. She'd rescued Ditty from the garbage and taken her home, and Ditty had been a better therapist than any of the real live people who wanted to help her. She'd spent hours talking to the mannequin in her bedroom.

Everything.

Her mind. Her body. Her life.

'Why did you take my file?' she asked Justin.

You already know the truth.

Peach picked up the thick folder and left it in her lap. It took her a while to open it. When she finally did, she turned to pages in the middle. Somewhere around age six, she'd broken two bones in her right wrist. Funny, she didn't even remember it. She waved her right hand as if she were a beauty queen in a parade, but her wrist worked fine, and she'd never noticed any pain there. Kids heal. She saw her mother's signature on release forms for X-rays. Thinking about it, she had a vague memory of wearing a cast and of Deacon writing FRUITY on it.

More pages. Physicals. She remembered the cold steel of a stethoscope on her chest and how she squealed. The wooden stick on her tongue. Ahhhhh. Dr Smeltz poking her in the belly button. '*You're as fit as a fiddle with a hole in your middle.*' Herself, giggling every time.

Weird rash. '*You shouldn't touch those plants, sweetie, they're poisonous.*'

Prescription for Amoxicillin for a bad ear infection.

Chicken pox. 'I've seen lots of tots with spots.'

Diarrhea.

Burn on her pinkie from touching a hot stove. She still had a whitish patch of skin there.

Pneumonia.

The notes on pneumonia were near the front of the file, because it was one of the last times she'd seen Dr Smeltz. She remembered getting sick in Tampa and Lyle and Deacon screaming at each other. She remembered the long drive home at night, the loud music, the weird sweet smell in the car, and then herself throwing up all over the back seat. Deacon, shouting at her.

The soft bed at Diane Fairmont's house. Dr Smeltz in the bedroom. '*You're lucky I was here, young lady. You are very sick, but I'm going to make you better. Okay?*'

She removed a page from the doctor's notes. His handwriting was awful. *Fever at 104. Taking immediate steps to bring temperature down. Delirium. Girl keeps repeating: Why is there so much blood?*

Peach blinked and read that sentence again.

Girl keeps repeating: Why is there so much blood?

She heard a voice in her head, but it was her own voice.

'What are you doing?'

'What's happening? I'm scared.'

'Why is there so much blood?'

Peach snapped the file shut. She stared at her hands and saw that they were trembling like leaves afraid to fall. She put the file back on the table in front of her, and she never wanted to open it again, never wanted to see it again. *You already know the truth.*

She closed her eyes. The thump of the storm became a thumping inside her head, pressing on the walls of her skull. She felt herself go somewhere else, somewhere long ago and far away. It was night. She was on a road, the world spinning. And then her brain, sounding like the kindly voice of Dr Smeltz, interrupted and pulled her back: *Don't you go there, young lady*.

Peach thought about Justin in the library at Lake Wales. She imagined him at the reception desk, smiling, being charming, asking the librarian to find a local address for Dr Smeltz. Before that, he'd spent hours among the microfiche carrels, copying pages from the newspapers ten years ago. She saw a stack of pages he'd left for her. Articles he'd copied from the microfiche.

Those pages looked scary to her now. She didn't want to see them, but she picked them up anyway. Most of the copies were from newspapers printed the day after Labor Day, featuring ugly black headlines about the murders. But not all. As she dug through the pages, she saw that Justin had gone further back, to the weekend when things began to go bad. When everything was different. When nobody was the same.

She saw an article about a political fundraiser in Tampa.

'Oh, Lyle, can I go, too? I want to see the city! And the zoo! Please please please please please.'

She remembered Lyle: stressed, angry, driving her and Deacon in the Mercedes to Tampa. Another argument. Deacon sulked the whole ride. He didn't want to go, not with his twelve-year-old sister, not as a babysitter. Lyle left them alone in the city; he had things to do, important people to talk to. She and Deacon went to Busch Gardens. She took rides; he smoked funny-smelling cigarettes and said not to tell Lyle about it.

On one of the rides, she noticed that her throat had begun to hurt.

By evening, she was in the hotel room in bed, burning up. Coughing. Sweating. Sobbing: *'I just want to go home, please take me home, I want to go home!'*

Lyle shouting at their brother: *'Goddamn it, Deacon, for once in your life, stop thinking about yourself, and do what I tell you! Get in the car, and drive your sister back home right now!'*

Peach picked up another article from the stack of copies Justin had made. She read the headline:

SEARCH CONTINUES FOR MISSING TEENAGER

Police and community volunteers scoured the woods surrounding Lake Wales yesterday, continuing the search for Alison Garner, 14, who was reported missing by her parents late Saturday evening.

No evidence of the girl's whereabouts have been discovered so far, and no witnesses have come forward with information about the disappearance.

Alison was believed to be riding her bicycle when she left the family home, which is located on Old Bartow Road in West Lake Wales. She was last seen wearing red nylon shorts and a white tank top . . .

No matter how many times Peach tried to read the article, she couldn't finish. She simply saw one name over and over.

Alison. Alison. Alison.

There was one page left that she hadn't seen. One more article that Justin had copied. She didn't want to pick it up, because she knew exactly what it would say. She knew how the story ended.

You already know the truth.

She turned over the paper.

TEENAGER BELIEVED VICTIM OF HIT AND RUN

The search for missing teenager Alison Garner came to a tragic end late yesterday, when two migrant workers found the girl's body hidden in a gully off the shoulder of Highway 60.

Police have concluded that the girl was struck by a vehicle on the highway while she was riding her bicycle, which was also found hidden near the body. The coroner reported that Garner was apparently alive for some time after the accident and might well have been saved if emergency personnel had been alerted.

'That's the terrible thing about this case,' said Lake Wales Police Chief Thomas Cappelman in yesterday's press conference. 'Whoever hit this girl simply dragged her off the road and let her die. He hit her, and then he hid her body and didn't tell a soul. This wasn't just an accident. This was murder. When we find the driver, that individual is going to prison for the rest of his life. I promise you that.'

'See the little white cross?' Peach told Justin. *'You have to be careful when you drive here.'*

51

Frank Macy looked surprised.

That was what Cab thought as he studied the dead man's eyes. Surprised that he had been conned. Surprised that a man who was smart, cool, and lethal could be played for a fool. Surprised that anyone would try to make him famous for a series of murders he didn't commit.

'Someone wants Macy to take the fall. That was the plan all along.' Cab pointed at the empty pistol case. 'Macy's prints are going to be on the gun and the clip,' he said.

He stared at the article pinned to the bulletin board and the message scrawled across it. All fake. This was never about revenge. It was all about misdirection. They'd been led down the garden path, led toward Frank Macy from day one. Someone wanted them to believe that history was about to repeat itself.

And it was. It was.

'Macy would have taken the blame for the Labor Day murders, too,' Lala said. 'No one would ever have found his body. Biggest manhunt since Booth, and all the while he would have been sitting inside some alligator's stomach.'

'He's in the house right now,' Cab said. 'He's going to kill Diane. That's the final play.'

He thought: *My mother's in there, too.*

The rain washed inside the open garage door like a wavy curtain. The wind was a loud, incessant whistle. He turned toward the door, but whatever was going to happen had already begun. Not even a block away, he heard the first bang, and then in rapid succession, he heard four more bangs, muffled but sharp. Gunshots.

Cab sprinted. The storm hit him in the face, as if he'd struck a wall. It nearly knocked him backwards off his feet. Lala ran, too, but he didn't wait for her. His feet punched through the standing water, down the driveway, onto the street. It was like running through molasses, the water grabbing his ankles, the slick mud making him slip. He was in slow motion, battling the wind.

He could barely see, not in the daytime darkness, not with his eyes slitted against the downpour. He couldn't hear anything except the storm roaring in his ears, as fierce and loud as a lion. He ran by feel, his fist clenched around his gun.

Fifty yards from Diane's estate, he spotted a lump in the water, like a whale breaching. When he knelt down, he saw a body face-down near the sidewalk. Cab felt the man's neck, but there was no pulse. He grabbed his shoulder and turned him over, and he recognized the face of the estate's security guard, with a bullet hole like a third eye squarely in his forehead.

Whoever had pulled the trigger was already on his way, heading for Diane. And Tarla.

Lala caught up to him. She tugged on his sleeve, pulling him to his feet. 'Come on,' she shouted. 'Cab, come on!'

They left the dead guard where he was. They kept running.

Cab charged toward the vine-covered walls surrounding Diane's house. The mop heads of the palm trees shot spikes through the air, forcing him to duck. The bay seemed to be coming for them, like an entire ocean slouching down the street. He reached the iron gates of the estate, which swung wildly, bouncing open and then snapping shut like the jaws of a giant turtle. He and Lala waited. When the wind split the gates apart, Cab grabbed Lala's hand and dragged her through the gap just before the heavy wing reversed course and took aim at them with the speed of a train.

They bolted up the cobblestoned driveway, but someone was in their path, blocking their way. A man waited for them on his knees. His arms drooped at his side, and when the man's fist emerged from the water, it held a gun. He didn't point it at them. Instead, the man's torso swayed, and the gun fell from his hand. His whole body sank sideways, and he went limp.

Cab and Lala ran forward. It was Garth.

The masseur's tanned face looked pale for the first time in his life, and watery blood pulsed from a scorched bullet hole near his shoulder. His brow and bulbous nose were contorted in pain, but he relaxed when he saw Cab.

'I chased him back here,' Garth mumbled. 'Bastard killed the guard. He got me, but I think I got him, too.'

'I'll stay with you,' Lala said.

'Forget me. He's heading inside.'

'Just one?' Cab asked.

'Just one guy. One guy with a big gun. Déjà vu, huh?'

The storm raged. The house shook.

Tarla and Diane sat on opposite sides of the sofa on the north wall. Caprice stood in front of the floor-to-ceiling windows, staring out at the garden. 'You'd think the eye of the storm would be coming across soon,' she said.

Tarla hoped that was true. They needed a break where the wind died and the rain stopped. Chayla seemed to become more violent as the hours passed. They felt as if they were in a cage, with zoo animals roaming free just beyond the black glass.

The room smelled of cranberry, like Christmas, an oddly comforting aroma in the hot summer. A fat scented candle burned unevenly on the table near the patio doors, and its liquid pool of wax glistened. A tapered white candle flickered in front of them, casting a shimmery glow on Diane's face. Otherwise, they were in the dark. With the power off, the air had grown hot and heavy.

'What's happening?' Diane asked. 'And where's Garth? How long has he been gone?'

'Do you want me to go look for him?' Tarla asked.

Near the doors, Caprice shook her head. 'I don't think we should go anywhere alone.'

Tarla wondered where Cab was. She told herself that soon enough, he would be here. Everything would be fine. He would stroll in, wet, smiling, hair spiky, and he would make a joke. There was nothing to worry about.

'Damn the phones,' she said when she tried to call him. No signal. She wanted to hear her son's reassuring voice.

Blown sand rapped on the glass, as if it were knocking, asking to come in. Tap tap tap, like a Morse code. Leaves slapped on the doors and stuck there. Water squeezed its way onto the tile floor in tiny puddles. Wind got inside the walls and wailed like a ghost pining for a lost love. Tarla experienced a strange sensation, and she didn't know what it was. It had been such a long time she'd felt anything like it, but something nameless wrapped itself around her body like a damp fog. And then she understood. It was fear. She was scared to death.

Tap tap tap, said the sand.

Slap slap slap, said the leaves.

My love, my love, my love, said the ghost in the attic.

Bang bang bang.

Tarla stood up immediately, her body tense. 'What was that? Did you hear that?'

Diane stared at her. 'I didn't hear anything.'

'That wasn't the storm,' Tarla said.

Caprice eyed the invisible garden. She went and got a candle from the table and held it near the glass, its light like a beacon. The storm assaulted the window, inches from her face. 'I don't see anything,' she said.

She turned around to face them. She still held the candle.

Tarla looked over Caprice's shoulder, past the dancing light, which reflected in the glass. One moment, nothing was there, and the next moment, something took shape outside the doors.

A man. A man in a hood.

Tarla screamed.

52

Peach drove.

She didn't care about the storm. She didn't care that everyone else had closeted themselves inside their homes to steer clear of the worst, furious hours. The wind threw her heavy car like a toy around the highway, but she drove and drove, past the beaches, across the bridge, into the desolate heart of Tampa. She wasn't aware of time passing or of debris pounding her windows or of her engine coughing out warnings as the water threatened to flood it. The bay could have swallowed her whole, and she wouldn't have flinched; she would have stared sightlessly ahead as she vanished under the waves.

She drove.

Her mind was a child again. Chayla was in the future. Her past rose out of the bay like a sea monster, winding its fingers around her throat. She remembered.

She remembered everything she'd buried for ten years.

The accident threw her body forward.

She was already dizzy from the sickness in her chest. Her clothes were glued to her clammy skin. She'd thrown up twice in a plastic garbage bag, but where she'd missed, she'd spit up over the back seat of Lyle's Mercedes. The car smelled like her puke, mixed with the nasty sweetness of whatever Deacon was smoking in the front seat.

She lay there, stretched out in the back, coughing, gagging, her chest hurting, wondering if she were going to die.

Then she was airborne. Metal hit metal. Tires squealed. She flew, rolling and slamming into the back of the front seat. Her head hurt. Her mouth bled. She found herself on the floor, staring at the roof of the car.

Deacon murmured something, like a curse or a prayer. 'Oh, my God.'

He got out and left her. She heard his running footsteps on the highway. She was alone. She hacked, and phlegm caught in her throat and bubbled onto her lips. She had vomit in her hair. She was scared, and she wanted to be home.

'Deacon?' she called plaintively, but he didn't answer. 'Deacon!'

She heard strange noises on the road, like when they were camping and Lyle scraped a shovel over dirt to cover up a fire. She pushed out her tiny hands, feeling for the door handle. When she pulled the lever, the door unlatched, and she dragged herself into the humid night. Her brain spun when she stood up. She thought she would throw up again.

Peach looked for her brother. It was as if he had disappeared – but no, there he was, behind the car, twenty yards away. The moon made him look like a ghost. The highway was empty, and empty highways made her think of wolves and owls and alligators and other things that had teeth and claws.

'Deacon? What are you doing?'

She shuffled toward him. Her feet were bare. The rocky shoulder poked at her skin. She wore only her little white nightgown, which flapped in the summer breeze.

'What's happening? I'm scared.'

He didn't notice her at all. She got up really close to him, close enough to see his wild eyes and his mouth hanging open like a dog's. He was breathing loud and sweating. He clenched and unclenched his fists. His hands were dirty.

'Deacon?'

She looked down. Splatters of red shined near his feet, like a map broken up by lakes. A big lake and smaller lakes. They made a trail along the asphalt and the dirt shoulder and down into the thick grass of the gully.

'Why is there so much blood?'

Her brother saw her for the first time, and his eyes widened. He sucked in his breath and bellowed at her. 'FRUITY, GET BACK IN THE CAR!'

She shriveled in fear. 'But Deacon, I–'

'GET BACK IN THE CAR AND SHUT UP!'

Peach ran to the Mercedes over the rocky ground and practically dove into the back seat. She took a fleece blanket she'd used and threw it over her head. She curled into a corner, hugging herself so tightly she thought she could squeeze herself into a ball and roll away. She waited, and she had no idea how much time passed before Deacon got into the front seat again.

She could feel him looking at her, even though she couldn't see him.

'I'm sorry,' he murmured. 'I apologize for yelling at you.'

She didn't dare say a word.

'We hit a deer. I freaked out.'

Peach let the blanket slip off part of her face, enough to free her eyes. Her voice muffled, she spoke into the fleece. 'Did it die?'

'Yes, it died.'

'Oh, no. Oh, was it a big deer or a little deer?'

'It was a big deer. It lived a long life. Don't be sad.'

'But what do we do–'

'We don't do anything,' Deacon told her. 'It didn't happen. Do you understand me? It never happened.' He leaned way far back, until his body was almost over the seats, and he was practically in her face. 'I mean it, Fruity. You never tell a soul about this. It's our secret. Okay? Promise me.'

'I promise,' Peach told him.

It was the promise of a scared little twelve-year-old girl, but she kept her word. She never told anyone. After a while, she even stopped telling herself. The accident became a kind of odd little dream from her pneumonia, something that might have been real and might have been a fantasy. It wasn't even until she and Justin drove to Lake Wales again, and she came upon that isolated section of Highway 60, that she even remembered that anything had happened.

Deacon hit a deer. Right there in that dangerous section of road. It had nothing to do with the little white cross.

Peach drove. She might as well have been flying, with Chayla lifting her on its wings. She kept hearing an echo of voices, as if they were stuck in the clouds, raining from the sky. Deacon's voice. And Lyle's voice, too. Arguing. They always argued, but this was much worse.

'*I can't protect you anymore*,' Lyle shouted. He didn't know Peach could hear them from her sick bed. That she was listening to things that made no sense.

Deacon: '*You're supposed to be my brother. This is my whole life!*'

'*Blame yourself, not me*,' Lyle told him. '*You didn't give me any choice. I'm sorry, but you have to face what you did. I talked to a lawyer. She says there's no way to escape this.*'

Except there was an escape.

With Lyle dead, it all went away.

Peach drove. And drove. She knew where she was going and who she had to see. She knew where Chayla was taking her, carried along by the winds at her back.

53

The patio door was locked.

The man raised his gun and fired two shots into the floor-to-ceiling window beside the door. The glass around the bullet holes became white frost, and cracks wriggled outward like lightning bolts. Wind punched loudly through the two holes, increasing the pressure on the weakened frame, and when he fired again, the window exploded inward in a hail of diamonds.

Tarla squeezed her eyes shut. Glass rained down on her hair. Her ears rang with the explosions. The air in the sunroom smelled burnt, and sheetrock dust made a cloud where the three bullets tunneled into the rear wall.

He stepped through the shattered window past jagged teeth clinging to the frame. The storm came with him, loud and uncontrolled. Curtains on both ends of the wall of glass began to dance. Ten feet away, Tarla felt spray soaking her face. With the window broken, the zoo cage had swung open, and wild animals poured inside.

The man with the gun was dressed as he had been ten years earlier, all in black. The hood covered his face, but seeing him, Tarla knew it was the same man. This time, she knew she wouldn't walk away alive, waking up in a hospital days later. None of them would. She had a vague curiosity about what it would feel like when he shot her, how much it would hurt, how long it would take her to die. She tried to swallow her regrets, which were numerous. Cab's smile filled her mind, as it had the first time.

Caprice stood next to her, stiff as a corpse. Her hair sparkled with fragments of glass. Her eyes were dark little stones, and her jaw was set, fiercely determined. She looked like a cat on the hunt, ready to pounce. Tarla wanted to catch her eye and say: *You won't win.*

Diane hadn't moved. This man had come for her, but she looked serene, as if the Chopin funeral march were playing calmly in her head, a piano serenade for the soon-to-be dead. For the first time in a long while, Tarla thought that her friend looked free. She realized it had been a terrible mistake for Diane ever to enter the election campaign. Politics changed you. It made you worse than you were. Now, with that burden lifted, she could simply be Diane again, if only for a few more moments.

Time hung in the air, the way a bubble floats, but every bubble has to pop eventually. The man took a step toward the three of them. He couldn't miss, not at this distance. Even so, he was hurt. His free hand clutched his side. Tarla could see a tear in the fabric, drenched red with blood.

'You don't need to hide this time,' she said. 'Who are you?'

He stopped, and it was as if, finally, he wanted them to know who he was. He took his gloved hand from his wound and grabbed a fistful of nylon above his forehead and slid the hood off his face. His red hair was flat and wet. His skin flickered with dark shadows from the candles. He was handsome and rugged, the kind of man who drew second looks wherever he went. To Tarla, he was so, so young – not even thirty – which meant that ten years earlier he had truly been no more than a boy. An eighteen-year-old, slaying his brother, like Cain killing Abel. Tarla realized that it was *youth* she had sensed behind the hood back then. Youth, that foolish time when emotion means everything, and consequences don't exist.

Diane said: '*Deacon?*'

'I'm sorry,' Deacon Piper said to her.

Tarla was close enough to see his face clearly. He wasn't sorry. He wasn't necessarily a killer in his heart, but he wasn't sorry. He was a man with a mission, who wouldn't stop until he was done.

'Why?' Diane murmured. As if it were nothing but idle curiosity. As if she were talking about the choice of paint on a wall. 'Why do this?'

'I have no choice,' Deacon replied.

'Don't tell me you're some kind of closet Nazi,' Tarla interrupted loudly. Somewhere in her mother-of-a-policeman brain, she thought: *Play for time*. Time made all things possible. Even rescue. 'One of those awful Alliance members out to make the world safe for fascism? That would be very disappointing.'

'I can do this, or I can go to prison for the rest of my life. That was my choice then. It still is.' He added: 'I don't take any pleasure in it.'

'Well, that makes me feel so much better,' Tarla said.

'Don't toy with us!' Caprice hissed, speaking for the first time. 'If this is who you are, then you have to live with yourself. If you think you can do this, then screw up your courage and do it.'

Deacon pointed the gun at Caprice. 'Do you want me to kill you first?'

'I don't care what you do.'

Deacon stared at her and said, 'Bang' – but he didn't fire. He swung the gun back to Diane, who showed no fear. She watched Deacon and the black barrel of the gun with a peculiar fascination. Deacon limped closer, arm outstretched, ready to shoot. No regrets or doubts. No hesitation. No second thoughts.

Tarla stepped in front of him.

She blocked his way, a human shield between him and Diane.

She wasn't going to let him kill her friend, not then, not now. 'I think we've been in this position before,' she reminded him.

'Yes, we have,' Deacon replied.

'I'm curious. Why didn't you kill me ten years ago?'

'Honestly? You were too beautiful to kill.'

'And now?'

Deacon actually smiled. 'You're still beautiful.'

He pointed the gun at her lovely face.

She thought: *So it's like this.*

A voice from the broken window interrupted them. It was Cab's voice, calm and deadly. It wasn't in her head, it was real. 'Deacon, put your gun down right now.'

Cab stood in the window between the sharp jaws of glass. Clouds of rain swarmed around him. He had both hands on the butt of his gun, his finger on the trigger. The wind made it hard to aim, but he fought the gales as he stepped through the wreckage of the window into the sunroom. He didn't blink as he stared Deacon down. Behind him, silently, Lala slid inside the house too, her own gun also directed at Deacon's face. Two against one.

Deacon eyed them quietly, but he didn't lower his weapon.

'It's over,' Cab told him. 'Kneel down, and lay the gun on the floor.'

Deacon still didn't move. He was a game-player, analyzing his options, deciding if there was a way to win.

'That's my mother,' Cab went on. 'If you kill her, I'll be forced to kill you.'

'Maybe that's what I want,' Deacon said.

'No, I don't think so. I don't think you're suicidal.'

Lala spoke to Deacon. Her voice was soft. 'We already found

Frank Macy's body. We know you were planning to frame him. The plot's done. You've lost. More killing won't change that.'

Deacon gave the barest shrug. He turned away from Tarla and squatted and laid the gun at his feet. When he straightened up, he lifted his hands in the air. 'What now?' he said.

'Lace your fingers on your head,' Cab told him. 'Turn around. Walk backward toward me slowly.'

Deacon did as he was told. He turned around. He took a step backward.

At that moment, with wicked timing, Chayla intervened.

The locked patio door shuddered. The sixty-mile-an-hour wind knocked on the door and then smashed it in, throwing the door on its hinges. It swung like a missile into Cab's back, kicking him sideways into Lala like a bowling pin. They both toppled; their guns skidded along the wet floor.

Deacon immediately bent down to scoop up his gun. He pivoted to aim at Cab, but Caprice dove across the short space, colliding with Deacon, who tumbled backward and rolled. Dizzied, he scrambled to his feet with his gun in his hand. Caprice grabbed Cab's gun from the floor, and together, simultaneously, they pointed the weapons at each other.

Deacon backed toward the open window. He held his side, which was bleeding profusely. 'Have you ever fired a gun?' he asked Caprice.

'No.'

He took a sideways glance at Cab and Lala, who were crawling on the slippery tile, trying to regain their balance. 'Do you really think you can?'

'Watch me.'

'You'll die, too,' he said.

'Maybe.'

Deacon took her measure, deciding if she was serious.

He tilted the gun barrel down as if to surrender, but then, with a smirk, he turned and ran. Caprice fired repeatedly after him. The bullets were like little bombs blasting between the walls. Windows cascaded outward, breaking and falling. The storm howled as if Caprice were firing into its belly. She kept shooting wildly as Deacon vanished, until the gun was empty and each new pull of the trigger ended in an impotent click.

Deacon was gone. Chayla folded him up into her furious heart.

Cab, who was still reeling from the impact of the door, jumped through the window in pursuit.

54

A searing pain burned like a lit cigarette on Deacon's back and made a trail of fire through his soft insides. As the bullet exited through the taut muscles of his stomach, he realized with a sense of wild surprise: *She shot me*. The impact kicked him forward, stumbling, but he righted himself. He put a hand on his abdomen, which was warm and wet, and pressed hard, feeling blood squirm between his fingers.

He was invisible in black. Behind him, silhouetted against the pinpoints of candles, he saw Cab Bolton scanning the grounds. The gardens hid Deacon. He lifted his gun and fired from the trees, and Cab ducked. He didn't think he'd hit him.

The distance to the foreclosure house felt like miles. He knew he wouldn't make it. He headed away from the main gate, following the vine-draped north wall through dense bushes that whipped into his face. The house loomed to his right, nothing but a black shape.

Escape was impossible. He understood that. He was dying from the hole in his abdomen, but it didn't stop him from using his last breath to get away. If he could get to the estate's garage, if he could steal a car, there was hope. As long as blood pumped, then his heart was beating, and he was alive. He'd learned that lesson a long time ago.

Why is there so much blood?

That one night, that one moment on the road, never left his head. He could still feel the bitterness gripping his stomach as he made the night-time drive from Tampa. He could feel his head swim with each joint, but the pot didn't relax him; it just fed his impatience. That night, he was an eighteen-year-old boy, hating the world, hating his domineering brother, hating his little sister puking in the back seat, hating his parents who had died. All of that rage made its way into his foot, dead-heavy on the accelerator. Seventy miles an hour. Eighty.

He was alone on the highway, and then he wasn't alone. Alison was with him.

Alison, who was nothing but a flash of blond hair in his headlights. Alison, who flew when the bumper of Lyle's Mercedes clipped her bicycle tire, whose head landed like a falling meteor on the asphalt.

He remembered the panic he felt. His body was bathed in sweat. His fogged head went around and around. He remembered running from the car to where she lay. He remembered staring at her on the ground, so small and limp, blood flowing, her eyes closed. He knew what to do. Call an ambulance, wait with her, hold her hand, whisper in her ear that everything would be okay. That was what he planned to do, even as he took her sneakered feet and dragged her off the road into the damp gully. He could imagine himself explaining the accident on the phone and giving the police his location, even as he covered her still-breathing body with dirt and leaves, even as he shoved her mangled bicycle under the cover of a flowering bush. *There's a girl, she's hurt*, he heard himself say, even as he screamed at Peach to get back in the car, as he told her never to say a word to anyone about what had happened.

He hit a deer. That was all. That became the truth.

If Lyle had left it at that, if he had let Deacon take the car to Jacksonville for repair, maybe his brother would still be alive. Lyle was no fool. He'd seen the headlines; he'd seen through the lie. And so he had to die. Strange, how simple the calculation was. He could talk to a lawyer and plead guilty and give up his life, or he could put a bullet in his brother's brain. Strange, how easy it was to do that. How good it actually felt, silencing that awful, judgmental voice forever.

He wasn't sorry. He hated Lyle. He only wished he could have told his brother to his face who the man of the family really was. Lyle was a coward who wanted big things but blinked at what it took to get them, who never understood that the ends justified the means. Not like Deacon. He wished his brother had known the truth. Then again, maybe he did. Maybe in that final instant, he knew who was putting that gun to his head.

Deacon emerged, bent and weak, from the trees. He staggered for the garage's rear wall and collapsed against it, breathing heavily. When he twisted the doorknob, it was locked, but he pressed his gun against the bolt and fired, busting the door inward. He fell inside. The three-car garage was sticky and dark, and he could see vehicles in each stall. He limped beyond the cars and threw open one of the big doors. Turning back, he spotted a door leading inside the house, and next to it were three sets of hooks, which glistened with car keys. He dragged himself across the concrete floor, trailing blood. He grabbed the keys and threw himself inside the closest vehicle, which was a monstrously sized ebony Cadillac Escalade.

He tried the first set of keys. They didn't fit. The second set made the engine growl to life. He shot backward, weaving, dinging the side of the Audi in the adjoining space. The rain swirled down as he backed into the cobblestoned turnaround, spilling over onto mud and brush. He gripped the wheel with one hand like a vise. His insides were a blowtorch that didn't cool when he shoved his other hand into the wound. He had to remind his brain what to do next.

He shoved the gear into drive. His foot jammed the accelerator, and the truck fishtailed. He couldn't keep straight. He fingered the dashboard and found the switch for the headlights, and the bright beams lit up the driveway like searchlights. Through the driving rain, he caught a glimpse of Cab Bolton running toward him across the estate's sodden lawn. Deacon headed for the iron gates, which snapped open and shut, and he crashed through them, tearing them off their hinges, skipping them like beach stones onto the street.

He was free. He swerved down the neighborhood street, throwing up waves, barely clearing the trees on either side. Debris clung to his windshield. He squinted to see. He felt the way he had a decade earlier, bitter, his head swirling, going faster and faster.

And then there she was. In the middle of the street. In his headlights.

Just like back then. An innocent girl, about to be thrown aside, crushed by the tons of steel. His foot lurched to the brake, and he heard a voice screaming in his head: *Stop stop stop stop stop stop.*

It wasn't Alison. He was in the present, not the past.

It was Peach.

She saw him coming, and she knew it was her brother. There was no doubt in her mind. He drove wildly, like a man trying to escape his crimes. The headlights of the SUV were dragon's eyes. The truck bore down on her, but she stood in the middle of the street, her hands at her side, the storm punishing her body, and she didn't move. She made no attempt to dive clear. She heard the whine of brakes, heard the tires slipping in the water, saw the back of the truck skid.

The Escalade lurched to a stop inches from her body.

She had to shield her eyes, but she could see him behind the headlights. The driver's door opened, and he climbed out. He clung to the window with one hand to keep himself upright, and he screamed at her.

'Fruity! Get out of the way!'

Peach simply shook her head and didn't move. The lights bathed her, making her feel small. Small, which was how she'd felt ten years ago, wandering in a haze onto the deserted highway. Deacon had screamed the same way then, in desperate terror, telling her to get back in the car.

He was the same man. Her brother.

'This isn't about you!' he shouted.

She walked around the corner of the SUV. She came close to the driver's door, and she could see that he was badly wounded. 'Not about me?' she said, but the storm was louder than she was. Hearing it try to drown her out, she raised her voice and shouted back. She was no longer a child.

'Not about me? You killed Lyle, didn't you? You killed Justin, too. It was you!'

Deacon raised his other hand. There was a gun in it, pointed at her head. 'Fruity, get out of here!'

'Sure, kill me! That's what you do, Deacon. You kill people.'

'I'm not kidding!'

Peach walked closer, until the gun was a beast in her eyes. Wild wind, wild rain, plunged from the sky. 'Neither am I! Do it!'

He was the young one now. He was still eighteen. His voice screeched. 'Goddamn it, Fruity! Don't make me!'

'I don't care! Do you think I don't know what you did? I remember the accident. I remember *Alison*. So now you have to kill me, too, just like everyone else, right? So pull the trigger!'

Deacon shoved the barrel against her forehead. It was hot; it burned. Over his shoulder, beyond the car, she could barely make out two people sprinting through the storm. They were fifty yards away, but they were getting closer. Two people. Cab. Lala.

Deacon glanced back and saw them, too. He pushed the gun into her face again, so hard it made her stumble.

'Go away! Just go away! I don't want to hurt you!'

Peach took both hands and wrapped them around the gun. His hand was cold against her warm fingers. His blood smeared her face. Their eyes found each other, and his eyes were lost and lonely. His skin was bone white, his red hair matted on his head. His whole body trembled.

'*Deacon, stop!*' Cab shouted.

Deacon wrenched away, ripping the gun from her grasp. He threw it into the gutter, where the weapon vanished under the rushing water. Slamming the door, pushing past her, he ran, but it was not a run at all. He tottered like a dirty drunk. Six steps later, he lurched to a stop, and his knees crumbled. He went down, sinking to all fours, and then his left side gave way, and he sprawled onto his back, twitching, spread-eagled. A river washed over him, deep enough nearly to cover his body.

Peach's breath stuttered in her chest, and she splashed toward him. She got on her knees and slid an arm under his limp neck and held him. His eyes were open but gray. His lips frothed with blood. She was vaguely aware of Cab and Lala drawing close, of them standing over her and touching her shoulder, but she didn't move. She waited, because the end was near.

She stared into his face, but it wasn't him she saw. He seemed to become everyone else she'd lost, everyone she'd never had a chance to hold. Her mother. Her father. Lyle. And Justin. Justin, with his porkpie hat swirling away in the water, his mustache drooping, but still with that grin, teasing her, loving her. She wanted to hold on to all of them forever. Keep them here. Keep them alive for another second.

But the man in her arms was none of those people. He was her brother. He was a killer.

'Oh, Deacon,' she said, but his eyes had already closed.

55

Chayla had fled.

The clouds scurried after her, leaving the detritus of the storm – cars pushed around like toys, trees downed, roofs torn away – to glitter wetly under a perfect sun. Steam rose from standing pools of water. Fish rotted on streets and sidewalks half a mile inland from the Gulf and the bay. The rumble of back hoes and dump trucks made a whine in the background as the clean-up of the region began.

The elegant landscaping of Diane's garden had been torn apart. A fallen palm tree lay across the grass, its shaggy top half submerged in the duck pond. A stone flamingo had been beheaded. Bushes were uprooted, and when the mild wind blew, they rolled like tumbleweeds. The floor of the gazebo, where Diane and Cab sat, was dirty with mud and branches.

They'd cleaned off chairs, and they sat with china mugs of pomegranate oolong tea. Diane didn't look at him; instead, she studied the disarray in the foliage, as if plotting its rebirth. She picked up a long strand of weeping willow that lay across the ledge of the gazebo. It was like seaweed plucked from the beach. She tried to bend it into a circle, but it didn't bend, and so she dropped it back to the earth behind the shelter.

'I haven't thanked you for saving our lives,' she told him.

'Thanks aren't necessary,' Cab replied. 'I'm sorry you were placed in such a frightening situation.'

'Well, nevertheless. I'm very grateful. I'm sure Tarla is, too.'

Cab smiled. 'I believe her exact words were, "Did you have to wait until the last second like this was the eighteenth sequel to *Die Hard*?"'

'That does sound like Tarla,' Diane said.

'She also mentioned that McTiernan wanted her in the original movie instead of Bonnie Bedelia, but she couldn't stand Bruce Willis.'

'So she's coping well with her second brush with death.'

'She is.'

Diane picked up her cup of tea, but then she put it down again, as if it had lost interest for her. 'I'm still shocked about Deacon. I do feel bad for him, despite everything. And for his sister.'

'Peach is strong. I like her. If it weren't for her, Deacon's plan might well have succeeded. Frank Macy's body would have disappeared into some deserted part of the Everglades. Deacon used the gun he got from Macy at Picnic Island, so Macy's prints would have been on it. All the evidence would have pointed toward Macy, not just now but for the Labor Day murders, too.'

'And toward me,' Diane added. 'Or Drew.'

'Yes, a lot of people would have believed that you or your son paid Macy to kill Birch back then. Neither of you would have been alive to protest. Meanwhile, Deacon would have reappeared a couple days later, having "escaped" from wherever Macy and his friends had been hiding him after he was supposedly abducted.'

'What about that young man Justin? Why was he killed?'

'Justin obviously put two and two together,' Cab told her. 'He connected Alison's death to Deacon and realized that Lyle was the real target of the assassination on Labor Day. Justin must have started following Deacon, and that led him to the foreclosure house. After being inside, he probably guessed what

Deacon was planning, but Deacon got to him before he could tell anyone.'

'The real mystery is why, isn't it?' Diane asked. 'Why did Deacon take it so far? Why kill me now?'

Cab nodded. 'Yes, that's the unanswered question. The FBI has been digging through his house and his computer records, but it doesn't look like he left much of a trail regarding his motive. For now, they suspect he was afraid of being exposed for his role in the original murders.'

'Do you believe that?' Diane asked.

Cab rubbed his suntanned chin. 'Oh, I'm sure that was part of it.'

'But?'

'But I think there's more to the story,' Cab said. 'The police discovered something curious. About six months ago, Deacon visited Hamilton Brock in prison.'

'Brock? Why?'

'No one knows. Brock isn't talking. He claims it's another conspiracy theory aimed at pinning a murder charge on him.'

'Are you suggesting that Deacon was secretly a member of the Liberty Empire Alliance?'

'Well, there was nothing in his personal effects to suggest he was harboring a radical ideology, and it's hard to believe he could have kept it hidden from Peach and others all this time. On the other hand, Deacon would have been a prime candidate for recruitment. An angry teenage boy. Parents dead. Disaffected. Maybe when he decided to kill his brother, he thought he could strike a blow for the Alliance by killing Birch, too.'

Diane looked thoughtful. 'Do you think we'll ever know the truth?'

'The investigation will continue, but no one in the Alliance has an incentive to talk.' He added: 'What about you? I saw the headlines. I saw the crush of press outside. You've dropped out of the race.'

Diane nodded.

'You've got a perfect excuse for doing so,' Cab said, 'after what you've been through.'

'Yes, but I'm not interested in excuses. I did something wrong. I've hired an attorney to negotiate a plea to cover my actions involving Frank Macy. I imagine I may see some time in Club Fed. Or not, depending on whether they take mercy on a distraught mother.'

'And on whether that bartender's death in Pass-a-Grille was really a coincidence,' Cab said. 'Some of my friends in the police think you and Deacon planned the whole thing to bring Frank Macy down.'

'I realize that. For what it's worth, it's not true. If Deacon killed him, he did it on his own, without telling me. I never would have been involved in murder.'

'I believe you.'

'Even so, this is the end of my public life. I'm out of politics. I'm resigning from the foundation, too. I told Tarla that she and I should take a long cruise somewhere, if I'm not playing solitaire in a women's jail.'

'She mentioned that. Somewhere with nubile brown men. She said once Garth is on his feet again, he could come along to apply the tanning butter.'

'Oh, Tarla,' Diane replied, shaking her head.

'I guess this means Ramona Cortes will get what she's always wanted,' Cab went on. 'With you out, it's a two-person race for governor. She's ahead in the polls. Everyone says she's going to win.'

'That's what they say,' Diane agreed. He saw a peculiar smile flit across her lips.

'You don't think so?' Cab asked.

Diane went back to her tea, even though it was cold now. 'I think the election is still four months away,' she said. 'Anything can happen.'

Walter Fleming nursed his Budweiser, which he drank from a long-necked bottle. The union boss had half a dozen more bottles soaking in ice in a silver bucket beside his deck chair. The blistering noon sun turned his high forehead pink. He wore an ugly yellow-striped bathing suit that he'd owned for years. His flip-flops lay in the sand at his feet. He wore black Ray-Bans that looked a lot like the sunglasses his father wore in the 1950s. Everything old was new again.

He sat in the sand behind his retirement home, which was near Carrabelle on the panhandle. The ground was flat, and the water hardly moved. A few teenagers splashed in the water, but this place was too boring for most of the kids. He spent weekends here with his wife. She lived in the house permanently, while Walter spent his weekdays in Tallahassee and in union halls around the state.

It was Monday, but he didn't feel like working. He was in a foul mood. His mood didn't get better when he saw Ogden Bush strolling toward him from the deck of his house. Ogden wore a dress suit and a fedora, which made him stand out like a politician shaking hands at a state fair. His black skin glowed with sweat, but he sported a cool grin, which nothing ever erased. He had a tan envelope scrunched in one of his slim hands.

Bush took off his hat and wiped his bald head. He stood on the beach, admiring the girls in the surf. 'Aren't you worried about skin cancer, Walter?'

'You're the only mole that bothers me, Ogden,' Walter replied.

Bush chuckled. 'Funny. That's funny.'

Walter took a swig of beer and wiped his beard with his sweaty forearm. Beside him, Bush settled into an empty chair. Without being asked, the political spy grabbed one of Walter's beers from the icy bucket, twisted off the cap, and drank half of it in a single swallow.

'Quiet around here,' Bush said. 'You really want to retire in this place? It would drive me crazy.'

'I like quiet. I don't get much of it.'

Both men finished their beers in silence. Walter flicked at a bee that buzzed around his head. His lips drooped downward in a perpetual frown.

'You look like Grumpy Cat, Walter,' Bush told him. 'What's with the gloom and doom?'

Walter dropped his empty bottle in the bucket. 'You've seen the polls?'

'Sure. They suck.'

'They suck all right. The Governor got no bump from the smooth response to Chayla. All the headlines have gone to Ramona Cortes talking about law and order and political corruption. She sits there and lumps the Governor's scandal in with the Common Way shit like it's a symptom of some bigger problem, and the national media eat it up. She's up ten points. Ten.'

'Cheer up,' Ogden told him. 'It's not the end of the world.'

Walter stripped off his sunglasses and jabbed them at Bush. 'See, that's what I hate about consultants. It's all a game to you. You win some, you lose some. At the end of the day, you don't care. Me, I think about a right-winger like Ramona Cortes sitting in the governor's office, and it makes me sick. It's a fricking disaster.'

'You'd rather Diane Fairmont?' he asked.

'Between the two of them? Yeah, I'd take Diane over Ramona, but that's not going to happen.'

'Nope,' Bush agreed. 'Diane's toast. She managed to look noble stepping down, though. People see her as a victim again. Lots of sympathy.'

Walter snorted. 'So what are you doing here, Ogden? You need a job?'

Bush shrugged. 'Yeah, kinda ironic, huh? Diane's out, so am I.'

'We're not hiring.'

'No? We've got a deal, Walter. I expect you to live up to it. I kept my end of the bargain. I was your spy.'

'A spy who couldn't deliver,' Walter snapped.

'Oh, don't be so sure. You're going to want to see what I brought you. Of course, if you'd prefer, I can simply burn it, and you can spend the next four years dealing with Governor Cortes.'

Walter's eyes narrowed. 'What are you talking about?'

Bush waved the tan envelope in the air. 'I have a little parting gift from our friends at Common Way.'

'Like what?'

'Like a nuclear bomb,' Bush said.

Walter frowned. 'What is it? Where did you get it?'

'It showed up on my desk. I don't know who left it there, but I can guess. Fact is, I think they suspected my divided loyalties. As for what it is – well, see for yourself.'

He handed the envelope to Walter, who dug out a pair of reading glasses from a canvas bag beside his deckchair. Walter undid the hook on the envelope and slid out a single sheet of paper. It was a copy of a ten-year-old invoice from an Orlando law firm, and the services rendered were described simply as 'Consultation.'

Walter recognized the name of the firm. It was an old-line white-shoe law firm with political connections and a practice that spanned corporate and criminal matters. He also recognized the name of the man to whom the bill was addressed.

Lyle Piper.

'What the hell is this?' Walter asked.

'Check out the date of the consultation.'

Walter did. The two-hour discussion between Lyle Piper and his lawyer took place a week before the Labor Day murders. 'Okay, so? I'm being dense here, but I still don't get it. It doesn't look like a bombshell to me.'

'Do the math, Walter,' Bush told him. 'Deacon Piper hit a girl in Lyle's Mercedes and dragged her off the road and left her to die, right? His brother figured it out. So he consulted a criminal attorney, because he wanted Deacon to turn himself in. This is the invoice.'

'Yeah, I know the story,' Walter said.

'Okay, but do you know who was a partner in criminal law at that Orlando firm ten years ago? And do you know who was also a friend of Lyle Piper's going back to their law school days?'

Walter's brow wrinkled in confusion, and then his confusion washed away like footsteps in the wet sand. He realized that Bush was right. The paper he was holding in his hand was radioactive. 'Son of a bitch,' he murmured. 'Ramona Cortes.'

Bush tapped his nose with his index finger. 'You got it.'

Ramona Cortes.

Walter shook his head in disbelief. 'She knew. She knew what Deacon Piper did to that girl. She knew it ten years ago.'

'Yeah, pretty convenient, huh? Ramona had Deacon Piper's whole life in her hands. One word from her, and he'd be behind bars for thirty years. Talk about having leverage over somebody.'

'She'll deny everything,' Walter said. 'The invoice doesn't list her name. It doesn't say anything about the nature of the consultation. We'll never be able to prove that she was involved in the plot.'

Bush shrugged. 'Who cares? Let her deny it all she wants. She'll spend the next four months answering questions about what she knew and when she knew it. The allegation alone will destroy her.'

That was true. This piece of paper would change the race. Ramona would lose. The Governor would win.

Or would he?

'Why would Common Way give this to you?' Walter asked.

'Obviously, they don't want their fingerprints on it.'

'So what's their game? Nothing's free with those slippery bastards.'

'They don't like Ramona. She's out to destroy the foundation. If they can't have Diane in Tallahassee, they'd rather see the Governor re-elected than a sworn enemy like Ramona.'

'I don't buy it,' Walter said. 'They're up to something. They're still trying to fix the race. You know what Ramona's going to do if this comes out. She'll throw it back in our faces and say this is another dirty trick from the Governor's campaign. It'll be ugly street warfare. That's what Common Way wants, isn't it? Let us pound each other for a few weeks, drive both of our numbers down, and then they step in and find a new candidate who vaults into the lead.'

'Maybe so,' Bush said, 'but do we have a choice? Without this dirt, there's no race at all. Ramona wins.'

Walter didn't like being between a rock and a hard place. He liked being the rock, banging on everybody else. Even so, he couldn't say no. He didn't trust Common Way, but sometimes you had to give your enemies what they wanted and hope you could still screw them tomorrow. 'Yeah, okay,' he said.

'We go nuclear?'

'We go nuclear,' Walter agreed.

'The roll-out has to be handled delicately,' Bush told him. 'It can't come from any of our usual sources. We've got to stay ten miles away from this. Everybody will suspect it comes from us, but we can't let anyone prove it.'

'Do you think I don't know that?' Walter asked. 'Don't worry. I know guys. We'll get the story planted. This thing will land like Pearl Harbor in Ramona's camp.'

Ogden stood up and laced his hands behind his neck, relishing the sun. 'Excellent. It's always a pleasure doing business with you, Walter.'

Walter didn't return the compliment. He studied the paper in his hand and took no pleasure in it. He was already anticipating the fallout, imagining the headlines, the press conferences, the claims and counter-claims. It would be a bloodbath, but elections usually were.

'So what do you think, Ogden?'

'About what?'

Walter nodded at the piece of paper. 'You think Ramona really did this? She was ready to have Deacon Piper commit murder to put her in the governor's chair? I can't stand the lady, but I just wonder if it's true.'

Bush's lips folded into an amused smile. 'Walter, you surprise me. This is politics. What the hell does truth have to do with anything?'

56

'Hello, Alison.'

Peach stared at the little white cross that was pushed into the ground near the highway shoulder. Pink flowers decorated it. Someone had slung rosary beads around the cross. It wasn't a grave, but if a ghost had to pick a place to haunt, this was a pretty spot. By all rights, Chayla should have unearthed the fragile memorial and trampled it, but God had made an exception for Alison. The cross had come through the storm unscathed.

She sat cross-legged in front of it. The ground was dry. Her Thunderbird was parked twenty yards away. A truck passed on the lonely highway, and the driver gave her a short toot of his horn. Paying respects.

Alison Garner. Fourteen years old. She was two years older than Peach had been that night, but two years was nothing.

'My name is Peach,' she said. 'You don't know me, but I was there. It was my brother who hit you. I mean, wherever you are, you probably already know that. I guess I knew it, too, but I never wanted to admit it to myself. It's funny what the brain can do. Anyway, I wanted to say I'm sorry. You should have had a life, and you didn't.'

Peach waited. She wasn't expecting an answer, but it was polite to let your words sink in. She'd always done the same thing with her mannequins. Talk to them, and then let them think about it. Annalie – Lala – would have said she didn't need to worry unless they started talking back.

'I saw your parents,' she went on. 'They miss you a lot, but they seem happy. I was afraid they would yell at me or something, but they cried and hugged me, and I started crying, too. They said I should stay for dinner, but I didn't want to impose. I asked to see some of your things, though. They still have a lot of them. You were a Britney fan, huh? I saw you had a concert program. She was never one of my favorites, but I could see where you would like her. They had a video of you, too, singing in church. You had a pretty voice. Me, I can't sing at all.'

Peach looked up at the sky. Birds flitted and called to each other in the trees. A month had passed, and the storm was a fading memory.

'I've been trying to decide whether my brother was a bad person,' she went on. 'I mean, I know he was. You probably hate him, right? It was weird talking to your parents, because I figured they would hate him, too, but they said Christians believe in forgiveness. They told me how sorry they were for me and how I must miss Deacon. They said they know how hard it is to lose someone you love, no matter how it happens. And the thing is, they're right. I do miss him. I still love him. I hope you won't think badly of me for that.'

She brushed a tear from her eye. Another one followed, and then there were too many to wipe from her face, so she let them flow.

'I hear you had a boyfriend. I saw a picture of you two going to a dance. Did he kiss you? Boys are funny about that when they're young. I never had a boyfriend until this year, and he's – well, he's gone now. We kissed. We never did more than that, because it's just not my thing. Sex just gets in the way. I liked kissing, though. I liked holding him and having him hold me. I miss him, too. I miss him a lot. I don't know, sometimes I think it's me. People who get close to me die. I don't really have anyone now. Nobody's left.'

Through her tears, she managed to laugh at herself. She'd never been a fan of self-pity. Things were what they were. Even so, here she was, with another imaginary friend. She was twenty-two years old, and she talked to mannequins and ghosts.

'Sorry,' she said. 'I'm making this all about me, when you're the one who's dead. Except, who knows, maybe you're already back. Or I don't know, maybe it takes a while. I think there are old souls and new souls. Do you know what I mean? Some people seem like they've been around for centuries even when they're young. Justin was like that. Other people feel like this is their first go-round. Oh well, I don't know. I probably sound crazy to you. Anyway, if you're back, and you see me, give me a wink, okay? I don't know what I'm going to do next. I quit my job. I'm sick of politics. But I'll be around.'

Peach got up from the highway shoulder and brushed the dirt off her pants. She dug in her back pocket and pulled out a slim volume of poetry. It was the book she'd found in Justin's safe house – the duplicate of the volume she'd given him of poetry by William Blake. She'd wrapped the book in plastic. She put it on the ground and propped it against the cross.

'I don't know how things work where you are,' she said. 'If you can read, I thought you might like this. If you see Justin, maybe he can read some of them to you. He was good at that.'

A gust of wind rose up and rattled the trees. To Peach, that felt like an answer from somewhere.

'Well, I should go,' she went on. 'I have a dinner party to go to. With a movie star. Can you believe that? Me! I guess that means I should change clothes.' She turned to walk away, but then she stopped. She bent down again, rubbing one of the flowers adorning the cross. 'Take care of yourself, Alison.'

She walked back to her Thunderbird, did a U-turn, and headed back toward Tampa.

57

'Do you think she's okay?' Lala asked.

Cab followed Lala's eyes to Peach, who stood on the balcony of his mother's condominium. The young girl leaned against the railing, staring out at the calm waters of the Gulf. For as young as she was, she looked older now. An old soul. He'd grown very fond of her, in the way a man does who has lost a daughter. She was quirky, but so was he. She had strange New Age ideas, and she was altogether too serious, but for someone who had lost as much as she had, she dealt with it well.

'Actually, I think she's fine,' Cab said. He added: 'It helps her to have a friend like you.'

Lala smiled. 'Are you being charming?'

'Always.'

She tipped her wine glass against his. He didn't think she'd ever looked more elegant. Lala, who lived in her black jeans and black T-shirts, wore a fuchsia cocktail dress that barely reached to her knees. A deeper crimson sash circled her waist, with a flowered brooch in the middle. The dress was sleeveless, showing off her lean, strong arms. Her tumbling black hair ended in broad curls below her shoulders.

'Did I mention you look beautiful?' Cab added.

'Tarla said formal.'

'She'll be jealous. She's not used to being outdazzled.'

'Smooth talker,' Lala said, but he knew she was pleased. 'Do I need to compliment you, too?'

'Yes, because I am so insecure about my looks,' Cab said.

'Very.'

He grinned. 'You'll stay the night?'

'You just want to see this dress in a pool at my feet.'

'I do.'

'We'll see,' she said. 'Some of us work for a living, you know.'

'Sounds dreary,' he replied.

He knew she had to be back home in the morning. It was an August weekend. Lala had joined him in Clearwater late on Friday, and it was Sunday now. Tarla had made herself discreetly absent for most of that time, but she had insisted on a dinner party before Lala returned to Naples. He suspected it was really more of a spying mission on his relationship with Lala.

'What about you?' she asked.

He understood the question. When would he come home? He lived on the beach in Naples, but he'd stayed here in the apartment next to his mother for more than a month. Lala was starting to wonder if he'd ever return or if he was now permanently under Tarla's thumb. There was no job to pull him home anymore. He'd already made good on his promise to resign from the Naples police. He was a free man, for whatever that was worth. He didn't know exactly what freedom entailed. So far, he wasn't in a hurry to find out.

'Maybe I'll come home with you tomorrow,' he said.

'Really?'

'I do miss my place. Plus, I should probably feed the cat, right?'

'You don't have a cat.'

'Well, that's lucky.'

She smiled at him. A smile deserved a kiss, so he bent down and kissed her. They were bad at some things together, and good at others, and they were good at kissing.

'Won't Tarla miss you if you go?' Lala asked.

'She misses me already. She misses me when I'm here.'

'Where is she, by the way?'

'Picking up Caprice.' He waited for her face to erupt with displeasure, and then he said quickly: 'Kidding. Kidding. You really don't like Caprice, do you?'

'No, I don't.' Lala added pointedly: 'Have you seen her lately?'

'No, but she's been pretty busy.'

'Do you miss her?'

'I've been thinking about her a lot,' Cab admitted.

'Wrong answer.'

'Not in the way you mean,' he replied.

Puzzlement crossed Lala's face, but she didn't press him for an explanation. She wandered toward one of the sofas and put down her wine glass on a walnut table. He came up behind her and stroked a bare shoulder.

'I tried calling Ramona,' Lala said, 'but I didn't reach her.'

'She's busy, too.'

'I don't believe what they're saying about her in the press.'

'As a cop or as a cousin?' he asked.

'Both. I've known her for years. She's a good person.'

'She admitted that Lyle consulted her about the hit and run,' he said.

'Only in general terms. Not about Deacon specifically or about the accident.'

'Ramona is smart,' Cab said. 'It's hard to believe she didn't make the connection.'

'If she did, she would have taken it to the grave. She's a lawyer.'

'I'm not sure I share your charitable opinion of lawyers,' Cab said. He kissed her neck, but she tensed. 'Sorry, I didn't say you were wrong about her. Sometimes I can't resist playing devil's advocate. It's a terrible flaw.'

She relaxed and turned around. 'I apologize. I'm the one who's being sensitive. You're right, I don't know the truth. I only know what I believe.'

'That's good enough for me.'

'You're buttering me up, but I still think you're more interested in getting my dress on the floor.'

'Guilty.'

Lala ran a finger along his chin. 'Would you really come back home with me tomorrow?'

'Yes.'

'That's an incentive, I'll admit.'

'Good.'

She picked up her wine glass again. 'So are you serious about taking up special investigative projects? Or are you going to stay unemployed and watch soap operas and knit sweaters for your cat?'

'I don't have a cat,' he said.

'Oh, that's right.'

'I am serious,' he said. 'In fact, I'm thinking of taking on a partner for my agency.'

Lala's eyebrows arched. 'You and me? I'm flattered, but don't you think that's a terrible idea? We don't exactly thrive when we spend all of our time together. A night here and there is more than enough. Besides, I'm a cop. That's all I ever wanted to be, and that's still what I want to be.'

'I know. I like you as a cop. I wasn't talking about you.'

She looked somewhat crestfallen. 'Then who?'

Cab nodded at the girl on the balcony, who continued to stare dreamily at the Gulf waters.

'Peach?' Lala asked.

'Peach,' Cab said. 'What do you think?'

'Actually, I think it's a great idea. Have you talked to her about it?'

'No, not yet. Will you put in a good word for me?'

'I will.'

They kissed again. Lala turned for the balcony and left him alone. He knew she would stay the night, and he would leave with her in the morning, and life, which had been on hold for a while, would begin again.

Lala slid open the patio door and went outside and closed it behind her. He watched the two women together, Lala and Peach. There was something close there, an intimacy of friendship, an easy familiarity. Peach hugged her. Lala smiled, and he saw genuine affection in her smile. Lala had a big family, and Peach had no family at all, but the thing about big families was that there was always room for one more.

Then there was himself and his mother.

'Penny for your thoughts,' Tarla said.

Cab jumped. He hadn't heard her arrive. His mother still had the ability to appear miraculously at his side out of nowhere. 'A penny?' he said. 'You can afford more.'

'I'm retired on a fixed income, darling. I'm economizing. Anyway, you look happy. Is something wrong?'

'Oh, it just occurred to me,' he said, pointing at Lala and Peach, 'that those two women are likely to be in my life for a long time.'

'Well, I hate to ruin the moment for you,' Tarla replied, 'but so will I.'

'Despite my best efforts?'

'I'm afraid so.'

'Just so you know, I'm going back to Naples with Lala tomorrow,' he said.

'Finally! No offense, darling, but you were starting to get on my nerves.'

She winked at him and patted his cheek. He looked momentarily dismayed, but then he smiled. Tarla was Tarla and would never change. She was dressed to kill, as she always was. She was beautiful, as she always was. The drive between Naples and Clearwater didn't take long in the Corvette. They still had things to talk about and things to work out.

'I have to go annoy the chef,' she said. 'Try to stay out of trouble until I get back.'

She tossed her blond hair and strolled away in her three-inch heels, leaving him alone. With nothing else to do, Cab headed for the balcony to drink up the evening sun, put his long arms around Lala's waist, and offer Peach a job.

EPILOGUE

Caprice Dean sat on a bench in the gardens of the Bok Sanctuary, under a sprawling ash tree that dripped with Spanish moss. Florida had never seen a more perfect December day. The air was dry. A noon sun was warm but not hot. The tower was at her back, its carillon playing a Shaker hymn that competed with the chatter of the birds. Her briefcase sat on the ground beside her. There was plenty to do, but she left it alone for now, so that she could enjoy the view across the green lawn and down the slopes into the orange groves.

She checked her watch. He was late.

She'd prepared carefully for the meeting with him. You had to approach every negotiation as a war, and all your weapons were on the table. Women were the hardest, because she'd always found them to be inherently untrustworthy around other women. You couldn't believe anything they said to your face. Men were easy, because they were creatures of desire. Senators or accountants, they were all the same. Undo a button, they were yours. He was no different.

The Shaker hymn ended. Another song began on the bells. It took a few notes, and then she recognized it. That song. That was the one. She stood up automatically. She didn't need to hear him to know he was behind her. She swung around, and he was watching her. Tall. Handsome. Ironic smile. Knee bent, hands in his pockets. She erased the memory of the song, even though every clang of the bells pounded in her brain, and she gave him a casual smile.

'Hello, Cab.'

'Caprice,' he said. He cupped an ear and cocked his head. 'Pretty, isn't it? I told them you had a special request.'

'Interesting choice.'

He came and sat down on the bench beside her. She sat down again, too. His arms draped around the back of the iron railing; she could sense his hand behind her shoulder. His legs jutted out, ridiculously long.

'I checked the concert program from the Labor Day event,' he said. 'This is the last song they played.'

'You've been busy.'

He listened to the music in silence. 'You know, Tarla's right. This sounds a lot like Supertramp.'

'It's not,' Caprice said. 'I picked it.'

'Yes, I know.' He smiled at her. 'You look gorgeous, by the way. Not that that's a surprise, you always do. They say politics ages people, but you seem to get younger.'

Normally, she would have flirted back. This time she didn't. He had her off her game, and she didn't like it. 'I appreciate your meeting me,' she said.

'Of course. This is a beautiful spot. Although it must hold difficult memories for you.'

'It does, but you can't change the past. This is one of my favorite places.'

'Even though your fiancé was murdered here?'

'Maybe I come here to think about him. Did you consider that?'

'Yes, but I don't think of you as the sentimental type.'

Caprice frowned. She wasn't accustomed to people playing games with her now. 'I've been keeping tabs on you,' she said. 'And on this new investigative agency of yours.'

'I'm flattered,' Cab replied. 'You've had a lot on your plate these past few months.'

'Well, you didn't give me much choice. I have sources who tell me that you've been scouring through my past. Talking to people who know me. Digging up college and law school friends. Finding staffers and volunteers who worked on Birch's campaign. Not just you but Peach, too. I'm used to reporters looking for stories and background, but when I saw your name, I couldn't help but wonder exactly what you were doing.'

Cab shrugged. 'You hired me.'

'And then you quit, as I recall.'

'Oh, I never really quit after I start something. I just change allegiances. I'm like a politician that way.'

'Funny,' Caprice said, but she didn't smile or laugh.

'I can't help but wonder why you hired me in the first place,' Cab said.

'You already know that. I suspected there was a threat against Diane. As it turns out, I was right, even if I didn't realize the danger was inside our own organization.'

'Yes, I saw your press conference,' Cab said. 'How you added security, hired a detective. Very noble.'

'I believe I credited you with saving Diane's life,' Caprice reminded him.

'You did. Thanks. That's good for business.'

'So what's the problem, Cab? The job is done.'

'It is, but I'm a little like a dog with a bone. I just keep going back to it when I should leave it alone.'

'That doesn't explain why you've been doing all this research on me.' She smiled, and she made love to him with her eyes. 'Why, I would almost think that you've become obsessed with me, Cab.'

'That would be easy for a man to do,' he acknowledged.

'Do you want back in my life? The door is still open.'

'Even now?'

'Even now,' she said. 'Nothing has changed for me as a woman. I'm still attracted to you.'

'And you always get what you want,' Cab said.

She grinned. 'Most of the time.'

'Look at Ramona Cortes. She was an enemy. She had the upper hand against Common Way in the election, but then she was neutralized. Destroyed. No charges, no crimes, just clouds of suspicion.'

'Charges can be proved or disproved,' Caprice said, 'whereas suspicion lasts forever.'

'Yes, how convenient. It cost her the campaign. It forced her to resign as Attorney General. The investigation into Common Way wound up dead in its tracks. You got everything you wanted. Yet again.'

'Apparently I did,' Caprice agreed.

'Almost as if it were planned that way from the start,' Cab said.

'Oh, now you're giving me more credit than I deserve.'

'Am I? I don't think so. I think it would be a huge mistake for anyone to underestimate you. You're brilliant, beautiful, and absolutely ruthless.'

'How nice of you to say.'

'The information about Ramona: you were the one who planted it, weren't you? After Lyle died, you would have had a copy of the invoice that the law firm sent to him.'

Caprice shrugged. 'If I ever saw it, I'm sure I didn't give it a second thought. No, I imagine some Good Samaritan inside the law firm had an attack of conscience. It's a big firm. Besides, does it really matter? The truth is what it is. Ramona knew about Deacon ten years ago.'

'But so did you,' Cab said.

'Me? Don't be ridiculous.'

'Lyle didn't tell you? His fiancée?'

'I'm sure he would have told me at some point, but Lyle was protecting Deacon. A tragic mistake, as it turns out, but Lyle always had integrity.'

'Yes, he did,' Cab agreed. 'You know, Rufus Twill told me something about Lyle when I met him. I didn't really think about it at the time, but I should have. I got too caught up with Drew as a suspect in the murders. My mistake.'

Caprice waited, a smile frozen on her face.

'Rufus said that Lyle called him shortly before Labor Day,' Cab went on. 'He said they needed to have a talk. Did you know anything about that?'

'No.'

'Do you have any idea what Lyle wanted to talk to Rufus about?'

'None at all.'

'Really? That surprises me, with the two of you being political partners. I mean, I can't see Lyle going to the press about his brother's hit and run. He was already in touch with a lawyer about that. On the other hand, I *can* see him deciding to blow the whistle on Birch Fairmont, can't you? He found out what Birch had done to Diane. He couldn't live with it. He knew his candidate was a monster, and he was going to slay him, regardless of the consequences to the Common Way Party. Regardless of the consequences to *you*. You said it yourself, didn't you? If Birch had been exposed, it would have been a disaster.'

'Where are you going with this, Cab?'

'Well, I just keep going back to the amazing fact that events always seem to work out exactly the way you want them to. Birch didn't get exposed. He got killed. He became a martyr. Common

Way became bigger than ever. Instead of losing everything, you wound up with even more power and money than you started with.'

'Only by losing the love of my life,' Caprice reminded him acidly.

'The love of your life? That's sweet, but I recall you saying your relationship was mostly political. And if Lyle talked, well, that would have been the end of his political usefulness, wouldn't it?'

'How dare you,' she snapped.

'I'm afraid emotional outrage doesn't become you, Caprice. It's not convincing. Isn't it remarkable that Deacon chose to kill Lyle because he was afraid of going to prison for the hit and run – and yet he chose to do it in a way that also took care of a huge political problem for you? Birch dead, Lyle dead, it was like winning the lottery, wasn't it?'

Caprice slapped his face. Hard. Cab touched his cheek, which bore the crimson mark of her hand. He laughed. 'Are those nails or claws? "Tyger! Tyger! burning bright / In the forest of the night / What immortal hand or eye / Could frame thy fearful symmetry?" Peach reminded me about that poem. I couldn't help but think of you.'

'Shut up.'

Cab smiled at her, completely unaffected. His calm drove her crazy. He reached inside his pocket and slid out a photograph. 'See this picture? I got it from an electrician in Ocala. He's a reformed member of the Liberty Empire Alliance. A true believer who ran out of anger. It's a picture he took outside an Alliance meeting in the spring ten years ago. They don't like pictures, but he was actually shooting a photo of where his car was parked because he was pissed that he got a ticket. Turns out he got a few of the Alliance members in the background of the photo. Anyone look familiar?'

She didn't look at the picture. 'No.'

'The kid with the red hair? Definitely Deacon Piper.'

Caprice shrugged. 'Good for you, Cab. You've discovered concrete evidence that Deacon had Alliance sympathies. That explains a lot. He killed Birch for the Alliance, and he killed Lyle for his own reasons. Ham Brock got him to do the same thing to Diane. Probably with Ramona's encouragement.'

'And once again, things work out perfectly for you.'

'I don't like your tone, Cab.'

'No? The thing is, I went to see Ham Brock again last week. I showed him the picture. He thinks Deacon was the mole inside the Alliance back then. And that made me think about you telling me how you always liked to have your own person on the inside, reporting to you. Did you use Deacon to spy on the Alliance? Were you already thinking the Alliance might be useful to take the fall if things went bad with Birch?'

Her first instinct was to give in to her agitation, but she held herself back. She knew he was baiting her. She wasn't going to let him win. Instead, she eased back on the bench without a care in the world. 'Ham Brock,' she said. 'You consider him a reliable witness, do you?'

'In this case, I do. Did Lyle know you were using his brother as a spy?'

'Of course not, because it's not true.'

'Just to satisfy my morbid curiosity, how far did the relationship with Deacon go? Did you sleep with him?'

Her head snapped around. 'You're on dangerous ground, Cab.'

'I just wondered if Deacon was in love with you. It seems like he was ready to do anything for you. He killed Birch. He almost killed Diane. He even made sure you wouldn't get blamed if he got caught. That's chivalry. Deacon meeting with Ham Brock a few months ago – that was a nice touch. Brock said Deacon spent half an hour bragging about everything that Diane was going to do against supremacist groups when she was elected. Were you hoping that Brock would put out the word? More rumors about the Alliance when Diane was killed? Of course, it didn't really matter what Deacon said to Brock. If Deacon got caught, the meeting alone would make people assume the Alliance was involved.'

Caprice said nothing at all.

'Not that Deacon planned to get caught,' Cab said. 'He intended to frame Frank Macy. But what was your plan, Caprice? Did you plan to kill Deacon all along?'

'Ashes to ashes,' Caprice said in the doorway of the garage.

Deacon had the gun in his hand and pointed it at her with a swift seamless whip of his arm. Instinct. She didn't flinch. Instead, she stood there, rain-soaked and wanton, her clothes like film on her body. The tiniest of smiles creased her face. Strange how she could smile knowing what was about to happen, but then, how could you not smile when you will soon have what you have always craved?

She came to him, dripping. 'Are you scared?'

'No.'

'It will all be over soon.'

'I know.'

Her fingers stroked the barrel of the gun, which was hard and long. She felt his excitement.

'I want to see the body,' she said.

He took her hand and led her to the car. He popped the trunk, and when she saw the dead eyes of Frank Macy staring at her, she quivered. It wasn't fear; it was arousal. She put a finger to the wound and let one of the corpse bugs climb onto her nail. She twisted her hand, making it run in circles around her finger, and when she was done playing with it, she crushed it under her thumb and dropped the carapace back among its brothers.

'Do you think this will work?' he asked.

'Trust me,' she said.

'There's a chance – I mean, it's possible that I won't make it. I've protected you if that happens. You know that, don't you?'

'I do. Thank you.'

That was the limit of her emotion. She'd always known his place in her universe. He was a useful tool to her, but if he died, if he was exposed, she would walk over him like litter in the street.

'There are days . . .' he began, but he couldn't finish his thought. He couldn't go there.

'We all make sacrifices,' she said.

She heard him try and fail to keep the bitterness from his voice. 'And what's yours?' he asked.

She put her hands on his face. He responded like that blind, dead insect, unable to stay away from her, despite the consequences of what lay ahead.

'Mine is living with who I am,' she said.

'You said you never fired a gun before,' Cab reminded her. 'Isn't that what you told Deacon in the sunroom? All those shots went wild. Except for the last one, which killed him. Dead in the center of the back. Perfect aim.'

'Luck,' Caprice said.

'Yes, you are a very lucky woman. Except I found a shooting range not far from where you grew up. They still remember you. The pretty teenage girl who was as sharp as a sniper. They're proud of you, by the way.'

'I hadn't fired a gun in years,' Caprice said. 'And I don't think I'm under any obligation to tell the truth to a murderer who's threatening to kill me.'

'That's true,' Cab said. 'You know, I really have only one question for you. There's one thing I'm not sure about. The whole plot with

Diane, that was you all along. That's why you hired me, isn't it? To point me down the path, to give the whole thing credibility. You used me from the start. I don't like being used, but I admit, you're good at it. As for the Labor Day murders, I wondered whether it was your idea or Deacon's, but come on. Deacon was a kid. You were the brains. Killing Birch and setting up the Alliance? Political brilliance. No, the only question I have is about Lyle. Did you know Deacon was going to kill him, too, or did he surprise you? I'd like to think you didn't know that was coming. I'd like to think you weren't acting your horror when he put the gun in Lyle's face and killed your fiancé. Sadly, though, I don't believe it. You told Deacon exactly what to do. Everything.'

Caprice took a breath in and a breath out. 'What a fascinating fairy tale.'

'Isn't it?'

'These are extraordinarily serious allegations to level against a woman with my power,' she said. 'You do realize that.'

'Yes, I do. And you do have power. That's what you always wanted, isn't it? I talked to your friends in college. They have exceptional admiration for you. They'd never met anyone so ambitious and so single-mindedly focused on achieving what she wanted. They all considered it to be one of your virtues.'

'I hope you don't plan to go public with these crazy ideas, Cab,' Caprice advised him. 'As far as I can tell, you don't have a shred of real evidence of my doing anything wrong, least of all the terrible things you've talked about. Not that you could, because none of it is true.'

'I'm not wearing a wire,' Cab said.

'In my business, everything is on the record.'

'Of course.'

'You really don't want me as an enemy, Cab. Trust me on that.'

'I think it's a little late for that,' he said.

'Yes, I think you're right.'

'Anyway, no, I have no plans to go public with any of this,' he told her. 'Not yet. I've been looking into it for months, but I can't find any useful evidence at all to prove anything. Even though I know you're guilty as hell.'

'Why are you so sure?' she asked.

'Honestly? Because my girlfriend really, really doesn't like you. I trust her judgment, but I suppose a prosecutor and jury would want something more. Which I don't have. So you win, Caprice. For now.'

'I usually do.'

'However, I'll be keeping an eye on you.'

'I bet you will.' Caprice saw an aide gesturing at her from near the beautiful tower. The music of the bells had gone silent. It was time to go. She stood up, and so did Cab, and the two of them shook hands. The security personnel who had hovered at a distance drew closer.

'Don't be a stranger,' she said to him. 'Goodbye, Cab.'

'Goodbye, Governor,' Cab replied.

AUTHOR'S NOTE

Cab Bolton first appeared as a character in my novel *The Bone House*. I planned the book as a stand-alone, but readers soon demanded to see more of that tall, rich detective. I hope you enjoyed his return. With this book, I now have two parallel series, one featuring Cab and one featuring Lieutenant Jonathan Stride of the Duluth Police. You can also look for my stand-alone *Spilled Blood*, which won the award for Best Hardcover Novel in the 2013 Thriller Awards.

You can write to me at brian@bfreemanbooks.com. I enjoy e-mails from readers and always respond personally. Visit my website at www.bfreemanbooks.com to join my e-mail list, get book club discussion questions, read bonus content, learn about meet-and-greet events in your area, and find out more about me and all of my books. You can also 'like' my official fan page on Facebook at www.facebook.com/bfreemanfans or follow me on Twitter, Instagram, or Tumblr using the handle **bfreemanbooks**.

I'd also like to ask a favor. I'd be grateful if you could do online reviews and post or tweet to your friends when you enjoy my books. That's a big help . . . thanks!

I lost a dear friend in the publishing industry as we were putting the finishing touches on *Season of Fear*. My agent Ali Gunn discovered me in 2004 with the manuscript of my first novel, *Immoral*. She was my agent, ally, friend, and supporter for all of the past decade. Ali passed away tragically and unexpectedly this winter, leaving a terrible hole for everyone who knew her. This book, like my other books, is in your hands because of Ali. I will always be grateful to her for shaping my career.

I'm fortunate to work with an amazing team in the publishing industry, especially everyone at my worldwide publisher Quercus. My thanks to David North, Rich Arcus, Nathaniel Marunas, Eric Price, Richard Green, and the entire Quercus team on both sides of the Atlantic.

This is my first book since *Stripped* to be set outside the Midwest. I'm very grateful to Mary and Roger Stumo, who allowed me and Marcia to use their condo in Indian Rocks Beach while we were doing research and scouting locations for the book. Most of the locales in this novel are real places, which you can find on Google Earth.

I have some wonderful readers who help me with feedback on early drafts of my manuscripts. They play an important role in shaping the final book. So big thanks to Marcia, Matt and Paula Davis, Terri Duecker, Mike O'Neill, and Alton Koren. Our three cats Heathrow, Gatwick, and Baltic also contribute to each book, but their 'help' typically consists of sleeping on my keyboard and in my chair.

Speaking of Marcia . . . you will see her on the first page of every book, and after thirty years of marriage, she's the most important person in everything I do. So if you enjoy my books, the thanks go to her as much as me.

Steven Hagu[illegible] for one of Eu[illegible] before he finally ma[illegible] his shackles and slip away under co[illegible] darkness. Having bade a life of financial security fare[illegible]ll, he got the crazy notion to embark on his lifelong dream to become a crime fiction writer, and the result of his wordsmithery is the exciting debut novel *Justice for All*.

Steven is 35 years old, and lives in Norwich with his wife, editor-in-chief and harshest critic Lisa, and his chocolate Labrador, Murphy. He is a sucker for all things Americana, and he's currently working hard on his next novel.

Find out more about Steven at
www.mirabooks.co.uk/stevenhague

STEVEN HAGUE

All the characters in this book have no existence outside the imagination of the author, and have no relation whatsoever to anyone bearing the same name or names. They are not even distantly inspired by any individual known or unknown to the author, and all the incidents are pure invention.

First published in Great Britain 2008 by Harlequin Mills & Boon Limited, Eton House, 18-24 Paradise Road, Richmond, Surrey TW9 1SR

ISBN: 978 0 7783 0198 1

58-0208

Printed and bound in Spain by Litografia Rosés S.A., Barcelona

For my wife Lisa,
who could see the light at the end of the tunnel,
and my dog Murphy, who dragged me towards it.

PROLOGUE

Three Months Earlier

VIKTOR DANILOV had killed more people than he cared to remember, in more ways than he cared to describe, and while he didn't take any pleasure from murder, he didn't take any pain either. For Danilov, death was just a way of life.

He stood motionless in front of the church, sporting a black rain slicker and wide-brimmed fedora. A tall man, at least six feet four, with a wiry frame that carried no excess fat, and skin that was almost translucent. The midday sun beat down on his shoulders but the heat didn't bother him. Nothing did. He was in the zone. Controlled breathing, slowed heart rate, his mind a blank canvas save for one thing. His target. In Danilov's experience, clarity of thought led to clarity of action.

He pulled on a pair of clear latex gloves, first covering the sickle on the back of his left hand, then the red hammer tattooed on his disfigured right, before pushing open the heavy oak doors and ducking inside. The church was empty, and a stifling aroma of dust and disuse hung heavy in the air. Etiquette demanded that he remove his fedora, but he left it on. He bolted the door then walked forward to claim a seat in the rear pew.

His eyes were drawn to the altar. The venerable old table was safely ensconced behind a communion railing, its pitted surface home to an ornate wooden cross and a jewel-encrusted reliquary. The railing annoyed him, providing so obvious a barrier between the priest and his so-called flock. What was the priest afraid of? Did he need protection from those that he sought to enlighten? Organised religion. A crutch for the weak. Praying to some unseen deity was for fools and savages. He checked the steel watch that encircled his wrist. It was almost time.

The door to the sacristy opened outwards and a priest emerged. He was garbed head to toe in a traditional black cassock, but the cincture was tied a little too low around his waist, which had the unfortunate effect of exaggerating his paunch. After casting a weary glance around the church, he shuffled over to the lone confessional booth and disappeared inside.

An old Russian proverb flitted through Danilov's mind—not all who wear cowls are monks. Maybe he'd toy with this one a little. He rose from the pew and headed for the booth, where he made himself uncomfortable on the faded kneeler. The small shutter in the dividing wall slid open to reveal a thin wire mesh.

'Yes, my son?' The priest's avuncular tone was perfect. How could a man not admit his failings to so friendly a voice?

'Forgive me, Father, for I have sinned,' began Danilov, his Russian accent as thick as molasses.

'How long has it been since your last confession?'

'I not remember.'

'Do not worry, my son, many of the flock become separated from the shepherd at some stage of their lives, but the important thing is that you're back on the path towards righteousness. What is it that you wish to confess to?'

'Murder.'

The priest stiffened on the other side of the booth. When he next spoke, his voice was measured and sombre. 'You have committed a diabolical act. The taking of life is a power that resides with God, and God alone. In what circumstances did this death occur?'

'Circumstances, Father?'

'How did it happen, my son? Was it an unfortunate accident of some sort?'

'*Nyet*, no accident. You not understand. Man not dead yet.'

'So you have yet to kill a man, but you intend to?'

'I have killed many men, Father, but they not important. I want forgiveness for man I'm about to kill.'

'I cannot grant forgiveness for such a deed ahead of its undertaking, for a man cannot be truly contrite for a heinous act he has yet to commit, only afraid, for he knows that he is about to set out on the long and lonely road to damnation. Put these dark thoughts from your mind, my son, stay here and pray with me, and together we will find succour in the healing arms of the Lord.'

'That I cannot do. Man must die. I must kill him. I leave now.'

The Russian rose to his feet and stepped out of the booth. His chest rose and fell with all the randomness of a metronome. A horn-handled stiletto appeared in his hand. When he thumbed the release catch, five inches of stainless steel sprang forth soundlessly.

In…out went his breathing.

He opened the door to the confessional. The priest half turned in the confined space to look up at him. His face showed surprise, then fear. The old man's mouth started to open but the time for talking was past. Danilov pushed on the priest's forehead to expose a mottled neck, then slashed left to right, cutting through folds of scraggly flesh to sever the carotid artery. Blood spurted out, a few splatters hit his rain slicker. No matter. The priest's eyes turned glassy while Danilov cleaned his knife on the holy man's vestments.

In…out went his breathing.

Just two more tasks to complete. He busied himself with the corpse for a few seconds then stood back to appraise his work. The priest's lifeless eyes stared no longer, having been covered by a black silk blindfold. Danilov let the door of the confessional swing shut to leave the body entombed in its upright coffin, then headed for the altar. Once there, he spread out twelve playing cards in front of the wooden cross—jacks, queens and kings, the three picture cards from each suit. Game over. Time to leave. He got as far as the main door then doubled back to the sidewall to light a solitary candle. It never hurt to cover all the bases.

His breathing went in…out, cool as you like. For Viktor Danilov, it had been just another day at the office.

CHAPTER ONE

ZAC HUNTER was nervous. Not scared nervous, but excited, as today was the big day. Things hadn't gone well for the prosecution thus far, but all that was about to change. He popped the muscles in his neck and shuffled his ass on the wooden bench. LA courtrooms weren't built for comfort.

The public gallery was rammed full, and it had been that way since day one of the trial. There was plenty of local interest in the case, but few people had more emotionally invested in the outcome than him. The room was dark, the atmosphere sombre. Oak panelling covered the walls while a scuffed tile floor ran underfoot. Wooden fixtures and fittings abounded, and they looked like oak too. A small forest had been cut down to outfit this place. There were no windows, which meant no natural light and no outside distractions. Instead, strip lights flickered overhead, their low wattage output bathing the room in a sickly glow. Lunch recess was almost over, and the air was alive with the gentle hum of a hundred murmured conversations, but Hunter was silent, his mouth too dry to talk.

Ahead of him, on the other side of the railing that separated the general populace from the business end of the room, were the attorneys' tables. To the left the defence, to the right the prosecution. Eight people were present, but Hunter only had eyes for one. He stared at the back of the defendant's head, his jaw set firm. Carlos Montero. Salvadorian immigrant. Kidnapper, pornographer, dead man walking. On trial for the abduction and murder of seven kids, and also responsible for screwing up Hunter's life. If looks could kill, Señor Montero would have required the immediate services of an undertaker.

The Salvadorian had been in the movie business. The snuff movie business. He'd plucked homeless kids from the city's darkened recesses, pumped them full of crack, then locked them in a room with nothing but a cheap video camera and a six-foot-six, three-hundred-pound paedophile named Bones for company. Six children had gone missing over a period of three months, each one resurfacing in a dumpster, their broken bodies tossed away like so much trash. Hunter had worked the case hard, harder than he'd ever worked any case before, putting in hour after hour, week after week, month after month, until time ceased to have any meaning, until life itself ceased to have any meaning other than bringing down the killer.

He'd become obsessed, working himself beyond exhaustion, until even sleep had failed to provide any refuge, his nights haunted by visions of the children's violated bodies, their screams of agony ringing in his ears each time he awoke. He'd kept a bucket by his bed, as he'd start each day by hacking up the contents of his stomach, his subconscious desperate to purge itself of the horrors of the night before. And the days—the fucking days—were even worse than the nights. Constant detective work with no clear leads, going from pillar to post without direction, feeling like nothing more than a fraud with a badge, all the while waiting for that terrible moment when another young body would be found stashed in some back alley. Tracking down the victims' families to deliver the terrible news. Attending funerals where lines of sobbing mourners watched tiny caskets being lowered into the ground. Then waiting for the whole damn cycle to start up again.

But just when he'd thought he might finally crack under the pressure, the abduction of Julie Delmar had broken the case wide open. She'd run away from home after a row with her stepfather, and had been missing for two days when the calls had started to come in. Just two days. When she'd quit home, her clothes had been clean, her hair had been tied in neat bunches, and her freckled face had been devoid of grime. Compared to the other street kids, she'd have stood out. Enough to be seen. Enough to be remembered. Witnesses placed her buying a foot-long chilli dog from a street vendor on Sunset, cadging for loose change outside Grauman's, and being bundled into the back of a white panel truck on Franklin. One sharp cookie had even had the foresight to make a note of the truck's licence plate, a plate that had led first to the paedophile Bones, and then to Montero.

The Salvadorian had initially denied all knowledge of Julie Delmar's whereabouts, but after thirty minutes of gentle persuasion his memory had returned. He'd led Hunter to a derelict steelworks on the edge of town, and once inside, up a flight of steel steps and along a walkway to what had formerly been the foreman's office. The windows had been boarded up, the wooden door padlocked top and bottom. Approaching sirens had begun to ring out their clarion call as Hunter had burst into the room to find Julie lying peacefully on a mildew-stained mattress. She'd looked for all the world like she was asleep, but this was one nap she wouldn't be waking up from. Hunter had been too late.

The memories of that day continued to haunt him. How he'd been so damn close to saving Julie's life but had still come up short. How he'd cradled the young girl's body in his arms, her eyes glassed over, her pale skin cold to the touch. How he'd failed her. How he'd failed them all. How someone had to pay.

He watched as Montero shifted around in his seat to look back over the courtroom. The Salvadorian's beady eyes flitted from person to person until they finally met Hunter's unwavering stare. The wounds on the guilty man's face remained prominent—a broken nose that kinked sharply to the left, a gap where his two front teeth had once resided. Hunter's blood began to boil. This case wasn't business, it was strictly personal. Just when he thought his fury had peaked, the Salvadorian tossed him a wide grin and turned back to his attorney.

Hunter's rough hands balled into fists. He forced himself to take ten deep breaths, just like the bullshit anger management classes had taught him, then looked back up to find that Montero's attorney was whispering into her client's ear. She was an attractive woman somewhere in her early thirties, wearing a black business suit with a crisp white blouse beneath. Power dresser. Her blonde hair was pulled back in a neat ponytail, and there was a pair of designer glasses perched on her freckled nose. The freckles made her look young and innocent. Hunter suspected she was anything but.

Her name was Rebecca Finch, and she'd led the prosecuting attorney on a merry dance thus far, objecting almost every time he'd had the audacity to open his mouth. She'd thrown doubt on the credibility of witnesses, argued that evidence was circumstantial or inadmissible, and bamboozled the jurors with so many legal technicalities that their heads were swimming with jargon by the end of each day. She'd made the case against the Salvadorian look weak. The confession that Hunter had beaten out of him hadn't been worth the paper it had been written on. Even the fact that Montero had led him to the very steelworks where the girl's body had been found had counted for nothing. Everything was inadmissible, as his interrogation technique was adjudged to have been overly energetic. The review board had called it 'use of excessive force' just before they'd stripped him of his badge and shown him the door.

So there was a lack of hard evidence. Montero had been careful to distance himself from the operation, leaving Bones to take all the risks. It was Bones who'd left a mattress soaked with DNA evidence at the steelworks, Bones who'd left his fingerprints on the digital video camera, and Bones who'd starred in the snuff movies found on the camera's memory card. Montero's Salvadorian hands were clean. And Finch had played on that Salvadorian angle. Hinted that institutionalised racism was at work. Suggested that her client might not have been in this situation if it hadn't been for his cultural background. She'd made him look good on the stand, his facial wounds suggesting victim rather than accused. He'd put on a real performance for the jurors. Given them shocked when he'd found out that Bones had been kidnapping street kids. Given them saddened when the police thought that he might have had something to do with it. Given them outraged when recounting how a rogue detective had beat him to within an inch of his life.

Hunter had watched the trial unfold with a growing sense of unease. Rebecca Finch was a hotshot. A real go-getter. But while there was little doubt she was winning the battle, she hadn't yet won the war. Thus far, the prosecution had been hampered by the fact that all of Montero's associates had developed a sudden case of amnesia. Nobody had a bad word to say about the Salvadorian. Nobody, that is, except Bones, the three-hundred-pound paedophile who'd left more than enough evidence at the steelworks to seal his fate. Bones was the guy who had the most to gain from cutting a deal. Bones was up next on the witness stand. The tide was about to turn.

CHAPTER TWO

THE DA had been working Bones over for weeks, first threatening, then cajoling, then shaming, until the dim-witted monster was ready to plea-bargain his soul down the river. Bones's testimony was going to implicate Montero in everything—the abductions, the snuff movies, the disposal of the bodies—every little thing. And his reward for making like a 24-carat Judas? Immunity from death row, jail time to be served in a psych ward instead of San Quentin, and a shot at parole fifteen years down the line. No matter that he was a child-murdering rapist on multiple counts. The DA wanted Montero, so Bones was going to talk his way out of a lethal injection. Everything in life came down to cutting deals. Even justice.

'All rise for the Honourable Judge Jackson. Court is now in session.'

A hush fell over the room as a small door midway along

the rear wall swung open. The judge emerged from his chambers brushing the last vestiges of lunch from his black robes. Hunter watched as he waddled to the bench, an aging, rotund man with a well-groomed beard and a tendency towards pomposity. He nodded once to the members of the jury, then nodded once more to the bailiff and court stenographer as he settled his ample rump into his seat.

After a brief shuffling of papers, he addressed the court. 'Case number 922, the People versus Carlos Montero, is now resumed. The charge is murder in the first degree, filed under section 189 of the Californian penal code. Are the People ready to call their next witness?'

'Yes, Your Honour,' the lead prosecutor, a stick insect who went by the name of Vidic, replied. 'The People call Bones.'

Hunter's heart rate accelerated a notch as Bones was led to the witness stand. He was huge, a bull of a man, towering over the guard alongside him and somehow wedged into a nasty checked suit. His dank brown hair was cut in no discernible style, three-days' worth of stubble sprouted from his saggy jowls, and his eyes jumped nervously around the room, looking everywhere except at the defence table. Hunter tensed up. Talk about mixed feelings. Part of him wanted to leap up and go throttle the sleazebag, while another part wanted to offer a round of applause. He tried to focus on the greater good. Bones's testimony was going to send Montero down. The plea bargain meant they'd get two sleazebags for the price of one. It was a start.

Bones arrived at the stand, shoehorned his fat ass into the seat, and stared studiously at the floor. Heavy beads of perspiration ran down his forehead. He wiped them off with the back of his arm.

'Please state your name, and spell your last name for the record.'

He had to lean forward to reach the microphone. 'Bones—B-O-N-E-S.' In marked contrast to his great size, his voice was high and squeaky, as if his balls were in a vice, which, metaphorically, they were.

'Your full name, please,' prompted the bailiff, failing to hide the note of impatience in his voice.

'Bones is my full name…got it changed…all legal and proper.'

Some sniggers rang out from the public gallery. The Bailiff elected to move on.

'Please place your hand on the Bible. Do you solemnly swear to tell the truth, the whole truth, and nothing but the truth, so help you God?'

'Yeah.'

Vidic approached the stand with something like a swagger, his confidence finally on the rise. After weeks of getting the run-around from Rebecca Finch, he was about to strike a blow for truth, justice and the American Way. He favoured the jurors with his most charming smile then turned to begin the questioning. The courtroom went deathly silent. Hunter leant forward in his seat and sent up a prayer for little Julie Delmar and the six other murdered children.

'Mr Bones,' began Vidic, 'how long have you known the defendant, Carlos Montero?'

'About three years,' Bones muttered at his scuffed black boots.

'Mr Bones, please direct your answers into the microphone stationed directly in front of you,' Judge Jackson cut in, 'and enunciate in a clear fashion. I can assure you that the court is very interested in what you have to say.'

The giant shuffled forward in his seat and adjusted the microphone, then raised his head until he was looking straight at Montero, a mixture of dumb fear and pure hatred burning in his eyes. A vein started to jump in his forehead. His fist clenched on the stand. Then he looked away.

'Once again, Mr Bones,' continued Vidic, walking grandly up and down in front of the jury. 'Can you confirm that you have been a friend of the defendant, Mr Carlos Montero, for the past three years?'

'Yeah. He used to be my buddy.'

'And how did you first meet?'

'At Co-Co's strip bar. He bought me a beer…'

'But Co-Co's wasn't just any strip bar, was it, Mr Bones? Didn't their dancers tend to be a little on the young side? So much so that the bar was busted fourteen times in a three-month period before the police finally shut it down?'

'Objection!' barked Rebecca Finch. 'Assumes facts not in evidence. The witness is not privy to police records.'

'I'll make an offer of proof on the string of violations that Co-Co's strip bar committed, Your Honour,' responded Vidic. 'In the course of this trial you'll hear testimony from an LAPD detective who will confirm that the bar was shut down fourteen times in the three months prior to its closure on June 10th of this year.'

'I'll allow it,' rumbled Judge Jackson.

'So once again, Mr Bones, were the dancers at Co-Co's underage?'

'If you say so.'

'I do say so, Mr Bones, as I want everyone present to realise what sort of a strip bar we're talking about here.' Vidic broke off and shuffled through some papers. 'After your first meeting with Mr Montero, how often did you subsequently meet at Co-Co's?'

'Once, maybe twice a week…till it got shut down.'

'And what was the main topic of conversation during your meetings?'

'Montero did most of the talking. Told me he was a film-maker, a real big shot. Asked me if I wanted to be in one of his movies, said I had star quality…'

'What sort of movies are we talking about here, Mr Bones? Hollywood action flicks? Literary adaptations? Romantic comedies?'

'No. Hard-core porn… He wanted to know how big my schlong was…made me show it to him in the john.'

'Thank you for sharing that tender moment with us, Mr Bones,' muttered Vidic with all the distaste he could muster. 'So Montero's movies weren't the sort you could get from your local rental shop? They were, in fact, only available to those in the know? Under the counter, that sort of deal?'

'I guess…' Bones shrugged his huge shoulders in tacit agreement, causing the flab on his chest to wobble.

Vidic walked back to his table, collected another sheaf of papers, studied them for a few moments, then returned to his position in front of the witness stand.

'I have in my hands your sworn confession, Mr Bones,' he began, holding the papers high to draw attention to them. 'In this sickening statement, you admit to the abduction of seven children in an unmarked white panel truck, you admit to the subsequent rape and murder of those seven children, and you admit to disposing of their bodies in back-alley dumpsters.'

'Yeah… I'm sorry for what I done… I'm gonna get me some help…'

Hunter sneered. It was too damn late for contrition. Way too late for those poor kids.

'But it wasn't you that chose the children, was it, Mr Bones?' Vidic continued. 'It wasn't you that found the abandoned steel warehouse, turned the old office into a cell, or set up the filming equipment that the police found inside? As your statement attests, you had an accomplice. A leader, in fact. The brains of the operation…Carlos Montero.'

A smile started to inch its way across Hunter's face. This was it. This was the moment when the jury would start to see Montero for what he really was. The moment when all the legal bullshit would stop and the truth would come out. Bones took a deep breath then stared straight at Montero as he answered through gritted teeth, 'I don't know nuthin' about no accomplice. Mr Montero dint have anythin' to do with it.'

A shocked intake of breath swept around the room as Hunter's smile morphed into a grimace of disbelief. What the fuck was this? Vidic froze in his tracks as the colour drained from his face and the confidence drained from his demeanour. His mouth hung open like that of a gawping fish and it took him a few seconds to remember to clam it shut, and a few seconds more to realise that he'd better move fast to undo the damage.

'Mr Bones, may I remind you that you are under oath, and that your deal with the State of California requires you to regale this court with an open and honest account of Mr Montero's involvement in this case. You find yourself in a very precarious position. Take your time...think it through before you answer...think about everything you stand to lose. Now, I ask you again, was Carlos Montero your accomplice?'

'No, sir. I done it all on my own. I was trying to make films just like Mr Montero. I wanted to be a big shot movie guy just like him. Those kids...I'm truly sorry about them, but Mr Montero had nuthin' to do with it. I'm sorry for all this trouble, but I got a family too...' Bones looked straight at the accused as he spoke. Hunter felt sick with rage. The courtroom erupted.

The judge banged his walnut gavel and called for order. As soon as the crowd had quietened down Rebecca Finch was smartly out of her seat.

'May I approach, Your Honour?'

A nod of acquiescence was swiftly forthcoming. Finch covered the distance to the bench in four athletic strides, with Vidic following dejectedly in her wake.

'If that's all the witness has to say, then these proceedings are over, Your Honour. Without his testimony, the case against my client is circumstantial at best.'

The judge stared down from on high at the lead prosecutor. 'Ms Finch has a valid point. I warned you about being over-reliant on your key witness during pre-trial, Mr Vidic. Without him, your case is dead in the water. What have you got to say?'

'I don't know what's happened here, Your Honour. Just give me a little time to speak to my witness. I'm sure I can get this all straightened out.'

'As it's Friday, I'll give you until first thing Monday morning. But if it turns out that Mr Bones has decided to retract his original statement, I'll have no option but to throw this case out of court. My time is precious—I can't afford to waste it on pointless prosecutions.'

The two attorneys turned away as the judge banged on his gavel. 'This court is in recess until nine a.m. Monday.'

Pandemonium broke out as people started to discuss the events they'd just witnessed. Some leapt to their feet to hurl abuse at Montero, the lawyers, and even the judge, but Hunter stayed right where he was, a feeling of disbelief washing over him. He bowed his head, closed his eyes, and dug his fingers deep into his temple. This couldn't be happening.

CHAPTER THREE

'SAME again...' Hunter growled, rubbing a hand through his short-cropped brown hair. Another Coors was quickly forthcoming—the barman knew better than to question him when he was in this kind of mood. The joint was dimly lit, the lights way down low, giving the place a seedy sort of feel, and an old-style jukebox in the far corner was kicking out 'Paint it Black' by the Stones. Apart from Hunter, who was perched on a stool, there were a handful of other regulars dotted around, each of them busy keeping themselves to themselves. Tommy's bar never had drawn much of a crowd.

Hunter sighed. An ever-growing collection of empty beer bottles sat on the oak counter in front of him. It was ten p.m. and he was blind drunk, but the booze wasn't helping. The whole legal system was a joke. You put a guy like Montero on trial, and even though everyone knew he was guilty, he was gonna walk. Months of painstaking investigation, weeks in court, and for what? Nothing. Call that justice? All Hunter wanted was a little quality time with the Salvadorian in a windowless room. No witnesses, no judges and, best of all, no lawyers. Swift verdict, appropriate punishment. Biblical. An eye for an eye. Montero's life for the kids'. He took another slug from his beer as a newcomer grabbed himself a spot at the bar two stools down.

'Whisky—Old Fitzgerald—leave the bottle.' The voice was gruff and commanding, as if its owner had issued countless commands over the years and had gotten used to most of them being obeyed. He knocked back the shot in a single gulp, replenished his glass, then pushed the bottle along the counter.

'Care to join me?'

Why the hell not. Hunter turned to the stranger and nodded. The guy was pushing sixty, with closely cropped salt-and-pepper hair that favoured the salt, a weathered face with a slew of broken veins in his cheeks, and a steely blue gaze that grabbed your attention and refused to let go. His build was stocky, like that of a prizefighter, but it was hard to tell if he was in good shape, swaddled as he was in a knee-length blue coat that had definitely seen better days.

'The name's Carson,' he began, gesturing at the empty tumbler. 'Knock yourself out...'

Hunter poured himself a generous measure and gulped it down. The whisky was smooth on the tongue but it kicked like a mule once it hit the back of his throat, and while the slow burn helped warm his guts, it did little to brighten his mood.

'Bad day, eh?' rasped Carson, as he retrieved a pack of red pistachios from somewhere inside his coat.

'The worst...'

'Saw you at the trial...'

'Trial? Don't make me laugh. I've seen more due process at

a lynching. Montero's gonna walk and he's guilty as hell. Christ, he admitted the whole damn thing to me, but would the court listen? Would they fuck! They'd rather have a kiddie rapist on the stand than an honest cop... Wait a minute, what were you doing at the trial? You're not a goddamn reporter, are you?'

'Fuck that. I'm a cop. Out of Robbery-Homicide Division.'

'Carson? The name's kinda familiar. Didn't you have some trouble with the desk jockeys over at IA a few months back?'

'Yeah—wrongful arrest beef. Forgot to get the right forms signed before I busted into some pimp's pad to ask him about a dead hooker. Whadya gonna do?' He shrugged. 'You're Zac Hunter, aren't you? I've been following your case for a while. All those dead kids...what a fucking tragedy. Musta bust you up inside. Hey...tell me something...when you were beating on Montero, was that business or pleasure?'

'Business...the little girl was still missing...' murmured Hunter, remembering the interrogation that had cost him his job.

'I don' know whatchu talking 'bout, I ain't seen no little girl. I's just a film director.' Montero grinned from behind his walnut-topped desk, while gesturing to the multitude of skin flick stills that lined the walls of his office.

'We got Bones, we got the truck, and we got you, so you're gonna tell me where Julie Delmar is, one way or another. Start co-operating—make it easy on yourself.'

Montero extended his middle finger. Hunter's patience snapped. He didn't have time for this bullshit. He leapt across the desk and threw a right cross straight into the middle of the pornographer's face. Thud. One broken nose. Blood and snot gushed from the nostrils.

'Muthaf—'

The curse went unfinished as Hunter's left hand closed around Montero's windpipe while his right fell from on high to slam into the Salvadorian's mouth. His fist hammered down a further three times, opening up wounds to the lip, cheek and temple, before he lifted Montero out of his seat and hurled him against the rear wall. After a moment's pause, the Salvadorian slid to the floor, where he cowered like a whipped dog.

'Where's Julie Delmar? Where's the girl?'

No response. He drew back his right boot and slammed it into Montero's ribs. A loud crack signified that at least one had been broken. Montero screamed and spat out two of his teeth.

'Where...is...she?' Hunter punctuated each word with another vicious kick. He lifted his boot and stepped down on the Salvadorian's throat. Montero's bloodied face looked up at him, his eyes bulging in fear, his veins standing proud as oxygen deprivation set in, and still Hunter kept shouting.

'Where...is...she?'

'So you beat the girl's location out of him, called it in, then dragged his sorry ass straight over to the warehouse. Sounds like good police work to me. I woulda played it the exact same way. Matter of fact, it reminds me of a time when I was back in DC, trying to track down a stash house in the projects. I nabbed a street seller and pounded on his sorry ass till the words flowed out of his mouth quicker 'n the blood. Took me an hour, and I damn near broke my left hand on his jaw,' Carson said, cracking his knuckles. 'But it goddam worked. Had the drugs impounded by sundown.'

'You worked in DC for a while?'

'Back in my younger days, before I moved out here.' The old man nodded in response as he poured them both another generous shot of whisky. Over in the corner, 'Sympathy for the Devil' faded out on the jukebox and 'Under My Thumb' kicked in. 'I'm almost done, though. Retirement's just round the corner so my caseload's pretty light. Been on the force the best part of thirty years and every damn day it gets a little bit harder. More red tape, and more rights for the accused. What about the victims' rights? Who speaks for them? We used to, but now they got us gagged, made us powerless. We're fighting our war on crime with a peashooter while the hoods are packing nothing but heavy artillery. And as for the lawyers? Don't get me started on them…'

Hunter nodded glumly in agreement. 'Did you see Finch in there today? Making her way in the world by keeping a child-killer like Montero on the streets, and I bet it didn't even prick her conscience.'

'Goddamned dyke. Lawyers like Finch are no better than the scum they represent. Her cheque's in the post, Montero's gonna walk, and meantime you're out of a job. What sort of world are we livin' in? Bet you'd do things a little different if you had your time over. Bet you wish you'd dished out some real justice when you had the chance.'

'Open it up!' Hunter yelled at the cowering Montero. The two men were at the steelworks, standing on a raised walkway in front of a padlocked door. A number of empty paint tins and rotting cardboard boxes were dotted around their feet.

'I ain't got no key,' croaked the Salvadorian.

'Bullshit!'

Hunter shoved his handcuffed prisoner to the floor then hoisted him up by the earlobes. Montero gargled rather than screamed, his larynx still feeling the after-effects of being on the wrong end of a size ten boot.

'Where's the damn key?'

'Go fuck yourself!'

Hunter spun the Salvadorian around, grabbed the back of his jacket, then pushed him over the balustrade until the forty-foot drop to the floor below loomed large.

'Trust me—I'm not fooling around…'

The growing wail of sirens began to penetrate the building's interior. Montero's face went scarlet as the blood rushed to his head.

'It's in da tin, it's in dat paint tin by the door…'

In a move he'd later regret, Hunter pulled his captive back from the abyss and tossed him along the walkway. The lid to the paint tin came off easy—inside, there were two stainless-steel keys. The keys turned in the padlocks and the door opened with a slight groan, as if disappointed to reveal its secrets. A funnel of light spilled into the room, reaching just far enough to illuminate the foot of a stained mattress.

'Where are the goddamn lights?'

'Generator…on your right…' Montero was through holding out. Maybe the prospect of a long fall to a certain death had helped loosen his tongue.

Hunter reached down and fumbled around in the shadows until he found the right switch. The machine buzzed to life, bathing the room in the harsh halogen glare of two industrial spotlights. The space was bare save for a digital video camera set up on a tripod plus the dirty mattress. The naked body of a small girl lay on the mattress. Julie Delmar. A sob caught in Hunter's throat. Time stood still for a second as a familiar feeling of helplessness washed over him, then he broke his paralysis to rush over to the child and reach for a pulse. Her skin was cold to the touch. A track of fresh needle marks ran up her forearm. He was too late. He collapsed to his knees and began to sob in heaving bursts, and with each passing second his anger began to build. He knew what had to be done.

He drew his Beretta and turned back towards the door. The

sound of a large number of men running along the walkway barely registered. He walked out to face the snivelling Montero, released the safety, and levelled his gun.

'No…please…no…'

Hunter's finger tightened on the trigger. A few more ounces of pressure were all that was needed. The faces of each of the seven murdered children flashed through his mind, each one crying out for justice from beyond the grave. Running footsteps clattered to a stop just behind him. The cavalry had arrived.

'LAPD! Lower your weapon! Put the gun down now!'

His trigger finger tensed. His whole arm started to shake. The sound of weapons being cocked rang out.

'Stand down Hunter! Stand down now!'

'Damn straight. I should have blown that cocksucker out of his shoes back at the steelworks, ended his sorry life once and for all. But I was too slow…' Hunter took another slug from his beer. 'Tell you one thing for free, though—I've still got a bullet with his name on it, badge or no badge.'

Carson digested that statement without comment, holding Hunter's gaze for a full thirty seconds before dispensing two more shots of whisky.

'And there's no chance that the prosecution's main witness, Bones, is gonna testify?' he asked, as he withdrew a credit card from his wallet and threw it down on the counter.

'Nope. I spoke to a friend at the DA's office and there's no way that sack of shit is going to change his mind over the weekend. He just keeps saying he's got a family to protect. Montero must have got to him. Threatened his wife and kids. Without his testimony we're sunk—the whole case is shot.'

'Tough break,' said Carson, downing his shot. When the barman brought over the cheque, he signed it with a flourish then rose to his feet. 'Been good talking to you, but my empty home awaits. And a word to the wise.' He lowered his voice. 'When it comes to Montero, do what you gotta do.' With that, he turned and was gone.

Alone at the bar once again, Hunter's booze-addled brain continued to buzz. Moving on with his life wasn't an option. There was no way he was just gonna wipe the slate clean and forget about the past. Seven kids were dead and the blood was on Montero's hands. It wasn't over. The so-called justice system might have blown its chance, but Montero was going to pay, one way or another—Hunter was damn sure of that.

CHAPTER FOUR

HUNTER'S ride was a classic. A 1970 Plymouth Barracuda, jet black, with a 426 Street Hemi under the hood. He eased the 'Cuda through the Monday lunch-hour traffic on Fifth Street until a stoplight forced him to come to a halt at the base of the Bunker Hill Steps. The steps were LA's answer to the more celebrated Spanish version that resided in Rome, and just for once modernism had given neo-classicism a run for its money. He glanced upwards to observe some tourists in matching red polo shirts being shepherded towards the summit, the group driven from one series of terraces to the next by an over-eager guide who barely paused to acknowledge the runnels of water cascading down the centre of the course. That was the trouble with city life—even when people were on vacation, they were in a hurry. He pulled away as the stoplight turned green, and drove on for a couple more blocks till he arrived at his destination.

The building was a mid-sized skyscraper with traditional red brickwork and blacked-out windows that glinted in the afternoon sun. It was set back from the sidewalk, courtesy of a chrome-plated wall. A polished concrete path ran though the middle of the wall and finished at the base of a series of gentle steps. On either side of the steps were expensive-looking steel planters housing mature Japanese maples. A series of chrome plaques were set to the right of the glass entrance doors. The third one down read 'Mitchell, Wallace and Flint, Partners in Law'. Swanky.

Hunter pushed through the doors and strode into the lobby, his desert boots barely making a sound on the terrazzo tiles underfoot. He ignored the main reception desk and followed a guy with wavy hair and an expensive suit over to the elevators, then waited for him to enter a pass code on the numeric keypad that was set into the wall. When the doors rolled open, he stepped inside with a nod of thanks. The law firm was spread over two floors, the eighteenth and nineteenth. He pushed the button for 18 and felt the elevator give a slight judder as it started its ascent.

Great. Another trip to a law office. The first he'd had to make since being booted out of the department a few weeks back, and one of the aspects of his old job he hadn't missed one bit. Talking to a lawyer was like trying to wrestle with a well-oiled snake, while reasoning with one was even more pointless. And they were spreading like a goddamned plague. The USA was now home to over a million practising attorneys and that number was set to rise as companies became ever more fearful of litigation. Nobody took responsibility for their actions any more—they were all too busy finding someone else to blame.

The elevator came to a gentle stop and the doors rolled open. A petite blonde looked up from her position behind the reception desk and gave him her best plastic smile, which quickly faded once she got a load of his attire. Faded Levi's and a scuffed leather jacket, with a black denim shirt underneath. He walked over to the desk, and by the time he'd got there the receptionist's fake smile was back in place, and he had one of his own to match.

'Good afternoon, sir, can I help you?'

'Afternoon…Jenny,' he replied, checking the nametag pinned on her chest. 'I'm here to see Ms Finch.'

'Your name, sir?' She reached for an appointment book.

'You won't find me in there, honey. Which way to her office?'

'I'm sorry, sir, but if you don't have an appointment, Ms Finch won't be able to see you. She's a very busy woman, booked solid all day—her next client is due in just fifteen minutes.' She looked back up and appraised him. 'If you'd like to leave your name and a contact number, perhaps I could get her to call you?'

'That doesn't really work for me… Tell you what, why don't we make full use of the spare fifteen minutes she's got now? Don't worry, we're old friends…I'll just head on up and surprise her.' He strode back to the elevator, noting with relief that pass-code access was only required at lobby level. 'Nineteenth floor, right?' he called over his shoulder. These executive types always went for the view.

'Er…yes, but you can't just march up there unannounced…'

Jenny was flustered. Maybe she was new to the job. He gave her his best winning smile as he pushed the call button. 'Trust me, we go way back…' The elevator emitted a ding as the doors slid open. He stepped inside the metal box before she could offer any further protest and gave her a nonchalant wave. The smile fell from his face as soon as the doors slid shut. He shifted his head from side to side during the ascent, popping the muscles in his neck. His sense of injustice had grown over the weekend, and he knew that if he was going to put things right, he only had a limited window of opportunity in which to do so.

He hadn't gone to the trial that morning. Why waste time on a sure thing? A local radio station had confirmed the worst—Bones had stuck to his bullshit story, the judge had thrown the case out, and Montero had walked free with a big smile plastered all over his face. Hunter knew what had to be done, but before he got down to business he wanted to have a quiet word with Rebecca Finch, the legal champion of smut-pushing, child-murdering paedophiles.

When the elevator doors opened, an empty hallway confronted him. He stepped out onto a dark blue carpet, his boots half sinking in the deep shag, then debated whether to turn left or right. Left first. As he walked down the hallway he checked the nameplates on each of the walnut doors, ignoring the framed modern artwork that hung on the eggshell-painted walls. Finch was behind the last door at the end. She'd bagged herself a corner office. Prestigious. He let himself in, walked straight past the startled personal secretary without a word and crashed into the inner sanctum.

Recessed bookshelves covered two of the walls, each of them filled with rows and rows of leather-bound law books, huge volumes that offered a guaranteed cure for insomnia, while the third wall was home to a number of framed diplomas, plus a large abstract painting featuring a series of monochrome rhomboids arranged in an intricate spiral. The fourth wall, if indeed you could call it a wall, was a window, a huge expanse of reinforced glass that ran from floor to ceiling to offer a panoramic view of the city below. In front of the window was an expansive cherry walnut desk with a dark leather inlay, and behind the desk, looking pretty hot in a tight white blouse, was Rebecca Finch.

'And just what in the hell do you think you're doing?' she asked.

The secretary poked her head around the door before he could answer. 'Should I call Security, Miss Finch?'

'Don't worry, Margaret, I can handle this. Take a seat, Mr Hunter.'

'I'd rather stand…' He waited for the door to click shut before continuing. 'Your main purpose in life is to keep criminals on the streets. Every day you do your utmost to ensure that scum like Montero are allowed to roam freely among us, spreading their poison wherever they choose. How the hell do you sleep at night?'

She looked back angrily and pushed her glasses up the bridge of her nose. Her eyes were a cool hazel colour and they bristled with indignation. 'Everyone's entitled to a legal defence.'

'Bullshit. You knew Montero was guilty, yet you did everything you could to save his skin. He kidnapped kids. He pumped them full of drugs and left them with that sick fuck Bones. He murdered them. What's it like, accepting blood money to keep a monster like that on the streets? Are you proud of yourself?'

Finch rose to her feet and walked around the desk, and Hunter couldn't help but notice how her skirt clung to her shapely legs. She stopped a yard shy of him and put her hands on her hips, her tone taking on a steely edge. 'The burden of proof falls on the prosecution. My client was released as there was a lack of evidence against him—largely on account of your violent behaviour in his apprehension, and your complete inability to follow legal protocol. If you want to apportion blame, I suggest you look to yourself in the first instance.'

'Save it for someone who gives a shit—I'm not buying.'

'Perhaps you need a refresher course on the sixth amendment—"The accused shall enjoy the right to a speedy and public trial by an impartial jury…and shall have the Assistance of Counsel for their defence". I'm just doing my job. How would you have it? Let me guess, a vigilante on every street corner? I know your background.'

'And what the hell is that supposed to mean?'

'Zac Hunter, aged thirty-four, former LAPD detective with a penchant for using his fists. My client wasn't the first man you beat to a near pulp, but with any luck he'll be the last. I've read your IA reports—I know how you operate,' Finch said, her blouse tightening across her chest as she took a deep breath. 'Diego Garcia, suspected gunrunner, 1996. Diego had twin fractures to his jaw and eye socket at the time of his arrest. Jimmy Walcott, suspected pimp, 1999. Jimmy was wheeled out of an interrogation room with a shattered patella and a compound fracture of his left tibia. And how about Omar Dupris, suspected drug dealer, 2002? When you brought him in he had two broken arms and six fractured ribs. Omar had to take his food through a straw for the best part of a month. And these are just some of your edited highlights, Mr Hunter. Quite frankly, I'm surprised that all your temper cost you was your job—you ought to be doing a little jail time yourself. But then again, the police department always has looked after its own.'

'I've never punched out anyone who didn't deserve it. Sure, I've sidestepped a few laws in my time, but at least I've got morals. Go talk to the families of the seven murdered kids then take a long hard look in the mirror. People like me exist to protect the world from people like Montero, whereas people like you are just out to make money—you're a bloodsucking leech who's only looking for her next buck. I'm through talking with you—I can see that I'm wasting my breath.'

He spun on his heel and stormed out of the office, almost colliding with Finch's next appointment in the anteroom, a handsome kid in his early twenties who had the long, blond hair of a Californian surfer.

'Stay away from my client, Mr Hunter,' Finch yelled after him.

He headed for the exit without a backward glance, stepped out into the empty corridor, pulled the door almost shut, then stopped dead. The sound of Finch's secretary uttering a stream of apologies fluttered out through the thin opening like butterflies on the breeze. After a few seconds the old girl re-appeared to escort the kid into the main office. Hunter hurried over to the Rolodex on her desk. He flicked through the section marked 'M'. Miguel, Mitchell, Morgan, Montero. Bingo. He was halfway through memorising the address when the cool tones of Rebecca Finch stopped him in his tracks.

'I think that's quite enough snooping for one day, don't you, Mr Hunter? Are you going to leave of your own volition, or should I have Security escort you out of the building?'

He left without a word.

'Please accept my apologies, Mr Ashton,' said Rebecca Finch, calmness personified, as she sat back down in the black leather chair behind her desk. The young man in front of her scowled, the sour expression spoiling his otherwise handsome features.

'I don't like to be kept waiting, especially by the hired help. Make sure you're on time for our next meeting. I'm not paying you to be late.'

You're not paying me at all, thought Rebecca. Your father's footing the bill. She gave him her most professional smile before continuing. 'It won't happen again.'

'It had better not…' Ashton leant back in his chair and rested his black Ferragamo shoes on the edge of her desk, his glare fixed firmly in place. 'Now, to business—remind me of what I'm up against?'

Rebecca stared pointedly at his feet until he removed them. This kid was a royal pain in the ass. Every pre-trial meeting they'd had thus far had panned out much the same. He'd swagger in with his film-star good looks—high cheekbones, blue eyes, and long blond hair—plus his designer wardrobe—today he was sporting silver Calvin Klein jeans and a ruby red Ralph Lauren polo shirt—before proceeding to piss her off in a way that only the super-rich and super-arrogant could ever hope to achieve.

'You've been charged with gross vehicular manslaughter under the Californian Penal Code Section 191.5, and if found guilty you face imprisonment in a state penitentiary for a term of up to ten years.'

'And what's it going to take to make all that go away?'

'If I'm being honest, a minor miracle. Things aren't looking too good,' she began, leafing through his case file. 'The prosecution has got too much hard evidence stacked up against you. There's a barman who says you were drinking champagne for most of the afternoon; you tested way over the limit when the cops breathalysed you; and some guy who was out walking his dog is going to testify that you went straight through a stop light before hitting the victim.'

'Victim!' snorted Ashton, running a hand though his flowing locks. 'How come everyone's getting so worked up about some dirt-poor Mexicano? It's not as if I ran down the state governor. He was only a fucking beaner, for chrissakes. Who the hell's going to miss him?'

'His parents, for a start,' answered Rebecca, her fingers tightening on the edge of the file.

'Watch the attitude…there are plenty of other lawyers in this town, although I've gotta admit that not all of them have your…qualifications…'

Rebecca stiffened as his eyes strayed southwards to run

over the contours of her blouse. She picked up the case file and raised it between them like a defensive wall.

'I graduated *magna cum laude* from the University of Southern California, one of the nation's top law schools, and I've amassed ten years' trial experience with two of LA's most prestigious practices, during which time I've recorded one of the best win-loss ratios in the whole of the city. We can talk about my credentials all day, Mr Ashton, but the fact remains that with the combined testimony of the police officers and eyewitnesses, you're in real danger of being found guilty of vehicular manslaughter. Unless someone changes their story, it's going to be a hard sell to convince a jury that you weren't to blame.'

'Don't you worry about the eyewitnesses,' he said, smiling for the first time. 'I've got a feeling they'll have a change of heart once they get to court. Without them, where do I stand?'

'Well, there's still the matter of the police evidence taken from the scene, the breathalyser reading, tyre marks, speed calculations and the like, but I could throw enough doubt over the accuracy of those numbers to get a jury to think twice about convicting. But what makes you think the eyewitnesses won't talk?'

Ashton looked at her like he was dealing with a child. 'Don't be so naïve. My father is one of the hottest movie producers in Hollywood. He works out problems every day of the week, and he'll work out this one. Just plan my defence on the grounds that there'll be no one with a bad word to say about me once we get to court, and I'll take care of the rest.'

'You can't just buy your way out of this,' warned Rebecca, as he started to walk out of her office.

'Wanna bet?' He smirked over his shoulder.

She waited for the door to slam before letting loose a loud

sigh. Inside her desk drawer was a small bottle of antibacterial hand gel. She squeezed some into her palms and started to scrub furiously.

'Give me strength,' she said, as she stared at the abstract painting that hung on the far wall.

CHAPTER FIVE

HUNTER slowed his Barracuda to take one of the sharper turns on Mulholland, then punched the throttle as he came out the other side, prompting the vehicle's 426 Hemi engine to roar. The acceleration was smooth and easy, but Hunter knew that the course of action he was planning to take would be rough and hard. If he went ahead, there could be no turning back. His life would change. Maybe for the better. Maybe for worse. At this point, he had no way of knowing.

He concentrated on losing himself in the winding road. Mulholland Drive was a magical stretch of blacktop. It was the point at which human ingenuity came face to face with the raw forces of nature, and he never tired of travelling along its twisted 52-mile length.

Twisted. Now, there was a good word to describe both Rebecca Finch and her chosen profession. And yet he'd definitely felt a spark of attraction during their confrontation, which irritated him deeply. Finch's cold-hearted ability to defend the scum of the earth went against all he believed in, so her hot body and pretty face didn't count for all that much. She was little more than a wolf in sheep's clothing. He felt his hands tighten on the steering-wheel as he turned onto one of the many side streets that snaked up into the hills like capillaries departing an artery. After travelling another couple of hundred yards, he swung the 'Cuda into his driveway and came to a gentle stop by the circular courtyard that adjoined the front of his house, a sprawling one-storey affair that had been built back in the 1960s out of adobe, the tightly compacted bricks of earth, clay and straw that had once been so prevalent across the whole of the southwest. Having climbed out of the car, he drew a series of deep cleansing breaths into his lungs, thankful to be back in the hills that ringed the north side of the city, high above the smog-filled mean streets that were squeezed into the over-populated valley below. The cast-iron gate swung noisily on its hinges as he entered the courtyard before clanging shut behind him. The hinges needed oiling, and they'd needed oiling for months—the Montero case had left him with neither the time nor inclination to keep up with his household chores.

He climbed onto the curved porch that led to the front door, entering the dappled shade formed by a latticework portico and its covering of fan ivy. Five strides forward, then his key was turning in the lock. The door opened onto a hallway that followed the shape of the courtyard. To the left, it led to two bedrooms and a small bathroom, and to the right, it opened out to reveal a living area that boasted high ceilings and a large south-facing wall made entirely of glass. A micro hi-fi unit sat inconspicuously in the corner, along with a framed photo of an auburn-haired stunner. Hunter felt a familiar pang of regret as he drank in her features. Her lips were full and sensual, while her heavily lidded eyes smouldered like a femme fatale's in an old Bogie flick. Skye. His ex. Back in Las Vegas, putting her curves to good use while earning top dollar as a showgirl at the Bellagio. She'd skipped out on him when his obsession with the Montero case had become too much to live with, and who could blame her? He'd left a message on her machine every week for the past two months but none of them had been returned. Maybe it was time he stopped calling.

He turned on the hi-fi, prompting the abrasive sound of hard-core legends Husker-Du to fill the room. Track one: 'Crystal', from *Candy Apple Grey*. A wave of frustration washed over him. Being a crime fighter was the only job he'd ever wanted, and now it had been taken away from him. The real pisser was that he'd been damn good at it. He'd taken on a heavy workload, and cleared lots of cases—tough cases at that. Sure, he'd let his temper boil over on occasion, but it was hard to stay cool when you had a succession of drug-peddling, whoremongering, murderous assholes to deal with. His thoughts turned back to the conversation he'd had with Rebecca Finch. People like her just didn't get it. LA's career criminals played outside the rules. The only way to bring them down was to fight fire with fire, and if that meant dealing out a little pre-judicial punishment every now and again, Hunter was more than happy to oblige. Unfortunately, the brass down at Parker Center hadn't seen it that way. They'd said that his *attack* on Montero had been a step too far. They'd said that they couldn't protect him from the PC lobby any longer. They'd said that he'd turned into a liability. So what the hell was he gonna do now? No job and no prospects, and the streets of LA were still a long way from clean.

He headed through the living area to the kitchen, where he

retrieved a bottle of ice-cold Asahi from the fridge, then set about fixing himself a salad and pastrami sandwich. Once the snack was ready, he walked over to the sliding glass doors that led to the deck, and stepped outside. The deck was rectangular in shape and it was fashioned from natural pine. Its simple balustrade was also made from pine, and on the other side of that balustrade was a sheer drop of around 150 feet. At the bottom of the cliff the land evened out and ran gently away to the valley that stretched out below. The scenery was breathtaking—the rocky foreground segueing into thick clumps of sagebrush and chaparral until civilisation began to take over, just a few outlying houses at first, and then more and more concrete blots on the landscape until homestead became suburb and suburb became city. The whole region had once been a vast wilderness that had been prime grizzly bear country—one great mass of towering Californian pines as far as the eye could see—but the trees had all but disappeared, either hacked down by the loggers or choked by the noxious fumes that billowed up from the metropolis. And what price for the destruction of the forests? The local ecosystem had been thrown into imbalance, resulting in a series of dangerous floods every time the storms broke in winter.

He sat himself down on the wooden storage box that served as the deck's only piece of furniture. The box's interior had a waterproof lining to protect its contents from the elements—it was where he stashed his climbing equipment. Five-Ten Anasazi shoes, a 100-foot length of kernmantle nylon rope, a harness, carabineers, belaying gloves, and so on—all within easy reach of his own private cliff in case he should suddenly get the urge to lower himself over the edge. When he was clinging to the rock face, all his troubles would just fade away. The combination of intense physical and mental exertion had a way of clearing his mind like few other pursuits, except maybe good sex, but sex wasn't something he'd been getting much of since Skye had skipped town, good or otherwise.

And now climbing had gone the way of his other short-lived hobbies. Biking, kayaking, canyoneering—he'd thrown himself into each of them, only to quit once police work had gotten in the way. His reasons for taking them up were mired in the past—he'd been trying to form a connection with the father he'd never had. Other than a sketchy description of his old man's violent death, pretty much all he knew about him was that he'd loved the great outdoors. Another Husker-Du track kicked in on the hi-fi behind him: 'Don't Want to Know if You Are Lonely'.

He took a bite from his sandwich and washed it down with a gulp of beer, his first since the alcoholic excesses of Friday night. Carson had seemed like a stand-up guy. Most cops had given him a wide berth since he'd been kicked out of the department, not wishing to be associated with the latest in a long line of black sheep, but Carson had pulled up a stool and bought him a drink. And the old guy had listened. And he'd understood. Understood that sometimes you had to step over the line to get things done. You couldn't reason with scum like Montero—the only language they understood was that of violence. They were a cancer, and you didn't treat cancer by talking the malignant cells out of the patient's body. No, you blasted those sons of bitches with high doses of radiation until they'd been wiped out. The trouble with the likes of Montero was that, just like cancer, they kept coming back.

He second-guessed himself for what felt like the thousandth time, but there was still nothing he wished he'd done differently with the case. No loose end he should have chased down, no clue he'd missed along the way, nothing. If he'd made a mistake, he was too dumb to see it. Whaling on the lead suspect had been the right thing to do at the time. When a young girl's life was at stake, the rulebook went out the window. He took another slug from his beer as he stared out into nothingness. Six tiny bodies had piled up over a three-month period but, despite his intense efforts, he'd drawn a total blank. Even after the lucky break that had led him to Bones and Montero, he hadn't been able to get to Julie in time. Even then, he'd been too late to save her. Next track on the CD: 'Sorry Somehow'.

He pawed at his eyes, trying to wipe the vision of Julie's violated body curled up on a dirty mattress from his memory, his mind once again returning to that terrible moment. In his dreams, her voice sang out to him from among a children's chorus, and while he could never quite remember the words, a sense of abject loneliness stayed with him when he awoke. She was lonely because she couldn't rest, and she couldn't rest until both of her tormentors were punished. The legal system had failed her by leaving the job half-done. Bones was going to rot in a ten-by-four cell until he got his lethal injection, but Montero...Montero hadn't even begun to pay for his crimes. Hunter knew what had to be done, and he knew that he was going to have to move fast, before his quarry had a chance to up sticks and disappear. As he looked out over the valley, he realised that his life had new purpose, and a quiet calm fell over him. He may not be able to give Julie life, but he could sure as hell give her peace. The track that was playing on the CD came to a close: 'Dead Set on Destruction'.

CHAPTER SIX

REBECCA groaned, rubbed at her eyes, then shuffled the legal papers that lay strewn across her dining-room table. A stack of files sat to her right, while a take-out Styrofoam carton sat to her left. The carton still contained some of the endive salad she'd picked up from her favourite restaurant on Bunker Hill before heading home. Her late-night food orders at Café Pinot were becoming so regular she was thinking of buying shares in the place.

She was wearing a pair of blue jeans and a plain white T-shirt, having shucked her business clothes as soon as she'd stepped in the door. Her hair, so neatly tied back during the day, now hung loose on her shoulders, and every now and again she'd brush a few stray strands away from her forehead. She was working late for the fourth night in a row, studying Ashton's case files, trying to get a handle on how the case would develop. Things weren't looking good for the kid. If the witnesses stuck to their statements he was facing a custodial sentence, and he wouldn't be serving his time at the county jail, no, sir, pretty boy Bobby had committed a felony, and felonies carried a stay at the state pen. Still, with time off for good behaviour, he'd probably be out within a couple of years or so. Not that she was writing the case off, far from it—she was going to do everything in her power to keep Ashton at liberty, starting with poring over the files one last time. She picked up the police accident report file. When it came to defending a client, you could never be over-prepared.

'Tired?' asked her sister from the far side of the room.

'I'm bored, Anabeth,' Rebecca replied, without looking up. 'I've been through these files so many times I could probably recite them off the top of my head.'

'And that's just as it should be. You've gotta know that stuff inside out before the trial starts. Every little detail. You don't want Ashton to get sent down through any lack of effort on your part. There's a lot riding on this one…'

'I know, I know, don't worry, I'm well prepared. They'll be no screw-ups from me.'

'There'd better not be.'

Rebecca looked at her sister. The physical similarities between them were marked—the same svelte figure, the same strawberry-blonde hair, and the same batch of freckles dotted across the nose—but when it came to fashion, the two of them were chalk and cheese. Where Rebecca opted for power suits that befitted her standing as a successful defence attorney, Anabeth preferred to slum around in an old jogging outfit that had gone out of fashion some time in the mid-1980s. Predominantly black, with a little white piping down the sides, it made her look like she was about to attend a wino's funeral, not that she ever left the house.

'How was Ashton at today's meeting?' asked Anabeth.

'The same as always—that kid elevates being arrogant to an art form. He's just about the rudest client I've ever had, and there's been some stiff competition for that title over the years. His bad manners are now so predictable they're almost boring. But there was a bit of excitement before he arrived, though. Zac Hunter, the detective who was fired for assaulting Montero, showed up to berate me for keeping "child-killing scum" on the streets.'

'What did you do?'

'Kept my cool and showed him the door.'

'Good. You don't need any distractions, not while you're working with Ashton.'

'I know. But Hunter is kinda cute, though. He's got that whole granite-jaw thing going on, and his eyes really sparkle when he's angry. Plus he was obviously in great shape—he could have lifted me out of my chair and thrown me across the desk any time he wanted,' said Rebecca, pretending to concentrate on the accident report as she imagined the frown on her sister's face.

'You can cut that out! What about our policy? No men. They just get in the way. You lose your focus. Remember what happened the last time you tried dating someone?'

'I lost a case.'

'Damn straight you did. And that can't be allowed to happen again. Especially now. Not when Ashton's about to take the stand.'

Rebecca smiled—winding up Anabeth had always been easy. She glanced out the window as the headlights of a slow-moving car caught her eye. Probably one of the neighbours returning from a night out at some exclusive eatery, or maybe just the security guys on a sweep. There was never that much through traffic as the street didn't really lead anywhere—it was shaped like a crescent, joining the main road at two points about three miles apart, with a maze of purpose-built condos in between. The condos were inhabited by members of LA's white-collar brigade, hence the private security firm, although Rebecca suspected they were more for show than protection, just a couple of old guys, Hank and Walt, who spent most of their time playing poker in the guardhouse over by the main entrance. Every once in a while they'd climb into their Crown Vic to drive around and play cop, but usually the card game would hold sway. These guys weren't exactly renowned for their dedication to duty.

The car with the headlights came to a stop a couple of houses down and cut its engine. Excitement over. Back to the case. She brushed some stray strands of hair from her face and moved on to the coroner's report. It made depressing reading. Ashton's victim had been pronounced dead at the scene. The cold, clinical description of the child's fatal injuries sent a chill to her heart. A young life ended so abruptly, robbed of its rightful time. A wave of melancholy washed over her. Memories, none of them good. A solitary tear leaked from the corner of her eye. She grit her teeth and wiped it angrily away. Emotion couldn't be allowed to cloud the issue. Not now. Bobby Ashton was her client, and he had the right to a defence. She was being paid to secure his freedom, and that was what she was going to do.

After another twenty minutes of shuffling papers her eyes had grown so heavy they were starting to shut of their own volition. She admitted defeat and began to clear the table—first, sweeping up her interrogation strategy notes for each witness, then collecting the three scientific research studies on breathalysers. The clock on the mantel struck one as she packed the last of the files in her briefcase. She stretched back and let loose a yawn that echoed around the room. Another long day, and you could bet your bottom dollar that Ashton wouldn't appreciate it. Still, she had important work to do, and if that meant a few late nights now and again, it was a price she was willing to pay.

'Hard work brings its own rewards,' said Anabeth, appearing at the doorway. 'Just think how you'll feel when the jury delivers a "not guilty" verdict…just think how I'll feel…'

The two of them had always been close, and they'd always been attuned to each other's innermost thoughts. Anabeth was the elder by a couple of years, and as they'd been growing up, she'd been the perfect big sister, the caring, sharing type that every little girl wished for but few ever got. When Rebecca had been struggling with her homework, Anabeth had helped, when she'd made the track team for the first time, her sister had been in the stands to cheer her on, and when she'd started dating, Anabeth had taught her the rules of engagement. In short, she'd always been there for her, in a supportive but never stifling, way.

'It's not gonna be an easy win, though,' mused Rebecca. 'There's a lot of strong evidence stacked up against him.'

'And that's why you've got to work doubly hard. Find the gaps in the prosecution's case…find a way out for your… client. But you've done well tonight, you've put in some solid hours. Now it's time to get some rest. You're gonna need to be at your best come trial time.'

Rebecca nodded, pushed back her chair and rose from the table. She'd barely covered half the distance to the door when the scene of quiet domesticity changed abruptly.

Crash! The window exploded inwards as a chunk of rock whistled past her nose to thud against the far wall. For a couple of seconds she stood motionless, then adrenaline kicked in and she dove for cover. Pain flared in her ribcage as she landed on the carpet, then she rolled towards the foot of the table, her heart pounding so hard it threatened to burst clean through her chest. Four more rocks sailed through the air in quick succession, each one the size of a large fist, bouncing off the furniture as they sought out a target. She balled herself up into a protective cocoon, her breath coming in ragged gasps, her arms shaking uncontrollably. Fresh tears welled in her eyes, and all she could hear was the sound of her sister's screams echoing inside her head.

CHAPTER SEVEN

HUNTER was dressed all in black—Levi's jeans and a crew-neck sweater underneath a leather jacket—operations garb. He checked his wristwatch. The time was 3.00 a.m. He let the Barracuda roll quietly out of his drive, and didn't start the engine till he was halfway down the street. No point in waking the neighbours at this late hour. The last thing he needed was someone witnessing his departure. The taillights of another vehicle stared back at him from a few hundred yards ahead, reminding him of the predatory eyes of a panther. He followed them along Mulholland for a while before taking the turn for the San Diego freeway, glad to be free of their accusing stare.

As the lonely blacktop slipped by, Julie Delmar's face appeared in his mind's eye, urging him to carry out his task. He turned on the stereo. The cheers of an expectant crowd filled the vehicle's interior, swiftly followed by a lone electric guitar playing the same line over and over again like a clarion call to arms. The crowd started to clap in rhythm, excitement hit fever pitch, then the drums kicked in. The lead guitarist's fingers danced across the fret, and a howl that could only originate from a throat sandpapered by a forty-a-day habit joined the fray. AC/DC's 'Riff Raff', taken from their 1978 live album *If You Want Blood, You've Got It.* Straight ahead rock and roll beyond compare.

After a brief spell on the freeway, he cut across the bow of a diesel big rig to exit onto West Sunset, which he followed all the way down to where it joined the Pacific Coast Highway. The speedometer touched seventy as he sped along the main strip at Malibu, beachfront bars and restaurants to his right, golden sands and the lonely ocean to his left, until he swung into Canyon Road to wind his way up into the Santa Monica Mountains. He was now among the homes of the rich and the infamous, the kind of people who could afford to pay top dollar for both the view and the proximity to California's best stretch of coastline.

He knew the area pretty well. He'd worked a case here a few years back, one that had involved the suspected kidnapping of an octogenarian's trophy wife, a five-foot-ten, silicon-enhanced bimbo who went by the name of Sherelle. The husband had been beside himself, although Hunter had got the distinct impression that his fear had been based more on the terrifying prospect of a large ransom demand than on concern for his missing spouse. As it turned out, Scrooge needn't have worried—Sherelle was found alive and well and living in a New Mexico fuck-pad with her tennis coach.

He headed further up into the hills, throwing an occasional glance at the houses set back from the road, most of which were clearly visible through the heavy wrought-iron gates that kept uninvited guests kicking their heels out front. Security was tight. Aside from the heavy gates, electric fences lined the tops of the boundary walls while strategically placed spotlights were ready to throw a harsh glare on the landscaped front gardens if so much as a stray cat were to cross the well-manicured lawns, not that there were any stray cats in this neighbourhood.

As the gradient became steeper, houses started to disappear behind kinks in the driveways and heavily planted front gardens. He killed the stereo and brought the 'Cuda to a gentle stop at the kerb. Montero's place was just around the next bend. From here on in, he was going to be on foot. He grabbed his rucksack from the passenger seat, then stepped outside and started to shiver. In a few more days the first of the winter storms would arrive. He threw a glance in both directions. All was quiet—he owned the streets. Nerves tingling, heartbeat on the rise, adrenaline kicking in—and, boy, it felt good. Now that he'd committed himself to a course of action, the pressure that had been building inside him finally began to drain away. He strode forward, and with each passing step he felt the reassuring presence of his Beretta under his arm.

Two large iron gates topped off with razor wire fronted Montero's residence. They were modelled on those that hung proudly at Graceland, although the silhouettes of the King had been replaced by a couple of sombrero-wearing mariachis. Sacrilege. To the right was a ten-foot-high security wall, but to the left no such protection had been deemed necessary, as a natural outcrop of rock towered some thirty feet overhead. The outcrop would have appeared nigh on impassable to your average Salvadorian smut peddler, but to any climber worth his salt it looked more like an open invitation.

Hunter had scoped out the route to the summit earlier that day and it had looked fairly straightforward. Of course, attempting a climb in the dark wasn't exactly wise, but he didn't have too much choice. He flexed the muscles in his hands and arms then went through a few warm-up stretches. Once he'd cinched his rucksack to his back, he cleaned the rubber soles of his climbing shoes. Any sand or grit would spoil the friction, and he didn't want to take any more chances.

The early going was easy, as the coarse sandstone offered plenty of grip for his feet while solid hand jams came courtesy of a twisting crack, but once he'd made it halfway to the summit things became more challenging. The dull glow cast from the nearest streetlight no longer reached him, so from here on in he had to rely on touch alone. He shut his eyes and envisioned the route, then reached up with his hand to find a seam of shiny quartz. Damn! The quartz was heavily split and friable, and it wasn't going to take his weight. He took a few seconds to think things through. If he remembered correctly, the seam narrowed as it approached the main gate, so if he couldn't climb over it, maybe he could go around?

He reached out with the tip of his right foot to find a thin ledge. The ledge carried him twenty feet to his right, then he stretched upwards to latch onto a small nub with his right hand, simultaneously shifting his foot higher to maintain his centre of gravity. The shiny seam of quartz now stared him directly in the face. The first beads of sweat began to pop on his brow as he searched above the seam for a hold. First a thin flake that he didn't dare trust his weight to, and then, success—a small sloping pocket—and when his left hand latched on with a resounding slap, he knew that the worst was behind him. The pocket marked the start of a thin chimney that carried him all the way to the summit. Piece of cake.

When he clambered over the top he found himself facing a wall of thick vegetation—palms, banana plants, giant ferns—one more step and he'd be lost in the tropics. He changed back into his desert boots, pulled on a pair of thin leather gloves, then started to work his way forward. Cicadas chirruped in the darkness while mosquitoes gorged themselves on any patch of flesh he'd left uncovered. This was fieldwork, in the true sense of the word.

After five minutes of hard-earned progress, Montero's house came into view. It was set well back from the treeline on the crest of a small hill, built in the style of a traditional Mexican hacienda—wooden beams, bare brickwork, primary colours—and it was swathed largely in darkness except for a dull yellow glow emanating from a second-floor window. Hunter drew his Beretta, released the safety, and screwed on a suppressor. Breaking cover, he ran across the well-tended lawn in a low crouch, then climbed onto the veranda. The blinds were drawn, but he ducked below the level of the sills anyhow. Better safe than sorry. Once he'd made it to the main entrance, he found himself facing a huge double door fashioned from gnarled and knotted timber. The door was full of character, unlike its owner, and it was also ajar. Interesting. His threat level ticked up a notch. South American criminals had plenty of character flaws, but a laissez-fare attitude to security generally wasn't one of them. He pushed the door open and stepped inside.

The entrance hall was grand, an atrium by design, with a circular skylight, an elaborate chandelier, and a white stone floor. A wide staircase, also made of stone, stood straight ahead. He considered checking for life on the rest of the ground floor, but his gut told him not to bother. Instead, he climbed the stairs to find that the balcony was carpeted in plush maroon. He smiled. The carpet would help mask his final advance. On his right was a shadowy hallway, on his left the same, save for the slight glow emanating from the base of the furthest door. Bingo. Either Montero was still awake, or he slept with the light on.

Hunter headed left, one cautious step after another, aware that any sound might alert the Salvadorian to his presence. His senses were buzzing. A sudden feeling that he was being watched washed over him. He stopped dead, trusting his instincts, then stilled his breathing and listened intently. Nothing. He spun around, eyes straining against the darkness, but all was still. Just a dose of healthy paranoia. He took a deep breath then moved on.

The thin strip of yellow light continued to ooze out from beneath the door. It was like a sign. A marker to guide him to his destiny. He crept to the end of the hall and grasped the doorhandle. He could almost sense Julie and the other children alongside him. Now was his chance to make restitution. Now was his chance to speak for those that had been silenced. Now was the time for justice to be done.

He crashed into the room, pupils constricting as they adjusted to the light, Beretta coming round in a controlled arc as it searched for a target. He was ready for just about anything…except for the scene that confronted him. A huge four-poster bed dominated the room, and on that bed lay a butt-naked Montero, and beneath him an equally naked Hispanic girl. The girl had long auburn hair and a little too much make-up. Her legs were wrapped around the pornographer in coital bliss. Neither the girl nor Montero bothered to acknowledge Hunter's presence, but both had a valid excuse. Matching bullet wounds, one to the back of the Salvadorian's head, the other through the girl's left eye. Montero and his whore were already dead. Hunter had been beaten to the punch. Once again, he was too late.

CHAPTER EIGHT

'THIS is ridiculous. How much longer are we going to have to wait?' Anabeth was getting impatient. Rebecca had phoned the police over two hours ago, but as yet no squad car had arrived. A call into the private security firm had been equally unrewarding—Hank and Walt hadn't seen a thing. What a surprise.

'As long as we have to.' Rebecca yawned. 'I guess the cops have got more important things to worry about than a bit of mindless vandalism. You can go to bed if you want. I don't mind waiting alone. It's not as if there's any danger—whoever threw those rocks is long gone by now.'

Rebecca was sitting at the small breakfast table in the kitchen, sipping from a mug of hot chocolate. At first, she'd tried waiting in the front room, but it had gotten steadily colder as the hours slipped by—broken windows were little defence against the chill night air. Anabeth had wanted to clear up the mess, but

Rebecca had insisted that they leave everything as it was. Defence lawyers knew better than to tamper with a crime scene.

'I'll wait up with you,' replied Anabeth. 'I don't think I could sleep anyhow, after all this excitement. Maybe you should ring our folks—let them know what's going on.'

'What's the point? They've got their own lives to lead. Living in their exclusive Manhattan apartment, hauling down six-figure salaries from one of the biggest law firms in the state. They're not interested in my problems any more. I'm lucky if I get so much as a card at Christmastime…'

'You shouldn't let what happened to me come between you.'

'Too late. It already has. But it doesn't matter—not as long as I've got you on my side.'

'You'll always have that.'

Rebecca nodded gratefully and started to compile a mental list of what would need to be done in the morning. First, they'd have to arrange for a glazier. Crime levels might be fairly low in her neighbourhood but that didn't mean you could leave gaping holes in your property and expect to keep your possessions. Then the mess would have to be cleaned up. She'd have to let the office know she was going to be late. Damn it! Tomorrow was the first day of the Ashton trial. She had to be in court. Clean-up would have to wait. A rap on the door broke her reverie.

'Finally!' said Anabeth in mock celebration.

'You watch that tongue of yours,' Rebecca warned her sister, who seemed to be spoiling for a fight. All she got in response was a grunt. 'Who is it?' she called out.

'Police. We had reports of a disturbance at this address.'

'That was some time last week,' shouted Anabeth. Rebecca shushed her, slipped the security chain into place and opened the door a crack. 'I'm going to need to see some ID.'

The officer looked a little put out as he fumbled for his badge. He was little more than a kid, barely out of his teens, his face still pockmarked with acne, his regulation buzz-cut doing little to improve his chances with the ladies.

'Thank you…' Rebecca strained to read the name on the card, 'Officer…?'

'Willocks, ma'am. Can I come in?'

Rebecca slipped the chain and held the door for him to walk in. She stared at him expectantly as she waited for the detecting to start. After thirty seconds or so of pretty much nothing, her patience ran out.

'Should I show you to the front room?'

'The front room?'

'Where the rocks were thrown through our window… remember? You do know why you're here?'

'Oh…sure…of course…'

She led the way, with Willocks following dutifully behind like a well-trained puppy. The drapes billowed inwards as a gentle breeze nudged them from the outside, a few chunks of vicious-looking glass clinging stubbornly to the frame. Five fist-sized rocks were dotted around the room, but Willocks ignored them and headed straight for the easel in the far corner.

'Er…what is it?' he asked, as he stared at the series of interlocking monochrome circles that stretched over one half of the canvas.

'It's an abstract, and it's not finished,' replied Rebecca. 'My sister's an artist, specialising in geometrically influenced designs.'

'Oh. It's…er…nice…'

'Yes—she's very talented.' She smiled at her sister then gestured to the rocks on the floor. 'Aren't you forgetting something?'

'Oh…yeah…of course…' he muttered, squatting down on

his haunches to get a closer look at one of the larger intruders. 'When did you say this happened?'

'Last month. We left them there as we thought they added something to the decor—gave the room a more rustic, outdoorsy feel,' Anabeth muttered. 'Plus the ventilation's improved no end…'

'About two hours ago,' said Rebecca, throwing a glare at her sister. Whenever Anabeth got scared, she got sassy, and it had been that way since first grade. 'Probably just kids messing around, but I thought I'd better report it.'

Willocks prodded one of the rocks with a pen. 'Oh, I doubt this was kids.'

'What makes you say that?'

'Well, this is a good neighbourhood and it was pretty late—most kids around here would have been in bed. Plus you're the only house on the block that's been hit. When kids start acting up, they tend to leave a trail of destruction. No…I don't make kids for this…it looks like you were targeted.'

'Well, that's nice to know,' groaned Anabeth. 'Any idea why?'

The sarcasm washed straight over him. 'Have you upset anyone recently? Any disputes with the neighbours, problems at work?'

'Nope, nothing like that,' started Rebecca, then her brow started to tighten at the memory of Hunter's intrusion into her office. 'Except…there was this one guy…'

'Go on,' he encouraged, rising from his haunches to take out a notepad.

'Oh, it's probably nothing, but an ex-cop by the name of Zac Hunter barged into my office this morning to berate me over a case.'

'A case? You some kind of private detective?'

'No, I'm a defence lawyer.'

'A defence lawyer? Why didn't you say so? You guys

make plenty of enemies—I guess it's kind of an occupational hazard. It's a wonder that something like this hasn't happened before. You working any delicate cases at present? Upset anyone in particular?'

'All of my cases are delicate.'

'Hmm… We'll keep an eye on this Hunter guy, maybe have a quiet word with him, but beyond that, there's not much we can do. You could consider taking out a restraining order against him, but I guess you already knew that, being a lawyer and all.'

'Well, thank you very much, Officer Willocks. You've been a great help.' Rebecca winced at the sarcasm that dripped from Anabeth's voice. 'It's good to know that our tax dollars are being put to such good use.'

'Anyhow,' Willocks continued, somehow immune to the insults, 'you were right to call us. I'll get this written up, then if something similar happens again, we can start to build a harassment case against him.'

'Thanks for your time, Officer,' said Rebecca, showing him to the door. 'We really appreciate it.'

Willocks gave her a confused look before spinning on his heel to go back to his squad car.

CHAPTER NINE

'YOU have the right to remain…dead,' muttered Hunter as the cloying smell of blood began to tug at his nostrils.

He stood transfixed for a moment, staring at the macabre sight before him. Two bodies, naked as the day they'd been born, intertwined and engaged in the very act of creating life at the time of their death. Murder most foul. Then again, maybe not that foul. Montero had deserved this plus a whole lot more. But who the hell had done it?

Hunter slowly approached the bed. The sheets were made of white silk, no doubt expensive, and they provided a stark, virginal backdrop for the bodies. The pillows, on the other hand, retained little evidence of whiteness beneath the lovers' heads. Instead, scarlet blooms mushroomed from the epicentre of death like some overly energetic algae. The smell of blood became overpowering as he examined the bullet wound on the back of the Salvadorian's head. Dark powder burns ringed the hole, meaning that the killer must have been close when he'd discharged his weapon. Real close. This guy was a pro. Some sort of assassin. Or at least someone who knew what the fuck they were doing. The wound was fair-sized, probably a .45, and there was no sign of the shell. He leant over to get a look at the far side of the body. A hypo was sticking out of Montero's left biceps, its plunger fully depressed. Interesting. Had the Salvadorian been mainlining when his bête noire had arrived, or had the killer inserted the needle? Maybe it was some kind of a message?

He ran a hand over his closely cropped hair as he turned his attention to the girl. What a way to go—with a dead child-killer's prick stuffed up your snatch. Her eyes were still open, an expression of shock on her face. She'd seen the killer coming but it hadn't done her much good. Blood continued to ooze from one socket, running down the side of her face to pool on the pillow below. There was no sign of coagulation, suggesting that her death had been recent. Her dark hair was coiffed to street slut perfection, while her make-up worked double time to hide the fact she was still a minor. Fucking Montero, cradle snatching till the end.

Hunter felt a burst of anguish as he realised that yet another child had died on his watch, then a sense of abject frustration began to well up inside him. It wasn't every day he decided to kill a man in cold blood. It had taken some deep thought and righteous anger to get to this point, only to find he'd been robbed of his purpose. Montero should have been his. He'd had his executioner's speech worked out and everything. Stealing another man's vengeance killing just wasn't on. Plus there was the young prostitute to consider. All her hopes for the future, all her dreams of building a better life, had been taken from her in the time it had taken the killer to pull the trigger. She'd deserved better. A whole lot better. But someone had thought otherwise. What he had here was a mystery. And who solved mysteries? Detectives. He'd been one of those.

His eyes darted around the room, looking for any little thing that might be significant. The bodies had told him all they were going to—if they harboured any more secrets it would fall on the coroner to reveal them. A plasma TV hung on one wall, with two freestanding speakers placed on either side. A chaise longue stood over by the window, looking both decrepit and expensive at the same time. A small open-fronted cabinet was stationed to the left of the bed, housing some dog-eared porno mags plus the remote control for the TV. A digital alarm clock sat on top of the cabinet, along with a few playing cards and a torn condom wrapper, which was kind of ironic, as Montero's last fuck had been a long way from safe sex.

On the other side of the bed, four full-length mirrors served as doors for a built-in wardrobe. Hunter strode across the room and pushed on the first of the doors. It yielded a little, gave a slight click, then opened outwards to reveal a Sony home entertainment system. The next cupboard contained a collection of Gianni Manzoni designer suits in pristine condition, along with some Klaus Boehler dress shirts of various hues. For a low-life pornographer, Montero sure took pride in his appearance. The third cupboard was packed with drawers, which in turn were packed with neatly folded cashmere jumpers, recently pressed polo shirts, and a large collection of white boxer shorts and jet-black socks.

In the fourth cupboard, he struck gold. A top-of-the-line Sony digital camcorder, tripod mounted, aimed straight at the bed. Strewn around its base were at least twenty miniDV tapes. He grinned as he noticed the blinking red light on the side of the camera. This case was gonna be over in a hurry.

He checked the inside of the cupboard door and, sure enough, it was a two-way mirror. The evening's events had been caught on tape—foreplay, intercourse, climax—although the money-shot in this movie would be of a prick getting blown away instead of just blown. Maybe Montero's career as a porn director was finally going to pay off.

He ejected the tape, stashed it inside his rucksack, then threw one last glance at the corpse.

'*Adios*, asshole. Burn in hell,' he muttered, and then he was headed for the exit, but just as he began to turn the doorhandle the boom of a shotgun stopped him cold.

Hunter had company.

CHAPTER TEN

DANILOV edged across the landing, vacating the bedroom that had been his sanctuary for the past couple of minutes. Montero's home was open house tonight. First of all, there'd been a girl with the target, and the boss hadn't mentioned any girl. She'd had her eyes screwed shut either in ecstasy or boredom right up until the moment he'd shot Montero, then suddenly her eyes had been wide open, pupils dilating in surprise, so he'd shot her, too, without hesitation. Once she'd seen him he'd had no choice. Not that there had been much to see, as his fedora had been pulled down to obscure his features, but it didn't pay to take chances. A pockmarked eighteen-year-old called Vasily had taught him that, many years before, and Danilov never forgot an important lesson.

And as if the girl hadn't been enough, another man had then entered the house just as he'd been ready to make his exit. Danilov had no idea who he was—all cats were grey at night—but the intruder had come in smooth and quiet, so quiet that the Russian had almost missed him. For a split second he'd thought about neutralising him, but the shot hadn't been a certainty, not from an elevated position fifty feet away and in near darkness, so he'd played it safe and backtracked into an empty bedroom, leaving the stranger free to go visit Montero and his dead whore.

This turn in events had been somewhat worrying. A guy like Montero had to have more than one enemy—in fact, there was probably a small army of people that wanted him dead—but why had one of them chosen tonight to come calling? The very same night that Danilov had been told to make his play? It was a pretty big coincidence, and the Russian didn't believe in coincidences, big or otherwise.

So the question was—had he been set up? He'd stayed put in the bedroom, pondering that very poser for a couple of minutes, his Glock trained directly at the door, ready to open fire if there was the slightest turn in the handle, but nothing had happened, so he'd found himself in the situation that the Americans liked to call 'shit or get off the pot,' and he'd decided to get off and go see about leaving the premises. Movement made sense, if for no other reason than it was bad luck to spend too much time in the same house as two dead bodies.

Danilov edged to the top of the staircase, put one foot on the first stone step, then froze dead in his tracks for the second time in the space of a few minutes. A slight movement downstairs suggested that yet another intruder had entered the premises. The discharge of a shotgun in his general direction confirmed it. He threw himself back behind the balustrade as the double-ought buckshot sailed harmlessly overhead to embed itself in the ceiling. Lucky for him his adversary had opted for short-range stopping power over medium-range accuracy. But who was this new arrival?

Scuttling backwards towards the relative safety of the hallway, he loosed off a couple of shots to cover his ignoble retreat, just as the first intruder stepped out of Montero's room to enter the fray with weapon drawn. With inhuman speed Danilov swung his gun towards the threat and squeezed the trigger. The Glock coughed twice…

Hunter waited behind the bedroom door as the shotgun blast reverberated around the house, his mind racing. If Montero's killer was still present, what in the hell was he shooting at? Before he could come up with an answer, two pistol shots rang out from somewhere on his level. A firefight, and that meant the assassin had company. Someone else had joined the party. But who? He eased open the door and ducked out into the hall to see if he could get a handle on events. The first thing he saw was something glinting in the moonlight on the far side of the stairs, and then he was throwing himself backwards just in time to avoid the two hard calibres meant for his head. Somebody wanted to play rough.

Three more shotgun blasts followed, each one progressively louder than the last, as the owner of the 12-gauge made his way up the staircase behind a wall of suppressing fire. Hunter heard chunks of plaster rain down after each blast, but he couldn't see them, so it seemed a fair bet that the guy was shooting at whoever was across the way. Hunter backpedalled to the built-in wardrobe, smashed one of its doors with the butt of his gun, then selected a shard of mirror from the debris—his next foray onto the landing was going to be a little more circumspect. With his back against the bedroom door, he angled the shard until he could see all the way to the shadows at the far end of the house. All was quiet.

'Hunter! That you up there?' yelled a vaguely familiar voice. He racked his brains as he tried to work out whether the owner of the shotgun was a potential ally or foe, and then it came to him.

'Carson?'

'In the flesh and twice as ugly,' came the shouted reply. 'I've got him pinned down in one of the bedrooms. Any chance of a little help?'

What the fuck? Hunter spun out onto the landing to find Carson edging his way up the last few stairs, cradling a police-issue Ithaca shotgun. The detective was wearing the same shabby coat he'd had on back at the bar, and his face was ruddy, either through cold, exertion, or a mixture of both.

Hunter got straight to the point, 'What the hell are you doing here?'

'I could ask you the exact same question. You ran your mouth off so much at the bar I figured you'd do something stupid, so I thought I'd check in on Montero's place for a couple of nights. If anyone asks, I'm just a cop investigating a disturbance.'

'Back-up on the way?'

'Nope, you're looking at a one-man army. Thought I'd cut you a break and keep this quiet, but I wasn't expecting anyone else to get caught in the crossfire. Who's the son-of-a-bitch hunkered down over there? Is it Montero? Or have you found someone dumb enough to call themselves your partner?'

'It's not Montero. He's back there with one hole too many in his head and, given that he was dead when I found him, I figure you can mark our mystery man down as the killer.'

'So you wanna go shake his hand and buy him a drink for services rendered?'

'No. Montero was mine. Plus he left another corpse—a

prostitute. Montero may have got what he deserved, but the girl was an innocent.'

'A prostitute? That's no great loss…'

Hunter angled his gun down the hallway. 'How'd you wanna play it?'

Before the grizzled detective could reply, a succession of shots rang out. Both men ducked for cover, but they needn't have bothered as the bullets hadn't been meant for them. Instead, the sound of crashing glass rang out, quickly followed by heavy footfalls on wooden floorboards.

'The window!' yelled Hunter. 'He's making a break for it!'

He sprinted down the hall, charged through the door, and skidded to a stop at the window, where he scanned the grounds for movement. There! A shadowy figure on top of the veranda. He loosed off two shots but they both missed high as the assassin leapt down then zigzagged across the lawn towards the cover of the treeline.

Hunter rested his arm on the window-frame, steadied his breathing, and went to fire, but just as he did so, the lights blazed on overhead, ruining his night vision in an instant. He loosed off six rounds in quick succession, but they were fired more in hope than expectation. The assassin had escaped.

'What the hell did you do that for?' he asked, rounding angrily on Carson.

'Sorry, wasn't thinking, but, then again, neither were you. Say you'd hit the guy—what then? You wanna explain what you were doing here tonight?' Carson paused for a moment to let him think things through. 'I reckon I did you a favour, and now I'm going to do you another one. All this gunfire will have drawn some attention. Get the hell out of here before my colleagues show up. You can bet your bottom dollar they won't be as understanding as me.'

The detective gestured for Hunter to leave, the Ithaca

hanging loosely by his side, but Hunter stayed right where he was.

'You should know that I take it kinda personally when someone fires a gun at me. Call me sensitive, but that's just the way I'm put together. I'm not gonna take it lying down. And Montero was mine. I put my life on hold to catch that bastard. Do you know what it's like to see a child's broken body laid out on a bed of trash? Do you know what it's like to feel powerless to do anything about it? Yeah, you know. Their faces have stayed with me, day after day, week after week, month after month. I had to deal with the nightmares, I had to deal with the pain. I had to tell their families, and I had to watch as the little caskets were lowered into the ground. I was the one that arrested Montero, so I should have been the one to exact justice on behalf of those kids. Whoever killed him tonight hadn't earned that right, not in the same way I had. And now another child's been killed—the prostitute back there lying in a pool of blood. This isn't over, no fucking way. I'm going after this guy, starting right here, right now.'

The detective shrugged his shoulders as if he couldn't care less.

'Yep, it figures—it's not as if you've got anything else to do. You wanna play at vigilante, that's your business. Now get the hell out of here.'

Hunter made straight for the exit.

CHAPTER ELEVEN

DANILOV was relieved to be back on home ground. Things had been going smoothly at Montero's until he'd neutralised the target, but after that there'd been complications, and he didn't like complications. He stepped out of the elevator and strode down the carpeted hallway, a Fed-Ex package wedged under his arm. When he came to a stop at the end of the hall, he tapped a four-digit electronic code into the numeric pad to the right of the reinforced door, waited for the steel bolts to disengage, then stepped inside his apartment. No old-fashioned key to fumble into a lock here, no old-fashioned anything, in fact, as the building was right at the forefront of modern technology.

'Lights—on,' he commanded, prompting the apartment's computer to illuminate the main living area, which still had the antiseptic scent of a new home despite the fact that he'd lived there for almost six months. A huge sofa made from the finest black leather sat straight ahead, while beyond that a high-definition plasma TV dominated the far wall. A low coffee-table fashioned from chrome and glass languished between sofa and TV, and two matching display cabinets, one housing a selection of history books, the other a selection of wolf sculptures, stood on either side of the main door. The remaining furniture nestled in the far corners of the room—a hi-fi unit on the left, and a computer desk on the right. The walls were painted a soft cream and the long drapes that covered the windows were burnished gold. All in all, it was very classy.

'Stereo—on.' The velvet tones of Frank Sinatra filled the room as he threw the Fed-Ex envelope on the sofa then headed for the adjoining kitchen. Custom-built beech cabinets hugged the walls, interspersed with lots of stainless-steel appliances, the most impressive of which was the Smeg refrigeration unit. He reached inside the freezer compartment and withdrew a half-empty bottle of Stolichnaya, poured himself three thumbs of the clear 80-proof liquid, then grabbed a jar of freshly salted cucumbers and headed back to the lounge to slump into the welcoming arms of his sofa.

Russian vodka in hand, Old Blue Eyes belting out 'Cheek to Cheek' on the stereo, and finally things were on the up, and after the night he'd had, it was about time. Complications. First the slut with Montero, then the sudden appearance of two well-armed men who'd had the gall to open fire on him. Not that he minded being fired on—in his line of work, it was something of an occupational hazard—but he didn't like to make a habit of it, which was why he planned each operation down to the very last detail. Maximise the preparation, minimise the risk was a motto that had served him well over the years but, despite all his precautions, things would still go wrong every once in a while, and that was when he really had to be on his game. How one coped in the face of adversity was the true measure of a man, and tonight he'd coped well. The operation had been a success, albeit a qualified one. Target neutralised, assassin unharmed. But the appearance of two armed men raised a number of questions, questions that needed answers.

He took a hit from his drink and devoured a slice of cucumber. Delicious. The best vodka appetiser bar none. He'd made a fresh batch yesterday, first lining a jar with sliced garlic and horseradish leaves, then adding the cucumber and some salted water, and in the proceeding twenty-four hours the flavours had melded together beautifully. He tuned the TV to CNN, then muted the volume so as not to disturb his big band pleasure, choosing instead to keep up to date with current events by reading the banner headlines that scrolled across the bottom of the screen.

Trouble at home, trouble abroad—everywhere you looked there was bad news, and the only way to judge the severity of any given situation was to see if the newsreader's expression morphed from fake smile to fake concern. He found himself wondering why he even bothered to pay attention to the outside world any more—the black deeds of the globe had no impact on him. Violent explosions in bloodstained Gaza, ongoing civil war in famine-torn Africa, psychotic serial slayings in the Mid-West, none of them were of any real import. He'd learnt years ago that the key task in life was to look out for number one, and he'd learnt it the hard way.

Deserted by his good-for-nothing parents at an early age, two losers who'd had more love for the bottle than they'd had for him, he'd been forced to grow up on the back streets of Moscow. Ulitsa Solyanka had been his home, Salt Street, notorious for its brothels, prostitutes and criminals in the nineteenth century, and not exactly a barrel of laughs in his youth. To the south lay the Moskva River, to the west the Kremlin, with its red brick walls and the golden domes of Uspensky Cathedral, and to the north the infamous Lubyanka Prison, home of the KGB.

As a juvenile he'd scratched out an existence within this small triangle of a great city, begging by day and turning to petty crime at night, when the drunkards' rouble-filled pockets had been walking currency caches for a boy with quicksilver hands and nerves of steel. Pretty soon he'd joined a street gang, mostly comprising other luckless urchins like himself, and headed by a pockmarked 18-year-old called Vasily. Life had been hard, the day-to-day struggle for survival further complicated by ongoing battles with rival street factions, many of them older, stronger and more adept in the use of violence. Vasily had been a great strategist in the turf wars, but he'd lacked the true stomach for a fight, a trait that Danilov did not share, and pretty soon he'd discovered he had stomach enough for the both of them.

Officer Alenichev had been the man who'd unearthed Danilov's propensity for violence. This fine, upstanding example of the Moscow police force had been as corrupt as they'd come, in bed with the local crime boss, figuratively speaking, and in bed with his sergeant's wife, literally speaking—he had been a man for whom everything had had its price. Danilov had first crossed paths with him when he'd been caught pickpocketing one cold winter's night, and his punishment had been a beating to within an inch of his life. It hadn't been the thieving that had upset Alenichev, more the fact that little Viktor hadn't been willing to hand over his ill-gotten gains.

While Danilov waited for his bruising to subside, his broken bones to heal, and his cuts to pucker and harden into scars, he let his hatred fester, nursing it deep in the very heart of him. Three months later he jumped Alenichev in a deserted alley, stabbed him twice in the neck with a rusty knife, then watched on as his nemesis died an ignoble death face down in the trash. As the policeman's lifeblood ebbed out across the cobblestones, Danilov recognised a self-truth that had changed his life—he didn't care. No spark of remorse, no twinge of guilt, no sick feeling in the pit of his stomach, not even a sense of satisfaction now that vengeance was his. He felt nothing. Nothing at all.

When it came to dealing in death, most of those who were proficient in the art warned that the first kill was usually the worst, but for Danilov the first had been no better or worse than any of the others. Countless deaths (he'd stopped keeping a tally once he'd passed the two hundred mark) spread over four decades and across two continents, and all had had but one common factor. They had been necessary, or at least Danilov had deemed them necessary, and his was the only opinion that mattered.

After a few years on the streets, his proficiency at killing got him noticed by the Russian mafia, where he rose quickly through the ranks as an assassin for hire. At first, he kept a tally of his executions, marking the occasion of his hundredth knife kill by tattooing a sickle on the back of his left hand and greeting his hundredth shooting with a hammer tattoo on his right. The sickle was for cutting, the hammer for hitting, and the sickle had come a whole year earlier as he'd always favoured the close-in work. To this day execution by knife still felt more real to him—he'd been planning to carve up Montero, but the presence of the prostitute had called for greater firepower.

The Sinatra CD had moved on to 'Witchcraft' by the time he'd finished his vodka. He'd been a fan of the singer ever since he'd heard a bootleg recording back in the 1970s. Sinatra had made it the hard way—going from musty dives on the streets of Hoboken to achieve worldwide acclaim, a fact that earned his respect. He went to the kitchen to replenish his drink, then returned to the living area to seat himself at the glass-topped computer desk, where he turned on his Dell PC and waited for it to boot up.

The computer was equipped with the latest version of PGP desktop, courtesy of a CD-ROM sent two months ago by his mysterious 'boss'. PGP stood for Pretty Good Privacy, and as the name suggested it was a program designed to facilitate secure messaging through the wonders of 256-bit encryption. According to the blurb in the instruction booklet, the sending computer would encrypt the message with a symmetric key, then encrypt that symmetric key with the public key of the receiving computer, which would then use its own private key to decode the symmetric one, before using the symmetric key to decode the message. Danilov had given up trying to understand the nuances of the process weeks ago. He logged onto the internet via a high-speed broadband connection to find a buddy icon present in his AOL instant messenger list. The boss was waiting for him, hungry for an update on the fate of Montero. A question popped up on the screen.

"Did our friend catch his flight?"

Danilov regarded the flashing cursor for a moment, took a quick sip from the ice-cold Stolichnaya, then started to type.

"Da. On red-eye to Boston, with girlfriend."

"Girlfriend?"

"Da. Scared of flying, but I got her to go."

"I didn't tell you to send his girlfriend. She was meant to stay home."

"She had to take flight. Bad for us if she'd stayed."

The cursor blinked for a half a minute. The boss was upset.

"You must NEVER send anyone to Boston, except for those I identify. NEVER. Under ANY circumstances. The slightest mistake could jeopardise all that I've worked for. NO extra passengers. Is that clear?"

"Da. Two other men also at meeting."

"WHAT? Your meeting was meant to be strictly confidential. Who were they?"

"You not know?"

Danilov's eyes narrowed as he waited for a response. As far as he could see, there was only one logical explanation for what had happened at Montero's, and if what he suspected was true, he was in mortal danger.

"The two men had nothing to do with me. The privacy of our work is of paramount importance. Did you send them to Boston? Did you recognise them? What did they look like?"

So many questions, but so few answers, thought Danilov. And all this shit about sending people to Boston. He had no idea why the boss had picked that as a euphemism for murder. And why bother with euphemisms when the messages were encoded? It made about as much sense as taking a samovar to Tula. The keys clacked as he responded;

"Men arrived late, missed most of meeting. Came separately, but teamed up. Refused to fly. Looked like professionals. Are you trying to replace me? If so, release me from contract. No need to send strangers to meeting. I don't like surprises."

The cursor flashed on the screen for over a minute before Danilov got a response.

"1) I did NOT invite these men to the meeting.

2) You cannot walk away. Remember, I've tracked you down before—there's NO place you can hide.

3) You remain my spokesperson until I say differently. Is that clear?"

It looked like he'd struck a nerve. *"Da. What next?"*

"You should have received a package containing background information on our next client. Look through the files, get to know him, then arrange a meeting, and make sure that this one stays private. In the meantime I'll see if I can find out who these two strangers were."

With that, the 'boss' was gone. The Russian scrolled back through the transcript of their conversation and read it once more from start to finish. Had the boss been lying when he'd denied all knowledge of the two men at Montero's? It was hard to tell when all he had to go on were the cold letters that beamed out from his computer monitor. No voice inflections, no nervous tics, no tells at all, just the bare bones of their chat with none of the tasty meat. Well, whoever those guys were, things were going to get trickier moving forward.

Having refilled his tumbler, he sank back into the leather sofa and stared at the Fed-Ex envelope. Another package from the boss. Another assisted suicide just waiting to happen. He ripped it open. Inside were a number of large glossy photos of a shaven-headed behemoth, some taken up close, others from more of a distance. He whistled to himself. The target must have tipped the scales at somewhere just shy of 350 lbs and it didn't look like there was too much muscle buried beneath all that blubber. His legs emerged from a pair of cut-off jeans like a pair of tree trunks, his torso was almost spherical, and his watermelon head sat balanced on a neck comprised of thick roles of concentric flab. This kid's idea of a balanced diet must have been a cheeseburger in each hand. Americans! Half of them were obese slobs who couldn't keep their hands out of the cookie jar, while the rest were stick-thin narcissists who lived for plastic surgery.

He shuffled through the photos until he came to a particularly arresting headshot. Babyface. This one was young, despite his huge girth. Kid Kong. Little more than a boy, or at least what passed for a boy on a physical level, but appearances could be deceptive. Danilov had robbed his first mark, lain with his first woman and taken his first life by the time he'd been thirteen. Maybe this kid was the same. Maybe he'd prove dangerous. But, then again, maybe not. The youth of America relied too much on firepower and too little on brains. Danilov could have solved LA's gang problems in a week if he'd had the inclination.

He stared at the photo for a while, drinking in the kid's pasty features. Shaven head, prominent ears. Thin lips twisted into a sneer. Angry eyes that stared back at the camera in a fuck-you challenge. His opponent was pissed, and pissed at the whole wide world. He put the headshot to one side, then leafed through the rest of the photos. Kong was alone in most of them. Maybe he had relationship issues. It was only by the last couple that he'd found any company, standing in the middle of a set of similarly attired youths, six in total, all sporting the same chrome-dome haircut and step-off attitude. Both pictures had been taken outside a biker bar, and the target and his companions didn't seem to be entering or leaving the establishment, just hanging out, a couple of them chugging down tallboys, the rest checking out a pristine Hog parked to the left of the main entrance.

He withdrew a typed report from the envelope and scanned it for info. Harold Ribecki. Another piece of the puzzle fell into place. Danilov always liked to have a name. Even years ago, when he had been operating on the frozen streets of Moscow, he'd made it his business to know the names of his victims whenever possible. He'd even asked a few of them for ID just before he'd cut their throats with a serrated blade. He glanced back at the headshot. Soon the name of Harold Ribecki would be added to his long list of victims.

The rest of the report provided a last known address for the target, a list of the bars and clubs he frequented, a couple of known associates, along with their home addresses, a couple of suspected associates with no addresses attached, and the name of his current girlfriend. Danilov tossed the papers onto the coffee-table, then leant back into the sofa. In the next half-hour he'd look through the package once more, commit everything to memory, then burn the contents in his kitchen trashcan, leaving only ashes behind. He glanced down at the collection of papers in front of him. A lot of ashes. When it came to compiling reports, the boss was nothing if not thorough.

CHAPTER TWELVE

HUNTER took another pull from the long-necked Asahi as he stared out across the valley. The lights of the city twinkled below him like something from a fairy-tale, although in his experience fairy-tales were in pretty short supply down there. He sometimes thought about quitting LA to head for the hills—some lonely spot among the mountain ranges of Nevada where he could be at one with nature and away from the evils of man—but he knew that he never would. It was the very presence of evil that meant he had to stay—after all, someone had to take out the trash. He leant forward against the balustrade and took some deep cleansing breaths of the oxygen-rich air. He could still feel the buzz of adrenaline in his system, but it was starting to subside.

Music wafted gently out of the sliding glass doors behind him, Swervedriver, an obscure Brit guitar band that specialised in sci-fi rock and roll. Soothing, almost ethereal, it helped calm his nerves. The stereo was dialled way down low—although the nearest neighbour was half a mile away, even the slightest sound travelled a fair distance on a still night. Another pull from the Asahi and more visions of death in his mind's eye. So Montero had checked out. For some people the pornographer's demise would have been vengeance enough, but Hunter wasn't some people.

With him and Montero it had been personal. No one else had earned the right to interfere. Black mark number one against the assassin. Plus the guy had left an innocent hooker dead at the scene. Black mark number two. And not to forget the clincher—he'd loosed off a couple of rounds in Hunter's general direction, and that was just plain rude. His mom had taught him to judge a man by his deeds, and he'd taken that lesson to heart—so as soon as those shots had been fired, the assassin had appointed him judge, jury and would-be executioner.

Three strikes, the assassin was out, and Hunter was in—in on the search to uncover the guy's identity and, more importantly, in on the quest to discover his angle. Why the hell had the assassin gone after Montero? Hunter's curiosity was piqued. Catching the bad guys had never been enough for him—understanding the motive for their actions was the key, as it was then and only then that he could start to make any sense of this fucked-up world. He'd been struggling to come to terms with man's capacity for casual violence for most of his life, ever since his mom had sat him down as a six-year-old boy to explain why he'd never met his father.

She'd told him that his dad, Joe, had been having lunch at a small diner when two stick-up kids had decided to rob the joint. Joe had tried to intervene, but all his act of heroism had earned him had been a fatal gunshot wound to the chest. His mom had said that Daddy was a hero, then she'd barely spoken of him again, saying it was better to let it go rather than wallow in grief. He'd pestered her for more details all through his youth, right up until she'd died of cancer just after his sixteenth birthday, leaving him alone and angry at the whole goddamned world.

His father's homicide had shaped the course of his life. From the moment he had been told about the tragedy he'd known that he'd wanted to join the LAPD, so he'd studied hard through school, signed up for the academy as soon as they'd take him, served his time on the streets, then aced the detectives' exam. His whole life had been dedicated to the pursuit of justice, but now he'd been kicked out of the department in disgrace. He'd blown everything.

His future, which had once been so clearly mapped out, had become a series of question marks. What was he going to do with his life? How was he going to get by? And how was he going to make sure that justice continued to be served in the City of Angels? For a guy with no job, no girl and no family, these were the sorts of questions that were best avoided. No point losing sleep when you didn't have the answers. Better to focus on the here and now—find something real to occupy the mind. Like the assassin. He retrieved the videotape from his rucksack and gave it the once-over. Just a standard miniDV tape with a blank label on its surface, wound about a third of the way through its length. Time for a late-night screening. He went inside, hooked up his camcorder to the TV, then pushed in the tape. After jabbing the rewind button he tossed the remote onto the sofa alongside some environmental magazines, then headed for the kitchen to fetch another Asahi.

The tape had rewound by the time he returned, so he shifted the most recent copy of *California Wild* out of the way and settled back to enjoy the show. The first twenty minutes or so consisted of Montero taking the young hooker every which way—her ears were the only orifices that seemed safe from invasion, and even they'd probably have come under fire had the encounter dragged on. The girl's feigned groans of pleasure and squeals of ecstasy filled the room, but the bored look in her eyes gave a more accurate reflection of her interest in proceedings. Nothing personal—just business.

As Montero thrust himself into the supine form beneath him, the girl screwed her eyes shut and bit down on her lower lip. Thirty seconds later a dull *phut* was caught on the soundtrack as his face exploded, showering the girl with red-flecked chunks of bone and brain. So that was how the scumbag had gone out. Shot from behind on the down stroke. Never even saw it coming. The girl's eyes sprang open in surprise then widened in terror. Hunter heard another dull *phut*, then her left eye disappeared and blood welled out of the socket. Game over.

After a few more seconds the assassin strolled into frame. He was tall, gaunt and unassuming, as if he wasn't quite sure whether to materialise in the room or not, and he was dressed all in black, right up to the fedora that obscured most of his face. Eccentric. Hunter allowed himself a half-smile. Eccentric might prove helpful. The assassin stood motionless for a moment, reviewing his handiwork, then he began to unscrew the suppressor on his Glock. There was some sort of mark on the back of his left hand, but it was semi-obscured by a clear latex glove. Hunter pursed his lips in frustration—a careful man was harder to catch. Once the gun had been returned to its holster, the assassin delved into his jacket pocket to retrieve a syringe and a vial of cloudy liquid. He unscrewed the cap on the vial, jabbed the syringe's needle through the seal, and drew up the plunger until most of the liquid was transferred. What the hell was this? It was way too late to be playing doctor.

The assassin moved to the near side of the bed, bringing

himself closer to the camera, where he proceeded to lean over Montero and administer some post-mortem medication to the pornographer's left biceps. Hunter jabbed at the pause button on the remote. Something had caught his attention. He wound the tape back a few seconds then advanced it frame by frame. As the assassin's hand began to reach over the bed, he froze the image and let his eyes drift casually over the picture. Sometimes it helped if you didn't look too hard. But not this time.

Whatever had piqued his interest refused to make itself known, so he moved on to stage two of the search process, mentally subdividing the image into six square sections then examining them one by one. He hit pay dirt on section five. The latex-gloved hand that was holding the syringe was one finger light. Pinkie finger. Hard to spot. The mark on the back of the assassin's hand was also a little clearer. Hunter walked over to the screen and slowly traced the mark's outline. Was it T-shaped? Maybe not. Either way, it was still a distinguishing feature. He returned to the sofa and resumed playback. Once the killer was done with the syringe, he headed out of frame for a few seconds then reappeared on the far side of Montero's body to deposit something on the bedside cabinet. Hunter closed his eyes and visualised the scene as if he were still there, until each item that had been sitting on the cabinet swam back into focus in his mind's eye. A digital alarm clock, a few playing cards and a torn condom wrapper. The clock was an unlikely parting gift, but the other two items were both feasible, if not obvious, things to deposit. But why? It was certainly something to think about.

When he looked back up the killer had disappeared again and this time he didn't return. After a few minutes of total inactivity Hunter watched himself appear on screen and walk over to the bed. The show was over. Montero's secret record of his last minutes on earth had provided a few leads that would need to be run down, plus a few questions that needed answers, and Hunter knew just who to ask.

CHAPTER THIRTEEN

'Now, remember what I said. Keep quiet, look sombre, but not so sombre that you look guilty, and let me do all the talking. OK?'

Having deposited her BMW 645Ci coupe at a nearby parking garage, Rebecca Finch was heading towards the courthouse. Bobby Ashton, her blond-haired Adonis of a client, was alongside her, and she was trying to give him a lecture, but Bobby wasn't paying too much attention as a couple of cuties on the other side of the street had caught his eye.

'Mr Ashton!' Rebecca exclaimed. 'May I remind you that you could be facing a custodial sentence if this trial goes badly—please listen to me.'

'Huh? Yeah, sorry, honey…whatever you want.'

Rebecca sighed in exasperation. It was going to be a real pleasure defending this asshole. She was glad to see that he'd taken her advice and dressed up for the occasion—a sharp Nino Cerruti suit to go with his Gucci loafers—but, truth be told, it wasn't his appearance that was causing her concern, it was his big mouth. While she had no intention of putting him on the stand, it wasn't going to be easy limiting his outbursts in open court, and as soon as he started to talk he'd mark himself out as an arrogant, spoilt brat, and there weren't too many juries in the land that warmed to that kind of individual. But at least she'd got lucky during selection, as the list of potential jurors had included a surprisingly high number of white-collar Caucasians. Through clever use of her peremptory challenges she'd been able to tilt the balance of the final twelve in their favour—given the nature of the case, the fewer dirt-poor Latinos sitting in judgement, the better. Now if she could just keep Ashton quiet long enough for her to mount a credible defence, she might be able to keep him out of jail.

She stifled a yawn as the two of them walked on in silence, Ashton's languid stride easily keeping pace with her staccato steps. The lack of conversation was providing her with some thinking time, and while she was trying not to dwell on last night's attack, she was mostly failing. She'd arranged for a glazier to repair the damage to the window later that day, but she still had no idea what the rock thrower had hoped to accomplish. Had it been an act of retribution related to one of her old cases? Or an act of intimidation, designed to make her think twice about taking on a new case? Well, whatever it was, one thing was for sure—she didn't scare easy.

The courthouse came into view as they turned the corner. It was an impressive piece of old-time architecture that had been constructed from heavy granite-faced blocks back in the 1920s. Six giant Corinthian columns projected from its façade, supporting a triangular pediment that featured sculptures of classical figures in bas-relief. At its centre was a large, glass-roofed rotunda to let light from the heavens shine down on the earthly pursuit of justice below. A long flight of shallow steps led up to the main entrance, and these steps were currently home to what looked like an angry mob.

'What the fuck is this?' Bobby Ashton hadn't been to court before. If he had, he would have known that angry mobs were pretty much par for the course.

Rebecca estimated that the protesters numbered somewhere around fifty, mostly Hispanic, with a few Caucasians and African Americans thrown in for good measure. Some held aloft placards bearing a beatific photo of a clean-cut teenager set among painted white roses, while others punched the air as they roared out a chant. When they caught sight of Rebecca and Ashton, the chant doubled in volume.

'Justice for Manuel! Lock Ashton up!'

What the chant lacked in style, it made up for with directness.

'Keep your head down, say nothing, and keep walking,' she whispered to Ashton, taking him by the arm.

'I'm not walking through that! Get me in some other way…' he snarled back. The prospect of having to confront the grieving friends and family of the boy he'd run down had caused all the colour to drain from his complexion. Penitent? Doubtful. Cowardly? Much more likely.

'There is no other way in. Just keep walking and keep your head down. I've run the gauntlet a million times, and through much bigger crowds than this, and if I can do it, so can you.' She quickened her pace and started to drag him along the sidewalk, and after some initial resistance he fell in alongside her.

'Yeah, you're right. Don't they know who I am?' he said, talking up his confidence. 'My father could buy each and every one of them ten times over. They should learn some respect.' He grew in stature as his arrogance overcame his fear, and by the time he'd reached the courthouse steps he was almost glowering with self-righteous indignation at the fact that some commoners had the audacity to challenge him.

'Justice for Manuel! Lock Ashton up!'

The chant rang out loudly from all sides as the mob surrounded them. Rebecca pushed on, trying not to see the hate and anger in their eyes. She felt the heat of strangers' warm bodies pressed up against her while the smell of their breath assaulted her nostrils. An old lady thrust a picture of the boy Manuel into her face and implored her to look, but she pushed it aside without answering. She knew from experience that this was neither the time nor the place to discuss a case, but that was one lesson Bobby Ashton had yet to learn.

'What the hell's your problem, buddy? It was an *accident*, it wasn't my fault.' He'd stopped to go toe to toe with a protester who'd got too close to his highly polished loafers. Big mistake.

'Mur-der-er!…Mur-der-er!' shouted the protester into Ashton's face, a dark-haired, middle-aged, blue-collar kind of guy who sported a pencil moustache and a straggly goatee. Pretty soon everyone else had taken up the slow chant.

'Hey! Cut that out!' yelled Ashton. 'I *said* cut that out!'

If anything, the volume increased. Ashton stood dumbfounded for a second, not used to being ignored, then his temper snapped and he made a lunge for his tormentor. Rebecca tried to intercede but the sea of protesters got in her way, and all she could do was watch as Ashton grabbed moustache guy by the lapels and started to shake him like a rag doll.

'Shut the fuck up, you dago son of a bitch!' he screamed, spraying the guy with spittle. For a split second Rebecca thought that the protestor was going to fight back, but then he reined himself in and opted for the non-violent protest approach, although he didn't stop chanting.

'For chrissakes, Ashton, let him go!' Rebecca yelled as she

struggled to force a way through the throng, but the human tide seemed to be carrying her in the opposite direction. This was a long way from good. Things were getting uglier by the second, and if Ashton was stupid enough to throw a punch, they'd be finished. Flashbulbs started to go off behind her. Great. Reporters. That was all she needed.

Summoning all her vocal might, she shouted out one last threat. *'Let him go now, Ashton, or I walk.'*

He looked around with a surprised expression on his face. Not too many people had ever threatened to fire *him* before. Must have been quite a shock for daddy's boy. He dropped his opponent's lapels, sneered at him one last time, then resumed his struggle up the steps towards Rebecca. After a few more seconds a brace of uniformed court officials showed up to ease their passage. Better late than never. But while the crowd parted like the Red Sea, the level of hostility remained electric.

'Idiot,' she muttered to Ashton once they reached the top. All she got in return was a smile. When they walked through the large wooden entrance doors of the courthouse, the chant of 'Mur-der-rer!' could still be heard from outside.

CHAPTER FOURTEEN

HUNTER took another mouthful of the pad Thai noodles, savouring their peanutty flavour, before tapping his empty bottle of Coors on the counter to get Tommy the barman's attention. It was early afternoon and he was back in his favourite haunt, an old-style joint that just reeked of history, and a pretty seedy one at that. It was the sort of bar that wouldn't just tell you its story, but would first sit you down, rap a .45 on the table and grab your shrinking balls just to make sure it had your full attention. The riff-heavy 'No One Knows' by QOTSA was playing on the jukebox and Hunter was tapping his feet to the rhythm.

Another beer duly arrived, so he took a long pull then raised the bottle in recognition of services rendered. The beer was crisp and refreshing, racing over his taste buds to wind its way steadily down to his gut. It was his third of the day if you didn't count the Asahi he'd downed before sun-up, and he didn't. Getting loaded whenever you felt like it was one of the perks of being unemployed, although over-indulgence had its price. He'd spent the morning trying to sweat out the toxins by first running through a vigorous routine with some free weights, then concentrating on cardiovascular fitness with a compound set of push-ups, pull-ups and pile squats.

He put the beer down and watched a bead of condensation make its slow descent from the bottle's neck to the aging oak surface below. Now, here was a proper bar counter, one that had been christened countless times over with splashes of beer, the sweat from a working stiff's palm, or sometimes the blood from that same sucker's split lip.

'How you like noodles, Hunter?' asked a young voice. He looked up to find that Dusit, Tommy's Thai apprentice, had emerged from the kitchen.

'Pretty good, Dusty, pretty good.'

Tommy had got fed up saying Dusit, so he'd nicknamed the boy Dusty, which was kind of apt, for when he wasn't rustling up some new Asian speciality dish out back, the kid was in charge of the cleaning. Dusty hailed from the Chang Mai region of Thailand, north of Bangkok, and he'd been hired on a trial basis till the end of the month. So far, he was working out well, although Tommy's grocery bill had rocketed as the kid was constantly buying exotic ingredients for his recipes, not that you'd hear Hunter complaining.

'I go fetch some Tom-Yum soup…'

Hunter rolled his eyes in mock resignation, then checked his watch. It had just gone two. Carson was late. He'd set up a meeting with the old cop to discuss the Montero assassination. The home-made porn flick he'd nabbed from the scene had raised some questions, questions that only someone inside the official investigation could answer. If he was going to catch up with the assassin, he was going to need some help, and that was where Carson came in. He had a feeling that getting information wasn't going to be easy, though, as old pros like Carson didn't just throw you a bone. No, this was going to have to be a quid pro quo sort of deal. The main door swung open to throw a shaft of sunlight into the bar's gloomy interior.

'About time,' he called over his shoulder.

'Yeah, well, some of us still have jobs to go to,' deadpanned Carson, bolting down the remnants of a greasy cheeseburger as he claimed a seat at the bar. 'Been busy tying up a few loose ends on a couple of old cases, trying to clear the decks ahead of my hard-earned retirement.' The detective was wearing a flecked grey suit that struggled to contain his broad shoulders, along with a plain white shirt that was in serious need of a visit to the laundromat. 'Now, what the hell did you drag me across town for?'

'Couple more beers here, Tommy.' Hunter waited for the drinks to arrive before continuing. 'I've got a few questions about the Montero death.'

'And why in the hell should I answer them?'

'Because I've got more on the assassin in the last few hours than you'll manage in the whole of next week.'

'Oh, yeah? Like what?'

'How about a pretty decent physical description for starters…?'

Carson let loose a soft whistle. Hunter figured him for impressed.

'I shouldn't really be sharing details of an ongoing investigation with you, but if you've got a description…' Carson mused, pulling out a fat Cuban cigar and a Zippo lighter that sported the Playboy bunny on its brushed aluminium surface. 'Lord knows, this case could do with a break. OK, give me what you've got, then we'll see about those questions.'

'Nope. Questions first…description later.' He met Carson's

gaze and the two of them went eye to eye for twenty seconds or so, then the older man shrugged, lit his cigar, and proceeded to cough up his guts before he'd even taken one puff.

'Jesus!' exclaimed Hunter. 'You don't sound so good.'

'I'll live,' muttered Carson. 'Now, how about those questions?'

'First up, was Montero wearing a condom when you pulled him out of the girl?'

'Why in the hell should that matter? It's not as if either of them need to worry about STDs any more.'

'Humour me.'

Carson held up his hands in mock resignation and continued, 'Yeah, Durex, as it happens, ribbed, for her pleasure. One of our techs was bitching about the removal process. What's the relevance?'

'It's more about the irrelevance—the presence of a condom means that the torn wrapper on the bedside cabinet had every right to be there.'

Carson gave confused. 'You're gonna have to help me out here, Hunter, cos either I'm missing your point or you don't have one…'

Hunter ignored him. 'There were also some playing cards on the cabinet—were they dusted for prints?'

'Yeah, them and everything else in the room.'

'And, unlike the condom wrapper, the cards were print-free?'

'Yep.'

'Didn't that strike you as kinda odd? Even if they were a virgin pack of cards, whoever put them there should have left at least one set of prints.'

'Correct,' said Carson.

'So that means the cards were left by someone wearing protective gloves—the assassin. But the big question is, why did he leave them in the first place? And as for that physical description, your guy's about six-foot-four and thin as a rake, he wears a fedora, has a T-shaped mark on the back of his right hand, and he's missing the pinky finger from that same hand. The murder weapon was a Glock, but you probably knew that already from the ballistics tests.'

'Ballistics test? I'll be lucky if I see them inside of a week. OK, hotshot, how in the hell do you know all that?'

Hunter reached inside his jacket for the miniDV tape, and slid it towards Carson, who nodded in understanding. 'The camera—'

'In the closet,' finished Hunter. 'The tape was still running when I got there. I've taken the liberty of editing myself out of the main feature—I figured it would spare us both a headache if my presence at Montero's remained unknown.'

'You figured right,' said Carson, pocketing the tape. 'You do realise it's a felony to remove evidence from a crime scene?'

'So go ahead and arrest me…'

Carson's eyes flared angrily for a moment, but he let it slide. 'How about those playing cards? Any insights? Is the killer sending us a message?'

'I don't know yet, but the one thing you can be sure of is that he's a pro. Not only did he take Montero out clean, he evaded us in the process. And the gimmicks—the fedora, the cards—this guy's a bit out of the ordinary. There's no way Montero was his first.'

'Bravo. We've found playing cards at three other murder scenes, and all of them remain unsolved. I've been chasing a shadow for the last three months—it's my last active case before I retire.'

'So you've got a serial killer on your hands. But what does Montero have to do with it?'

'Search me. Maybe the killer wanted some publicity—Montero's been all over the news. Or maybe he just took an instant dislike to the guy—he wouldn't be the first. There's no link between any of the victims, least not one I can find. I only went to Montero's to keep you out of trouble, I was shocked as hell to find anyone else at the scene, then doubly shocked when I saw the playing cards.'

Both men took a pull from their beers before Carson continued; 'Anyhow, enough of this bullshit. What is it that you really want?'

Hunter's eyes went steely. 'I want in on this investigation. I want to know everything you know, as soon as you know it. I want to take this guy down.'

'Why? When he killed Montero, he saved you a job.'

'Maybe so, but he hadn't earned the right. Plus he killed a young hooker—she didn't deserve to go out like that. This guy's out of control. He's got to be stopped.'

'What is this? Disgraced cop takes one last shot at redemption? You looking for your old job back?'

'Call it what you want, but I want a piece of it. Besides, I've got plenty of time on my hands, as you're happy to keep pointing out.'

'And what's in it for me?' Low tones, time to get serious.

'You get someone working 24-7 on the case, someone who's not bound by rules and regulations, someone who can go in where angels fear to tread. Check out my file—I made a lot of cases—my instincts are good. I had one of the highest clearance rates in the city last year. If it weren't for Montero, I'd still be playing inside the system, but maybe things have worked out for the best—I can get a whole lot more done as a freelancer. What do you say?'

'You're gonna go ahead with this regardless, aren't you?'

'Damn straight.'

Carson appraised him for a moment. 'Hell, I like you, Hunter, you're my kind of guy. And I already pulled your file—you're right, you were a good cop. You want my opinion, the department's given you a pretty bum deal. Back in the day when I was first coming up, beating on the likes of Montero would have gotten you a citation, not the goddamn boot. Maybe you deserve another chance. Plus you won't have to worry about all the rules and regulations that have got the rest of us so damn hogtied. Lord knows, I could do with a fresh perspective. What the hell, I'd rather have you on my team than running around the streets like some loose cannon. Least that way I can keep tabs on you. Tell you what, I've gotta head over to Parker Center now, but how about you come around my place later on tonight so we can discuss the case? I've got some files back there I think you'll find interesting. It'll be our little secret, *capisce*?'

Hunter gave a nod then raised his bottle and chinked it against Carson's. He'd got himself a partner and a purpose. Things were looking up.

CHAPTER FIFTEEN

HAROLD RIBECKI had a bunch of flowers in his hands and a big smile on his face as he squeezed his giant frame through the doorway to enter the fleapit motel room. The smile, which wasn't an expression he employed often, made him look even dumber than usual, but for once he didn't mind. Harold was excited. Today was a red-letter day: for the first time in his twenty odd years on the planet, he was finally going to get some.

He walked over to the bed, his cut-off jeans rustling softly as his thighs rubbed together, and pushed one of his ham-like fists into the mattress to test its strength. It creaked a little, but held firm. Next, he checked out the sheets, and while they were a long way from pristine, they were clean enough. No sense in getting too prissy at a time like this. Besides, personal hygiene had never figured that high on his list of priorities. When you tipped the scales at 362 pounds, body odour was a fact of life.

He checked the digital display on his watch. It was 4.30 in the p.m. Not long now. Jenna's note had said that she'd be at the motel by five. Old man Margetson must have let her leave the mini-mart early today. She didn't usually clock off till six, even when things were slow, which was pretty much every damn day of the week. Harold delved into his pocket and pulled out Jenna's wrinkled note. He'd read it so often he almost had it memorised. Key phrases leapt off the page at him. 'We got something special… Time to heat things up… Meet me at the Mill Road Motel.' His heart rate ticked up a notch.

He laid the note on the bed alongside the bunch of red tulips he'd lifted from someone's front yard, then glanced around the rest of the room. A small TV was bolted high in one corner, while a ratty old chest of drawers was pushed back against the far wall, sporting a swivel mirror that was laced with hairline cracks. He lumbered over to check himself out. The pasty face that stared back at him was blotched red with excitement. He ran a hand over his shaven head and felt the first rough shoots of stubble sprouting through his scalp. Maintaining the pose, his eyes strayed downwards to take in the large damp patch that had blossomed under his arm. He raised the fabric of his swastika embossed T-shirt towards his nose, took a deep sniff, then lowered it. Not too shabby.

This was gonna be sweet. In the two weeks he'd been dating Jenna she'd only ever let him get to first base, so tonight was gonna be something special. She was a few years older than him, a big girl, all woman, in fact, with dyed red hair and about twenty assorted piercings through lips, nose and eyebrows. All that facial steel didn't do much for Harold, but the ample rack just to the south of it certainly did. He felt his loins stir at the prospect of finally seeing her in the buff. Maybe she'd been testing him, keeping him waiting to make sure he was for real. He grinned. She'd find out soon enough.

This motel thing was a pain in the ass, though. Why the hell had she picked one in the shittier part of town? It had set him back thirty bucks, cash that could have been put to much better use at Billy's Biker Bar. And it had really pissed him off when he'd had to hand over his hard-earned dough to the spook at the front desk. Talk about rubbing salt into the wound. Still, if this was where Jenna wanted to make it, this was where they'd make it. No point in quibbling over money when the stakes were this high.

A delicate knock at the door broke his reverie. Christ! This was it. An unsightly bulge started to grow in the front of his jeans. He froze for a moment as the next half-hour played out in his mind's eye, until a second knock prompted him to burst into action. He straightened his T-shirt, retrieved the bunch of tulips from the bed, then clumped across the room with a stupid grin spread all over his face.

'Big Daddy's a comin', Jenna, I hope you're ready for him…'

He slipped the deadbolt and started to turn the doorhandle. This was it. Harold Ribecki was about to get fucked.

Danilov had the motel corridor all to himself, and he looked somewhat out of place, his immaculate appearance jarring with the less than salubrious surroundings. His right arm was extended and the Glock in his hand was pointed straight at the door to room 17. As the handle began to turn, his finger eased down on the trigger, slowly upping the pressure until breaking point was just a hair's breadth away. What happened next happened fast. The door swung inwards, Harold Ribecki's grinning face loomed large, Danilov's gun coughed twice, and two 9 mm bullets burrowed deep into Kid Kong's cerebral cortex.

Ribecki stood motionless in the doorway, the grin now stuck for ever to his face. His eyes glazed over and a trickle of blood ran down the bridge of his nose. Danilov took one pace forward to bring the barrel of the Glock into contact with the behemoth's forehead. Ribecki fell backwards into the room and landed with a dull thump, his impact on the threadbare carpet sending up a small cloud of dust to mark his passing. Having retrieved his spent shells, the assassin glanced left and right to check that his work had gone unnoticed, then stepped inside and eased the door shut.

'Not what you expecting, no?' he asked, as he bent down to stare deep into a pair of unblinking eyes. 'Life is just one big disappointment.' He touched the rim of his fedora then rose to his feet. Time to get busy.

He decided to work on the corpse right where it had fallen. Not that he had much choice. It would have taken a small crane to manoeuvre it anywhere else in the room. He unscrewed the suppressor on his Glock, pocketed it, then slid the weapon back into its custom-made shoulder holster. When his hand reappeared from inside the confines of his jacket it held a small tub of black shoe polish and a scrap of rag. He opened the tub, daubed the rag, then began smearing the polish over Ribecki's lifeless face.

'That is better. Now you have bit of colour, no?'

He worked quickly, rubbing the polish into all the nooks and crannies before moving upwards to cover Ribecki's bald dome. After a couple of minutes he stepped back to admire his handiwork, nodding once in recognition of a job well done. The kid now looked like a seriously overweight Al Jolson. Once he'd spread the twelve playing cards out on the bed, he let himself out of the room, took a couple of steps down the corridor, then doubled back to hang an ancient 'Do Not Disturb' sign on the doorhandle.

Even corpses needed their rest.

CHAPTER SIXTEEN

HUNTER parked his Barracuda behind a beat-up Nissan truck that sat rusting by the sidewalk and stepped outside. Following his meeting with Carson at lunch, it was now a little after 7 p.m., and he'd come to visit the detective on his home ground. Carson lived in the Little Armenia district of East Hollywood, so called because of the large number of Armenian stores and businesses that had opened up there in the past few years. The area had been pretty seedy prior to the Armenians' arrival, with low-rent hookers and well-armed drug dealers on every street corner, but the immigrant community had worked hard to clean things up, and their persistence was slowly starting to pay off.

'Nice car,' said Carson, nodding at the 'Cuda as he emerged from his house. 'Need a new one myself—my truck's on its last legs. Why don't you come inside?'

Hunter locked the 'Cuda and walked towards the detective's

house, a modest, stuccoed affair with a ramshackle red-brick garage stationed alongside it. The front garden was a haven for the local wildlife, while the flagstone path that led to the door was laced with cracks and choked with weeds. Hunter smothered a smile. Maybe the Armenian clean-up campaign hadn't made it this far yet.

'Make yourself at home,' muttered Carson, gesturing for him to enter.

He stepped inside and glanced around. The hall was bare, save for a lonely umbrella stand that housed no umbrellas and a pair of eight-by-ten colour photos in budget-price frames. The photos were of two middle-aged woman: a sour-looking brunette and a nondescript blonde.

'What you've got there is mistake number one and mistake number two,' said Carson, noting his interest. 'One on the left is my first wife—married her back in DC but she left me after a few years—said I spent too much time at work. After that, I spent even more time at work on account of the fact I had no home to go to, till I got stuck with this new lieutenant who was a stickler for rules and regs. I lasted about three months with him before I put in papers to come out to LA, where I met and married mistake number two, a police administrator who put up with me for a while before walking out a few months back.'

'You still in touch with her?'

'In a manner of speaking. Anyway, how about I fetch us a coupla beers?'

'Sure thing, Pops.'

Carson took off his coat, threw it on the hardwood newel at the bottom of the stairs, then headed for the front room, which was almost as sparsely decorated as the hall, although a tired-looking sofa, a dilapidated armchair and a modest entertainment centre did their best to fill the space. A stack of magazines sat on the sofa, along with a couple of old pizza cartons that were emitting a musty smell. The beige carpet was worn thin along the walkway to the kitchen, while a few stains and cigar burns reinforced the general feeling of disrepair. It looked like Carson had let things slip after his divorce. This place definitely lacked a woman's touch. A large photo of an old log cabin stationed right on the edge of a grey lake took pride of place on the main wall. Hunter walked over to get a closer look. In the foreground, Carson was standing with a fishing rod in one hand and a serious-sized bass in the other.

'It's Miller time.' The detective lobbed an unopened can in Hunter's general direction. 'God's country,' he proclaimed, when he saw Hunter in front of the photo. 'The cabin belongs to an old pal of mine. I head up there with my rods whenever I feel the need for a bit of solitude. Reminds me of when my dad used to take me out on the Potomac as a kid in DC. There's nothing like hauling down a big fish with your own hands on a clear winter's morn.'

'I wouldn't know,' replied Hunter, turning around and getting straight to the point. 'So how about those files?'

'Cool your horses, we got plenty of time. Let me get a start on this beer. I'll go fetch my files in a minute,' grumbled the old man as he proceeded to light up a Cuban. Pretty soon the whole room was choked with a thick cloud of acrid smoke, and Carson was engaged in another long coughing fit.

Hunter put a lid on his frustration and kept schtum. He'd come to the detective's house in order to get a look at his personal files on the assassin. Montero's murder had taken the number of deaths to four, and Carson had documented them all, supplementing the official reports with some off-the-clock legwork of his own. Hunter was itching to get a look at the info, but for some reason Carson was playing hard to get.

'Right,' began the detective once he'd stopped hacking his

guts up, 'here's how we're gonna play this. I'll give you the skinny on victim one, then you go dig around and see what you can turn up.'

'Now, wait just a goddamned minute…' spluttered Hunter. One case at a time? What the hell was this? 'You gotta be shitting me…'

'Calm down and hear me out. If I show you everything at once, you'll get so lost in the big picture you might miss something. This way, you'll come at each murder from a fresh angle, approach 'em with a clear mind. Maybe you'll pick up on something I missed.'

'But what if the something you've missed is hidden in the big picture?'

'Then you'll get to that in a few days' time. This isn't open for negotiation, Hunter. I'm risking my pension if anyone finds out about our little arrangement, so I'm calling the shots.'

Hunter didn't like it, but he didn't have much choice. 'OK, one at a time. So who's first?'

Carson wandered off down the hall. A door clicked open somewhere further back in the house, then a few seconds later it clicked shut. When the detective returned he was carrying a manila file under one arm. The file didn't look that full.

'Take the weight off…' Carson shifted the pizza cartons off the sofa, leaving Hunter to relocate the pile of magazines. The one on top was entitled *Lesbian Lust* and it featured two lithe young women locked in the sixty-nine position. He threw Carson an enquiring glance.

'Research,' muttered the old man in reply, as he bagged himself the armchair, opened the file, and started to read. 'Victim number one, Father Henry Mulrooney, found dead in his confessional booth at the Church of St Lawrence, his throat cut from ear to ear.'

'A priest?' Hunter gave surprised.

'Yep. And get this—he'd been blindfolded. Maybe our perp is a little kinky. Other than that, the scene was clear. No fingerprints, no witnesses and no hidden video camera. If it hadn't have been for the playing cards left at the altar, I'd have never tied it in with the others. Here, take a look for yourself. I've gotta go take a leak.'

He took the file from Carson's outstretched hand and leafed through it. Inside was a full description of the crime scene, along with the official forensics report, a fairly sparse background check on Father Mulrooney and a four-page history of the Church of St Lawrence. As soon as he heard Carson's footfalls on the landing overhead, Hunter rested the file on the sofa, rose to his feet and hurried out into the hall. There were two doors beyond the foot of the stairs, one closed, one open. Hunter headed for the closed one and ducked inside.

Carson's study. The desk by the window was home to an antique IBM computer that was so old it probably operated on a weights and pulleys system, while a bunch of papers were strewn in front of the PC. In addition, there was an easy chair under a standard lamp, plus a huge bookcase jammed with files and reference books. The wall to the left of the door was dominated by a large corkboard, although not that much of the cork was visible, buried as it was beneath a mountain of photos, scribbled notes and press clippings. Hunter stepped forward to take a closer look. Four headshots were pinned to the board, each one marking a point on the compass. The late Father Mulrooney was positioned at west, while Montero was at east. A bandana-sporting black man and a scrawny-looking white guy held down north and south respectively. At the epicentre of the four photos was a blank space, from which hand-drawn lines in heavy black ink ran outwards to attach themselves to the deceased.

'My, my,' muttered Hunter. 'Haven't you been busy?' It was the same sort of dedication he'd shown back when he'd been working the Montero case. Impressive. Somewhere overhead a cistern flushed. He dragged himself away from the corkboard and left the den in a hurry. By the time Carson had returned, he was back on the sofa, reading through the Mulrooney file.

'You wash your hands?' he asked.

'Very funny. Learnt much about the good Father?'

'Plenty on how he died, but not a lot on how he lived. Haven't you got any more background on this guy?'

'The rest's down at the station,' said Carson, settling back into his armchair while taking a draw on the Cuban. 'I'll dig it out for you. Anyways, all you really need is right there—a name and address. First thing tomorrow you can head over to the church and ask a few questions—that way you'll start to build up a picture of your own. And spare a thought for me while you're off having fun—I've got a goddamned media briefing on Montero's death scheduled for 9 a.m.'

'Sure thing, *boss*.' Hunter gave sarcastic. It was just like being back on the force, but without the pay and the pension. Still, at least he'd wake up with a purpose, and purpose was the one thing that had been sorely lacking in his life of late. A burst of excitement coursed through his being. Tracking down killers was what he did best. Some people defined themselves by their looks, others by their possessions, but for Hunter it all came down to how many murderous sons of bitches he could take out of the game, and come sun-up tomorrow, he'd be looking to add another one to his tally.

"We may have a problem."

Danilov stared at the words on the screen and scratched his chin. In the preceding ten minutes he'd filed his report on the death of the human blimp Harold Ribecki, then fielded a few straightforward questions from his invisible boss, and now that the formalities were out of the way it looked like they were getting down to business. So. The boss had a problem. As far as Danilov was concerned, this whole situation was one big problem from start to finish. He'd have given almost anything to return to Moscow, but that, unfortunately, was out of the question. He started to type.

"Da?"

"I've identified the two men that appeared at Montero's house. One of them you needn't concern yourself with—he's a cop by the name of Bud Carson who's probably just counting down the days to retirement. But the other's a little more worrying. Zac Hunter. Recently kicked off the force for excessive brutality during Montero's arrest, so he probably wasn't there to congratulate the Salvadorian on his acquittal. If Hunter takes your intervention personally, he might just start sniffing around."

The solution was obvious to Danilov. *"I send him to Boston?"*

"No. First we have to ascertain if he's a threat. I want you to tail him for the next few days and see what he gets up to. Where he goes, who he talks to, that sort of thing. His home address is 42 Longview Terrace, which is up in the hills off Mulholland Drive."

"Then Boston?"

"NO. He's to be left alone unless I give the order. I want a daily report on his movements, starting tomorrow. You provide the info; I'll make the decisions. And play it safe—I can't afford any slip-ups."

Danilov snorted. The boss's lack of faith was enough to dent his professional pride. *"Ex-cop is no threat to me."*

"Just be careful. And make sure that you're ready to move fast if I give the word."

And with that the boss was gone, leaving Danilov alone at his computer. He headed for the kitchen to fix himself a sandwich, his thoughts turning to the boss's instructions. Follow the man called Hunter, like some lone wolf stalking an unsuspecting elk across the icy wastes of Siberia. He snorted to himself for the second time in as many minutes. The thrill of the chase was all well and good, but without the payoff at the end, it was all for nothing.

He carved off some salo and placed it on a thick slice of rye bread, before proceeding to liberally smother the dry-cured pork fat in hot mustard. The salo came from a small Ukrainian deli a few blocks over, and if its rich smell was anything to go by, it was good quality. He took a bite and smiled his thin smile. The pork fat had been salted and smoked to perfection. But the smile soon fell from his face. He didn't like the thought of some ex-cop on his tail. It was bad enough that he had to put up with a mysterious boss that knew his every move, but the thought of someone else closing in on him was totally unacceptable. Things would be a whole lot simpler if this Hunter was just removed from the equation. Maybe a chance would present itself while he was watching him. The boss need never be the wiser. Accidents happened all the time.

CHAPTER SEVENTEEN

AN INSISTENT bleep brought Rebecca out of her slumber. She rolled over with a groan and shut off the alarm clock. The house was as quiet as a morgue. She fantasised about going back to sleep but knew that it wasn't an option, as another day in court awaited her. Clients didn't just defend themselves. Even arrogant asshole clients like Bobby Ashton.

She threw back the duvet, rose to her feet, stretched once, yawned twice, then pulled on her robe. Shower first, then coffee, or the other way around? Decisions, decisions. Maybe a caffeine injection will get me going, she thought, stifling another yawn. She entered the kitchen to find Anabeth sitting at the table, wearing her customary Adidas sweatsuit. The blinds were still drawn, but shafts of sunlight cut through the slats to throw a striated pattern on the floor.

'Morning,' said Rebecca, heading straight for the coffee-machine.

'Morning. So how'd it go in court yesterday? That drunk driver anywhere closer to freedom?'

'It went as well as could be expected. I caught a break on the judge—old man Wharton was appointed and I'm three-and-oh with him. He's getting more and more liberal as he approaches retirement. As for Ashton's chances, it's too soon to say. I'll have a better idea once we hear from the prosecution's key witnesses—the barman, the arresting officer and the like.'

'You know how you're gonna combat them? Got a strategy in place?'

'I've got a couple of tricks up my sleeve. Plus Ashton reckons that some of them might reconsider and change their stories.'

'Yeah…that figures. Rich kid greases some palms and everything turns out OK.'

'Apparently.'

'Well, it doesn't matter how you get a "not guilty" verdict, as long as you get one.'

'The end justifies the means?'

'Exactly. This is a big case. You've worked hard for it. Now you've just got to make sure you get the right result.'

The percolator finished its cycle, so Rebecca poured herself a cup then pulled on the cord that opened the blinds.

'What the…?'

Half the neighbourhood was clustered out on the sidewalk, staring straight at her. Some were huddled together in small groups while others were trying not to point. A few of the youngsters looked like they were laughing.

'What is it?' asked Anabeth.

'There's a bunch of people gawping right at me.'

With coffee-cup in hand, she headed for the front door, slipped the security chain and stepped outside. Her arrival caused all conversation to come to a halt. A small boy at the front of the throng had his arm stretched out, frozen in place, pointing at whatever had drawn these people to her home. Rebecca followed the direction of the gesture and felt the air drain out of her.

The word BITCH had been painted on her lawn in bright red letters. She took a couple of steps forward in a daze. When she glanced back for reassurance from her sister, she discovered that more hate messages had been scrawled on the side of her house.

ASHTON = KILLER

FINCH = WHORE

JUSTICE FOR MANUEL

The night before last, rocks through her window, and now this. For the next few seconds everything seemed to happen in slow motion. The coffee-cup slid from her grasp as her hands flew up to her temples. The crowd watched on in silence as the cup fell end over end towards the ground. The cup smashed on impact to send hot liquid and chunks of white porcelain flying outwards in all directions. Then time sped back up as the crowd sparked back to life, shouting a hundred different questions all at once. A local TV news van came screeching to a halt at the kerb. Its rear door slid open and a bearded man jumped out with camera already running. Rebecca spun on her heel, ran back inside her house and slammed the door. Anabeth looked at her enquiringly.

'What's going on?' she asked.

'I don't know,' replied a shaken Rebecca, 'but I sure as hell intend to find out.'

Hunter had woken up early, excited at the prospect of starting his search for the assassin. As he'd lain there, he'd realised that his life finally had purpose again—something constructive to do with his time—and that had made him feel good. He'd pulled back the sheets and climbed to his feet, stretched, then headed for the bathroom, where he'd drained his bladder before taking a long hot shower to relax the tension in his shoulders. Once he'd dragged a straight razor across his face, he'd pulled on a pair of jeans and a lightweight black sweater, then rustled up a plate of ham and eggs, which he'd quickly devoured, before sitting himself in front of the TV with a cup of freshly brewed coffee.

Carson was due on any moment now. He tuned to a local channel just in time to watch the blonde news anchor hand over to a live feed from a pressroom inside Parker Center. As the camera panned around, he saw that the room was full of assembled media types, some waiting with pen poised just above pad, others staring through lenses at the small dais at the front of the room. Three people sat behind the desk on the raised platform—a young, smartly dressed man on each flank and an older, scruffier individual in the middle. Carson. Hunter allowed himself a smile. The detective's lack of sartorial elegance had probably caused someone in the department's public relations office to have a fit. He took a sip of his coffee and listened as the media briefing got under way.

'Thank you for attending this briefing,' began the smartly dressed officer on Carson's right, 'which has been called following the deaths of Carlos Montero and Catalina Suarez two nights ago. In just a moment I'll hand you over to the lead detective in the case, Bud Carson, who will read a short statement before taking a few questions from the floor. OK—are we all ready? Then I give you Detective Carson.'

Carson grimaced as a few flashbulbs went off, threw an angry stare at the room of people, then began to read from a sheet of paper, his gruff voice amplified by the small microphone placed directly in front of him.

'Carlos Montero, a native Salvadorian who has lived in Los Angeles for the past three years, was found dead at his home in the Santa Monica Mountains on 24th November. Mr Montero was forty-two years of age, single, with no dependants. His body was discovered in the early hours of the morning following reports of suspicious activity on his property. At the time of the discovery of Mr Montero's body, a second corpse was found, that of Miss Catalina Suarez, a fifteen-year-old illegal immigrant from Mexico. Miss Suarez was well known to the LAPD's vice squad, and is believed to have been present at the Montero residence that evening for purposes relating to her line of work. As yet we have been unable to notify Miss Suarez's parents of her death, although our colleagues in Mexico are doing all that they can to track them down. The cause of death in both cases was a gunshot wound to the head. Preliminary ballistics tests suggest that the weapon used was a 9-mm handgun, probably manufactured by Glock. As a result, the deaths of both Carlos Montero and Catalina Suarez are being treated as homicide.'

Hunter watched as Carson turned over the sheet of paper and continued to read.

'As you are all aware, Carlos Montero was recently on trial for the abduction and murder of seven children. The collapse of that case left Mr Montero a free man. The LAPD will afford the same resources to the murder of Mr Montero as it would to the murder of any other individual within our jurisdiction. Homicide is homicide, and we will do everything in our power to bring the killer of both Mr Montero and Miss Suarez to justice. I will head the investigation, with a focussed team at my disposal. After this briefing, any media enquiries should be directed to my assistant on the case, Detective Eduardo Rios. That is the end of the statement. I will now take a few brief questions.'

A hand shot up from the front of the audience. 'Hector Perez, *La Opinión*. Have you got any leads, Detective?'

'As yet our crime-scene analysts have been unable to find much in the way of physical evidence at the scene. As for motive, Mr Montero was strongly suspected of involvement in a number of criminal activities, and I believe that this involvement may have somehow led to his death.'

'In what way, Detective?' shouted a voice from off camera.

'Deal gone bad, power play by a competitor, failure to pay off a debt…take your pick.'

'John Walters, *LA Times*. I've heard rumours that Mr Montero's death might be linked to some other homicides in the city. Have we got a serial killer on our hands, Detective?'

'Absolutely not.' Carson glowered from the dais. 'At this stage there is nothing whatsoever to link this double homicide to any other death in the city.'

'So there's no truth in the rumour that you were picked to head this investigation as it has similarities to some of your other cases?'

'I'm a homicide detective. I handle a lot of cases. The only thing they have in common is that they all involve stiffs. People die in LA every day of the year—they're not all linked.'

'Will you be interviewing the parents of the children that Montero was suspected to have killed, Detective?' pressed Walters.

'No. As I said a moment ago, I shall focus our attentions on Mr Montero's suspected criminal associates. One thing I have learnt over my long years of police service is that if you're looking for a killer, look in all the dark places first. When it comes to carrying out violent acts, criminals are best qualified. Right…I'm done… No further questions,' barked Carson, as he rose to his feet and walked out of the back of the room.

Hunter reached for the remote as the TV footage cut back to the news anchor in the studio.

'Well...that was Detective Bud Carson speaking direct from Parker Center, briefing us on the recent murder of Carlos Montero,' she began, quickly recovering her composure following the abrupt end of the feed. 'And in related news we can now go live to our correspondent Amy Chung at the home of Rebecca Finch, who you may remember was the lead defence lawyer in the case against Mr Montero. Amy? I hear there's been some excitement. What's going on down there?'

Hunter replaced the remote on the coffee-table and watched as the image on the screen changed to that of a pretty young Asian reporter standing in a nice suburban neighbourhood.

'I'm here in South Pasadena, outside the home of leading defence attorney Rebecca Finch who, as you can see, has come under personal attack this very morning,' said Amy Chung, stepping aside to allow the camera to focus on the house behind her. Hunter was startled to find that a number of aggressive messages had been daubed on the walls of Rebecca's house, while the word 'Bitch' had been painted on the lawn in bright red letters.

'The graffiti is thought to be related to Miss Finch's next case,' piped up Amy Chung, now back on screen, 'that of Mr Bobby Ashton, who is due to stand trial for the vehicular manslaughter of Manuel Ortega, an eleven-year-old boy who died in an automobile accident on South Rodeo Drive earlier this year. With this attack on Ms Finch's home coming so soon on the heels of the murder of her previous client, Carlos Montero, one can only wonder as to Miss Finch's current state of mind. Wait a minute, I think I see movement inside the house. Perhaps she's coming out...'

The front door opened and Rebecca Finch appeared.

Hunter thought she looked good—she was wearing a smart black business suit that had been cut to flatter her figure, her hair was pulled back in a neat ponytail and her pretty face sported a neutral expression. He watched as she locked the front door behind her then walked quickly over to the silver BMW that was parked in the driveway. Before she could make it to the sanctuary of the car, Amy Chung and her cameraman had moved smartly to intercept her.

'Miss Finch—Amy Chung, news reporter from Fox affiliate KNBC 4. Have you got any thing to say about the attack on your home?'

'No comment,' responded Rebecca, as she tried to get to her car.

'The graffiti appears to be linked to your decision to defend Mr Bobby Ashton against a vehicular manslaughter charge. Given that you have now come under personal attack, will you consider dropping the case?'

'Absolutely not,' she said icily, managing to elbow the reporter aside and get her key in the lock.

'Have you anything to say on the murder of Carlos Montero? In a roundabout way, it seems that your efforts to keep him out of prison may have resulted in his death.'

Rebecca stopped dead and turned to face the camera, her face filling Hunter's TV screen, her expression as cold as ice.

'The case against Carlos Montero was dropped due to a lack of evidence. He was therefore a free man. An innocent man. His murder was a vicious and terrible crime. I fully expect his killer to be brought to justice. I have complete faith in the abilities of the Los Angeles Police Department, and I look forward to hearing that they've apprehended Mr Montero's killer in the very near future. That is all I wish to say on the subject.'

With that, she climbed inside her BMW, started the engine

and pulled away. Hunter retrieved the remote and clicked off his TV. He was annoyed to find that Finch was still defending Montero even after the scumbag's death, but he had to grudgingly admit to having acquired a newfound respect for the lawyer's toughness. She'd woken up to a nightmare—aggressive graffiti, aggressive TV crew, the whole nine yards—but she'd handled it all in her stride. Pretty impressive.

He finished the rest of his coffee, rose to his feet, then made for the front door, collecting his leather jacket and Beretta en route. Thoughts of tough, pretty defensive lawyers would have to wait—it was time he set out on the trail of the assassin.

CHAPTER EIGHTEEN

HUNTER eased down on the brakes of his Barracuda to come to a gentle stop outside the Church of St Lawrence. The church was situated in the aptly named Temple City, a small community in the west San Gabriel Valley that was predominantly Caucasian, although it had recently begun to attract a glut of Mandarin-speaking Orientals. He'd never had cause to visit the area before, but he was vaguely aware of its layout, as he had a working relationship with one of the Taiwanese residents—a bank teller named Jimmy Chang who was happy to delve into the financial records of anyone Hunter was interested in, no questions asked. He'd caught Jimmy's teenage daughter buying some uppers in a bar on Sunset three years ago, but he hadn't put her through the system, a decision that had left Jimmy eternally grateful.

Before he climbed out of the car, he reached over to the

passenger seat to collect a nine-by-twelve envelope that contained ten colour photos of the assassin—five full-length shots and five of the hand with a T-shaped mark and no pinky. He'd had a small photographic studio pull them off stills from his copy of the miniDV tape in the hope they'd prove useful, but he wasn't holding his breath.

Sweat popped on his brow as soon as he hit the street. The weather was shaping up to be hot, one of those freak days in late fall that made you think you were still stuck in the height of summer. The asphalt was beginning to heat up and small patches had already become glutinous underfoot. The same thing would be happening city wide, turning LA into a giant heat island, its miles and miles of concrete helping to trap the sun's warmth and raise temperatures, and higher temperatures meant more air-con, which in turn meant more pollution. Urban life sucked.

He hurried over to the heavy wooden doors that marked the entrance to the church and went inside, glad to get out of the sun's oppressive glare. There was a small white noticeboard in the porch. He gave it a perfunctory scan but found nothing of interest. The inside of the church was gloomy. As he strode down the central aisle he recognised the interior from a dozen different crime-scene photos. A priest emerged from the sacristy laden with blue hymnbooks. For a man of the cloth, he looked kind of young. He stopped dead when he saw he had company.

'Can I help you?' he asked in a clipped tone.

'I sure hope so. I'd like to ask you some questions about your predecessor, Father Mulrooney.'

The priest's expression hardened. 'I feared as much. You're just like all the others. Get out! I've no desire to go through this all over again with another one of you parasites. Shame on you. Go on, get out! You ghoul!'

Hunter was momentarily taken aback by the verbal onslaught. He raised his hands in a conciliatory gesture and tried to claw back some of the lost ground.

'Hey, calm down there, Father. I think you might have misjudged me. My name's Zac Hunter and I'm helping the police with their enquiries, going over the details of Father Mulrooney's death in the hope that I turn up some new evidence. I just need a few minutes of your time then I'll be on my way.'

'Oh…well…I guess that's OK…' he said with a smile that failed to extend to his eyes. 'I'm sorry to fly off the handle, but every day brings another set of callers that have some sort of morbid fascination with the late Father's death, God rest his soul, and I'm through being polite to them.'

'Don't sweat it, Father—no harm, no foul. Anyway, can't say I blame you. Some people are drawn to violent deaths like moths to a flame. Used to see it all the time when I was on the force—we called 'em vamps, shorts for vampires.'

'You're an ex-cop? So what are you now? A private investigator?'

'Yeah, something like that. Anyway, Father, about those questions…'

'Of course, of course, just give me a second to lay out these books… Please, take a seat.' The priest nodded towards the nearest pew then hurried over to the choir stalls where he proceeded to lay out the hymnbooks, five to each row. 'Fire away,' he invited on his return.

'First up, did you know Father Mulrooney?'

'A little. I'd come and help out here from time… Father Mulrooney was an old man, and sometimes he'd need assistance.'

'What sort of assistance?'

'Oh, you know, lifting, carrying, that sort of thing, plus I'd stand in on the occasional service if he didn't feel up to it.'

'How could you spare the time? Don't you have a flock of your own?'

'Oh, no, not yet. I'm still learning the ropes, as it were, but I'm hoping that St Lawrence's might turn out to be my first full-time position. I was asked to stand in here after...well, you know...and three months later I'm still here, so fingers crossed.'

'In the days prior to the Father's death, how did he behave? Did he seem out of sorts at all? Was anything troubling him? I know the police will have asked you these kinds of questions already, but think back—sometimes things become clearer with the passage of time.'

The priest paused before answering, his lips twitching slightly. 'No, nothing like that, he was just the same old Father Mulrooney. His only care in the world was being the best priest he could be. He believed that his role on earth was to offer spiritual guidance to those that came looking for it.'

'And what about those that didn't come looking?'

'Everyone comes looking in the end, Mr Hunter. Some just take longer than others.'

How enlightening. Hunter pressed on. 'So there was nothing in his personal life that might have caused someone to murder him? No enemies? No one nursing a grudge?'

The priest looked away as he answered. 'No. Nothing like that.'

'Any idea why the killer blindfolded him?'

'None at all.'

'Did he have any friends or family that I can talk to?'

'No, not really. His family's back in Vermont, and as for friends, well, I guess you'd say that he got all the friendship he needed from the Lord.'

'OK. How about this guy?' he asked, pulling the murky

photos of the assassin out of his envelope. 'Have you ever seen anyone hanging around the church that looked like this? Tall, skinny, well dressed? What about that T-shaped mark on the back of his hand? Maybe that's familiar?'

The priest took the proffered pictures and gave them a cursory glance before handing them back with a shake of his head. 'I'm afraid not. Your photos aren't very clear, are they?'

Hunter arched an eyebrow. Everyone's a critic.

'Well, if there's nothing else, Mr Hunter, I'd like to be getting on. To be honest, we're all trying to put what happened to Father Mulrooney behind us.' The priest rose to his feet. 'Such a terrible thing when the forces of evil strike down a servant of God.'

'You seem to be handling it quite well…'

'The Lord moves in mysterious ways, Mr Hunter. I believe that the Father's passing is just another small part of His grand design.'

'Must be nice to be able to rationalise everything like that. Back when I was a cop, I saw things that would curdle your blood, and I saw 'em on a daily basis, but I sure as shit never saw any grand design.'

'Maybe you just weren't looking hard enough… Well, if there's anything else I can do, just let me know,' said the priest, ushering him out.

'Mind if I put these on your noticeboard?' Hunter asked, holding up two pictures of the assassin.

'Be my guest.'

He wrote a short note asking for information on the base of each photo, along with his cellphone number, then pinned them to the board. The priest hovered behind him, almost nudging him towards the exit, until he took the hint and stepped out into the sunshine. 'Thanks for your time.'

'Good day, Mr Hunter.' With that, the priest was gone, back

to shuffle blue hymnbooks around an empty church. Hunter climbed inside his Barracuda and replayed their conversation in his head. Something wasn't right. The priest had been nervous when he should have been sad. Jumpy, when he should have been morose. And his answers had been too bland. Too noncommittal. Like they'd been rehearsed. Maybe the priest had something to hide. Hunter could smell a cover-up, but that didn't come as any great surprise. It sure as hell wouldn't be the first time that the church had closed ranks to protect one of its own.

Danilov put the Zeiss binoculars back in their case and hurried down the street. He stepped inside the church porch, gently humming 'My Way' as he checked out the noticeboard. His heart rate, usually so reliable, actually skipped a beat. The washed-out ex-cop had left two photos of him for all to see. Where in the hell had he got them? He folded the glossy pictures into quarters, buried them deep inside his jacket pocket, then patted his shoulder holster. If Hunter was intent on looking for trouble, he'd come to the right place.

CHAPTER NINETEEN

HUNTER slowed his Barracuda and craned his neck to take a look at the Watts Towers. Whenever he was in South Central he made a point of checking them out, as he'd always found them inspiring. The seventeen interconnected structures climbed above the surrounding low-rises to sparkle in the sunlight as if they'd been encrusted with precious jewels. It had taken an Italian construction worker thirty years of his life to build them, first fashioning the main armatures from steel pipes, wire mesh and mortar, then using whatever scrap materials he could find for decoration—porcelain, ceramic tiles, seashells, broken glass and the like. Thirty years of collecting trash and turning it into art, and now one man's dedication echoed down the ages as an example to all. The Towers were a shining beacon of hope in a shithole of despair.

Hunter left them behind with a tinge of regret, drove on

for a few blocks, then pulled up in front of 147 Hickory Street and killed the engine. The place looked pleasant enough—white picket fence, well-tended lawn and a recently swept path that was marked with pots of flowering geraniums—it was all very welcoming. The house itself was similarly neat, its faux wooden sidings having been freshly painted to add to the impression of wholesomeness, although the presence of security bars over both the front door and the windows rather spoilt the mood. After his blow-out at the church Hunter had called Carson and bullied him into providing some background info on victim number two. The detective had dispatched him to the home of Eileen Schaeffer. Eileen was sixty-three years old and she'd been widowed for the best part of a decade, and up until a few months ago she'd been a loving mother to her only son, Marty. Hunter ran a hand over his close-cropped hair and checked his face in the rear-view. The bags under his eyes were surprisingly large. He rubbed at his forehead and took a few deep breaths. This interview was going to be delicate. Marty Schaeffer hadn't exactly gone out in a blaze of glory…

Marty stumbled down the street, a scrawny man in his early forties with a gaunt face, a nose that was too long and eyes that stared out in an expression of permanent surprise—for some reason, he'd never been a big hit with the ladies. As he veered to his right, a sonorous belch escaped his lips, followed by a high-pitched giggle.

The moon was high overhead, semi-obscured by the dark clouds that scurried across the night sky. He hadn't been out this late since…well, since ever. What a night. A little slow at first, sure, but once he'd gotten a few drinks inside him things had really taken off. The bar had been packed with so many girls he hadn't known which way to look. And they were all so young! Some of them looked like they'd only just graduated from high school, despite all the make-up. He'd lost his co-workers at around 10 p.m., but that hadn't bothered him any. He hadn't needed company to watch the floorshow. Man, what a night. He was going to have to do it again. Get out more. See the sights. But not tomorrow. Tomorrow was Ma's bridge night and he was in charge of refreshments. Maybe he'd hit the town at the weekend.

Another stumble, this time to his left, straight into the fender of a beat-up Oldsmobile parked at the head of a dark alley. His stomach flipped over, his head swam. Maybe he should just hang out here for a while, get his breath back. Too late. Something was coming up. Marty's mouth flew open as he blew chunks all over the hood of the Olds. Once the worst was over, he retched a few times then tried to spit the sour taste from his mouth. Goddammit—projectile vomiting had not been part of the plan.

He closed his eyes and went to put his outstretched hands on the hood, then half fell as one of them slipped in his own mess. His stomach churned, his throat hurt, and there was a sharp pain building in the centre of his forehead. All he wanted to do was go to sleep, but he was still a few blocks from home, and the way he felt right now a few blocks might as well have been a few miles. When the voice first called out, he was so wrapped up in his own physical discomfort he didn't even hear it.

'Hey!' it said again, slightly louder.

And this time it got through. A guttural sound, like the owner's throat was full of phlegm. Marty turned around slowly, his head still in a spin, to see who'd called out to him. The street was deserted, empty in both directions. He screwed up his face in confusion.

'Hey!' barked the voice again, and Marty realised it was

coming from the alley. He took a couple of steps forward to peer into the shadows, his alcohol intake overriding his natural cowardice. A dumpster sat halfway down with a pile of rubbish alongside it, while a few overturned trash cans were dotted around to further sully the ambience. Overhead, a sole streetlamp threw out a feeble arc of light while telephone wires snaked their way into low-rent apartments.

'Who's there?' he yelled, squinting against the gloom. The pile of rubbish next to the dumpster moved.

'Spare some change?' said an accented voice. A hand reached out from the shapeless mass, palm facing upwards. One of the city's homeless after a free dinner. Screw that, thought Marty. Can't this bum see I've got problems of my own? He staggered and reached out for the wall as more bile rose in his throat. By the time he'd done retching, the beggar had crawled two-thirds of the distance towards him, his hand still outstretched.

'Fuck off,' said Marty, wiping some drool from his chin, but the beggar kept coming, his shaven head glinting in the moonlight. 'Can't you see I'm sick?'

The smart thing to do would have been to just walk away—some of these bums carried all manner of diseases—but Marty's legs had temporarily turned to jelly. He hawked twice, spat on the ground, and came to a decision.

'OK, OK…hold up… I'll get you some change…' He delved into his hip pocket to retrieve a few wrinkled bills, which he quickly threw down at the mass of old blankets in front of him. As the bum's left hand shot out to gather up the cash, Marty noticed some sort of weird birthmark just below the knuckles.

'Now, give me some space, here, I ain't feeling so hot…'

Waves of nausea rolled over him again. He shut his eyes tight and took a few deep breaths, willing his head to clear.

Once he'd regained some sort of control over his innards he looked up to find that the beggar was now just a yard away. He opened his mouth to complain but that was as far as he got. The bum leapt to his feet and something shiny flashed in front of Marty's eyes, then something pleasantly warm ran down the front of his neck. He reached for his throat and felt the blood pulse out through his fingers as his life force ebbed away. His legs gave out from under him and he slumped to the ground, his hand still locked in place. As he lay among the rancid garbage, he tried to splutter one last word, but all that came out was a gurgle, and then it was over. Marty Schaeffer was dead.

Danilov looked down at the lifeless body without feeling then wiped his knife clean on the dead man's slacks before retracting the blade and returning it to his jacket pocket. He checked the street—all clear. Time to set the scene. He smiled—this guy was skinny. He liked skinny guys—they were easier to move.

'All are not cooks that walk with long knives, my friend,' he said softly. 'Now we go on little trip.'

He grabbed the corpse by its ankles and dragged it deeper into the alley, bouncing the head off the asphalt every few steps. No matter—this guy was long past complaining. Once he'd made it to the far side of the dumpster, he dropped Schaeffer's legs and turned to fetch one of the stray trashcans.

The nearest one was half-full, lying just outside the arc of light thrown down by the spluttering streetlamp. He emptied the can, then carried it over to the dumpster and rested it on its side, before turning his attention back to the corpse. First, he removed the wallet from Schaeffer's hip pocket and checked its contents. Driver's licence, forty bucks and a couple of credit cards—Diners and Amex. Big score. He pocketed the money and threw the rest away. Next, he unbuckled the dead man's slacks and dragged them down to expose two pipe-cleaner legs that glistened white in the moonlight. Schaeffer was wearing a pair of K-mart's own-brand boxer shorts that sported a large damp stain on the front. Danilov snorted—this guy had gone out like a little girl, pissing himself at the moment of death. Be glad of small mercies, he told himself. At least the coward's bowels had stood firm.

He rolled the body onto its front, hoisted it over the trash-can, then dragged down the boxer shorts to leave Schaffer's bare ass pointing skyward. Not a pretty sight. Spinning on his heel, he walked over to the dumpster to retrieve the canvas rucksack he'd stashed there earlier. It contained two items—a ten-inch black rubber dildo and a small tub of lubricating jelly. He unscrewed the tub, slathered his hands in jelly, then gave the dildo a generous coating—this was no time to skimp on the raw materials. Emotionless as ever, he spread Schaffer's ass cheeks then jammed the fuck-stick up as far as it would go.

'How you like that?' he asked the dead man.

The scene looked good, like some outlandish piece of modern art, but there was still one thing missing. Danilov pulled twelve playing cards from his pocket and proceeded to spread them out around the corpse. A quick nod of satisfaction, then he peeled off his latex gloves and stashed them inside the rucksack, quickly followed by the old rags he'd worn during the attack. One last look around the alley to check that he'd left it clean, and then he was gone, walking off into the night like a vengeful shadow. From start to finish, the whole incident had taken place in under three minutes. What a pro.

Hunter heard raised voices from inside the house as he climbed up onto the stoop. The security gate wasn't locked.

Maybe things only turned really bad around here once the sun went down. He straightened his leather jacket and brushed at his jeans. The gate swung outwards with a creak. He rapped twice on the door then took a step back, doing everything he could think of to appear non-threatening, but when the door opened, he wondered why he'd bothered.

Eileen Schaeffer was not your typical sixty-three-year-old divorcee. Her bleached blonde hair was swept back in an impressive pompadour that towered overhead like a monster wave that was just about to break, and with a hairdo like that there was no point scrimping on the make-up, and Eileen hadn't. Heavy blue eye shadow, a thick layer of rouge and electric red lipstick—by the looks of it, half the cosmetic industry's annual profit was tied up in this one face. Her blouse was cut dangerously low and her ankle-length skirt was figure hugging—she'd gone all out for seductive, but all she'd managed was grotesque. Hunter was tempted to turn tail and run, but he decided to tough it out.

'Can I help you?' she asked, as her eyes roved hungrily over his muscular frame. Her voice was deep and throaty with a slight foreign accent. Maybe she'd been watching too many Dietrich films. He explained why he was there then followed her inside, trying not to notice the way that she swung her aging hips from side to side as she walked.

The front room was decorated like something out of the glamorous 1950s, all deep red tones, soft fabrics and heavily lacquered furniture. The raised voices he'd heard from the stoop were emanating from a small colour TV set back in one corner. It was tuned to the *Jerry Springer Show*, where some trailer trash tribe were airing their sordid grievances in front of a nationwide audience. Eileen hit the off button, collected a picture frame from the credenza, and offered it to him.

'My poor, poor Marty. Such a terrible thing... Please, take

a seat.' Hunter took the frame and got his first good look at Marty Schaeffer. Middle-aged, greasy-haired, goggle-eyed. No wonder he'd never left home.

Eileen lowered her creaking bones onto the chaise longue and patted at a spot just next to her, but Hunter decided to play it safe and go with the high-backed armchair four feet away. A brief look of disappointment crossed her face before she continued.

'Such a sweet, sweet boy, he never had a bad word to say about anyone, but now he's gone and I'm left here all on my own in this horrible neighbourhood. It used to be OK, you know.' She dropped her voice to a conspiratorial whisper. 'Till the darkies moved in.'

'Was Marty having any trouble at work? Any financial worries?'

'Oh, no, everyone loved Marty. And as for money, well, we got by well enough.' She leant forward slightly to allow Hunter a glimpse of her wrinkled cleavage, and though he looked away quickly, the damage was done—yet another gruesome image seared onto his retina.

'Have you got any of Marty's financial records? Credit-card statements, anything like that?'

Eileen left the room for a few minutes and returned carrying an ornate silver tray that she rested on one end of the chaise longue. On top of the tray were two goblets of sherry and a batch of documents held together with an elastic band. Hunter accepted the papers with interest and the sherry with trepidation. He took a quick sip to be polite, hoping that the old girl didn't have access to Rohypnol. The papers were a mixture of Diners and Amex card statements in no discernible order. He scanned down the columns, searching for anything out of the ordinary, any large one-off payments, unexplained travel expenditure or out-of-town purchases, but there was nothing.

'What about his friends? Any arguments? Maybe with his lover?' If it wasn't money related, maybe there was a partner involved.

'Oh, no, nothing like that.' Eileen fluttered her eyelashes. 'Marty steered well clear of girls. I always told him that they were nothing but trouble.'

'I'm sorry to have to ask this, Mrs Schaeffer, but are you sure that Marty was interested in girls? The way his body was found in that alleyway would seem to suggest…'

'Don't you go talking about my Marty like that!' she snapped. 'He was a good boy, and whatever happened to him in that godforsaken alley was none of his fault. He's gone now, and you should all just leave him be.'

Hunter rose to his feet. 'I'm sorry to have upset you, Mrs Schaeffer, but I'm just trying to find out what happened. If you'll excuse me, I'll be on my way.'

'Oh, no, no, you haven't finished your sherry… I didn't mean to shout, but it's all just so upsetting…'

'I really must be going, I've got other people to see.' He pushed on towards the front door despite the restraining presence of Eileen's hand on his arm.

'You'll help my poor Marty, won't you, Mr Hunter? You'll find out who did this to him? He didn't deserve to die as he did. The last few months of his life had been hard enough…'

Hunter stopped dead. 'In what way?'

'There was some trouble last year…with a girl…a no-good lying bitch who had it in for my Marty.' Eileen's eyes flared. 'Made up stories about him, said that he'd…' she swallowed as she struggled to say the word '…touched her. Cost him his job at the auto plant. Put him through hell. But he was innocent. Innocent!' she crowed defiantly.

Interesting, thought Hunter. Maybe Marty Schaeffer wasn't as squeaky clean as he'd first appeared. Of course, had he been allowed access to the official police files he could have saved himself a trip. He shrugged off Eileen as politely as he could, stumbled out of the house, then headed back to his car, failing to notice the tell-tale glint of sunlight on binocular lenses two blocks down.

CHAPTER TWENTY

IT WAS just before five when Rebecca left the courthouse to head back to the parking garage. The second day of Ashton's trial had been eaten up by a whole host of drawn-out discussions on points of law, and she'd raised most of them herself. The strategy came straight from chapter three of her playbook—when in doubt, try and bore the jury into a 'not guilty' verdict. At least Ashton had managed to keep his mouth shut thus far—maybe she'd bored him into submission, too.

The handsome asshole was still upbeat about his chances and his confidence was starting to rub off on her. If Ashton's movie-producer father had paid off the key witnesses then he might yet avoid having his name added to the list of 160,000 inmates that were currently locked down in California. With 33 penitentiaries and an annual budget of over five billion dollars, the state now ran the largest prison system in the western world, but if you had enough money, there were still ways you could still slip through the net.

She quickened her step, swinging her leather briefcase from side to side, eager to get home to her sister. Anabeth had been stuck there all day, doubtless having to endure more media intrusion along with a host of unwelcome stares from the neighbours. Rebecca had tried to organise a clean-up crew to remove the painted slogans from the side of the house, but the earliest they could come was the weekend. On the plus side, at least the lawn had been done, as the local gardener, Pedro, had been round in the afternoon to dig out the offending patches and lay some fresh turf.

She ducked inside the cool interior of the parking garage and felt an immediate shiver race down her spine. The central space was bright, well served by the powerful strip lights, but the sidewalls were shrouded in shadows. She reached for the can of mace she kept in her handbag, then squinted into the gloom. Once thirty seconds had passed without incident, she resumed the journey to her car, although she continued to throw an occasional glance towards the inky depths. Some people would have viewed her jumpiness as a weakness, but she looked on it as simple self-preservation—ten years as a criminal defence lawyer had taught her to always be on her guard.

She bypassed the lifts in the centre of the structure and headed further along the ground floor, returning the mace to her handbag as she fumbled for her exit ticket. Her silver BMW 645Ci coupe sat halfway along the inner bay, nestled between a beat-up white panel truck and a mud-streaked Buick. Having shimmied down the thin gap between the Bimmer and the truck, she rested her briefcase on the roof of her car, then went to unlock it.

As she pushed her key into the lock, the door of the panel truck screeched open and two gloved hands seized her roughly from behind, one around her waist, the other over her mouth to choke off her screams before they'd even begun. She tried to pull away but her assailant was too strong, then her feet were off the ground as she was hauled into the truck's cargo hold. Her eyes widened in terror and she let loose another scream, but the hand over her mouth kept the noise to a minimum. Her kicks grew weaker as the truck's engine roared to life, then a strangely pleasant smell danced over her scent glands and everything faded to black.

When she came round, the first thing she realised was that her mouth was dry and she had a dull headache. Plus her back hurt. She was lying down on something cold and metallic, and that something was moving, rocking her from side to side. The sound of an engine thudded in her ears. Memories of the parking garage came flooding back. She'd been dragged into the back of a truck. A wave of fear washed over her. She opened her eyes and blinked against the glare of a flashlight.

'So you awake? Good. Now we talk.' The voice was Latin American, the tone serious. 'Here, drink this, it take away the taste of the chloroform.' The beam of light wavered for a second then a bottle of Evian was thrust towards her. She unscrewed the top, took a mouthful, rinsed it around, then spat it back in the general direction from which it had come.

'*Puta!* What you wanna do that for? You one dumb white bitch… I make it a rule to never hit no woman, but for you, maybe I make an exception…'

'Let me go, and I might not press charges.' Belligerent. Fighting fire with fire. Her career had taught her to confront aggressors with aggression—in court, signs of weakness were like drops of blood to the circling prosecutors. As her eyes adjusted to the light she saw the outline of a man sitting on his haunches, his build short and muscular, his features obscured by the black ski mask pulled tight over his head.

'You in no position to cut a deal, Miss Big-Shot Lawyer. You gonna listen to what I got to say, and you gonna listen good. And you ain't goin' nowhere—ain't no recesses in the back of my truck.' No chuckle accompanied the wisecrack. This guy meant business.

Rebecca crossed her arms and tried not to shake. She couldn't allow her kidnapper to realise she was scared, and scared bad. He had enough of an upper hand as it was. 'What do you want?'

'You gonna drop the case with Ashton. That boy don't deserve no legal representation. You gonna quit first thing tomorrow and leave him to rot.'

'If I quit, then he'll just appoint someone else—maybe someone better,' she said, struggling to keep the fear out of her voice. Come on, girl, pull it together. This is just another negotiation, and you've cut countless deals before.

'Mmm…maybe you got a point…' The man behind the flashlight thought things through for a few seconds. 'OK, you still his lawyer, but you gonna screw up the case, make sure his ass gets sent down.'

'But that's not how the system works—he's entitled to a fair trial, and if he's found guilty by the jury, then he'll serve a sentence.'

'That cocksucker entitled to *nada*!' shouted her captor. 'He guilty as sin and you gonna make sure there's no miscarriage of justice…otherwise…' He pointed a snub-nosed revolver straight at her, cocked the hammer, then pulled the trigger. Her whole body tensed at the click of the dry-fire. 'Otherwise, next time this be loaded…'

The masked man rapped his knuckles against the sheet metal that divided the cargo hold from the cabin, prompting the driver to swing over to the kerb. As soon as the truck had stopped, he yanked open the side door and gestured with the gun.

‘Get out, an’ remember what I say…’

She staggered onto an unfamiliar side street and walked away with as much dignity as she could muster, her muscles tensed against the prospect of a farewell bullet to the back of the head. When the truck door clanged shut, she started to cry.

CHAPTER TWENTY-ONE

'SO THE vicar was a dead end, but you found out that Marty Schaeffer had woman problems?' asked Carson, as he leant forward to grab some more red pistachios from the pack he'd left on the bar. The carmine dye used to colour the nuts had rubbed off on his fingers, making it look like he'd washed them in blood.

'Yeah, albeit slightly historic ones. I did some digging around into the girl who accused Schaeffer of rape, but she seemed to have moved on with her life. She's married now, with a couple of kids. There was no sign she was nursing a grudge. I don't make her for a suspect.'

It was early evening and Hunter was back at Tommy's bar to update the detective on his meagre findings. The two men were sitting at the counter, splitting a pitcher of Coors and chewing the fat. In the background, the opening bars of

Led Zeppelin's 'Kashmir' rumbled ominously out of the jukebox.

'Of course, you already knew about Marty and the girl…' Hunter muttered.

'Yep,' agreed Carson, lighting another of his fragrant cigars, 'and you'll be pleased to know that I came to the same conclusion you did.'

Hunter gave exasperated. 'What's the point of all this? I'm chasing your goddamn tail—running down leads you've already run down. It's a waste of time. Why don't you throw me a bone—give me something to get my teeth into?'

The detective returned his stare for a few seconds, then reached down for the carry-case that rested against the foot of the bar.

'How 'bout this?' he said, throwing down a file on the counter. 'Rhythm Ray, former head honcho of the 16th Street Renegades, last seen splattered across the centre line of a neighbourhood basketball court one block south of 42nd and Dalton.'

'What's his story?'

'What up, niggah? Yo punk ass is late, and I don't likes to be left hanging.'

The two men faced off against each other in the middle of the neighbourhood basketball court, a place where the inner-city kids usually dreamt of becoming the next Shaquille O'Neill or Lebron James, but today the sight of an important gang meeting. Guards were positioned around the fringes of the playing area, one staring outwards every ten yards plus two groups of three stationed at the north and south entrances. Each man wore a uniform of Nike Shox basketball boots in black and metallic silver, pristine black Levi's, plus the infamous shirts of the Oakland Raiders. Up top, some sported bandanas while others went with the strategically shaven look, but they all had one thing in common—each man packed serious heat.

The court was surrounded by low-rent apartments on three sides and by the city street on the fourth. The balconies were devoid of people but crusted in pigeon shit. The residents knew better than to venture outside when a gang meet was going down. Stray bullets could do a lot of damage. The street, like the balconies overhead, was deathly quiet. A few parked cars were dotted around, some of them so beat up that they'd probably been abandoned, but there was no through traffic and no pedestrians, except for one old beggar who'd found himself some shade at the top of a stoop.

The guy who'd been accused of showing up late went by the moniker of Rhythm Ray. Music filled the silence as a beat-box started to pump out some old school Public Enemy—'You're Gonna Get Yours'. Rhythm, as his nearest and dearest liked to call him, wasn't late at all, in fact, he was ten minutes early, but that didn't matter. His accuser was just looking to gain an edge, maybe spark off some drama. Damn hothead was always spoiling for a fight. If things didn't get off on the right foot, bloodshed was a distinct possibility.

'It don't mean no nevermind, I'm here now, let's get down to business.' Rhythm kept his face neutral as he spoke and made a point of holding his palms outward in a gesture of reconciliation. He was the leader of the 16th Street Renegades, well, co-leader to be precise, as his twin brother kept reminding him. The guy standing opposite him was the boss of the Heaton Park Hollow Points and he went by the name of Paleface. This chump dressed like a brother, spoke like a brother, hell, even smelled like a brother, but, as his name suggested, he didn't have much of a tan. Nine times out of ten that lack of colour would have thrown a serious hitch into his aspirations to make it to the top of an all-black inner-city gang, but Paleface had got himself a trump card—he was straight up psychotic. He'd do anything to anyone given the slightest provocation, so Rhythm had to tread carefully, especially as he'd entered the lion's den without back-up.

'Frisk this dumb muthafucka! And if he's strapped with anything more dangerous than his dick, send him to his maker.'

Rhythm stood motionless as two Hollow Points patted him down. They could check all they liked, but they wouldn't find a thing. He was unarmed.

'He be clean.' The lieutenants backed off to take up positions on either side of their boss.

'So what is it you be wantin', boy? Why you done call this meeting?'

Rhythm got straight to the point. 'A truce, bro. Effective immediately.'

'We ain't kin and I ain't your bro! Why da fuck should Hollow Points break bread with your raggedy-ass crew? Renegades be buggin' out? Streets be getting too hot?'

'Things be getting hectic. Citizens be dying, bitches and shorties. Last time you rolled you murderised a lil cuz that was just eight years old. Killings gotta stop, for the sake of both our communities. Ya feel me?'

'You gotta lotta heart for a cocksucka. Rollin up in my 'hood, givin' me orders… Y'all think that sounded like a motherfuckin' order?' Paleface got grunts of support from his crew. 'Man, that kinda shit just rubs me all wrong! I don't take no orders from no muthafucka. You'd best remember that next time you got something to say.'

'Hey, chill da fuck out, it ain't like that—I ain't here to hand out orders, I's just got suggestions. Let's keep to our own turf for a while. We don't got no call to be beefin'—there's enough game to go around for all us niggahs.'

'That it? Let me think on it some…'

Paleface whistled to one of his soldiers who responded by tossing over a basketball. He dribbled down court, pulled up twenty-five feet short of the hoop and sent down a three-pointer, swish, all net. White boy got game. One of the guards behind the backboard retrieved the ball and tossed it back, then Paleface drove down the lane and laid up for two. Rhythm tried not to look frustrated. This was no time for sports. After a couple more shots, Paleface called time and wandered back over.

'You got an answer for me?' Rhythm asked.

'Yeah…fuck all dat shit! Hollow Points ain't never gonna cosy up to no Renegades. Tell this sucka our motto, boys…'

'Only good Renegade's a dead Renegade!' Paleface's crew barked out, except for the three guards over by the north entrance who'd been distracted by something at their feet.

'You betta step off and check yo'self, muthafucka. Gotta be loco showin' up here with no back-up. We been gunnin' for you and your no-good brother for months, then you just walk right in like it was no big thing. Shit! You makin' it too damn easy. Now I'm gonna have to make a mess of my nice clean court. Someone toss me a nine…'

Rhythm tasted bile as one of Paleface's lieutenants threw him a gun.

The 1969 Chevy Camaro was stationed directly opposite the basketball court but, despite its pristine condition, the car wasn't attracting much attention. It had a wide, ground-hugging appearance, and sported a classic bumblebee-style paint job—jet black, save for a wide yellow stripe that ran from hood to trunk along the top of the vehicle. Its six-spoke alloy wheels shone brightly in the midday sun, while its taillights glowed red, as if possessed by some demonic entity.

The reason why the Camaro wasn't attracting much attention was quite simple. Hardly anyone could see it. The car was 17 inches long, a little more than 8 inches wide, and it sat just 5 inches off the ground. This particular Camaro was an RCV, a remote-controlled vehicle, with an impressive top speed of 75 miles per hour, which wasn't that far short of its big brother's capabilities. It edged away from the kerb, slowly at first as if checking for traffic, then more confidently, full of purpose. Having crossed the street, it bumped up onto the sidewalk and executed a sharp turn to face left, before accelerating along the fence that surrounded the basketball court, its little wheels spinning furiously. It came to an abrupt stop a few yards shy of the three guards that were stationed at the court's north entrance.

'Hey! What da fuck?' asked the most observant of the gangsters.

His two companions broke off their conversation and looked up.

'Old-style Camaro—pretty fly.'

The observant guard took a step forwards. The Camaro instantly retreated.

'Who's runnin' this thing?' asked the guard, glancing around.

'Don't know, cuz, it's all quiet an' shit…'

'Hey, shorty! Come on out!' The three men looked up and down the deserted street. 'We ain't gonna hurt ya…'

When no answer was forthcoming the guard made a sudden lunge at the car, but it evaded his outstretched hands to leave him grasping at nothing but thin air. The Camaro sped away, apparently through playing for the time being, but as soon as it had covered two-thirds of the court's 94-foot length it stopped once again, then shifted around until its grille was aimed squarely at the chain-link fence that enclosed the playing area. Had there been a miniature driver behind the wheel, he would now have been staring directly at a small hole in the fence, not the sort of ratty hole caused by general wear and tear but a nice, neatly clipped hole that, as luck would have it, was just large enough for the RCV to squeeze through.

Rhythm Ray and Paleface were the only two people that didn't see the Camaro coming as they were still engaged in their high-stakes pissing contest at mid-court. Paleface was in the process of levelling a Glock at Rhythm's head when the little car stopped right at their feet. 'What da fuck…?' began Paleface, but that was as far as he got.

The odourless block of Semtex hidden inside the Camaro detonated, sending shards of the RCV flying outwards in a murderous blast. Both men's lives came to an abrupt end as their weak flesh was vaporised in the explosion. The two lieutenants who'd been standing nearby didn't fare much better, although at least their relatives would have something to bury—a forearm, a chunk of torso, half a leg—random body parts that were thrown clear of the blast zone to lay forlornly on the concrete.

For a few seconds there was complete silence, and then all hell broke loose as the soldiers stationed around the outside of the court came to life. Scurrying around like headless chickens, albeit headless chickens armed with automatic weapons, they aimed inwards, outwards and upwards, but to little avail as no threat could be found. The beggar watched on from the shaded stoop. Once he was certain that no one was looking, he tossed a small remote-control unit into the clump of bushes on his right, then peeled off his latex gloves.

'Two…for the price of one…' muttered Danilov, as he shuffled off down the street.

Carson took another hit of beer and followed it up with a lungful of cigar smoke before giving Hunter some background on the Renegades.

'The word on the street is that they were fighting a turf war with the Hollow Points. Things were getting out of hand, lots of drive-bys, lots of dead bangers, heavy losses on both sides, and all that killing was starting to eat into business—no one dared walk the streets at night, and if no one's walking, no one's buying. Anyhow, Rhythm Ray set up a parley with Paleface, the Points' main man, to call for a truce, but neither of them got much further than saying hello before they were blown six ways to hell and back. Someone sure as hell didn't want that meeting to take place…'

'So how'd you tie that to our boy? Surely it had gang-hit written all over it?'

'That's just what I thought till I found a bunch of jacks, queens and kings taped to the front of the apartment building across the street.'

'The assassin's calling cards…'

'Yep.' Carson downed his beer and reached for the pitcher. 'Top-up?'

'Sure,' replied Hunter. 'So where do I fit in?'

'We didn't get much from the gangs on this one. Oddly enough, they weren't that keen to co-operate. Maybe you can convince them of their civic duty and get them to open up, what with you being a citizen and all. They might know more than they're letting on.'

Hunter paused as Dusty arrived to deposit two bowls of Masaman curry on the table. He took a mouthful of the fiery dish then nodded in approval. The kid went back to the kitchen with a smile on his face. 'So who do I talk to?'

'Ray's brother, calls himself Furious on account of his temper. Since he's been in charge, he's taken the Renegades to a whole new level. They own the streets now, wiped out the Hollow Points in little more than a month. That cat's straight up crazy.'

'Sounds like a fun date. Count me in.'

'You'll find him at the self-same basketball court where the hit went down. Furious has made it his base of operations, turned it into some sort of shrine for his dead brother. Step easy, though, cos these boys are trouble.'

'Oh, Carson,' deadpanned Hunter, 'I never knew you cared.'

CHAPTER TWENTY-TWO

DANILOV was all alone in his pristine bachelor pad, and he was a little frustrated. Sure, he'd been forced to endure a boss before, but never an invisible one, a spectre that couldn't be reasoned with. His latest spell at the computer was proving to be a waste of time. He'd spent the last five minutes trying to convince his boss that Hunter was a legitimate threat, but thus far he'd failed. The conversation had gone something like this.

Danilov—Hunter went to the church and the Schaeffer residence.

Boss—Don't sweat it.

Danilov—Hunter's handing out grainy photos of me.

Boss—It's not your concern.

Why wouldn't the fool listen? It was all very well for him to be so relaxed about the ex-cop's ongoing investigation—after all, it wasn't his neck that was on the line—but the least he could do was show a little professionalism. It was no good burying your head in the sand and hoping that things turned out for the best. Problems like Hunter didn't just resolve themselves. He started to type.

"Hunter must be stopped. I put him on plane to Boston. Easy for me. Hunter is bum. Spends all day in bar."

"No. If Hunter had dug up anything worthwhile, we'd already know. He's not a threat."

"But first I find him at Montero's, then church, then old woman's house. Getting close. Must be stopped."

"No."

"Then I quit."

"You can't quit."

"Arrangement is over. You are weak. That puts me in danger. Hunter has links to cops. If you let him live, you throw Viktor to wolves. Like Judas. Sell me out. Maybe I send you to Boston."

"Are you threatening me?"

His fingers tensed, hovering just above the keyboard, but this time he refrained from answering. Fresh lines of text appeared on the computer screen.

"You can't hurt me, as you don't know who I am. You may be a first-rate marksman, but you can't shoot what you can't see. And you know what happens if you fail to fulfil your contract…

—First, I contact the police and reveal your involvement in the recent spate of brutal murders.

—And second, I broadcast your location to Igor Krupchenko's son. Do you remember Igor? The Russian mob boss you betrayed to secure your freedom? I think you'll find that being in the witness protection programme isn't worth shit if your enemies know where to find you.

So I suggest you think twice before threatening me again. How about you shut the hell up and do exactly as you're told?"

Seeing the name Igor Krupchenko on the screen sent a cold shiver down Danilov's spine. Much as he was loath to admit it, the boss had a point.

"So I leave Hunter alone? Until I am caught?"

"No. His meddling has to stop. Here's what I want you to do..."

From the moment Hunter had set foot inside his home, he'd known that something was wrong. Not obviously wrong, like finding a three-hundred-pound gorilla in the hallway, but wrong nevertheless. There'd been a slight nagging doubt in the back of his mind telling him that all was not as it should be, and if he hadn't have been so goddamned drunk, he might have taken more notice.

Carson had kept him company at the bar long after closing. The old man had downed a heroic amount of beer while Hunter had matched him drink for drink. Two guys on a real tear-up, both trying to lose their demons in an alcohol-induced fog. So instead of listening to his sixth sense he stumbled towards the kitchen to fix a strong black coffee. Didn't bother to turn on the lights, just navigated from memory. The fine ground Colombian beans were in an airtight container at the back of the fridge. He shovelled two heaped teaspoons into the glass cafetière he kept out on the worktop, filled the kettle with water, then waited for it to boil. Fetched himself a bag of dry wheat crackers from the cupboard and started to chow down. Finished the bag, fetched another. Then and only then did he turn on the lights.

And there it was again. The little niggling doubt that said something wasn't quite right. He looked around the room, trying to place the source of his discontent, but nothing shrieked out at him. The sound of water bubbling in the kettle began to compete for his attention. When it hit boiling point, the appliance clicked off. With a half-shrug he turned back to the job at hand, sloshed the hot liquid onto the coffee, and dumped three large spoonfuls of sugar into a mug.

His vision swam in front of him. Phew. That Carson could sure put it away. He knew from past experience that most cops were hardened drinkers, especially the older ones, probably on account of the fact that they'd had more time to see more horrors. Alcohol served as an emotional crutch—a way to help numb both the pain and the memories. He'd hit the bottle pretty hard himself while he'd been drowning in the horrors of the Montero case, and plenty of his former colleagues had similar stories to tell. Picture this—an average shift might involve investigating a triple homicide, offering crumbs of comfort to a raped schoolgirl, or cleaning up after a pregnant junkie who'd just OD'd. How were you meant to go back to the wife and kids after a day like that? How were you meant to lead a full and balanced life when everywhere you looked all you could see was the horror that humans were capable of inflicting on each other? There was no escape. Every place you went held a memory. The bright new shopping mall out in Pasadena? Spate of violent muggings in the car lot. Your favourite restaurant in West Hollywood? Dismembered body found a block away in a dumpster. That sports bar on Olympic? Korean storekeeper burnt alive by arsonists four doors up. It wasn't the sort of stuff you could just forget about. And although alcohol wasn't a wonder cure, it did at least help you to cope, especially when it was taken with a large side order of cynicism.

Hunter depressed the cafetière's plunger and poured himself a mug of joe. Being drunk and alone in the early hours of the morning always left him maudlin. His ex-girlfriend, Skye, had always made herself scarce when he was in this sort of mood, and she was pretty scarce now. Back in Las Vegas, doing the showgirl thing. Moving on with her life. Just like he ought to. He added a dash of cold water from the tap then took a couple of gulps. The coffee was rich, aromatic and sweet—just what the doctor ordered. His thoughts turned back to the bar. One thing was for sure—Carson definitely had some issues. Waves of bitterness had rolled off the old man all through the evening, especially when talk had turned to the assassin. The detective had admitted that the official investigation was headed nowhere fast. They'd released the assassin's physical description and immediately been inundated with hundreds of reported sightings, but thus far they'd all proved false. Carson was pissed at himself for not having caught the guy yet. He was probably pissed at Hunter, too. Call it displacement.

By the end of the evening Carson had even started to ramble on about his private life, as he'd turned his anger on ex-wife number two. His second marriage had come to an abrupt end for the same reason that the first one had failed—hours on the job—only this time he hadn't worked enough of them. He'd come home halfway through a shift to find his wife in bed with the 'new-age artsy-fartsy muff diver' that had moved in next door. His wife had coolly informed him that she'd decided she was a lesbian, then she'd packed her bags and walked out. As Carson had recounted the sorry tale his pain and resentment had come through loud and clear, although his blue eyes had glinted when he'd said he was working on a plan to straighten her out. Hunter took another gulp of coffee then rose to his feet. Time to turn in. With any luck, a good night's sleep might just put a dent in tomorrow's hangover. A sonorous belch escaped his lips as he threw his half-finished bag of crackers onto the worktop. He killed the light in the kitchen and made his way through the main living area, then bounced off the walls of the curved hallway until he arrived at his bedroom door. As he started to push down on the handle, the little warning voice in his head sparked up yet again, and although it finally managed to make itself heard, his reactions were so shot he was long past the point of being able to respond.

The door… his inner voice warned. You never shut your bedroom door…

Too late. As soon as the door swung inwards he heard a soft *phut*, then felt a sharp pain in his upper chest. Someone had shot him. He fumbled for his Beretta and stumbled into the bedroom, eyes straining against the gloom. What the hell was going on? The room was empty. Icy tendrils started to lace their way across his chest, winding outwards from the epicentre of the wound. He swayed on his feet as his vision grew blurry. Familiar objects morphed in and out of shape, then the breath caught in his throat. Darkness reigned as he slumped to the floor.

CHAPTER TWENTY-THREE

DANILOV stepped out of the closet and walked over to look at the supine form in the middle of the room. The whole thing had been surprisingly easy. Circumventing the alarms, gaining access to the house, shooting Hunter from close range—all accomplished without a single hitch. He'd been hoping for more of a challenge.

He started humming 'Strangers in the Night' as he grabbed the unconscious man under the armpits, dragged him across the floor and propped him against the foot of the bed. Hunter was heavy. There had to be a lot of muscle buried deep within that wiry frame. The Russian crouched down and took a good look at his adversary. Mousy-coloured hair, cropped short, and a tanned, clean-shaven face. Plus he stank of alcohol. No wonder the ambush had been so easy—Hunter had been out on his feet.

Not so tough now, he thought as he slapped the unconscious man's cheek to draw an angry red blotch. It was a shame he couldn't finish him off while he had the chance. But orders were orders. Still, maybe this little episode would help convince the ex-cop to keep his nose out of other people's business from now on. He rose to his feet and walked calmly over to the sole chest of drawers where a serving tray awaited him. Resting on the tray were a single sheet of paper and a small metallic object that stood upright on one end. As he retraced his steps the object overbalanced and rolled towards the edge of the tray. He veered instinctively to his right in an attempt to stop its progress and slammed his foot into the base of the bed.

'Fuck your mother!' he barked, closely followed by a string of Russian profanities.

Trying to ignore the steadily escalating throb in his big toe, he fumbled around on the floor until he'd retrieved the object, then placed the tray on Hunter's lap, who by now had started to make some faint groaning sounds. He checked his watch. Almost time to leave. The feathered dart that stuck out of Hunter's chest came free with a slight tug. He held it up for inspection, then laid it gently on the tray.

OK, my friend, he thought, rising to his feet, this is your last chance. Learn your lesson and learn it well. Because the next time I come looking for you, you're going to end up dead.

When he first came to, Hunter was blessed with all the mental faculties of a three-year-old. After babbling and dribbling for a spell, he finally managed to string a cohesive thought together, that thought being—Am I dead? And while he was puzzling over the answer, another observation popped into his mind—Christ, my head hurts. And not only did it hurt but it also appeared to have trebled in weight. He tried to lift his chin off his chest, and was rewarded with a burst of shooting white pain across the front of his skull. His mouth was dry, his lips were stuck together, and when he opened his eyes, his head swam and everything looked fuzzy around the edges. He clamped his eyes shut again. Maybe self-induced blindness was the way to go. What the hell had happened? The last thing he remembered was getting shot, but if this was heaven, it was one hell of a disappointment.

After taking a series of deep breaths for around ten minutes or so, he started to feel a little better. Not right, hell, a long way from right, but better nevertheless. As the blood began to flow back to his addled brain, his thought processes kicked into a higher gear, cutting through the mental fog that had first enveloped him on regaining consciousness. First task, check for a wound. He ran his hands over his chest, but everywhere was dry. No gaping hole, no oozing blood. Well, that was a relief. At least he wasn't sitting on the floor with his eyes shut tight while his life force dribbled away like so much sand through an hourglass. Next, he concentrated on his ears, straining to hear the slightest sound, but although he was greeted with total silence, that didn't mean he was alone. For all he knew, his attacker could be waiting patiently in the next room, ready to give an encore performance. Hope not, he thought, getting shot once per day is my personal limit.

As the minutes ticked by, memory fragments started to clamour at him from the darkened recesses of his mind, chief of all the noises he'd heard while semi-conscious. The sound of someone moving around the room. The sound of someone cursing. He concentrated on hearing that voice again but the words refused to form in his head. The harder he tried the more garbled they became—nonsense words, guttural sounds, they made no sense. So how about the voice itself?

Male, for sure, neither low- nor high-pitched, but with…with an accent. That was it! An accent. He couldn't understand the words because the intruder had been speaking in a foreign language. Something Caucasian. Interesting.

He stiffened in surprise. Now that the feeling had returned to his legs, the nerve endings down there were cheerily informing him that there was something resting on his thighs. He reached out and ran his hands around the edge of what felt like some sort of serving tray. Sitting on top of the tray was a folded sheet of paper and an object that was both plastic and feathery. Steeling himself against the inevitable wave of nausea, he opened his eyes.

Tranquilliser dart. Now, that explained a lot. Out for the count? Yep. Woozy and disorientated on waking? Yep. Splitting headache? Yep. He had all the symptoms. At the far edge of the tray was the one item his hands hadn't strayed across—a serious-sized bullet. A .308 Winchester Silvertip, if he wasn't mistaken. Sniper's round. He unfolded the paper. The typewritten words swam in front of his eyes but their message was clear enough.

> Cease your investigation into Montero's death. It does not concern you. Stop interfering, or I will be forced to use the bullet instead of the dart.

He read the note through again. Hmm. The author must have come over all shy as he hadn't even signed his name, but as he'd left such a nice friendly warning, Hunter felt obliged to track him down and offer his personal thanks. Stubbornness ran in his family, and the one thing that was guaranteed to harden his position was a threat.

CHAPTER TWENTY-FOUR

'I WANT to buy a gun.'

Seb finished stacking the cartons of .40 Smith and Wesson hollow points in the glass-fronted display cabinet then turned to look at the woman on the other side of the counter. Now, that makes a refreshing change, he thought as he gave her the once-over. The average customer in Defence of the Realm was male, middle-aged, going to seed and generally a bit harsh on the olfactory department, whereas this one was female, in good shape and decked out in a smart business suit, plus she smelled kind of flowery.

Seb was a sprightly fifty-two-year-old, and he'd been running the store for almost twenty years. He'd always liked the name, mainly because it sounded English, and anything that sounded English sounded classy. Selling guns was his one true calling in life. He'd gotten into the trade at a young age and had stayed put ever since. The day he'd bought the store still rated as an all-time great in his book. Talk about a sound business proposition. Ever since the founding fathers had first given their citizens the right to bear arms, Americans had rushed out to tool up. Sure, things had been tight in the early years while he had been making a name for himself, but these days business was booming. He put it down to the climate of fear that everyone was living in. It didn't bother him, though, because when it came to the weapons trade, fear equalled profit.

The woman cleared her throat, prompting Seb to take his eyes off the swell of her breasts and move on up to her face. She was pretty. Her blonde hair was pulled back in a ponytail, her cool hazel eyes shone with intelligence, cute freckles were dotted across the bridge of her nose, and she hadn't overdone the make-up—just a little mascara and a soft peach lipstick to highlight her features. He pretended to fiddle with something under the counter in order to buy himself enough time to work the wedding band off his index finger. The wife hadn't put out since she'd turned fifty. Maybe his luck was about to change.

'So you're looking for a gun?' he asked, flashing his best salesman's smile.

'That's what I said.'

Abrupt. Looked like this little madam was in a hurry.

'OK. Why'd you need one? Recreation or self-defence?'

'Do I look like someone who goes hunting on the weekend?' she asked, holding her hands up in a 'check me out' kind of gesture. Seb took the opportunity to grab another lingering look at her figure.

'Self-defence it is, then,' he said cheerily. 'Can I have a look at your hands?'

'Why? You want to read my palm?'

'No, ma'am.' Seb smiled. 'Need to see what sort of fingers you've got. Different fingers need different triggers. For instance, if your fingers are short and stubby, then you'll need a compact gun with a short trigger reach.'

The woman held out her hands for inspection. Her fingers were long and tapering, like those of a pianist. Seb took a good long look while humming and hawing as if he was doing some sort of complex mental arithmetic, but all the while he was imagining those hands wrapped tight around his schlong. As the fantasy took hold, he got carried away and reached out to touch her, but before he could make contact she pulled her hands away. When he looked up, there was a flicker of amusement in her eyes.

'Right, let's see what we've got.' He unclipped a large set of keys from his belt and began to unlock some of the counter display cabinets, whistling an off-key tune as he went about his business. When he'd finished making his collections, three firearms were laid out for inspection.

'First up, the Smith and Wesson 36LS—better known as the Ladysmith. A five-round revolver, carrying .38 Specials, nice and small, nice and light. Set you back around four hundred bucks. Next, the Colt 1911A. Takes a .45 calibre, so it's got a bit more stopping power than the Ladysmith, plus it holds seven rounds instead of five, which can come in handy if your aim's a little off. Retails at six fifty. And lastly the Browning Hi-Power. Ten-round magazine that takes pretty much any 9 mm or .40 cal cartridge ever made. Trigger's got a light pull on it, and the grip's great in a smaller hand. The Browning would be my recommendation.'

'How much for the Browning?' asked the woman as she picked up the gun and pointed it experimentally at the clock up on the wall. Dollar signs flashed in front of Seb's eyes.

'Usually goes for seven hundred, but I can let you have it for six fifty. Plus I'll throw in a couple of cartons of ammo. Call it a one-day special.'

The woman smiled politely as she checked out the gun. He kept quiet and gave her some time. A good salesman knew when to talk, and when to shut the hell up. Besides, once the Browning was in the customer's hand, it usually sold itself.

'I'll take it.'

'That's great. Cash or charge card?'

'Charge.' She fumbled in her handbag for a few seconds then handed over an American Express platinum card.

'OK. If you fill in your details on this here form, I'll ring up the sale, carry out the background checks, then give you a call as soon as you're clear to collect the weapon.'

The woman glanced around at the empty shop, ran a hand through her hair, then lit up the room with a dazzling smile.

'Come on, do I look like trouble? I don't do drugs, I'm mentally competent, and I'm certainly not a convicted felon—in fact, I'm a lawyer. How about I take the gun before you run those pesky background checks? There's been a spate of burglaries in my neighbourhood recently, and it'd make me feel a whole lot safer if I knew that I had some form of protection.'

'Well, it's against the rules, but I sure wouldn't want anything to happen to you while I was doing the paperwork. Go ahead, take it, and maybe you'd like to join me out on the range some time so I can give you a little training? Owning a weapon is one thing, but knowing how to use it is a whole 'nother ballgame.'

'I might just take you up on that.'

Seb cracked a broad grin, then boxed up the Browning and stashed it in a carry bag, along with a couple of cartons of ammo. Once he'd rung up the sale, he pushed the receipt across the counter and watched as the woman signed with a flourish.

'Pleasure doing business with you,' she said with a smile.

'The pleasure was all mine. Now, how about that training?' Seb asked, but she was already headed for the exit.

* * *

Rebecca left Defence of the Realm with a newfound feeling of security. It was kind of odd, the impact that a small piece of machined metal could have on your self-confidence. She'd never owned a gun before, as she'd always thought that they invited trouble into your life rather than drove it away, but ever since her abduction, she'd been feeling more than a little jumpy.

The whole incident had reminded her that she was operating in a dangerous line of work, where emotions ran high and events sometimes spiralled out of control. For the first time in her life, she'd felt the need for a little protection. She hadn't gone to the police. There'd been little point. She had no evidence that she'd been kidnapped other than her own testimony and, besides, it wasn't as if the cops were going to go out of their way to help a defence lawyer. As far as those Neanderthals with badges were concerned, Rebecca and her ilk were the enemy. Part of the problem, not the solution. Talk about misguided.

Of course, the kidnapper was almost certainly a relative of Manuel Ortega, the kid that her client, Bobby Ashton, had run down after an afternoon champagne binge. You couldn't blame the Ortegas for being angry—they had every right. Rebecca knew how they felt as her sister Anabeth had once been through a similar trauma, but the Ortegas couldn't be allowed to interfere with her work—it was far too important. The carry box containing the Browning Hi-Power bumped against her thigh as she walked across the car lot to her BMW. From now on, if anyone tried to mess with her, she'd be ready.

CHAPTER TWENTY-FIVE

NOPE, not that one. Hunter hit the eject button on his car stereo and out popped another language CD. He'd bought ten of them from a Borders first thing that morning in an attempt to identify the native tongue of the assassin, and thus far he'd listened to various strings of incomprehensible gibberish from the Netherlands, Belgium and Scandinavia, without any luck. He pulled his Barracuda onto the Harbour Freeway and accelerated past a diesel big-rig in the inside lane. The rig was headed for the port, belching a thick cloud of carbon monoxide into the atmosphere as it went. Thousands of trucks made the same journey each year, so LA's smog wasn't likely to clear any time soon.

The warning he'd received late last night had done little to quell his desire to close the case, although it had shaken him up a little. For a few minutes he'd been totally at the assassin's mercy. But why had he been spared? Whatever the reason, he couldn't allow himself to get caught cold again. From here on in, he had to be at his sharpest. He popped another foreign language CD into his stereo. He'd ruled out France, Spain and Italy from the get-go as he figured he'd have recognised the sound of those languages, if not the words, but that, unfortunately, was the sum total of his linguistic abilities. So next up was the rest of the Baltic states. Voices from far-away lands reached out to him as the streets went by in a blur. Estonian and Latvian weren't what he was looking for, but he was getting closer. Lithuanian was a maybe, as was Russian. Polish also resonated, but something about it wasn't quite right. And that was the last of the CDs. So was it Lithuanian or Russian?

The Soviet Union. Now, that was one for the history books. All those years of Communism, and where was it now? Capitalism had arrived, corruption had flourished, and the countryside dachas had swapped hands from the privileged bourgeoisie to any low-life criminal who'd mastered the thriving black market. Good sporting nation, though. At one point, their trips to the Olympic podium had been so frequent he could almost have hummed along to the Rodina as the Red Flag had billowed overhead. The Soviet flag…now, why had that prompted alarm bells to go off? He visualised it—all red, with a gold hammer and sickle crossed in the upper left corner. The hammer! That was it. Another link in the chain. The T-shaped tattoo on the back of the assassin's hand was a hammer. And that made him a Russian.

He eased off the throttle and swung over to the exit ramp, headed for the Compton district of South Central. Of course, you weren't supposed to call it South Central any more, just South LA, as the city had decided that the original name had become synonymous with criminality, but changing the name hadn't made it any less dangerous. Take Compton—it was on its way to becoming the murder capital of America, with a homicide rate ten times higher than the national average, all thanks to street gangs just like the one that Hunter was about to visit.

The basketball court where Rhythm Ray had been executed was only a couple of blocks away. Traffic was light, which didn't come as any great surprise, as the drive wasn't overly scenic. Tired-looking apartment buildings loomed large to block out the sun. Half the ground-floor windows were boarded up. Indecipherable graffiti was spraypainted across any spare patch of brickwork. Surly-looking kids loitered on stoops, blasting out angry gangsta rap from their oversized beat-boxes. All things considered, you had to be a bit desperate, or a bit crazy, to roll into this neighbourhood without an invitation.

Hunter's eyes skipped from alley to doorway on the lookout for trouble. Compton had been bad news for some time, so bad that the LAPD had pretty much given up trying to police parts of it, and now that the psychotic Furious and his Renegades were in control, it looked like things had taken a turn for the worse. As he crossed the corner of Chester Avenue and Cypress, he cut the car's speed to a near crawl. Traffic went from light to non-existent. The streets were empty, save for a couple of youths stationed on opposite sides of the block. They each wore black jeans, black shirts and black shades—come dusk, they'd be almost invisible. Both kids had red bandanas tied loosely around their left wrists—the only splash of colour in their otherwise monochrome ensemble. As soon as they realised that Hunter intended to drive on through, the bandanas were raised high overhead to flutter in the breeze like flaming torches. The kids were lookouts, the bandanas a warning signal, which meant that Furious and his men would be waiting up ahead. Hunter tightened his grip on the wheel. There was only one way to find out what sort of reception they'd laid on.

* * *

'Ain't life sweet.'

Furious took a long draw on his oversized blunt, followed it up with a swig from his magnum of Cristal, then raised his pockmarked face to the heavens to wallow in the warm morning sun that fell from on high.

'Fo' real, boss,' chorused three of his lackeys. If there was one thing he never grew tired of, it was their fawning adoration, particularly as he knew that it was based on a healthy undercurrent of downright fear. When it came to keeping your men in line, fear was the only way to go. A man that respected you would go so far, a man that loved you like a brother still had his limitations, but a man that feared you would do whatever the fuck you wanted him to, otherwise he'd have to face the consequences.

Furious was sat in his favourite easy chair while his three lieutenants lounged around him like courtiers before their king. One of them, Slice, was leaning against a large tribal drum, his dreadlocks pulled back in a ponytail. More men were stationed around the edge of the playing area, each within touching distance of the chain-link fence. Niggahs on sentry duty. Hard-ass muthafuckas toting guns on full auto that were there to keep the general populace at bay, not that the general populace had any business here, but Furious wasn't one to take chances. He had the whole block sewn up tight. First line of defence—the lil gangsta wannabes acting as lookouts on the street corners. Next line—the aforementioned sentries. And the last line—da bunker.

Da bunker was an eight-by-ten cinderblock structure slap bang in the centre of the court. Its walls were reinforced with one-inch-thick steel plate, and its roof was made from the same material. You entered in a half-crouch through a gap at the rear, and once inside you tried not to die through dehydration, cos on a hot day it heated up like a muthafucka. But da bunker hadn't been built for comfort—its primary purpose was one of defence. At the first sign of a drive-by, Furious was buried deep inside those four walls like a rock-hard cock in a whore's warm snatch.

Its erection at half-court had been no accident. When construction had begun, Furious had decreed that the bolthole was to be built on the very sight where his brother, Rhythm Ray, had bought it. So da bunker's secondary purpose was to serve as a shrine. Photos of Ray adorned the walls and stolen church candles burned slowly down to the wick in each corner. Two of the younger members of the crew were tasked with the responsibility of making sure that these eternal flames never went out. Lucky them. Truth be told, da bunker was becoming more shrine than defensive stronghold nowadays, as there was no one left to stand against Furious.

His enforced succession to the Renegades' throne had resulted in a bloodbath of biblical proportions amongst the neighbourhood's gangs. A bloodbath that he'd initiated. Whole crews had been wiped out by the brutal war, the pussy-ass competition surprised by both the velocity and ferocity of his attacks. He'd waited a long time to lead the Renegades, and he sure as shit planned on making the most of it. Ray, God rest his soul, had been a good boss, but he'd lacked the requisite cruelty to be great, which was one brotherly trait that Furious didn't share.

'We gotta delivery coming in from the coast tonight, boss. You want me to take care of it?' The sonorous tones of Slice, his gargantuan first lieutenant, broke Furious out of his reverie. If you asked Slice about his moniker, he'd tell you that he'd earned it with the aid of the Bowie knife that was strapped to his leg, although it probably had more to do with the vicious scar that ran the length of his jaw line.

'Na. Don't sweat it. I be there.' Furious liked to take a

hands-on approach when it came to the product, and if that made him a control freak, then so be it. Besides, tonight was important, there were ten keys of powder coming in, 100 per cent pure, and once that shit was cut up for street consumption it would equate to a whole lot of green. He took another long hit of skunk and sank deeper into the easy chair. Man, that was good weed. Just as he was about to doze off, a shout from one of the sentries caused his eyes to snap open.

'Heads up! Heads up! We gots company…'

Slice started to beat out a staccato rhythm on the tribal drum as Furious jumped to his feet and stared outwards towards the source of the commotion. Red bandanas were flying a block down the street and that meant danger. His well-trained men had formed a defensive perimeter just back from the fence, each of them down on one knee with weapon at the ready. He felt a fleeting moment of pride—those muthafuckas were like a well-oiled machine, ready to lay down a wall of fire at the slightest provocation—and then he was making for the sanctuary of da bunker in double quick time. No point in having protection if you weren't gonna use it.

Hunter rolled past the bandana-waving kids at low speed with his hands digging into the top of the wheel, taking care to ensure they remained plainly in view. How young were those sentries? And why weren't they in school? Still, he guessed they were getting an education of sorts. The sound of tribal drums started up somewhere in front of him, their insistent rhythm bouncing off the surrounding buildings to take on a hypnotic quality. Jesus, he'd heard of the urban jungle, but this was ridiculous.

A burst of movement from the apartment block on his right caught his eye. He looked up to discover an elderly lady staring back at him from one of the second-floor windows. More faces began to appear, men, women, and children, until almost half the windows were occupied, the residents drawn to the show by the beating drums. Goddamn ghouls. The whole block was starting to feel like some kind of Roman amphitheatre as Hunter marched out to face Furious and his hungry lions.

Guards were stationed along the rooftops overhead, but they were more for show than defence. As Hunter rolled forward the basketball court came into view. It didn't look like much b-ball was played there any more—you'd need one hell of a crossover dribble to get past the strange little building at half-court. He pulled over to the kerb, cut the engine, and took a quick head count. Fifteen serious-looking guys packing heavy calibre, all of it aimed in his direction. This was shaping up to be one of his more challenging interrogations.

He opened the door and climbed out, both hands raised high above his head. When no bullets came flying in his direction, he shucked off his leather jacket to reveal the Patriot shoulder holster strapped underneath. Using just thumb and forefinger, he withdrew the Beretta from its rig and deposited it on the hood of his car. When you were this outgunned, it was wise to play at subservient. Sometimes, making friendly with the natives was the only way to go.

'Da fuck you want?' shouted the nearest of the Renegades. As opening gambits went, it wasn't the most polite.

'Take it easy, I just wanna talk.' Hunter walked over to the court and quickly found himself surrounded by a ring of angry faces.

A huge guy with natty dreads and a nasty facial scar got up close and personal. 'You trippin', boy, ain't no one here wants to talk to you.'

'Figure he's 5-O, Slice, figure he's come to stir up some

shit,' whined a voice to his right. 'We gots to in-ter-ro-gate him, make him talk.'

The ring closed in and someone spat at his feet. He ignored it and stood his ground. This wasn't going well. Time to lay on a little more of his patented charm.

'I think we might be able to help each other out.'

'Don't need no help, less you wanna come suck on my dick,' said Whiny Voice. Laughter rang out from the rest of the crew.

'Sure thing. Anyone lend me a straw?' Hunter deadpanned. The laughter stopped dead, the aggression level went off the chart. Hmm. Maybe that wasn't the best of wisecracks, given the circumstances.

'Dumb muthafucka axin' fo' it, Slice,' slurred another one of the guards. 'You gonna cut him up? Murderise the muthafucka?'

The guy called Slice withdrew a huge Bowie knife from the sheath that was cinched tight to his right thigh. He raised it skywards in a clenched fist. The sunlight glinted off the serrated blade as his knuckles stood proud. Two Renegades stepped forward to take a firm grip of Hunter's arms. He didn't put up a fight—now wasn't the time. The knife danced in front of his face, then he felt its point press into the soft skin just under his left eye. A warm trickle of blood ran down his face. He forced himself to stand still. Slice's voice rumbled out like a warning from the gods.

'I'm gonna fuck you up bad…'

CHAPTER TWENTY-SIX

DANILOV felt his heart rate quicken as the knife drew blood from Hunter's face—was his adversary about to be removed from the equation? The assassin was huddled up on a stoop, dressed as his alter ego, the beggar, and he was watching the scene unfold through a Hensoldt sniper scope. The scope had been separated from its usual partner in crime, the SIG Sauer SSG 300, which was safely stashed in the trunk of his BMW X5.

Of all his disguises, the beggar was the one he liked the best. No one stared too long at someone who was down on their luck, society preferring instead to pretend that he wasn't there, for fear that if they should acknowledge him, they would somehow be acknowledging their part in the burgeoning homeless problem. Being a beggar was like being invisible, and the gift of invisibility was more than a little useful in Danilov's line of work.

He'd been tailing Hunter ever since he'd left home that morning, keen to see if a tranquilliser dart to the chest had dented the ex-cop's desire to investigate. The first thing his quarry had done was pull in at a Borders, where he'd emerged clutching a plastic bag. Maybe he'd bought some books—a few Dostoevsky novels to help while away the time now that his investigation was over—but, then again, maybe not. Danilov figured Hunter for the relentless type. The ex-cop wasn't just going to fade away—he'd keep on coming until he was stopped.

His suspicions about Hunter's persistence had been confirmed by midmorning, when he realised that the Barracuda was headed towards the site of another one of his assassinations—the basketball court. He'd found himself feeling a little nostalgic despite the circumstances. The miniature car bomb was one of his favourite devices—not only did he get to use his munitions expertise, he also got to play with an RCV. It was a method of dispensing death that brought out the child in him.

As soon as he'd known where Hunter was going, he'd quit the tail and parked his BMW down a quiet side street. Leaving the expensive vehicle in so downtrodden a neighbourhood wasn't ideal, but the local kids would probably assume it was a hustler's ride and give it a wide berth. Once he'd donned his disguise, he'd shuffled off towards the court. When he'd passed the two sentries en route, he'd started to cough and splutter and paw at his eyes. Neither boy had tried to approach him—probably for fear they might catch something.

So now he was back on the self-same stoop from which he'd detonated the RCV, dressed in foul-smelling rags and panhandling for loose change, although every few seconds he'd subtly raise the Hensoldt scope to his eye to keep track of events across the street. The last of these magnified glimpses had coincided with a huge gangbanger pushing a knife into Hunter's face. A burst of excitement had gripped him, tinged with a hint of jealousy. Excitement because one of his problems was about to be erased, jealousy because it wasn't going to be him that got to do the erasing. He shrugged it off. Either way, he was going to come out ahead. A trickle of blood started to run down the ex-cop's face. This was it—any second now…

'Time to make you pretty, boy…' said Slice, brandishing the Bowie.

'Do that, and you'll never find the guy that killed your boss.'

That seemed to get the gangster's attention. Slice lowered the knife and looked back expectantly at the cinderblock structure in the centre of the court, and a few seconds later a figure emerged. A tall guy, six feet plus, wearing a sleeveless vest to display his glistening biceps and cradling an ugly MAC-10. His hair was done in cornrows, his eyes burned with animal intelligence, and his neck sported enough gold chains to dry out a South African mine.

'Mr Furious, I presume?' inquired Hunter.

'Who da fuck are you, and what you be sayin' 'bout my brother? You answer me quick, boy, or I gonna turn these niggahs loose.'

'The name's Hunter and I'm on the trail of an assassin. This guy's taken out four people so far, and I'm pretty sure your brother was one of them.'

'I tole you boss, muthafucka's 5-0, and we don't be dealing with no 5-0. Can I do him, boss, can I?' the banger with the whiny voice interjected. Furious fixed him with a cold hard stare then turned back to Hunter.

'How about it, boy? You a cop? If you is, you must have some kinda death wish to be settin' foot on Renegade land.'

'I'm no cop. I'm just a private citizen that's got a personal beef with the assassin.'

'An' why you be thinking this dog killed my cuz?'

'Because he left his calling card at the scene.'

'How you know all that if you ain't 5-0?'

'I've got an in on the force. I've read the official files. And I can promise you this much—it wasn't a gang hit that killed Rhythm Ray.'

Hunter waited as Furious appraised him through heavily lidded eyes. He kept his expression neutral, knowing full well that to show any sign of weakness now would be tantamount to signing his own death warrant.

'Dis white boy cool. You niggahs get back to your posts. We gonna talk some bidness.' The circle dispersed and Furious led the way over to half-court. 'I knew it weren't no gang hit. Only muthafucka crazy enough to pull a stunt like that was Paleface, and he went up in the same damn explosion. You want some Cristal?'

'Bit early in the day for me.'

'Ain't never too early for Cristal.' Furious chuckled. 'Dassa problem with you cornbreads—don't know how to live.'

'Back up a minute—you just said that Ray was killed in an explosion? I thought he'd been shot?'

'Den yo research ain't for shit. Ray was blowed up by an itty-bitty car.'

'A remote-controlled car?'

'Believe. Little muthafucka blew cuz halfway into next week. So how we gonna find this killa?'

Hunter digested this new information for a second before moving on. 'Let's start with you giving me some background on the hit. What was Ray doing that day?'

'Damn fool trying to make peace with the Hollow Points. Had a meeting with a crazy-assed white niggah, called himself Paleface. If I'd known what Ray was planning, I'd stopped him. When you in the game, peace don't come through talkin', it come through actin'—with one of these.' Furious lofted his MAC-10 to make the point.

'Why the sudden need to make peace? I thought turf wars were a way of life?'

'Damn straight. But Ray thought there was too much drama. Been a lot of drive-bys, lot of niggahs gettin' dead. Few months back, Paleface and his crew wasted a woman lived right across the street from our crib. Ray took it hard—old lady was like mom to us when we was shorties. Trigger-happy fools just be firing wild as they went by.'

'And I'm guessing that the police weren't too bothered by this woman's death? Just wrote it off as another gang hit?'

'You guessed wrong. Old lady's husband seen the whole thing from his window. He'd been waiting for her to get back from the market, she was carryin' bags up the drive when she got popped. Husband had the balls to snitch Paleface out. Raised hell till the muthafucka got arrested.'

'Did it get as far as a trial?'

'Hell, yeah,' said Furious, draining the bottle of Cristal, 'But it dint mean no nevermind. Paleface skated, walked out of court a free man. 5-0 found the car, but it was all burned to shit, and Paleface had a long line of niggahs swearing he be somewhere else on the night in question. But a couple of his crew did take a fall—dumb-ass niggahs that got caught holdin' the murder weapons. Forensic science shit did for them.'

'But they wouldn't roll over on Paleface?'

Furious snorted in response. 'Say what? That'd be like cutting their own throats. Ain't nobody that dumb. So what you know bout the bitch that killed my cuz?'

Time to tread carefully. If Hunter gave too much away, he'd run the risk that the Renegades would take care of the assassin themselves and leave him out in the cold. This shit was personal, and he wasn't going to give it up easy. He flexed his shoulder muscles and popped the muscles in his neck, buying himself a few seconds of valuable thinking time before phrasing a response.

'First of all, I need to find a tall, thin white guy—a Russian—with a missing pinky finger and a tattoo of a hammer on the back of his right hand.'

'He the muthafucka that killed Ray?'

'Nope—just a link in the chain. Put the word out on the street, use your contacts. I figure a guy answering that description is gonna stand out some.'

'Say I find this Russian. Then what?'

'Give me a call and I'll take it from there.'

'This ain't the old days and I ain't your slave, massa!' Furious snarled. 'Just so we be clear, I want a piece of the cocksucka that killed my kin. He got to get got. Don't you be thinkin' you can have him all to yo'self. You sure as shit don't wanna fuck with me!'

'Chill—we'll work as a team. You find the Russian, I'll find the killer. Soon as I do, you'll be the first to know.'

'Team, huh? Like some ebony and ivory bullshit? Yeah, I can dig it.' Furious held out his hand and the two of them shook on it.

Jeez, thought Hunter, guess this is what it feels like to climb into bed with the devil. 'Here's my cellphone number. Give me a call as soon as you hear anything, no matter how small. How can I get in touch with you?'

'Slice—give da man some digits.' The scarred lieutenant was quick to oblige. 'Any time you wanna face to face, I be here most days. Feel free to roll up—you gots yo'self a temporary pass.'

Hunter nodded once then spun on his heel and headed

back to his car. Mission accomplished. With one of the city's most powerful gangs in tow, now he had eyes on every street corner looking out for the Russian. Now all he needed was a bit of luck. In the meantime, he felt the urge to solicit some spiritual guidance from a recent acquaintance. The young priest at the Church of St Lawrence had fed him a pack of lies the last time they'd met, and he didn't take kindly to being bullshitted.

Furious wore a pensive expression as he watched Hunter walk away from the court. Growing up in a war zone had helped him hone his survival instincts to an impressive degree. He'd realised from an early age that the dog-eat-dog nature of the street meant you had to be on your guard twenty-four seven. Even the slightest mistake was liable to leave you playing guest of honour at a casket party. His life was littered with the deaths of those nearest and dearest to him, and he had no intention of joining his fallen comrades any time soon. When danger was all about, you had to have a nose for trouble. You had to know when the shit was gonna go down, and you had to know in advance, otherwise that shit was gonna land slap bang on top of you. And as he watched Hunter climb into his car, Furious was sure of one thing: Honky didn't smell so good.

It wasn't that every word that came out of Hunter's mouth was a lie, no, he'd been way too smart for that, using just enough truth to cover over the bullshit. But Furious knew something wasn't right, and when those alarm bells started ringing, he was quick to pay attention. Still, one thing was for sure, Hunter must have been packing a set of cast iron balls to show up unarmed. It wasn't every day that a white man fronted up to the Renegades and lived to tell the tale. Matter of fact, it wasn't *any* day.

'Yo, Slice,' Furious murmured, sitting back down, 'I got a job for yo' black ass.'

His scarred lieutenant lumbered over. 'What gives, boss?'

'I don't trust white boy. He's layin' down a line of bullshit and I ain't buyin'. I want you to watch him for a coupla days, see if he's righteous.'

'Undercover shit?'

'For sure.'

'You thinkin' he's 5-0?'

'Maybes. Or working for some other gang.'

'Ain't no gang strong enough to take us on, boss. Hollow Points all gone, Varrio Flats all messed up, West Side Mafia layin' low. You wiped 'em all out.'

'Maybe, maybe not. White boy might be linked to that new Armenian crew we be hearin' about. Take the Hummer, get on his ass, see what's occurring.'

'I'm on it.'

Slice nodded, then spun on his heel to begin the surveillance, leaving Furious to ponder who Hunter was and what he was after. Now that he'd made it to the top of the pile, he had no intention of getting knocked off through lack of effort. If some muthafucka was planning to make a move, he was gonna be ready. Let 'em come.

CHAPTER TWENTY-SEVEN

THE church of St Lawrence was just as quiet and empty as Hunter remembered it. He headed for the sacristy and barged straight in without knocking. The priest was behind a small desk with his back to the door, busy stacking up the same hymn books he'd been lugging around on Hunter's last visit. When he spun around, his fine ginger hair went flying in all directions.

'Ah, Mr Hunter, isn't it? What can I do for you?' he asked, taking a seat behind the desk, a rosy red colour rising in his cheeks.

'Why was Father Mulrooney blindfolded when he was killed?'

The young priest's eyes flicked away. 'I told you before, I have no earthly idea. Anyway, I'm afraid that I can't really talk now…I'm very busy…'

'Tough shit. Why was he blindfolded?'

'Please, curb your language, Mr Hunter, you're in a place of worship. Anyway, I'm not sure I like your tone, so I'm going to have to ask you to leave.'

Hunter took a step forward. 'The blindfold?'

No response. The priest's bottom lip started to quiver. Hunter reached over the table and grabbed him by his vestments, half yanking him out of the chair until they were nose to nose. The reek of his fear was palpable.

'Last time I was here you lied to me. That's not going to happen again. I'm gonna ask you one more time—why was Mulrooney blindfolded?'

'T-to stop him s-seeing…' the priest stuttered, flinching as Hunter drew back a fist. 'To stop him…watching.'

'Watching what? What did he like to watch?'

The priest threw a frightened glance over Hunter's shoulder as if he expected someone else to come crashing through the sacristy door. A backhanded slap to the face quickly refocussed his attention.

'What was it that he liked to watch?'

'They'll fire me if I tell you…' Snot dribbled out of the young man's nose. He wiped it away with the sleeve of his cassock. So much for cleanliness being next to godliness.

'Right now, your job prospects are the least of your worries.'

He cast his eyes downward. 'There were some…problems… with a couple of the choirboys…'

Hunter's fist clenched tighter on the priest's robes. 'What sort of problems?'

'Father Mulrooney used to encourage them to take showers together,' he choked out in a near whisper. 'Told them that they had to wash the sin from their bodies.'

Rage flared inside Hunter's chest. 'So that's what passes

for spiritual guidance in the Catholic Church nowadays? A paedophile with a bar of soap? You people make me sick.'

The priest flinched at the words but pressed on—now that he'd begun to recount the sordid tale he seemed eager as hell to get through it. Probably hoped that by telling the truth he'd somehow achieve absolution—maybe ditch the boulder of guilt that had been chained to his ankle ever since he'd agreed to keep quiet.

'One child's parents started to complain once they discovered what had been happening, but the Church hired a lawyer, then made a substantial out-of-court settlement to ensure it was all hushed up.'

Hunter stared at the priest in naked disgust. Here was a young man sworn to carry out the duty of the Lord. A man who was meant to educate the masses as to what was morally right and wrong. And what had he done when he'd found out that his predecessor had had a predilection for small boys? He'd kept schtum. Played his part in the cover-up. And the fact that he appeared ashamed of his actions somehow made it worse. It made Hunter want to bury his fist in the freckled face that sat before him, but instead he released his grip on the priest's robes and stepped back.

'I think it's time you considered a career change—you're obviously not suited to this line of work. Next time I come around you'd better be gone. You want to help make things right, go tell the cops all you know. Mulrooney's name should be dragged through the mud, along with all those church leaders that turn a blind eye to him and his kind. You do that, maybe you'll be able to look yourself in the mirror again.'

The priest bowed his head. With a final snort of derision Hunter spun on his heel and exited the church. He stood outside for a few moments, savouring the sun's cleansing warmth, until a call on his cellphone brought him back to reality.

'Hello?'

'Hunter? It's Carson.' He was pleased to hear the detective's gruff voice. Now, there was a guy that was steeped in morality. 'I've got something to show you. Meet me downtown, at the Mill Road Motel on Crocker Street, first thing tomorrow—say ten a.m.'

'Sure. What's the story?'

'You'll find out tomorrow. Catch you later.'

The phone went dead in his hand. Carson wasn't in the mood to swap pleasantries. Hunter was intrigued.

"Hunter ignored warning. Went to basketball court, spoke to gang leader. Went to church, spoke to priest. Must be stopped."

Danilov leant back from the keyboard and awaited a response. Of all his secure internet conversations, this one was the most important. If the boss still refused to sanction a hit after today's developments then he was pretty much giving Hunter a clear run. Not that Danilov was scared by the prospect of facing the ex-cop one on one—in fact, he'd welcome it. But why wait for the inevitable? Wasn't it better to remove obstacles in your path as soon as you were aware of them, rather than wait till they caused you to stumble? Hadn't the boss ever heard of forward planning?

And now that Hunter had made friendly with the Renegades he was even more dangerous. Having a stubborn ex-cop on your case was bad enough, but having a bunch of heavily armed thugs combing the streets for the merest hint of your presence was a whole lot worse. If Danilov's ability to pass through the masses unseen was compromised then his effectiveness as a killing machine would be reduced, and that could have very serious implications indeed.

He topped up his tumbler with some more Stolichnaya,

then rubbed the bridge of his nose between thumb and forefinger. If the boss came back with a no he'd be left with only two options. Option one—he could arrange for Hunter to suffer a little accident and hope that the boss didn't take it too badly. Option two—he could go on the run. Neither was particularly appealing. To rely on the boss's mercy after he'd disobeyed a direct order was little more than a crapshoot, and Danilov wasn't one to gamble with his future. And as for pulling a disappearing act, well, the boss had tracked him down before, and he'd made it pretty clear what would happen if he were forced to do so again.

Danilov considered himself a brave man, but the prospect of meeting up with the son of Igor Krupchenko scared even him. Krupchenko had once been his employer, but he was now doing life up at Folsom. When the Racketiry had expanded into the US, Danilov had been sent over to help eliminate the competition, and he'd been doing just that when things had gone wrong. He'd dispatched a target the old-fashioned way, face to face, always happy to employ the personal touch when dealing out death, but as he'd turned to leave the Feds had swooped in from all angles with enough firepower to start a small war.

The target had been under surveillance on suspicion of being a major new player in the heroin trade, which incidentally was the very same reason that Danilov had been dispatched to kill him—all that fresh product was lowering street value and hitting Russian profits. So the Feds had him right where they wanted him. They'd even filmed the hit on videotape, taking great delight in playing it to him over and over while reminding him of the joys of a lifetime's incarceration.

When they'd offered him a deal, he'd listened. He'd known that it wasn't a smart move to betray Krupchenko, but the prospect of spending the rest of his days in the pen was a nonstarter—when it came to making difficult decisions, he was nothing if not practical. But his disloyalty had carried a price; disloyalty brought shame and, as a proud Russian acknowledging that a blood debt was due, he'd cut off his little finger and mailed it to Krupchenko's son.

So for one small appendage and a little bit of information he'd managed to trade his cell for a spot in the witness protection programme. For the past three years he'd lived under the radar and everything had been going just fine, right up until an unmarked envelope had arrived at his old apartment five months ago. The envelope had contained each and every detail of the life he'd left behind, along with some glossy photos of his first target and a crystal-clear warning as to what would happen if he didn't carry out the termination. His first instinct had been to run, and he always listened to his instincts. In a little under a month he'd gotten himself a whole new identity and a change of address, but he'd barely had time to unpack before another envelope had shown up at his door, its contents almost identical to those of the first, except for one thing—a bold-typed message that said if he moved house again it wouldn't be Fed-Ex that came knocking but the Russian mob.

Thus Danilov had got himself a new boss, and that boss had him by the short and curlies. Since then he'd spent every waking moment trying to work out the blackmailer's identity, but thus far he'd drawn a blank. He drummed his fingers on the glass-topped table, fully aware that he could soon be faced with another difficult decision. Five minutes had passed since he'd reiterated his view that Hunter needed to be dealt with. What was taking so long? There was only one logical way to move forward. Finally, a line of text appeared on the screen.

"Send him to Boston."

Danilov smiled.

CHAPTER TWENTY-EIGHT

'ALL rise for the Honourable Judge Wharton!'

'Case number 1247, the People versus Robert Ashton, is now resumed,' began the judge. 'The charge is gross vehicular manslaughter, filed under section 191.5 of the Californian penal code. Are the People ready to call their next witness?'

The prosecutor wasted no time in answering. 'Yes, Your Honour. The People call Dwayne Sharpton.' The courtroom doors opened, and a scruffy-looking youth walked up the aisle to take his place on the stand.

'Do you swear to tell the truth, the whole truth and nothing but the truth, so help you God?' bellowed the clerk, keen to make the most of his speaking part.

Rebecca put on her game face. Today was Bobby Ashton's big day in court. Over the next few hours he was going to be tried for the manslaughter of Manual Ortega and judged by twelve of his peers. She used the word 'peers' in its widest possible sense—as far as she was aware, none of the jurors had a multi-millionaire for a father. The courtroom was packed to the rafters with people who wanted to see Ashton pay, people who wanted to see him go free and people who just wanted to see. Professional spectators. Every big case attracted its fair share of them. Like flies around shit. And this case was bigger than most. And shittier.

Ashton was turned out in an immaculate grey Hugo Boss suit, a white linen shirt, and a spiffy-looking tie. His clean-cut image was a plus—the jurors would respond well to it, on a subconscious level at least, and that could only aid his cause. It might have been a small point, but Rebecca had a feeling that her client was going to need all the help he could get. Come to that, maybe she would, too, if she managed to get him off. Her abductor had been pretty clear about the consequences of mounting a successful defence, and he hadn't sounded like a man making idle threats, but she couldn't let that worry her now. This case was too important.

She turned her attention back to the kid on the stand. He was the first major witness for the prosecution, and he went by the name of Dwayne Sharpton. She'd already leafed through Dwayne's background file to get a handle on his personality, but that was for due diligence as much as anything else—they were called background files for a reason. If you really wanted to know how someone was going to react to the pressure of testifying in court, the only surefire way to find out was to be there when it happened. Some witnesses became ultra-confident in their eagerness to tell the world their version of events, while others just wilted under the spotlight, and young Dwayne looked like a wilter.

He was somewhere in his early twenties, with grungy clothes and a pockmarked face, and he wore a pained smile beneath a towering jet-black quiff. Every few moments he'd run his hands through his elaborate coiffure as if to check it was still there. The courtroom remained in stasis as it waited for him to respond to the clerk's opening question. After a five-second pause he finally found the courage to answer.

'I do.'

An expectant hush fell over the room as the prosecuting attorney rose from his seat. Rebecca watched as he strutted past the jurors, giving them his best 'we're in this together' smile, trying to gain an advantage. Alongside her, Bobby Ashton leant in close to whisper in her ear.

'Don't worry, I've got it covered,' he whispered, squeezing her thigh. She elbowed him away and directed her attention back to the stand, where Dwayne had begun to drum his fingers on the oak block in front of him.

'So, Mr Sharpton,' began the prosecuting attorney, 'please can you state your occupation for the court?'

'I work at the Blue Light Bar…on Copthorne Boulevard.'

'And how long have you worked there?'

'Just over twelve months.'

'OK, Mr Sharpton, now, according to your boss's time cards, you were working on the afternoon of the 14th of June?'

'Yeah, I guess so, if that's what the cards say,' mumbled Dwayne, shuffling in his seat.

'During that afternoon, did the defendant, Mr Robert Ashton, frequent your establishment?'

'Frequent…what…? I'm sorry, I don't understand…'

'Did Mr Ashton drink in the Blue Light on that afternoon?'

'Er…yes.' Dwayne ran his hands through his quiff again. 'I think he was there for most of my shift. Ordered a big plate of sandwiches from his booth in the corner, and he had a couple of young girls in tow. Both of 'em were smokin' hot. They looked like models.'

'I'm not interested in the female company that Mr Ashton was keeping, rather the amount of liquor he imbibed. What was he drinking on that afternoon?'

Dwayne scratched the side of his face, plumed his quiff and glanced around the court as if looking for reassurance. His eyes lingered on Rebecca for a split second before moving on to Ashton, and although she couldn't be sure, she thought that the cocksure defendant alongside her offered a quick nod of encouragement.

'Uh...let me think... Yeah, I remember. Mr Ashton was drinking Virgin Marys...yep, he was on them all afternoon...'

'Virgin Marys?' The look on the prosecutor's face was priceless.

'That's right. Tomato juice, Worcestershire sauce, Tabasco, lemon juice, salt, pepper and a bit of celery,' Dwayne spoke up, gaining in confidence now that the lie was out in the open.

'I know what's in a Virgin Mary, Mr Sharpton!' the prosecutor almost shouted. 'Can I take this opportunity to remind you that you provided a sworn affidavit stating that Mr Ashton was drinking Moët & Chandon champagne on the afternoon in question. I believe that your exact words were that he was "downing it like it was going out of fashion." May I also remind you that the State of California considers perjury to be a very serious crime, punishable by a prison term of up to four years.'

'Er...yeah...about that... Couple of days ago I remembered that there was this other guy in the bar, looked a lot like Mr Ashton, and it was him that was drinking the champagne. I'm sorry if I've caused any trouble.'

'Trouble? You're a disgrace, Mr Sharpton—'

'Counsellor,' the judge cut in. 'Please, curb your comments.'

'Sorry, Your Honour. No further questions. Your witness.' The prosecutor slouched back to his seat, shaking his head at the jurors en route to let them know what he thought of Sharpton's testimony.

'No questions, Your Honour,' Rebecca called out in a bright, clear voice, keen to give off a positive vibe—cases had been won or lost on such trivialities as mere personality before.

The hum of conversation struck up behind her as the courtroom reacted to this turn of events. She looked around and the first faces she saw were those of Manuel Ortega's family, right up close in the front row, each and every one of them trying to remain stoic in the face of this early disappointment.

'Order!' called the judge, banging his gavel.

Rebecca stiffened as Ashton leant in close once again, his breath hot and sticky in her ear. 'Amazing what can be achieved with a little financial incentive,' he whispered, before flicking his tongue against her earlobe.

CHAPTER TWENTY-NINE

WHEN Hunter pulled up at the Mill Road Motel the following morning, Carson was already there. The cop looked even older in the cold light of day, his skin as weathered and craggy as the cliffs at Yosemite. He'd ditched his trade-mark knee-length coat in favour of a suede sports jacket and a pair of jeans, and he held a white A4 envelope in one hand and a half-eaten doughnut in the other.

'What time d'you call this?' he spluttered, as he polished off his doughnut.

'Nice to see you, too, oldtimer,' responded Hunter, climbing out of his car with two cups of coffee. 'I stopped off en route, figured you might appreciate a caffeine injection.'

The detective wedged the envelope under his arm and reached for the proffered beverage.

'What's in there? Crime-scene photos?' asked Hunter.

'Not exactly… Remember I told you I had a plan to get ex-wife number two back? Well, this is it. Photos of Carson Jr. If these don't straighten her out, nothing will.'

'I didn't know you had kids.'

'I don't—there's nothing childish about Carson Jr,' he said, grabbing his crotch and letting loose a laugh that sounded like an outboard motor trying to fire.

'Man, that's one set of photos I don't want to see.'

'Can't say I blame you.' Carson took a sip of coffee then nodded at the building behind him. 'Ain't this joint a beauty?'

Hunter took his first good look at the motel. It was set back from the road, a ground-floor affair, comprising one long row of rooms that stretched from the check-in cabin by the entrance to the crumbling brick wall at the far end of the lot. A sign by the cabin said that rooms were available by the week, day or hour. The only way in was through a heavy fire door at one end of the building. Paint was peeling from the façade in a number of places, a couple of the windows were boarded up, and litter had been allowed to collect by the walls, enabling the reek of rotting refuse to further impact its AAA rating. It was the sort of place that even cockroaches thought twice about inhabiting.

'Delightful,' deadpanned Hunter. 'I hope you haven't got us a room…'

'As a matter of fact…' Carson pushed open the fire door and led the way down a dingy corridor that was untouched by natural light, illumination coming instead from the cheap strip lights that fizzed and crackled overhead. The door to room seventeen was covered with yellow crime-scene tape. The detective started to tear it off.

'Guess our boy's been busy again?' asked Hunter.

'If there's one thing you can't fault him on, it's his work rate.' Carson finished ripping at the tape, opened the door and entered the room. 'A maid found the victim yesterday morning. She hadn't been in to clean for a few days as the killer had very thoughtfully left the "Do Not Disturb" sign hanging out front. She was more than happy to comply with that request until another guest started to complain about the smell. Got the shock of her life when she opened the door.'

Hunter followed him inside. The stench of decomposition hit him straight away. He covered his nose with his hand. This was one fragrance Dior wouldn't be bottling. The room was sparsely furnished, offering a tired-looking double bed for the cost-conscious traveller, a ratty chest of drawers in which they could stash their meagre belongings, plus a small TV set for their viewing pleasure. But the real point of interest was the large dark stain on the threadbare carpet. Hunter knelt down for a closer look. Dried blood. This was where the assassin's most recent victim had bled out.

'You got a name yet?' he asked Carson.

'Fat kid by the name of Harold Ribecki. His mom reported him missing a couple of days ago. It looks like he was lured out here on a promise—we found a note on the bed and a bunch of red tulips on the floor. Spoke to his girlfriend, a Jenna Williamson, who denied all knowledge of the note, the meeting, the motel, pretty much everything.'

'Were the playing cards present?'

'Yep, he left 'em on the bed.'

'Got a forensics report yet?'

'Yep. They've been and gone. Thought I'd wait till they'd cleared out before I invited you along. Wouldn't want you meeting any of my colleagues, given your off-the-books status in the investigation. Anyways, forensics said we got lucky with one of the slugs. Went straight through the kid's head and buried itself in the wall opposite. But that's where our luck ran out. Nine-mil bullet got chewed up by a steel strut—ballistics reckons that even if we find the murder weapon it's unlikely we'll get a match that'll stand up in court. As for the body itself, there were twin wounds to the forehead, both showing signs of compression and stippling, so we figure the shooter was up close when he pulled the trigger.'

'And what had he done to the victim?'

Carson offered a rueful smile. 'Covered him in boot polish. Blacked him up. It looked fucking surreal, fat kid lying there with shiny white eyes staring out of a jet-black face.'

'So Ribecki was a racist…'

'Kid had some ties to a half-arsed white supremacist group. How'd you know that?'

Hunter ignored the question and pressed on. 'And at some point in the not so distant past this Ribecki had a run-in with the law?'

'Don't know. Haven't had time to run a full background check on him yet,' Carson replied gruffly.

'Bet you a buck he's got a rap sheet.'

'OK, Hunter, what's going on? You've obviously got something spinning round in that head of yours—why don't you just spit it out?'

'Let's look at the victims one by one. Carlos Montero—found with a needle in his arm. He got street kids high then put 'em in smut films. It took me months to finally bring him down, then he walked out of court a free man. Montero's the reason I'm here. Father Mulrooney—found blindfolded. The good Father liked to watch his choirboys take a shower, but the Church made sure it was hushed up. Marty Schaeffer—found with a dildo up his ass. Marty skated on a rape beef. And now this kid, Ribecki, a known racist found covered in boot polish. You look hard enough, you're bound to find that he got away with something.'

'And what about the gang leader, Rhythm Ray? How does he fit into your theory?'

'Ray wasn't the target, he just got caught in the crossfire. The assassin was after the guy Ray was meeting—some chump called Paleface, boss of the Hollow Points. Paleface took part in a drive-by that killed an old lady. He dodged jail time when his crew backed him up with a false alibi. The assassin took him out with a car bomb. See how it works? The punishment fits the crime. Our assassin is delivering his own very special brand of justice on those whose crimes went unpunished. But you already knew that.'

Carson sat down on the bed and lit up a cigar. 'Not all of it—the stuff about Rhythm Ray and Paleface was news to me—but, yeah, I'd pretty much figured out the rest. And as for Ribecki, he was up recently for assaulting a black kid. Left his victim confined to a wheelchair. Ribecki got off when the kid refused to testify at the last minute. Prosecutor assumed that someone threw a scare into him.'

Hunter felt his anger start to build. Everything he'd done thus far, every place he'd visited, every person he'd spoken to, all felt like one big waste of time. Carson could have clued him in from the get-go instead of sending him around town on some wild-goose chase. From now on, he was through wasting time.

'I'm done working with you unless you start sharing information. I've had enough of going over the same goddamn ground that you covered weeks ago. You're treating me like I'm some wet-behind-the-ears kid just out of the academy, and it's got to fucking stop. What's the value in "coming at things from a fresh perspective"? While I'm wasting time chasing down cold leads, the assassin is out killing another innocent.'

'I'd hardly call Ribecki an innocent,' interjected Carson.

'Give me a break! You think this assassin's on the side of the angels? What about the young hooker that was found with Montero? Did she deserve to die? Or even Rhythm Ray, come to that, as it sounded like he was about to become a force for good on the streets.'

'Dead hooker, dead gangbanger—my heart bleeds.'

'I'm warning you, Carson, copy me in on your files or I go it alone,' snarled Hunter, his eyes blazing.

Carson gave him a bored stare, shrugged, then raised his hands in defeat. 'Sure, whatever you want. You've already covered all the hits I know about anyhow. Maybe it's time you saw the bigger picture. Lord knows, this case could do with a break. Tell you what, I've got a couple of things to do, but once I'm through, I'll go home and fetch my files, then I'll meet you at Adriana's Diner over by Union Station. Say midday?'

Hunter nodded in relief. Finally, he was getting somewhere. Maybe there'd be something in the files that would help identify the assassin. Some little clue that had been overlooked. He'd already come up with a decent physical description and a motive without too much help from the cops. Once he got the official line on the killer, finding him ought to get a whole lot easier. How many tall, skinny, Russian assassins with hammer tattoos and a missing pinky finger could there be in this town? He followed Carson out of the motel with a renewed sense of purpose.

CHAPTER THIRTY

OFFICER WILLIAMSON had been on the force for little more than a year, and it hadn't exactly been the best twelve months of his life. He'd joined up to make a difference, but already he'd begun to question the wisdom of that decision. He'd had no idea of what he'd been letting himself in for when he'd first donned the uniform. Sure, he'd heard all about the rising level of crime, but no one had warned him that it was rising so fast it threatened to engulf the city in a tsunami of lawlessness. As far as he could make out, everyone seemed to be on the take. Petty crime, white-collar crime, domestic crime, violent crime—you name it, he'd responded to it. Often two or three times in the same day. It was enough to get anyone down.

So when the chance to make a clean bust came along, Williamson went after it with both hands. It didn't matter how small or insignificant the misdeed was, he'd chase it down as hard as he could in an attempt to fight the burgeoning feeling of helplessness that was threatening to finish his new career before it had really got started. But while these small victories gave him a boost, it never lasted for long. Let's face it, arresting the neighbourhood flasher was like chipping away at the tip of a gargantuan iceberg. What he really needed to do was catch himself a whale. Someone big enough to make him feel important. Someone that would help convince him he was making a difference, even if deep down he suspected he wasn't. Someone like a drunk playboy who'd climbed behind the wheel of his overpriced sports car to mow down a little kid. Yeah—that sort of collar would definitely cheer him up.

His fists clenched as he looked over to where Bobby Ashton sat grinning alongside his attorney. When he'd first arrived at the scene of the 'accident' Ashton had been slumped over the wheel of his Porsche, the front fender wrapped around a streetlight. The son of a bitch had been mumbling incoherently, suffering from nothing more serious than a mild concussion and a few cuts and bruises. Unfortunately, little Manuel Ortega hadn't got off so lightly. The poor kid had bled out on the sidewalk with a whole slew of internal injuries. Little Manuel had never stood a chance.

So Officer Williamson had been eagerly awaiting the start of the trial for the last few weeks, and now that he was on the stand, he could barely contain his excitement. This was his big chance to tell the world how he'd been the one to administer the breathalyser test, his chance to let everyone know just how over the limit Ashton had been, and he intended to make the most of it. He'd already sailed through the prosecution's questions with ease. Next up was the cross-examination. He could still remember the playboy's reaction to being told that he'd just killed an innocent child—he'd shrugged it off like it didn't matter, like all he'd done had been to step on an ant or something. An ant—that was probably how the spoilt brat viewed anyone that wasn't hauling down a seven-figure salary. Well, screw him, because today the little man was going to have his say. Williamson straightened in his chair as Rebecca Finch, the defence attorney, approached.

'Good afternoon, Officer Williamson. As we've heard during the first part of your testimony, when you were questioned by my esteemed colleague,' she began, nodding towards the prosecuting attorney, 'you were the first patrolman to arrive at the scene of the accident.'

'Yes, I was.' He started to relax. If all her questions were that easy, this was gonna go fine.

'At which time you administered a breathalyser test,' she continued, referring to her notes.

'Indeed I did.' He nodded sagely.

'And how long would you say had passed from the moment of your arrival to the administration of the test?'

'Five minutes, maybe ten at the most.'

'And may I ask why you didn't carry out the test immediately?'

'Because I was too busy checking on both the minor injuries to your client,' he spat in Ashton's direction, 'and the dead child that he'd left in the street.'

'And would you say that Mr Ashton's reading was abnormally high?'

'Yes, I would. Highest I'd ever seen. It was almost off the scale. He musta had more alcohol than blood in his veins on that afternoon.'

'An abnormally high reading. In your own words, it was "almost off the scale." How often have you seen readings that high, Officer?'

'Never before and never again. That son of a bitch was so drunk he was practically dead to the world.'

'Officer, please desist with your more colourful comments and just answer the questions,' the judge interjected.

'Sorry, Your Honour.' Gotta keep a check on my emotions, thought Williamson. Focus on the facts, make sure that my story's heard.

'Do breathalysers ever give incorrect readings, Officer?' asked Finch with a butter-wouldn't-melt look on her face.

'Objection!' interjected the prosecuting attorney. 'The witness is not qualified to answer that question. He has no scientific knowledge on the inner workings of breathalysers.'

'Overruled. I think the officer has enough experience in these matters to have a valid opinion. Please answer the question,' directed Judge Wharton.

'Er…well, yes, occasionally, but as a rule they're highly reliable.'

'But they're not one hundred per cent reliable? They aren't infallible, are they, Officer? Sometimes they go wrong?'

Finch's voice had morphed from warm and alluring to cold as steel in an instant, and Williamson was starting to feel like a mouse that had been cornered by an alley cat. Talk about having to watch what you say. He phrased his next answer carefully.

'Well, sometimes, but not in this case… Ashton was drunk as a skunk, he could barely string two words together without slurring or giggling.'

'Are you aware that there are over a hundred different compounds present in human breath at any one time, and that up to eighty per cent of them can be falsely detected as alcohol by breathalysers as they contain the methyl group structure?'

'Er…'

'Did you know that eating bread can cause an alcohol-free subject to give a breathalyser reading of 0.05, which is perilously close to the state's legal limit of 0.08? We already have it on record that Mr Ashton had eaten a plate of sandwiches at the Blue Light Bar while imbibing nothing stronger than a Virgin Mary. Did you also know that exposure to lacquers, paint removers, gasoline or cleaning fluids can cause erroneous breathalyser results?'

'Well, no, I didn't, but—'

'Are you aware that breathalysers are very sensitive to temperature and will give false readings if not properly recalibrated for the ambient conditions? Did you recalibrate the device before you took Mr Ashton's reading, Officer?'

'Now, wait a damn minute. He was drunk, it was obvious…'

'Let's just examine the facts here, Officer. You took a ridiculously high reading from a piece of machinery that has proven to be defective on numerous occasions in the past, therefore suggesting that an error may well have been made. When talking to my client, you found him incoherent, struggling to express himself and full of wild emotions. Given that he'd been involved in a fatal car accident just moments earlier, isn't that exactly how you'd expect him to behave? He's hardly likely to make much sense, now, is he? Mr Ashton was obviously overcome with grief, suffering from a severe traumatic reaction to the tragedy that had just occurred. As a matter of fact, he's been suffering ever since, and has recently checked himself in for counselling. In many ways, Bobby Ashton was as much a victim of this awful accident as poor Manual Ortega.'

'But that's not how—' Williamson started up, but Finch cut him off.

'Thank you, Officer Williamson. No further questions.'

'But—'

'You are excused, Officer,' intoned the judge.

Williamson took his leave from the witness stand and slouched out of the courtroom. Shit. How in the hell had that happened?

CHAPTER THIRTY-ONE

DANILOV removed his fedora and smiled as he looked out of the third-storey window. Perfect. He had a clear line of fire to his target. The Russian was downtown, holed up inside one of the rooms at the Excelsior, a hotel directly opposite Adriana's Diner. He'd tailed Hunter there, waited a few minutes until he was certain his quarry was going to stay put, then scouted around for somewhere to set up the shot.

The Excelsior had been heaven sent. An elevated position with a great field of vision, it allowed him to look down on both the diner and the adjacent car lot while also offering the requisite privacy that was desirable when carrying out a daylight execution. As much as he'd have liked to handle this one up close, logic had dictated he take the sniper's long-distance approach as there was a real danger that Hunter might have recognised him face to face.

He'd entered the Excelsior via its service entrance and marched straight in as if he was there on important business. No one had given him a second glance. If you looked like you belonged, you invariably did. He'd cut through the kitchens with rifle safely ensconced in its carry case and headed up the stairs to the third floor, passing just one elderly gentleman en route, who'd seemed more concerned with negotiating the steps than remembering the distinguishing features of a Russian assassin. His fedora had helped mask his face while a pair of latex gloves had covered his hands.

Relying on his internal compass, he'd made his way to the front of the building, aiming for the room that would provide the best view across the street. Something had told him that number thirty-seven would fit the bill, so he'd let himself in with the aid of a master key that he'd swiped from an unattended maid's trolley, then paused to listen for signs of life. When the sound of running water from behind a closed door had become apparent, he'd laid down the carry case on the unmade bed, drawn his Glock and stepped into the bathroom.

An attractive blonde had been taking a shower. As she'd spun around to confront him, he'd shot her between the eyes. After turning off the water and checking that she was dead, he'd returned to the bedroom in order to ready himself for the main event, but the fact that everything had happened so quickly had troubled him. When given a target, he liked to research their daily routine, get a handle on what made them tick, identify their weaknesses, but with Hunter he couldn't afford the luxury of time. No, this assassination had to happen fast, as with every passing second the ex-cop's investigation brought him closer to the truth.

He studied his surroundings. The bedroom was painted an off-cream colour and, judging from the lack of any marks on the walls, the paint job was relatively recent. It was adequately furnished, with a faux mahogany wardrobe and chest of drawers opposite the king-size bed and a high-backed chair over by the window. A pile of clothes sat on the chair, while a half-packed suitcase lay on the floor alongside it. Danilov allowed himself a half-smile—if the blonde had been getting ready to leave, her checkout had come a little earlier than expected.

Some impressively skimpy undergarments lay on top of the pile of clothes. They were made of silk, white silk to be exact, and they smelled strongly of perfume. He threw them down and opened the window, replacing the sweet scent of the dead woman's undergarments with the not-so-appealing fug of everyday city life, then walked over to the bed, released the two clasps at either end of the carry case and started to take out the constituent parts of his sniper rifle.

The SSG 3000. A bolt action, magazine-fed killing machine, crafted by the skill of the Swiss and the precision of the Germans. The 23.4 inch barrel slotted into the main body of the weapon with the aid of six interlocking lugs, and the stock was made from McMillan fibreglass. The magazine held five .308 Winchester Silvertips—heavy-duty rounds that promised deep penetration and controlled expansion. The gun had already been calibrated to his own exacting standards, and it was accurate in the 0.5 minute-of-angle range, meaning he could hit a half-inch target at 100 yards. When he picked it up, it felt like an extension of his arm.

He'd been schooled in the black art of sniping by Yuri, an ex-Spetsnaz member, in the countryside outside Moscow. Yuri had found himself out of a job in the late 1980s after the Red Army had been downsized to help pay for Gorbachev's economic reforms, but fortunately for him, the Racketiry had been crying out for a man with Yuri's skills—two tours of Afghanistan and black-ops work all over Eastern Europe made for an impressive CV. Danilov had been a natural, and under Yuri's expert tutelage his talent had blossomed, until one day the apprentice had surpassed the master.

He threaded the rounds into the magazine, pushed it home, then locked the bolt, before taking his place at the window. It took him a minute or so to settle on a shooting position as he searched for a comfortable stance that would provide a solid base for the gun, but once he was happy, he rested the barrel on the frame and looked down the Hensoldt scope.

The diner was popular. He could see a pretty waitress scurrying from table to table, and there was a steady stream of new clients pulling into the lot to replace those on their way out. It looked nothing like his favourite eatery back in Russia that had always been half-empty—a small, family-run joint, with wolfskins nailed to the walls and hunting trophies perched on the shelves. He'd have killed for a bowl of their piping hot bosartma right now, but as the chances of getting any Azerbaijani stewed lamb seemed pretty remote, he popped a stick of gum into his mouth instead.

Hunter had got himself a spot by a window, and for a split second Danilov thought about shooting him there and then, until the ex-cop leant back in his chair to ease himself out of the frame. The assassin took a deep breath and relaxed his trigger finger. No point in taking a risky shot. Better to wait until the target came outside and walked across the parking lot, where the light conditions would be that much better and the risk of someone blocking his shot would be that much less. He made some minute adjustments to the scope to bring the image into sharp focus, then angled it towards the lot to check where Hunter had left his car, sending the crosshairs flashing over an old guy in a pick-up truck plus a couple of Negroes kicking back in a Humvee. A large billboard provided the backdrop to the scene, on which a half-nude anorexic movie star was draped around an oversized bottle of overpriced perfume. These Americans and their celebrity culture. They'd buy anything just to make themselves feel closer to their idols.

He traversed the scope back towards the diner to find Hunter conversing with the waitress. Once again the target's head was lined up bang in the middle of the crosshairs. The waitress handed Hunter a dog-eared menu then slopped some coffee into a plain white cup. Meal for one? No, he was checking his watch. Maybe he'd been stood up. Had fate been cruel to his adversary? Another half-smile. Even the condemned man shouldn't have to eat alone.

Hunter took another look at his watch. It had just gone 12.30 p.m. Carson was half an hour late. Much more of this and his patience would start to wear thin. A raven-haired waitress in a red and white checked uniform bustled by on her way to a nearby table. She was on her own and she had her work cut out. Adriana's was busy, stocked with an assortment of loners, couples, business folk on their lunch-breaks and travellers en route to nearby Union Station, which augured well for the quality of the food.

He'd gotten a spot by the window so he could enjoy an unrestricted view of Alpine Street. Not that Alpine was overly scenic, but he liked to have a handle on who was coming and going. Call it a cop thing. Plus it helped to distract him from his memories. Whenever he was in a diner all he could think about was his dad, who'd been gunned down in a similar kind of place. His pulse quickened as he glanced around the room, imagining how it might have played out all those years ago. Two stick-up kids barrelling though the front door, guns in hand. Screams from the diners as panic takes hold. Gunmen head for the till, teller reaches for the sky. His dad sees a chance, rises to his feet. Charges the gunmen from their blind side. They sense the attack, spin round and fire. Dad slumps to the floor.

'You OK there, sug?'

Hunter jumped at the sound of the waitress's voice. The raven-haired serving girl stood just behind him with a coquettish smile on her face.

'Yeah...I'm...fine,' he mumbled, wiping the sweat from his brow.

'Can I get you...anything?' she asked, giving his shoulder a gentle squeeze.

'Give me a minute?'

'Sure,' she murmured. 'And if you're still hungry after lunch, I get off at three.'

She walked off, wiggling her ass in his general direction. He admired the view for a few seconds then took a few deep breaths before rereading the menu for the umpteenth time. The salsicce with polenta sounded good. Or maybe the meatballs. Or maybe the waitress's ass. His stomach rumbled as he took a sip of coffee, then he winced at the sour taste and hoped that Carson's timekeeping didn't turn out to be as tardy as his appearance. There were few things he found more annoying than having to sit and go hungry while waiting for someone to arrive, especially when you were waiting on your own, although to be fair, he wasn't exactly on his own. Two gangbangers were sitting out in the car lot, presumably despatched by Furious to keep tabs on him.

He'd picked up the tail not long after he'd left the Mill Road Motel. Would have been kind of hard not to, though—they'd insisted on going bumper to bumper with him for most of the journey. He'd driven around for a while just to see how serious they were about following him, and while they obviously lacked any sort of rudimentary surveillance skills, they seemed serious enough. He'd recognised the big guy in the passenger seat as Slice, one of the higher-ranking Renegades, which presumably made the driver one of their foot soldiers. He checked his watch again, then rang Carson's cellphone, but all he got was his voicemail. Typical—never a cop around when you needed one. He rolled his eyes and came to a decision. So much for all this sitting around in a place filled with bad memories. Maybe it was time to go see what those bangers wanted.

With sniper scope pressed firmly to eye, Danilov watched Hunter throw down the menu and rise to his feet. This was it. He was coming out. Time to get in the zone. The assassin slowed his breathing to a snail's pace until his chest barely moved, giving him almost total control over his heart rate, then he focussed his mind, clearing it of distractions until all that was left was the connection between eye, finger and the trigger of the SIG Sauer 3000. As soon as Hunter disappeared from view, he traversed the rifle over to the diner's main entrance, snicked off the safety and readied himself for the kill shot.

Ten seconds, then twenty, then thirty passed, but the door remained shut. Doubts began to surface in his mind. Another half-minute ticked by before he was forced to acknowledge that something was amiss. He eased off the trigger. Where was Hunter? Maybe he'd gone back to the table? *Nyet*, the table was still empty. He checked the front door again. No change there. He decided to risk a quick sweep of the building. Nothing of note was visible on the street-facing side, and nothing untoward was happening on the near side. The fire door that served as an emergency exit to the car lot was closed, while the three windows dotted further along the wall were barely big enough for a child to wriggle through. But why would Hunter be looking to slip out unnoticed anyhow?

Unless he'd realised there was a bullet with his name on it sitting snug in the breach of a sniper rifle across the street. Impossible, snorted Danilov, no one spots me on their tail, not until it's too late.

Wait a minute. Was that fire door open maybe just a crack, or were his eyes deceiving him? He concentrated intently, looking for the slightest movement, the merest suggestion of activity, but when movement came, it was anything but slight. The door flew open and Hunter exploded out in a half-crouch to race across the gravel. Danilov fought the urge to loose off a round. Fast-moving targets were harder to hit. He swung his rifle around to reacquire the target. Hunter had come to rest against the rear bumper of the Dodge stationwagon he'd spotted earlier, which just so happened to provide excellent cover from any third-floor assassins situated on the other side of the street.

'Fuck your mother,' muttered the Russian. How had Hunter got wise to his presence? Now he had a decision to make—stay or go? Logic dictated that he should leave. The assassin's greatest weapon was the element of surprise, and once that was gone, the playing field took on a much more level appearance. The last thing he wanted to do was get embroiled in a firefight, because that would attract the cops, and once they showed up, making a clean getaway would become more of a challenge. But he did have the advantage of an elevated position, and he was blessed with far superior firepower—two factors that were not to be taken lightly. As he deliberated, his target broke cover and scurried out from behind the Dodge to dash over to a Ford pick-up in a half-crouch, leaving his head plainly visible above the truck's rear cargo area. All thoughts of retreat were instantly dismissed from his mind. Now was his chance. He eased down on the trigger and broke through the pull to send a lethal projectile arrowing straight towards Hunter's defenceless forehead.

CHAPTER THIRTY-TWO

REBECCA straightened her papers on the defence bench as she waited for the next witness to make his way to the stand. A shaft of sunlight fell through the skylight above to bathe her in a warming glow. Her confidence was on the rise. Although Ashton had been drunk out of his mind and driving a high-powered sports car when he'd killed a child, there was now a real chance she could get him off. The prosecution's main witnesses had backfired on them spectacularly. She'd always hoped to cast some doubt on the accuracy of the breathalyser test but Officer Williamson had made it a whole lot easier than expected. And when the barman had changed his story to exonerate Ashton, well, that had been nothing short of heaven sent. On second thoughts, maybe the wealth of Ashton's father had more to do with it than some higher power, but the effect was much the same.

So now it was time for Rebecca to show the jury her softer, caring side, while she questioned her own key witness. Walter Polson—a down on his luck vagrant who'd miraculously stepped forward at the eleventh hour to cast doubt on the veracity of the prosecution's claims. For a street bum, Walter looked pretty swell. Nice blue Brooks Brothers suit, shiny leather brogues, crisp dress shirt, and to top it all off he'd been freshly shaved and given a sharp new haircut. Amazing how a day in court brought out the best in some people.

'Mr Polson,' she began, 'can you remember where you were on the afternoon of the 14th of June?'

The old fella straightened up in the witness box and answered in a loud, clear voice. 'Of course. I was on the corner…of Rodeo and Olympic…taking a walk. It was a nice day…I remember it well.' His delivery was so stilted he may as well have been reading from an autocue.

'And were you present at the time of the automobile accident involving Mr Robert Ashton and Manuel Ortega?'

'I certainly was.' He nodded to the court. The old guy was doing well—she'd told him to keep his answers simple, as that way there was less chance of him becoming flustered and making a mistake.

'And did you have a good vantage point from which to view the accident?' she continued.

'Yep.'

'Is your eyesight good, Mr Polson?'

'Yep—twenty-twenty. I could read the writing off that girl's T-shirt in the back row if you'd like?'

'That won't be necessary, sir. If you remember, you sat an eye test for me just last week. I have the results here, and you passed with flying colours. If opposing counsel has no objections, defence would like to admit them as exhibit nineteen, Your

Honour,' said Rebecca, holding up a sheet of paper. The judge nodded. 'Could you now describe the accident, Mr Polson?'

'Well, I noticed Mr Ashton's car first, as it was such a nice vehicle, all sleek and classy looking. He was driving down the street at a fairly gentle speed, doing nothing wrong at all, when a young lad suddenly dashed right out in front of him. Came out of nowhere.'

'When you say out of nowhere, where exactly was that, Mr Polson?'

'Right off the sidewalk. The kid ran out from between two parked cars. Mr Ashton tried to avoid him, ended up swerving across the other side of the road, but he never stood a chance. Poor kid went up in the air like he'd been shot out of a cannon.'

There were a few cries of pain from the Ortega family at that. Rebecca gave Polson a withering look. This was no time for theatrics.

'So, in your considered opinion, Mr Ashton did all that he could to avoid hitting Manuel Ortega?'

'Yes, ma'am, he certainly did. It wasn't his fault. The whole thing was just a terrible accident,' he said, clasping his hands together in front of him as if in prayer, inadvertently revealing he had a chunky new Rolex strapped to his wrist.

'Thank you, Mr Polson. No further questions, Your Honour.' Rebecca felt another small rush of triumph. This was going great. When she turned to go back to her seat she found that the whole Ortega clan were staring daggers at her. She kept her face neutral and looked quickly away.

CHAPTER THIRTY-THREE

Now that Hunter was outside the diner, thoughts of his father's violent death had started to fade. He worked his way along the side of the pick-up truck at a snail's pace, using slow and steady footsteps to mask the noise of his boots on the gravel. He was coming up on the Humvee from behind, which in his experience was generally the safest way to approach two trigger-happy gangbangers, who thus far remained oblivious to his presence. The Humvee was huge—a real brute of a vehicle. Compared to the other cars in the lot it looked like a small tank. Slice and his henchman were chilling out, passing a brown bottle back and forth, taking major-league slugs from whatever alcoholic beverage was hidden within. In all his years on the force, Hunter had never seen a stakeout that looked anything like this. He took another step forward, marvelling at the two men's total disregard for surveillance etiquette, when—*Boom!*—the next track on the car stereo cut in. Ice Cube, an oldie—'When Will They Shoot?'

The popularity of Adriana's diner meant that there were plenty of cars parked out in the lot, which made it a relatively easy task to approach the Renegades without being seen, although he quietly loosed the clasp on his shoulder holster anyhow. He may have just been popping over for a friendly chat, but some people only understood the most basic forms of communication. The Humvee and its gangsta-rap-loving occupants were now just ten yards away. He kept his eyes fixed firmly on the backs of their heads, both of which were bobbing in perfect synch to the heavy bass. Slice took another long pull on the bottle then held it aloft and shook it from side to side. Hunter's sixth sense kicked in. What happened next happened quickly.

He threw himself forward just as Slice turned to lob the bottle onto the rear seat. Pain flared as he wrenched his right ankle in a pothole. A low sonic boom accompanied his swan dive, then the sound of shattering glass added a sweet tinkle to proceedings as the truck's cab window blew out overhead. The wind was forced from his lungs in a sudden whoosh as he made hard contact with the ground, and the fact that someone was firing a high-powered sniper rifle at him had barely had time to register before three more low booms intruded on his thoughts, each bullet puncturing the pick-up's flimsy side panel to whistle just inches overhead. He hugged the dirt, his mind racing. His ankle was on fire, his knee throbbed painfully, and his hands stung from a tiny thousand pinpricks, but other than that he was OK. But for how much longer? Because one thing was for sure—he was pinned down behind some pretty poor cover, and whoever was firing at him meant business.

So he was faced with a choice. He could either hunker down and try to dodge the bullets, or he could risk all by making a break for it. Neither option was particularly attractive. There seemed little doubt that the guy taking pot shots at him was the same stone-cold killer that had left a slew of unsolved executions in his wake, so coming out from behind the pick-up would probably amount to little more than suicide. Besides, there was nowhere to run—the fire door that led back into the diner had swung shut—but staying put and leaving everything to chance wasn't exactly his style. He tugged his Beretta free of its holster and loosed off the safety as another projectile whined dangerously close overhead. Nothing else for it. Time for Hunter's last stand. He pushed one hand into the dirt and tensed his muscles to spring upwards, but before he could make a move, a pair of automatic weapons roared to life.

'What the fuck?' he yelled, hugging the ground once again, only to realise that he wasn't under attack. He slithered towards the front of the truck to find out what was going on, but the truth dawned on him before he'd made it clear of the tyre arch. The Renegades. No self-respecting gangbanger was going to sit around and ignore a good old-fashioned firefight. He risked a peek across the lot and, sure enough, Slice and his buddy had exited their Humvee to shoot wildly at some hotel on the other side of the street.

As Hunter watched, Slice's partner got so caught up in the moment that he started to walk forward, seemingly labouring under the misconception that his very presence would be enough to scare off whoever was firing from on high. Big mistake. A sniper bullet caught him in mid-stride, blowing the top half of his head clean off, spraypainting the gravel with an interesting mix of blood, bone and brain. The banger's lifeless body managed one more step before it fell to the ground in a crumpled heap, where it would remain for the next couple of hours as a reminder to any passing kids to stay in school. Having witnessed the demise of his companion, Slice redoubled his efforts to shoot holes in the hotel, albeit from the relatively safety of behind the Humvee. The big guy wasn't stupid. Hunter scanned the windows across the street for signs of life and awaited his chance.

Danilov disassembled the sniper rifle and stashed it back inside the confines of its carry case. He'd already lingered way too long, as his desire to halt Hunter's troublesome investigation had encouraged him to spend a few extra seconds at the window in the hope that another clear shot would present itself. That, and the fact that his professional pride had taken a hit. Hunter had made him miss, and missing wasn't something that he was overly accustomed to. As soon as he had time, he was going to take the rifle apart down to its last screw and spring, check for signs of metal fatigue, then steam-clean the trigger mechanism thoroughly.

He collected the spent shell casings, slipped on his fedora, and hurried out of the hotel room. Hunter must have the gods on his side. The ex-cop's head had been right in the centre of the scope, but just as he'd pulled the trigger, his target had dived forward and disappeared from view. He'd known that he'd missed before the bullet had even left the barrel, but there was precious little he'd been able to do about it except flick the bolt, ram home another .308, shoot at the vehicle, then repeat the process, all the while praying that one of the projectiles would find its mark.

He took the stairs two at a time. The cops would be here soon. How the hell had he missed those two gangbangers? He shook his head as he entered the lobby. They'd been sitting in a Humvee on the far side of the lot and he'd barely registered their presence as he'd been concentrating too hard on the primary target—a mistake he'd made in his youth. Back on the cold streets of Moscow, he'd been so devoted to dispensing death that events on the periphery had sometimes passed him by. How galling that he should choose today of all days to fall back into bad habits.

The double doors that led to the hotel kitchens were up ahead. He pushed through them without pause and realised that he was vaguely annoyed. It wasn't often he left the scene of a hit empty handed. Wasn't ever, in fact. Although he could argue that one confirmed kill was better than no kill at all. He allowed himself a cold smile. That banger's head had exploded like a ripe watermelon. Not that it counted for anything. Little more than a waste of a bullet. His smile faded away. He had failed—Hunter was still alive. His arms tensed as he dodged around a surprised chef who was busy chopping fresh basil with a gleaming nine-inch blade.

'Hey! What da hell you doing?' shouted an Italian-sounding voice from the far end of the kitchen. He ignored it and pressed on. The back door stood open before him, wedged in place by an empty trashcan. He barrelled through and emerged in a deserted side alley. Exactly two minutes and twenty seconds had elapsed since he'd packed away the rifle. To turn right was to head back to the main street, so he went left, making his escape via a quiet route that he'd checked out earlier. As he strode off into the shadows, the sound of multiple police sirens began to swell up behind him.

CHAPTER THIRTY-FOUR

'WILL the foreman of the jury please rise?'

The courtroom went deathly silent as a well-groomed man sporting a neat suit and tie combo rose from his seat in the jury box. He stiffened when he realised that all attention was focussed solely in his direction, brushed himself down, then tried to avoid returning any of the stares that were arrowed his way.

'Has the jury reached a verdict?' asked the judge in his most sombre tone.

The foreman cleared his throat before responding; 'Yes… Your Honour.' The first word came out slightly squeaky, the second two more sonorous as he over-compensated.

'On the charge of vehicular manslaughter, how does the jury find the defendant?'

Rebecca felt herself tense. This was it. This was why she worked her butt off. This was why she pulled all those long hours at the office then left for home burdened down with case files that she'd stare at well into the small hours of the morning until the words became little more than a meaningless jumble of letters on the page. This was why she didn't have a social life. This was why her sister's face was the only one she ever saw on the other side of the breakfast table. In short, this was why she made sacrifices. Sacrifices she didn't begrudge for a second. All the weeks of hard work she'd put in on the Ashton case came down to this one moment.

Moments like this were why she'd become a defence lawyer. She watched Ashton out of the corner of her eye. He sat ramrod straight in his chair, looking resplendent in his Hugo Boss suit while glowering defiantly at the foreman of the jury, as if daring him to deliver a guilty verdict. Her client certainly appeared confident enough. Then she noticed the tell-tale bead of sweat that glistened on his upper lip. Maybe he'd finally realised that there might come a day when even Daddy's millions wouldn't bail him out.

The foreman cast his eyes to the floor as he delivered the verdict.

'We find the defendant not guilty, Your Honour.'

For a second there was silence, then Manuel Ortega's mother let loose a shriek of pure anguish. At the other end of the reaction spectrum was the now at-liberty Bobby Ashton, who leapt out of his chair to punch the air in delight, his cool-as-a-cucumber façade falling away to reveal the nerves he'd kept hidden deep within. A hundred voices rose as one, the words becoming lost in the general ruckus, though you could tell from the tone that the mood was ugly—one thing was for sure, there weren't too many people in the courtroom that were happy with the decision.

'Goddamn you! You're gonna pay! You're gonna pay for what'chu did to my little boy!'

The sight of Ashton in celebratory mode was too much for Mr Ortega to bear. The father of the deceased was now straddling the railing at the front of the viewing gallery, desperate to get to his son's killer. Two court officials were trying to restrain him, and they were having one hell of a time as Ortega senior was a heavy-set guy with broad shoulders and bunched muscles, the sort of muscles you got from putting in long shifts on a construction site. His eyes had taken on a demonic glow, and veins popped furiously in his forehead. In the face of such righteous anger Ashton had stopped celebrating to retreat to the far side of the defence table, and he was right to be scared. Mr Ortega would probably have torn the young playboy limb from limb given half a chance.

Other members of the clan leapt up to follow their patriarch's lead, but just as it looked as though the court officials would be overwhelmed, reinforcements arrived. Scuffles broke out between the grieving family members and the strong arm of the law, punches were thrown, batons were drawn, and all the while old Judge Wharton banged away on his gavel, demanding that order was restored.

'*Puto!* Murderer! Cocksucka!'

Furious cries emanated from the throng as drops of blood started to sully the scuffed tiled floor. Rebecca grimaced. If this continued, someone was going to get hurt. She grabbed Ashton by the hand and half dragged him across the room to the door that nestled inconspicuously on the back wall.

'Das right, Ashton, run you muthafuck, but one day we gonna find you!' Ortega senior bellowed after them.

Rebecca pushed her client into the judge's chambers, but before she could close the door, he turned back and surprised her.

'Thanks,' he muttered. In all the time they'd spent together, it was the first time he'd ever been gracious.

'I'm not doing it for you,' she snarled, shoving him away

and slamming the door in his face. She took a deep breath then turned to confront the Ortegas, whose struggle to reach the front of the court had started to abate now that the object of their wrath had been hustled from sight.

'He's gone,' she began in a conciliatory tone, 'so why don't we all try and calm down—this isn't helping anyone. I'm sorry for your loss, I truly am, but nothing you do will ever bring your son back.'

An uneasy truce developed between family members and court officials as the two fighting factions disengaged to leave a no-man's-land of little more than a yard between them. After sucking down a few deep breaths, Ortega senior was the first to speak. His voice was sombre and tinged with bitterness.

'We came for justice, lady, but what did we get? That scum is walking out of here a free man, back to his fancy car, fancy home, fancy life, while our little Manuel is cold and alone six feet underground. You call that justice?'

'Everything occurred as it should, Mr Ortega. Evidence was studied, witnesses came forward, the jury made their decision. Due process was followed, protocol was obeyed. It was a fair trial.'

'But was it justice, Miss Finch?' he asked bitterly, 'Was it *justice*? I don't think so. It was a travesty. An abomination. And you played your part in it.' He pointed a stubby finger straight at her. 'You helped him hide from the truth. You helped him escape. How'd you live with yourself? How'd you look in the mirror?' he asked with a slow shake of his head, seemingly stupefied.

Before Rebecca could answer, the throng parted to allow Mrs Ortega to walk forward at funeral-procession pace. She was dressed all in black, her long dark hair pulled back in a tight bunch, her eyes only just visible behind a heavy veil. She walked right up to the railing, one heavy footstep after another, until she was little more than three feet from Rebecca, then she paused and studied the younger woman with a sad regard.

Rebecca had no words for her, no legal terms to hide behind, no explanations, no crumbs of comfort from one woman to another. Now was neither the time nor the place for empty talk, so instead she waited, holding the mother's gaze, readying herself for another verbal onslaught. The seconds ticked by as everyone waited for something, anything, to happen. And then it did. Mrs Ortega spat directly into her face, then turned and walked out of the courtroom.

CHAPTER THIRTY-FIVE

Now that the altercation was over, Hunter had gone back inside the diner, as it was a whole lot safer than hanging around outside. No one seemed to be paying him much attention. Either the sound of the gunfight hadn't made it through the walls, or the patrons considered it none of their business. Before he'd returned, he'd offered his tail cum guardian angel a quiet word of thanks, which Slice had accepted with a shrug. Participating in shootouts was no big deal for a gangbanger.

Hunter had ditched his sour cup of coffee for a hefty shot of ten-year-old cognac, which the waitress had delivered with a cute smile, no doubt hoping he'd turn out to be a big spender. The cognac was smooth on his tongue and warm in his belly. When it came to soothing the nerves, nothing hit the spot quite like a drop of Hennessy and, boy, did his nerves need soothing.

Although he'd come under fire on more than one occasion in his somewhat colourful past, it had never been at the hands of a world-class sniper, and the experience hadn't been one he'd found overly enjoyable. The worst thing had been the feeling of helplessness. The sniper could see him, but he couldn't see the sniper. Pinned down, with nowhere to go, just waiting for the bullet that would turn out the lights. From start to finish, the entire episode had lasted for less than a minute, but it had felt like a whole lot longer. He'd been scared as he hunkered behind the pick-up truck, and he wasn't ashamed to admit it. Fear was healthy—a built-in survival mechanism that kept you alert. The important thing was how you dealt with it. You had to stay calm and channel the adrenaline rush into action.

As he took another sip of cognac, he vowed to himself that from this day on, he was going to do his level best to keep on the good side of any snipers he had the misfortune to run into, notwithstanding the one that had just tried to kill him—for that guy, he was willing to make an exception. He shifted position in his seat and winced as another explosion of pain shot through his ankle. The damn thing was twisted up good. On the walk back from the lot he'd discovered that it would just about bear his weight, but any kind of lateral movement was out of the question. Son of a bitch. The last thing he needed was an injury now that he'd made it to the top of the assassin's shit list. Still, at least his investigation into the string of unsolved killings was getting close enough to prompt a response. First there'd been the warning note back at his house, free tranquilliser shot included, and now this. The assassin was definitely rattled.

When Hunter had been with the department, he'd made it a personal goal to piss off as many bad guys as possible. The best way to judge a detective was to take a headcount of his enemies. Forget all that bi-monthly appraisal bullshit—if you wanted to find the star performer, just look for the cop with the highest street bounty on his head. Law enforcement wasn't a popularity contest, despite what the politicos would have you believe. And now that he was working freelance, he'd managed to piss off a serial assassin. He cracked a grin. It was nice to know he hadn't lost his touch.

He looked up as a familiar bout of violent coughing signalled Carson's arrival.

'Whoa there, oldtimer, sounds like you're trying to hack up your innards. Much more of that and your upcoming retirement might come earlier than expected.'

'Won't be as early as yours… Just give me a second…' spluttered Carson, as his police radio started to squawk. He retrieved it from his jacket pocket and pushed the respond button.

'Yep… Uh-huh… Oh, for Chrissakes, I'm busy. I told you you'd get that report in the morning, and that's when you'll get it. Now, go back to arranging paper clips or sticking your dick in the pencil sharpener, or whatever it is you people do…'

He cut the communication short and pocketed the radio. 'Goddamn desk jockeys down at Parker Center—never give me a moment's peace… Now, what gives?' he asked, taking a seat.

'What gives? Where the hell have you been? I've been trying to get hold of you for the best part of an hour.'

'Been busy. Some of us still have paying jobs. What's your problem? Can't sit around and kill a little time?'

'Kill a little time? You're shitting me—the only thing around these parts that almost got killed was me.'

'You run into some trouble?'

'You could say that. The assassin showed up and started taking pot shots at me with a high-powered rifle.'

'You nail him?

'Nail him? I never even saw him. I was too busy trying to bury myself in the dirt to even think about returning fire. If it hadn't been for a couple of trigger-happy Renegades I'd have been in deep shit. You might want to get a forensics team over to the Excelsior.' Hunter gestured to the hotel on the other side of the street. 'Our guy was set up in one of the street-facing rooms.'

'I'll get right on it. But don't hold your breath. He's never left any evidence behind before. Hey, wait a minute—did you say that some Renegades bailed you out? You gone and made yourself some new friends?'

'Something like that. Guess they must have warmed to my sunny disposition.'

'Humph,' snorted Carson. 'Can't see it myself. But the bottom line is you're OK?'

'Yeah, for now, but that's the second time the Russian's had the drop on me and you can bet your ass I won't survive a third. Come to think of it, you'd best watch your back as well, cos if he knows about me then it stands to reason that sooner or later he's going to find out about you.'

'I'm not sweating it. It'd be suicide for the guy to take out an active cop—a move like that would bring half the force down on his head.'

'Yeah, well, consider yourself warned. I'm starting to get the feeling that if we don't get him soon then he's gonna get us. This guy's playing for keeps. Anyhow, where are those damn files you promised me?'

'Forget about them—there's been a development. While you were playing hide and seek with our elusive friend, I was busy doing some grade-A detective work. I spread the word around a few of my sources, told 'em I was on the lookout for a tall, white Russian that was shy one pinky finger with a hammer tattoo on the back of his hand, and whaddya know, I finally turned up a lead. A guy answering that description is a regular at Witchcraft, an old-style piano bar just off Sunset.'

Hunter felt a burst of excitement course through his veins. 'How good's your snitch?'

'Solid gold. I got a real nice feeling about this one.'

'So how do we play it?'

'I say we go stake out the place tonight and see if anyone that looks like our boy shows up. Assuming you're game?'

'Just try and stop me. It'll make a refreshing change to be the hunter instead of the hunted.'

'Yeah—maybe you can start living up to your name. There's a parking garage opposite Witchcraft that'll make a great place for a stakeout. Meet me on the roof at 7 p.m. It's time we put this case to bed.'

Hunter nodded in agreement. His heart rate was up, his nerves were tingling. The assassin had just tried to kill him, but soon the tables would be turned. With a little bit of luck, tonight was gonna be all about payback.

'For chrissakes, have some more wine and get over it. We got what we wanted,' said a voice from the shadows.

Rebecca sat alone at the kitchen table. Her black Prada suit hung loosely off her shoulders, and thin trails of mascara ran from the corners of her eyes. The mood was sombre; the lights dialled way down low. She'd been dead to the world ever since she'd returned from the courthouse, musing on the terrible loss the Ortega family had suffered. For some plaintiffs a not-guilty verdict turned out to be the final straw—she'd seen ordinary people destroyed by a trial on more than one occasion. Shell-shocked individuals who'd come looking for answers, hoping that the legal system would go some way to right the wrong that had been done to them, only to be let down at the final hurdle. What these people had needed was a sense of closure, but all they'd got had been a sense of despair. The world could be a cruel place.

She reached across the table for the bottle of Rioja. The wine hailed from north central Spain by way of her local supermarket. According to the advertising blurb on the label it was a cheeky little number with the ability to light up any occasion, but thus far it had done little to improve her mood. She took another gulp. Maybe she just hadn't drunk enough yet.

'You were doing your job. The jury made the decision to let Ashton walk free, not you. The Ortega family are pissed, but they'll get over it. And so will you.'

Anabeth didn't have much time for self-pity. Ironic really. If anyone had the right to moan about the hand they'd been dealt it was her, but she'd never once complained. Rebecca smiled wistfully as she took another sip of the wine.

'There, that's better—if I'm not mistaken, that was almost a smile,' goaded her sister. 'Knock back another glass and you might be back to normal, or at least what passes for normal in your case.'

'Very funny,' Rebecca muttered, although she appreciated what Anabeth was trying to do. They'd been through this situation a few times before. Every now and again a case would hit home harder than the others, and each time it would take her a couple of days to snap out of her funk. It wasn't easy knowing that you'd just played your part in helping a guilty man walk free, it wasn't easy at all. Particularly when that guilty man was a spoilt brat like Bobby Ashton, a guy with fewer redeeming qualities than a sewer rat and all the moral fibre of a stick of wet celery. But when it came down to it, she was just doing her job.

'Get much painting done today?' she asked, gesturing at the half-finished canvas of interlocking monochrome circles that had been relocated from the living room. 'This one seems to be taking for ever…'

'You can't rush great art. Anyway, you must be famished…

Why don't we call out for pizza? I'll bet you haven't eaten in hours.'

'I could use some food,' Rebecca allowed, heading for the kitchen counter. She raised the cordless phone from its cradle, tapped in a number from memory, then held the receiver to her ear.

'What the...?' A confused look crossed her face. 'Phone's dead,' she muttered, after repeating the process.

'Try your cell.'

'It's on charge in the bedroom. I'll go get it...'

But before she could move the door crashed open as two masked men burst into the kitchen. One held a snub-nosed revolver while the other carried a length of electrical wire. Both were dressed in black jeans and crew-neck sweaters. The room went silent for a moment, then Rebecca let loose a piercing scream, just as the leader of the two men yelled, 'Don' make a sound, don' make a sound!' in a frighteningly familiar voice.

'Get out of our house!' Anabeth yelled. 'Get the fuck out now!' The two intruders completely ignored her.

'Rico...go take care of her...quick!' ordered the gunman, prompting his partner to stride across the room with electrical wire at the ready.

'Leave my sister alone!' shouted Rebecca, jumping forward. She managed three steps before the butt of the gun crashed down on her temple, bringing her forward progress to a sudden halt. She tottered on the spot, then her eyes rolled back in her head as she slumped unconscious to the floor.

'That bitch is loco,' said Rico, staring down at Rebecca's prone body.

CHAPTER THIRTY-SIX

'NICE spot.' Hunter nodded. It didn't get much better than this for a stakeout.

'Glad you approve,' muttered Carson.

The two men were sat on the top floor of a parking garage, their eyes trained on the building opposite. Witchcraft—the piano bar frequented by the Russian assassin. About fifty yards below them was the bar's main entrance, while off to the right was a small side door that opened out onto the parking lot, where three cars, a white Toyota Supra, a Chrysler LeBaron and a dark green Jeep Cherokee, were parked. Witchcraft was on Hacienda, just a stone's throw away from the scene on Sunset Strip, although it was light years away in style. The only access was via the front of the property, and the road was clear in both directions. Perfect. Now all they had to do was wait for the assassin to show up.

'I used this spot once before, years ago, back when the bar used to be a meat-packing plant that doubled as a front for the Mob,' Carson reminisced, resting his Leupold binoculars on the sidewall to light up a Cuban. 'Sat up here every night for two weeks straight, bang in the middle of winter. Talk about a laugh a minute.'

'The Mob using a meat-packing plant as cover? Bit of a cliché.' Hunter rolled his eyes and leant back in one of the detective's fold-away chairs. Finally, a chance to rest his injured ankle.

'Back then, half the meat trade in the city was run by guys called Sal or Vinnie. Those Eye-talians…no imagination.'

'Your snitch give you any idea what time the assassin might arrive?'

'Nope—we're just gonna have to sit tight.'

Hunter groaned.

'Don't worry, son, you're in the hands of a master. I learnt the art of patience when I was an itty-bitty kid back in DC, sat out on the Potomac with my pa, waiting for a fish to bite. Hell, I remember this one time—'

'Spare me,' interrupted Hunter. 'Enough already with the recollections. Let's focus on the job at hand.'

He turned his attention back to Witchcraft. An ornately carved sign bearing the bar's name hung over the double glass doors that served as its entrance. The sign was lit up with some subtle spotlighting—no garish neon here—the joint looked kinda classy. Four large picture windows, two on either side of the doors, added to the feeling of quiet opulence. The heavy velvet drapes that hung in the windows were pulled back to reveal circular booths, and inside each booth was a highly polished mahogany table. It was the sort of place that was members only, with a waiting list a mile long. No membership, no admittance—the two heavy-set goons stationed either side of the entrance made sure of that.

'Fancy a snort?' asked Carson, dangling a small pewter hip flask under Hunter's nose. 'It'll help keep the cold out.'

'Don't mind if I do.' It wasn't much fun being stuck on a garage roof while looking down on a place of such warm refinement. The flask contained whisky, probably single malt, and it was way better than coffee and doughnuts any day. 'So where's the back-up?'

'You're it,' said Carson, taking back his flask.

'You flouting authority again, Detective? Standard operating procedure dictates you should have additional manpower when apprehending a dangerous suspect. Not that I'm too disappointed, mind. I was kinda hoping for first crack at him.'

'Get in line, buddy,' the older man snorted. 'I've been on this guy's ass for months, and that means I'm gonna be the one to take him down.'

'You might have been working this case for a while, but I was the one that got shot at, and that gives me equal claim. Plus when he killed Montero, he stole my chance to avenge seven dead kids.'

The conversation paused as Carson was hit by a burst of violent coughing. After thirty seconds of what sounded like someone trying to hack up their small intestines, he spat out a shiny globule of blood and phlegm then wheezed for breath.

'Jesus!' exclaimed Hunter. 'You seen anyone about that cough?'

'There's no cure for old age, son,' spluttered the detective, wiping his chin on the back of his sleeve.

'Maybe you should cut back on the cigars?'

'And maybe you should mind your own goddamned business. Anyhow, about that back-up. I thought I'd make sure it's our boy before calling in the cavalry. I'd look kinda stupid if

I dragged a SWAT team all the way down here to arrest nothing more than a bunch of martini-sipping Sinatra fans.'

'Your call. I'm just along for the ride—a concerned citizen doing his bit to keep the streets safe. You're the one that stands to lose his pension if things turn to shit.'

'Big deal,' muttered Carson. It looked like a healthy retirement fund wasn't top of his list of priorities.

The two men lapsed into silence as they stared at the entrance to Witchcraft. It was early evening, around 7 p.m., and the flow of customers was little more than a trickle. As the minutes ticked by Hunter found himself thinking about the brief conversation he'd had with Slice outside Adriana's diner. While there was no disputing the banger's violent tendencies, it was clear that he had a pretty sharp brain hidden under his natty dreadlocks. It was a damn shame when a guy like that ended up running with a street gang—he had so much more to offer. Still, it was no great surprise. A hustler's lifestyle looked pretty sweet to a ghetto kid—fast cars, fast women, easy money. When the only other employment on offer was minimum wage at McDonald's, you could see why so many fell victim to temptation. Hunter checked his watch. Thirty minutes had elapsed without a single customer entering Witchcraft.

'Man, we could be stuck up here all night,' he said.

'Yeah, you've got a point,' replied Carson, as he rose to his feet and arched his back. 'Maybe I should head on down for a closer look.'

'Eh?'

'For all we know, this assassin might have started his evening early. Say he's already inside, we're gonna be sat out here for hours waiting for him to reappear. The blood could freeze in my veins by then. I figure I'll go down, have a nose around and see if there's anyone that fits the description.'

Hunter gave incredulous. 'You're shitting me?'

'Where's the harm? I'll only be a couple of minutes.'

'Where's the harm? What if he sees you first and makes you for a cop? You could blow everything as soon as you put one foot inside the place.'

'Ain't gonna happen.' Carson shrugged. 'A face like mine hardly screams law and order.' The old man had a point. With all those busted red corpuscles under his eyes he looked more like a career wino than someone who was paid to protect and to serve.

'Well, if you're going in, I'm coming with you.'

'No dice, son. I need you up here to let me know if he enters from the street and, besides, he's already seen your face on at least two occasions, so there's no way you can go anywhere near him. You got your cellphone?'

Hunter nodded.

'OK. We'll keep the line open, then that way I can give you a running commentary on what I see. Soon as I find our guy's not there, I'll come back up.'

'Just make it quick,' said Hunter, conceding defeat. This sure as hell wasn't standard surveillance procedure but, then, Carson wasn't a standard sort of cop.

CHAPTER THIRTY-SEVEN

REBECCA got a big dose of déjà vu when she came around in the back of the white panel truck for the second time in the space of a few days. The same cold hard floor, the same engine drone, the same rocking motion. Her wrists were tied tight behind her back, her mouth was gagged with a sour-tasting piece of cloth and her head thudded painfully as a result of its recent collision with a gun, but other than that she was OK—at least in the physical sense—although she was more scared than she'd ever been in her entire life.

She tried to calm down and think things through. First and foremost, she was still alive. If they hadn't killed her yet, maybe they didn't plan on killing her at all. She flexed her wrists against the bonds but there was no give in them. Whoever had tied her up had known what they were doing. If there was no chance of escape then she'd have to talk her way out, but that wasn't going to be easy—she'd been gagged. How was she going to convince her captor to grant her the gift of speech? She took a couple of slow, deep breaths to compose herself, opened her eyes and shuffled into a sitting position.

'So…you awake!'

It was the same Latin American voice, but something told her that this time she wasn't going to get off with just a warning.

'You know why you here, eh? Course you know. Man, you one dumb bitch. I tole you what would happen if you helped keep dat cocksucka out of jail, I tole you, didn't I? But you didn't listen, and now you gonna pay da price.'

The masked man reached for a battered rucksack. Rebecca tried to speak, but all that came out were a collection of grunts.

'Yeah, das right, you keep on talkin', jus like you did in court. Talkin', talkin', talkin', and every word a goddamned lie! You nuthin' but a whore, a dirty, no-good whore—takin' dat rich boy's money to help him hide from justice. Well, he ain't gonna be hidin' much longer. Cocksucka thinkin' he's so special—I got news for him. He pull his pants on one leg at a time, just like da rest of us, an he gonna suffer, just like we all suffer, when I catch up with him. And you? Well, you gotta pay too…'

Rebecca's eyes widened as her captor pulled a bottle of rotgut whisky out of the rucksack, along with a small foil wrap.

'I bet you worried about dat sister of yours right about now, hey?' he continued. 'Dat's good. Worryin' about your *familia*. Dat's what's important. Lookin' out for your own. It's why we're here. Someone gots to look after da memory of Manuel. Someone gots to make sure justice is done, and dat someone might as well be me. And don't you be worryin' 'bout your sister. We never touched her. She gonna be fine. Dat's da difference between us—we not animals. We got *values*. But you…' He shook his head slowly. 'You help an evil man to escape. Makes you no better than him. No better at all.'

Rebecca's heart was racing. She knew that if she could only talk to this man, spend just five minutes explaining everything to him, then she'd have a shot, but it didn't look like she was going to get the chance. She made one last attempt to command his attention, giving him a beseeching stare as she coughed out some garbled words, but it was to no avail—her captor didn't want to know.

'First of all, we gotta mess you up a bit…' She tried to sway back as he leant in close, but there was nowhere to go. 'Let's start with the hair…' His breath was hot against the side of her face and it reeked of spicy food. As his hands reached out she threw a kick at him, landing a solid blow to his shins that elicited a grunt of pain.

'Bitch!' he cried, as he grabbed her by the shoulders and slammed her down to the floor of the truck, then locked her in place with a knee to her sternum. 'Now let's see you move…' Her skin crawled as his rough, callused hands first tugged at her hair, then rubbed at her face to smear her make-up.

'There, dat's better,' he said, leaning back to admire his handiwork. What the hell was all this about? Call her an optimist, but it didn't feel sexual, despite the fact that his knee continued to press hard between her breasts. 'Now you gonna have a little drink…'

He retrieved the whisky and broke the seal. She tossed her head from side to side as the neck of the bottle approached, but he grabbed her jaw and held it steady. The amber liquid splashed onto her face, soaking the gag with its sharp taste.

'Hold still…' he ordered, as he slopped some more cheap

booze down the front of her blouse, causing the fabric to cling to her skin. 'Now we get da party started…'

He unwrapped the small foil package to reveal its contents—a shiny new syringe along with an ampoule of dull white solution. Her heart sank. He was going to make her OD!

'You better keep still, lady…'

He ripped the right sleeve of her silk blouse and took a firm grip of her arm. She watched in despair as the tip of the needle punctured her skin and slipped easily into a vein. As he depressed the plunger, she howled in terror.

CHAPTER THIRTY-EIGHT

'OK…I'M crossing the street…you see me from up there?' Carson's gruff voice came through loud and clear on the cellphone.

'You're pretty hard to miss,' said Hunter as he watched the detective amble towards the front of Witchcraft. 'How about picking up the pace a little, Pops? The sooner you get this done the better.'

'Give an old man a chance. Takes me a while to get going these days. Hang on, let me talk my way past these bouncers.'

The sun had all but disappeared over the horizon, helping the two burly men on the door to cast a pair of imposing shadows halfway down the street. Hunter listened in on the open line as Carson explained that, no, he wasn't a member of the private club but, yes, he was a cop, and if he didn't gain access to the joint in precisely five seconds he'd have it shut down on suspicion of underage drinking, facilitation of prostitution, or maybe even harbouring an untuned grand piano—the bouncers could take their pick. They waved him straight through. Even the hired muscle knew not to upset a crotchety old lawman.

'So what do you see?' asked Hunter, his heart rate quickening.

'Coat-check girl…pretty little thing…'

'Stop messing around and hurry up.'

'Right…I'm in the main lounge area,' Carson said in a hushed voice. 'There's a long bar over by the back wall, plus a lot of tables and chairs dotted around the place. Lighting's dialled way down low, and right in the middle of the room they've got a grand piano… Hey, the guy that's playing is pretty good. You want a listen?'

The strains of an instrumental version of 'Strangers in the Night' suddenly grew in volume. Goddamn it! This was no time for goofing around.

Carson came back on the line. 'Nice, huh? You like Francis Albert?'

'Some other time. Who's there? Anyone that looks like our boy?'

'Hey, wait up. Let me get myself a drink—it'll help me blend in. 'Less you want me to just walk around eyeballing everyone in the joint? I wouldn't advise it, though, as it might look kinda suspicious,' he muttered. 'Hey, barkeep? Whisky on the rocks. Old Fitzgerald. Make it a double. And get one for yourself. I hate drinking alone.'

'Boozing on the job, Detective. Whatever would your captain say?'

'He'd probably tell me to write it up and file a report. OK…I've got myself a seat at one end of the bar and from here I can pretty much see everyone in the place. Hmm…'

'What? What do you see? Is it him?'

'Nah…cool your horses. At the other end of the bar there's a couple of silver-haired gents, all dressed up for a night on the tiles, but I'm sorry to say that neither one of 'em looks like our Russian. Got a few people sitting over by the piano, couple of tables, one home to a sweet young couple, the other housing a lone female, and believe me, buddy, it's no accident she's alone—she's gotta weigh at least three hundred pounds and she's downing margaritas like Prohibition's about to make a comeback. And for the grand finale we got a bunch of young guys over on the far side, stockbroker types, all suited and booted, probably celebrating another killing on the Dow.' A tinge of contempt crept into his voice. 'Fucking creeps. I'd like to haul them all in just for pissing me off. But as far as the Russian goes, it looks like we struck out.'

'So far.'

'Yeah, so far,' Carson allowed. 'I'm gonna take a leak then I'll be straight back up.'

'Hurry the hell up, will you? I'm stuck up here on a cold roof while you're knocking back shots in a warm bar. Hope you enjoyed your whisky…'

'Like a duck enjoys water.' The sound of the piano slowly faded as Carson made his way to the john. 'A day doesn't go by that I don't treat myself to a drop of Old Fitzgerald. Call it my last remaining vice. Anyhow, this is Carson signing off as he enters the can…' Hunter heard a heavy door creak open. ''Less you want a running commentary while I take a piss? Hey…wait a minute… Take it easy…back the fuck up…'

There was a sudden clunk followed by sounds of a struggle.

'Carson!' yelled Hunter. 'What the hell's going on?'

The phone line went dead.

* * *

Rebecca felt dog-tired and very drunk. Her head was way too heavy for her neck, and she didn't seem to be in full control of her body. She went to rub her forehead and poked herself in the eye. Had she been straight, she might have recognised these symptoms as those brought on by a modest dose of PCP in a first-time user, but straight was the one thing she wasn't.

'Where we going? What we gonna do? What's your name?' she slurred. Everything seemed to be happening in slow motion. Her armed captor stood on her left, his partner on her right, each of them grasping an arm as they guided her down a quiet back street. Her restraints had been removed, but the gun was still present, pushed hard against the underside of her ribcage.

'You jus' keep walkin', lady, we almost there…'

Buildings loomed large on either side, most of them industrial and most of them boarded up. Meaningful commerce had long since departed, ceding the real estate to a handful of junkies that frittered their lives away one day at a time. Half the streetlights had failed to come on, while brown rats nosed hungrily at the mounds of trash that lay against abandoned storefronts. A small mini-mart waited up ahead and, judging from its façade, it was just hours away from going belly up.

'We going there? That place? I could use a drink…yeah, a drink would be good… Come on…let's all get a drink…' Rebecca muttered, waving her arm in the general direction of the mini-mart.

'Yeah, honey, dat's where we going,' said the gunman. 'You jus' keep putting one pretty foot after another and we'll be there soon enough.'

Truth was, her feet were about the only part of her that could still be classed as pretty. In addition to messing with her hair and make-up and showering her with cheap booze, her consorts had torn her blouse off one shoulder and ripped a large gash in the front of her skirt.

'Here, take a sip of this.'

The bottle of whisky was dangled in front of her. She made a pathetic lunge for it, missed, then grabbed hold on the second attempt. Took a long swig, coughed, then took another. The two men laughed and urged her onwards, finally bringing her to a stop just outside the store.

'What we gonna buy? Why we here? My head hurts… hurts so much…'

The lead kidnapper put two rough hands on either side of her face and looked deep into her eyes. 'Listen close, honey, dat guy in there—he's a thief.'

'A thief?'

'Das right, a thief. He robbed you. Took all your money. Now you gotta get it back,' he said in a low, mellifluous tone, his voice taking on a hypnotic quality.

'Took my money? All of it?'

'Every last cent. So you gotta get it back. Right now.'

Rebecca pointed towards the door. 'We're going in there?'

'Yeah, honey, in there. Das where he is, an he's a bad man. You got to stand up to him—do what's right. Here, take this—it'll scare him…' The masked man winked as he drew a pistol from his waistband and handed it to Rebecca.

'Gotta get my money back,' she slurred, her mind made up. Justice had to be done. She'd always been a great believer in the rule of law.

'Den let's go do it.'

The thinner of her two escorts held open the door and gestured inside. She didn't need to be asked twice. With an objective now implanted in her mind, she stumbled towards the counter.

'Can I help y—' started the old guy by the register, before

trailing off into silence when he saw Rebecca's masked accomplice. He ran his left hand over his bald pate, smoothing down hair that had long since departed, while his right hand slipped slowly beneath the counter.

'Ah-uh,' warned the masked man, his gun arm rock steady. 'Keep 'em where I can see 'em. Jus' take it easy and no one gonna get hurt.'

'I want my money back!' slurred Rebecca, as she levelled her gun.

'Better do what she says, mister, she a regular Annie Oakley. Here—put da cash in this.'

With a weary shrug, the shopkeep opened his register and emptied its meagre contents into the proffered canvas bag.

'Here—that's all I've got. Takings were low today.'

'Like every other day, I bet?' the masked man sympathised. 'No matter, hand it over.'

'Yeah—give me my money,' demanded Rebecca, half losing her footing. Once the bag was safely in her grasp, her face lit up like a child's on Christmas morn. 'We going to arrest him now?'

'No, honey, we gonna let this guy off with a warning. He ain't no repeat offender, are you, old man?' Another wave of the gun.

'No, sir,' came the reply. The shopkeep plainly had no idea what was going on, except that he was being robbed. Again.

'Now wave goodbye to dat pretty camera, honey, den we can get going.'

The masked man gestured towards the small surveillance cam bolted up on the back wall. Rebecca smiled and waved. Mission accomplished.

Just under a minute had passed since Carson's cellphone had gone dead and Hunter was starting to panic. He swung the binoculars from the entrance to the windows then back again. Something was up, and he knew that he ought to head down there, but negotiating six levels of parking garage might take too long.

A ray of light spilled from the side of the building. Hunter panned across the parking lot, straining to penetrate the gloom, until a tall man in a fedora loomed large in his vision. The assassin! Son of a bitch! He shifted his binoculars to the right and the picture got worse. Carson stumbled forward with his hands on his head, throwing the occasional glance up at the garage, doubtless praying for a rescue that wasn't going to come.

Hunter reached for his Beretta and drew a bead on the Russian, but he knew damn well he couldn't make the shot. Not from this range, and not in this light. At best he'd spook the guy into blowing Carson's brains out. Best to hold fire. Think things through. Carson was still alive, so maybe the assassin planned on using him as a bargaining chip. But to bargain for what?

The two men bypassed a white Toyota Supra and came to a stop by a dark green Jeep Cherokee that faded in and out of the gloom like a mechanical mirage. The plates were Californian—4 BBA…something…55…maybe 9? Hunter swung the binoculars back to the two men just in time to see Carson lean forward, open the rear door of the Cherokee and lower his head to climb in. It was at that moment the Russian chose to strike.

Three paces forward, gun pushed up close to the back of the detective's head, one shot fired. Blood splattered across the interior windows like spraypaint on a ghetto wall as Carson fell headlong into the vehicle. The assassin fired two more shots at his prone target then slammed the door shut and jumped into the driver's seat. Hunter took careful aim with his Beretta and squeezed off a burst, but only succeeded in dinging the hood. The Cherokee's engine roared to life, then its tyres spun on the gravel as it thundered away. Another futile burst from the Beretta, and that was that. Carson was gone.

Fuck, thought Hunter, a feeling of numbness washing over him. So much for my hostage theory.

CHAPTER THIRTY-NINE

REBECCA groaned and rubbed at her head. It was pounding so hard she was starting to wonder if someone was trying to jack-hammer their way out from the inside. To add to her woes her mouth was sawdust dry, the foul-tasting gag was back in place and her whole body shook uncontrollably, but at least her hands were untied. She'd been curled up in a foetal ball for what felt like hours, her eyes shut tight, waiting to come down, and while she wasn't totally compos mentis as yet, she was alert enough to realise that her ordeal was far from over.

When she opened her eyes and blinked through the flash-light she discovered that she was back in the same truck she'd started the evening in. The masked man was in his usual position, resting on his haunches with weapon in hand. Her first thought was to remove the gag, but her captor quickly discouraged her with a wave of his gun.

'Ah-uh—I ain't got time to listen to your bullshit.'

'Wha-da-ell-di-u-giv-me?' she slurred, hoisting herself into a sitting position and crossing her arms for warmth. The truck jolted around another hairpin curve, throwing her against the side panel to add a bruised shoulder to her list of ailments. Some night this was turning out to be. She dug her fingers into her arms, trying to encourage the blood flow and force some life back into them, because now that she was untied there was only one thing on her mind. Escape. She had no idea why she'd been given back some of her freedom. Maybe the kidnapper had decided she was no longer a threat. Maybe he thought that a bottle of rotgut whisky followed by some vein-injected narcotics would be enough to knock the fight out of her. Well, if he thought that, he thought wrong.

She gauged the distance between them at about four feet, then spent the next thirty seconds watching the gun barrel to see if it wavered. No such luck. Launching an attack seemed out of the question, but what choice did she have? Better to go out in a blaze of glory than wait for a bullet to the head.

The truck wobbled over some potholes as she flexed the muscles in her thighs and made some minute adjustments to her position, looking for a little more leverage with which to thrust herself forward. Surprise was her only weapon. Her handbag and its contents were still at home, which meant that her brand-new Browning Hi-Power was also at home. As the truck took another sharp bend, she went back to kneading the muscles in her arms, wincing as her fingernails cut into her skin.

That was it! Her fingernails! Ten little pointed weapons just waiting to be unleashed. But how to put them to best use? His eyes. She had to go for his eyes. Poke them, gouge them, claw at them till he was as blind as a newborn. Knock his gun arm out of the way, get inside, then go for those eyes. Right, you son of a bitch, she thought, tapping into her primal blood lust, I'm gonna tear out your eyes and pound your head to a pulp. Now was the time. Her muscles tensed.

'Watchu thinkin' 'bout?' asked her captor, shuffling backwards and cocking his weapon. The click stopped Rebecca in her tracks. 'Don't you go getting any ideas. Not now we so close to the end.'

Her heart sank. He'd read her mind. The fight dribbled out of her like water through a widening crack in a dam—slowly at first, then ever faster as the hopelessness of her position sank in.

The masked man checked his watch as the truck screeched to a sudden stop. 'OK, now you gotta take off wha's left of dat blouse…'

Fight flickered within her once again. Death was one thing, but she wasn't going to be sent to the afterlife having meekly submitted to rape. She shook her head violently, her eyes glaring with defiance.

'Jus' hurry up,' he commanded. 'Turn around if you want—in fact, it's better if you do, and stop worryin'—I ain't gonna lay a hand on you. If you think I wanna touch the woman who helped keep Manuel's killer outta jail, you even dumber than I thought.'

He looked at her with a mixture of contempt and amusement, then gestured with his gun when she refused to comply. 'Take da blouse off or I shoot you in the gut—you know how long it takes to die from a gut wound? You know how much it hurts? Well, unless the blouse comes off, you gonna find out…'

Rebecca was backed up into a corner and she knew it. At least Anabeth wasn't involved in this god-awful mess. She'd already suffered enough. She kept her eyes trained on her captor, then started to unbutton her blouse, before changing tack and ripping the whole thing off in one motion. Not much point trying to save a garment that was already hanging off both shoulders.

'Das good,' he muttered, his eyes instinctively drawn to her pale silk bra. 'Now da skirt.'

She reached behind her, unhooked the clasp, and wriggled out of her skirt, then found herself wishing that she'd picked out something more substantial than a thong when she'd gone to the closet that morning. She felt the masked man's eyes wander over the contours of her body and realised she had one more weapon to use, the same one that women had been using ever since the war of the sexes had first began. Her femininity.

She sat up straight and arched her back, thrusting her breasts towards her captor like a pair of sacrificial offerings. No point in playing demure now, that just wasn't gonna cut it.

'Put 'em away—a pair of titties ain't gonna buy your way outta dis, *chica*. Besides, I got my own *señora*—I'm a happily married man. Now turn around.'

Rebecca didn't know whether to feel aggrieved or insulted. Her hitherto much-admired body didn't seem to cut it with aging Mexican kidnappers. It was bad enough that she was facing her own death, but to have to do it with a newfound inferiority complex…

Her black humour helped distract her from the thought of what was to come. She turned around, lowered her head and started to pray for her sister. Everything she'd done, she'd done for Anabeth. No regrets. No remorse.

'Now hold still…' Her executioner's breath was hot on the back of her neck. Her time was almost up. She rocked back and forth, finding some strange solace in the movement, until a hand grasped her clavicle to restrain her. Tears began to well in her eyes as something cold and hard pressed into her back. This was it. Time to die.

CHAPTER FORTY

HUNTER opened the front door of his house, ducked inside and reached for the light switch. His ankle throbbed with a dull ache, while his head reeled at the fate that had befallen Carson. As he'd headed back to his home on Mulholland, endless reruns of the detective's death had played out in his mind, and with each one his role as spectator had become ever more frustrating, until the first pangs of guilt had begun to gnaw away at him, even though he knew there was nothing he could have done.

The old man had been the closest thing he'd had to a friend, and seeing him killed in cold blood had brought back a lot of memories, none of them good. Carson had been a stand-up guy, one from the old school, and he was going to miss having him around. If he'd had time to waste on a shrink, he probably would have heard a load of psychobabble about him searching for a father figure, and maybe he had been. It hadn't been easy growing up without a dad, and although his mom had done her best, she'd also been taken from him way too soon.

He headed for the kitchen, grabbed a cold one from the fridge and drained the bottle in one long pull. Once he'd popped the lid on another, he wondered what to do next. He'd already left an anonymous tip with the LAPD switchboard, reporting the Jeep Cherokee containing Carson's corpse as stolen, but he didn't expect it to be found any time soon. The assassin was way too clever to get caught with a dead detective in the back seat—he'd probably dumped the SUV in one of LA's darkened recesses by now. There were plenty of unscrupulous junkyard owners who specialised in making things disappear.

But that didn't mean that the SUV had to be a dead end. He got straight on the phone and punched in a number.

'Yo, this is the Scorpion. Speak, if you wanna be spoken to.' The voice that answered was reedy and thin despite the street patois.

'Danny?' asked Hunter. Danny Green was a nineteen-year-old high-school dropout with a two-time bust for marijuana possession, who also happened to be the best computer hacker that Hunter had ever laid eyes on.

'Who wants to know?'

'Hunter. And you can cut out that tough-guy bullshit—it's not fooling anyone.'

'Hunter! My man! How's it hanging?'

'No time to play catch up, *amigo*, I need a little help, and the clock's ticking, *capisce*?'

'Loud and clear. You caught me just in time—I was just about to defenestrate a PC. Anything you need—like I told you before, I'm your man. The Scorpion always remembers his friends.'

Hunter had helped the kid plea-bargain his way down from dealing to possession a few months back, figuring that the favour would pay off one day down the line, and it looked like that day had just arrived. 'I need you to get inside the DMV database and run a plate for me.'

'That's it?' Danny failed to mask the disappointment in his voice. 'Man, can't you give me something more challenging? Hacking the DMV is a one-banana problem—it's strictly for code monkeys…'

'The plate is 4 BBA 559, out of California. This is important, Danny—I'm on a case.'

'Didn't you get busted? I thought LAPD showed you the door?'

'Yeah, it's the damnedest thing, turns out that being a citizen is no obstacle to being a detective. Just cos I've lost my badge doesn't mean I've lost my balls.'

'I hear that.' The youngster laughed, as his hands danced over a keyboard. 'Now, what was that plate number again? Hit me with it, I'm ready to rock 'n' roll.'

Hunter repeated the licence number and waited for the results, drumming his fingers on the kitchen worktop as the seconds ticked by. In a little under a minute he had his answer.

'Hire car. Hertz. Give me a second, I'll go deeper into the rabbit warren. Got it. Checked out this morning to a Mr V. I. Lenin. Home address listed as number fifty-four, Red Square, Burbank, LA. Hey, wasn't he in the Beatles?'

'Nah—that was John Lennon, numb nuts. The guy we've got here is Vladimir Ilyich Lenin—former leader of the USSR, which means that the rental name's false, along with the address—Lenin's mausoleum is in Red Square. Don't they teach you kids anything at school these days?'

'I sorta left early, remember?'

Hunter wasn't listening. 'No matter what I do, this guy's

always two steps ahead of me. Oh, well, thanks anyway, kid—it was worth a try.'

'Don't thank me—thank the wonders of the World Wide Web. Anyhow, I should be thanking you for giving me a little excitement—my parole officer's got me working nine to five in a salt mine with a bunch of pseudosuits. Hang loose, Hunter.' With that, the phone line went dead.

He took another pull on his beer and examined his options, which didn't take long as he was pretty much out. With no way to trace the rental car, the assassin had disappeared yet again, only this time he'd taken Carson's corpse along for the ride. What a fucking waste. Carson had been a good cop, a shoot-first-ask-questions-later kinda guy. The sort of detective that got things done, and didn't worry about the ramifications of his actions till after the event. Actually, scratch that—a guy like Carson *never* wasted time worrying about the fallout. His kind got results in the war on crime because his kind knew that it *was* a war, and in a war you didn't take prisoners.

Hunter took another sip from his beer as the seriousness of his position sank in. The assassin had killed an active cop, and that meant the gloves were off. Until he caught up with the Russian, he was living on borrowed time, stumbling around in kill-or-be-killed territory, and he had no intention of winding up in a casket. But how the hell was he going to track down his adversary? The Witchcraft tip-off had been his first solid lead, and look how that had turned out. What he had to do was get back to basics—plough through the paperwork, work through the assimilated data, in the hope that something would turn up, and that meant getting hold of Carson's files. The files he was supposed to have brought to the diner. The files that might contain some sort of clue. It was a long shot, but it was all he had.

He checked his watch—it was ten p.m. Dark outside, low cloud cover. It would be gone eleven by the time he got to Carson's pad in East Hollywood—people would be turning in for the night. Bottom line, he needed those files—and when it came to breaking and entering, there was no time like the present. He drained his beer and headed for the bedroom to collect the flashlight he kept stashed in the base of his closet, but when he threw open the door, the scene that awaited him stopped him cold.

Holy shit! Someone had redecorated. He yanked his Beretta out of its holster and stepped into the room. The once magnolia walls were now hidden beneath an avalanche of newspaper clippings, grainy monochrome photos and hand-scrawled slogans, giving the room a crazy, claustrophobic feel. Up above, the ceiling hadn't fared much better, as an inverted pentagram had been painted directly over his bed in blood-red paint. Hunter started to pace around the edge of the room, examining his new wallpaper with growing horror. A photo of Father Mulrooney, the kiddie-fiddling vicar, standing outside the church of St Lawrence. An article on inner-city gangs and the death of Rhythm Ray. An exposé on the rise of Nazism among LA's disenchanted youth that featured a snapshot of Harold Ribecki. An editorial diatribe on the acquittal of Carlos Montero and the associated failings of the judicial system. And more, so much more—all of it punctuated with the rabid sloganeering of a deranged mind, vicious messages hand-scrawled in red straight through the assembled evidence, for evidence was what it was. Hunter's bedroom now resembled the inner sanctum of a serial killer. Someone was trying to frame him.

CHAPTER FORTY-ONE

REBECCA stiffened as she felt something press into her shoulder blade. The side panels of the truck closed in on her as the beginning of the end loomed large. Of all the wondrous places on earth, this was where she was going to die. Trapped inside a claustrophobic metal box. Tears trickled down her cheeks.

'Now keep still—I don' wanna make no mess,' warned her captor, who she pretty much had figured for Manuel Ortega's father, not that it made much difference. Had she been able to speak, she'd still have had a shot at survival, but the sour-tasting gag in her mouth meant that her wish for one last meaningful conversation looked destined to go unanswered.

She clenched her teeth, readying herself for the end, all the while thinking that it was so damn unfair. Her work was only half-done, and there was no budding apprentice waiting in the wings to step up and take over. Her sister would be left disappointed.

And then something strange happened. Her captor started to draw whatever he was holding across her bare shoulders in long languid strokes, strokes that were unmistakable in their purpose. Pen strokes. He was writing something on her back. A word. Hope flared in her again. Maybe that word was salvation.

As Hunter continued to walk around the room he discovered more and more damning evidence linking him to the string of unsolved murders. A carton of playing cards, each pack still in its Cellophane wrapper. A collection of surveillance photos of the Schaeffer house, former home to the rapist Marty. A matchbook from the Mill Road Motel. A hymnbook from the Church of St Lawrence. All in all, it was quite a collection.

But it wasn't until he looked under his bed that he stumbled across the mother lode—enough weapons to start his own paramilitary organisation. A collection of knives, ranging from serrated hunting blades through chef's carvers to easily concealed Italian stilettos. And guns. Lots of guns. Full autos, semi-autos, old-fashioned revolvers, even a sawed-off pump. Someone had gone the extra mile to set him up, and that someone was the assassin.

You had to hand it to the guy—he'd moved fast to take out the two thorns in his side on the very same night. Frame one, kill the other. Very neat, very tidy. His eyes rolled over the assorted collection of firepower. One of the guns might even have been used to shoot Carson. That way it would look like the crazed serial killer had discovered that the lead cop on the case was getting too close, so he'd decided to remove him from the equation. Despite the seriousness of his predicament, he felt a grudging respect for the assassin. This was a move of pure genius. But how was he going to counter it?

First of all, his bedroom needed one hell of a spring clean. He may have respected the Russian's Machiavellian scheme but that didn't mean he had to like it. He started to tear at the paper on the walls. A few minutes later he became aware of the growing pile of rubbish strewn about his feet and decided to re-evaluate. He fetched a holdall from the closet. This stuff had to be packed away for transportation.

He started to scoop up the mess, but the holdall was barely half-full when a piercing light blasted through his bedroom window, a light so pure, so all-encompassing it felt like an impromptu celestial visit was on the cards. He dropped to the floor and buried his face in the carpet just as a bullhorn shattered the silence.

'Zac Hunter! This is the police! Your house is surrounded! Come out with your hands up! You have one minute to comply!'

So much for getting shot of the evidence. Now he was just gonna get shot. Hauled downtown with his fingerprints smudged all over the newspaper clippings and surveillance photos. At least he hadn't touched the guns. He crawled over to the window and risked a quick peek though the glass. High-powered mobile lights were trained directly on the front of his house, and through the glare he could make out a swarm of shadowy figures in full tactical gear. There was nothing the department liked better than to come down hard on one of their own—it made the chief look tough on corruption. As he lay there on his bedroom floor, cradling a Beretta that he dared not use, one word pounded in his head. Trapped.

CHAPTER FORTY-TWO

'DAS perfect,' muttered the masked man as he stared at Rebecca's back. 'Now you get out. Party's over, lady. Time for you to take a walk.'

The truck's side door opened with a metallic screech. Dare she believe that her nightmare was almost over? She shuffled around in the confined space to find that she had a new window on the world. A row of shallow concrete steps stretched out before her, and at the top of the steps was a large, well-lit building. The front of the building was made from glass, and inside a security guard patrolled Reception. Her heart leapt. Civilisation was just a hundred yards away.

'C'mon, get cho ass in gear… Get out—now!'

For the first time that night her captor sounded a little nervous. Her clothes sat alongside him in an untidy pile. She gestured at them more in hope than expectation.

'You won't be needin' 'em. Get outta my truck, climb those steps, then go in that building. Tha's all you gotta do.'

She shuffled towards the opening then clambered out into the chill night air. Goose-bumps reared up on her almost naked body, prompting her to cross her arms across her chest. The first step towards freedom was the hardest, but with each passing footfall her confidence began to grow, infinitesimally at first, then faster and faster, until it matched the speed of her forward progress. When the truck's engine roared to life behind her, she barely heard it as her head was filled with the sound of her sister's voice roaring her on towards safety. Ten steps higher, then twenty, then thirty, and she was almost there.

A large sign hung over the building's main entrance. It read CHANNEL NINE NEWS in bold black letters that were ten feet high. As the guard in Reception became aware of her approach, he morphed into a slack-jawed yokel, suggesting that lingerie-clad babes were something of a rarity on the front steps, but by the time she'd stumbled inside, he'd regained enough composure to talk into his radio mike.

'This is Carter in Reception—I'm gonna need a little help.' His eyes roved up and down Rebecca's body as he listened to the response. 'You wouldn't believe me if I told you. Are you OK, ma'am?'

'Jesus—what's that say on her back?' asked a voice from off to one side. She spun around to find a youngster in an ill-fitting suit ogling her from his position at the front desk, a chrome and glass affair that squatted like a futuristic bug on the right hand side of the lobby. 'Hey? Don't I know you from somewhere?' he asked, his pimply face lighting up in recognition. 'Yeah, you're that hotshot lawyer who got Montero off. Oh, boy, Henry's gonna love this!'

She started to tear at the foul-tasting gag, but the kid was already shouting into his desk phone, clamouring at the aforementioned Henry to get his ass downstairs for a major scoop.

'Call de police…' she slurred, finding that the combination of whisky and narcotics had done little for her elocution.

'Hey—would you look at that,' said the guard with no small sense of wonder, having just had his first glimpse of her back.

Rebecca stumbled towards him and held out her hand. 'Gimme your jacket.'

'Aw, man, she stinks of booze!' he exclaimed, pulling away.

A soft electronic ding signalled that an elevator had arrived. The doors swished open and out tumbled a dishevelled newsman clutching a digital-camcorder.

'So where's the fucking fire?' he asked the kid at the desk, before letting loose a 'Holy shit!' when he saw Rebecca. The camera was up, running and trained on her before she even had time to think about covering up. She spun away and shielded her face, but that only succeeded in eliciting a comment of 'Beautiful…' from the experienced TV journo.

'Told you it was a major scoop, didn't I, Henry? She's that hot-shit lawyer, I'm sure of it.'

'Leave me alone…' sobbed Rebecca.

Just great. She was gonna be headline news dressed in nothing but her undies. And then she finally understood. The whole night had been about making her a laughing stock, finishing her career through public humiliation. She'd never been in any real danger, despite how it had seemed at the time. The Ortegas had set out to ruin her, but they only knew half the story. They'd acted on their perception of events rather than the cold, hard facts. If they'd only let her talk, none of this would have been necessary. Everyone deserved a last chance. An opportunity to atone. A chill swept over her as she realised what that meant. She was going to have to make some changes.

'You getting a close-up on that?' asked the kid behind the desk.

'Sure am,' muttered Henry, as he zoomed in on the word that was scrawled in indelible ink across Rebecca's bare shoulders.

WHORE.

'Zac Hunter—you now have forty seconds to comply. Come out of the house with your hands above your head. There's no need for further bloodshed. Your situation is hopeless—there's no chance of escape.'

The guy was back on his bullhorn. Damn! Only forty seconds left? Well, didn't time fly when you were having fun? The police thought they had him cornered, all clustered around the front of his house like a bunch of big-game hunters, for that was what he'd become in their eyes, big game, an ex-cop gone bad, a killer on the loose. A glimmer of an idea began to form in his mind. He shimmied away from the window and exited the room on his belly. Once he was out of the spotlight, he jumped to his feet and hobbled through the main living area, fully aware that time was of the essence. You could forget the countdown crap the guy with the bullhorn was pulling—an amped-up SWAT team with itchy trigger fingers was going to come hammering inside any second now.

He eased open the glass doors that led to the deck, stepped out into the night, then locked the doors behind him. When he glanced over the edge of the railings there was no sign of life. Cool. The police had counted on the natural barrier of the cliff to pen him in. Bad call. He opened the deck's wooden storage box and withdrew the necessary equipment—his Adidas rucksack, Five-Ten Anasazi climbing shoes, leather belay gloves and a 100-foot length of nylon rope. He took off his jacket, stashed his desert boots in the backpack, then hurriedly slipped on the belay gloves and Anasazis. The guy on the bullhorn had been quiet for a good twenty seconds and that could only mean one thing—he was almost out of time.

He padded his right shoulder with his jacket, looped the rope around the railings, then stepped over the edge and straddled the doubled line. With the anchored end held tight in his left hand, he wound the rope under his right ass cheek, up across his chest to his shoulder, then down his back to his right hand, leaving him ready to make a body-rappel. He leant back from the edge, letting his ass take his weight, then began to walk backwards, favouring his good ankle, while feeding the line through his gloved hands. The going was tough—although his leather jacket helped shield his shoulder from the worst of the friction, his ass took a hammering. Once he'd gone about fifty feet down the face, he rested on a thin ledge, unwound the rope from his body, then pulled it free of the railings with a sharp tug.

It took him a few moments to mentally prepare himself for the rest of the descent. Ordinarily the climb would have held no qualms as he'd soloed it on countless occasions, but this time he had a bad ankle to contend with. He lowered himself off the ledge and searched around with his left foot until he'd found a solid toehold, and then it was time for the fun part. Pain shot through his right ankle the moment he asked it to take his weight, but he grimaced and rode out the wave of nausea, telling himself that the discomfort was nothing more than an unnecessary distraction.

He'd covered another ten feet when the silence was broken by the sound of a door being driven off its hinges—the SWAT team had invited themselves into his house. Flashlight beams spilled out of the glass doors above, crisscrossing in the night sky like a downmarket laser show. He redoubled his efforts at the sound of muffled shouts. Sweat ran down his brow to burn his eyes while his ankle sang out in protest, but he kept on moving until pretty soon terra firma was coming up beneath him.

He flexed the muscles in his shoulders to work out the lactic acid, while his chest rose and fell as he sucked in oxygen. When he glanced back up, there was no sign of activity on the deck. With any luck, it would take them a while to work out how he'd escaped—those action men weren't exactly the sharpest tools in the shed. As he stumbled down the slope towards the nearest set of house lights, his thoughts had already turned to his next objective—getting Carson's files.

CHAPTER FORTY-THREE

CARSON'S house looked deserted. All the lights were off, there was no sign of movement, and it was quieter than an AIDS-infested brothel. Hunter had made the drive over in a nondescript Dodge he'd boosted from outside a juke joint, reasoning that he was probably saving the owner a DUI charge. The Dodge hadn't been much of a catch, though, as it stank to high heaven of stale sweat and greasy fast food. Even with the windows wound down, Hunter had spent most of the journey trying not to gag.

He left the car by the kerb and hurried up the weed-strewn driveway, heading straight towards the red-brick garage. The door rolled up smoothly and then he was inside. He pulled down the door and flicked on the lights. Carson's old Nissan truck was parked in the centre of the space, waiting forlornly for an owner that would never return. A workbench ran along the length of the rear wall, while access to the main property was through a plain wooden door midway along the wall.

He hurried past the car to the workbench, where he rummaged around until he found a claw hammer and a heavy-duty pry bar. He positioned the tip of the bar just above the lock, then drove it into the soft wood with the hammer. When he leant on the bar, a section of the door buckled and splintered, sending a flurry of white paint flakes falling to the floor. He repeated the process underneath the lock, then knocked out the entire mechanism with one heavy blow. The door swung open on its hinges. Carson's house wasn't exactly Fort Knox.

Hunter hurried inside and found himself in the kitchen. Dirty dishes were stacked in the sink, while cartons of take-out Oriental were sat on the table. The detective had enjoyed a rich Chinese curry for his last meal if the lingering smell was anything to go by. Signs of life in a dead man's house—the scene was strangely macabre.

Leaving the kitchen behind, he made his way down the hall past the photos of the two ex-wives, before entering the study. Everything was as he remembered—computer desk by the window, easy chair under a standard lamp, and a huge bookcase jammed with files and reference volumes. The corkboard remained to the left of the door, with photos of Father Mulrooney and Montero pinned at east and west, and the now recognisable images of Marty Schaeffer and Rhythm Ray at north and south. The assassin's fifth victim, Harold Ribecki, had yet to be added.

Hunter shut the blinds, flicked on the lamp and sat at the desk. He leafed through the papers that were strewn in front of him. Most of them were assorted press reports on the victims' untimely demises. Nothing new there. Move on. He gave the computer a miss and went to open the desk drawer, figuring that an oldtimer like Carson would favour paper filing over electronic. The drawer was locked, but that didn't pose too much of a problem as it wasn't the sort of lock that could withstand a sudden assault from a claw hammer. Inside was a collection of unmarked manila folders. With growing interest, he pulled out the first of them and started to read.

Jackpot. A detailed file on Carlos Montero, containing information on his criminal background, full transcripts from his court case, the crime-scene report from his house, plus a preliminary autopsy report. Hunter flicked through the rest of the files to discover similar goldmines on the other four victims. Why the hell had Carson stalled on handing these over? This was exactly what he'd come looking for, but now wasn't the time for a cramming session. He battened down his curiosity, scooped up his bounty, then headed back to the borrowed Dodge. Somewhere in those files was a clue to the assassin's identity. Carson might not have been able to find it, but Hunter was determined he would.

Danilov deposited the padded envelope on the coffee-table and stretched back in his leather sofa, his stomach heavy from a good meal. Zharkoye had been on the menu tonight, a traditional Russian stew consisting of roast beef, potatoes, onions and carrots, and the scent of the rich dish still hung heavy in the room. Warmth and energy coursed through his being as the carbohydrates and fats designed to combat his homeland's harsh winters had their effect.

He tapped his fingers and tried to relax. The music emanating from the stereo usually helped sooth his soul, but for once his devotion to Old Blue Eyes was not quite total as his eyes kept straying back to the envelope. Another communiqué from the boss, Fed-Exed direct to his apartment. His situation was akin to that of a puppet on a string, and he didn't much care for it. He tore open the package with one smart pull, then began to study his next target.

This one was handsome, but that wouldn't last. He held up an eight-by-ten colour headshot and studied the subject's features until every last detail was etched into his subconscious. Another man marked for death by some unseen hand, another man whose time left on earth could now be counted in days rather than years. He wondered what the target was doing at this very moment. Dining on a prime cut of steak, slowly savouring each mouthful of the succulent meat, unwittingly devouring the condemned man's last meal? Making love to a beautiful woman, burying himself inside her, thrusting harder and faster until his passion was spent? Had he known what awaited him, would the steak have tasted juicer? Would the orgasm have been more intense? Probably not. Fear was usually an unwelcome distraction from the base pleasures of life.

Danilov had no idea why this man had been marked for execution, but it wasn't his place to know. The target's name was as unfamiliar as his face. He could have been anything from a grade-school teacher to a serial killer. The purest lamb or the blackest sheep, it mattered not. Either way, he'd be dead before the week was out. Whether he deserved to have his life cut short didn't come into it. The role of the assassin was hangman, not judge and jury—those elevated positions were saved for the men who paid the bills or made the threats in the boss's case.

Danilov put down the photo and began to read through some of the background information. He was halfway down the second paragraph when his telephone started to ring. His brow furrowed. He'd had three friends in his entire life, and none of them knew where he was. Dmitriy and Sergei were back in Moscow, getting rich on the thriving black market, while Vasily was ten years dead, buried in an unmarked grave in the Siberian wilderness. His social life had been moving in ever-decreasing circles for some time now as his betrayal of the Racketiry meant that he could never return home—instead, he was imprisoned in the United States, a spoilt, childish nation that wasn't fit to suckle at the teat of his beloved Russia.

The phone continued to ring. He regarded it with some suspicion, took a sip of vodka, then slowly lifted the receiver.

'Is Viktor there?' The tone was high-pitched and innocent, the voice of a child.

'Da,' he allowed, his eyes narrowing.

'I've got a message for you. There's been a change of plan.' The words came out slow and stilted as if the kid was reading from a script. His young voice ran through some simple instructions before asking Danilov if he'd understood.

'Is someone with you? Put them on the line.' He held his breath.

'Hey, he wants to talk to you,' the kid piped up.

The boss was there! Danilov's heartbeat ticked faster. This was his first chance to make direct contact with the man who'd treated him like a slave from the *gulag*. Months of fruitless searching had led nowhere, but now there was just the length of a phone line between them. He stiffened as he heard the receiver being handed over. Waiting for his boss's first words felt like waiting for an edict from God. And then…silence. It looked like it was up to him to get the ball rolling.

'What is wrong? Lost your tongue? Nothing to say?' he said softly. 'Are you coward? No matter, hear this, hear it well. One day you must release me from arrangement. Let me live life out from under shadow. Let me be free. Otherwise…' As he indulged himself in a dramatic pause, the phone line went dead.

He pursed his thin lips. It was as close as he'd ever come to discovering the boss's identity, but in truth he was still a million miles away. And now this change in the plan. This break with tradition. Why? He sat back and considered the possible reasons for a while, then a smile made its way across his gaunt features. Only one likely explanation existed. An explanation that would play straight into his hands. Finally, his wish had been granted.

CHAPTER FORTY-FOUR

HUNTER stretched back in the booth and massaged his neck. With home comforts temporarily unavailable he'd been forced to spend the night in the stolen Dodge, and now he was paying the price. He'd pulled into the rear lot of Tommy's bar at a little after two a.m., swapped the Dodge's plates with those of an old Caddie, then tossed and turned in the passenger seat till dawn. The sudden licence change wasn't likely to upset the Caddie's owner as the car had been collecting nothing but rust and vermin for the past four years. Tommy kept threatening to restore it, but his grand project was yet to get off the ground, largely on account of the fact that Tommy knew jack shit about cars—he couldn't even drive.

The failed auto-restorer wandered over and deposited a steaming mug of coffee in front of him. 'Dusty'll bring breakfast over in a couple of minutes,' he muttered.

Hunter felt safe at the bar, despite his fugitive status. Other than Tommy and his Thai apprentice, the only other people who knew he frequented the joint were a couple of regulars who spent most of their days blind drunk. He took a gulp of the coffee. It was strong and sweet, providing a much-needed wake-up call to his system. He took a few more gulps to shake off his lethargy then turned to the job at hand. Carson's files. Five manila folders lay spread out on the table in front of him, and inside those folders were thousands of words typed on hundreds of pieces of paper, and somewhere within those words lay the answer. A clue to the identity of the Russian hit man. The hit man who'd robbed him of his vengeance on Montero. The hit man who'd come gunning for him. The hit man who'd killed Carson in cold blood. He reflected a moment on the fate of his friend. Where had the body been taken? The sooner he found the Russian, the sooner he'd know. The least Carson deserved was a proper burial.

'I bring food,' Dusty interrupted his reverie. 'Noodles, bean sprouts, pak choi, broccoli and a little chilli.'

Great. Just what his digestive system needed to start the day—spicy food. He took the proffered bowl and shovelled down a mouthful, nodding his thanks to the expectant young Thai, who responded with a broad smile before spinning on his heel to return to the kitchen. He ran a hand through his closely cropped hair then started to read from the first of the files.

'While Harold Ribecki had clear ties to the white supremacist movement, he was not believed to be a major player in their affairs. His immediate circle of friends limited their activities to regular acts of vandalism and the occasional beating, and although he was often seen in the company of Charles Noughton, a leading local racist suspected of waging a terror campaign against the city's black population for the past three years, Ribecki's obvious lack of brainpower would suggest that Noughton looked on him as little more than hired muscle…'

Just the occasional beating, thought Hunter. Well, I guess that makes it OK, then. He skimmed on until he came to the section detailing Ribecki's unprovoked attack on a young black male, an attack that had left the victim confined to a wheelchair and Ribecki standing trial.

'Ribecki left the victim, an Andre Noble of 15 Parmelee Avenue, lying unconscious in the street, suffering from severe head trauma, ten broken ribs, a shattered kneecap and a number of serious flesh wounds to the face and torso. Had the paramedics not arrived promptly, Mr Noble would most likely have died. The attack was believed to be racially motivated, a charge that Mr Ribecki did not go out of his way to deny…'

Any sympathy Hunter may have had for Harold Ribecki was fast evaporating. Sounded like the kid had got exactly what was coming to him. Yeah, sure, maybe he'd had a rough childhood, maybe his daddy had run out on him when he was young, or maybe Pops had stayed home and beat him every night, but as far as Hunter was concerned, whatever excuses the psychologists wanted to dredge up, they were just that—excuses. It was all about personal responsibility—if you could look yourself in the mirror at the end of each day, knowing you'd tried to do the right thing, then that was all that could ever be asked of you.

He moved on to the transcripts from Ribecki's trial. Legal jargon jumped off the page as the defence lawyers ran through the holy trinity that had been pounded into them at law school—procrastinate, obfuscate and discredit—all aimed at convincing the jury that reasonable doubt existed. Who were these vultures? He glanced back to the notes at the top of the page—Mitchell, Wallace and Flint—then read on. It wasn't until he'd closed the file and got halfway through the next one on Father Mulrooney that he realised the name of the law firm sounded familiar. 'Mitchell, Wallace and Flint.' He closed his eyes and leant back in the booth, visualising the three words in his head until they began to morph from black type on the page into fancy etching on a chrome plaque, and suddenly he knew where he'd seen the names before.

With growing excitement he searched out the transcripts from Father Mulrooney's court case and looked for the name of his legal representation. 'Tolliver and Associates.' His heart sank. That couldn't be right. He threw down the file and made a grab for the one on Marty Schaeffer, racing through the pages until he found the name of the rapist's defence team—Tolliver and Associates again. That made two for Tolliver and Associates and two for Mitchell, Wallace and Flint.

'Tommy—I gotta use your phone,' he cried as he hurried to the end of the bar.

'Be my guest.'

He called up information, obtained the number for Tolliver and Associates, then asked to be connected with their personnel officer. A well-spoken woman came on the line, and after a brief preamble Hunter asked just one question. When the answer came back, his face lit up. Holy shit. His first major break in the case. A possible link across all the killings. Now all he needed was motive. What would drive someone in the suspect's position to eliminate these people?

He redialled Information and asked to be put through to the legal firm Mitchell, Wallace and Flint. A young woman answered on the second ring.

'Hi,' began Hunter. 'I'm Jon Rawles from the leading Californian legal newspaper *The Recorder*, and I'm looking for some background information on some of your staff to see if they're suitable for a story we're going to run in the next issue…'

Within five minutes he'd found what he was looking for.

CHAPTER FORTY-FIVE

THE woman's head bobbed to the music as she jogged down the street, causing her light blonde hair to bounce on her shoulders. She looked good and she knew it—her black Adidas sweatsuit with its funky white trim was all the rage—but she ignored the admiring glances and focussed instead on the glorious blue sky that reigned overhead. Her long confident stride ate up the sidewalk, one foot following the other in a rhythmic progression, each one falling bang in time to the beat. She was listening to Madonna. High tempo. Upbeat. Perfect for a workout.

'Not hungry?' asked Rebecca, as she buttered her toast. Her sister shrugged. She never had been one for breakfast. After the horrors of the night before, Rebecca had called in sick, an event that was almost as rare as a solar eclipse.

'How are you feeling?' her big sister fussed for the thousandth time.

'Trust me, I'm fine.' Rebecca yawned, her lethargy caused by having spent half the night being questioned by the cops. The two detectives assigned to her case, Hallenbeck and Griggs, had initially seemed a little sceptical about her abduction story, although all that had changed once her preliminary blood sample had tested positive for phencyclidine, which was more commonly known as PCP. She took a gulp of freshly squeezed orange juice then glanced up at the portable TV that sat on the counter.

Yet another local affiliate was running a report on her fall from grace. She'd already sat through two lots of footage of her semi-naked appearance at Channel Nine News, the first clip dubbed with a serious voice-over, the second played more for laughs. She wondered what angle this next one would opt for.

The woman slowed her pace as a junction approached. She came to a halt just shy of the kerb and jogged on the spot to maintain the momentum of her exercise regime. Cars passed in front of her as the Walkman skipped to the next track. One of her favourites—'Papa Don't Preach.' The lights turned red for oncoming traffic, so she set off across the blacktop. She never saw the souped-up Firebird come careering through the intersection at a million miles an hour, and never heard the warning shouts from passing pedestrians. She never saw the car's back end flip out or heard the screech of its brakes or smelt the burning rubber, but she sure as hell felt the grille slam into her legs, and she felt the wind race through her hair as she was catapulted upwards into the blue sky, and she felt her spine crunch against the road once gravity reeled her back in. And then…she felt…nothing.

* * *

The news report came to an end. Rebecca had to hand it to them. It had been a thoroughly professional hatchet job. They'd postulated that her career as a lawyer was as good as over as no one would ever take her seriously again. A silver-haired anchorman had stared out gravely from the screen and informed his audience that the ability to command respect was a key skill of any good lawyer, a skill she now lacked. He'd then gone on to postulate that more revelations could yet come to light, as there were rumours of security camera footage that showed Rebecca holding up a mini-mart at gunpoint.

'I don't know why you keep putting yourself through it,' Anabeth said softly. 'In a couple of days the whole thing will probably have blown over.'

'Fat chance,' she replied morosely.

'Once the cops bring in old man Ortega and sweat the truth out of him, everyone will know what you went through, and things will go back to normal.'

Rebecca pursed her lips. Her next sentence wasn't going to go down too well. 'I'm not pressing charges.'

'What?' Anabeth exploded. 'You've gotta be kidding me. This guy takes you at gunpoint, pumps you full of drugs, strips you to the bone, scares you half to death, then humiliates you in front of the whole damn city, and you still don't want to press charges? Mind telling me why the hell not?'

Less than half an hour after the road accident, an experienced police officer was swiftly dispatched to the University of Southern California to interrupt a lecture on the rights of the accused during criminal trial. He stood outside the classroom for a few moments, gathering himself for the worst part of his job, then knocked once and marched stiffly inside. Thirty or so youthful faces stared down with curiosity at him from on high. After a few hushed words with the lecturer, the officer cleared his throat, then asked for one member of the class to accompany him. A pretty, bespectacled young woman stood up and made her way down from the back of the room, unaware that the course of her life was about to change for ever.

'Mr Ortega has just lost his son,' Rebecca said softly. 'He's been through enough.'

'That's no excuse! What he did to you was barbaric—totally unacceptable. You have to press charges.'

'Just stop for a moment and try to see it from his point of view. His little boy gets run down in the street. The driver's a rich brat who's so drunk it's a miracle he could even find the steering-wheel, let alone turn it. So the Ortegas go to court, expecting justice. But money talks and the rich brat walks. The Ortegas go through hell for the second time in as many months. And who helped the rich brat stay out of jail? Me. That's right—me. Little wonder Ortega wanted some revenge.'

'It wasn't your fault. You were just doing your job. The jury listened to the evidence and they made their decision. Not you. The jury. If old man Ortega needed to vent, he should have gone after them. He can't see the bigger picture. He never should have messed with you. Your work's too damn important.'

'What he did was understandable, and I'm not going to see him punished for it,' Rebecca said firmly, putting an end to the conversation.

The steady bleep of the heart monitor was the only sound in the room. The law student sat beside the bed, unable to take her eyes off the broken body that lay before her. She'd put in a call to her parents, who were all the way over on the eastern seaboard, but she hadn't been able to get hold of them. As she'd sat in the squad car en route to the hospital, the police officer had told her that her only sister had been involved in a serious road accident. The shock had hit her like a sledgehammer. Her blood had run cold, and somehow, just for a second, the world had stopped turning. The officer had gone on to explain how a hit-and-run driver had collided with a jogger at an intersection before accelerating away from the scene of the crime. Several witnesses had already come forward to state that the driver had been going way too fast when he'd gone through a stop light. The police already had him in custody. His cowardly flight had ended three blocks later when he'd crashed into the rear of a slow-moving semi. When they'd picked him up, he'd been drunk as a skunk.

The heart monitor bleeped and the student dabbed at her tear-stained cheeks as she sent up another prayer, begging for divine intervention. Her breath caught in her throat as the beep morphed into a constant, high-pitched tone. Medical staff came bursting into the room. One administered a shot of epinephrine and started mouth-to-mouth, while another weighed in with chest compressions. The monitor gave out the same high-pitched tone. A third wheeled over a crash cart, charged up the defibrillation device, attached the paddles, and hit her sister's body with a bolt of electricity. The line stayed flat. He tried again. No change. The law student sank to her knees and started to pray.

Her only sister was pronounced dead at 10.48 a.m. on Monday 4th September 1989. The student sobbed silently, and as the tears streamed down her face, she vowed that the killer would be punished. The burial was one week later, but it took the student another six months to realise just how far she'd go to honour her pledge, because on 5th March 1990, in a small county courtroom in downtown LA, the hit-and-run driver was sentenced to just four years in jail for the vehicular manslaughter of Anabeth Finch.

It was then, and only then, that Rebecca first knew what she had to do.

CHAPTER FORTY-SIX

'WILL somebody get that fucking door? Maria—shift your fat ass!' Bobby Ashton shouted.

Where the hell was that maid? Probably slacking off with Federico the gardener out back. Damn lazy beaners never put in a full day's work. Why his father still insisted on employing them was a complete mystery. He stretched back in the plush leather sofa and returned his attention to the *Baywatch* rerun that was currently playing on the TV. His hand strayed towards his crotch as Erika Eleniak bounced onto the screen, her perfect breasts somehow restrained by a skimpy red bikini that just didn't look up to the task. The front door could take care of itself—Bobby had more pressing matters to attend to.

The bell rang again. He decided to ignore it. Since when had he been the hired help? Greeting guests was one of the many things that didn't appear in his job description. Not that he had a job description—when your dad was as filthy rich as Bobby's you sure as shit didn't need anything as menial as a job. He reached for a can of cola, chugged down some of the sickly sweet fluid, then extended his middle finger in the general direction of the jerk out front who didn't know when to quit. Five seconds passed before the bell rang again. Another five seconds, another ring. The son of a bitch obviously couldn't take a hint. Someone was gonna have to straighten him out.

'Aw…Jesus Christ,' whined Bobby, as he stood up and adjusted his slacks in a futile attempt to hide the bulge in his crotch. That Erika Eleniak had a lot to answer for.

The bell rang once more as he slouched across the parquet floor of the reception hall, its insistent chime further stoking his anger. What the hell was going on? He'd already been forced to answer the phone just thirty minutes previously, when some idiot had tried to convince him that he'd ordered a pepperoni pizza with extra anchovies. Pizza? Get real. And he didn't even like anchovies. By the time he'd made it to the door he was just about ready to explode. He swept his hands through his wavy blond hair, glued his best sneer onto his chiselled features and decided to let whoever was out front face the full force of his wrath.

'Where's the fucking fire?' he shouted as he pulled open the door.

A tall guy in a set of white coveralls stood on the porch, the sort of guy that Bobby liked to describe as a long streak of piss. His head was half-bowed, a wide-brimmed hat obscured most of his face and he was cradling an unmarked cardboard box that was about three feet in length. A white panel truck sat directly behind him, with the words IN BLOOM stencilled on its side in cartoon letters.

'Sorry to disturb, sir,' he said softly. 'I come with flowers for Mr Ashton.'

The voice was accented, maybe European. Great. That was all Bobby needed. If it wasn't enough that he had to put up with the Mexican help all day long, now he had to deal with some immigrant from another continent. Why couldn't they stay in their own damn countries?

'What fucking flowers?' he barked.

The deliveryman pushed the cardboard box forward as he spoke. 'I have flowers right here, two dozen lilies ordered by Mr Ashton.'

'I didn't order no fucking flowers. There's gotta be some mistake.'

'Maybe your father order? You check, please? If I don't deliver flowers, I lose job.'

'That's your problem—you think I give two shits about your goddamn job? Besides, my dad's at the golf course, and I'm sure as shit not going to interrupt his round to see if he ordered any goddamn flowers. Now fuck off and stop breaking my balls...'

'Your father not here? Anyone else?' the deliveryman pleaded. 'Maybe maid knows about flowers?'

'The maid's gone missing, and for the last fucking time, I don't want your flowers. Now get the fuck off my property.'

'I leave on porch. That way, I make delivery, maybe keep my job.' He bent down and rested the box against the main wall of the house.

Bobby rolled his eyes heavenward. 'For crying out loud, have you got some kind of hearing problem? Just take your flowers and—'

But before Bobby could complete his insult the deliveryman had exploded out of a half-crouch to send a fist arrowing straight into the base of the younger man's jaw. Pain flared as his teeth came together with a sickening crack, then he found himself flying backwards into the reception hall where he landed with a dull thud. The deliveryman was quickly on him, restraining him with a knee to the chest as he clamped a sodden rag over his face. Bobby gagged as the stench of thick chemicals invaded his nostrils, and within seconds a series of black dots began to bloom in front of his eyes.

One last thought crossed his mind before he passed out.

Fucking immigrants.

Danilov stepped inside the entrance hall and looked down at Ashton's body with a knowing smile. Killing this one was going to be a pleasure. His conversations with America's wealthier inhabitants had become so infrequent he'd forgotten just how rude some of them could be. If punching Ashton in the face had given him this much of a rush, just imagine the fun to be had when severing his jugular.

He retrieved the cardboard delivery box from the porch and tore it open. Inside there was nothing that resembled a floral display—instead, there was a black zip-lock body bag just waiting to receive six feet of anaesthetised brat. Its surface was spotted with a number of strategically placed breathing holes, as his orders had been clear—keep the target alive. He unfurled the bag on the parquet floor, pulled the zip, then rolled Ashton's body into position. After two minutes of fumbling with four remarkably pliant limbs he had him wrapped up nice and tight.

He left Ashton where he lay and hurried around to the rear of his truck. Well, to be fair, it wasn't exactly *his* truck. He'd 'borrowed' the vehicle from a moustachioed deliveryman named Miguel, and Miguel was going to wake up with one hell of a headache about three hours from now with no clue as to what had happened. Miguel could consider himself lucky—there weren't many people that survived a confrontation with Viktor Danilov. He pulled open the truck's double doors then went back inside the mansion to retrieve his new-found travelling companion. Thanks to the slavish addiction to appearance that ran rampant amongst the LA movie set, Ashton's body was comparatively light, and he had little trouble in hoisting it over his shoulder.

'Strong as ox,' he muttered, as he threw the body into the truck—threw, rather than placed, as the boss had specified alive, not unharmed—then hurried forward to the cab. The engine spluttered to life on the second attempt, making him yearn for the throaty roar of his BMW X5, and then he was rolling down the right hand side of the U-shaped driveway, heading towards his next destination. He checked his watch as he waited for a gap in the traffic. Good. There was still plenty of time. The boss had told him to be at the warehouse by three p.m., but he planned on being there a whole lot earlier than that. This was one party he didn't want to be late for.

Hunter drummed his fingers on the steering-wheel in time to an old Guns 'n' Roses track entitled 'Mr Brownstone', a joyous ode to the myriad delights of heroin addiction. Those LA rock stars certainly knew how to live. He was sitting in the uncomfortable Dodge, the unwholesome smell of its previous occupant still assaulting his nostrils, parked up on Oxford Way in Beverly Hills. On the other side of the street was the Ashton mansion and, yeah, mansion was the only word you could use to describe the place—even the ducks wandering across the front lawn looked like they had a superiority complex. It was probably worth ten million dollars, but while the colonial architecture was undoubtedly impressive, Hunter found himself reminiscing about a time when civilisation had yet to encroach on the region, when antelope and wild horses had run free and geese had gathered in the *ciénaga* at the base of Coldwater Canyon. But those days were gone. Mankind had vanquished nature, bringing elaborate concrete structures, acres of asphalt and choking pollution along with all the other evils that money could buy, and it was evil that had brought him here that afternoon.

Once he'd discovered that Rebecca Finch was the link across all the revenge killings, establishing her motive hadn't been hard. Delving into her past, it hadn't taken long to find out that her sister, Anabeth, had been killed in a hit-and-run accident years earlier. When the driver of the vehicle had been apprehended, he'd been bombed out of his gourd, but despite that he'd been given a pathetically lenient jail term—it was enough to make anyone mad.

As far as Hunter could make out, Rebecca had then dedicated her life to punishing the guilty. As the justice system had failed her so completely, she'd taken matters into her own hands, setting herself up as a defence lawyer to ensure that she was in the best position to establish guilt, before helping the worst of her clients to walk free in order to keep them away from the vagaries of judicial sentencing. She'd then unleashed her pet assassin, who'd left twelve playing cards at the site of each execution—jacks, queens and kings—to signify a jury sitting in judgment. As he'd uncovered the truth, Hunter had been forced to reappraise his opinion of the lawyer. Each and every day the dregs of society were allowed to cause more pain and suffering on the street. At least Rebecca's revolutionary approach guaranteed a drop-off in repeat offenders. Only problem was, her methods were flawed.

Guessing the likely identity of her next target hadn't been much of a challenge either. Bobby Ashton. A drunk-driving spoilt brat who'd (a) killed a small kid, and (b) just walked out of court a free man with Rebecca's assistance. One plus one didn't always equal two but on this occasion he was willing to bet his left nut that the standard laws of mathematics would apply. As for the identity of the assassin, that remained an unknown. Probably someone Rebecca had represented in the past—the idea of turning the animals on each other would hold a certain appeal—but it didn't really matter at this point, as Hunter expected the Russian to come for Ashton any time now.

After placing a bogus pizza call to make sure that the kid was safe and sound inside his palatial home, he'd spent the next uneventful hour waiting for the assassin to show up. Some people might have considered using the kid as bait as somewhat unethical but, as far as Hunter was concerned, Ashton had it coming. Besides, how else was he going to track down the cold-blooded killer that had made two attempts on his life and whacked his friend? Hold out for a dinner invitation? Nah, better to catch the guy in the act and pounce on him when he least expected it, although the plan had been much the same at Witchcraft and look how things had turned out there. Poor old Carson—all the guy had wanted was to cut through the bullshit and clean up the streets, but now he was gone and it was left to Hunter to see things through.

At last, some action. A flower delivery truck turned into Ashton's driveway and sidled up towards the main house. Hunter wasn't sure how to react. Sit tight and wait to see what happened, or go in all guns blazing and hope he didn't end up with a dead delivery schmuck on his conscience? There was also Bobby Ashton's safety to consider. But not for long. Protecting unrepentant child killers didn't figure high on his list of priorities.

He set his jaw. His mind was made up. Maybe it'd be best to ride this one out. Give it a few minutes, see if anything out of the ordinary occurred. He checked his watch—it was almost 1.30 p.m. He killed the car stereo and watched as the truck pulled up in front of the main entrance. The driver climbed out. He looked kind of tall, so his height was ballpark OK for the assassin, but it wasn't what you'd call a positive ID. Hunter clicked his tongue in annoyance. Desperate though he was to bring the Russian to justice, putting a bullet in the head of anyone over six feet seemed a little extreme.

As he watched on, the driver hustled around to the rear of the vehicle, where he pulled open the double doors, ducked inside and emerged with a rectangular-shaped box under one arm. Excitement over. Looked like he was going to deliver some flowers after all. He clicked the stereo back on to return to the joys of Axl Rose and his crew of long-haired rockers, and the opening strains of 'Paradise City' began to fill the car. His eyes drifted back to the mansion as he willed the deliveryman to hurry up and get the fuck out of there, and as if on cue, the man in white coveralls strode back into view, only this time, something didn't look quite right. Maybe it was the full-sized body bag that was draped over his shoulder. Unless Hunter was very much mistaken, flower firms dropped off rather than collected. His adrenaline surged as he realised he was only a few hundred feet from his nemesis. The assassin tossed his cargo into the rear of the truck like it was nothing more than a sack of potatoes and got ready to depart.

Hunter gunned the Dodge's engine and went to race across the street, but the traffic was against him. By the time enough of a gap had opened up, the truck had already left the driveway and pulled out onto the road. He cracked a shit-eating grin and dropped in a few cars behind. No matter. He'd just follow the Russian and bring him down at the first opportunity. Jeez, if he got really lucky, the guy might even lead him to Finch for a double collar. Now, wouldn't that be sweet?

CHAPTER FORTY-SEVEN

HUNTER pulled up at the kerb as the delivery truck came to a stop in front of a disused warehouse, its nose pointed directly at a large industrial door. About an hour had passed since he'd left the Ashton residence and the journey across town had proved uneventful. He'd played it safe, keeping a three-car gap between himself and the truck at all times, eager to see what developed. The warehouse was somewhere in Inglewood, just south of the Forum, and it was pretty rundown—the crumbling brickwork was covered in graffiti and the window at the far end was boarded up. The only thing that looked new was the shiny metal chain on the industrial door. When the assassin climbed out of the truck he was carrying a pair of heavy-duty bolt cutters. The chain never stood a chance. Once he'd rolled back the door, he returned to the truck and drove through the opening. Seconds later, the door clanged shut.

Hunter crossed the street and approached the warehouse. He couldn't go in the front—it would be too damn noisy. His eyes skirted along the façade until they settled on the boarded-up window at the far end. Windows usually signified the warehouse office, and offices generally had doors. He limped to the end of the building and peeked round the corner. Bingo. The presence of a small side door put a smile on his face, and that smile broadened when the door opened with a gentle nudge. The lock had been smashed, probably by some passing vagrant in search of shelter. He slid inside and waited for his eyes to adjust to the gloom. A ratty old chair with most of its stuffing torn out sat in front of him, along with a cheap metal desk that was covered in dust. To his right were a couple of battered filing cabinets, and above them were a series of posters featuring wafer-thin models in tight-fitting jeans. The panel wall opposite had space for two large windows that would once have overlooked the warehouse floor, but the panes of glass were long gone, having been replaced by lightweight chipboard.

He crept over to the door, stilled his breathing, and listened intently. All was quiet, but the assassin had to be in there somewhere. To step through the opening was to present himself as a target, but he had no intention of backing out now. He eased open the door and swivelled out in a half-crouch, eyes flicking around the cavernous space, gun following suit.

A glass ceiling was set in the centre of the roof, its panes half-choked with grime, although the sun still managed to penetrate in places to bathe the centre of the warehouse in a sickly glow. Some empty metal clothes racks sat to his left, while flat-pack boxes were stacked high by the wall to his right. The white panel truck was just ahead of him. He slid forward on the balls of his feet, then worked his way steadily down the far side of the truck, his desert boots silent on the dusty floor, his heart hammering in his chest. Sweat ran down his brow while his ankle throbbed steadily. Once he'd reached the cab, the assassin and Ashton came into view.

The kid had been lashed to an old wooden chair—staked out invitingly under a shaft of sunlight with the empty body bag at his feet. He stiffened when he saw Hunter, and although the gag in his mouth kept him quiet, his eyes stared out beseechingly. The assassin was facing the other way, double-checking the knots, while hundreds of tailor's dummies leant against the far wall, giving the scene a macabre backdrop.

'Hands on your head! Now!' barked Hunter, his voice gaining gravitas as it echoed around the chamber. The assassin slowly complied.

'I leave Ashton here, just like you say. Leave him to starve to death, no? Just like you wanted…'

'I don't think Ashton's gonna be feeling hungry any time soon,' muttered Hunter as he eyed the truck. 'Now, turn around, nice and slow…'

'I wait many months for this moment…then you arrive early and trick me…but at least now I finally see your face…'

When the assassin turned around, Hunter felt a chill course through his being. The Russian had an otherworldly quality about him, an aura of death. His skin was pale and drawn, stretched taut over angular cheekbones, while his eyes were little more than slits, grey chips of ice that betrayed no flicker of emotion.

'Step away from the kid,' Hunter ordered as he emerged from the cover of the truck to drive the assassin back towards the office. 'Now, reach for your gun, real slow, and toss it away…'

The assassin's expression was one of utter bewilderment as he pulled back his coveralls to reveal a Glock 18. The gun made a clattering sound as it disappeared into the shadows.

'You? *Nyet*…it cannot be. You are the one? Sent me targets? Makes no sense… I tried to kill you…'

'And when that didn't work, you tried to frame me,' retorted Hunter. 'You left a bunch of stuff back at my place that makes me look like some kind of psycho. Why the hell did you pick me to take the fall?'

'What you mean?' asked Danilov.

'Don't give me that! All the news clippings and insane graffiti you left in my bedroom, and all those weapons. The police are combing LA for me as we speak.'

'You are mad.'

'Well, if it wasn't you, it must have been your boss.'

Danilov was still confused. 'So you're not boss?'

'What? You think I'm your boss? Of course I'm not.' Wait a minute—what gives? The assassin thought that he'd been sending the targets. Another piece of the puzzle fell into place. 'Let me get this straight—you're just some mercenary that kills on command? And you don't even know who's paying the bills?'

'Payment! I get no payment! I kill because I have to, otherwise boss would throw me to wolves.'

'Talk about ironic. All this while you've been one step ahead of me, but now I'm finally one up on you!'

The assassin's eyes narrowed. 'You know boss?'

'Yep.'

'Give me name!'

And it was at that point that things got really interesting.

'Rebecca Finch,' said a woman's voice from deep inside the shadows that hugged the mannequin-lined wall. 'Drop the gun, Hunter, and back the hell up!'

CHAPTER FORTY-EIGHT

THE Beretta in Hunter's hand implored him to respond with a hot chunk of lead, but sometimes you had to know when you were beat. Ashton made a whining sound alongside him, shaking his head forcibly from side to side, almost upending his chair.

'Shut up, kid,' Hunter muttered as he laid down the gun and gave it a gentle kick towards the front of the truck, all the while fuming at himself for having walked straight into a trap. Shit. An idiot and his weapon were easily parted.

'*Nyet*…it's not possible,' said an awestruck Danilov, his sallow face bleached of what little colour it had once possessed. 'You were my lawyer…'

'That's right, Viktor,' responded Rebecca, as she emerged from a pile of mannequins with Browning Hi-Power in hand. 'How else do you think I get to make the acquaintance of lethal killing machines?'

'You put me in witness protection programme...'

The Russian was having a hard time getting his head round the turn in events. The poor guy was so dumbstruck he probably hadn't even started to consider the precariousness of his position, something that Hunter was all too aware of. Only one person was likely to walk away from this mess and, as things stood, Rebecca Finch was in the box seat.

'What the hell is all this about, Rebecca?' asked Hunter in a low voice. 'I knew you lawyers were ruthless, but what you're doing seems a little extreme.'

'Extreme? How? I've been representing scum like him...' a nod towards Ashton '...for the past five years. I've seen the pain and agony they've caused, I've seen them convicted, I've seen them sent down, then a few years later I've seen them released to do it all over again. Some people never learn from their mistakes, no matter how long they're locked up for. And some are just plain evil—every breath they take is an affront to human decency. The legal system doesn't know how to cope with them. Murderers walk free on technicalities. Rapists get to whine about their, oh so difficult childhoods in counselling. Drug dealers get time off for good behaviour. It's got to stop.'

'And that's where you and laughing boy come in?'

'Viktor Danilov was a gift from the gods. I had to wait a long time for someone with his skills to cross my path, and when he finally did, I knew that some higher power was at work. It was a blessing. A chance to strike back. A chance to make a difference. So from then on I made damn sure that I kept the worst of my clients out of jail, just so they could meet Viktor. That way, they got *justice*. Real *justice*. I'd expect a man with your past to understand.'

'You blackmail me for months,' Danilov snarled. 'Keep me at hand like dog on leash—'

Hunter cut the Russian short. 'Pipe down, buddy. We'll deal with your wounded pride later. Right now there's more pressing matters to attend to. Like where do we go from here?'

'The way I see it, there are only two options,' said Rebecca. 'Either you're for me or against me. I'd hope that someone like you would understand. Why don't you sign up for the cause? Just think of the power we'd have if we worked together…think of the good we could do…'

Hunter looked her dead in the face. Her belief in what she was doing was evangelical, but she'd already gone too far. She'd allowed innocent people to be killed. She'd sanctioned the hit on Carson. She'd tried to frame him for all the vengeance killings. But despite all that, he had little choice but to play along. This was going to be the toughest job interview of his life—the consequences of failure didn't bear thinking about. He looked at the barrel of the Browning and wondered if it had ever been fired. Had Rebecca ever killed anyone? Subcontracting to assassins was one thing, but pulling the trigger yourself wasn't as easy as it looked in the movies. It took a certain kind of moxie to dispense death, especially when it was in cold blood. Maybe she wouldn't be up to the task.

'Well, let me put it this way. All those guys you had killed—there were no tears of sorrow from me,' he began. 'And I gotta admit, your approach would go some way to putting the brakes on the growing prison population.'

'But why you here? Why now?' rasped Danilov. 'Never got hands dirty before.'

'I was going to give Ashton one last chance to show some remorse. One last chance to make his peace.'

'This case is personal for our esteemed lawyer,' interrupted Hunter. 'Some idiot killed her only sister, Anabeth, in a DUI years ago, and now she's looking for some payback. Ashton's drink-driving has dredged up a lot of bad memories—that's why he's lined up with the grille of that truck. You're gonna mow him down, aren't you, Rebecca?'

Ashton whimpered through his gag as a tear rolled down Rebecca's face.

'Not dead…Anabeth's not dead… She's OK…still OK…'

'Rebecca, you've gotta face it—she's gone,' said Hunter in a soft voice. 'She was killed at a Hollywood intersection back in 1989, then laid to rest in Holy Cross Cemetery. I can take you to the gravestone if you like…'

Rebecca let loose a wail of despair that chilled him to the bone.

'But she'll never leave me… I told my parents, but they didn't understand…they said I was keeping the pain alive…they said I had to let go… Now they barely return my calls. But why should I let go? Anabeth still comes to me…she gives me advice…she keeps me strong…' Her voice trailed off and she stood silent for a few seconds until she'd regained some of her composure. 'Ever since her accident I've known what had to be done. The guilty have to be punished, and who better to ascertain guilt than defending counsel? Montero was a child killer. Schaeffer a rapist. And the others…they all deserved to die. Ashton has to suffer for what he did. For my sister. For Anabeth. It's all been for Anabeth. I want to see him beg for mercy. Viktor was meant to leave him here, but once you showed up, I had to step in.'

'Because my presence meant that I knew too much.'

'Ah-huh,' she said as she wiped away the tears. 'So, how about it? Are you going to join my crusade? We could do great things together. We'd make a great team—you, me and Anabeth.'

Hunter watched as her face took on a crazed expression, wild-eyed, beseeching, dangerous. All that talk of advice from her dead sister meant Rebecca wasn't playing with a full deck, but she was holding an automatic pistol, and that wasn't the best of combinations. How the hell was he going to get out of this?

'The way I see it, even if I say yes, there's still a problem. What about Ashton?'

'There's two problems, actually—how can I trust you?' She thought it through for a moment, then shrugged. 'Two problems, one solution. Help me kill Ashton to prove your loyalty.'

All her attention was focussed on Hunter as he came to a decision. Big mistake. Danilov's hand whipped out from the back of his white coveralls brandishing a switchblade. In one smooth motion he cocked his arm and sent the weapon hurtling towards the unsuspecting lawyer. Maybe the assassin got lucky, maybe it was all skill—but either way the knife found its mark, burying itself deep in Rebecca's throat. Her eyes widened in surprise, then her gun clattered to the floor as she reached for the hilt.

CHAPTER FORTY-NINE

TIME stood still for a few seconds as Rebecca grasped the knife handle that protruded from her neck, a look of disbelief on her face. Blood began to bubble out of the wound, slowly at first, then faster, until a red river ran down the front of her blouse. She coughed once, then her eyes rolled back in her head as she slumped to the floor, and that was the signal for all hell to break loose.

Hunter hurled himself headlong towards his Beretta. Danilov dived for his Glock. The two men reached their weapons simultaneously, leaving the delivery truck directly between them. Hunter rolled into a crouch alongside the truck's front fender, swung the barrel towards the assassin, and loosed off two quick shots, but Danilov was already on the move, sprinting towards the safety of the office. Bullets punctured the thin panel walls to mark the Russian's progress, then Hunter was firing again, peppering the doorway with lead. The last bullet clipped the fleeing man's shoulder, but before Hunter could start celebrating, he came under return fire as Danilov loosed off a burst of his own. Hunter hit the deck as a pair of 9-mm rounds exploded into the truck, then waited for the barrage to subside. Rebecca started to cough up blood. He was wondering whether he could drag her to safety when the Russian's voice rang out.

'Hunter…it is over. Let me go…I have no argument with you. Lawyer was blackmailing me… I go back to quiet life…away from here…away from you.'

Hunter reloaded his gun. There was no way he was going to start negotiating.

'You hear me?' Danilov continued. 'Let me go. That way we both live…'

Hunter skirted around the far side of the vehicle, eased open the door and climbed inside. The keys were still in the ignition. The engine caught at the first time of asking, then he wrenched the gearshift into reverse and stamped on the accelerator. The truck flew backwards like it had been shot from a cannon, slamming through the thin panel walls of the office like a charging rhino before coming to an abrupt halt against the warehouse's brick exterior.

Hunter peeled himself off the steering-wheel, cut the engine and pushed at the door. Dust hung heavy in the air. He flailed with his Beretta in search of a target. The office looked like it had been through an earthquake—the aging chair and desk were now buried beneath sections of panel wall, while the filing cabinets had been damaged beyond repair—but there was no sign of the assassin. The door stood wide open and the side-alley was empty—Danilov had gone. The urge to follow was almost overwhelming, but Rebecca needed help. Hunter doubled back to the warehouse floor where she lay in a pool of blood. Her eyes stared up at the heavens. Her breath came in shallow gasps. Her forehead was cold to the touch. All in all, it didn't look good.

The assassin's knife was still embedded in her throat, her feeble attempts to remove it having failed, and blood continued to run down the contours of her neck to pool by her side. It looked like severe trauma to the carotid artery. He gripped the handle and withdrew the blade in one smooth motion, prompting a burst of arterial spray to arch from the wound. Her chest rose and fell as she took another shallow breath. He ripped off his shirt and pressed it against her neck, but within seconds it was soaked with her blood. There was nothing he could do. She didn't have long. He brushed a strand of blonde hair from her face then held her close as she tried to speak. Her words came out in a barely decipherable gurgle.

'For me...

'For Anabeth...

'For justice...'

Her eyes glazed over, her hand fell limp, and then she was gone. He gently rolled down her eyelids then rose to his feet, feeling a burst of sorrow for someone who'd tried to do the right thing but had gone about it the wrong way. She was a beautiful woman whose mind had been twisted by grief. In another life, the two of them might have been partners, but in this one things hadn't worked out that way. Rebecca had been a white-collar vigilante, a voice for the silent majority, and he was more than sympathetic to her cause, but her mistake had been to delegate the assassinations to a stone-cold killer like Danilov. When it came to wet work, you had to have the guts to take a hands-on approach, otherwise things could get out of hand. The wrong people got eliminated. Innocents like Carson got caught up in the crossfire. Mistakes were made.

And talking of mistakes, what was he going to do with the bound and gagged affront to humanity that sat tied to a chair in the middle of the floor? He couldn't just leave him there. He retraced his steps and went to work on the gag, taking care to avoid the puddle at the kid's feet and trying not to breathe in too much ammonia.

'Nice, real nice,' he muttered. 'Isn't it about time you were potty trained?'

'Fuck you,' whimpered Ashton as soon as the gag was free. 'I could have been killed.'

'Believe me, we'd have coped with the loss. Now, listen up. You've been given a second chance here today, a chance to make up for all the shitty things you've done with your life up till now. If I were you, I'd think very seriously about taking it.'

'And just who the fuck are you to tell me what to…?' The kid's voice trailed off when he saw the Beretta dangling from Hunter's right hand.

Hunter decided to stop wasting his breath. Rebecca had been right—some people would never learn.

'Be seeing you, kid,' he muttered, heading for the exit.

'Hey! Wait a minute! You can't just leave me here.'

'Wanna bet?' said Hunter, turning back to fix the kid with an ice-cold glare. 'You can stay there and think about what you've done. Think about the child you killed. Think about the pain you've caused. And while you're doing all that thinking, I suggest you do it quietly, otherwise your Russian friend might decide to come back.'

Sermon over, he spun on his heel and walked away. He was done wasting time on the likes of Ashton and, anyhow, he had far more pressing matters to attend to.

Now that he'd had a little time to reflect on the last few minutes, one thing wasn't making much sense. Why had Rebecca asked him to join her crusade? Why the hell would she want to team up with the man that she'd just tried to frame? For all she knew, the police had a BOLO out on him at this very moment. And since when had she crossed over from punishing the guilty to framing the innocent? His brow furrowed as he pondered these questions for a moment, then everything suddenly became clear. He knew what he had to do. The hunt was on.

CHAPTER FIFTY

HUNTER was back at Tommy's bar, sitting at the far end of the counter, nursing a shot of whisky. The phone sat in front of him, his first call having just come to a close, when he'd anonymously informed the police of the whereabouts of the warehouse that contained both Bobby Ashton and Rebecca's corpse. As things stood, he was still the number-one suspect for a string of unsolved killings, but the kid's testimony ought to go some way to getting him off the hook. This factor, and this factor alone, had helped him resist the temptation to leave the spoilt brat to rot. Sometimes he was all heart.

Tommy was the only other person present, and he was busy emptying a case of Budweiser into one of the fridges behind the bar. Hunter took another sip of whisky as he readied himself for his next call. A female voice answered on the third ring in a clipped, professional tone. When he asked to be transferred to one of her colleagues, there was a slight delay before she returned to report that the person he'd asked for was on vacation and wouldn't be back for another two weeks.

He replaced the phone in its cradle. Vacation—yeah, he guessed you could call it that. His next call was to Hertz, the rental car company whose Jeep Cherokee had last been seen leaving Witchcraft with Carson's corpse on the back seat. He drummed his fingers on the table as he waited for an answer.

'Good afternoon, Hertz rentals. How can I help you?' asked a young male voice.

'Yeah, this is Detective Zac Hunter.' He reeled off his old badge number and hoped that Hertz employees didn't keep up to date with the hirings and firings of their local police department. 'I've got a couple of questions related to a Jeep Cherokee you leased to a Mr V. I. Lenin on the 23rd.'

'Sure thing, Officer, anything you need. Just give me a second to call it up on the system. Yep…here it is… Fire away.'

'OK. Does your system tell you what time the Cherokee was rented?'

'Yes—it was rented at two-thirty in the afternoon.'

'Right. How about you read out the names of all those people who rented vehicles five minutes either side of the Cherokee?'

'You got it.'

Hunter listened intently as the clerk quickly ran down a list of names, but none of them jumped out at him. He thought things through for a moment, then asked the clerk to search for one name in particular, broadening the time period to the previous three days. When the clerk next spoke, another piece of the puzzle fell into place.

'Here you go—the individual in question hired a four-wheel-drive Ford Explorer on the 23rd, the same day as your Mr Lenin got his Cherokee.'

'Can you give me the licence on the Explorer and the details of the credit card that was used to book it?'

Hunter scribbled the information down on a beer mat and asked when the car was due for return.

'Hmm, let me see. Says here the Explorer's due back in two weeks' time.'

He thanked the guy for his help, rung off and ruminated on his next move. Credit-card usage. That was the way to go. The quickest way to trace someone in the modern world. He took a deep breath. If he got a hit this time, whatever lingering doubts he had regarding the identity of the person who'd framed him would fly out the window.

He picked up the phone and stabbed at the buttons with his fingers, placing a call to one of his contacts at Bank of America. Jimmy Chang, the Taiwanese immigrant who lived out in Temple City, near the Church of St Lawrence. Jimmy was good with numbers, which was probably why he worked in a bank.

'Hey Jimmy, I'm after a favour.'

'Aren't you always? And, boy, it must be important seeing as how you've skipped the pleasantries—no how you doing, no how's the wife and kids. Hell, you're lucky my ego don't bruise easy…'

'Sorry—how is Li Meng? She keeping out of trouble?' he said, offering a gentle reminder of how he'd let Jimmy's daughter skate on an uppers bust three years ago.

'She's fine, and I'd like to thank you once again….'

'Yeah, Jimmy, you can thank me by running a credit card. It's an Amex—you guys deal with them, don't you? I'm after any card usage that shows up on your system during the last couple of days.'

'No problem. What's the name and number on the Amex?'

Hunter reeled them off and waited for a response. Jimmy had an answer for him in under a minute.

'I found your card, and I've got three hits on it. First, from a gas station on I-10 just outside San Bernardino late last night, then another an hour later from a roadside diner on Highway 18. The last one occurred first thing this morning, from a mini-mart in someplace called Pine Ridge.'

'Pine Ridge? Isn't that up near Lake Gregory?'

'No idea, buddy. I don't vacation in the rural backwaters. You'll have to get yourself a map.'

Hunter didn't need a map. The more he thought about it the surer he was. Pine Ridge was right by a lake—and that made a whole lot of sense.

'You need anything else?'

'Nope—that's about it. Thanks, Jimmy, you've been great.'

He cut the call, the first seeds of a plan beginning to form in his mind. He checked his watch—it was four p.m. Just enough time to make a couple more calls to set things in motion. Once that was done, he'd grab a few hours' shut-eye somewhere safe before heading up into the mountains. If he was going to pull this off, he'd need to be at his sharpest.

CHAPTER FIFTY-ONE

THE mountain road was long, winding and lonely, the last pair of trailing headlights having blinked out ten miles back. California pines towered on either side and dark stormclouds were gathering in the night sky overhead. The heavy winter rains were just around the corner, waiting to bring three months of floods to LA, which was kind of ironic for a city that imported $150 million worth of water every year. Hunter stepped on the gas and watched the speedometer edge higher. The solitude gave him comfort. It gave him time to think. To remember everything that he'd been through recently.

How his girlfriend, Skye, had dumped him after the hunt for the missing children had taken over his life. How his violent apprehension of Montero had been followed by the pornographer's acquittal in a windowless courtroom. How the Russian assassin, Danilov, had thwarted his need for vengeance. How he'd teamed up with Carson to bring Danilov down. How he'd found the link across the assassin's executions to reveal that Rebecca Finch had been pulling the strings. How he'd been set up to take the fall for Danilov's executions. And how he'd watched Rebecca die. It was all going to come to an end somewhere just up ahead.

Things were going to get messy. Lines were going to be crossed. Old allegiances were going to fail, new ones were going to be formed. Sometimes you had to get your hands dirty in the pursuit of justice. Hunter understood that better than most. But you had to make sure you could wash the worst of the dirt off at the end of each day, otherwise you were no better than the animals you sought to cage. He knew what had to be done, and he hoped he could live with the consequences, because after tonight there could be no turning back.

As his tan Dodge spluttered onwards, an old logging track loomed large on his left. Judging by the height of the weeds, it hadn't been used in some time. A mile further on he passed a few small cabins set back from the road, each one situated far enough away from the next to suggest that personal space was a highly valued commodity around these parts. As the cabins flashed by, an occasional light shone out from a window, an odd plume of smoke puffed from a chimney—meagre signs of life in an otherwise desolate environment.

He'd been on the road for the best part of three hours, so when he finally arrived at his destination it was with no small sense of relief. On first impressions, Pine Ridge was a one-horse town, and that horse had long since departed. If it weren't for the rusting metal sign that confirmed his arrival, he'd have sworn he was still lost in the woods at the ass-end of nowhere. Only a lifelong hermit would have had the temerity to call this place a thriving metropolis. The sum total of buildings was one wooden saloon, one small mini-mart, a modest boarding house with a sign out front saying it was closed till next spring, and around ten or so rundown brick dwellings that looked barely fit for human habitation. It sure as hell wasn't anything to write home about. The only signs of life came from the saloon, where a dull light shone behind slatted blinds and a bass-heavy beat thumped out to frighten the passing wildlife. The building was fashioned from pine, the lumber doubtless harvested from the surrounding woodland at some point during the town's more prosperous past. It was the kind of place that managed to look both welcoming and ominous at the same time. A hand-painted sign hung over the door. It read PINE RIDGE TAVERN. The owner must have had one hell of an imagination.

Hunter pulled into the lot, bounced over some ruts in the dried mud, then coasted to a halt alongside an old Chevy pick-up. The first drops of rain began to splash off his windscreen as the storm broke. Parked directly opposite was a vehicle he found instantly recognisable. His back-up had already arrived. Everything was falling into place. He killed the engine and climbed outside to brave the weather. Large droplets of water pummelled him from above. The gods themselves were crying tonight, and with good reason. He threw a quick glance around the lot to confirm that no four-by-four Explorers were hidden among the fifteen or so other cars that sat idly by, then strode up to the bar's front door and yanked it open. The thudding bass line immediately morphed from mild annoyance to ear-threatening assault. Jesus. If he spent too much time in there he was gonna wind up deaf. Still, at least the loud music would guarantee a little conversational privacy.

A rock band consisting of three shaggy-haired no-accounts were playing in the far corner of the joint, and playing badly. The overweight drummer seemed more intent on pounding through his skins than creating anything that resembled an actual rhythm; the bassist's performance was hampered by the fact he was so drunk he could barely stand; while the lead guitarist sang like he was being disembowelled and played like a man who was still waiting for the gift of opposable thumbs. Mercifully the number came to an end, allowing the singer to thank his female fan club of one—a slutty blonde who burst into wild applause from her position down front at a rickety table. She might have been his sister, his girlfriend, or both—Pine Ridge looked like the sort of place where incest would pass as entertainment on a cold winter's night.

As the band launched into a gut-wrenchingly awful cover of the Ramones' 'Blitzkrieg Bop', Hunter checked out the rest of the bar. On his left, four old guys sat propped up at the counter beneath a dense cloud of smoke, taking occasional puffs on some foul-smelling cheroots. The central aisle was filled with circular tables, but only two of them were occupied—one housed a rough-looking couple who were busy sucking on each other's faces in between taking hits from a bottle of Wild Turkey, the other was home to a group of bleary-eyed men who'd been there for most of the night if their collection of empty pitchers was anything to go by. The rest of the clientele hung out on the right hand side of the bar, getting wasted in the relative comfort of the high-backed booths that ran the length of the side wall.

He made his way down the middle of the room until he caught sight of his two new partners in one of the booths. They stood out like roadkill on a desert highway, but no one was bothering them and, besides, they could look after themselves. He offered them a nod that was swiftly returned, then made his way over to the counter to grab himself a beer. The barman was old and crotchety, with a straggly grey beard that reached halfway down his chest. He dug a bottle of Bud out of the fridge, shoved it across the counter, then went back to cleaning his gums with a dirty toothpick. Talk about service with a smile.

Hunter bagged himself a booth, his back to the bar's main entrance to ensure that any new arrivals would be unaware of his presence. In the next half-hour, two things happened. First, the so-called rock band wound up their set and cleared the stage, much to the relief of any music lover within a five-mile radius, and, second, Hunter finished his beer and ordered another. As he was taking a pull on the long-necked Bud, a creak from the main door signalled that someone had come in from the cold. He sat the bottle down, released the safety on his Beretta, then thrust the gun inside his jacket pocket. Was this the moment he'd been waiting for?

He sat dead still as his pulse raced, somehow resisting the urge to lean out past the end of the booth for a better look. Within ten seconds a man appeared at the counter. He was dripping wet from the storm, with a hat pulled tight to his head, but despite his bedraggled appearance there could be no mistaking him. Same weary gait, same heavy blue coat, same barked order for fine-brand whisky. The guy who'd framed him for murder. The guy who'd stood back and left him to die. The guy who had played him like a grand piano from the very first moment they'd met. Hunter had found him—the end game had arrived.

CHAPTER FIFTY-TWO

CARSON—back from the dead—and, boy, did he have some explaining to do. Hunter felt a cold fury descend as he slid out of the booth. This guy was meant to have had his back, but instead he'd been intent on stabbing him right between the shoulder blades from the get-go. Hunter's desert boots made no noise on the wooden floor as he closed the distance to his erstwhile partner, his rage growing ever stronger with each passing step. By the time he'd crossed the room he was just about ready to explode.

'I'll have a Bud if you're buying…'

The old man stiffened, his drink frozen halfway between the counter and his mouth, his plans for a quiet evening fast evaporating.

'How'd you find me?' he asked, turning around slowly with his hands in clear view, his expression a mixture of surprise and resignation, like on some level he'd expected to be caught.

'Shouldn't have used your credit card, Carson. Dead men don't keep spending. Once I'd realised that Danilov and Rebecca had nothing to do with framing me, you were the only person left with both the means and the opportunity. No one else knew I was involved in the case. So I started to wonder if your whole death had been staged for my benefit. When I discovered that you'd booked a vacation and a rental car on the very same day of your apparent demise, I knew that something was up. And when I got a pal of mine to see if there'd been any credit-card usage in your name over the last twenty-four hours, guess what he found? Bud Carson was alive and well and buying groceries in some town called Pine Ridge.'

Carson ignored him as his eyes strayed downwards to Hunter's jacket. 'I don't suppose there's any chance that yonder bulge means you're pleased to see me?'

'I'm pleased enough, oldtimer, pleased enough, but, trust me, you don't wanna get me over-excited. Come on, I've got us a nice booth over by the far wall. Why don't you grab yourself a seat and tell me all about the afterlife?'

Carson led the way across the bar, took off his hat, settled down into the proffered seat and rested his hands on the table.

'So my credit card led you here, and good fortune led you straight to this bar?'

'Something like that. I assume your pal's fishing cabin is around here someplace?' Carson nodded, prompting Hunter to continue. 'Hiking through the woods in search of some old cabin didn't appeal to me, so as soon as I found out that Pine Ridge had a watering hole, that seemed like the best place to start. You were bound to show up here sooner or later.'

'Yeah, well, you know me, I like a drink, but I don't like to drink alone. Had me a few good nights in here over the years.'

'I'll bet. Anyhow, enough of this chitchat. How long have you known about Rebecca Finch?'

The old man rubbed at his jaw before responding. 'A few weeks. Got it from the playing cards left at the scene of each crime. Took me a while to realise that those jacks, queens and kings represented a jury, but once that happened, the legal angle led me straight to her.'

'Then you started to work with her?'

'Nope—I've never even spoken to her. But I could see the value in what she was doing, so I decided I'd leave her be—stand back and let nature take its course. Well, not exactly take its course. I've falsified evidence and buried key facts to keep her out of the spotlight for as long as possible. And why? I'll tell you why. I gave my whole life to police work and all I got in return were a couple of messy divorces and a shit load of frustration. When my second wife walked out on me, the job was all I had left, but in recent times I've come to realise just how goddamned useless the modern-day cop is. What's the point of spending weeks on the trail of a killer if they're gonna walk free on some legal technicality at the end of it all? Cleaning up the dregs of society is important work, and Finch's methods were a whole lot more effective than those employed by the so-called justice system. Only trouble was, if an old drunk like me could follow the clues, so could someone else. In the end, she was always gonna get caught. So I started to watch out for a patsy—some guy with a grudge that I could pin the assassinations on.'

'Someone like me,' Hunter snarled.

'Yeah, you fit the bill to a T. Disgraced cop, just been booted off the force with a string of IA investigations behind you, each one detailing how you took the law into your own hands to break a case. Your track record marks you out as a violent man. Have you read your file? According to the shrinks, you're borderline psychotic. Plus you're a loner. Parents long gone, and you've barely held down a girlfriend for more than a couple of months at a time. You know what your psych profile resembles? A serial killer. You made the perfect patsy, and your involvement in the Montero case was the clincher, as I'd already guessed he'd be next on Finch's hit list. All I had to do was link you with the other victims then feed you to the department. Sure, the case might not have stuck, but I figured that I'd buy Finch another couple of months at the least—give her more time to carry on the good work.'

'Yeah—let's talk about that "good work". Assassinating child killers and rapists is one thing, but what about all the innocents that got caught in crossfire? People like the young hooker with Montero? Or Rhythm Ray? Hell, at one point I even thought you were a victim.'

'Go cry me a river. They were nothing more than collateral damage. Small price to pay. Take Montero, for instance. Cost us one dead whore. If he'd lived, how many kids would have gone on to die in some snuff movie? Way I figured it, a whore's life wasn't worth fretting over, not in the big scheme of things.'

And there it was in a nutshell. The reason why the revenge killings had to stop. As soon as you started accepting civilian casualties and whining about the greater good, you'd lost all moral authority. You'd lost all perspective. You'd turned yourself into everything you most despised. A murderer. A common killer. The enemy.

Hunter's eyes narrowed. 'And the whole fake death thing, that was just for my benefit?'

'Yep. You were starting to get a little too close to the truth, so I planted the evidence at your place off Mulholland. Some of it was pretty convincing—one of the knives actually had Ribecki's blood on it—then I set up my fake death at

Witchcraft with the help of an old buddy of mine who used to work in special effects for Universal. He went along with it, no problem—thought he was in on a retirement prank. Posed as the killer, set up blood squibs and everything. I figured that with me out of the picture you'd have no one to back up your story once you got hauled in. Plus you'd come across as crazy—claiming to be a secret part of the investigation, telling everyone I'd been killed. So once I was dead, I left an anonymous tip about you with the cops, then headed up to the mountains to do a little late-season fishing. Only problem was, you escaped from your pad, then set about solving the case. How'd you do it so fast?'

'Broke into your place and stole your private files…you know, the ones that contain all the background info on each victim. They gave me the link to Rebecca—each of the assassin's victims had enjoyed legal representation, and Rebecca had worked for all the firms at one time or another.'

'Shit. I guess I shoulda got rid of them. They're a darn sight more complete than the official ones down at Parker Center. But it really shouldn't have mattered. If the cops I'd sent to arrest you had just done their jobs, you'd be in lockdown right now.'

'You son of a bitch.'

'Whatever.' The detective shrugged, sliding towards the end of the booth, 'Anyhow, it's been nice catching up, but I figure it's time I made myself scarce.'

'Where the fuck do you think you're going?'

'Come on, son, face it—you got dick. I'm just an incompetent old drunk headed for retirement—you'll never prove that I worked out what Finch was doing then stood by to let it happen. No one in their right mind's gonna believe you. The only option you've got left is to shoot me down in cold blood, and if you were gonna do that, you'd have done it already.

Deep down, you're torn, because you hate our shitty legal system just as much as I do, but you don't have the guts to do anything about it.'

'Yeah, maybe you're right,' allowed Hunter, taking a slug from his beer. 'Maybe I haven't sunk as low as you have. At least, not yet. But before you leave, there's a couple of guys I'd like you to meet. Fellas, it's time to say hello.'

Two dark faces appeared from the other side of the booth to loom over Carson, one contorted with rage, the other sporting a vicious-looking scar that ran the length of his left cheek. Gold chains hung heavy over black shirts while huge rings lined raised knuckles. These guys never left home without their bling.

'Carson—I'd like you to make the acquaintance of Furious, leader of the 16th Street Renegades, and his pit-bull of a first lieutenant, Slice. Furious is kinda new to the leadership business, having only recently taken control of the gang after the untimely death of his brother, Ray, who spontaneously exploded in the middle of a basketball court. You remember Rhythm Ray? He was one of those innocent bystanders you deemed collateral damage.'

'Time's up, muthafucka, you gots to pay,' whispered Furious through clenched teeth, as Slice slid around the side of the booth to jam a gun into Carson's ribcage. 'You might not have killed my bro, but you sure as hell left him to die…'

'Hunter…you can't…' spluttered the detective, a look of fear creeping into his eyes.

'I damn well can. You wanted street justice—now you've got it. Go explain yourself to them, because in this fucked-up world I don't know what's right or wrong any more. I think I'm gonna do just what you did—stand back and let nature take its course.'

'Let's go, muthafucka,' whispered Slice, grabbing a chunk of Carson's coat and dragging him out of his seat.

'But, Hunter…they're animals…' Carson shouted, turning a few heads in the bar.

'Y'all stay out of this,' warned Furious, as the four heavy drinkers stationed at the nearest table started to rise. ''Less you wanna wind up perforated. This ain't none of your god-damn business.' A wave of his Uzi was enough to get them to sit back down in a hurry.

As Slice dragged the bellowing Carson outside, Hunter leant back in the booth and took a long, hard pull on his Bud. He didn't know it then, but the detective's last words would stay with him for years to come;

'Call this justice? I'll see you in hell, Hunter! I'll see you in fucking hell!'

And then it was over.

CHAPTER FIFTY-THREE

HUNTER took a couple of minutes to finish his beer before standing up to leave. While he'd have liked nothing more than to kick back in the bar and wait for his emotions to cool, that wasn't an option. Something told him if he stayed put for much longer the locals might start asking questions, the sort of questions he was in no mood to answer. As it was, he'd only managed to maintain his privacy thus far by resting his Beretta on the table.

He scooped up the gun and strode quickly across the room, keen to leave the dubious delights of Pine Ridge far behind. Once he'd barrelled through the front door to return to the storm, his conscience decided to kick in, prompting Carson's craggy face to appear among the surrounding pines. He blinked hard and banished his mental demon. He'd done the right thing. The old guy had turned a blind eye as the innocent victims had started to mount. He'd even tried to frame *him* for all the vengeance killings. One way or another, Carson had to pay.

The sudden roar of a powerful engine dragged his attention back to the here and now. The two Renegades, Furious and Slice, were about to depart in their big black Humvee. He gave the two gangsters a nod of acknowledgement as he walked over towards his Dodge, which was now sandwiched between a Chevy pick-up and a BMW X5. This whole business had left him with some strange new friends. If anyone had told him a couple of weeks ago that he'd end up making nice with some gangbangers, he'd have had them committed. The Humvee's tyres kicked up the mud as it rumbled towards the exit. Hunter watched as the vehicular monster swung out onto the road and set off for LA. He was still standing there when he heard the ratcheting sound of a pump action shotgun from just behind him.

'Danilov,' he stated, without looking around, his heart sinking like a stone. 'How's that shoulder bearing up?'

'Fine, my friend, fine—flesh wound. Throw down gun, raise hands.'

'I thought you'd left town?' Shit. His mind was racing. How the hell was he gonna get out of this? The slightest move would invite a slew of steel pellets to eviscerate him from behind. He removed the Beretta from its holster and hurled it away, his stomach sinking as the weapon disappeared into a puddle with a resounding plop. Talk about feeling emasculated. His eyes snapped back to the departing Humvee in the hope that the Renegades might be able to bail him out, but they'd already swung out of the lot to head south.

'Leave town? Without saying goodbye? Impossible. Now, get inside car,' Danilov ordered. 'I even let you drive.'

While his heart told him to make a break for it, his head overruled it—running wouldn't save him now. He stepped forward and climbed behind the wheel of the BMW, well aware that this next ride could turn out to be his last. He craned his head to watch the Russian emerge from the gloom with a sawn-off Mossberg cradled in his arms. Danilov opened the rear door, clambered in and jabbed the gun barrel hard into the back of the seat.

'How the hell did you find me?' snarled Hunter. 'I had no idea I was coming here myself until a few hours ago.' It was time to start asking questions—his only hope was to get the Russian talking then wait for an opening.

'The horse may run quickly, but it cannot escape its own tail. Tommy's bar—the one you spend so much time in—I wait for you to arrive, then follow when you leave. It is good you come out to country—now we can complete our business in peace. Start engine, go south.'

He pulled on the restraining belt, twisted the key in the ignition, found the switch for the wipers, then manoeuvred the BMW across the bumpy lot. When he hit the main road, he turned south to head back towards LA, although he didn't expect to make it that far. Once they'd gone a few hundred yards, he tried to strike up another conversation.

'Look, there's no need for this—our business is over. Finch was blackmailing you into carrying out the executions and you had no choice but to comply. You're not the first guy that tried to kill me and you won't be the last—I don't hold grudges. You can go anywhere, do anything, and you have my word that I'll never come looking for you.' As he spoke, he stepped on the gas.

'I am sorry, my friend, but you are loose end, and Viktor does not leave loose ends. You should be honoured. As worthy adversary, I decide to kill you up close, old-fashioned way, then I be sure you are dead.'

'You'll have to excuse me if I don't share your enthusiasm for my imminent demise, but I was kinda hoping to live a little longer—about sixty years, to be precise.' The speedometer edged above fifty.

'Ha!' came the snort from behind. 'You Americans—always so funny.'

The last of the lonely log cabins flashed by on his left. How much longer did he have? Were they headed towards a prechosen site for his execution, or was the Russian just waiting to get beyond the scope of Pine Ridge's prying eyes? He coaxed the BMW up to sixty, but the road was still pitch black in front. Where in the hell were those gangbangers? Ten seconds later he got his answer.

The abandoned logging track was just ahead, but something wasn't right. Hunter eased off the gas. The weeds! There was a fresh path through the weeds. Something had flattened them. A sudden blur of movement in the forest caught his eye, then he was bracing himself for impact, locking his arms against the wheel, setting his feet against the floor. A split second later the Renegades' Humvee roared clear of the trees to slam into the side of the BMW with a bone-crunching smash. Hunter stiffened as a burst of pain shot through the right side of his body, a pain that was so pure, so exquisite, he thought he was about to die.

The screech of metal on metal seared the silence as the smaller vehicle was sent flying across the rain-slicked surface at a rate of knots, the world spinning by in a blur until instinct took over and he stamped on the brakes. The air was driven from his lungs as the restraining belt tightened painfully across his sternum, then the vehicle came to a halt. Black spots danced in front of his eyes. His entire right leg felt numb. But he was still alive.

He took a deep, whooping breath then slowly twisted his head to check on the Russian. Danilov had definitely come off worse—he hadn't even seen the Humvee coming. The impact had catapulted him across the rear seat and straight through the far window to leave him hanging half in and half out of the car. The Mossberg had fallen harmlessly to one side. Hunter tried to turn around, but the restraining belt was jammed tight. He beat on the release mechanism and threw another worried glance over his shoulder. Blood poured from a gaping wound in Danilov's forehead, and his right arm was covered with multiple flesh wounds, but was he dead? Probably not.

As if to prove his fortitude, the injured man emitted a low groan and began to haul himself back inside the vehicle, raking his chest over the last few shards of glass in the frame to open up a deep gash, not that it seemed to bother him any. This guy was a fucking machine. Hunter redoubled his efforts with the restraining belt, pounding the release mechanism for all he was worth, until suddenly it popped free, and then he was dragging himself through to the rear of the car, his dead leg following gamely behind.

The shotgun—that was the key. Two desperate pairs of hands closed around the Mossberg at the exact same moment, and then they were wrestling for control, grunting like animals, Hunter half on top of the Russian, fighting for his life, the intensity of their frenzied struggle somehow amplified in the enclosed environment. He tried to yank the gun free as he stared into the face of his would-be executioner, a demonic face that was covered in blood, sporting eyes as cold as a Siberian winter, and then those eyes lit up—Danilov had slipped his finger through the trigger guard.

Slowly, inexorably, the barrel of the gun began to tilt down in Hunter's direction, and though he tried to fight back, Danilov was strong, so strong, and he had superior leverage. The barrel's small black opening crept into view with its promise of instant escape from all worldly cares, but Hunter wasn't quite ready to die. He drew himself back and slammed his forehead straight into the bridge of the Russian's nose, and the feeling of bone demolishing cartilage was good, so good that he let fly again.

Primal instincts now unleashed, he pounded down repeatedly, the taste of blood spurring him on, his vision coming through a thick red veil. Six times, seven times his head rose and fell, but still the Russian refused to relinquish his grip on the gun. Eight times, then nine, until Danilov's face was little more than a sodden mass, and finally Hunter felt his foe's grip begin to weaken. Sensing his chance, he grabbed for the trigger and threw all his weight at the Mossberg. The shotgun discharged just as the barrel touched the Russian's cheekbone. The sound was deafening, the effect spectacular. Danilov's head vaporised, showering the rear seat of the car with chunks of blood, brain and gristle, and leaving a headless corpse where once had been a ruthless assassin.

Hunter clambered out of the BMW, spat the coppery taste from his mouth, then fell to his knees and started to retch. The nerves in his right leg sang out as feeling returned. Two pairs of sneaker-shod feet came to a halt in front of him, signalling that the Renegades had made it to the site of the crash. He looked up at Furious and watched his lips move, but all sound was lost to the ringing in his ears. After a couple of minutes the effects of the shotgun blast began to subside.

'Looks like I owe you my life,' Hunter said gratefully, rising to his feet and holding out his hand, which Furious accepted with an insouciant shrug.

'Ain't no thang. My man, Slice, noticed you'd got yourself caught up in some shit as we pulled out of the bar, and seeings how you'd just done me a solid by flushing out Carson, I figured I owed you.'

'Try not to leave it so long next time.'

'Full-frontal assault was out. Muthafucka had you in his sights. So I had to get creative. Use some tac-tics. Play it cool. Who was that cat?'

'The man that killed your brother.'

Furious stared at Danilov's prone body for a moment, hawked twice, then spat forcibly onto the bloodied corpse. 'So we all done?'

'Yeah—it's over. Sorry about your Hummer,' Hunter said, gesturing to the stationary vehicle that sat a hundred yards back in the middle of the road.

'Don't sweat it—muthafucka's built like a tank. Probably just need a paint job. Anyhows, I can always get hold of another. Wanna ride?'

'Sure.'

'Your life always this hectic?'

'I made a few career choices recently and things seemed to have livened up.'

'What's next?'

'Well, I guess with a little bit of sweet talking I could get my old job back, but I think I'm done with the department. Something tells me I'll be a whole lot more effective if I stay freelance.'

Yeah, that was the future, thought Hunter—self-employment.

Watch out, world, here I come.